I0636517

Acknowledgements

As a child the last thing I would have ever imagined doing with my life, was to write a book. My goal in life at the time was to become a professional soccer player, but that road ended, in 2001, after winning a division III national championship with The Richard Stockton College of New Jersey, men's soccer team. After that pivotal moment in my life, one door shut, a new one opened, and a new path awaited me. Where it would take me I didn't know, but one thing I knew for certain, was that I was going to live my life as an artist. Since soccer and the arts were, and are the two passions of my life; since the phase of my life as a soccer player had ended, it was now time to pursue the arts.

From athlete to artist, after graduating from college with a Bachelor of the arts, in art history, and after experimenting with and learning many different art mediums, writing was the form, I felt I was best at, and enjoyed doing most. Painting, graphic arts, photography, and film making are all art forms I have experimented with, enjoyed, and hope to master, but writing seemed to be the heart and soul of all, which I am currently devoted to.

Writing has changed me in so many ways, and the path I have taken and the people I have met, since, June of 2007, when Esperanza was only a thought in my mind, and I wrote that first word, hope; no matter how difficult, burdensome it has been at times, or how many drafts and notebooks I have filled up, I wouldn't change anything about the experiences I had, with writing Esperanza.

Esperanza is my first official book, and even though it may not be perfect, or written to the standards of the literary world, it is a part of me. Like one of my children, I have nurtured, I have grown with the creation of Esperanza. And if it is considered a failure, that's ok, because in my eyes to get to this point is success. So, if there is anyone out there who dreams of writing a book, or says that they can write one, well then, stop talking about it, stop procrastinating, and don't be afraid to, even if you find yourself held back by the confines of life, make excuses, or have a lack of talent, DO IT. I dared to, and I did, even if I didn't have a clue how to from the very beginning. So, if I was able to write and publish a book, then so can you. I encourage it, and I hope that what I have written inspires you, and others to write a book or pursue whatever it is you dream of doing, but may fear beginning.

And if there is any kind of advice to give, then it is that living life is what got me to this point. I have and still go with the flow of life. A fool some may say, but the currents I took, and the tides I've climbed have brought so many different, challenging, and amazing people into my life, who have changed me in some way. The ones who have come and gone, the ones who ignored me, mocked me, insulted me in any way, or judged me without knowing who I am, all of their laughter at me, negative words directed at me, and all of the pity, doubt, and disbelief I saw in their eyes, even you, the wicked ones, the shallow ones, and the ignorant ones, were a part of this journey I have taken. But it were the ones I have created everlasting bonds, and relationships with, the ones who taught me, and the ones who loved me, who have inspired me, and drove me to the edges of what can and can't be done, to carry on and finish what I have started. There are too many to name, but the important ones deserve my gratitude.

For Mom, Dad, Domenick III, Joey, grandparents, aunts, uncles, cousins, nieces, nephews, in-laws, extended family, in-laws in Mexico, friends, teachers, coaches, teammates, colleagues, café companions, my editor Mr. Carlyle Van Thompson, Casey Carpenter for your honest feedback, Eliza Dee for copyediting and polishing Esperanza up into a final draft, my brother Joey Tutalo for designing and making the book cover, those who inform, who helped me awaken and find truth, strangers and single serving friends, and for muses, but, above all else for mi niña, Sofia, and mi esposa, Gabriela. For the real Gabriela, who I met, after the fictional Gabriela was thought of and created; you are the manifestation of my imagination, my light, my guide, my passions drive, you give me reason to live, and carry on, even if there seems to be no end, or disaster further ahead; because of you I live life, and I write.

Esperanza

By:

Tommy Tutalo

I

Failure is the absence of faith

Prologue

All that remained were the ghosts and the echoes of everything that once was. The dilapidated apartment, left abandoned throughout the years, was no longer home but a window into the past. As sunbeams shone through the broken window and the howling winds blew in through the emptiness, life seemed to have slipped away between the fabric of space and time.

Although the years had come and gone, all that remained of a life forever lost was preserved in the pages of three aged brown leather journals that Sarita began to unwrap. They were all she had left.

The journals were resting on her lap, wrapped in brown paper, securely laced together by two pieces of slightly shredded twine. Sarita was no longer a shy yet mischievous girl, but now a young, beautiful adult in her late twenties, all alone in search of meaning and direction towards a new path.

Sarita's mesmerizing eyes beamed with anticipation as she stared at the three journals. She reflected on all the stories she had been told and contemplated whether she wanted to tarnish the stories told by her mother, Gabriela, or relive them all, and perhaps a little bit more, via the written word.

The internal wounds from the loss of her mother were still fresh, but would soon begin to heal. Sarita began to scan through the first journal, periodically pausing at random words, keenly observing that portions of pages were filled from top to bottom.

The array of words were only fragments of the mind, glimpses of a life lived to the fullest that had suddenly been cut too short. But each page was so full of emotion and extraordinary experience that it felt liberating, yet like a disturbing prison manifested by the truth found within the pages.

Some things were never meant to be known, but all that had been found was now a key to open up the mind and free the soul. Amidst the clouds of darkness still lingering, Sarita found solace within the pages filled with a life battling fear, doubt, disbelief, yet thriving with passion, desire, love and happiness. It seemed no matter how many times there seemed to be failure within the heart of darkness, Gabriela's life and words were able to comfort and inspire Sarita, providing a beacon of hope.

~Esperanza~

Hope, where would we be without it? Hope is one of the most essential things in a person's life, yet we still find ourselves as lost souls, sitting here all alone, gazing out the same old window that once was. Whether it was the love we once had, or the messengers sent to guide us through the darkness, to the other side and back again, the journeys we take and the people we meet along the way change us.

For better or worse, we are no longer who we once were, or at least not who we thought we were. But one thing is sure, one thing is true—that out of all the messengers and saviors sent to soothe the pain or guide us through, we will always remember that time, that moment that changed our path, and changed our lives. Most importantly, we will always remember those who kept us on our feet, guided us when we were blind and gave us hope.

Even as I continue to sit here in the silence, I can still clearly remember that time and that moment that forever changed my life. Standing in darkness on the banks of America—that was the beginning of all that I now have. My home, my life, my hermosa.

The spark of imagination became my reality, and as for the experience— well, it changed me. I never imagined being where I am now, but that's the way life is. It surprises us, puts us in situations that test us, and brings people into our lives who challenge us. Everything changes—the places, the faces, and even my own face in the mirror.

When I lost faith in God, and doubted that God even existed, I was given the most unexpected gift and became alive. It wasn't until the night I risked everything for a dream that I regained my faith in God, believing that God existed in us all and helped those in need.

I can still feel the essence of emotions from that night, feel the cold, muddy waters, and jagged desert rocks. I was lost and all alone. I could hear the screams from within the darkness of that night. It was that night that I realized, God, no matter how flawed, brought me to the banks of freedom, guided me and showed me the light. It was the voice from that night, her voice, that I will never forget. I can still hear it echoing deep within my ears. "Open your eyes, open your eyes . . ."

#

"*Abre tus ojos* . . . open your eyes . . . Gaby, open your eyes." Fabiola Flores spoke softly as she shook Gabriela's shoulder. "We're here."

In the darkness, Gabriela opened her eyes. She was sacred and lost. At first, she felt like she was blind. Sweat slowly poured down her forehead, burning her eyes. She could only sit there in pain, as her arms were pinned up against the other scared migrants who sat in the same tight cramped circle. But soon after her eyes adjusted, Gabriela was able to see the eyes of the other migrants.

She was not alone, and together they were about to take a leap of faith from within the dark abyss in which they found themselves. It was so hot inside that it felt like the sixth circle of hell. The dark Chevy van constantly rocked them back and forth, up and down. They were unable to move of their own accord. For the moment, there was nothing they could do. Even if all the migrants seemed to be in a hopeless situation, their eyes showed glints of hope. They had faith. Even with the suffocating sounds of a baby crying and the roaring of the engine. No matter what awaited them, they knew that once they arrived at their final destination, they would become the authors of their own fate.

Soon after the engine seized, there was silence except for the crickets that lurked in the night. No one dared speak. Before Gabriela had a chance to whisper to Fabiola, the back doors of the van creaked wide open. Two coyotes appeared in the moonlight and began to hustle everyone out of the van.

To balance herself, Gabriela firmly pressed one hand against the window and the other on the ceiling as she stood up. She felt numb and remained stoic as she watched the others get out. This was it, no turning back. This would be her first and last chance at freely crossing the border to live the American Dream. All thanks to Fabiola, who began to step out. Fabiola took Gabriela by the hand, guiding her out to join the others.

"*Todos escuchan.* In five minutes, the border patrol will leave to switch with the night shift. You'll see the lights from the truck as they leave. Then you'll have twenty to thirty minutes to swim across the river, climb up the ravine and then run fifty to seventy-five yards to the road, where the black van with the other coyotes will be waiting for you. They will then drive all of you to freedom," the coyote announced.

"How far do we have to swim to cross the river?" One of the migrants asked.

"About twenty-five yards," the coyote answered sternly.

"*Ay, Dios mío,*" Elena, the *gordita* woman with the baby cradled in the *rebozo*, cried out. She held her baby tight and made the sign of the holy trinity. One of the other migrants rubbed her shoulder.

"Listen, *mujer*, stay close to me," Fabiola said. "Swimming across that river will be the most difficult thing we'll have to do tonight. So make sure you stay strong mentally and focused so that you can make it across quickly. The faster we swim, the more time we'll have to get up that ravine." Although she was unappealing, even with her jagged teeth, it was Fabiola's inner passion and drive that convinced others to follow her call. Gabriela was one of many.

"I'll try, but I . . . I can't swim too well." Gabriela's body quivered all over.

"Don't worry, *amiga*, tonight you will. Just keep your eyes on the other side." Fabiola put one hand on Gabriela's shoulder.

Even though Gabriela smiled, she swallowed a wad of anxiety. Being on the banks of freedom was beyond her imagination. Before she had a chance to express how she felt with words, across the river, the lights from the border patrol truck flashed.

"Okay, *muchachos*, into the water, *vamos*," the coyote instructed.

All of the migrants stepped into the river. At first the chilling water caused most of them to grumble out explicit words. But after they got their bodies two-thirds into the rancid water polluted with garbage and oil, their determination warmed them. Elena began crying out in prayer while the baby wailed.

"Shut up . . . shut that baby up!" One of the migrants yelled out as he struggled to swim, provoking Elena to go back. Gabriela, who was about fifteen yards out, stayed adrift for a moment to watch Elena.

Although all the migrants were strangers chasing the same dream, in the eyes of Gabriela, they were as one: a family who needed each other's support. She felt that the van ride together and their experience had created an everlasting bond amongst the migrants, one that she wasn't willing to see fall apart. Gabriela wasn't a great swimmer, but she swam back for Elena and the baby.

"No, *mujer*, don't go. It's not your problem. Leave her," Fabiola called out.

"But, the baby," Gabriela pleaded as she turned to face Fabiola.

"Forget the baby! You'll never make it back in time!" The two shared an unsettling stare before Gabriela turned away and began swimming back for the hopeless woman. Fabiola turned and began to swim towards America.

Each breath was suffocating, and each stroke Gabriela took was burdensome. As the soulless migrant who had scolded Elena swam by Gabriela, he taunted her for going back. Gabriela became strengthened. She felt liberated and swiftly swam up to Elena.

"*Tranquila, Elena, tranquila*," Gabriela said as she tried to turn Elena around in the waist-deep water.

"No, no, leave us. I-I can't make it with *mi chiquita* . . . you go, go—take care of yourself." Elena struggled to stay afloat with each breath.

"No, Elena. I won't let you and your baby stay behind, not after you got this far." Gabriela held Elena afloat as she encouraged her. "Remember our conversation on our way here? Remember what you told me? You gave me strength. Now I'll give you mine. C'mon, hurry!"

Gabriela turned Elena around, unwrapping the rebozo to free the baby. She then rewrapped and tucked it inside of Elena's backpack, which floated on top of the water. Gabriela then put the backpack back on Elena with the baby securely kept inside, only its head sticking out of the unzipped top.

Gabriela took Elena by the hand and began to walk back out into deeper waters. Elena began to cry out in prayer once again, but she and the baby started to settle down. Gabriela squeezed her hand tightly as they swam out into the darkness. She felt dragged down by the weight, but seeing some of the other migrants standing on the banks of America infused Gabriela with a rush of adrenaline.

Voices echoed out across the river, from the coyotes and the migrants. Their reassuring words filled Gabriela with confidence to keep moving, faster and faster, helping her overcome the pain in her arms and the polluted water that was gargling in and out of her mouth.

"Almost there, Elena, . . . almost there." Gabriela struggled to speak but never slowed down or lost focus. With Elena by her side, she swam towards the migrants standing on the shores of America with open arms and words of encouragement.

"*Vamos, vamos!*" One of the migrants yelled out as Gabriela came within ten yards of the river's edge.

Just as Gabriela and Elena touched the muddy bottom of the river and began to walk in the waist-high water, two-thirds of the migrants began to run up the ravine. Only a third stayed behind to help Gabriela and Elena get out of the water. It was no surprise to Gabriela who had left her and the others behind, but it hurt to see Fabiola walk away and watch her reach the shore from afar. Fabiola was her friend, her ticket into America. Once on the banks, none of that really mattered.

Gabriela helped Elena catch her breath and took the baby out of the backpack. She wrapped the rebozo back around Elena, securely cradling the baby. "You see, Elena, you see? Dreams come true. We're here in America, together."

"*Gracias, Gabriela, gracias.* I . . . I wouldn't have made it here without you," Elena gasped while breathing heavily and running her fingertips through Gabriela's hair. Gabriela did the same, caressed the baby's head, then turned with Elena and they began the walk up the ravine together.

"*Vamos, mujer, vamos!*" Fabiola demanded, as she walked up the ravine ten yards ahead of Gabriela while looking back. Gabriela looked up at Fabiola and then back down at Elena, who was gasping for air.

"Go, Gabriela, don't wait for me. I'll meet you at the top." The look in Elena's eyes encouraged Gabriela to turn around and quickly walk up the ravine to catch up to Fabiola.

"Agh, *mujer*, I told you not to go back. *Mira*, there's only about five minutes left before the border patrol come back. Half of the others are already at the road where the van is parked."

Gabriela didn't say a word; she just ignored Fabiola's selfishness and continued to walk beside her to the top of the ravine with the other migrants. Before going any further, Gabriela paused to look back across the river at the Mexican border from the top of the ravine. She saw before her a vast, empty desert wasteland of America.

She looked up at the night sky. She was not alone, and felt the presence of God. Gabriela closed her eyes and imagined a better life. Her dreams were unfolding.

"*Por* Mamá." Gabriela's last breath brought a sense of peace. One of the migrants called out, and there was a flurry of excitement.

"*Mira . . . mira*, the van, they're here. Hurry so they don't leave us!"

Gabriela opened her eyes and saw two headlights moving in the distance. She began to trot across the desert towards the road with the others, but then stopped.

"No, no, *muchachos*. They're moving too fast, and towards us. It's border patrol!"

A spotlight on top of the truck shined out across the darkness and illuminated Gabriela and the other migrants, causing them to run away in all directions. Half ran into the desert, while the others went back down the ravine. Gabriela stood frozen but was dragged down the ravine by Fabiola, who guided her along the river's edge.

"Vamos, amiga, vamos!" Fabiola shouted as she dragged Gabriela alongside her.

As they ran along the ravine, they passed by Elena, who Gabriela grabbed by the hand and dragged along with them.

"No, no, *mujer*! Leave her! She's slowing us down!" Fabiola yelled.

Gabriela grabbed both their hands even tighter, only to have Fabiola shake her off and run ahead with three other migrants, but all were confronted by two border patrol agents.

"No te muevas! No te muevas! Abajo, en el piso, ahora!" They yelled with guns drawn.

Fabiola and the other migrants ran back towards Gabriela and Elena. Gabriela turned and began to run up the ravine with Elena, only to have Elena trip, fall and roll down. Gabriela ran back down for her and the crying baby, but as Gabriela stood over her, Fabiola and one of the migrants ran past.

"Vamos! Amiga, hay vienen, vamos!" Fabiola screamed, causing Gabriela to look and see one of the border patrol agents running up towards her from about thirty yards away.

"Alto! No te muevas! Quédate donde estás!"

Gabriela reached down and grabbed Elena to pick her up, but she pushed Gabriela away. Elena unwrapped the baby from the rebozo and handed it to Gabriela.

"Go, Gabriela, go. Don't worry about me, you can still get away. Here, take the baby with you. She's better off with you. Give her the opportunities I promised I would provide for her. Go, now!" Elena cried out.

"I'll miss you." Gabriela looked Elena in the eyes one last time, then turned around with the baby cradled in her arms and sprinted back up the ravine across the desert, never looking back. Gabriela could hear Elena scream out as she blindly ran into the darkness.

"Over here, *mujer, vamos!*"

Gabriela could now hear Fabiola and the other migrants, as well as the border patrol agents yelling, but couldn't see them. Only the echoes guided

Gabriela towards Fabiola. Fabiola was standing on the edge of the road only twenty yards away from the black van filled with the other coyotes and the few migrants who had made it. Fortunately, they had patiently waited for Fabiola and Gabriela.

As Gabriela ran towards her, Fabiola was ambushed by two border patrol agents who tackled her down to the ground. The van began to drive away. Gabriela jumped out in the middle of the road, forcing the coyotes to stop.

As she stood with her arms held in front of her face at the bright headlights, the others slid the van's side door open, dragged Gabriela and the baby in, and then peeled out past the two border patrol agents who stood over Fabiola, who lay with her wrists bound.

The agents fired their guns at the van. Bullets pierced the back and side of the van, deflecting off the sides and ricocheting around inside the van, wounding one of the migrants. Everyone was in an uproar as the van drove off the road into the desert, bouncing around as it drove faster, away from the border patrol truck that chased them and into the heart of darkness, to freedom…

<u>1</u>

The sunlight from the heavens shined down through the open window, illuminating Gabriela's hands and fingers as they gracefully combed through Sarita's beautiful long, thick dark hair, while Gabriela softly sang a Spanish lullaby. The essence of tranquility relaxed her and created an escape from thinking about her haunting past.

Although, time ceased to exist at the moment, it was the night Gabriela crossed the US-Mexico border, which reminded her how far she had come since taking a risk to chase a dream. At the time it seemed so daunting and foolish, but it was the path that had brought Gabriela to New Jersey, and all which had spawned from the synchronistic experiences and other paths Gabriela had chosen in life.

"Mama . . . Mama?" Sarita turned her head to see why Gabriela wasn't responding. "Mama, Mama, is everything okay?"

"Sorry, Sarita, but I was, just, ya know, daydreaming." Gabriela struggled to find the right words. She then stopped combing Sarita's hair.

Sarita turned around in her chair. "It's okay, Mama , um, sometimes that, that happens to me too," she said with a smile.

"Yes, Sarita, it does, to all of us. Sometimes when we least expect it."

"So, um, did, did you go someplace exciting?"

Before responding, Gabriela admired her little *hermosa*, her light; the love of her life. Without her, Gabriela was all alone.

"No, but the path I chose, no matter how dark it seemed to be, eventually led me to someplace that is much better now, much brighter." Gabriela held Sarita's head in her hands and gave her a kiss on the forehead, running her fingers through Sarita's hair.

"Oh, *Chor-tee*, what would I do without you? You're the reason for all of this." Gabriela's accent made some of her words sound peculiar, like Sarita's nickname, Shorty. Gabriela scanned the small, modest apartment filled with hardly any possessions; Sarita looked around as well until eventually their eyes aligned once more.

"Am I really?"

"Yes, you came into my life and gave me hope when I lost faith in myself and in God. With hope, you can become or do anything you want with your life, just as long as you believe in yourself."

"Um, well, maybe someday when I become a famous actress, like, like Anne Hathaway, I'll be able to buy us a big house to live in, with a ton of rooms. Um, one that has a toilet that actually works, a washer and dryer, and a backyard, that has grass and a pool. And I could also get you a really nice car, like . . . like a Ferrari, so that you don't have to take the bus anymore. And I'll get a scooter, a red one, for me to ride around and take me wherever I wanna go."

Gabriela smiled. "Someday, Chor-tee, someday. Anything is possible. But for now, why don't you go outside while the sun is still out? It's a beautiful day. Keep yourself busy while I finish dinner."

"Okay, Mama." Sarita got up and walked towards the door.

"Hey, Chor-tee, *venir ven aquí y dame un beso antes de que te vayas.*" Sarita came back to give her mother a kiss.

"Have fun, but behave. Remember, I can see you from the window."

"I will, Mama."

Sarita turned around and trotted out the door, which she pulled shut behind her. Gabriela watched with a smile, contemplating how taking that leap of faith many years ago and boldly going down many unexpected paths from Mexico to America had brought her not only to where she was now in life, but her greatest gift—Sarita.

$\underline{2}$

As Sarita stepped out into the dimly lit hallway of the Clearview apartment complex, she was engulfed with mustiness. The wooden floors were rotted and creaked. The green paint on the walls of the narrow hallway was faded, cracked and chipped. Even if it was home, Sarita was unfazed by the decrepit interior as she walked towards the stairwell at the end of the hallway of the horseshoe-shaped building.

After Sarita made her way down the five filthy flights of stairs, she ended up in the courtyard, which was laid out with bricks and weeds. Along the sides of the courtyard were sitting areas with benches, chairs, and small round tables, while in the center was a big old circular stone fountain. Beyond that was an area filled with dirt and patches of grass, where an old rusty swing set with a slide was.

As Sarita walked from the lounge area to the back, she looked down and tried to hide behind her hair, since the same people were outside all day, every single day. They never seemed to leave. Mostly the people there were ones whom Sarita didn't really like. Especially the ones Sarita called the three *brujas*, or witches: Mona, the landlord of the building, and her two cronies, Martha and Mable.

The three of them were widows, and it was no surprise to Sarita why, especially Mona. Mona made the devil seem like a saint. Mona's late husband, the former landlord, had killed himself because he couldn't put up with her anymore. The poor man had hung himself in the bathroom. Even after his death,

Mona showed no remorse. She accused him of being selfish by leaving her all alone. As for the other two, they had given their husbands heart attacks, and now the three did nothing but complain. They complained about their dead husbands, as well as everything and everyone in the world, always trying to throw their misery onto everyone else.

"Hey, *señorita*, when's ya motha gonna pay me my goddamn rent. Ya know she hasn't paid in *dos* weeks. Why don't ya do yourself a fava, and tell ya motha that she owes me *mucho dinero* each day she's late from now on, because if not, tha both of ya will be living in tha streets, *comprende!*" Mona croaked in her hoarse voice as smoke from her cigarette slowly rose languidly from her mouth and lingered in the dense air. Mona was middle-aged, but her wrinkled, shriveled-up skin made her look like she was in her seventies. She wore a nightgown with clear plastic slippers. Her hair consisted of a frizzy blond afro, and her makeup was colorful, smeared across her face. Sarita thought Mona looked like a circus clown with a hangover. Martha and Mable dressed similarly, except they were shorter and chubbier, not tall and thin like Mona.

"*Sí, señora*," Sarita answered. She spoke to them only in Spanish just to avoid talking to them because she knew they wouldn't bother if she didn't speak English.

"*Sí señora?* When's this poor child gonna learn some goddamn English? This is America she lives in, not south of tha border. And I don't care how old she is either, she should be speaking English," Mona stated.

"You're right, Mona, it's a goddamn shame. I blame tha motha. It should be tha motha's responsibility to teach her. Instead she sends tha poor thang outside to play all day. Now she should be upstairs with her motha learning English every single day. And what does she allow her daughter to do? She lets her go outside and play around in tha dirt like an animal," Martha added.

"Hmm, I agree, Martha. It's tha motha. Not only does she not teach tha poor girl any English, but she is lazy. Why doesn't she get a real job, so she can buy tha poor girl some new clothes? Look at that raggedy old outfit, all shredded, with holes in it. I mean, muay God, look at it. It looks like she's been in a whar," Mable ranted.

"Forget the clothes, she better pay me my goddamn rent," Mona scorned.

The three brujas then went off into one of their ridiculous debates about what department stores have the best sales. After leaving the three *brujas* behind, Sarita made her way to the swing set, passing by Ramona, the little old Hispanic lady who would scare Sarita with stories from the Old Testament and Revelation. There were no other children outside today, so Sarita ended up sitting on one of the swings all alone.

She rocked gently back and forth and grazed her feet around in the dirt. When not in the company of friends, Sarita's escape from the world around was found deep within the eye of her mind. It was a safer place. Even though Sarita was alone on the swing set, in her mind, Sarita was never really alone. It wasn't the people lounging around in the courtyard or some higher force, but someone else nearby. As Sarita sat on the swing like she had many times before, there would always be a sudden sense of fear that would emerge and consume her.

On the fifth floor, there was a window at the end of the building that faced out towards the swing set. Inside the apartment lived a man—a mysterious, reclusive man. No one had ever seen him go in, and no one had ever seen him go out. Many stories floated around Clearview about the enigmatic man living in apartment 515. Some of the stories were good, but most were bad.

Every time Sarita was alone on the swing set, she realized that during this time, she could see a silhouette of him watching her from the window. Not only did this scare Sarita, but she was even more frightened that the man lived right next door to her.

"Sarita, *ven acá que vamos a comer!*" Gabriela stuck her body halfway out her apartment window as she shouted. Sarita got off the swing and slowly walked, keeping her eyes on the man in the window.

# # #

From inside apartment 515, the mysterious, reclusive man watched Sarita walk through the courtyard. As he cracked open the curtains with his paint-stained fingers, he smoked a cigarette. He sat poised. His piercing crystal-blue eyes, scruffy face, and long dirty-blond hair hanging down around the sides of his face was that of a tainted artist. As he had done many times before, he mused over Sarita's innocence. There was a radiance that he was drawn towards, which helped to eradicate the darkness of his life and his past.

# # #

Once inside, Sarita sprinted up the stairs, stumbling on the laces from her scuffed-up untied red high-top Converse All-Stars. In the hallway, she crept backwards towards her apartment. She stared at the mysterious, reclusive man's apartment door, knowing that he was probably on the other side watching.

"Sarita, que estás hacienda? Ven para acá, entra a la casa, ahora!" Gabriela called out, her face peeking out the apartment door into the hallway.

Sarita slowly turned around, faced Gabriela and then ran into her apartment. Gabriela looked out into the hallway, stared at the mysterious, reclusive man's door, and then shut her own.

<u>3</u>

The luscious aroma of *mole poblano*, chicken drenched in a spicy dark brown sauce, with a side of *arroz rojo*, made with tomatoes, onion, a little garlic and salt, along with warm, crisp corn tortillas filled the atmosphere. Gabriela locked the multiple locks on the apartment door and then walked into the kitchen, where Sarita was waiting at the table. Gabriela joined Sarita, and the two held hands, said grace, and then began to eat.

"So, what did you do outside?" Gabriela questioned Sarita as she began to fish around for pieces of chicken hidden in the sauce-filled mole poblano bowl.

"Um, nothing, just—just sat on the swing." Sarita shoveled a spoonful of mole poblano into her mouth.

"Were any of the other children outside with you?"

"Um, no. Just all the same people who are always outside. Like, like the three brujas, and that scary old lady who always talks about the end of the world and El Diablo," Sarita said, mimicking the way Ramona acted and spoke.

"Be nice, Sarita. How many times have I told you to just ignore Mona and the other two? Ramona isn't scary. She's a sweet old woman who used to babysit and look after you when you were younger."

"Um, yeah, I know. She used to talk to dead people all the time and cast spells on me. I, I used to always have nightmares when she babysat me, 'specially after staying at her apartment. It was so creepy. She had all these crosses and scary religious pictures hanging up all over the place, and, and she used to talk about her dead relatives that she kept in coffee cans." Sarita emphasized her words with her hands.

"Oh, please, Sarita, you exaggerate way too much. Ramona doesn't keep her dead relatives in coffee cans. They're called urns. And she isn't some witch who cast spells, either. She just likes to read from the Bible a lot and read psalms, okay?"

"Um, well, if they're urns, then she has a lot of relatives named Maxwell," Sarita muttered.

"Sarita!" Gabriela lashed out, causing Sarita to lower her head to just above her bowl while she ate. Sarita looked down at her bowl, then up through her strands of hair.

"Um, Mona, she told me to tell you that—that you owe her *mucho dinero*."

"That *bruja*, I told her I was going to be late with this month's rent and that I will pay it with next month's!" Gabriela slammed her spoon down.

"Um, she, she said that for every day that goes by without you paying, you will have to pay more for each day." Sarita continued to look down at her bowl.

"*Perra hija de puta!* She still keeps harassing you, Sarita, and doesn't have the respect to come up here to tell me! *Maldita bruja!* Next time she harasses you, let me know right away, because I'll walk down there and make her wish she never said anything to you at all. The same with the two fat ones! *Puta!*"

Sarita laughed and choked on her food.

"This isn't funny, Sarita. You don't understand what this lady is like, how she made this place worse. Her husband was a good man. He liked and took care of everybody. Frankie kept the place clean, always checked up with everyone to see if everyone was okay or if they needed anything. This *bruja, nada!* She sits out there rotting all day and doesn't care about anyone or anything, just her goddamn rent! God bless Frankie's soul, he was a good man. I hope that *puta* rots in her chair and burns in hell for all eternity!" After venting, Gabriela calmed down and continued to eat her dinner.

"All done, Mama."

"Already, Chor-tee? You have to learn to slow down when you eat. You eat way too fast. It's no good. One day you're going to choke on your food."

"I know, Mama, I'll try to." Sarita chugged her glass of milk and wiped her mouth.

"Well, try harder! You say that all the time."

"I will, Mama." Sarita got up and gave Gabriela a hug and a kiss. She then cleared her side of the table, walked over towards the sink and cleaned her dish and utensils. "Okay, Mama, all done. I'll be in my room."

"Okay, Chor-tee."

Sarita found comfort in her bedroom. After putting on some indie rock music, Sarita searched for something to occupy her mind. Within the vicinity of Sarita's fingertips was an endless library of books, magazines, comic books and graphic novels, crammed onto a multilevel bookshelf and scattered all over the room in various stacks.

There were also Sarita's seven blue neon guppies, named after each day of the week, which she fed. Sarita's bed was pressed up against the back wall, adorned with the Mexican flag and a collage of self-made drawings and paintings, posters and pictures from magazines.

She reached underneath her bed and pulled out an old wooden cigar box, resting it on the floor in front of her knees to open. Inside were a variety of homemade friendship bracelets, both hers and ones given to her, photographs of her, her mother, relatives from Mexico and friends, candy, letters, and notes. Sarita then added some loose change she'd found earlier in the day to her savings of coins and crumpled-up dollar bills.

Sarita stepped towards an old storage trunk. Inside were coloring and sketchbooks, old magazines, crayons, markers, drawing paper, and other art supplies. After digging around, Sarita pulled out crayons, coloring pencils, and a sketchbook.

She set herself up at her desk with all her art supplies. Alongside her desk was a small table set up with all of her still lifes. There was a human and a horse armature, empty wine bottles, vases filled with plants and flowers, and a variety of Barbies, whose blond hair were dyed black to make them look Mexican. Some were even tagged with self-made tattoos and others painted and dressed like gothic beauties or corpses, like the Corpse's Bride. There were also decapitated dolls, some without limbs, voodoo dolls and traditional Mexican

Day of the Dead dolls, along with a variety of stuffed animals, and characters, which helped fuel her imagination.

A door mirror rested against the wall next to the still lifes. As Sarita sat composed like Frida Kahlo, she observed every aspect of herself intently, eventually taking the beauty of the feminine and gracefully transferring all she saw onto paper. Sarita's beautiful hair that flowed down and around her shoulders, her dark eyes, pouty lips and innocent face of curiosity, were all carefully sketched with painstaking attention to detail. Although Sarita wasn't a master artist, her talents weren't wasted. She always drew or painted whenever she could or acted out, always indulging in the arts and life.

Gabriela continued to sip her wine, her mind occupied by everything there ever was, had been, and would be. She turned and gazed out the open window, the illuminating light from the setting sun shining in and blinding her. That was when the past, her past, awakened.

<u>4</u>

Within the emptiness of an undisclosed holding room, Gabriela sat in bondage with her head bowed, while staring up through her strands of hair into the blinding ceiling lights. At the moment, Sarita, all that Gabriela desired, and the years spent in America were gone. All that remained were the memories to hide within to nullify Gabriela's present state of captivity and wash away the pain.

Unfortunately, though, Gabriela sat all alone, while running her fingertips along the scarring on her wrists and the cold metal handcuffs securing them. Behind closed eyes, Gabriela was consumed with a variety of scenarios and unanswered questions, such as who her captors were, why she had been taken and held in bondage, where Sarita was, how Sarita was and how she would get out of her present state of servitude and safely reunite with Sarita. Even though there were so many questions left unanswered, Gabriela still had faith.

Soon, Gabriela sensed a malevolent presence. There was a slow amplification of stomping boots that echoed out in the distance. Gabriela listened as the pounding got closer and closer, and then heard the clinging and clacking of bolts and locks just a few feet away. With the creaking sound of a door slowly opening and closing, Gabriela opened her eyes.

She focused on a pair of boots worn by the unknown individual who stood before her. As Gabriela observed the well-polished black boots, which illustrated status and success within the ranks of the military-industrial complex, she was reminded of the many pairs of shoes she had worn since coming from

Mexico, and how far she had come in life.

The boots then disappeared from Gabriela's frame of vision as the stranger began to pace back and forth in front of her. She found the strength to look up to get a glimpse of the identity of her abductor. He was tall, well-defined, dressed in solid black unmarked military attire, yet he wasn't military. Unbeknownst to Gabriela, he was in fact from a branch of law enforcement.

Gabriela was only able to get a glimpse of his profile as he continued to slowly pace back and forth, studying Gabriela's essence of beauty like da Vinci, as she silently sat there like a shackled Mona Lisa. Gabriela was lost within his piercing dark eyes, as he gazed at her like a raven staring at its prey. His hair was short and black, coated with streaks of gray, his chiseled middle-aged face painted over with gray scruff.

As tension and discomfort began to build up within the room, the man came to a sudden halt. For a moment, there was an overcast of uncertainty and anticipation as Gabriela waited for her tormentor to impose his final judgment. A sudden ripple of words tore through the silence.

"You know, someone as pretty as you really shouldn't hide behind her hair."

The man spoke with a slight Spanish accent and then patiently waited for Gabriela to respond. There was nothing, neither a verbal nor a physical response from Gabriela. Only silence, which triggered the man in black to continue.

"There's no need to be afraid. I'm not here to hurt you."

The man in black took notice of the handcuffs on Gabriela's wrists. He reached into his back pocket for a key, then stepped towards Gabriela, unlocked the handcuffs and removed them. Gabriela caressed her wrists.

"You're welcome."

Gabriela remained silent. The man in black was willing to play along in order to overcome Gabriela's present state of withdrawal.

"Well, now that you're free, you shouldn't be afraid anymore. You can relax. Like I said, I'm not here to hurt you. I'm here to comfort you. I'm Ignacio." As Ignacio introduced himself, he reached out his hand to shake Gabriela's.

Even though Gabriela remained still, Ignacio continued in hopes that Gabriela would open up to him. He wanted more information about her and her life, to relay back to his superior.

"I know. I understand that if I were in your shoes right now, I wouldn't talk either, especially after being brought here against your own will and having to sit in here all alone in handcuffs for quite some time now. But that's okay, because we have plenty of time to spend together, to get to know each other better."

Ignacio began to pace back and forth again.

"I'm sure that you have a lot of questions that you would love to have answered right now. I can see the vulnerability and curiosity in your eyes. You have the look of a child, who wants to hear and know so much, all at once. A child who is dependent and lost without being given answers. I also see courage, strength, and a fire burning in your eyes. Even with the curiosity of a child and the heart of a lion, I can also see deep within your eyes that you're still searching for the truth, for meaning in all of this, in life and the world we live in. You're still trying to figure out what your purpose in life is, why you're here."

Ignacio paused, and then smiled as he continued, "Aren't we all? And the question I'm sure you're asking yourself right now is, why me, why have I ended up here, why now, what led me to this?"

Ignacio gestured dramatically.

"I sometimes ask myself the same thing. And what I always end up thinking about are the choices I made in life, the choices that filled me with love and joy, the choices that ruined and scarred me, the choices that molded and defined me. And even though they are just memories now, to hide within, for an escape, I still imagine what my life would be like now if maybe, just maybe, I had chosen a different path at some point in my life. Maybe things would have been different, or maybe they would have been better . . . or worse. Either way, what always seems to overshadow the choices made and dictate the outcome of a path taken is fate. Do you believe in fate?"

In Gabriela's eyes, fate was an accepted aspect of life. It was something that was as routine as the sun and moon rising and falling from dusk till dawn, in perpetual motion throughout an ever-changing cycle of the seasons. Fate was a grand illusion, a series of many different prepaved paths laid out from birth to death, which were then taken by choice. Gabriela accepted her fate. She also understood and accepted that she was the one with the free will to choose her path. Most importantly, though, Gabriela had faith, within herself, and would remain silent.

"The idea of someone controlling every aspect of our lives seems redundant to me, but then again, there seems to be no coincidences. Everything always seems to fall into place, no matter how tragic or fortunate, like pieces of a jigsaw puzzle. In essence, though, it seems to me that we forget that we are the creators of our own existence, that we are the ones who put the puzzle together, that the whole idea of fate, the choices we make, and all the coincidences within our lives, as a collective whole, are nothing but figments of our imagination. To live a life of fear and fall victim to this collective whole is blindness. We need to open our minds and live from deep within, to not be afraid to take risks in life, that it's best to fly into the light and burn out rather than hide in the darkness. We need not be afraid to risk everything for a dream. You know all about that, I'm sure, to risk everything for a dream. Isn't that the answer to your question, why you're here, now, at this moment?"

Gabriela remained frozen as she listened to Ignacio's rhetoric. Even though she somewhat agreed, which suddenly fueled her, Gabriela refused to give in to Ignacio's shrewdness. After Ignacio spoke his final words, he came to a sudden halt, observing Gabriela's presence, like a master artist, philosophizing about the divine essence of art and beauty and life within a world of heaven and hell. Ignacio then resumed pacing back and forth, emphasizing his words with his hands once again.

"You know, I once knew a man who took great risks in life. He was a man who came from nothing, who accepted every aspect of life and lived each waking day to the fullest. He never limited himself. He would go beyond all shadows of doubt to experience every aspect of life and every opportunity that came to him, and never allowed anyone or the opinions of others to get in his way. In the eyes of others, he was the face of boldness, a genius who made decisions on intuition and always lived in the moment. He always embraced failure with open arms and would find a way to turn his failures into success. He was a restless soul who rarely slept, who was always hungry for knowledge, to learn about everything and everyone in life, the world around and beyond the infinite of the universe and all that seemed to be myth and legends."

As Ignacio continued, the passion within his voice began to slowly build up like an uprising of a distant storm. Gabriela, who was being entranced by such soothing deception, began to refocus her thoughts.

"He lived a life of poverty, a life of comfort, and a life of fortune. What he had experienced and seen with his own eyes are what other men only know from books and stories told. His life was that of which he seeks, a life of myth and legend. This is a man who'd traveled the world by foot, twice. He had once been a prisoner of war, who escaped and went back into the gulags to free others, a man who turned loose change into a fortune, which he soon lost and eventually won back on a bet he couldn't afford, tripling what he once had. He eventually turned a small chain of businesses into an empire and became an honored guest of kings and queens. He was a lover of both man and beast, a fairy-tale romantic who could woo a woman of any age with the glance of an eye, a man who once lived amongst a pack of wolves and spent three years in a wilderness of exile. But his greatest feat was that of passion and tragedy. He once killed a man for love with his bare hands, and after looking death in the eyes, he successfully delivered his firstborn in the heart of the Amazon, on the same night. And after all he experienced in life and all he gained in life, he left it all, just because. It was that feeling, that burning desire of emptiness, that hunger to live, that he missed so much. He eventually traveled the world again, to live amongst the unfortunate, becoming a humanitarian, a godly figure in the eyes of those he helped and lived with in third-world countries."

Ignacio paused for a moment, once again studying Gabriela, who still remained idle, before continuing to speak.

"He never returned. Word got out that he died. His wife and children eventually grew old and disappointed, never knowing the truth. As for me, I never accepted his death. I had faith in him. And then one day, my curiosity was answered. It was on a day when I was sitting outside a café on the street of an old European city, filled with despair, until . . . a presence approached. At first, I didn't believe what stood before me; I thought that I was seeing a ghost. But as I became lost in his eyes once again, I could see the fire to live life, which was still passionately burning deep within his heart. After catching up, I had the courage to ask him what was his secret. What was it that drove him beyond fear, doubt, disbelief, beyond all boundaries and limitations? There was a long pause, and then he simply said, 'In life, you have to be true to your heart, because your heart is the voice of truth and all-knowing. It's the only truth, and with it, you need patience . . . but in the end, if all else fails, all we have is hope.'"

Ignacio's final words rang in Gabriela's ears like church bells. Gabriela was instilled with a spark of life, an awakening that remained even as Ignacio continued to speak.

"So, what was it like, to leave everything you've ever known far behind, all that safety and security, to risk it all and blindly follow in the shadows of so many, to live out a fantasy . . . a dream? When you first came here, what was it like?"

After Ignacio questioned Gabriela's motive in life, she found the strength to look up into his eyes. In his eyes were the ghosts from her past, and after seeing that Ignacio was just another malicious person, she looked up into the blinding lights that opened up the doors to a tainted past, a dark path taken with an optimistic heart.

<u>5</u>

All around, there was a sense of amnesty and assertiveness within the streets of Los Angeles. The protesters who blindly filled the streets by the thousands, protesting sovereignty for legal and illegal immigrants and renouncing all those who came from foreign lands, kept the sheep mentality in full effect. In the eyes of the globalist, the illusion of freedom was a necessity to control, deceive and divide all those who came from beyond borders and all those who lived within the empire of lies.

America was a political battlefield in which those who sought freedom and a better life were just pawns, used in a bureaucratic game of power and control. It was a game of illusion, filled with good and evil, that kept all of the people in place. Even if all those stuck in the middle of a politically charged uprising seemed free, the perception of perspective was a necessity for those from both sides of the border, and for all those living within the illusion of lies to distinguish their own sense of identity, beliefs and reason. The illusion of freedom kept those from both sides of the border blind to their God-given right of freewill; those who had faith and sought truth in order to live a better life, such as Gabriela, would find it.

As a mass of people continued to protest and fight amongst each other, Gabriela rode on a crowded bus, silently gazing out the window. Though Gabriela was lost in America, hearing the unrecognizable English language, she was still consciously aware of her surroundings and had the courage to carry on down a dark path.

Eventually the bus came to a stop, and the doors opened. Gabriela emerged onto the streets of Los Angeles. She held her bag tightly and looked around while she walked through the crowded streets of the urban jungle. Gabriela was no longer a modest girl. She was now an advocate of those with corrupt souls who used her for profit and gain. In the eyes of Gabriela, the unconventional path was a sacrifice that brought her from Mexico. It was her only way in, a temperamental stepping stone to get started in America, before she would leave it all behind to live the American Dream.

As Gabriela continued to walk along the storefront-filled streets of a run-down Los Angeles neighborhood, she walked with a sense of attentiveness. Living in shadows was a necessity for Gabriela's way of living and a way to secure her freedom. In America, being incognito for the time being was a requirement to preserve her livelihood.

Gabriela was one of many who had come from Mexico to live a life as a mule. For many, it was a way to get in or get started, but for some, it was all they had. This life lived in shadows was never a life Gabriela had imagined or dreamed of living. It had found her, and fate seemed to have guided and brought Gabriela down a challenging path in order to provoke and test her as she tried to discover herself in an attempt to fulfill her destiny.

As Gabriela walked into a restaurant used as a front for criminal activities to drop off a brick-sized package of cocaine she kept in her handbag, she constantly looked over her shoulder and wouldn't look anyone in the eyes. She hid behind her hair. The life was unpleasant for Gabriela, but having courage was what kept her vigorous.

After dropping off the last package for the day in an undisclosed location within the restaurant, Gabriela left and returned to the Mexican barrio where she lived. This was the product from one of Gabriela's friends, who had become her ticket into America.

6

Sonora State, El Norte, was now home. The past was left far behind; Gabriela's home in Tehuacán, her mother, her brother, her modest life, friends, and family. At first it was extremely difficult for the naïve eighteen-year-old to leave her mother, but Gabriela's mother, no matter how fearful she was of the north and border cities, respected Gabriela's ambitious desires to start over and live a better life. Unbeknownst to her Gabriela had bigger plans, her eyes were fixed further away, beyond the desert, somewhere over the border, in America. Deep inside her soul, she felt and knew that she was destined to be there. Making it to El Norte was only the beginning.

For now, though, Gabriela sat on a stone wall overlooking the zócalo, observing her new home, and its people. She began writing in her journal all that she felt and saw. The world seemed bleak and unpleasant, but Gabriela was able to see the beauty in everything: a child, a smile, laughter, or even a simple kiss. Even within the lonely people, both the old and young who walked anonymously within a sea of faces, Gabriela was able to see oceans of love and peace. It was uplifting for Gabriela, who was also one of many characters playing out their unscripted roles in this so-called game of life. Where the road would go, Gabriela didn't know, but she was willing to follow it. Ultimately the road carried on into the vast street markets filled with a variety of vendors, bodegas, and an array of cafes and cantinas.

As Gabriela strolled through the market, she was fixated with the artisanship and appreciated the Mexican ideals and styles that had been passed down from generation to generation. The craftsmanship of all the handmade Mexican products she observed filled her heart with a sense of pride for her heritage, as she continued to meander and haggle with local artisans. As time began to take control of Gabriela, she maneuvered her way through the congested labyrinth of the street market until she reached her final destination.

Café Solano was a bohemian nook filled with local artists, musicians and writers. It was a relaxing place to settle into and drift away from all the troubles in the world. Its cozy modern-day Mexican interior décor, and the musician's rhythmic Spanish guitar riffs and soothing lyrics that echoed throughout the café, created a pleasant cove of solace. All Gabriela needed now to complement the setting and mood was a freshly brewed cup of Mexican spiced coffee. It was here where she would meet an old friend from her past, someone who would be able to help Gabriela achieve her dream of getting into America.

After Gabriela got her coffee, she settled down at a table in the back of the café. She checked her watch and smiled. There was still time to kill before her friend arrived, enabling Gabriela to enjoy the cup of coffee, good music and dive into her journal again. Gabriela was in heaven as she sat all alone, lost in her thoughts while she observed her surroundings. The simplicity of life was what Gabriela needed. Time seemed to stop. It seemed just as soon as Gabriela became completely immersed in her thoughts, her friend appeared.

"*Hola, amiga. Cómo estás?*" Fabiola Flores said as she stepped before Gabriela.

"*Hola, amiga. Bien, bien, y tú?*" Gabriela stood up and gave Fabiola a hug.

"*Bien, bien.*" Fabiola sat down beside Gabriela.

Fabiola was a short eighteen-year-old with short straight jet-black hair, full, lush lips, jagged teeth, dark eyes, and thick eyebrows. She wore a red V-neck t-shirt underneath a black hoodie, with the sleeves pulled up to reveal her right forearm tattoo of a black-and-red heart-shaped locked padlock.

"So, what's all this? It looks like you have a lot on your mind." Fabiola took Gabriela's open journal, only to have Gabriela pull it back across the table and close it.

"It's my writing, just . . . just something I enjoy doing in my free time, writing down my thoughts and what I do each day. Ya know, something to look back and reflect on."

"Interesting, but I don't understand why anyone would want to remember what they did in the past. Besides our childhood and all those happy moments, aren't we supposed to forget about the past and move on?" Fabiola provoked Gabriela.

"Well, yes and no. Even though the past could be filled with good and bad experiences, those experiences are what we learn from to help us do better with our lives in the present and in the future." Gabriela emphasized her words with her hands.

"I see. Well, good or bad, I never want to look back." Fabiola sat up straight, took out a loose page from Gabriela's journal, and began to recite Gabriela's words. "'Even in times of distress, and in times of joy, I sometimes wonder what is it all for, this life, this path, this journey I seem to forever be lost on . . .' Very powerful words. So, are you lost at the moment?" Fabiola said with a slight smile.

"Perhaps, but that's why you're here now, to help me find my way."

"Yes, yes, I know, but let's talk first, ya know, we haven't seen each other for a while. Let's talk about other things, like what you've been doing in Tehuacán since I moved, this boyfriend that left you, and other stuff, before I explain how we'll get into America." Fabiola handed Gabriela the loose page.

"Okay, but what do you want to hear about first?"

"This boyfriend of yours, I'm sorry, ex-boyfriend. What's his name again?" Fabiola leaned in close.

"Hernando."

"Hernando. I don't like that name, but go on, tell me more about Hernando."

"Well, he was my first love, a musician. He used to play the guitar and sing to me all the time. We were perfect together, always happy. He was gentle with me, took care of me and was funny. He always made me laugh, but . . ."

"So, what happened? Hernando cheated on you?" Fabiola incited Gabriela.

"No, well, I'm not sure if there was another girl, but he just left one day, to go and play with a band. He didn't even say goodbye. He just left me with a letter."

"Ah, men. Never trust men. Men are evil, and weak-minded fools. Men are weak like children and live like animals. It's so easy to manipulate and use men, 'cause men only think about one thing—many women. Just tempt them, and they are in your control," Fabiola said passionately, causing Gabriela to laugh.

"Yes, *amiga*, yes. Especially after what happened with me. Anyway, I don't even want to talk about it right now. How about you? How have you been since we last spoke, before I moved up here to live with my aunt and uncle?"

"Free. It's different living up here near the border. Your dreams seem more alive and achievable, being this close to America. That's why I can't wait until we go. You see, *amiga*, we have a reason to go. Some people work on a farm, some people work in a *cocina*, some people work in an office or a school, others for corporations or some work in the streets, struggling to sell whatever they can. Ya know, I've never wanted to do any of that, to have to work, and work, and work, like some mule on a farm, for what, just to make enough money in order to feed and take care of my family. That's not life, that's not living. To live like some slave, constantly working all day and all night, being told what to do, how to do it, being so exhausted by the end of the day that you don't have the energy to think straight or play with your children, and in the end never making or having enough money. Humans were not put on this earth to work! No, humans were put on this earth, for . . ."

"For what?" Gabriela asked as Fabiola searched for the right words.

"To be happy; happiness is living."

"Yes, I agree, happiness is the key to living a better life."

"Mexico is one of the most beautiful places in the world. Our roots run deep, and our land is filled with so much beauty and history. I cherish it and hope to someday pass it onto others and the next generation, not only here, but further away in the United States and foreign lands, where people don't know Mexico or its people. The road to happiness is what you and I are now on, which has led us to the north. It isn't the end, it's the beginning. Don't you agree, *amiga?*"

"Yes, but tell me more about these people who are going to help us get into America, and what exactly we have to do."

"They're a couple of *coyotajes* I met in a bar one day. Not too handsome, but they're alright, they mean well. They're always looking for people like us who are desperate to get into America," Fabiola stated.

"Yes, I'm definitely willing to do whatever it takes to get into America so that I can start over and live a better life, but I don't think I'm desperate. I'd say I'm more ambitious. Ya know, to take the riskier path in order to get to where I want to get."

"Yes, I agree, but they see it as being desperate and try to take advantage, so don't take it too personal, and stay strong. Don't worry, either. I made it very clear to them that the both of us aren't some ignorant girls, desperate to get out of the poverty we live in."

"So, what did you tell them?"

"The truth, that both of us are good students who can't afford college, were denied a visa to get into America, so we looked at the best options for us, which was to go in without having to pay a fee."

"I blame myself for not being able to get the visa. I'm terrible with interviews; that's one of the reasons I haven't been able to get a decent job. And not having a father in my life for so many years didn't look good when I applied for my visa either," Gabriela said.

"Yeah, well, what's done is done, and now we have to make the best of our situation. Just think of the better opportunities we'll have in America. I hear that what the average person makes in a month here, you can make in one day in America."

"Really? Wow. Explain to me again what it is we have to do?"

"Well, first of all, it's better than staying here, trying to make the money to pay some other coyotes we don't know, or waiting for the *la bestia* to come with the Central and South Americans, and other Mexicans, to bring us to the border or find someone else to help us. Normally, coyotes would cost around thirty thousand pesos or so. That's a lot of money, and considering we don't have that kind of money to pay them, that's why it's best we cross the border as mules."

"A mule?"

"Yeah, a mule. Ya know, someone who transports drugs into the United States."

Gabriela choked on her coffee. "Drugs? And how will we do that?" Gabriela struggled to speak as she cleared her throat. She then began to fiddle around with the pages of her journal.

"Well, from what these coyotes told me, you and I will have to have the drugs taped to our stomachs and then, after crossing the border, we'll have to bring the drugs to some organized gang living in California. As compensation, we'll have to work for them. But don't worry, it's not forever. The coyotes made it clear that they'll let us go once they feel we've worked off our debt for being brought to the United States."

Gabriela turned away. Feelings of regret began to consume her. Fabiola reached out to hold both of Gabriela's hands and looked her in the eyes.

"Hey, listen, if this is starting to feel too dangerous for you, if you want out, you're free to go right now. I can find someone else to go with me. If you still want to get into America on your own, know how difficult it will be to go back living in poverty, trying to make the money on your own to pay for some other coyotes, or get on the train with all the others, trying to get to the border, who end up getting robbed and assaulted by gangs, or end up caught by border patrol or dead by trying to walk through the desert. If that's what you want, good luck. Right now we both have a free ticket in. The way I see it, we're lucky, because usually mules have to go on an airplane or drive through border checkpoints, and a majority of the time, they get caught and sent back. We just have to have the drugs taped to us when we cross the border with the coyotes."

"Yeah, you're right about this being better financially, but I don't know."

"Hey, listen, chasing dreams isn't easy. Sometimes you have to take chances in life. Being poor is a setback, and not being eligible to get a visa has been frustrating, but we can't let failures hold us back. This is an opportunity we both have now. And yeah, it's risky, but the way I see it, we'll get in. That's all that matters."

Fabiola's words left Gabriela in a contemplative state. The worst possible scenarios plagued her mind, but Gabriela knew deep in her heart that it was now or never. Fabiola squeezed Gabriela's hands tighter.

"Okay. So, where do we have to meet the coyotes before they take us in?"

"We have to go to Tijuana, stay there for one day, and then they'll take us and others into California, at night."

"That's pretty far away from here. So I guess we have to leave early in the morning?"

"Yeah, but not too early. The bus station is right down the street."

"So are you going to spend the night with me at my aunt and uncle's?"

"Yeah, just like we spoke about. Did you tell them yet?"

"No, not yet. I'm not too sure how to tell them, especially since they'll tell my mother right away. I think I'm just going to tell them what you told me to say, that I'm going to travel with you for a while, or just leave them a note instead."

"Well, if you want, I can talk to them with you."

"No, you won't have to do that. I'll be fine. Okay, *amiga*, how about we go to the bus station now to get the tickets, before there are no more seats left?"

"Okay, yeah, if you're ready to go now, let's go."

"Yes, let's go, *amiga*."

Fabiola let go of her hands. Gabriela then picked up her journal and cup of coffee and stood up alongside Fabiola.

The two *amigas* left the café. Even if the road ahead was risky, it felt liberating. El Norte, the gateway to America, was now an open book waiting to be written.

7

Gabriela sang a Spanish lullaby while beams of light from the rising sun shined in through the open window. The rays lit Gabriela's hands as she packed away memories from her past, along with the necessities for the future, into her bag laid out on her bed. The unscripted path that lay ahead would be unpredictable. As Gabriela prepared to depart, she was filled with courage and perseverance for the open road ahead. There was hope in the United States of America. But before leaving her past and those she loved, Gabriela wrote and left a farewell letter for her Tío Emilio and her Tía Rosa, and another for them to send to her mother back home in Tehuacán.

That was it. Without hesitating or looking back, Gabriela walked out the door with Fabiola and headed to the bus station, where the two got on the bus bound for Tijuana.

Tijuana was an impoverished, run-down, crime-infested border city, occupied by various gangs and drug cartels. It was here, within the heart of the city, where Gabriela and Fabiola would begin their exodus to America, but before departing, they would first go to Casa Roja.

Casa Roja's architectural features were of the traditional Mexican Pueblo style, with a façade coated with aged layers of clay and plaster smeared with faded red paint. It was a mediocre cantina, used as a front for criminal activities. Gabriela crept in behind Fabiola, who led the way through the vast cantina filled with the scum of Tijuana. It was a diverse blend of criminals, whores, the poor, and outcasts who found solace in the company of sin and live Spanish *guitarra* music. There was a sense of anticipation for the unexpected. Gabriela had never imagined being within such an immoral place. She turned away from the belligerent eyes that observed her from the shadows.

Gabriela and Fabiola were approached by a rugged-looking bandido, walking down a flight of old, creaky wooden stairs.

"*Hola, muchachas.*" Of average height, the man had a poorly aged, scruffy face, with an eyebrow piercing and two gold-capped teeth. He spoke with a raspy voice.

"*Hola, Juanito, cómo estás?*" Fabiola greeted him with a smile.

"*Bien, bien,*" Juanito said, brushing his ungroomed dark hair back. He looked from Fabiola to Gabriela, who turned away.

"*Ven, ven, vamos, muchachas.*"

Juanito gestured with his hand, beckoning Gabriela and Fabiola to follow him up the stairs. Gabriela could see Juanito's gun, which was tucked in the back of his jeans and hidden underneath his shirt, as she climbed up the stairs.

After ascending to the second floor, which overlooked the entire cantina, Gabriela and Fabiola followed Juanito through the private area to the back, where another young, rugged-looking bandido and an older robust individual awaited them at a table. The younger man was the first to stand up and greet both Gabriela and Fabiola, introducing himself as Julio. He pulled out chairs for both of them. After taking a seat, Gabriela and Fabiola were introduced to, and modestly greeted by, Señor Mariano Cruz, who was the head of operations.

A haze of cigarette smoke filled the dense air, together with clicking noises from the slowly rotating ceiling fan, faded voices, and the echoes of Spanish *guitarra* music. Cruz remained seated and only greeted Gabriela and Fabiola with his gaze and a nod while he smoked his cigarette and sipped his mezcal. Cruz was of average height and build. He had piercing dark eyes, a wrinkled Pug face, and well-groomed thick white hair that complemented the white chest hair sprouting out from his loose-fitting button-down cabana shirt. He was an orderly and very methodical individual, a modest businessman who was wise beyond his years. Mariano Cruz also had ties with affiliates of the crime syndicate Nada Mas during its infancy. Everyone patiently waited for Cruz to speak. Meanwhile, Gabriela observed her surroundings.

Juanito and Julio's guns rested atop of the table as they socialized with Fabiola. Over Gabriela's right shoulder, towards the back, inside a door left slightly open, were two young women sitting down next to tables filled with scales, measuring utensils, plastic baggies filled with cocaine, and bowls filled with some sort of liquid. A taste of things to come.

"So, these are the two girls?" Cruz's voice was deep and calming. Gabriela turned back towards the table and clutched her bag on her lap.

"*Ay, sí, estas son Fabiola y Gabriela.*"

"*Bien.* So, Fabiola and Gabriela, it is my understanding that the both of you are willing to work as mules?"

"*Sí*, Señor Cruz. We're both willing to do whatever it is you need us to do."

Fabiola spoke as if she really cared for Mariano Cruz and his business. Unfortunately, her words weren't worth the effort, since Mariano Cruz was already suspicious of Fabiola and Gabriela. They were like most of the young girls willing to work for him—strangers who represented a possible benefit or a possible liability. Cruz keenly observed Gabriela fidgeting with her fingers and her feet.

"Okay, okay, *mija*," Mariano Cruz silenced Fabiola. He turned to Gabriela. "And how about you, *mi ángel tímida*. Are you willing to risk everything and make the necessary sacrifices?" Cruz looked down at Gabriela's hands clutching her bag, causing Gabriela to loosen her grip and remove her hands.

"*Sí, sí, señor.* Whatever you need me to do, I'm willing to do it. I feel very thankful to be in the position I'm in now." Gabriela sat up straight and looked Cruz in the eye. He smoked his cigarette and studied her and body language.

"Those eyes, my God, such strong, beautiful eyes. Filled with so much ambition and desire. I like that. Deep within those beautiful eyes, I can see a courageous heart and soul, determined to conquer all that awaits her. Pisces?"

"Um, *sí, sí*, I'm a Pisces."

"Creative, sensitive, mysterious, but most importantly, adaptable. In life, it's not the strongest or the fittest that survive and evolve in the wild, it's the most adaptable." Cruz took a sip of his mezcal and turned towards Juanito and Julio. "I think she'll be fine. I see ambition in those eyes." He turned towards Fabiola. "Lucky for you, *mija*, I see desire in your eyes as well."

Cruz took a drag from his cigarette and continued to study his mules. A haze of smoke billowed up between himself and Fabiola. She turned towards Gabriela, who sighed. Fabiola smiled, putting Gabriela a bit more at ease.

"But, before I make my final decision and put all my trust into the both of you, I want to tell you a little bit, not only about myself, but also about how I run my business, and what to expect. Unlike others in this business, I'm a compassionate and extremely reasonable man. I understand the nature of this business, and how those who do the dirty work are seen as expendable little pawns. I only hope for the best of my mules. You're like my children, my little *niñas*, whom no father would ever consent to throwing out to the wolves."

Cruz looked away from Fabiola's tainted face and jagged teeth. He admired Gabriela's perky breasts, her beautiful dark eyes, and observed her hands, which still tightly clutched her bag, while he continued to speak.

"Your only job for me is to transport drugs into the United States, and then deliver them to my associate in California. After that, two other mules who are already with my associate, who've already walked down the same path before you, will be sent back with additional profits, not wired to my account. After spending three to six months paying off your debt, the choice is yours to come back here with other mules, or stay in the United States. It's my gift to those who work for me—freedom."

"Ah, now, who is my associate you'll be working for until your debt for being brought into the United States is paid off? His name is Salas. Along with his drug trafficking network, he also runs a prostitution ring. But don't worry, you two will not be forced into that. It has been made very clear to Salas that my mules are only mules, and not whores. "

"I warn you, though, Salas the Mexicano may be a tyrant, especially if you do not follow his strict rules. He has a thing with being on time. Among other things, it seems to be one of the few attributes we share, along with discipline, the number one rule we both abide.

Cruz paused, took another drag from his cigarette and then a sip of his mezcal.

"Now, here are some positive aspects. *Primero*, since I have a special place in my heart for those who are willing to make the necessary sacrifices and risk everything, just to get into the United States, to live a better life, you will be provided with a free ride and safe passage into the United States as compensation for working for me. As a Mexicano, I feel that not only have we been robbed out of our land by the United States, but our people deserve to live freely on stolen land that is rightfully ours. "

"Of course I understand the pros and cons of leaving Mexico to live in the United States, that those Mexicanos who go may end up with more money, but no soul. Although there are many opportunities in the United States to live a better life, you may never see your family again. So I also ask myself the same question every ambitious Mexican asks themselves before they venture out across the border, into the unknown of the United States: is it worth it? "

"But before you answer that, you must first understand that there is always that temptation of America, to be sucked into a black hole of mass media manipulation, losing your heart and soul and becoming robotic. A product of corporate America rich with abusing and taking advantage of its immigrants, especially illegal Mexicanos, the backbone of America's way of living. Without our services, such as working long hours for minimum wage, Americans would no longer have their comforts, clean homes, child care, exquisite meals at fine restaurants, well-built homes, and well-kept lawns and gardens. "

"That's why, before I cast my innocents out into the evil empire to live amongst the wolves, I want to make sure that those I am helping reach their dream are mentally strong. Not only do you have to be mentally strong to work for me as mules, but you also need to be mentally strong to live in the United States. I'm telling you this because I care not only for the well-being of my mules, but for all Mexicanos and Latin Americans I traffic into the United States with my network of coyotes. Life is a gift and very precious. Without a strong mind, you'll be lost. "

"Please don't feel misled by all I say about this unconventional life I live and, yet, how I speak so compassionately and negatively. It's all part of the game I play: to be a saint and a sinner."

Gabriela loosened her grip on her bag. Mariano Cruz smiled.

"As for this drug trafficking business, it's new to me. It's just a favor for my associate, Salas, since he knows my system is flawless. Not only do my coyotes have a secure passage to take across the border, but they are in sync with the border patrol time shifts, which creates a window of opportunity to make it into the United States, undetected by the few agents who have their backs turned. Knowing there should be no worries when crossing the border, he made me an offer I couldn't refuse. As for you two transporting drugs for me— once you're in the United States, sorry, *niñas*, you're on your own."

After Cruz finished his long rhetoric, there was a sigh of relief. Fabiola looked at Gabriela and smiled. Gabriela returned her smile and glanced at Cruz, who smoked his cigarette and continued to speak.

"It all sounds so simple and easy, but here's where it gets interesting, and we test my trust in you. Of course, both of you look like two lovely, trustworthy girls, but as compassionate as I am, I can also be a tyrant if my trust is broken. That's why, before we continue any further, as a precaution I must first have all the names and addresses of your closest family members. If the two of you decide to run off with my supply or happen to lose it and not show up at Salas's door, or later on, after you're free, my name or this business is ever mentioned, those close to you, who you love so dearly, will have to be terminated."

Mariano Cruz's daunting words sent chilling waves of fear throughout Gabriela's body. Thoughts of her mother, brother, Tío Emilio and Tía Rosa inundated Gabriela's mind. The worst fate imaginable could befall her family. Gabriela tightly grasped her bag.

"That's just the way business is, *niñas*. Now you should ask yourselves, how badly do you want to get into the United States, huh? Is the blood of those close to you, like Mamá or Papá, worth it? Think about that for a moment before we proceed."

Gabriela pondered. Was it worth it to risk the lives of those she loved just so she could get into America and live her dream? Fear of the unknown awaiting her told her no, but the support she saw in Fabiola's doe eyes convinced Gabriela to continue. Without Fabiola, Gabriela wouldn't be where she was now, with a "free" ticket into America.

"So, do we understand each other?" Cruz asked firmly.

"*Sí, sí*, Señor Cruz," Fabiola said. Cruz turned towards Gabriela.

"*Bien.* And how about you, *mi ángel tímida?*"

Gabriela looked away while clutching her bag once again. She remained idle and hesitant while she contemplated her final decision. After imagining the worst possible outcome, she slowly looked up to find consolation again in Fabiola's eyes.

"Listen, *mi ángel tímida*, and listen good. What you're about to embark on is not for the weak. It's okay if you're not sure and do not want this. You're free to go back home to Mamá and Papá."

Gabriela turned away from Fabiola and pulled her bag closer to her body. Cruz was able to read Gabriela's insecurities and weak persona like a book. This caused him to begin reconsidering using Gabriela as a mule, but he admired the ambition and burning desire he saw in Gabriela's eyes, causing him to provoke her once again, in order to get what he wanted.

"And if you choose to not go with my supply, the price for my coyote services is thirty thousand pesos, with a wait of three to six months. Knowing your financial situation, I would think you're sitting on a winning lottery ticket."

Fabiola turned towards Gabriela and encouraged her with convincing doe eyes. They cleverly exchanged nonverbal vows while Cruz patiently observed his two prospective mules giving their final consent. All were involved in the same situation, but it was Gabriela who felt the tremendous pressure most. She had to battle with having second thoughts about her involvement as a mule. She didn't want to tarnish her friendship with Fabiola. She also didn't want to diminish her own dreams of crossing the border to live a better life in America and have the opportunity to help provide for her family in Mexico.

"Know what? There's other girls waiting to fill your shoes. Julio, why don't you go get one of them now?" Cruz said nonchalantly. He turned towards

Julio, who began to stand up but stopped midway.

"*Espera*, I can do it," Gabriela answered as she continued to look deep into Fabiola's eyes. Fabiola smiled and turned towards Mariano Cruz, while Julio sat back down.

"*Bien, mi ángel tímida*. Let me give you a little advice before we begin. Your body language is weak. You're a very pretty girl who could use her beauty in America to take advantage of others and help you get what you want. The way you sit there, so nervous and scared, is a sign of weakness and vulnerability. You will need to work on that. People will take advantage of you, especially those you will be associating with. Whether you're carrying my supply or carrying for Salas, police will pick you out in a crowd, just like that. And we don't want that. Lucky for you, I see fire in your eyes, a strong spirit hiding inside such a fragile eggshell, waiting to break free. All you need is a little more push."

Mariano Cruz then picked up his .45-caliber revolver, cocked it and pointed it at Gabriela. As Gabriela looked down the barrel of the gun, a sudden surge of terror flowed up her spine. Just as she looked away, Cruz slid the gun across the table.

"Here, take it."

Gabriela hesitated, then grasped her bag and looked at the gun in confusion.

"Here, I'll make it easier for you." Cruz picked up the gun, emptied the bullets, and handed it to Gabriela, who let go of her bag to grab the handle of the gun. Gabriela slowly pulled the gun towards herself. Cruz studied Gabriela's demeanor. It was a test that Gabriela didn't understand. She began to feel more at ease the longer she held it.

"Get used to seeing guns, because the people you'll be working for will always have them. They will not hesitate to impose fear upon you or even use it before you on another, or God forbid, on you. And maybe, just maybe, at some point, if you find yourself in a desperate situation of, say, life and death and you have access to one of these guns to take and use, I wouldn't want you to hesitate and be too fearful to pick one up and use it. It's just the nature of the beast within us all. You need to walk like the lion I see in your eyes."

Cruz reached out to take the gun back from Gabriela. Her hands were moist and tense. Before Gabriela even had a chance to compose herself, Cruz stood up and beckoned the two girls to follow him.

"*Ven, ven, mijas*, I think we're done here, time for the preparations before your departure."

Mariano Cruz walked towards the closed door located in the back, followed by Gabriela and Fabiola. Inside the adjacent room were two other mules, a table filled with prepackaged cocaine, and an empty table to which Gabriela and Fabiola were escorted.

After Gabriela and Fabiola sat down, they were given a piece of paper and pen to write down the names and addresses of their closest family members. Gabriela hesitated again before writing down her mother's name, but the thought of a better life motivated her to continue writing. A rugged *hombre* walked towards Gabriela and Fabiola with the prepackaged cocaine and instructed both of them to take their shirts off. Fabiola took her shirt off with no sense of hesitation, while Gabriela momentarily stared at the man's childish smile before slowly removing her shirt. Once she had exposed her feminine curves, the hombre began to tape the prepackaged cocaine to each of their torsos. Gabriela cringed with disgust and discomfort as the unwelcoming hands grazed her breasts while the tape was wrapped around her torso like a Burmese python. After being strapped with the drugs, Gabriela and Fabiola put their shirts back on.

"How's it feel, *mijas*? Like a lover's arms wrapped around you? You better get used to it, because you're gonna be like that for a while."

Gabriela finished writing down her family's contact information. She and Fabiola handed the pieces of paper to Cruz, who curiously observed each one.

"*Bien*. Let's hope I never have to visit any of them," Cruz threatened as he put the papers in his pocket. Then he handed both of the girls an envelope.

"These are for you two. Inside you'll find all the necessary information: Salas's contact number and address, which is where you will deliver my supply. There is also an emergency contact number to call if one of you ends up in some sort of trouble. Part of my coyote network is based in Los Angeles, where you will be. They will help you with anything. As a treat for my pretty little mules, there's also fifteen hundred American dollars. Try not to spend it all at once!"

Gabriela and Fabiola looked inside their envelopes. Gabriela ran her fingers through the money. The cash was beyond any amount she had ever had.

"Now, do either of you have any questions before we finish?"

There was silence as the girls counted the money. They looked at each other with concern. The expectations of them were higher than what they had initially expected.

Mariano Cruz enjoyed the happiness he saw on the faces of the new wave of Mexican migrants whose services would provide him with much financial gain. Their happiness was a key to his success as a businessman for the people. Without them, Cruz wouldn't have a business, and without him, they wouldn't have an opportunity to pursue a better life.

"*Bien*," Mariano Cruz concluded.

Once Gabriela and Fabiola were properly equipped with instructions and guidelines to follow, they left Casa Roja with Juanito and Julio for an undisclosed location. There they would meet with the other migrants who would also be crossing into the United States. There were eleven Latin Americans from South and Central America. Most of them were young. One had a baby, and there was also one who was as old as an *abuelito*, who had nothing to lose. In their passive eyes and their tired faces, Gabriela could see the hardships they must've gone through already in life. She could also see the anticipation of living a better life in America. After being herded together, the migrants were loaded into a van, and in darkness, underneath the night sky and the full moon, they were brought to the undisclosed border crossing.

<u>8</u>

On the second floor of the Over the Rainbow daycare center, there was one of many business establishments used throughout Los Angeles as a front for drug trafficking and prostitution operations. It was here where Gabriela would pay off her debt for being brought to America. Although she had finally reached her destination with some of the other migrants, she was all alone. Fabiola Flores, unfortunately, had been detained and sent back to Mexico. All Gabriela had now were those who worked for her new benefactor, Salas.

The sight before her was now routine. A crew of four gang members cut, weighed, and packaged kilos of cocaine while the babies wailed. The two minions, Mendez and Munoz, overlooked the operations. Three illegal Mexican women who also worked as narcotics mules comforted the babies. One of the whores was escorting a customer up the stairs to the third-floor brothel. They comprised the malevolent atmosphere of which Gabriela was now an integral part. It was her temporary prison until she was able to pay off her debt. Once paid, she would be able to leave it all behind, with no strings attached. At least, that's what Gabriela had been told.

For now, she had to accept the reality of loading handbags with personal items and narcotics as a way for mules to smuggle drugs, as well as loading diaper bags with bricks of cocaine or taping baggies of cocaine around the torsos of the babies to hide underneath their clothes. The babies used weren't kidnapped, but brought across the border, or came from illegal immigrant women who were used as breeders. As for the mules, they would pose as the babies' mothers or nannies and carry them along with the hidden narcotics to drop-off locations that were usually in the bathrooms of restaurants or retail stores.   After Gabriela watched two of the three mules each get handed a baby and a diaper bag, she became lost in Munoz's eyes. Munoz seductively licked his lips and stared at Gabriela. She looked away and down while the two mules with the babies and diaper bags walked by. After they left, Gabriela and the other mule stood before Mendez and Munoz, who handed them their handbags. As Gabriela grabbed her bag from Munoz he continued to lustfully stare at her, blowing Gabriela a taunting kiss. Gabriela looked away, took the handbag, then turned around and walked out the door to make her daily drop-off.

Gabriela walked incognito. Even though Gabriela's life in America was very dark, criminal and unpredictable, for her safety, she kept her illegal status anonymous. Fortunately for her, the organized gang she was working for was disciplined: a branch of Nada Mas. Each day Gabriela was sent out, she would make two to four drop-offs, depending on the quantity of narcotics being exchanged. Drop-offs were usually made in undisclosed locations and left for other mules or drug dealers from other gangs who did business with Salas's organization. It was a flawless system, diligently mapped out.

Although walking through the streets as an illegal immigrant carrying narcotics was very daunting, the moment she walked into the bathroom stall of a restaurant, making the final drop-off for the day, Gabriela felt relief. Each day, she lifted up the cover of the toilet's tank, took out the brick of cash and replaced it with a brick of cocaine, and put the toilet tank cover back on, brought closure to a day filled with caution and fear. Afterwards, Gabriela would stop at a nearby park to relax before returning.

The park was one of the few places where Gabriela found peace. Although the handbag filled with bricks of cash reminded her of the dark life she now lived, a mother and a child strolling through the park hand and hand gave her a reflection of the better life she yearned for. Unfortunately, time was scarce, so Gabriela would savor what little time she had left before heading back.

After Gabriela walked through the second floor of the daycare, past crying babies, whores and gang members, to a back room, she was unexpectedly confronted by Salas.

Salas the Mexicano, also known as Pelochas, was a dictatorial tyrant who didn't accept any excuses—unsurprising, given his association with Nada Mas during its infancy. He sat tense and flushed. Gabriela could see the sweat marinating on his bald head. Deep within his cold dark eyes she could see that she was the source of his infuriation.

Finding strength, Gabriela began to walk towards Salas, Mendez, and Munoz. Each step reminded her of how Salas treated women who disrespected him: who didn't do their job, tried to steal, or tried to leave him and the criminal lifestyle. Some of the women bore scars from cigarettes, knives or sulfuric acid, while others joined the faithful departed. Gabriela knew she had to stay strong.

All sense of composure was surpassed by Salas, as Gabriela stepped before the table where he sat smoking a cigarette. Gabriela stood stoic. She focused on his cigarette, the excess smoke and ashes raining down into an ashtray, until Salas pointed to Gabriela's handbag and gestured for her to take out what was inside.

Gabriela removed the bricks of cash and placed them down on the table, waiting patiently as Mendez and Munoz counted the money with a cash-counting machine.

After Mendez and Munoz finished, Salas motioned to Gabriela to take a seat.

"*Cómo estás?*"

"*Bien.*"

"*Bueno*, so, where have you been? You're over an hour late."

Gabriela hesitated. It wasn't the first time she was late when returning from drop-offs, but it was the first time that Salas was the one to confront her. Usually Mendez or Munoz would discipline her, or anyone else who had broken or disobeyed strict protocols. Gabriela could see in Salas's eyes that he wasn't going to be lenient.

"Making my drop-offs. The buses were running late today, and then I . . . I stopped to eat, because I was hungry and—"

Salas smacked Gabriela across the face. Gabriela held her bruised face within the palms of her tear-filled hands.

"Three! Three times you've been late! You know how strict I am with being on time! Every time you're late, you have an excuse! This time it's the bus being late, and you're hungry. Next time you starve like the mule you are, because when you're late, I get a feeling that you're up to no good, you selfish little whore."

As Gabriela sobbed, Salas signaled Mendez and Munoz to leave. Gabriela looked at the fiery red tip of the cigarette he held out before her.

Gabriela tensed up as Salas stood up to condemn her with his cigarette and open hand. Mendez and Munoz walked out of the room, closing the door behind them, leaving Salas and Gabriela alone in the dark.

9

Inside a safe house on a cool midsummer's night, Gabriela woke up and crept out of bed. In the room were other illegal immigrants sleeping on mattresses laid out on the floor. It was a way of life for those who lived in shadows. Gabriela had walked the same path in order to get into America, and it were their differences, the individual struggles they all experienced, that created a bond and inspired them to carry on, no matter what barriers they faced.

Gabriela walked into the bathroom. She felt relaxed as she relieved herself. While she washed her hands, she looked at her reflection in the mirror. Along with the cigarette scars burned into Gabriela's forearm, the left side of Gabriela's face was still bruised from Salas's confrontation. It was a reminder of the dark life she lived. As Gabriela ran her fingertips through her hair and down to caress the bruise on her face, she knew that she was one of the fortunate ones whose life had been spared. She also knew that with one more mistake, she would end up dead.

For now, Gabriela remained poised. She walked into the kitchen, where an illegal immigrant woman held a crying baby while singing a Spanish lullaby. Gabriela walked by, smiling at the woman while she headed towards the sink for a glass of water. As Gabriela sipped her water, she shivered, sensing a disturbing presence. She stood still and listened carefully as she put the half-filled glass of water on the counter, then crept into the front room, peeking through the curtains and out the window.

Gabriela's eyes lit up. She turned to run away. ICE officers came crashing in the front door on one of their unannounced roadside raids. Before Gabriela had a chance to wake any of the others, ICE officers stormed into the safe house. Illegal immigrants began to panic and run in every direction.

Gabriela dashed up to the third floor alone. Out a window she flew, down a fire escape and through the darkness of an alleyway, only to turn a corner and be stunned by a light.

# # #

"Mama, Mama, it's okay, it's just a dream, it's just a dream."

Sarita embraced Gabriela as she woke up in a cold sweat, panting. The two sat close together in the bed. After Gabriela calmed down, she held Sarita in her arms, pulling her in closer. Sarita lay on her mother's lap as Gabriela ran her fingers through her hair.

"It's gonna be okay, Mama. It was just a nightmare, you're safe now."

"I know, Sarita, I know. I'm sorry if I scared you."

"Um, it's okay, Mama. We all have nightmares sometimes."

"Yes, we do, but don't worry. I'm fine now, so you can go back to bed."

"I will, Mama, I will." Sarita closed her eyes, and Gabriela continued to run her fingers through Sarita's hair. She began to sing a Spanish lullaby.

Then there was silence as Gabriela and Sarita lay limp on the bed. Just as they dozed off, the two were awakened by banging and someone screaming.

Sarita jolted up. "Mama, what's going on?"

"Shh, shh. It's okay, Sarita. It will be gone chor-teely," Gabriela said while caressing Sarita's head.

"Is he okay? What's going on over there?"

"He'll be fine, Sarita, he'll be fine."

For about two minutes straight, the reclusive man who lived next door screamed while throwing and breaking things and banging on walls. It wasn't a surprise to Gabriela and Sarita, because it wasn't the first time. They just never knew when to expect it. What was more disturbing for Sarita than not knowing who he was or what was wrong with him was the fact that she had never seen or met him. He lived right next door.

10

Sarita walked along the curb of Newark Avenue in front of Oasis Daycare, while trying to keep balanced with outstretched arms. Each attempt to successfully walk the length of the daycare storefront with her eyes closed was a struggle, and she often stepped on the edge of the curb and landed in the street. But her persistence was strong. She was attempting to occupy time as she waited for Gabriela to arrive.

Unbeknownst to Sarita, Gabriela smiled as she watched her antics from the opposite side of the street. The innocence of a child somehow always seemed to bring about a constant state of bliss. It were the little moments in life that Gabriela cherished.

After admiring Sarita from a distance, Gabriela strolled across Newark Avenue. As she furtively got closer, she could hear Sarita softly singing a Spanish lullaby as she continued to take slow, unbalanced toe-to-heel steps with her outstretched arms. After many unsuccessful attempts to walk the length of the curb in front of the daycare building, she was finally within a few steps of reaching the end. Gabriela stepped onto the sidewalk beside Sarita while greeting the two daycare counselors who were standing in front of the entrance doors with two other children.

Gabriela watched Sarita bite down on her bottom lip as she slowly stepped forward, closer to the end. To watch Sarita take small leaps of faith in life alone was sometimes hard, but it was also comforting to Gabriela, because it showed that Sarita was bold enough to take risks. There was hope, and Gabriela knew that one day Sarita would evolve and blossom like a butterfly that would audaciously fly out into the world all alone. Gabriela knew to enjoy every moment of Sarita's life. To let her experience life and take small leaps of faith on her own every so often, so that she could evolve into someone independently strong.

After watching Sarita struggle and fail many times, Gabriela finally had the pleasure to witness Sarita successfully conquer the length of the curb. After Sarita landed her final step, she opened her eyes with a smile and then spun around. Standing behind her with an even bigger smile was Gabriela.

"Mama!" Sarita called out. She leaped off of the curb onto the sidewalk. Gabriela stood with arms outstretched for Sarita, who in turn ran towards her. After they embraced, Sarita stepped back and looked up at Gabriela. Gabriela ran her fingers through Sarita's hair.

"So how was your day, Chor-tee?" Gabriela asked as Sarita twisted her right foot into the sidewalk while she looked around.

"Umm, umm, we, we painted and then, and then we played this game and, and . . . it was so much fun, you should've been there!" Sarita's voice gradually rose.

"Well, it sounds like someone had a really good time today. I wish I could say the same. I especially wish I could've been there for this game."

"Um, well, maybe next time you could come."

"Well, we'll see, Chor-tee. If the boss gives me the day off next time, I'll be there. Until then, you could tell me all about this game and the rest of your day on the way home, okay?"

Gabriela reached around Sarita's left shoulder while she turned around to stand beside Sarita. As they stood side by side, they said their goodbyes to the daycare staff and other children and began the walk home.

After walking to the end of Newark Avenue, Gabriela and Sarita turned to start down Central Avenue, which led them to The Heights District of Jersey City, where their home was. They walked beside a rising wall of stone that ran along the western sidewalk of Central Avenue and led them to Leonard Gordon Park, also known as Mosquito Park. By the time they got to the park they were so exhausted from the summer heat that they took a moment to rest on a park bench before continuing the walk home.

Both felt at peace. As Sarita sat kicking her feet back and forth, just a few inches above the ground, Gabriela reached down to rub her sore feet. Suddenly from out of nowhere, a butterfly came and landed on Sarita's fingers. They both froze with awe as they felt the spiritual presence the butterfly brought. As the butterfly rested on Sarita's fingertips, while flapping its wings Sarita moved her hand slightly, but the butterfly did not fly away. Gabriela slowly reached down and lifted Sarita's hand, holding it up before Sarita's eyes.

"Beautiful, isn't it?" Gabriela softly said with a smile as she admired Sarita.

"Um, yeah, I like it," Sarita said with a smile.

The Monarch butterfly was fully grown and symmetrically covered with patterns of black, orange, red and yellow. Sarita was entranced as she tilted her head from side to side, trying to get a closer look at the butterfly from every angle. The little things in life and small encounters brought a sense of peace and harmony. For a child's eyes, it brought more than comfort; it illustrated another side of life, one filled with mystique and possibilities. As Sarita continued to observe the butterfly, Gabriela leaned in closer and whispered into her ear.

"Butterflies are one of God's most amazing creatures. They are so small, yet filled with so much beauty—enough beauty to make people as big as us stop to appreciate the little things in life. They are also very brave. They start off as tiny eggs and are born as little caterpillars that have to go out into the world all alone. They travel great distances through vast fields of grass, up enormous trees, all the while being an easy target for their many predators. Eventually they find their destination, and then they hibernate in little cocoons, and then they are reborn. When they finally break free, they are no longer who they once were but someone else. Their experiences in life have changed them into something new, something beautiful, and they are able to fly off into the world all alone as beautiful butterflies. This one is a Monarch. Monarchs are very special because not only are they from Mexico, but they are able to fly from Mexico all the way to the far ends of America. Without faith, this little butterfly wouldn't be. So you see, Sarita, always have faith. Never give up or lose hope, no matter how far or hard the road ahead might be, and someday you will change and evolve like the butterfly."

The two smiled as they watched the butterfly fly away, and then stood up to begin their journey home.

Home in Tehuacán, Mexico, was a special place. Not because it was where Gabriela was born and raised, or because it was the safest place in the world to be, but because there was magic. In the eyes of Gabriela, who was seven years old at the time, the walls weren't as big or strong as the walls of Castillo de Chapultepec, and within those modest walls was a lack of material possessions, but simple lives held together with love. And located within the heart of the *casa* was an energy, which was above all else.

There was a magical aura of peace within the open patio space filled with life such as various plants and flowers, caged parakeets chirping and flapping their wings, and loose chickens clucking and roaming around. Even the soothing breeze that blew in from above, where there was no roof, enabled Gabriela to admire the sun and the moon ascend and descend, the clear blue sky and the billions of stars that filled the night sky creating an enduring sense of euphoria. Overshadowing it all was an awe-inspiring presence that created the magic with rhythmic guitar riffs and a gentle voice, singing sweet lyrics of adoration.

Francisco, Gabriela's father, was a stern yet sappy romantic, a man of average height, with mocha skin, short black-and-gray hair, and a well-aged face that was hard to read. He was a musician who played the acoustic guitar and passionately sang "Mi Niña" to Gabriela, entrancing and beckoning her like a magician to follow the hypnotic tune. His stage was the patio, and his devoted audience was Gabriela. Like the illusionist Francisco was, all he revealed was only a glimpse of all the love he had for Gabriela, and a little bit more that

Gabriela was blind to.

As Francisco's fingertips pressed down on the strings and stepped along the chords, Gabriela slowly walked into the patio area and hid behind the leaves of plants. From Gabriela's perspective, she was alive and free. Francisco's voice continued to seduce Gabriela's heart and soul while she peered out between the open spaces between the leaves. Eventually, she became lost in Francisco's eyes and drawn out into the open space. The exchange of energy between the two was beyond anything the eye could see. It was magic. Francisco sang the final verses and strummed the final chords, wooing his daughter.

"*Hija, hija,* my little butterfly, *ven, ven.*" Francisco beckoned Gabriela to come closer with his open hand. He then used it to caress Gabriela's head. "Before there was you, *hija,* this world, this place, this life . . . everything seemed to be so cold and dark. But God brought you into this world, and with you came light and warmth. God gave you wings so that you could fly."

"Um, really?" Gabriela said ardently with a smile.

"*Sí.* Can't you see your wings, like a butterfly's, so that you could go wherever you want to in the whole world? So, where would you like to go, *hija?*"

As Francisco spoke his final word, Gabriela finished looking back over her shoulder for imaginary wings and turned back around. She twisted her right foot into the ground and swayed her hips, both hands behind her back, as she thought of the perfect destination.

"Um, America," Gabriela said as she gazed up into her father's eyes. He continued to caress the side of her head and run his fingertips through her hair.

"America? How come you want to go to America?"

"Um . . . I don't know." Gabriela looked around, and then returned her gaze to meet her father's eyes.

"That's not true; there must be a reason why. How about you close your eyes and think, think real hard?"

"Um . . . I see a better place."

"Ay, *sí,* and now that you have your wings, you can fly to America, like the Monarch butterfly. But first, you're forgetting one thing."

"Um, like what?"

"Since you're such a young butterfly who may get lost, you'll need a guide."

"A guide?" Gabriela's voice rose slightly with exuberance.

"*Sí*, someone to show you the way." Francisco reached out to caress Gabriela's head and run his fingertips through her hair again. Gabriela looked around and then at Francisco.

"Um, would you be my guide?"

"*Sí, hija, sí*, but first, you have to pack your bags. Remember, this is our little secret. You can't tell anyone where we're going—not your friends, not your brother, and especially not your mother. You will have to wait for Papa to come home."

Gabriela nodded with a smile.

"Where are you going?"

Francisco leaned in closer towards Gabriela again to comfort her with his hypnotic words.

"Well, first Papà has to meet some people and discuss business. Ya know, music stuff, and then we will need supplies for our journey. I will need to get the necessities, like some water and food. Ya know, stuff like that."

"Um, okay. Well, don't forget to get lots of water, some tortas, and some galletas, 'cause those are my favorite."

"*Sí, hija, sí*, we will need those too." Francisco stood up.

Gabriela looked up into his eyes with a slight smile. She had never been beyond the neighboring towns. She was completely overwhelmed with happiness because her father was willing to bring her to America. In the eyes of Gabriela, America was a mythic place, a utopia where anything was possible and dreams could come true.

"Remember, *hija*, Papà loves you very much, and I will always love you, never forget." Francisco caressed the side of Gabriela's head and then ran his fingertips through her hair as he spoke.

"Um . . . I love you too. Do you promise to come back and take me to America?"

"I promise."

As Francisco declared his love and devotion, he looked into Gabriela's eyes, reaching out to hold the sides of her head with both his hands, leaning in to give Gabriela a kiss on both cheeks and then on her forehead. Gabriela closed her eyes and imagined a better life.

Even though it was only a matter of seconds, it felt like an eternity. Francisco stepped back and looked into Gabriela's eyes. There was trust there, while in Francisco's eyes, there was sorrow and regret.

As much as Francisco loved Gabriela, it was his inner demons that would drive him away. Francisco's addiction to the night life, women, and drinking was what would ultimately drive him away from his family, friends, and most importantly the light of his life, Gabriela, his little butterfly. Francisco caressed Gabriela's head and ran his fingertips through her hair one last time. He slowly stepped back, turning around to walk away. Gabriela was left by herself with his abandoned acoustic guitar leaning up against the waist-high stone wall that cradled a bed of roses.

After Francisco left, Gabriela packed her bags and waited for her father to return. She spent the rest of the day sitting on the curb in front of her house with her packed bag beside her, her head held in her hands. There was no more magic—only shattered dreams, a heart of emptiness, and broken promises.

<u>12</u>

In the eyes of Gabriela, she was in heaven. The naïve eighteen-year-old lay back in bed in the likeness of Bernini's statue of The Ecstasy of St. Teresa. Her eyes were rolled back, mouth slightly opened while moaning in exhilaration as her boyfriend Hernando passionately penetrated her sacred womb. The numbing sense of euphoria flowed throughout Gabriela's body, up her spine, and out her crown chakra. It was an electrifying experience, difficult to describe, but one that would never be forgotten. Even as their two hearts pressed together there was a burning sensation; a volcanic eruption of emotions and an internal surge of love flowing throughout their hearts and souls. It was as if two wandering souls, lost in a world filled with so many, the likeness of twin flames, had found each other and joined as one. Gabriela was convinced that Hernando was the one, her everlasting love. After having sex for the first time, Gabriela and Hernando cuddled before venturing out into the world together.

Love would continue and bring Gabriela and Hernando to the cliffs. It was an isolated area, located on the mountainside of a mountainous region on the outskirts of Tehuacán. The winding road lined with homes snaked up the edge of the mountain. This was where Hernando guided Gabriela by the hand, all the way to the last bend in the road, which led to the mountaintop. Off the side of the road, in a ravine nestled on the mountain's edge, was a great big boulder, hidden in vegetation and trees, which stuck out over the edge of the mountain like a natural platform. From this spot, Gabriela and Hernando were hidden from the world around, yet they had a bird's-eye view of Tehuacán and the vast open mountainous region of Mexico, as far as the eye could see, all the way to where the heavens kissed the earth.

As the two adolescent lovers sat side by side, Hernando sang and played "Tres Regalos" by Trio Los Panchos on his guitar, while Gabriela mused and admired her true love. Hernando was tall and thin, a frail romantic who had shaggy dark hair and a smooth baby face. His strong green eyes could woo and hypnotize any man or woman with his conquering gaze. His cunning smile and charming ways were able to seduce any audience or female. Although Hernando had the voice, the talent, and the sex appeal of what could be considered or misunderstood as a typical womanizing musician, that wasn't his style. He was very modest and gentle with Gabriela. He loved Gabriela just as much as she loved him, except music possessed Hernando's heart and soul. After finishing the final verse, Hernando put his guitar to the side. He leaned in closer to kiss Gabriela while holding and caressing the side of her head. He gently pulled back.

"*Mi amor, mi* little butterfly."

"*Te amo, mi amor, te amo,*" Gabriela answered as she gazed deep into Hernando's hypnotic green eyes, completely entranced by his seductive gaze. At that moment, there was nothing that could come between Gabriela and Hernando. Their auric field of love was firmly bonded together. Gabriela leaned in for another kiss, and then pulled away to speak, the energetic circle of love stayed together. "I feel so happy with you, *mi amor*. I don't want to separate from you, ever."

"I'll never let you go, *mi amor*. You'll always be close to my heart, no matter where we go in this life or the next." Hernando's cunning words pierced Gabriela's heart like Cupid's love-stained arrows.

"So, where will we go?"

"Definitely not Durango. It's too boring. It would have to be someplace far away, someplace exciting, someplace people dream of going to. Like . . . like . . ."

Gabriela admired Hernando's coy demeanor and turned to look out across the horizon. "America," Gabriela said confidently. It was someplace she desperately desired to go to someday.

"Yes, America, where we can go to Hollywood and see the movie stars. Or to New York, Newww Yooork"—Hernando opened up his arms and sang dramatically like Sinatra—"and eat lots of pizza and fast food!" He said the last words very quickly, like a television commercial, and Gabriela covered her mouth while she laughed out loud at Hernando's banter.

"Besides all the healthy food we can eat in America, there's more to see there than just Hollywood or New York, like . . . like Disneyland."

"Yes, how could I forget! The home of Mickey Mouse and Donald Duck." Once again, Hernando spoke in a very animated and mimicking manner, causing Gabriela to laugh again. Hernando paused to admire Gabriela's presence, and then said in a more subtle tone, "But, in all seriousness, someday I would love to take you to America, but . . ."

Hernando's final word overshadowed Gabriela's high emotions and brought her laughter and enquiring voice down to soft words.

"But? What is it, Hernando?"

"I was given an opportunity to play in a band, a really good band, Los Corazones Locos." Hernando elaborated with his hands and leaned in closer.

"That's wonderful, Hernando, I'm so happy for you! Why do you seem so . I don't know... so nervous?" Gabriela keenly studied Hernando's introverted body language and sensed that something was wrong.

"It's just that... you know that I love you very much and would give the world to you. But if I play in this band, this . . . what we have, I don't know how to say . . ." Hernando struggled to find the right words as he looked away and scratched the back of his head.

"I don't understand. What is it? What? You'll leave me just to play in some band with your friends?"

"No, it's not like that. This band travels a lot, not only in Mexico, but all around Central and South America." After Hernando spoke, there was an awkward moment of silence. Neither Gabriela nor Hernando looked at each other. Both looked out across the horizon while contemplating, searching for the right words.

"So you tell me, what will happen with us if you play in this band?"

"Listen, *mi amor*, I don't mean to put you... us... in a situation like this, but you know that music is my passion and all I can do. While Enrique and Armando are leaving to go to university, this is all I have," Hernando said passionately in an attempt to explain and smooth things over with Gabriela.

"Oh, yeah, well, what about me? What do I have? You know I can't afford to go to university, or get a good job. Hernando, you're all I have and all I've ever loved. I love you. Please, tell me you won't leave me." Gabriela began to choke up with tears in her eyes. Hernando saw the pain in Gabriela's eyes. He tried to heal her hurt with gentler words.

"Listen, I'm not making promises, but as of right now, I haven't yet made a decision."

"So, when will you, huh? And what if I'm pregnant, Hernando? Have you thought about that, huh? What will you do? Stay? Or will you still leave and go off with your band?" Gabriela's voice cracked with sadness. The only response Hernando could provide was to embrace her.

"No, *mi amor*, no."

"So, then there shouldn't be anything to think about." Gabriela's soft, provoking words caused Hernando to release her from his embrace and stand up.

"Agh! This is what I'm always talking about with you. You always put me on the spot and point the finger at me when I have vision and opportunity."

"That's not true, Hernando. That's not true. Please, *mi amor*, sit. Sit down so we can talk. Love and peace, *mi amor*, love and peace."

In a desperate attempt to keep the man she loved in her life, Gabriela turned around to gaze up into Hernando's eyes and plead for forgiveness. Hernando saw the love in Gabriela's eyes, which instantly brought his infuriated emotions back down. As Hernando began to speak, he pulled Gabriela into his arms once again.

"I love you, *mi amor*, very much. *Mi vida*, my everything, you know that, and no matter what happens, this, what we have, will never end. That I promise."

Hernando began to kiss Gabriela. They cuddled and gazed out across the open vastness. After sharing the moment of sweet embrace, Hernando got up, grabbed his guitar, and reached out his hand down towards Gabriela.

"I really need to get going now, *mi amor*, I have to play at the café. C'mon, let's go!"

Gabriela gazed up into his eyes one last time before looking down at his hand. She turned away and silently gazed out across the horizon. "No, *mi amor*, no, you go. I wanna stay here a little longer."

"Okay, *mi amor*, I will miss you." Hernando gave Gabriela one last kiss and warm embrace as a final farewell. "I will call you tonight, if I don't get home too late. If not, you know where to find me tomorrow—right here in our special place. Okay, my little butterfly. Don't go fly away from me, okay?"

Although Gabriela tried to remain stern with Hernando, who showered her with all his love one last time before departing for the evening, she couldn't resist his charming ways. She had to hold back a smile, which fought to come out. She had to stay strong and show Hernando that she was serious about him. She didn't want him to leave her for a band, like her father had done.

After Hernando left, Gabriela stayed and spent some time alone to think about her relationship with Hernando and her future. Tomorrow was another day. She would wait until she and Hernando were together again to express her deepest desires. For now, she looked out across the horizon while caressing her stomach, imagining living with Hernando in America with the unborn child that they would have someday.

As the day withered away into the night, and the sun ascended into the dawn of a new day, Gabriela returned to the cliffs, only to find disappointment. Hernando wasn't there waiting for Gabriela, like he had promised. He had abandoned her like her father. However, she found a rose and a message in a bottle.

Mi amor,

Even though this world is divided with good and evil, filled with so many and so much, as people, we find ourselves constantly struggling to survive and live life. No matter who or what has come into my life, there was always and only you. You were able to make me feel alive and free, my love, my life, my little butterfly. You always kept me grounded, and inspired me to live life. I am truly free knowing that you came into my life.

Our love is an ocean, large and vast, mutable and strong, and like multiple oceans joined together with our differences, our hearts are bonded together as one. Like the ocean, our love is constantly changing with the tides. Where we go from here, I don't know, but what I can say is that no matter which path we choose to take, and no matter the distance of separation between our two hearts, our love for one another can never be broken.

That's why I have chosen to take the path less traveled, to follow my heart down the musical path and dance my way through life. Just because I am embarking on the musical journey alone, mi amor, it doesn't mean that our love for one another has to end. If anything, it will grow with distance and time.

This sacrifice I have chosen for you. When I become a successful musician, I will be able to take care of you and our future children, and maybe someday bring you to America, where we could live free. Remember, mi amor, even though our hearts will be divided by distance, our love will stay strong and evolve over time.

For now I will miss you and never forget you. Stay strong, because even though we will be separated, you will be alone to chase your own dreams. My little butterfly, your wings are strong, so no matter what you choose to do, follow your heart, because with your wings you will be able to fly to the edges of the universe. My life, my light, my little butterfly. Never forget what we had and all we shared. You will be missed but never forgotten.

Te amo y besos,

Hernando

As Gabriela read the final words of Hernando's farewell letter, there was an internal storm of love and hate. Her heart became corroded over with hurt. Life seemed to be so cruel and painful as she stood alone filled with misery. Gabriela's heart was broken. As she stood sobbing, while gazing out across the open vastness, she crumpled up the letter, burying her past in the palm of her hand. She imagined living a better life someplace far away from home—where she had nothing left, someplace over the border, in America.

<u>13</u>

A haze of smoke wafted into the air from a half-smoked cigarette held between the fingers of Ignacio's left hand. Ashes sprinkled down onto the concrete floor as he sat on a folding chair in front of Gabriela. Although time seemed to have slowly elapsed by a matter of only a few minutes, in Gabriela's mind, there was a time loop of the past, which played out like a film montage, revealing glimpses of sporadic chronological sequences of her life.

"You know, your silence right now may be a sign of happiness, or who knows, maybe even a little bit of disappointment. I'm sure there are some bad memories in there, which cannot be ignored. But your scars, they paint a picture of pain. They seem to be permanent tokens that cannot be ignored, or covered with happiness."

Gabriela began to caress the cigarette scars on her forearms, imposed by the hand of Salas. Although the scars had faded throughout the years, leaving only subtle pigments that could be noticed by very observant eyes, the emotional stain from their manifestation was everlasting. Gabriela was left in a stoic state of being. Ignacio finished his cigarette and dropped the butt on the floor. He stepped on the butt with his boot, took out his pack of cigarettes, put one between his lips and then held the open pack of cigarettes towards Gabriela. Gabriela remained idle. Ignacio put his cigarettes away, took out his Zippo, and lit up his cigarette.

"So, was it worth it? All that pain? All that you lived through? Were you as disappointed as the others, when you first came here?"

If Ignacio only knew the reasons why Gabriela had chosen the path she had. If he only knew how she really felt, what the life she'd lived through was really like, maybe then he wouldn't look down on Gabriela with pity and doubt, like so many before. Maybe he would understand that any opinions of the life Gabriela had chosen to live depended on the perception of perspective. In the eyes of the blind, crossing the border to live the life Gabriela had, to work and live like a slave in poverty or be sent back, was a disappointment. *No* was Gabriela's answer to all her critics, which eventually fueled her to find the strength to look deep into Ignacio's cold, dark eyes.

"If you must know—no, I wasn't disappointed. I have no regrets about leaving the people I knew and the life I had in Mexico to live the life I chose to live here in America. It was worth all the pain."

Ignacio studied Gabriela's sudden change in demeanor while taking a refreshing drag of his cigarette. "Hmm, you know, I believe you. I could see the distance in your eyes; you have lived through a lot. You understand pain, that pain builds character. Emotional, physical, public humiliation, it doesn't matter, because all pain creates a sense of security in oneself, to never be afraid, to accept yourself for who you are and have the strength to live in a world that is so blind and daunting. To be able to experience life without fear of others, fear of choice, fear of the unknown, fear of love, fear of death."

Ignacio took another drag while he observed Gabriela, who was filled with visions of the love, pain and suffering she had lived through, and the death she had come face-to-face with.

"Love . . . *amore*. Love is what we all hope for in life. Whether it's the love we receive from another or the love we give, love is what drives us and what binds us. Love is art, love is beauty. Love opens our eyes, so that we can see, yet love also blinds us. Love stands beside death in the grand echelons of life experiences."

Ignacio paused for a moment, and Gabriela was left in silence to ponder her own dances with love and disappointment.

"Love and death, they mend like fear and desire. And like Romeo and Juliet, we would sacrifice one for the other. Yet no matter how fearless we may assume we are, still we fear both."

Ignacio then began to speak with dramatic hand motions, all while holding his cigarette between his fingers. He continued to humor and amuse Gabriela with his alluring words.

"And even though love may seem everlasting; an immortal part of life, love, like other life experiences, can be avoided or overshadowed by fear, by hate, but most importantly, by choice. You have the free will, the choice to love or be loved, yet, out of all life experiences, the one that is inevitable, that we can never avoid, no matter how fearless we are, is death—something not even free will can overcome or avoid. Even if some may be able to look death in the eyes and cast it away, sooner or later, death will return to collect what is rightfully his."

There was a moment of silence as Gabriela and Ignacio gazed through the haze of smoke lingering in the air between them. Ignacio smiled after seeing the vulnerability within Gabriela's eyes. She remained silent, while thoughts of the past filled her with fear and pain.

"So, tell me, since you've been here, and knowing how love has been nothing but disappointment for you in Mexico and in the life you've lived here—was it the love you were looking for? Was it worth everything to live a life of sin? Even when you had to look your child in the eyes and tell her you loved her, was it worth it? The pain and sin you've found here, does it compensate for the loss of all the love you once had, that you now hide, for the love of your child? Love is blind indeed, yet I can see that the love you want is still absent. Maybe it's death you want instead?" As echoes from Gabriela's dark and haunting past filled her mind, she gazed down into nothingness, through her strands of hair, back up into Ignacio's eyes and then back down again, as Ignacio continued. "Have you ever looked death in the eyes? *Mire me.*"

Ignacio's final words triggered a sudden sense of déjà vu, like a splinter in Gabriela's mind. She began to focus and try to understand the significance of her situation, and why she felt as if she had been in Ignacio's presence before, yet, also a reflection of the fear she had once felt from a dark and haunting past suddenly developed within her mind.

14

Faintly echoing out from the vents on the second floor was lascivious moans from a whore being barbarically fucked on the third floor by another satisfied client, and laughter from children playing in the first-floor daycare.

Gabriela patiently waited within a world of heaven and hell for one of the sinful to finish packing away bricks of cocaine into diaper bags for her and the other mules. It was the beginning of another ordinary day. The dissonance of the sounds of sex and innocent laughter no longer poisoned Gabriela's mind; nor did the excess of cocaine being cut, weighed, and packed away before her eyes disgust her.

Gabriela's modest shell was now completely shed away. All she now had was a coating of integrity and the mules who sat beside her. Not only had the mules gone down the same path as Gabriela, but they also shared the same dream—that this dehumanizing and degrading life they now lived would eventually lead them to a better life. In the meantime, Gabriela just focused on the hands of the sinful—who continued to pack bricks of cocaine, the babies having baggies of cocaine taped to their torsos, and on Mendez, Munoz, and Salas, who stood behind the sinful while discussing their daily objectives.

Munoz, who would always seductively stare at Gabriela, did so now, licking his lips while he listened to Salas. Gabriela looked away and focused on her shoes. She thought of the many miles she had walked in them to get to where she was now. After the supply of cocaine was packed, Salas summoned the mules over towards the table.

Each mule was handed a bag filled with cocaine and a baby laced with baggies. All the other babies cried, but not Gabriela's. Cradled in Gabriela's arms was Elena's baby, who sadly was also being used to transport narcotics. Gabriela felt guilty for bringing Elena's baby into such a terrible world, even if it was against her own will, but she had made a promise to bring the baby with her when she left, to care for her and raise as her own, in a better place. For now, Gabriela would do whatever it took to protect the baby.

After Gabriela and the other mules were handed their list of the daily drop-off locations, Munoz again blew Gabriela a taunting kiss, causing Gabriela to look away. Salas sternly stared at Gabriela. His intimidating presence spoke more than words, leaving Gabriela and the other mules with a sense of accountability as they all slowly walked away and left to make their daily drops.

After finishing all the drop-offs, Gabriela softly sang a Spanish lullaby within the walls of an obscured bathroom, while changing the diaper on Elena's baby. Inside the final drop-off location, Gabriela felt relaxed. She was now free from her daily life of sin and knew that the remainder of the day was hers. Before venturing out into the world, Gabriela finished putting the diaper on the baby and then began to wash her hands.

Soon after, as Gabriela glanced down to finish washing her hands, she felt an unsettling presence in the bathroom. Before Gabriela even had a chance to look back up, the reflections of two anonymous thugs filled in the mirror, as they silently stood behind her.

All at once, like the break of a storm, one of the thugs, Alejandro, his hair done in corn rows, tightly grabbed Gabriela around the waist, pulled her in close with one hand, and covered up her mouth with the other while the baby cried out. The other thug, Chato, who had sleeve tattoos of an array of religious symbols, then walked over towards the baby to calm it down, while Alejandro whispered into Gabriela's ear.

"*Dónde está la mierda?*" Gabriela was hesitant and only angered Alejandro with her silence. "*Dónde está?*" Alejandro raised his voice.

Gabriela looked over towards the bathroom stall, causing Alejandro to look back over his shoulder at Chato, who was trying to quiet the baby by shushing it and rubbing its head. Alejandro motioned with his eyes for Chato to check the bathroom stall for the drugs.

At first Chato looked down, up and all around, until he focused his attention on the toilet. He removed the toilet tank cover and took out the brick of cocaine.

"Got it, let's go," Chato said as he walked out of the bathroom stall with the cocaine.

"Good. Check the bag, see if there is any more in there," Alejandro directed.

Chato checked the diaper bag, and to his surprise, the bag was filled with five bricks of cash, each worth $50,000.

"Holy shit! Look, there's a shitload of money here!"

"Really? Then take the bag with the money too."

"What about the girl and the baby?" Chato asked as he held the bag.

"Maybe she knows where there is more. Is there more money and drugs?" Alejandro twisted Gabriela's wrist behind her back. "Answer me!"

Gabriela tensed up and hopelessly watched the anger in Alejandro's eyes.

"We don't have time to sit around and ask questions, just take her with us. She'll talk for Rosario," Chato insisted.

"All right, let's go." Alejandro began to walk Gabriela towards the bathroom door, where Chato was now waiting. Gabriela squirmed in an attempt to break free. She was so desperate that she managed to free one of her arms and then pulled Alejandro's hand down from her mouth far enough so that she could yell out.

"No, no . . . wait . . . wait! Please—" Gabriela yelped out, causing Alejandro to stop and struggle to get ahold of her. He managed to cover her mouth again and continued to drag her.

"Agh, *puta madre!*" Alejandro cried after Gabriela bit his fingers. He slapped Gabriela upside the head, and then dragged Gabriela towards the bathroom door. Chato followed behind with the bag filled with cash and a brick of cocaine.

"Wait, wait! You can't leave the baby there all alone!" Gabriela yelled out as she stopped, frustrating Alejandro, who held her and pushed her forward. She now stood before Chato, who looked at her with a sense of sympathy.

"Go, get the baby . . . hurry up," Chato said.

After Gabriela picked up the baby, the three walked out of the bathroom.

<u>15</u>

Gabriela silently sat in the back of a beat-up red two-door 2002 Honda Civic, gazing out the window with the baby cradled within her arms. Even in the mist of darkness, she imagined a better life. No matter how far down the desolate path Gabriela was being brought by her two abductors, there still seemed to be a sense of hope. After driving around Los Angeles, all roads eventually led to Jefita's, a Mexican bar and restaurant known for its exquisite and traditional Mexican food. Alejandro, Chato, and Gabriela, with the baby tightly held close to her heart, got out of the car and walked into Jefita's with the diaper bag filled with cash and the brick of cocaine.

Jefita's Mexican-inspired décor and mariachi band of three created an authentic Mexican setting. Inside Jefita's, the vast rectangular floor was filled with multiple tables and patrons. Even the bar located in the heart of the restaurant was full. The mariachi band played on the far end of the restaurant near the bar, nestled four steps below the dining area, which overlooked and wrapped around the perimeter of the bar area.

The three approached and joined another Mexicano, sitting at a table on the edge of the dining area. The table was strategically picked out, since it was positioned at the end of the extending entrance path leading into the restaurant. Next to the steps that led down to the bar, it rested alongside the well-defined carved wooden waist-high dividing wall that wrapped around the perimeter of the bar area. From this particular table, there was a clear view of the entire restaurant, the entrance and exit doors, the bathrooms behind the bar at the end of the restaurant, and all those within the restaurant.

"*Hola, cómo estás?*" Chino said, standing up to greet Alejandro, Chato and Gabriela. He was an unfit, pudgy Mexican of average height, with curly hair, a scruffy face, and fucked-up teeth that stuck out from underneath his lips. He looked like a rat.

"*Mucho gusto, amigo,*" Alejandro said.

"*Amigo, cómo estás?*" Chato said with a smile.

"*Bien, bien,*" Chino said, embracing both Alejandro and Chato. He turned towards Gabriela with a creepy smile. Gabriela turned away and tried to keep her distance as Chino pressed his smelly unfit frame up against her body and attempted to kiss her on the cheek. She cringed as Chino's foul breath wafted across her cheek and felt relieved when he pulled away. All four sat down at the table.

Alejandro sat on the inner side of the table, next to the dividing wall to his right, with Chino sitting across from him. To Alejandro's left, Gabriela sat with the baby in her arms. Chato sat across from Gabriela. As the four Mexicans settled in, a waiter greeted them and took their drink orders. The three Mexicanos each ordered a *cerveza*, while Gabriela asked for a glass of water, and Alejandro requested an extra chair. The chair was placed at the head of the table for another friend who would eventually join the four. The atmosphere within the restaurant was full of energy, but Gabriela felt sedated, filled with confusion and anticipation. She remained silent while Alejandro, Chino and Chato socialized.

"So, how'd you find this place?" Chato asked Chino as he looked around.

"You know Chi-Chi, who works with our crew sometimes?"

"Yeah, the *camarón*," Alejandro added.

"Well, I asked if he knew a good Mexican restaurant in the area, ya know, since we go to Mexicali and Rio Grande all the time."

"Yeah, because those are the best places to go to in L.A., man, everyone knows that," Chato stated.

"*Claro, claro.* Hey, it's about time you did something right," Alejandro replied.

"Ay, please, man. Anyway, that's one of the things about this place. Chi-Chi said it's the best kept secret in L.A., man. As busy as this place gets, not too many people know about it."

"*Muy bien, muy bien,* just what we needed."

"Yeah, well, let's hope that the food is as good as this place looks," Alejandro said.

"I wouldn't worry. If Chi-Chi said this place is good, I can guarantee the food is good. You know Chi-Chi, man, he's never wrong. He's like a *psíquico* or something."

"Oh yeah, is that so? Is that why you lost twenty-five hundred dollars on the Mexico-US friendly last week?" Chato joked with Chino, provoking Alejandro to laugh.

"*Puta madre!* Fucking Americanos! *Dos, dos* goals in the second half! If Dos Santos would've put away his chances in the first half, the game would've been over, three to zero. He had two open netters."

"Even with Clint Dempsey and Tim Howard both playing injured, the Americanos still won in Mexico City," Chato said, adding fuel to the fire.

"Motherfuckers were so lucky!" Chino lashed out like a child.

"I guess Chi-Chi was wrong with his inside information this time," Alejandro said as he laughed with Chato.

"Ay fuck, I don't wanna talk about it anymore. I'm too depressed, man. Anyway, what's a beautiful woman like you doing with a bunch of *idiotas?*" Chino settled down, leaned in towards Gabriela, and ate freshly homemade tostaditas with guacamole and salsa.

"You don't have to speak with Chino over here. He thinks he's papi chulo."

"*Think?* You're crazy. No way, man. With all the women I have, please."

"Nice first impression, telling a woman you just met that you have many women," Chato added nonchalantly as he looked at the menu.

"Yeah, one, two, three, four, five *señoritas* right here," Alejandro said, raising each finger, one at a time, then closing his fist and making a jerking off motion. Chato covered his mouth as he laughed, while Gabriela shyly turned away to hide her smile from Chino, who continued to shake his head and look at everyone before speaking.

"*Pendejos, pendejos, pendejos.* Anyway, where's the shit?" Chino said more sternly.

Alejandro slid the diaper bag filled with cash and cocaine under the table to Chino's feet. Chino looked around the restaurant and bent down. After looking inside the bag, Chino jolted up.

"Where did all this come from? I thought there was only going to be one package, not all this . . ." Chino paused, looked all around, and then lowered his voice as he leaned in closer towards Alejandro. "All this cash."

"Well, that's why *bonita* is here with us now." Alejandro turned towards Gabriela. "She's gonna tell us everything, right?"

All eyes were now on Gabriela as she rocked the baby. The sinister glare she had seen in Alejandro and Chato's eyes when they'd abducted her matched Chino's malevolent demeanor. Gabriela, who was still unsure how to respond or present herself in such a blind, unpredictable situation, remained silent. Fortunately for her, the waiter returned with their drinks and began to take their food orders.

"Water for the lady, and *cervezas* for the gentlemen. So, is everyone ready to order?" the young Mexican waiter asked, and then patiently waited while Alejandro, Chato, and Chino scanned their menus, scrambling to figure out what they wanted.

"Why don't you go first?" Alejandro told Gabriela.

"I'm not hungry," Gabriela replied.

"Order something, you need to eat."

Gabriela could see anger in his eyes, but it was Salas she was more concerned about. All his trust in her would now be gone.

"Okay. I'll have the *Jefita especial con pollo y salsa roja*," Gabriela said, hoping that going along with the situation would be safest for now.

"And for you, sir?" the waiter asked Chato.

"Just the seasoned *bistec.*"

"Let's see, um . . . I'll have the chimichanga," Chino said.

"And I'll just have the beef burrito with salsa verde combo," Alejandro requested.

The waiter then collected the menus and left.

"What about Rosario? Does he know about all this?" Chino asked after sipping his beer.

"Nah, not yet," Alejandro answered while Chato remained silent and focused. He was keenly observing his surroundings and studying Alejandro and Chino.

"You know this is huge. Once we let Rosario know about this and he tells Suarez and lets him know what we got—know what I mean? This is a fucking big score we made. This compensates for the last payment we fell short on, and any more debt we have with Suarez. No more riding lawnmowers and working in yards on hot summer days."

"I know, I know. Let me call Rosario now." Alejandro took out his cell phone while Chato sipped his beer and looked around. Gabriela noticed Chato's distant demeanor.

He didn't seem like the other two. He had an unfitting presence. Even when Chato had abducted Gabriela, he seemed out of place. Gabriela had noted his sleeve tattoos, a collage of biblical scripture, crucifixes, Jesus, the Virgin Mary, the Virgin Guadalupe, and a very distinctive tattoo of the Archangel Michael slaying the devil on the inner side of his left forearm. It all seemed out of place for someone with criminal intent. She compared it to the tattoos of the other criminals and thugs, who were inked with gang symbols, erotic female images, and images of death. Chato's tattoos were modest and appealing. Whatever was going on in Chato's mind or the others' at the moment didn't matter, criminal or not, though; Gabriela knew that she needed to find a way to get away from the three of them. For now all she was able to do was play the waiting game. She listened to Alejandro speak to a friend on the phone as she looked around, hoping to find an open window.

"Amigo, cómo estás? . . . Bien, bien. Listen, Chato and I are at the restaurant now with Chino . . . Yeah, everything's here . . . So, where are you now? . . . Okay, perfect . . . You want us to get you anything, some food, a *cerveza*? . . . You sure? . . . Okay, see you soon." Alejandro hung up the cell phone. "He said he's not far from here and that he should be here in about five to ten minutes."

"*Bien*, five to ten minutes; it's Rosario, so he should be here in about twenty to thirty minutes. That gives me time to go out for a smoke or two. Any of you want to join me?" Chino finished eating some tostaditas, dripping salsa onto the table. He sipped his beer, stood up, pulled out his pack of cigarettes, took one out and placed it in between his lips.

"No, *amigo*, no, I'm fine," Chato stated.

"Go and hurry up, *amigo*," Alejandro said.

"Ay, *sí*, and what about the *chiquita*? Would you like to join me? You can leave the baby with these two *pendejos*." Chino gazed deep into Gabriela's eyes and smiled. Gabriela, disgusted by Chino and his fucked-up teeth, turned away.

"No, thank you. I don't smoke."

Chato and Alejandro laughed.

"*Pendejos, pendejos*, go ahead and laugh, I'll find someone else to smoke with outside."

Chino left. Gabriela continued to rock the sleeping baby in her arms while she listened to the mariachis playing music and singing, along with the dissonance of voices and sounds echoing throughout the restaurant. The unscripted path of unpredictability was wide open. Everywhere Gabriela looked in the restaurant, she saw open windows and open doors. Besides the many people within the restaurant Gabriela could go to for help, there were also the isolated bathrooms in the back of the restaurant near an emergency exit door. There was also an atmosphere in the restaurant in which Gabriela could make a scene that would put her abductors into an uncomfortable situation. Gabriela also noticed two other unlikely sources of help.

<u>16</u>

As Alejandro and Chato engaged in small talk, Gabriela looked down towards the bar and focused on Mendez and Munoz, Salas's men, who coincidentally were sitting at the bar. Even though they were Gabriela's masters, being in a distressful situation Gabriela now found herself, the two were her only hope. Gabriela was able to clearly see Mendez and Munoz. She hoped that they would glance over in her direction and recognize her, or she would be able to slyly walk across the bar area to the bathrooms and get their attention. Only time would tell. Before Gabriela even had a chance to conjure up an idea, Alejandro turned towards Gabriela and startled her with a question.

"So, *chiquita*, why don't you tell me a little bit about yourself?"

Gabriela shied away. She wasn't ready to reveal anything, not yet.

"Don't be so shy, *chiquita*, I'm not gonna hurt you. C'mon, why don't you have some tostaditas? They're good. Maybe you'll loosen up a little."

Alejandro slid the bowl of tostaditas towards Gabriela. Alejandro's peace offering seemed humble. Gabriela remained cautious as she looked down at the tostaditas, across the bar area at Mendez and Munoz, and then at Alejandro. Chato sipped his beer, fiddled around with his cell phone, sending text messages, and looked around the restaurant as well. Gabriela knew the game and knew to expect the unexpected, especially now, with Mendez and Munoz possibly in the picture. She especially knew Alejandro's character all too well. She could see deep within his eyes that he was a mere amateur. No matter where he would try to bring her from here, she would be ready, and play along.

"Don't worry, it's not poison. Chino ate half the bowl and he's still alive. Here, *mira*," Alejandro said as he reached over to grab a tostadita.

As Alejandro ate, Gabriela reached down to grab one. After tasting how good it was, she helped herself to more, along with salsa and guacamole. The baby woke up and began to cry. Gabriela began to rock the baby while Alejandro reached over to rub the baby's head.

"*Tranquilla, tranquilla.* Ya see, there's no need to be scared of me, I'm not such a bad guy. Life can be so cruel to people like you and me. Especially to someone like me, who's chosen the life I now live. A lifestyle I'm sure you know very well. Isn't that why we're both here now, because of what we do, just to survive? It's a shame, though, that people, especially Americanos who are so judgmental of migrants like us, ya know, how they discredit us, and point the finger and say that's tha bad guy ova there. No, no, no, *preciosa*. Yo *y mi amigos*, we're like you. We came to a place where we are not wanted, yet we are needed. We came to a place where we struggle to survive, where we are considered minorities, yet we are in fact the majority, a suppressed majority who strive on stolen land. And why do we strive? We strive because we are not afraid to take chances."

After Alejandro finished, Gabriela keenly observed his soft façade. Alejandro's childish facial features, along with Chato's childish antics, still sending text messages, painted a clearer picture for Gabriela to see. Their worn-out construction boots, dirt-stained jeans and t-shirts were those of landscapers, modest blue-collar migrants caught up in a game of wolves. The same wolves Gabriela was associated with, like Mendez and Munoz, who now looked across the bar area and saw Gabriela.

As Gabriela looked past Alejandro, she was lost in Mendez's eyes, who looked at her with bewilderment. Mendez began to stand up, but was stopped by Munoz, who held him down by the shoulder. Mendez and Munoz studied Gabriela, and before she could attempt to communicate with them in any nonverbal way she could, Alejandro began to speak again.

"So, what's your name?"

"Gabriela. And you?"

"I'm Alejandro, that's Chato, and as you already know by now, the chubby one is Chino. So, Gabriela—Gabriela, like my sister. Ya know, the name Gabriela suited my sister very well. It means 'God is my strength.' She looked up to and loved God, devoted her life to God, and God—God answered. He turned her into an angel, like the Archangel Gabriel; the messenger of God sent down to look over and guide those down here on earth. Like Gabriel, my sister was an angel, a messenger, who not only cared for me and my two brothers, but my mamá, my papá, and both my *abuelito* and *abuelita*. She did it all, she worked two jobs, day and night, she cleaned up after and inspired us. So, with the name Gabriela like my sister, I'm curious. Do you feel that you have a similar personality?"

"Perhaps a little, but where is your sister now?"

"She's dead." Although Alejandro's final words engulfed Gabriela with dismay, she was able to remain focused and coyly change the subject.

"So, where are you from?"

"Oaxaca."

"Oaxaca, really? I'm from Tehuacán in Puebla State, but I lived in El Norte, Sonora State, before I came here."

"Viva Puebla." Alejandro's words put a smile on Gabriela's face.

"*Claro*. And my friends and I, we used to go to the beaches of Oaxaca, like Huatulco or Puerto Del Ángel, all the time. During July, we would go to La Guelaguetza."

"La Guelaguetza. As a child I used to enjoy going. I miss seeing the mountains, especially driving through them with my father. It was like driving through heaven, seeing the way the mountains rose up so high into the clouds. It felt good, peaceful. I also miss the band who usually played each Sunday in the church, Cristo Rey. It was so, so, amazing."

As Alejandro spoke and opened up about his childhood, Gabriela could see more of a desperate, fragile and vulnerable soul deep within his eyes. His decisive mask of intimidation was beginning to crack and crumble. Alejandro was the polar opposite of Mendez and Munoz, intimidating thugs. Gabriela noted their continual glances in her direction, trying to get a feel for the situation. Chato continued to play with his cell phone, yet stayed alert.

"You're so far away from home now, how come? Don't you miss it?"

"Like I said, I left and did what I had to do to help take care of my family."

Even though, Alejandro's path was similar to that of Gabriela's life path and ambitions, she remained poised in order to play Alejandro and win him over. "How come you chose to do bad things, running around with guns, stealing and selling drugs? You're from Oaxaca. It's a peaceful place, with nice people."

"How come? Everybody wants to know how come or why? Does it matter? What matters is that I'm here. Like so many before me, I chose to be here. I chose to find a way to get in, and it doesn't matter if the path I chose was right or wrong. Besides, between the black and white of it, we're all gray. And for those who judge, well, they should be judged. They don't understand how . . . how desperate we become sometimes, just to make it in this world. People back home, in Mexico, starving, struggling, dying, for what? Why should they suffer and we forget? That's the problem with the people here in the United States, they forget that we come here illegally for them; for family, for friends, back home in Mexico. We struggle for them. We choose to live a life of crime, for them. We sacrifice for Mexico, yet we are not considered saints, only sinners."

"It's okay, I understand, I—"

"No, no, you don't. You don't know what I left behind, what is forever gone, and, why, why I do what I do now!" Alejandro tapped hard on the table with the tips of his fingers. "You think I enjoy this? I only do it for them, *mi familia* back home, because I know this will get me what I need to care for them. After I get what I need and what I want, then I won't need this anymore. I prefer to take what I earn and go back home, to Oaxaca."

As Alejandro's emotions spilled over and came back down, Gabriela watched him. Mendez and Munoz were extremely focused on and engaged by what was going on. She glanced at Chato, who was now taking notice of Mendez and Munoz. After seeing how fragile and unstable a person Alejandro was, Gabriela was ready to make the right moves to get more information for her own benefit.

"So, how did you know I was going to be in the bathroom with the drugs and money?"

"From a close friend of mine who works in the restaurant; he cleans. He told me that one day, before stepping into the bathroom to clean, he called out to make sure no one was inside, and a woman answered. While he waited for the woman that was inside the bathroom to leave, he heard the lid of the toilet put back on before hearing the toilet flush. He became curious after that, so he decided to check, and that's when he found the cocaine. Next time he checked there was money, lots of money. After he found the money, he told me it was the same woman who would drop off the drugs each time, and that she was beautiful, very beautiful."

Alejandro seduced Gabriela with his eyes. Gabriela followed along and played the game well, biting down on her bottom lip while slowly unbuttoning the top few buttons of her blouse, which exposed her voluptuous cleavage.

"You're not scared of the people you stole from?" Gabriela looked past Alejandro at Mendez and Munoz again, then back into his eyes. Chato watched Gabriela, Mendez and Munoz looking at each other once again, and became even more curious.

"No, because, we only stole this one time from the restaurant. Lucky for us, the timing was perfect. Let's just say we have some debts we have to pay off. So we took advantage of the situation. As for the people you work for, they're no threat. With the score we have, we can cash out and be gone before they even find out who we are. We plan on going back home, to Mexico, to live like kings."

"So brave, I like, but what I like even more is something else you have."

As Gabriela mesmerized Alejandro with her eyes and teased him with her cleavage, she reached down under the table to caress Alejandro's leg and then his crotch. Alejandro reached out across the table to caress Gabriela's cheek and run his fingertips through her hair. As an aura of lust slowly built up, Chato remained focused on Mendez and Munoz, who continued to keenly observe Gabriela.

After studying the two, Chato turned towards Gabriela and Alejandro, who continued to flirt with each other. Something wasn't right. Chato could sense it. Not only was he cautious of who Mendez and Munoz were, but he was very wary of Gabriela, who was clearly playing Alejandro. As aroused as he was, and as much as he wanted to engage further with Gabriela, Alejandro knew he couldn't. Not now; he needed to find the strength to control his hormones. Alejandro pushed Gabriela's hand away and began to stand up.

"Excuse me, but I need to use the bathroom."

Alejandro walked away from the table and through the bar area, towards the bathroom. As Alejandro walked past the bar, Mendez and Munoz turned to watch where he was going. Mendez began to get up once again to follow Alejandro, but was held back by Munoz, who insisted they keep their eyes on Gabriela. Gabriela could now see the fire in both their eyes as they stared at her like crows on a wire, stalking their prey. Mendez then had the audacity to lift his shirt to Gabriela, slightly revealing his gun as a warning. After getting a taste of their fear-mongering, Gabriela turned back towards Chato. Chato also turned away from Mendez and Munoz, and looked into Gabriela's eyes with a slight smile.

17

As Chato studied Gabriela, she looked away. Gabriela turned to Mendez and Munoz again, but glanced away like an obedient dog, faced with conviction.

"It must be uncomfortable for you," Chato said.

"What do you mean?" Gabriela asked Chato, who then leaned forward.

"Ya know, to be as beautiful as you. It seems that no matter where you go, you'll always have unwanted men staring you." Chato smiled. Gabriela turned to look away at Mendez and Munoz, once again, then back at Chato.

"Perhaps, but I try not to let it bother me."

"That's good, but"—Chato took a sip of beer—"your two fans over there, they seem like they know you," Chato said, looking at Mendez and Munoz. Gabriela then turned as well to look at them, and then turned back.

"I don't know who they are, I've never seen them before. Maybe they've mistaken me for someone else." As Gabriela spoke, the baby woke up and began to cry. Gabriela rocked and shushed the baby until it settled down.

"So, is that your baby?"

"No, no, it's someone else's baby."

"So, whose is it, a friend of yours?"

"No, no friend, just some woman I came to United States with. She never made it over the border, so she gave her baby to me to take care of."

"Is that so? So, who did you come here with?"

"I came with a couple of coyotes from Tijuana, who work for a man from Mexico that does business with the man I work for now."

"I see. So, who is it you work for?"

"I'd rather not say."

Chato could see tenderness, a lost soul caught up with atrocious people who was now stuck in the middle of a difficult situation. As for Gabriela, who shyly looked at Chato, then away, and then back again, she could sense that Chato wasn't the bad person he posed as, that there was benevolence beneath the thuggish exterior.

"C'mon, you can trust me." Chato flashed Gabriela a wink, filling her with caution and curiosity. As Chato continued to speak, he leaned forward, resting both elbows on the table, and began to speak with dramatic hand motions. "I'm what some may call a guardian angel, without the wings, of course."

Gabriela now focused on Chato's sleeve tattoos. They seemed to speak to her. Jesus, the Virgin Mary, the Virgin Guadalupe, the Archangel Michael slaying the devil, and pieces of scripture, scribed within the collage of religious images. Whatever the universe or some higher force was trying to tell Gabriela, she felt that there was something beneficent about Chato.

"Well, if you're such an angel, how come you steal money and drugs and kidnap people with a gun, hmm?" Gabriela humored Chato, who smiled, and then elaborated.

"Sometimes the lamb has to wear wolf skin, to roam with the wolves, in order to capture and remove the big bad wolf from power; the one who threatens the lives of all the other little lambs."

"So, if you're not one of them, then who are you?"

The waiter returned with everyone's food, and then Chato and Gabriela silently began to eat. Gabriela ate her Jefita's *especial* chicken meal, while Chato meticulously sliced his steak into small portions. Chato began to eat one piece at a time, chewing multiple times and grinding his food down to shreds. As he continued to eat while looking down, Gabriela turned to watch Mendez and Munoz once again. They seemed to be very frustrated and began to try to nonverbally communicate with Gabriela, with body language and lip synching. Gabriela couldn't understand what they were trying to tell her. As Gabriela turned away, Chato turned back as well, looking away from Mendez and

Munoz. After Chato finished chewing, he confronted Gabriela.

"Listen, I know you know those two men down there, and if I had to take a wild guess, I'd say they are connected with you and all that you have in your bag. Maybe it's a coincidence, blind luck, or fate, as to why they're here now. That really doesn't matter right now, because I can see that you're in a very difficult situation as to who you can trust and leave this place with. What I can say now is, if you listen to me and stay close to me, I guarantee you'll be safe and won't have to end up with those two men over there, or these two clowns we're with."

Chato's words opened more doors. Gabriela keenly studied Chato's estranged persona and thought about Chato's words and who he could be.

"Are you a policeman?" Gabriela inquired.

Chato leaned back and nodded while rubbing his nose.

"Okay, I see, but what's going to happen with me and the other two?"

"I wouldn't worry. Alejandro and Chino are just a couple of landscapers who got caught up with the wrong people. A friend of theirs works for this drug trafficking network, known as Nada Mas. Even though it's in its infancy, it's big. It's slowly growing, and it's involved in a lot more than just drugs. Without getting into too much detail, it's been creating a lot of problems within the border states, especially within the universities and colleges in the area. It's also creating problems because it is connected to and does a lot of business with small-time and big-time gangs, both domestically and internationally, mostly with Mexican, Central American, and Colombian drug cartels. Anyway, one of our informants told us about Alejandro and Chino's involvement and how we would be able to easily use the two to get intel and get closer to people involved with Nada Mas, and use a mole such as myself to get inside this network and start breaking it down from within."

"So, what do I have to do with this?"

"I don't know—you tell me. All I know is that Alejandro had a friend who knew you were gonna be in that bathroom dropping off drugs. So, you tell me who you're working for, and who those two over there are, and I can guarantee you immunity."

Gabriela turned away. She thought about her past, the present, this current predicament and her future. Even though everything Gabriela dreamed of fulfilling in America seemed to be in jeopardy, there was hope seen in Chato's eyes.

"Okay, but if I tell you everything, how am I gonna get out of here?"

"As long as you stay calm and go along with everything, you're gonna be fine. Don't worry about Alejandro and Chino, or those two over there. I'll make sure no one harms you. For now, just be patient until the time comes when I'll be able to get you out of here safely, okay?"

Alejandro and Chino returned. Chato gave Gabriela a smile, then looked past her at someone sitting in the restaurant, another federal agent in street clothes, who nodded. Gabriela looked back over her shoulder, then back at Chato, who held his chest and adjusted his shirt.

"All right, perfect timing," Chino said as he began to eat his chimichanga.

"I guess the food is that good, you two couldn't wait for us," Alejandro said as he began to eat.

Gabriela smiled. As Alejandro, Chato, and Chino ate, Gabriela looked past Alejandro at Mendez and Munoz. She focused on Mendez, who was signaling Gabriela to go to the bathroom. At first Gabriela hesitated. She now knew Chato was possibly an authority figure who could help her. But even so, she felt the need to play both sides of the field, since it wasn't guaranteed Chato could be trusted, or would be able to definitely help her.

"I need to use the bathroom," Gabriela said.

"Hold it in," Alejandro said firmly.

"Not me, the baby. I need to change the diaper."

Alejandro stopped eating, slammed his fork and knife down, and then wiped his mouth clean.

"Take whatever you need out of the bag."

After Gabriela took out the necessary supplies from the bag, Chato stood. "I'll take her to make sure she doesn't try to leave out the back door," he said.

"No. Chino, you go," Alejandro said as he looked at Chato, who froze and sat back down, and then over at Chino, who quickly chewed and swallowed his food.

"Me? C'mon, man, I just started eating," Chino complained.

"Quiet, I don't want to hear it. Go, quickly before Rosario gets here."

Chino then childishly put his fork and knife down, stood up alongside Gabriela and began to escort her to the bathroom. Mendez also got up and walked towards the bathrooms. Munoz remained seated at the bar and watched Alejandro and Chato. As Chino and Gabriela walked away through the bar area, past Munoz, towards the bathrooms in the back, Chato watched nervously, knowing that the other stranger, Mendez, was in the bathroom alcove—which branched off from the bar and couldn't be seen from the dining area—waiting for her.

<u>18</u>

After Chino and Gabriela walked into the alcove, Gabriela walked to the end of the hallway and into the women's bathroom. Chino waited in the hallway, occupying himself by staring at an exotic woman talking on her cell phone, who turned away from him. Once inside the bathroom, Gabriela looked underneath each of the three stalls. She did not see any feet; there was no Mendez. She then went into the last stall to change the baby's diaper and wait for Mendez.

Unbeknownst to Gabriela, Mendez was standing on top of the toilet inside the middle stall and quietly crept up behind her. He placed his hand on Gabriela's shoulder, which terrified her. She turned around with the baby held tightly in her arms. Mendez grabbed Gabriela by the back of her bicep, forcing her out of the stall, into the open, where the sinks and wall mirror were, and locked the door.

"Who are those men you're with?"

"I-I don't know. When I was dropping off the last supply of cocaine, in Papá Chicano's, they came into the bathroom with guns, threatened to kill me and made me go with them!"

"Where's all the money?"

"They have all of it, and the last supply of cocaine."

"*Puta madres!* Where are they gonna go from here?"

"I don't know. All I know is that they're waiting for a friend to show up, someone named Rosario. I think they're gonna give him all the money,"

Gabriela looked down and around, then up at Mendez.

"Who the fuck is Rosario?"

"I don't know. He works for the same gang as the other three, some gang called Nada Mas." Mendez suddenly became calm.

"Nada Mas?" Mendez asked, a cautious tone in his voice. He looked around to contemplate the current situation, before continuing, "Okay, listen, don't tell those fuckers who you work for, and don't even think about telling them you know me and Munoz." Mendez spoke with an overpowering tone, then took out his gun and pointed it at Gabriela. "Because if you do, I'll kill you before they even have a chance, *comprende?*"

Gabriela stood still as she looked down the barrel of the gun.

"*Sí, sí,* and what about me, huh? What am I supposed to do?"

"You stay with them. Don't worry about the bag of money, because that is not leaving this restaurant, with them or anyone else." Mendez gestured with his gun that he would kill them in order to get the money back. "Go, go back before they get suspicious."

Mendez sternly looked Gabriela in the eyes as she quickly walked by with the baby tightly cradled in her arms. As she stepped out of the bathroom, Chino impatiently gestured to her to hurry up. Gabriela played along and apologized as she approached Chino, following behind him through the bar area. Munoz turned and watched as Gabriela walked by. He blew her a kiss. Gabriela cringed, looked away and continued to follow Chino until they returned to the table.

"So, what took you so long?" Alejandro snapped.

"I told you I had to change the baby's diaper," Gabriela said as she looked into Chato's eyes. Chato was eating his food, with a slight smile. She turned towards Alejandro. "Whatcha think, I was in there peeing like a man?"

Alejandro stopped eating.

"Ha-ha-ha, I like this *chiquita!* Hey, speaking of peeing like a man, I have to go take a piss now." Chino quickly finished eating, then stood up and began to walk away.

"Listen, you should be grateful you're sitting with us right now." Alejandro took out his gun and pointed it at Gabriela under the table. "Don't make me have to use this on you, okay? Have some respect."

Gabriela looked down at the gun and then up into the fire in Alejandro's eyes. Even though Alejandro tried to act like a tyrant keeping Gabriela in line, she could see how vulnerable he was and played along with his theatrics.

"Okay, I'm sorry. I didn't mean to disrespect you."

"Good, don't let it happen again."

"Easy, *amigo*, easy, the girl was just kidding with you." Chato smiled.

"Yeah, that may be, but now's not the time to be joking around. Rosario will be here soon. All of us need to get serious and be on the same page, okay?" Alejandro looked angrily at Chato, who responded by becoming more serious and playing along.

"Don't do it again. No more wise remarks from you. If you act out of line again, it's not Alejandro you will have to fear, it's me, okay?" Chato looked sternly at Gabriela as he spoke. Gabriela could see that Chato was acting, but played along with the script.

"Okay, okay, I'm sorry, to the both of you."

As Alejandro, Chato, and Gabriela made peace and began to eat in silence, Chino walked through the bar area towards the bathrooms. After he walked past Mendez and Munoz, Munoz got up and slowly followed him into the bathroom.

Once inside the bathroom, Chino talked to himself as he ran his fingers through his curly hair and adjusted his shirt.

"She doesn't know what she's missing. She don't know, she could have all this, all this machismo. *Mujeres* love Chino, it's that simple. Chino walk down the street, *mujeres* come to Chino." Chino then paused and smiled as he admired his unfit frame in the mirror. His fucked-up teeth stuck out further like a horse the bigger he smiled. "Downtown, that's how I do. *Mujeres* know when Chino dives down, they stay down, moaning for more."

After Chino creepily spoke about muff diving on a woman, he flicked his tongue and then walked away from the mirror to go and take a piss. Piss splattered all over the floor and on his clothes. As Chino continued to relieve himself, Munoz walked into the bathroom, locked the door and walked over towards the three urinals. He chose the middle one, which was next to Chino.

As Munoz pretended to relieve himself, Chino looked homophobically at Munoz, then stepped closer towards the urinal, turning his back towards Munoz. Munoz continued to stare at Chino until Chino turned to look at him again. Munoz began to look Chino up and down and flashed him a smile. Filled with disgust, Chino turned away and mumbled as he cut himself off midstream and began to zip up his pants.

"Fucking faggot, Chino don't suck dick." Just as soon as Chino turned his back on Munoz, Munoz turned around as well and wrapped a piece of chicken wire around Chino's thick, flabby neck. Chino reached up for the wire and tried to shake off Munoz. Munoz struggled to contain Chino's oversized physique, but managed to force Chino towards the sinks. As Munoz firmly held the chicken wire while holding Chino up against the sink with his body, he looked into the reflection of Chino's eyes in the mirror.

"What are you gonna do with all the money you stole, huh?"

"Pha, pha, phuck you, you phaggot—"

Munoz smashed Chino's face down onto the edge of the sink, knocking out multiple teeth. The teeth rattled around in the blood-filled sink and then down the drain. Munoz pulled Chino's head back up by his hair. Four front teeth were missing from his blood-filled mouth. Chino stared at the blood pouring out from his fucked-up mouth, filled with broken teeth, as Munoz pulled on the chicken wire even tighter.

"Tell me, tell me, you pig-face motherfucker, where are you and your friend Rosario going with all the money?"

"To—to pay phor your whore of a sister—" Chino answered, forcing out insulting words as he smiled, provoking Munoz to become filled with rage.

Munoz dragged Chino away from the sink into the last stall. The unsanitary toilet in the stall overflowed, full of an excess amount of shit, mostly diarrhea. This was where Munoz dragged Chino, plunging his face into the toilet bowl. Chino squirmed around, trying to breathe within the bowl of feces.

"Who's a faggot now, huh, you fuck?" Munoz said. He brought Chino's head back up to the surface. Chino began to gag and spit up shit. "You don't look so pretty now, motherfucker. Tell me where you're taking the money!"

"To that bitch of a mother you have—"

Munoz pulled the chicken wire even tighter, piercing the skin on Chino's neck and causing it to bleed. Chino tried again to reach up and pull the chicken wire away, but didn't have the strength. In a heat of rage, Munoz pulled on the wire with sharp brute force. Chino took his final breaths, then fell limp, face first into the shit-filled toilet.

"*Puta madre!*" Munoz said with shock and surprise, since his intention hadn't been to kill Chino without him revealing any useful information. He lifted up Chino's unfit overweight body and sat him on the toilet. Munoz locked the stall from the inside and then climbed over the top. After leaving Chino in the stall, Munoz cleaned up all the blood from the sink and then left the bathroom.

<u>19</u>

As Alejandro, Chato and Gabriela continued to eat, Rosario showed up. He was a middle-aged Colombian with a brownish skin tone, a roguish poker face, and well-groomed straight dark hair, which was brushed back. He wore a white designer button-down shirt with the top three buttons left undone and open, designer jeans, and black leather designer boots. Rosario's diamond pinky ring, cufflinks, and gold chains and bracelets revealed status and high rank within Nada Mas. His presence overshadowed the day laborers, Alejandro and Chato, who greeted him. They stood, showing their respect.

"Amigo, amigo, cómo estás?"

"Bien, bien," Rosario responded and then sat down at the head of the table.

"So, do you want some food or a *cerveza, amigo*?" Alejandro asked as he leaned in closer across the table towards Rosario. Rosario was observantly scanning the entire restaurant and all those within, before looking back at Alejandro.

"No, no, *amigo*, I'm fine. Plus, I'm not gonna be here for that long. Anyway, where's—what's his name, the fat one?"

"Chino. He's here, he just went to the bathroom. He should be back soon."

"Okay, well, we don't need to wait for him, so let me see what you got."

"Of course, of course, *amigo. Mira, mira abajo*." Alejandro reached down and slid the diaper bag filled with cash and cocaine towards Rosario's feet. Mendez and Munoz both sat up as they watched. Gabriela could see the fury in their eyes and then turned back, along with Chato, who then both watched

Rosario. Rosario observed his surroundings once again, then slid his chair back a little and bent down to look in the bag. As he did, Chato looked out past Gabriela at the other federal agent, in street clothes, sitting at a table all alone, who he then nodded to. After Rosario counted all the money, he sat back up.

"It's a lot more than I expected."

"*Sí.* So with all that we have to give to Suarez, this should cover our debt, right?" Alejandro asked with concern.

"Well, your debt is between you and Suarez. You two know how Suarez operates. He doesn't like irresponsible people. Neither do I, because if you fuck up, I get the heat from Suarez. After I give this to Suarez, I'm sure he will be more than happy, and you no longer will have to worry about me hassling you for payments anymore, or your debt with Suarez," Rosario said sternly.

"*Bien, bien.* So when will we be able to see Suarez and speak with him, ya know, about our cut?"

"Right now I don't know. He's a very busy man, but as soon as I give this to Suarez and speak with him, I will contact you."

"*Excelente.*"

"So, where did all of this come from?"

"Why don't you ask the girl?" Alejandro suggested. Rosario turned towards Gabriela, who comforted the baby and then shyly looked up into Rosario's hollowed eyes.

"So, girl, what are you doing with all of this? Who gave this to you?"

Gabriela shied away and looked at Mendez and Munoz once again, who now began to stand up at the edge of the bar with their drinks. There was ferocity within their eyes. Chato once again watched, then turned back towards Rosario, along with Gabriela. Rosario took notice of Mendez and Munoz, cautiously watching them, and then vigilantly looked at Chato and Gabriela.

"I—I can't say who." Gabriela's words aggravated Rosario, who then leaned in closer.

"Listen, girl, you're in no position to keep quiet. You tell me who gave you all this, and who you work for. If you choose to make matters difficult, I will take you someplace right now. Believe me, you don't want that, because when I'm done with you, you won't recognize your reflection in the mirror."

Gabriela could see in his eyes that he wasn't joking. She had seen that psychotic look once before in Salas's eyes and knew to expect only the worst. The beneficial thing was that Gabriela was in a very good position. If necessary, she could reveal Mendez and Munoz, or even give up Chato's cover, if it came down to it. For now, though, Gabriela, would play along.

"Hey, why does it matter who she works for—" Chato stated.

"Why are you speaking? Who told you to speak? This is between your friend and me, and this girl, who is the reason we are all here now." Rosario turned towards Alejandro. "Is this your new friend, who started working with you?"

"*Sí*, he started working with us about a year ago. He was one of the new landscapers who started working with our crew. Remember? I told you."

"Well, I don't like your friend," Rosario said sternly. He looked at Gabriela, who looked at Mendez and Munoz, and then he turned back to look at Chato, who he caught glancing over at Mendez and Munoz. "And I don't trust him either."

The baby then started to cry, and Gabriela began to rock and shush the baby.

"Would you shut that baby up and keep it quiet, girl!"

"I'm trying! She's getting hungry, I need to feed her." Gabriela fumbled around with the baby and tried to pick small portions of food from her plate to feed her, only to accidentally knock over her glass of water, which spilled all over the table and her food. Rosario slid his chair back in an attempt to avoid getting wet, but became enraged as water flowed off the edge of the table and down onto his expensive jeans.

"*Puta!*" Rosario lashed out as he wiped his jeans with his hand and a napkin. "Clumsy bitch, look what you did!" Rosario then smacked Gabriela upside the head.

Mendez and Munoz became concerned for Gabriela. They stepped away from the bar but stopped in order to keep a safe distance. Rosario took notice of them. He was now convinced that they knew Gabriela and Chato, who he had already caught looking in their direction.

"C'mon, that's not necessary. To hit a girl over a spilled glass of water?" Chato said, but this only enraged Rosario more.

"Didn't I just tell you not to speak? Do you think I'm kidding and this is a fucking game we're playing over here?" Rosario turned towards Alejandro. "You need to keep these two in line, especially if you want Suarez to compensate you for all you have here today."

Rosario periodically glanced over his shoulder at Mendez and Munoz, who now began to separate and move towards their table. Rosario turned towards Chato again, again catching him watching Mendez and Munoz, and someone else sitting all alone in the back of the dining area, behind Gabriela.

"What is this? What's going on?"

"What—what are you talking about?" Chato said.

"Don't play dumb with me—your friends over there. The ones who have been watching us since I came in here."

Chato looked over at Mendez, who stood at a single chest-high round bar table, and Munoz, who remained at the bar. Alejandro took notice as well, but turned back towards Rosario.

"Easy, Rosario, easy, they're nobodies. They're probably just checking out the girl here like everyone else in this place has been doing since we got here. Relax, Chino had this place checked out before we came here. Everything is fine."

"Speaking of Chino, where is that fat fuck? I want him here right now."

"Okay, okay, I'll go get him." Alejandro stood up. "He's probably taking a shit." Alejandro then began to walk away.

Rosario continued to watch Mendez and Munoz as Alejandro walked through the bar area towards the bathrooms. Mendez and Munoz took notice of Alejandro, but remained in the bar area since they could see that Rosario was aware of their presence. As Rosario, Chato and Gabriela silently sat at the table, Gabriela continued to comfort the baby while looking at Chato, who again looked past her at the federal agent, sitting in the dining area behind.

"I need to speak to Suarez, so the both of you keep quiet." Rosario took out his cell phone, called Suarez's number and patiently waited for him to answer the phone.

Gabriela glanced over at Mendez and Munoz. She could tell they were on edge and willing to do whatever was necessary to get the bag of money back, especially now that Mendez was on his cell phone. Gabriela inferred that the call Mendez was making had to be to Salas, knowing Salas, Mendez and Munoz would surely get the okay to strike at any moment.

# # #

As Alejandro walked into the bathroom and someone else walked out, the overwhelming smell of shit caused Alejandro to cover his nose as he approached the last stall.

"Hey, Chino, are you almost done, man? Rosario's here, and he's waiting for you. You know how that paranoid asshole gets . . . hey, Chino, you all right?" After Alejandro got no response, he looked underneath the stall. He could see Chino's feet, but he could also see shit and blood on the floor around his feet.

Alejandro jolted up, kicking in the door. He froze when he saw Chino's limp body resting on the toilet. The ring of blood around Chino's neck, his mouth full of blood, slowly flowing out—all confirmed Chino was dead. Alejandro took his gun out, stepped back and then left the bathroom.

# # #

"*Sí, sí*, just a bunch of amateurs . . . As soon as the other one comes back, I'm gonna get out of here . . . No, no, no problems, just concerns, nothing major . . . Well, of course, when I see you later we'll talk in more detail . . . Okay, *amigo*, see you later."

After speaking, Rosario then slid in closer towards the table and noticed Alejandro speed-walking through the bar area and back to the table.

"We need to get outta here, right now!" Alejandro was agitated.

"What's the problem?" Rosario asked.

"Chino's dead!"

Rosario reached down for the bag filled with money and cocaine. As he did so Chato gave a nod to the other federal agent sitting in the dining area, then turned towards Rosario and took out his gun. Rosario noticed the federal agent communicating with Chato and instantly turned towards Chato. When he saw him reaching for his gun, he picked up a steak knife and stabbed Chato's hand.

Chato screamed as the steak knife pierced his hand with such force that it penetrated three inches into the table, pinning his hand down. Simultaneously, an explosion of fury and rage broke out. Mendez, Munoz, Rosario, Alejandro and the other undercover federal agent all drew their guns.

As a storm of gunfire blasted throughout the restaurant, patrons panicked, screamed and began to take cover, scattering and stampeding out the door. Alejandro had his back to Mendez and Munoz. He was the first to get shot as he took his gun out and turned towards them. They shot at Rosario. Bullets pierced Alejandro's chest, splattering blood everywhere and onto the floor, where Gabriela dropped down with the baby cradled in her arms to take cover underneath the table.

As Chato attempted to take the steak knife out of his hand, Rosario shot him in the chest, only to be shot in the right shoulder by the other undercover federal agent. Unfortunately, the undercover agent was mistaken as a threat by a civilian who exercised their Second Amendment right to carry a firearm. The agent was shot by the civilian, who then turned towards Munoz, who shot and killed him.

Rosario held his wound and continued to fire into the bar area, hitting a woman running for cover and one of the mariachi players. Mendez hid and peeked out from around the bar table, only to be shot in the head. After Munoz saw that Mendez was dead and he was all alone, he dove for cover behind the bar. Rosario used the moment to quickly reload his gun, lift up Gabriela, who was still holding the baby, and use her as a human shield.

Munoz popped out from behind the bar with guns blazing. Even though he noticed Gabriela was in a hostage situation, he shot to kill. Munoz's eyes were fixed on the bag of money. During the split second Munoz took his eyes off Rosario, he was shot three times in the chest and once in the face.

After the storm of bullets ceased, the haze of gun smoke was left lingering within the restaurant. The remaining patrons continued to scream and run out of the restaurant.

"Get the bag, hurry up and get the bag!" Rosario ordered Gabriela, forcing her down to the ground. Sobbing, Gabriela picked up the bag with the crying baby tightly held in her arm and stood up beside Rosario, who once again held her close to him like a human shield.

"Leave the baby, leave the fucking baby!" Rosario struggled to hold on to Gabriela while he quickly walked backwards, scanning the entire restaurant with his extended arm, and gun in hand.

"No, I'm not leaving the baby!" Gabriela said, her voice cracking, tears in her eyes. She tried to escape from Rosario, but he pulled her in closer and quickly headed for the exit.

"Fucking bitch!" Rosario yelled as he dragged Gabriela through the restaurant and out before police and more federal agents showed up.

20

As Gabriela gazed out the passenger-side window of a black two-door custom 1970 Pontiac Firebird with tears in her eyes, Rosario weaved in and out of cars as well as oncoming traffic. While the chaos unfolded around her, Gabriela remained in shock. She did not hear the screeching tires or honking horns, but instead her inner voice, telling her everything was going to be fine. Rosario's ferocious outbursts woke Gabriela from her sudden state of unconsciousness, bringing her back to the nightmare unfolding before her.

"¡Cállalo! ¡Calla ese bebé! ¡Maldita sea! ¡Cállalo!" Rosario violently lashed out.

The roaring car engine echoed, sporadically shifting and accelerating, the sounds laced with the dissonance of honking horns, screeching tires, Rosario yelling out and the cries of the baby; it all played out like a symphony of chaos.

No matter where the road ahead led, Gabriela would try to remain calm and have faith. Even as Rosario continued to dramatically lash out at her and the world around him, she would not submit to fear.

Within the mist of chaos and disorder, Gabriela's attention was drawn towards a pen, left rolling around on top of the dashboard. Everything since coming from Mexico lay within such a simple object, a pen.

Gabriela turned her attention away from the pen to take one final look at the blood flowing out of Rosario's open wound and at the fear painted on his face. She then looked deep into the eyes of the baby. Deep within them, she could see and feel the love that motivated and fueled Gabriela to sacrifice everything for the well-being of the baby.

"¡Maldita sea! ¡Calla *ese bebé, antes de que yo lo haga, carajo!"* Rosario reached over to grab Gabriela's hair and slap her, trying to smack the baby too. Gabriela cradled it tighter for protection. She was able to get off a few defensive smacks, catching Rosario in the eye and causing him to pull back.

Rosario screamed, holding his eye with one hand while trying to drive with the other. The baby continued to cry. Knowing the vehicle had no airbags, Gabriela anticipated the situation. She strapped her seat belt around herself and the baby, then lunged forward while tightly cradling the baby within one arm, grabbing the uncapped pen from the dashboard with her other.

Gabriela lashed out across the center console of the car, stabbing Rosario in the throat. As blood began to spurt out from his ruptured artery, Rosario reached up for the pen sticking out of his throat. Just as Rosario pulled the pen out, the car began to swerve out of control. Gabriela then held the baby even tighter, bracing for impact.

Like a pinball being smacked around, the Firebird rammed into the rear of a Cadillac Deville and careened into the left lane, where there was a Ford F-150 pickup truck, which crashed into the driver-side door. The impact pushed the Pontiac across all three lanes to the opposite side, head-on into a lamppost, which twisted, bent and came crashing down on traffic, stopping the car.

After Gabriela regained consciousness, all that could be heard was the baby crying, a long continuous car horn screeching, and the subtle crescendo of police sirens echoing out in the distance. Gabriela slowly wiped away blood from her forehead and then looked over at Rosario, who lay face down, his head on the steering wheel. Blood slowly dripped down his face onto the floor. Gabriela unstrapped her seat belt, forced open the damaged passenger-side door, and carried herself and the baby out of the twisted wreck.

As pedestrians approached and tried to comfort Gabriela, police sirens became louder. Gabriela was in a daze. Someone attempted to take the baby away from her. She became fully conscious and pulled the baby back, tightly cradling it in her arms as she limped away from the scene.

~Addendum~

Even during times of strife, one must stay strong and carry on, no matter how cruel the confines of life can be. Have the fortitude to conquer all that tries to destroy your dreams; keep chasing, keep seeking, keep living, for there is prosperity that awaits you at the end of the road. . .

<u>21</u>

Life is an enigma, an endless dance with fate. Most people's lives seem written and laid out as prepaved paths to be taken or guided by unknown forces, from birth to death, but no matter how lost or alone, everyone has the choice and free will to discover and fulfill their own destiny.

Ten years ago, after Gabriela blindly ventured out into the unknown, being led and guided by a series of synchronistic events down an unforeseen path, she didn't find her purpose. It found her.

Ten burned-out purple candles rested on top of a half-eaten birthday cake, covered with vanilla icing and filled with strawberry and banana cream. On the table beside the cake was torn wrapping paper and a framed picture of Gabriela and Sarita standing in Liberty State Park in Jersey City, with the New York City skyline in the background, illuminated by the setting sun. Next to that was a leather sketchbook, with Sarita's initials embossed on the cover.

"So, what did you wish for?" Gabriela asked after eating her last forkful of cake.

"Um, sorry, but it's bad luck to tell," Sarita said as she chewed her portion of cake.

"Well, I hope it was something good."

"Don't worry, it was."

"Well, hopefully it comes true, and you know what, I almost forgot. I have one more gift for you, a special one." Gabriela got up and walked into the bedroom. Sarita watched her leave the room with a devious smile and then reached across the table, grabbed Gabriela's glass of red wine and took a big gulp.

"Sarita! Didn't I tell you before that you're too young?"

"Sorry, but it, it reminds me of the blood of Christ from church. So, um, is that for me?"

"Yes, Sarita, just be patient, okay?"

Gabriela sat down, placing the present on the table in front of Sarita. It was a small flat square box, wrapped with purple-and-green Feliz Cumpleaños wrapping paper. Sarita reached out for the gift and removed the wrapping paper. Gabriela adored Sarita.

Sarita's gift was an ornate, polished wooden rosary. Sarita held it out with the rosary beads intertwined between her fingers, so that the cross dangled down before her and Gabriela. As she held it in her hand to admire, Gabriela got up and knelt down next to Sarita. Gabriela then reached out and held it up and leaned in closer to whisper into Sarita's ear.

"Do you like it?"

"I love it, Mama. It's pretty," Sarita whispered back. "So where did you buy this?"

"Buy? No, Sarita, this wasn't bought, it was made. It's worth a lot more than any rosary you can simply buy, because this was not made by some jeweler or craftsman. This was made by my grandmother, your great-grandmother."

As Sarita glanced over her right shoulder at Gabriela, her smile grew bigger.

"Um, really, my, my great-grandmother from Mexico?"

"Yes. So you see, not only was this rosary made by the hands of one of your blood relatives from Mexico, but there is so much history behind the rosary. It has been passed down from generation to generation, from Mexico to America, and now to you. I was given this rosary when I was ten years old, just like you are now, which is why I am giving this to you as a gift. It also has special powers."

"Really?" Sarita glanced back at Gabriela with a smile and then back at the rosary.

"Yes, really. It was blessed by a spiritual healer from Mexico, someone who was believed to be a modern-day saint. It brings good luck and good health to whoever possesses it. Whenever you feel alone, lost or sad, if you hold it have faith and pray, it will bring you comfort. It's worked for me many times before, and now it's yours."

Gabriela picked it up, put it over Sarita's head, and brought it down around her neck. Sarita touched the rosary, and Gabriela reached around to hold her hand over Sarita's.

"Happy birthday, Sarita." Gabriela and Sarita then silently sat beside each other. Gabriela had one arm around Sarita and the other on Sarita's hand with the rosary. Gabriela closed her eyes and began to softly sing a Spanish lullaby.

22

Her eyes closed, Gabriela softly sang a Spanish lullaby while cradling Elena's baby. Since fleeing, Gabriela had been living underneath a bridge within the heart of Los Angeles.

After she stopped singing, Gabriela lost herself in the baby's eyes. Deep within, she could feel an escape from all her misfortunes. Gabriela lived at the peak of the incline, just underneath the belly of a bridge. All she had and ever needed were the little things. Things of art and beauty, such as the initials of lovers placed within hearts, smiley faces, graffiti art and even numbers, such as the number thirteen, and 11:11. It was what filled Gabriela with a sense of persistence while she slowly dozed off into the night.

Waking up to the dawn of a new day, Gabriela would continue to carry on with her life, like a gypsy, in search of a place she could permanently settle. Living like a vagabond wasn't a major problem. Trying to provide and take care of the baby was difficult, though. Elena's baby lay calmly on the ground in front of a dumpster, wrapped within a cocoon of salvaged blankets. Beside her was a white plastic convenience store bag, which had a yellow smiley face and the slogan Thank You Have a Nice Day, filled with their possessions. Gabriela searched for food through the garbage cans beside the dumpster.

After fleeing the scene of the car accident and leaving the diaper bag filled with cash behind, Gabriela had no money to acquire necessities such as food and water, which was hard on the baby. Stealing from convenience stores or farmers' markets wasn't a sinful act in Gabriela's eyes, but instead an act of survival. Sometimes she would have to resort to garbage picking.

After finding leftover bread, half-eaten sandwiches and scraps of chicken, Gabriela sat on top of a three-foot-high cinder block wall in the back of an alleyway between two restaurants and fed the malnourished baby. As she did, she softly sang a Spanish lullaby, which seemed to cleanse the sense of misery and despair. Gabriela and the baby made the best of their situation.

Suddenly, Gabriela was drawn away from the baby's eyes and lost within the comforting eyes of a stranger. The English words were unrecognizable to Gabriela, but when the kind woman began to speak in Spanish, Gabriela felt safe. Veronica would become Gabriela's savior.

# # #

After being whisked away by Veronica, Gabriela found herself in a better place. She cleaned a countertop in the kitchen of a restaurant with a wash rag while softly singing a Spanish lullaby, but then suddenly, all sense of calmness was overshadowed by a thunderous uprising of unrecognizable vulgarity.

"Where the fuck is she? Where the fuck is the new cleaning girl? Hey, you, new girl, get over here!"

Gabriela didn't move. She was oblivious to the words being yelled out to her from across the kitchen. At first Gabriela was confused, but she was soon able to tell by the uprising tone that her short, fat, scruffy-looking restaurant owner boss wasn't in a pleasant mood. He continued to repeat himself in a loud and furious voice, storming into the kitchen.

"Hey, new girl, I need you, right now!" As the owner continued yelling for her, he came up behind Gabriela. She turned around, bumping into a waiter who walked by with a tray filled with entrees, which came crashing down and shattered all over the floor.

"Now look what you did, you clumsy little Mexican whore! This mess is coming out of your paycheck, and this—you see this? Look, *mira!*" The boss took the glass he held and pressed it up against Gabriela's face hard on her cheek near her eye.

Gabriela didn't move. Tears began to trickle down her face. He took the glass away from her face and held it in front of her, pointing to the lipstick stain.

"*Mira, mira, puta!* This isn't the first time this has happened, and I'm sure that it won't be the last! I'm only telling you once. If it happens again, you're gone. You can go back to sweeping floors and sucking cock!" The boss threw the glass to the floor. "Now, that's coming out of your next check as well! Veronica, come here and translate for her! Make sure she understands! Then have her clean up this mess!"

"Okay, *señor.*"

The owner turned around and walked out of the kitchen, leaving Veronica with Gabriela. Gabriela stood with tears in her eyes as Veronica cleaned up the mess. After cleaning up, Veronica stood up and embraced Gabriela.

"*Tranquila, no te preocupes. Es tu primer día en este trabajo, ya aprenderás,*" Veronica said as she wiped tears away from Gabriela's face. She ran her fingers through Gabriela's hair and then rubbed her shoulders. "Soon, Gabriela, you will be in a better place than this, I promise. For now you just need to be patient and not lose faith."

"Why is he always so mean to me? I try so hard but he's still so mean and never forgiving. I . . . I can't wait until I learn enough English so that I can leave this place and go to a better place, so far away from here. I thought America was supposed to be better, but it feels like I'm in hell." Gabriela sobbed, choking with each breath.

"America is a better place, Gabriela, in time you will see. For now, you must stay strong and never give up on your dreams. You will learn English, and soon you will end up in a better place and have a better life."

"*Eso espero, Veronica, eso espero.*"

Soon after the tears were gone, Gabriela sat on a bus, leaving behind a day of misery and misfortune. All Gabriela could hear on the crowded bus was unrecognizable English words. She looked out the window. Within a world of heaven and hell, filled with gods and demons, there seemed to be no sense of morality or peace. America's façade seemed dark, but Gabriela was determined to remain poised and have the faith to carry on.

As the days, weeks and months passed, with Veronica's financial and emotional support, Gabriela would become unwavering. Eventually, she grew confident. She felt in her heart that it was time to move on, leaving all she had experienced so far in in Los Angeles far behind. Gabriela was ready to venture further out into America. Veronica would send her to a friend to begin her next chapter.

23

The ever-changing façade of America flashed before Gabriela's eyes through the window of the bus as it drove from the Californian metropolis to the deserts of Nevada, Arizona, and New Mexico, and then to the rural plains of Texas. After traveling a great distance, Gabriela ended up in Texas.

Upon arrival, Gabriela was taken in by Diego. Like Veronica, Diego was a caretaker for illegal Latin American immigrants. Diego's ranch became a sanctuary for Gabriela, a place of solitude where she developed the skills needed to carry on with life in America.

In Gabriela's eyes, life was beautiful; each waking day was a blessing. Gabriela was a part of the Ochoa family. Diego's five children reminded her of Elena's baby that she had left behind with Veronica. There was Salvador, eleven, Rodrigo, five, the twins Felicia and Fernanda, seven, and little Tito, three. They all ate breakfast together as his wife, Cristina, cooked. Diego quickly ate his breakfast before getting up to kiss everyone goodbye and leave to start work for the day. The simple life on the farm was a reminder of everything Gabriela had left far behind in Mexico. It was comforting, and the perfect setting for Gabriela to learn and slowly evolve before continuing on with her life.

Gabriela arrived during the time of the summer solstice. Other illegal immigrants whom Diego cared for worked on the farm, while Gabriela spent the summer months indoors doing chores and caring for the children. Although school was out for the children, it was in session for Gabriela.

Caring for the children was not only fulfilling, but it was a way of shedding away the skin of who Gabriela had once been, slowly reeducating herself and evolving into someone else. The time spent with the children was a joy, and watching cartoons and movies on the television, reading children's books along with the bilingual children, was not only entertaining but very educational. Not only was Gabriela getting a glimpse of American culture through different mediums, but she was learning the English language. The children became Gabriela's teachers, along with Cristina and Diego. Diego's home was even turned into a school. There were labels written in English, placed on many different objects in various rooms of the house. There were even times when Gabriela was made to ask for things in English, which helped her skills.

Life, death and rebirth seemed to constantly come and go in cycles. It was evident that Gabriela's time on the ranch wouldn't last forever. Eventually, it would fade away. Gabriela would evolve like the butterflies that flew around Diego's ranch. Six months after she arrived, it was finally time to leave the ranch and move on. Diego decided to send Gabriela to Miami, to live under the care of a friend.

<u>24</u>

After leaving the Ochoa ranch, Gabriela arrived in Miami around the time of the winter solstice. She was presented with promising opportunities and the helping hand of her new guardian, Carlos.

Carlos was a Cuban immigrant who owned a successful nightclub, Carlitos, nestled deep within the heart of Miami. It was one of many nightclubs Carlos owned up and down the East Coast. He also had many important business associates and contacts connected to Nada Mas; like Carlos, these associates not only helped take care of illegal Latin American immigrants, but also organized and ran a branch of the gang.

Gabriela was always provided with support and love since arriving in America, but something was missing. She missed having close, trustworthy friends of her own age, and a social life. Carlos would provide Gabriela with not only comfort and a full-time bartending job in his nightclub, but friends as well. Claudia, Yvonne and Yannina, who also worked at Carlos's nightclub, became Gabriela's friends.

For the next two years, Miami felt like heaven. The bliss it brought reflected within Gabriela's beautiful dark eyes as she dolled herself up in front of the mirror in the bathroom, within the apartment she shared with Claudia, Yvonne, and Yannina. The *amigas* were all getting ready to go out and enjoy the Miami night life.

The girls ended up dancing within a sea of people on a dance floor of an exclusive Miami nightclub. As hypnotic, trancelike techno music exploded from the DJ booth, the shots and mixed drinks flowed like an endless stream, fueling the hearts and souls of the four young *amigas*. As the four blissfully danced the night away, Gabriela's beauty mesmerized the male suitors dancing around her.

In time, Gabriela chose one lucky individual to dance with intimately. His well-toned arms, gentle eyes, and affectionate lips made Gabriela feel safe. Three years after coming from Mexico, she felt like she was finally home; she had found a blind sense of peace and happiness. Continuing her path to New Jersey was no longer an option. Gabriela felt that she had found her bliss and would sow the seeds of the American Dream in Miami.

However, in the middle of a warm midsummer's night, three anonymous thugs came storming into the apartment in search of pharmaceutical drugs and cocaine—part of a Nada Mas shipment the other three girls held on to and kept secret from Gabriela. They woke the four *amigas* and confronted them with guns drawn.

The thugs dragged the girls out of their bedrooms into the living room. Gabriela, Claudia, Yvonne, and Yannina knelt beside each other in submissive servitude, frozen, whimpering, with tears in their eyes. The leader, a brute, pointed his gun at each girl.

"Dónde está la mierda!"

Echoes from a dark past Gabriela thought she had finally left behind flashed before her eyes. Before any of the girls had a chance to control their emotions, the thug pressed the barrel of the gun up against Yvonne's forehead.

"Dónde está la mierda!"

The four *amigas* were still unable to compose themselves. Their eyes were filled with tears. The leader lowered his gun in front of Yvonne's face, forcing the barrel of the gun into her mouth.

"Arriba! Arriba enséñame donde está la mierda, antes de que te rompa tu madre!"

Yvonne remained still. She gazed up into the thug's psychotic eyes with her moist mouth wrapped around the barrel of the gun. Trying to find her balance with the gun in her mouth, she stood up and guided the leader into one of the bedrooms. He continued to hold it between her lips as he shuffled beside her.

The other two thugs admired the three *amigas* who remained kneeling, whimpering hysterically. Yvonne eventually returned to the room along with the leader, who followed behind her with a gym bag in one hand and his gun in the other, pointed at Yvonne's back. She was forced to kneel back down beside the other three *amigas*.

Gabriela felt betrayed and expendable. She was blind to what had happened because the three *amigas* had kept this secret from her. She watched as the leader and the other two thugs took stock of the drugs in the gym bag.

As the four *amigas* waited for their unfortunate demise, the three thugs admired the beautiful women and plotted their final act before making their departure. The leader stepped forward in front of the four. He cocked his gun and aimed it at the *amigas*, pointing it to each of their foreheads, one by one.

"De tin marin, de dos pingué cucara macara títere fué, yo no fui, fué tete, pégale, pégale al quien fué." As he spoke his final word, he stopped before Gabriela, who was looking down through her hair.

The leader ordered Gabriela to stand, but she remained still. He pulled her up by the hair and forced her into a bedroom at gunpoint. She felt like she had been selected first for execution.

She was then filled with a sudden surge of confusion and uncertainty as she watched him place his gun down on top of the dresser. It seemed as if her life would momentarily be spared, but she still feared the worst. She was forced onto the bed, pinned and held down while the leader began to grope and take advantage of her. Her resistance was overcome by his masculine wrath.

There were then three gunshots sounded with three-second intervals. Gabriela quickly reached out towards the nightstand, grabbed the statuette of the Virgin Guadalupe and smashed it against the leader's head.

As the leader lay limp on the bed, unconscious, Gabriela quickly grabbed a bag and filled it with clothes and money from both hers and Claudia's secret stash. The other two thugs knocked on the door. When there was no response, they came storming into the bedroom with guns drawn and fired at Gabriela, who was already half out the window. Gabriela fell two stories onto the roof of a stationery truck. She crawled off the roof, and quickly limped away through the parking lot as the thugs continued to fire at her.

Eventually, Gabriela found refuge at a secluded area near the beach. She sat leaning against a brick wall, whimpering, while tightly holding on to her rosary. Tears dripped onto the ground into an ocean of tainted hopes and dreams.

25

After Gabriela finished sharing the beauty and the horrors she had faced since coming to America, she sat idle. Her audience of one, Ignacio, sat dignified, smoking his cigarette. He was filled with sympathy and respect as he observed her tainted demeanor. As the two silently sat before each other, while ashes trickled and cigarette smoke drifted, a calmness was felt by both.

"You know, I find it quite amazing how fragile life is. All the hurt, all the pain, and yet compensated by so much love and desire. You must be so broken and confused inside. And even though your emotional scars may run deep, they seem to be only fragments of a life and soul that is forever changing, and forever evolving. Your words have painted a better picture for me. Now I can clearly see how someone like you has blindly leaped into a fountain of unpredictable dreams and experienced such horrors. Seeing the bigger picture now has truly opened my eyes to a life filled with so much courage, yet a life which has also experienced so much love and hate and seen such horrors as death. But even when death surrounded you, it seems that your life has been spared. Maybe it's fate, maybe it's luck. Or maybe . . . it's karma, the idea that the life you now live is just part of a grand scheme of keeping all in perpetual balance." There was a long pause as Ignacio took a drag.

As Gabriela focused on the ashes dropping, she was filled with a symbolic sense of death and rebirth. Once she had gathered her thoughts, she looked up and brushed her strands of hair to the sides so that she could look Ignacio in the eyes.

"Perhaps it was what you say… karma… that my life has been nothing but a continuous cycle of experiences. Both good and bad, being relived and recycled until I figure out and understand this life and reason for being here."

"So, what is it you miss most? What happened next?"

Echoes from Gabriela's past resurfaced, including both the haunting nightmares and the most illuminated dreams. Although she was all alone at the time, there always seemed to be a lingering sense of a presence, as if she was surrounded by angels sent from below and above. In her eyes, remembering a time that appeared daunting was worth reviewing, not for the horrors, but for an unexpected gift which would change Gabriela forever.

"It all, even though things got worse, as if I had started all over again, like when I first came to America. Similar people and similar experiences came back into my life. It found me. I have no regrets, because what I relived, no matter how horrible it was, brought me the greatest gift anyone could ever ask for . . . life."

<u>26</u>

After arriving in New Jersey, Gabriela settled down in Newark Penn Station. Her shoes were a reflection of the miles of heartache and pain, all the sacrifices made with each step from Mexico to New Jersey. She found herself sitting like a pawn, with no options and no place to go. Even if she had followed in the shadows of a Monarch butterfly, Gabriela felt that she was at the beginning of her journey, still wrapped up within a cocoon.

Lurking in the darkness of the lobby was Ángel, a hustler who admired Gabriela. In the eyes of others, Gabriela appeared modest, but in the eyes of Ángel, she appeared as a *mamacita* who was in distress. Gabriela's beauty was a reminder of all he possessed, and her fear was a reminder of all he controlled.

As Gabriela looked through the crowd, blind to the predators of the night, Ángel began to creep across the vastness, pausing slightly with each step, like a panther stalking its prey, and then gradually increasing his pace the closer he got. Ángel's body shivered with ecstasy; his excessive appetite for sinful exploitation was beyond morality. Before Gabriela even had a chance to take notice of Ángel, she was lost within his piercing green eyes, entranced by his smile and clever mask of deception. Gabriela was brought underneath the wing of Ángel, and taken away.

# # #

After Gabriela was whisked away by an angel sent from below, Ángel humored her as he drove her through Newark to the Tops Diner, located on Passaic Avenue, across the Passaic River in east Newark on the Harrison border.

It was here where Gabriela would be catered to.

As Gabriela ravenously ate her cheeseburger and french fries, Ángel sipped his bottle of light beer. His gold claw pinky ring that adorned his right hand pointed up in the air, and he tapped his elongated fingertips on the top of the table with his left hand while he savored Gabriela's beauty. After Gabriela finished her meal, Ángel set his beer down. He began to caress his sunken cheeks while biting and sucking his bottom lip as Gabriela reached out with both hands to grab her glass of water.

"So, baby girl, hows long have yous been living like a scared little mouse?" As Ángel spoke he reached out his right hand to brush Gabriela's hair to the side so that he could see her face. After Gabriela set her water back down, she brushed aside Ángel's hand and tucked her hair behind her ears.

"What do you mean?"

"C'mon, baby girl, your life is no secret to Ángel. Like eyes told yous before, baby girl, eyes only here to help yous out. So, where yous coming from again? 'Cause the ways eyes saw yous before, yous looked lost, like yous just crossed the border."

"Mexico, but I lived in California, and I spent some time in Texas and Miami."

"So, how come yous moved around so much, baby girl?" Ángel rested both his elbows on top of the table with his hands clutched together.

"Because, things just didn't work out for me."

"Eyes see. So, any particular reason why living in Jersey would be better, baby girl?"

"No, it's just that I wanted to get as far away from Mexico as I could."

"So, what's yous running away from, baby girl? What are yous, in some type of trouble or something? Or yous just searching for the American Dream, baby girl?"

"No, no trouble, just like you said, searching for the American Dream."

"Shiiiiiiiiiiiit, don't yous know that the American Dream is a myth, baby girl? That yous just wasting yous time? Shiiiiiiit, the American Dream don't exist, baby girl, yous just like the rest of those damn fools who come to America searching for the American Dream. Yous all delusional, searching for the wrong thing, baby girl. Know what happens, baby girl? Yous all spend yous whole lives in America living in poverty, struggling more than yous did back home, working long hours like a slave for nothing, baby girl. Whats kinda American Dream is that, to live and work like some slave?"

Ángel raised his voice slightly as he leaned forward, reached into his pocket, and pulled out a wad of hundred-dollar bills. He sat up again and leaned forward to count the bills. "Now yous sees, baby girl, this is what the real American Dream is all about, money, power, playing God, baby girl. Yous don't get this by living like some slave. Now eyes know yous want a piece of this. Shiiiiiit, seeing the ways yous are now, and hearing the ways yous got to Jersey, eyes know yous weren't being helped or living with just friends."

"What—what do you mean? I don't understand."

"Well, baby girl, with a beautiful face like yous, I have a feeling that yous weren't just sweeping floors or making soup of tha day to survive in America. Eyes also have a feeling that some of yous friends are like me. And by the way yous looked at my money, baby girl, eyes know for certain that yous had this type of money flashed before yous eyes before. Yous have that instinct and look in yous eyes to do whatever is needed to get this money from my hands. So what's it gonna be, baby girl? Yous gonna speak truth and let Ángel take care of yous, like yous friends before me, or yous still gonna play these silly games and force me to go get my friends in the blue suit and blue hat sitting ova there in that booth to take care of yous? Right now, baby girl, eyes all yous got. Without me, yous be back in the streets, abandoned and all alone with nothing and no one, or yous will probably end up doin' what eyes providing for yous right now, or worse, end up dead in some gutter in the street. So what's it gonna be, baby girl?"

Although Gabriela wanted to turn the other way, since she had no one and nowhere to go, she was willing to take the risk in order to get settled in and eventually move on with her life.

# # #

Illuminating light from lightning sporadically flickered and flashed within the darkness, while thunder banged and flood rains poured down from a passing storm, echoing in the distance like a symphony of the night. Gabriela silently leaned against the corner with both her arms crossed in the shadows of a two-family home used as a front for providing an excess of sex, drugs and gambling.

Inside, a haze of cigarette and marijuana smoke filled the dimly lit room, filled with an array of businessmen and blue-collar guys, accompanied by a variety of legal and illegal Latin American whores. At the center of the cesspool of sin, filled with greed, lust, slothfulness and excessive amounts of mindless self-indulgence, was a poker table, occupied by seven of the blind souls.

Ángel stood on the opposite side of the room and admired Gabriela. For the past six months since being brought here by Ángel, Gabriela had lived for free as his trophy girlfriend. It wasn't a moral path. Deep within Gabriela's heart, she had faith that she would find a way out, once she mapped out her future.

Ángel approached Gabriela. He guided her through a crowd of people and took her away into another room. As Gabriela followed behind Ángel across the vastness, from a table occupied with a group of artists, she felt a wave of bliss that pierced through her heart like Cupid's love-stained arrows.

Gabriela froze and gazed up through her hair to see what brought such delight in such a terrible place. It wasn't an object of affection but one of the artists, named Dante.

Dante looked up into Gabriela's eyes. Deep within his crystal-blue eyes, Gabriela saw an ocean of tranquility. And just as suddenly as a taste of heaven blanketed over all of Gabriela's pain, it was forever gone. Ángel whisked Gabriela away.

Before they would meet again, Gabriela stared at her reflection in the mirror while Ángel lay passed out in the nude on the bed behind her. As Gabriela stood naked, tears began to trickle down her cheeks.

27

Clouds slowly drifted across the warm summer night sky. The luminosity from the full moon shined in through the open window, illuminating Gabriela as she silently gathered her clothes and belongings, in the nude. After six months of living as an advocate of sin, Gabriela was finally in a position and well-balanced state of mind to leave it all behind, as Ángel was left passed out on the bed.

Before her departure, Gabriela stealthily removed a floorboard from the corner of the bedroom and took cash from Ángel's secret stash. Although it wasn't much, just enough to live off for a month, it would be Gabriela's insurance and the driving force behind her great escape out the window.

Gabriela would carry on through the industrial landscape of North Jersey, eventually ending up in Elizabeth. It was here where Gabriela would settle down into a studio apartment and reseed the roots of her American Dream. At first, living in Elizabeth was refreshing, as Gabriela was able to live a life of solitude, beyond the bounds of the system.

Living in poverty was nothing new, but in Gabriela's eyes, to finally be able to live a pure and simple life on her own, for the first time since coming to America; to live life and watch the world from a different perspective; to sit back from daily routine and not be enslaved by time or someplace to be; and not to consume, not to be in a survival state of mind—for now, this was being rich and free beyond borders.

Unfortunately, though, every day was a ritualistic routine of searching for work, and trying to find someone trustworthy enough to become a possible companion or friend. Each day was exactly the same. As the days passed by, Gabriela was unable to find a job, or a single soul with the potential to become a benefactor or true friend. What made matters even worse for Gabriela was that her financial security was beginning to fade away. Gabriela was running on empty, with only a month and a half left before being evicted. Gabriela felt her only escape was to be on the streets in the hope that the right person would magically come into her life. After spending a long day roaming around the streets of Elizabeth, unbeknownst to Gabriela, she was being stalked by a predator of sin who followed her in the shadows to her apartment.

The soulless male was dressed in black. He hid his face underneath the darkness of his hood. He wasn't out prowling around in the night for money or material goods. He was on the hunt for sweet and fresh pussy. Recently released from a ten-year sentence at Essex County Jail, the criminal with a history of assault, misdemeanors and rape, and ties to Nada Mas, was craving a female counterpart. Gabriela just had the misfortune to cross paths with the criminal right as dusk set in. No matter how many times Gabriela cautiously looked back over her shoulder, she was unable to detect her approaching attacker, who came up behind her as she approached her apartment door. He muffled her mouth, tightly grabbed her around the waist, and forced Gabriela into her apartment.

Inside the apartment, the attacker pinned Gabriela face down on the floor. He sadistically ripped the clothes off her frightened body, gagged her with her own belt and bound her wrists together with an electrical cord before feeding his sexual appetite. The thickness and girth of the unwanted phallus forcefully penetrated Gabriela's tight womb from behind. His act brought tears and crippling pain to Gabriela as she hopelessly gazed out across the scuffed-up wooden floor while crying out for help. For what seemed like an eternity in perdition, eventually it slowly faded away as Gabriela passed out from the emotional and physical pain. The rapist had finished conquering his first female since being released into society. He left Gabriela all alone on the floor, like a dying dog.

When Gabriela awoke, she spent the rest of the day scrubbing and cleansing her physical wounds in the shower while resting in the bathtub in a fetal position. Blood slowly trickled down the drain from her bruised vagina. Gabriela cried out and prayed for the pain to go away and for God to heal her wounds.

Gabriela's damaged heart and soul were corroded over with black and blue, and broken dreams. During the remaining days before being evicted, a cloud of depression arrived and permanently parked itself over Gabriela. She became completely possessed by demonic forces, pulling her along a downward spiral into a dark abyss. Fear consumed her, and because she feared losing her sovereignty in America, Gabriela wouldn't report the incident to the authorities. Instead she submitted to the darkness of keeping her emotions bottled up. She tried to move on with her life, but the trauma of being raped was so overwhelming that Gabriela gave into the demons. She submitted to her suicidal tendencies, spending her final days in a bathtub filled with blood and water.

# # #

As above, so below. As the persistence of time became nonexistent, from beyond the darkness of heaven and hell, behind closed eyes, a soothing voice echoed out in the distance.

"Tranquila, tranquila, relájate, tu estás a salvo ahora, todo estará bien."

Gabriela slowly opened her eyes to the blinding lights. At first, she was only able to vaguely see two angelic figures. Eventually the images manifested into a woman and a man. Gabriela's vision adjusted to the light and focused.

"Dónde . . . dónde estoy?"

"Estás en el hospital. El dueño de la casa te trajó aquí después de encontrarte en la tina del baño."

"¿Por qué? ¿Por qué estaba en la bañera?"

The nurse didn't say a word. She just looked into Gabriela's eyes and down, along with Gabriela, at her bandaged wrists. Gabriela caressed them, and as she did, the doctor began to speak.

"Do you understand English?" the doctor asked. Gabriela was unresponsive as she continued to caress her wrists. Finally, she looked up.

"Yes."

"Good, I'm Dr. Surasdevas. First of all you're a very lucky girl thanks to your landlord, who found you when he did. And also, you shouldn't worry, it was a failed attempt; you cut your wrists the wrong way. It seems that you've been through a lot. You shouldn't worry, though, because we're here to help heal your wounds, both physical and emotional. Everything is going to be okay. You'll be able to stay here for a few more days so that you can recover. Eva and I will be here to look after you, so you're in good company. What you should do now is get some sleep, rest. After conducting a few tests, we've found that your body has been through a great deal of trauma. I wish that I could stay a bit longer to be with you, but duty calls. You'll have Eva beside you for the time being. Oh, and one last thing before I go. I have some more good news for you. You're pregnant."

Gabriela's eyes lit up and her body became numb. "When did I become pregnant, and by whom? Was it Ángel or the rapist? Hopefully not, but what will I do? I'm all alone and have no money." After Gabriela was able to gather her thoughts, tears began to form and roll down her cheeks. In the eyes of the doctor and nurse, Gabriela saw happiness. She was able to force a smile to her face. She then reached down to caress her stomach. Deep within was a rebirth of life. Whose child it was, was disturbing, but no matter where the road ahead led, Gabriela would no longer be alone.

28

The thought of Sarita filled in the void. A haze of smoke slowly faded away and Ignacio began to speak.

"Mamá, how poetic that after all you have been through, you were left with a child, *una niña.* Becoming a mother during such desperate times and being able to independently overcome such hardships and horrors as you— you've lived a revolutionary life, indeed."

Ignacio then took a drag of his cigarette. Gabriela focused on her stomach while caressing the emptiness within—remembering how it had once been filled with Sarita.

"Nothing else compares to the sacred bond between a mother and child. Like heaven and earth, the infinite love shared seems to be the only truth. Even after living the life you have, shedding away all the tainted skin of sin you've fallen into advocating, the love you have for your child still remains. Knowing how sacred your bond is with your child, and how much you love her, what seems to interest me most is that your child, who is the love of your life, has come out of such a damaged womb. So, being the curious individual that I am, I must know—how does it feel when you look your child in the eyes to tell her that you love her?"

Ignacio's enlightening dramatics suddenly changed like the tides, to a subtle tone of taunting despair. The everlasting impact pierced through Gabriela's heart like a jagged spear, instantly causing her to lift her head and look up into Ignacio's cold, dark eyes. Deep within was the true face of

Ignacio—a deceiver, a man whose only purpose was currently to provide his enslaved female with humor and lies. Gabriela experienced another sudden sense of déjà vu. Once again, it was as if Ignacio and she had shared a moment once before, but an inner fury slowly built up from deep within.

"How do you think I feel? It hurts. Every time I look her in the eyes, it haunts me. Not because of who I once was or the life I've lived, but because I know what's out there waiting for her. I've seen such haunting and disturbing things. I have even looked death in the eyes. I know how evil the world is and how cruel it can be. Does she know the life I once lived? No, of course not. She's only a child. If anything, I give her glimpses. Will I ever tell her the truth, when she's old enough to understand? Absolutely. And whenever I do look her in the eyes, no matter how haunting it is when I tell her I love her, that love, no matter how flawed, is everything. It's my heart and soul. My love for her is forever."

As a haze of smoke filled in the air between Ignacio and Gabriela, the two shared a moment of silence once again.

"Your love for your child is strong and everlasting, a love that overshadows all that once was of your life lived in darkness. Yet I still seem to have this sense of pity and respect for you. I pity how your child has come from such a damaged womb, yet there is also a great sense of respect for the path you chose and the life you've lived. But what seems to interest me most is seeing how the past and present have now come full circle. How you seem to have blindly overcome such negative influences. I respect the patience you seem to have possessed throughout the horrors of it all. You have the patience of a saint, yet you've lived a life of sin, which fuels my curiosity even more. So I must know, especially seeing how your child hasn't manifested from a virgin birth— who's the father?"

"Does it matter?" Gabriela answered with a slight smile, in the likeness of the Mona Lisa.

Ignacio removed the cigarette from his lips to flash Gabriela a grin. Gabriela looked down and held her stomach, still remembering how it had once been filled with Sarita. Sarita was no longer by her side, but Gabriela only had to close her eyes to imagine her presence. From behind her closed eyes, Sarita was alive and well, and knowing this provided Gabriela with all the love she needed to endure her state of captivity.

29

The police state was in full effect. Federal authorities had put downtown West Orange, New Jersey, on lockdown while authorities from various agencies, both federal and local, went door to door in search of their suspect. They eventually located him and held him in a highly secured location. A run-down two-family home was now the center of a child abduction situation.

Dimitri Romanov, a broad-built Ukrainian who was an ex-Siberian special forces militant, was tightly held down on the second floor of a two-family home tucked away at the end of a dead-end street. He was held by local police officers, Essex County Sheriff's Department officers, New Jersey State Police officers, and an FBI task force who had been on the hunt for Romanov for the past four months.

The hunt had culminated in a hostile situation that had slowly manifested from the final stages of Romanov's heated divorce from his ex-model wife, Alana, and his refusal to accept the fact that he would never be allowed to have custody of, or even see, his seven-year-old daughter, Sasha. Amongst the mayhem and the media circus were the two FBI agents in command of the FBI task force: Special Agents Alec D. Donovan and William W. Walsh.

Donovan hurried with a yellow Have a Nice Day smiley face stress ball tightly clutched in the palm of his hand. He was a thirty-five-year veteran of average height, slightly overweight, with a short ten-dollar haircut. He had salt-and-pepper brown hair and a scruffy face, and he found relief in cigarettes and Xanax.

Special Agent Walsh childishly followed behind Donovan. He was in his early thirties, of average height, thin and fit. His short, dark hair was cut in a fifteen-dollar fade. Walsh was beginning his third year as an FBI agent and his second year as Donovan's partner—thanks to the demise of Donovan's former partner, Special Agent Wilson. Wilson and his entire task force had fallen victim to a horrific tragic accident involving an abandoned house, a stray dog, matches, fireworks and a leaky gas line.

Donovan and Walsh were the only two survivors left from the task force. Walsh had quickly moved up the ranks to become Donovan's partner and second-in-command of their new task force. Donovan had once been skeptical of Walsh, but now accepted and appreciated being his mentor and having him serve as an apprentice.

"What a goddamn mess. It looks like a fucking zoo over here! C'mon, Walsh, keep up!" Donovan weaved in and out of federal and local officers, agents and vehicles, Walsh staggering behind him.

"Hey, who's in charge here! Why in the hell are officers still hanging around like we're having a goddamn street fair over here?" Donovan yelled as he approached two high-ranking officers, one from the West Orange Police Department and the other from the Essex County Sheriff's Department.

"Whoa, whoa, settle down big guy," said De Meo, the high-ranking West Orange police officer.

"Big guy? Ya hear this fucking guy?" Donovan muttered under his breath as he turned towards Walsh, who now stood beside him. "Listen, I'm FBI Special Agent Alec Donovan. I'm the one who authorized the lockdown of this whole area, and the one in command of the federal agents on site. I will now be taking over command of this whole situation."

"Is that so? Well, way to be on time," Mullen, the high-ranking Essex County Sheriff's Department officer said to Donovan, who reacted by tightly squeezing his stress ball. "Listen, the show's all yours. Just in case you haven't heard yet, after this Dimitri Romanov guy shot and killed his ex-wife's boyfriend, who was watching the daughter at the time, he abducted her and has been on the run for the past four months. He was seen trying to get some money from a friend in a park in Irvington—"

"Yeah, our informant," Donovan cut in.

"Yeah, well, he's your dead informant now. After Romanov picked up on your boys watching the money exchange, he shot his so-called best friend in the fucking face and ran off with his daughter. He pistol-whipped some senior citizen for his Buick, then fled the scene, which led to a high-speed pursuit up 280 to downtown West Orange, where he then lost control and crashed into the Edison factories down on Main Street. He fled the scene with his daughter, shooting at and wounding two West Orange police officers, and ended up in that house over there across the street. Right now, he's bunkered down on the second floor. All we know is that he's armed and the girl is with him. As far as hostages, it's still unclear whether or not there was someone on the second floor; we're still trying to make contact with the suspect, who we haven't been able to get a visual on yet."

"Listen, I'm aware of Romanov, his past, and everything unfolding now. I've been on this case for the past four months. What I'm unsure about now is why there aren't gunmen on the rooftops. The entire perimeter should be secured by now."

"There's a chopper."

"I can see that, I did two tours in Nam. I know what a chopper looks like, and I also know that a chopper can't see inside that house!" Donovan snatched the walkie talkie out of Walsh's hand. "Smitty, you there? . . . Good, everyone's here, right . . . Okay, this is what I want. Get me two gunmen on the rooftops of each flanking house, one on each of those three houses across the street, and two gunmen on the rooftop of that building. That's about, um, twenty, thirty . . ."

"Looks like it's fifty yards away," Walsh added.

"I know that—fifty yards behind the house. I want a secure perimeter from all angles, that's as tight as Suzy on prom night. In and out, no blood tonight, boys."

All units, both federal and local, then began to move in, stealthily positioning themselves up on top of the rooftops. Still with no visual of Romanov, Donovan had no intention of sitting back and waiting for the fugitive to make the first move. He was a card hustler waiting for the right moment to put all bets on the table. The high-ranking officers both renounced Donovan's actions, warning him that blindly walking into the situation was a fatal mistake. Donovan continued to squeeze his stress ball while conducting his orchestra of defiance.

"Don't try and come in here, you phuckin' cop, or I kill . . . I kill all you wit my bare hand!" Romanov yelled psychotically out the front window of the second floor while standing in the open with no shirt on, gun in hand. All officers took cover and aimed their weapons on him.

Walsh took cover behind an unmarked SUV while Donovan grabbed a bullhorn from one of the other FBI agents and stood out in the open.

"Listen, Dimitri, no one here wants to hurt you. We're all here to help you, but in order for that to happen, we need cooperation from you. We just want to talk with you, talk about what you want and what we can do for you . . ."

"No phuckin' way. No, no, I trust no cop or man. Phuck you all, I just want leave wit my daughter, that's all. I want leave here wit my daughter and go home, back to Ukraine."

"I understand your feelings, Dimitri. I understand where you want to go with your daughter. But before we can talk about what you want and what we can do for you, first we need you to calm down and then calmly come out of the house with your daughter . . ."

"Don . . . Donovan . . . we . . . we . . . ," an FBI agent's voice suddenly disrupted Donovan, followed by static.

"What . . . what was that, Walsh?"

More static came through the walkie talkie as Walsh held it closer to his ear. "I'm trying to listen." As Walsh adjusted the frequency knobs, Donovan stepped towards him, snatching the talkie while Romanov continued to yell out explicit words.

"Smitty, is that you? . . . Smitty?"

"Donovan . . . I've got a visual of the girl, repeat, I've got a visual of the girl . . . the girl is all alone and quickly moving to the back of the house."

Donovan drew his gun and commanded all officers to enter the house from the rear.

"Back door is clear. Back door is clear. All units enter from the rear, the girl is in the clear! Here, Walsh, you're on the horn, keep Romanov busy for five minutes." Donovan handed Walsh the bullhorn, then ran up the street to go around to the rear.

"But, but . . . what do I say?"

"Tell him you love him."

"What in the hell do you think you're doing? Are you fucking crazy? Blindly going in without knowing if there's any hostages!" Mullen yelled while Donovan ran across the street to join the other officers raiding the house from the rear. All the other officers remained in position at the front of the house on standby while Romanov continued to yell out the front window.

"Look at all you phuckin' weak mans, I break you all like matchstick, phuckin' weak American mans, you!"

"Um...you shouldn't say that. We're—we're here to help you, be-because we love you." Walsh shivered as he stuttered into the bullhorn, causing Mullen to snatch the bullhorn away. After Mullen demoted Walsh, he proceeded to use the bullhorn to speak with Romanov, who was now no longer seen standing on the second floor in front of the front window.

The old wooden steps of the back stairwell creaked and cracked like rolling thunder. Federal agents stampeded up the stairs in tight formation with their guns drawn, followed by Donovan, who came sprinting up the rear. Romanov finally realized his daughter, Sasha, had left his side. Frantically, he raced through the length of the second floor to the back.

"Sasha . . . Sasha!" Romanov ran into the kitchen, only to be confronted by federal agents. The remaining agents quickly filed into the kitchen in strategic formation with guns drawn, provoking Romanov to take aim and stand his ground.

"Drop your weapon! Drop your weapon!"

"Down on the ground! Down on the ground, get down on the ground now!"

"Phuck you, you phuckin' mothaphuckas. Go ahead, shoot. Shoot, you phuckin' pussy mothaphuck!"

As an uproar of chaos unfolded, federal agents firmly stood in position with their guns pointed at Romanov. Romanov stood his ground, with his outstretched arm frantically scanning and pointing at each federal agent, while apishly beating his bare hairy chest with his other bear paw. Romanov's itchy trigger finger discharged the gun, which shot one round into a federal agent's thigh. Four other agents, including Donovan, unloaded their clips on Romanov.

Soon after the barrage of bullets and gun flashes cleared away, there was an overcast air of gun smoke, along with bullet casings scattered across the grimy tile floor. Romanov's blood was splattered all over the kitchen walls and floor, his body now lying limp in a pool of blood. Before any of the other units were notified, one agent checked the wounded agent while the other two searched the rest of the second floor for the daughter. Donovan scanned the whole scene, while he spoke on the walkie talkie.

"Donovan here. Suspect is down, repeat, suspect is down. Second floor is clear, send up other units."

The other two agents searching for the daughter returned. "All other rooms are clear, and no sign of the girl."

"The girl's gotta be in here somewhere; keep searching. How's Ortiz?" Donovan took out his smiley face ball.

"He'll be fine. Right, Ortiz?"

"Yeah, once this fucking pain goes away. Fuck."

"Agh, stop whining. I got three licks while patrolling in the bush for four months in Nam, two in the shoulder, and one in the gut. You young bucks need to toughen up." Donovan keenly observed the kitchen, approaching the kitchen sink and then kneeling down before the cabinet door, which was left slightly open. He opened up the door to find the daughter, curled up in a ball with her eyes closed, squeezing a teddy bear.

Donovan didn't say a word, just smiled as he put his stress ball away. He ran his fingertips through Sasha's hair, caressing her face to calm her down, which caused Sasha to open her tear-filled eyes. Her eyes were as white as eggshells, while she remained crouched, shivering all over.

As more federal agents entered the kitchen and began to secure the scene, Donovan reached in, pulled Sasha out from underneath the sink, and stood up with her cradled in his arms. Once again in Donovan's thirty-five-year career, he walked away unharmed, with an abducted child safely in his arms, unscathed.

30

The window booth inside a well-kept family-owned Jersey diner was now the humble setting for FBI Special Agents Alec D. Donovan and William W. Walsh. After bringing closure to the Romanov case, Donovan and Walsh were now free from further engagement on another high-profile case for the first time in many months. All they were left with was paperwork. They needed to follow up on previous cases and conduct further investigations, keeping a watchful eye on high-profile pedophiles and other sex offenders.

For now, Donovan ate his bloody, rare bacon cheeseburger, one hand doused in blood and grease while simultaneously checking text messages on his smartphone. Walsh ate a BLT and onion rings. As he ate, he kicked his feet back and forth, alternating his gaze between the view out the window, the fully occupied diner and Donovan. Walsh reached across the table to take ketchup-drenched french fries from Donovan's side plate, while he waited for Donovan to continue with their conversation.

Donovan smiled while slamming his smartphone down on the table. "Thirty-nine texts and fifteen voice mails," he said with his mouth full of ground beef. "I swear, the older I get, the more she has me by the fucking balls. I got no more breathing room, Walsh. You'll see, one day when you get married. The suffocating begins as soon as you say 'I do.' That's when the beast comes out from within them. From then on, they control everything: your home, your car, your bank account, your sense of style, and even your thoughts and opinions. I'm not making this shit up, Walsh, you'll see. And just wait until you have to deal with all the nagging and the bitching and moaning. I swear, even when you're right, you're wrong. Enjoy your youth, Walsh. You have an ocean of PTA out there waiting for you." Donovan bit into his bloody bacon cheeseburger again, leaving Walsh in a confused state.

"PTA?"

"Yeah, pussy, tits and ass. I mean, my God, look at that brunette over there."

Walsh turned around to look, but turned back after making eye contact with a young, voluptuous college girl wearing short shorts and a tank top.

"Um, yeah, she's okay."

"Okay? Just okay? You're not gay, are you, Walsh? Ya know, you're not pole surfing or drive shafting, are ya? It's okay if you are, but I'm just saying, PTA's much better."

"Na, nooo, no way."

"Good, good. So, you still going steady with—what's her name?"

"Bobbi Jo." Walsh stated, causing Donovan to pause; he then elaborated, "It's a she. Nah, no more. Things weren't working out, so I'm single now."

"Back in the game, that's what I wanna hear."

"Yeah, I guess."

"Anyway, where'd we leave off? Where was I?" As Donovan spoke, pieces of chewed hamburger meat fell down onto the table and his lap.

"Romanov's connection to various pedophilia rings and drug trafficking networks."

Donovan continued ravenously eating his bacon cheeseburger and ketchup-drenched french fries, reaching across the table to take some of Walsh's onion rings. He shook salt onto his food.

"Yeah, Romanov, the Siberian Bear, what a piece of work this fucking guy was . . . goddammit. Damn ketchup bottle. Hand me some napkins, Walsh! C'mon, hurry up. It's all over me!"

Walsh quickly handed Donovan napkins. The quarter-filled ketchup bottle had sprayed ketchup everywhere because Donovan hit it on the bottom with the palm of his hand. Donovan wiped down his ketchup-stained white shirt and cobalt-blue tie and the table top.

"My wife's gonna kill me. These stains will never come out! Dammit!"

"Easy, Donovan, calm down. Did you take your meds yet?"

"Agh, forget the meds!" Donovan crumpled up the napkins into a big ball, tossed it to the side, then pulled out his stress ball. "Anyway, Romanov's no fucking teddy bear, know what I mean? He was involved with a lot of shit and connected to a whole lot of POS's."

"POS's?"

"Pieces of shit. I mean the fucking scum of society, involved with pedophilia, drug trafficking, and human trafficking. Romanov had his hand in everyone's pocket: dirty old men, young perverts, bankers, politicians, teachers, dirty cops, even CEOs of high-profile companies. I mean he was hustling and providing for all these kinds of people, any drug of your choice, cocaine, marijuana, crystal meth, heroin, pharmaceuticals, Internet porn, children and young girls from Ukraine, China, and Mexico, and providing for pedophiles from all over the country. Good thing we got to him when we did. If we hadn't, he'd probably be pimping out his own daughter, the sick fuck."

As Donovan paused to eat some french fries, Walsh reached across the table to grab Donovan's pickle.

"So, who's running all these different networks that Romanov was working with?"

"Well, what I can say is that each network is its own entity. You got the drug trafficking coming from various drug cartels, both domestic and international, various pedophilia rings and human trafficking rings. As for Romanov, he was just a smart and successful business partner providing for all these different networks. But, lately from the intel I've been gathering on my own throughout the years, and what other agencies have been picking up on, is that all these different networks, the drug trafficking, the human trafficking and the pedophilia, are all conducted and controlled by one source. Some domestic cartel known as Nada Mas. I mean this thing is fucking big. Its tentacles reach all the way down to the tip of South America, which is not a whole lotta global mass, and nothing new, but its impact and influence on politics, corporate

America, and banking are fucking enormous."

"So, who's controlling all this?"

"Well, no one knows for sure. Even the CIA and NSA can't figure it out. Whoever it is, they're untouchable. But I'm sure there's someone out there who knows something and knows who and where the source is. Anyway, as long as no more children are being abducted or hurt by anyone connected to this monster, I'll be able to sleep at night."

After Donovan spoke, there was a moment of silence. Donovan was filled with an array of emotions and visions from his past.

"The children—ya know, since I don't have any, any case I'm on and any case I've been on for the past thirty-five years, I take personally. Each abducted child I'm looking for and trying to protect, I see them as if they were my own. It's my calling, to protect children from such evil people. You're young, Walsh, you haven't seen anything yet. Some of the cases I've worked on and the suspects I've dealt with make any horror movie you've ever seen seem like a Disney classic. In my thirty-five years on the job, I've saved and protected hundreds of children. No fatalities under my belt, except for this one time."

Donovan paused to sip his soda.

"It was my fifth year as an agent and my first high-profile case. My task force at the time got called in to handle a kidnapping and a shooting in some small town out in the Midwest. But that wasn't the worst of it. The suspect was some schizophrenic father who lost his job, whose family was falling apart. After getting divorced and losing custody of his daughter, one day he woke up and decided to murder his ex-wife. "

"When she came home after dropping their daughter off at daycare, he shot her in the fucking face with a shotgun, right as she came walking in the front door. He left her bloody mess in the house and went to the daycare to get his daughter. He just walked right into the daycare, unnoticed. He first shot the custodian who confronted him in the hallway and then walked into the room his daughter was in. Before the daycare counselor even had a chance to gather the children, he shot her down, took his daughter and left the scene. "

"He fled to a nearby house after forcing his way in. We arrived, had a visual and made contact. Then he allowed me to come in to talk to him. He had his daughter standing in front of him in the kitchen. What I remember most was the look in his eyes. They were as black as night. Even the whites of his eyes were black. There was no one home. He was very robotic, as if he was possessed. And the girl, she was terrified, trembling with fear, tears in her eyes, all choked up and trying to speak. 'Help me, help me,' she kept trying to say. "

"The suspect's name was Gary. He was calm and spoke very soft and clear. I remember having good, calm communication with him for about twenty minutes. I was even able to get him to give up his gun. Unfortunately, the gun wasn't the concern. I smelled gasoline. Gary and his daughter were standing in a puddle of gas. "

"Before I even had a chance to make a move, in a very calm manner, he just took out a small gas can out from under the sink behind him, and—and . . .'"

Donovan choked up and paused before continuing.

"Without warning, he doused himself and his daughter with gasoline and lit his Zippo. I—I hesitated and just panicked. I froze up and watched as they burned up in a blazing inferno . . . I could see their skin melting. I could hear the girl screaming in agony, I . . . I'm still haunted to this day by the girl's screams," Donovan said softly.

There was a moment of silence. Walsh looked away and down.

Donovan continued. "Besides the girl's voice I still hear in my head all the time, one of the things I remember most is the little girl's eyes. She had these big, gorgeous blue eyes. Every case I've been on since, I always recall the look in the girl's eyes: hopelessness. And I tell myself, I never want to see a child in a situation like that ever again. I still have nightmares from that day, and I hope I never have to be in a situation like that, ever again." Donovan finished his soda and sat back.

"Well, you only have a few more months until you retire, Donovan. After this Romanov case, it looks like you'll be in the clear and end your career on a positive note."

"I hope so, Walsh, but then again, anything can happen in the next few months. All you need is someone in a desperate situation with a motive to abduct a child. Anyway, I'm all done, you done yet?"

"Um, yeah, I'm good, ready to go?"

"Yeah, let's get outta here and head back." Donovan slid the bill across the table to Walsh, who began to put his jacket on. "All yours, Walsh."

"I paid last time, remember?"

"Whoa, not from what I recall. Don't get cheap on me, Walsh."

Donovan looked down upon Walsh as he stood up, put his jacket on, and ate the remaining french fries. After Walsh paid, both Donovan and Walsh were free from any further child abduction case. Donovan was in the clear to end his thirty-five-year career and retire on a positive note. There was still a window of time left, though, for anything to happen.

31

As the world slept during the night, hidden somewhere in the most desolate region of the Americas, gathered within an undisclosed meeting room, were the key players from Nada Mas. Inside the bare charcoal-stained metallic modern décor meeting room, sitting around an oblong conference table, were all the alpha males, the head figures from the various branches within Nada Mas, socializing and scheming while they waited for their most significant host to enter the room and begin the meeting.

Present at the meeting were the three major bosses of the drug trafficking branch of Nada Mas, each their own separate entity. There was Suarez, a firm swashbuckling Colombian who conducted drug trafficking operations on the West Coast. The two Cubans—Don Fernandez, a broad-built boss, and Carlos, an older, unfit, humble boss—worked up and down the East Coast. Beneath them on the pyramid were the two Mexicans: Salas, a short, bald tyrant with Napoleon syndrome, and Mariano Cruz.

Although both were involved with drug trafficking on the West Coast, with Salas based in California and Mariano Cruz based in Mexico, it was Cruz who was also part of the human trafficking branch of Nada Mas, whose coyote system, based in Mexico, trafficked migrants from South and Central America across the US-Mexico border.

The other bosses involved with human trafficking were Viktor Vyhovsky, a neurotic white-bearded Ukrainian who trafficked Europeans and Eastern Europeans across the Atlantic in cargo ships to the East Coast; and Gang Gao, a frail, quiet, yet strong and fierce Chinese man who trafficked Asians across the Pacific in cargo ships to the West Coast.

Along with all the Asian, European, and Latin American bosses, all the important power players from the United States of America were also present. There was Timothy T. Townsend, an American entrepreneur born into a bloodline of wealth, whose family had founded and still ran one of America's biggest pharmaceutical companies, Curatio. Townsend's role within Nada Mas was to supply the various drug trafficking branches with pharmaceutical drugs to be sold on the black market.

Also representing the American branch of Nada Mas was Jeffrey Rothstein, an important player in the entertainment industry, with links to major Hollywood studios, record companies, social media networks, and various production companies. Besides Rothstein, there were the political and legal forces within Nada Mas: Calvin Coughlin, an American investment banker and politician with ties to D.C. and Wall Street; and Eric Edwards, who was connected with all the American government's federal agencies. The Reverend Jefferson C. Collinsworth from South Carolina was present too, a broad six-foot-five African American with a well-groomed black-and-gray head of hair and beard and an empowering presence and voice, associated with many ministries and Christian sects and the NAACP, a civil rights activist with ties to the FBI and CIA. Randel Rosenthal, Nada Mas's official lawyer, was in attendance. Sitting amongst the powerful kinsmen with big egos was the most significant piece of the whole structure: Sven Schaffert, the banker who kept the hard-earned money of all the bosses and high-ranking members of Nada Mas safe in a Swiss bank.

The council of fourteen was together for the first time. It was the official birth of Nada Mas, and tensions were high as to who controlled what, who worked alongside who, who could be trusted, and most importantly, who Benny, the mastermind behind Nada Mas was. The high-ranking members only knew Benny through highly secured e-mail exchanges and brief phone conversations in which his voice was disguised, and through a network of messengers. Benny was the ultimate shadow figure, a man of myth people only knew through word of mouth. The atmosphere in the room was filled with anticipation, since it was rumored that the mystery man behind the curtain was ready to reveal his true identity. Only time would tell. A series of multiple bolts and locks unlocking and an industrial-sized steel door opening and closing could be heard beyond the metallic walls of the undisclosed meeting room. Each member of Nada Mas fell silent and turned towards the front of the room, where a side door began to slowly open up.

Marta Mendoza, also known as La negra corazón, slowly walked into the meeting room and stepped before the head of the oblong conference table. She was a chubby five-foot-tall Mexican woman in her forties with short dark hair, who wore lots of makeup and a one-piece black-and-white business dress. She controlled the Mendoza drug cartel from Mexico.

There was a sudden gasp and then silence. Marta Mendoza was used to the look of shock seen on the faces of men. Marta stood in front of the egotistical men of power and smiled as she set a leather business handbag down on top of the table. She opened it, took out packets and placed them in two stacks, which she handed to Don Fernandez and Suarez, who both sat at the front of the table, to pass out to the others. After all the packets were handed out, the men scanned through their packets like children on the first day of school, fearful, yet curious as to what to expect and who their headmaster is.

"Boys, welcome, to the first official meeting with all of the pioneers of Nada Mas. As you can all see, I am not Benny; I am Marta Mendoza. For those of you who don't know, after the sudden death of my twin brother, Martin, due to cardiac arrest, I am now in control of the Mendoza drug cartel in Mexico, my homeland. Some of you here might have heard of the Mendoza syndicate. And probably now what you are all wondering is, 'Why is this woman standing before me? Where is Benny?' Well, truth be told, since Benny started out working for and with the Mendoza family, I am now not only the only one he trusts, but the one he has chosen to organize, unite, and oversee the operations conducted by all of you. I am proud to welcome all of you, for being not only the seeds, but the life force behind what is now Nada Mas."

Marta Mendoza's hoarse, raspy voice flowed out like a soothing breeze, seducing all of the alpha males, yet provoking some with resentment.

"What tha fuck is this shit? A fucking woman, telling me what to do!" Suarez slammed the packet down on top of the table. Salas turned the other way in exasperation as he sucked his teeth.

"Easy, Suarez, easy, give the woman a chance to speak," said Don Fernandez, who sat across from Suarez.

"Easy, are you kidding me? Do you see what stands before us now?" Suarez said with his arms spread open, looking up and down the table at the other bosses.

"Would you please let the woman speak so that we can all listen to what she has to say first, before we jump to conclusions? Remember, we're all in this together."

Eric Edwards was a well-fit and toned retired Marine sergeant major, with ties to the CIA and other federal agencies, firmly stated. He sat at the head of the long conference table, on the far end next to Sven Schaffert.

"Now one of the gringos supports this woman! Why am I not surprised?"

"A gringo who has helped you, your parents and your family cartel smuggle drugs into my country and money into yours," Edwards lashed out in defiance.

"Please, please, Suarez. Please, would you be quiet and just listen so that we can move on with all of this?"

Cruz, who sat beside Suarez was becoming annoyed, calmed Suarez's ferocity, along with the threatening looks all the other members gave Suarez. Once Suarez settled down, Marta then continued.

"Thank you, gentlemen. As for the boy, I sure hope that you're done now, because, believe me, with an attitude like that, you will not last long within this circle or any other, that I can guarantee. It's a shame your parents aren't still alive to discipline you. Your attitude is an insult to their humbleness and loyal devotion to Nada Mas," Marta stated. Suarez arrogantly smirked.

"Now that we are through with the nonsense, before we begin, I will say that although the packet which you all hold is big, we will not be discussing everything contained within it in detail at this meeting. At the end of this meeting, these packets will need to be returned in exchange for your cell phones, which were collected at the door. Now, what I have to say is of importance, but will be short and sweet."

As Marta Mendoza spoke, the bosses scanned through their packets. Each contained a pyramid chart of Nada Mas, an outline of operations for each branch of Nada Mas, the order of operations regarding the process each branch conducted individually and with others. It also contained inventory, finances and the flow of money, the official Nada Mas philosophy, contact information, and a message from Benny.

"As you can see, every branch within Nada Mas is its own entity, yet cannot function without the others. It was made this way deliberately so that no one will be able to go rogue and break free, causing all the other branches to fail while the lone wolf is able to move on alone and succeed in a manner where they will become a monopoly and gain such power that none of the other branches will even be able to exist. This was Benny's vision from the very beginning. Following this vision is why Nada Mas has become what it is today, and why it will continue to move on in this manner and evolve into a global network of dominance."

As Marta spoke, half of the bosses gave Marta their full attention, while the other half continued to scan through the packet.

"So, basically we're all working hard and risking our own lives in order to feed this machine that one man controls from behind the curtain?" Jeffery Rothstein asked.

"I agree," Timothy Townsend said. "While we're all out in the fields, working hard, in a state of fear, producing and making money for this mystery man we only know from emails, disguised voice mails and word of mouth, we're supposed to remain loyal. We were coyly brought together and now put in a position where we need one another in order to continue with what we do. He remains anonymous, but we must now bow down to this Wizard of Oz."

"He's right. How do we know that our identities will be kept safe, and our finances will remain secured? No offense, but I hardly know any of you, and you, mister money man—how do I know you won't play around with my hard-earned money?" Salas neurotically lashed out.

"Please, please, I am professional banker who handles many important man's finances. Along with Randel Rosenthal over there, we're the two who are protecting not only all of your finances, but all of your legal situations."

"He's right. So if there is anyone who is skeptical of this whole operation, what I can say is that I was at least able to be in the same room as Benny. Although I wasn't allowed to see him, I did speak to him. I assure all of you that not only are your finances safe, and your legal status, but that as long as all of you remain loyal to Benny, Nada Mas and its philosophy, you will all be fine."

"Fuck this bullshit. Now the Jew Americano is trying to tell me everything is going to be fine and we can all trust each other and dance naked together in a field of daffodils! Fuck this shit! I hope you all know that Nada Mas was once my parents', a Colombian ideology! Benny, this fucking gringo stole the whole concept!"

"Silence, Suarez, because since the beginning, as loyal and respectful your parents were when Benny was working for me and my brother at the time of his rise to power, their ideologies were very cynical. Remember, it was Benny who masterminded the drug trafficking operations for your family's Colombian cartel. With that said, isn't Benny the reason your family cartel has been able to succeed and you were able to rise to power after the sudden death of your parents? So, enough of this childish nonsense, okay? Can any man here now say that they haven't become successful financially and grown their operations within the past few years of all of us working together under Benny for Nada Mas? Anyone?"

Silence filled the room. Marta had gained the respect of the majority, and even though Suarez had been a thorn in the side of Nada Mas since the beginning, it was his rise to power and his successful drug trafficking operation that now gained him respect amongst the others.

"Pardon me," Carlos said calmly, "but before you continue, I'd just like to say that I was very skeptical in the beginning as to who I could trust and whether this scheme of all of us working together as one entity to gain more profits and power would succeed. But being where I am now, I'm glad to say that I'm a happy man. I may not know all of you personally but I do understand that we are all pieces of a bigger picture, and that without one piece, the picture will not come together."

Don Fernandez gave him a pat on the shoulder. All the other bosses looked at Carlos as he spoke and gave him a nod, except for Suarez and Salas.

"All this that I see in here, I agree with, along with what some of you have said about becoming more profitable and growing bigger together. I agree very much with this project and its philosophy," Viktor Vyhovsky said as he scanned through the packet.

"Excuse me," Calvin Coughlin interrupted, "but just to add to all you have stated—Viktor, correct?"

Viktor nodded.

"Okay, well, being in the position of power that I am, in the United States, what I can add is that this project that we are all a part of is actually bigger than I think some of you may even be aware of." Calvin looked sternly at Suarez and Salas, who remained silent, yet poised.

"This network that currently operates only within the Americas will eventually grow into a global network, which will not only benefit us, but will be able to manipulate global markets, governments, and write the course of history. We are in a position where we can grow to achieve world dominance, which will be able to change all of humanity, based on our influence over world affairs."

"Keep speaking truth, brotha, 'cause that's the way I see it. This, all of this which we have created together, is more than just a money-making machine and temple of power. It is something more, something that can break down barriers and unite all of humanity, all depending on how we channel this power and influence that we possess. We are at a point where we can take the machine we've created and use it to either benefit humanity in a benevolent manner or, with corruption and abuse of power, use this in a malevolent way to control all with a whip and an iron fist," Reverend Collinsworth said passionately, filling the hearts and minds of the other bosses with pride.

"Thank you to both of you for seeing what I have stated before, that the original intent of Nada Mas was to benefit humanity," Marta responded. "Even though it sounds contradictory, since what we all do is corrupt, illegal and sinful. But, beneath the surface of it all, for those who can see, we are giving people a product they want, and no matter how dangerous or terrible our services appear to be in the eyes of the corrupt politicians and corrupt legal system we stand against, we are, in fact, givers. Givers who understand that there is corrupt competition within the whole structure of society, which we are trying to defy. The facets within the American government who corrupt and control all with corporate monopolies, government puppets, the banking system, a plethora of lobbyists, and imperialistic policies—we, Nada Mas, are the cancer to the American crime machine. It has corrupted and controlled not only its own people since it's been hijacked by very powerful men of influence, but all of humanity throughout the world. It's time that we give back. And, I warn you, Nada Mas was created in such a way that, if one of you becomes corrupt at heart and manipulated into becoming a loyal servant of our predecessors, which Benny foresaw could ultimately happen, you will be silenced."

Everyone listened as Marta spoke. Suarez and Salas spoke to each other in defiance of the Robin Hood image Marta created about Nada Mas. Before Marta was able to continue, Gang Gao began to slowly stand his brittle frame up, with a little help from Viktor Vyhovsky and Jefferson C. Collinsworth.

"To Nada Mas, and all that we will create with strength and honor, not only for ourselves, but for all of humanity. To the idea that we, as a people, can strive beyond the servitude of corrupt men of power, by slaying the dragon with its own sword."

Gang Gao's soft words laced with a thick Chinese accent pierced the hearts and minds of all like a spear of inspiration and hope for the sovereignty of humanity, provoking all to stand up and show their respect to the old wise man. All except Suarez and Salas, who remained seated. All the bosses then sat down, and Marta concluded the brief meeting of Nada Mas bosses.

"Thank you, Gang. You don't know how much your words truly mean to all of us, and to Benny, who I will inform of your devoted loyalty to this project and its ideologies. I feel that everything that needed to be said today has been said. Although this meeting is now over, we will continue with this week's conference later today at the Mendoza Chateau, where all of you will be accommodated and safe to spend some time freely roaming around the exquisite grounds. Not only do I expect to see all of you at our follow-up meeting later today, but I hope to see all of you at our traditional banquet dinner. There will be music and entertainment for all of you. Gentlemen, it has been a pleasure. For now I bid you all farewell."

After Marta spoke, she packed up her handbag. Don Fernandez wooed Marta with his gaze. Marta returned a flirtatious smile before leaving. Upon Marta's exit, all the bosses began to socialize and scheme as they stood up to leave. Suarez and Salas were left sitting unamused as they spoke amongst themselves. Although Suarez and Salas were the thorns in Nada Mas's side, Nada Mas would strive, with or without them, only time would tell.

<u>32</u>

As sporadic beams of sunlight shined in through the open window, the gentle wind blew in through the curtains, the wind chimes, and the oscillating fan, which all melodically echoed out. All around the apartment, there was a wafting scent of garbage, paint, and alcohol, and everything within was left unkempt. The paint on the ceiling and walls was cracked and spiderwebbed throughout. All the used furniture, such as a couch, a cot, a coffee table, a tiny kitchen table and a bookshelf, were crammed together on one side of the apartment.

The entire kitchen was skeevy. Water dripped down from the leaky faucet into the sink filled containing a week's worth of dirty dishes, and there was a pile of garbage on the floor that had fallen from the overflowing garbage can that had been left abandoned for days. The tile floor and stovetop were grimy, and empty bottles of beer, liquor, and wine filled the countertop.

On the other side of the apartment there was an assortment of paintings. Hanging on and leaning against the walls were beautiful abstract portraits, landscapes, still lifes, and contemporary paintings. Lying all over the paint-stained floor and resting on top of a studio desktop were empty paint cans, dirty brushes, and stacks of sketches and paper. Near the open window was an easel with an unfinished painting.

The unfinished image resting on the easel was an esoteric masterpiece, and lying in the dimness on the decrepit couch was its creator, the mysterious, reclusive man. His outstretched half-naked body lay facedown on the couch, illuminated by the beams of light that stretched across the apartment. As he lay there like a demigod, wearing nothing but a pair of old paint-stained jeans, awaiting his destiny, his calling, his well-defined, chiseled, toned upper body was a reflection of Dionysus, as if he was created and carved by the hands of divinity.

He lay unconscious within his arms, while his long dirty-blond hair hanging down over his face. As the wind chimes resonated blissful tones, the mysterious, reclusive man began to adjust his body. After he woke up, there was a great disturbance, an intensified banging like a percussion of rolling thunder, slowly building up to a crescendo. It felt like hammers banging steel within his head.

At first, he remained still, but then found the strength to sit up and hold his head as he tried to sober up. Unfortunately, though, the banging became louder and louder and made the pain in his head worse. And as the banging became even more forceful, he turned to see the door moving from the impact. A painting hanging on the wall near the door came crashing down.

The mysterious, reclusive man grabbed an empty wine bottle from the coffee table to arm himself before getting up to go open the door. But before he even had a chance to get up, there was a voice.

"Wake up! Wake up! Dante . . . Dante, for God's sake, wake up!"

Hearing the familiar voice, Dante put the bottle back down on the coffee table, got up and then staggered over towards the door. As Dante opened the door, he held his head with his other hand.

"Jesus Christ! You're completely plastered again! For God's sake, get yourself together!"

A short, stocky man wearing a suit, with slicked-back curly hair and a mustache, came storming into the apartment. After Dante shut the door, the man walked around, kicking empty bottles and garbage as he shook his head, threw his hands up in the air, rested them on his hips, and then threw them up in the air again. As the agitated man paced around, Dante made his way to the refrigerator, pulled out a bottle of beer and began to drink it.

"Well, I guess this goddamn mess explains what you've been up to for the past month, and why you never answer your phone or return any of my messages! I can see that you have gotten more drinking done than painting! You were treading water, my friend, and now it looks like you're drowning in booze! You had it all, Dante—talent, success, you had what other struggling painters only dreamed of, and what do you do? You ignore the fact and piss it all away! I'm the reason you have a one-man show after being in exile for the past thirteen years, and I'm also the one who is protecting you from your past, and this is how you repay me! This is your last chance, Dante, your last chance to lift yourself up from the shithole you came from and be back on top in paradise . . . *paradiso,* my friend. And now it seems like it's lost, *perduto!*"

Dante stumbled around. Greco stood before all of Dante's unfinished paintings as Dante stepped up behind him and mumbled while he pointed to a painting with his beer in hand.

"That one's almost done."

"What! That one's almost done! Which one? Because to me, Dante, they all look like they're almost done! In fact, it looks like you just started every one and they aren't even half-finished! You do realize, Dante, that you have one month! *Uno!* One! That's thirty-one more days to have thirty paintings completed. It looks like it's going to be your last one-man show, because before me right now, all I see are about ten unfinished paintings!"

Dante pointed to one on the easel.

"Wait! Wait! Hold the auction. I'm sorry, ten and a half. Ten and a half unfinished paintings that are now worth shit! You do realize that this last show will make or break you? Dante, please give me some kind of a response that you're still alive and can hear what I'm telling you!"

Dante, stood with his head bowed down while sipping his beer, and then flicked his hair back so his face was visible. He looked up at Greco with his hazy bloodshot eyes.

"Yes, Greco, I understand what you're saying. It's just that lately I've been going through some hard times, but I'm over it now. I'll be fine. The paintings will be done by the end of the month. Remember my second show at the Galleria Azul? I only had fifteen days to complete thirty paintings. Remember what happened? I finished them all with three days left, and that was one of my most successful shows. I sold out, remember that, Greco?"

Greco shook his head back and forth.

"Remember! Remember! Want to know what I remember. I remember you were a young, cocky, very talented painter who wasn't stuck at the bottom of the bottle, who had many women and not one of them distracted you from your work. You could paint around thirty paintings in six months, better and faster than any other painter who had a year! Do you want to know what else I remember? I remember you let a woman come into your life, who got too close, and you ended up becoming too attached, and eventually fell victim to her spiderweb! I remember you running away to the bottom of the bottle, like always when you find yourself in distress, but this time it was a girl who got the best of you. And it's ironic, because this time you weren't the one who left, leaving someone with a broken heart! I remember this time, you were the one left behind with the broken heart, and now I see a sad, sad man who is drowning in booze, and if he doesn't get himself together and try to swim back up, he may drown and end up dead at the bottom of the bottle, with nothing but a broken heart by his side!" Greco turned around and began to walk out the door.

"Get it together, Dante! Start swimming! And get yourself out of this mess! I'll call you in two weeks to check up, you better answer!" Greco kicked empty bottles and garbage as he walked out, slamming the door behind him, causing another painting to fall.

"Fucking asshole," Dante mumbled. He took another sip before going into the bathroom to wash his face and look into the mirror. His reflection was someone he didn't recognize anymore. He had once been an aspiring painter who traveled the world and became successful in other countries, only to come back and lose it all. Dante's reflection was that of a hopeless man who knew that all he had left would be gone if he didn't get himself together. But he also knew that there were other paths he could take instead to preserve his legacy.

Only time would tell. Dante slowly walked through the mess in the apartment, put on a shirt and then lit up a Lucky Strike. Each drag felt refreshing. And as Dante continued to smoke, he paced around and studied all his finished and unfinished paintings. All Dante had in life was before him, and what was left wasn't what it used to be. They were the remnants of an aging artist with nothing to live for. Dante knew he had to find the fortitude to complete what was left, but there was still a shadow that forever lingered over him.

The past was Dante's never-ending nightmare. Nada Mas, and all he had been connected to, was what haunted Dante night and day. No matter how many years had passed since Dante had left and gone into hiding, he knew that someday it would find him. Especially because lately, Nada Mas had been slowly crumbling apart. Dante had made a commitment to Greco, but he had already made a bold decision to leave it all behind without warning.

Attached to the refrigerator door was a plane ticket. After Dante studied his paintings, he walked into the kitchen and removed the plane ticket to look at it. As Dante continued to smoke his cigarette, he stared at the plane ticket for Aero Mexico flight 1203 from JFK Airport to Mexico City. The plane ticket was Dante's escape from his past, and Mexico was freedom. No matter how much Dante wanted to leave, there were still remnants which emotionally held him back: Gabriela and Sarita.

Their detachment was anomalous, for their protection. Dante walked over towards the open window, grabbed a stool and brought it over to his easel. There was an unfinished painting on it. He wanted to savor what was so sacred to him. Dante put his cigarette out in an ashtray, then grabbed a half-finished old bottle of warm beer resting near the easel. He took a sip, and then held a paintbrush in his hand while looking out the open window. Outside the window was the courtyard, which was filled with the usual people, and over by the swing set were children, amongst them Sarita. Even though Dante's true and everlasting love, Sonya, the one who had broken his heart, was forever gone, it was Sarita who above all else was his light of inspiration, which seemed to have healed Dante's broken heart and keep him close to home.

<u>33</u>

There was a buildup of laughter which soon faded away as Steven pointed out the mysterious, reclusive man in the window.

"There he is again, watching us from the window," Steven said as he stood behind Sarita and Tatiana, who sat on the swings, slowly rocking back and forth. They stopped to look up at the mysterious man watching them from the window, along with the other children.

"I heard that he's a child molester who kidnaps children and keeps them locked up in his apartment," joked Matty, who stood beside the swing set, next to Tatiana.

"Nah, I heard he's a serial killer. That's why he never leaves during the day and only at night so no one can see him. All those murders that happened lately, I bet he's the killer."

Sammy stood beside the slide, which the twins, Maria and Magdalena, were silently sitting on, cringing with fear mixed with a slight smile. Steven then leaned in closer to Sarita as he whispered into her ear.

"He's watching you, Sarita. He's waiting for you to go home so that you'll be all alone in the hallway, so that he'll be able to get you and lock you up in his apartment, forever." As Steven backed away from Sarita, Tatiana turned around.

"Dang, yo, why y'all all up in her Kool-Aid?" Tatiana loudly said.

"I wasn't even talking to you."

"Well, y'all must be, since Sarita's tha only one ain't scared to go knock on that damn fool's door. Ain't y'all tha one who lost tha bet wit Sarita? And now y'all acting like y'all bad and all. Shou eyes know what y'all trying to do, y'all trying to make another bet wit Sarita, so yous can try and get y'all money back. Don't listen to that fool, Sarita. He's still all upset and all, 'cause yous won all his money." Tatiana turned around to face Sarita as she dramatically spoke her final words.

"Um, yeah, I know, and, and you shouldn't worry about your money, Steven, 'cause I keep it in a safe place," Sarita responded, turning around to face Steven with a slight smile.

"Well, the only reason you're not scared of him is because you live right next door."

"No, that's not true." Sarita slowly turned around to look up at the man in the window. "Even though I live next door to him, I've still never seen him before, and, in the middle of the night, when it's quiet, I can hear him through the walls, talking to himself, and sometimes he screams, and breaks stuff."

"Maybe there really is someone inside with him," Sammy added. Maria and Magdalena embraced each other.

"Well, what about your mother? Has she ever seen him before?" asked Matty.

"Um, *nunca* . . . never."

After Sarita spoke, there was silence as all the children looked up at the mysterious, reclusive man in the window. Even though Sarita had some blind insight as to who the man might be, she, like all the other children, still feared the unknown.

"*Sarita, ven acá que vamos a comer,*" Gabriela yelled as she leaned out the window.

"Um, I—I have to go. Bye." Sarita got up off the swing and began to walk away from the other children.

"Hey, Sarita, watch out for the serial killer."

Sarita stopped, turned around to face the children, and then turned back around and gazed up at the mysterious, reclusive man's window as she continued to slowly walk home.

34

Curiosity consumed Sarita as she walked up the stairwell. Stepping into the hallway, she stood before the mysterious man's door. She imagined who he really was. After taking a big breath, she stepped towards his door, stopping only an arm's length away. Sarita then lifted up her arm and stretched it out until her fingertips were touching the door, and then attempted to knock.

"Sarita, cuantas veces te tengo que decir que no molestes a ese pobre hombre? Déjalo en paz. Ven aquí ahora mismo."

Sarita paused with her fist held before the door. She opened her eyes, sighed, stepped back, turned around and ran past Gabriela and into the apartment. As Gabriela shut the door behind Sarita, she ran towards the kitchen to sit at the kitchen table for dinner, where an aroma of authentic Mexican spices and food filled the atmosphere. After Gabriela joined Sarita, the two prayed and then began to eat chipotle chicken taquitos.

"I hope you weren't going to play knock and run again."

"Um, maybe," Sarita said with a slight smile.

"Sarita, why can't you just leave the poor man alone?"

"Um, I don't know. I'm—I'm curious, since I've never seen him before, only when I'm outside and he looks out the window. But even then, I really can't see him well enough."

"Well, I still don't understand why you're worried about the poor man. He doesn't bother anyone. He's harmless, and he keeps to himself."

"But, but Mama, aren't you curious at all? You've been living here longer than I have. You, you can't expect me to believe that not only have you never seen him, but that you aren't curious at all, even after all these years?"

Sarita opened up doors to Gabriela's past, a past Gabriela knew would someday have to be revealed.

"Maybe a little, Sarita, but . . ." Gabriela struggled to find the right words.

"But . . . but what, Mama?" Sarita enthusiastically said while she leaned forward in her chair. Gabriela finished her glass of wine, poured more, and took a sip. Even though there were many doors to Gabriela's past, the one that was now slowly opening up was filled with remnants from the dark path she had taken into America long ago. All those criminals connected to Nada Mas, with whom Gabriela was associated, and Dante, the mysterious, reclusive man. All aspects of Gabriela's life that she wanted to keep hidden from Sarita, if only for her protection. Gabriela felt that glimpses would keep Sarita's curiosity asleep.

"Sarita, before you were born, as you already know, I lived here in this apartment when I was pregnant with you, thanks to Eva, the nurse who was with the doctor when I found out I was pregnant. Eva was so generous, she let me live with her and took care of me until she was able to help me get a job and this apartment. When I first moved here, I had no friends. I was all alone and worked every day and every night, so that I could make more money and have a lot more to save, so that when you were born, I would be able to comfortably provide for you. So after living here for about three months or so, before I met anyone else in this building, I met the man who lives next door."

"Mama, you know the man from next door?" Sarita eagerly yelped out.

"No, no, Sarita, I never said I knew him. I only said I met him."

Sarita leaned in closer. "And?"

"Well, one night, very early in the morning, just before the sun came out, I was coming home from work. As I walked into the hallway from the back stairwell, I noticed that the man's door was left slightly open. Ever since I'd moved here, I'd always assumed that no one lived there, so I was curious. I opened the door and looked inside."

"So, was he there? And—and what was inside?"

"Shhh, easy, Chor-tee, listen. So, I opened the door and looked inside.

161

There was no one in there, but even though it was dark, I could see that the whole place was filled with paintings, blank canvases, drawings and paint. I said hello, hoping someone was inside in another room, but there was no answer, so I shut the door. As I stepped back into the hallway, just as I turned around, there he was, standing right behind me. I was so frightened that I froze up, thinking he would be very angry and do something to me, for looking in his apartment. But he didn't do anything. He just quietly stood there and then said hi. Then he walked around me and into his apartment. After he shut the door, I went to my apartment. Before I went inside, I looked back at his door, which he slightly opened to peek out into the hallway. Once he saw me still standing in the hallway, he shut the door again and then went back inside."

"And?"

"And, that's it, Sarita. I never saw him again."

"*Nunca?*"

"*Nunca.*"

"Well, what—what did he look like?"

"Since I was so frightened and the hallway was too dimly lit, I didn't get a good look. All I remember is that he is tall, thin and has long hair that hangs down over his face, that's all."

"That's all. And you never tried knocking on his door, to say hello, after that?"

"I did, Sarita, many times, but he never answered the door. So I gave up and never bothered anymore. I ignored the fact that he lives there."

"That's it?"

"That's it." Sarita couldn't believe what she had just heard, and became even more curious to know who the mysterious, reclusive man was.

"Um, what about all the screaming and noises he makes late at night sometimes?"

"When I first lived here, that never happened. Only a few years ago it started. That's a complete mystery to me, Sarita."

"Really?"

"Enough. I'm done, Sarita. I think that I filled your head with enough nonsense for tonight. I hope you don't go telling those other children ghost stories."

"Um, don't worry, I won't," Sarita said with a smirk as she looked away.

"I sure hope not," Gabriela said with a stern look on her face.

Sarita and Gabriela then continued to eat their dinner. Moments later, though, it would be Sarita who would once again nullify the silence.

"Um, Mama, what about when you first came to America, from Mexico? Um, you still never told me the whole story. 'Member? You promised you'd tell me one day."

"Yes, I did, Chor-tee, but not until you're older. Like I've told you many times before, there are just too many things I've done and lived through that you're too young to hear about and wouldn't understand."

"Um, but, but what about all the people you came here with? And 'member, you told me you came in a van and swam across a river?"

Sarita persisted, forcing Gabriela into a stalemate. Gabriela gave in and began to open up and reveal glimpses.

"It was very cold, ya know, the river I had to swim across, but being in that situation, the cold didn't bother me. You . . . you don't think about such things when you're risking everything for a dream. I had nothing to go back to. Well, that's what I thought at the time. I was so young, I allowed my emotions to take me away from what I now miss so much. But I have no regrets, because now I have you."

Gabriela turned to look Sarita in the eyes and then took another sip of wine. Sarita then sat up and leaned in closer.

"It's funny, because my whole life I dreamt of going to America, and I never imagined getting here the way I did. It was like it was meant to be, like God sent the right people to me at the right time in my life, who were able to help me get here. Although they were strangers, without them I wouldn't be here now with you. Before I even got anywhere near the river, I had to sit in a van for many miles, with twelve other people."

Once again, Gabriela paused and looked away with a slight smile.

"I can still clearly remember their faces. All of them looked as if they were awaiting their own deaths, yet, in their eyes . . . in their eyes, I could see hope. I could see that, deep down, they believed they would all make it. After traveling many miles, when we arrived at the river, it—it was like Christmas morning. The fear on everyone's face quickly vanished. Even though it was very dark, you could still clearly see America across the river, shining in the moonlight, reflecting off the water."

Gabriela's voice simmered down to a near whisper as she spoke her final words. The suspenseful tone filled Sarita with a craving for more as she attentively soaked in each word like a model student.

"For me, the swim across the river was the most difficult part of the night. Not only was I not a very good swimmer, but there was this one woman, a little older than me, who had a baby with her. Elena. She was so kind to me in the van, and helped keep me calm. And it's funny now, because in the van I was terrified, and she was fine, but once we got in the water, it was her who became scared, and me who stayed calm. After getting into the water, she was only about three feet in when she began to go back. I don't know why, but even though I was halfway across the river, I felt that I couldn't let her go back. I was willing to risk my chances of getting into America, just to help Elena and her baby swim across the river."

"How did you help them swim across the river?"

"Honestly, still to this day I'm not sure how I did it—ya know, where the strength came from to keep Elena and her baby afloat and swim her across the river with one arm. But when you're in a situation with nothing to lose, and it seems as if there is no chance of making it, as long as you have faith, and you believe in yourself, anything is possible, miracles happen. Somehow, I made it across the river with Elena and her baby. Unfortunately, that was as far as Elena got in America."

"Why? What happened next?" Sarita sat up on her knees.

"Easy, Sarita, easy. Relax, okay? I'm just about to get to that." Gabriela put her glass of wine down. "By the time we made it across the river, most of the others had already made it up the hill, across the desert, and gotten to the van that was waiting for us. It was just me, Elena, a few others, and . . . and,

Fabiola."

"Um, who's Fabiola?"

"An old friend; not someone I really want to talk about right now, but she is the reason I'm here now with you. Unfortunately she, Elena, and most of the others didn't make it out of the desert. After crossing the river, border patrol came and caught most of them. I still wonder to this day why I'm one of the lucky ones who made it."

"And—and what about the baby?"

"Elena gave the baby to me to take when we were all running away from the border patrol. Elena fell down and knew she wasn't going to make it, but she didn't want that to stop her baby from living in America, with the opportunities that she wanted her to have. I took her to California with me, and eventually left her in good hands. She's safe and in a better place now." Gabriela leaned forward and ran her fingertips through Sarita's hair. "Everything happens for a reason, Sarita, everything."

"Um, wha—what happened next?"

Gabriela sat back and took another sip of wine.

"What happens next is for when you're older," Gabriela said with a smile.

"Noooo, p-please, tell me, *dime*, pleeaaassssse."

"Sorry, Sarita, not now. You're too young, okay? What I can say is that after all these experiences and living through all that I have, life, it seems to me now, isn't that complicated. Faith, love, hope and if you believe in yourself, you can overcome any barriers in life, and do and become whatever you want, the end."

"Tha—that's it?"

"That's it, Sarita. No more stories. Finish up, okay?"

Sarita retreated into a cocoon and began to eat. Gabriela sipped her wine and observed Sarita's childish demeanor while she ate and kept readjusting herself on the chair. It was the little things in life that mattered most. To sit in silence and admire Sarita meant the world to Gabriela. Everything happened for a reason, and bonding with Sarita reminded Gabriela that even though she had taken a path through hell, it were the little things in life that gave Gabriela strength when she needed it and helped Gabriela make it. Little things like watching Sarita continue to eat and softly hum sweet nothingness while constantly readjusting her body always seemed to blanket Gabriela with adoration, and remind her that being where she was now, with Sarita, all of it, was worth the risks.

35

As remnants from Gabriela's past slowly faded away, Ignacio ignited the cigarette held between his lips with his Zippo and then took a drag. The bond between Gabriela and Sarita that Gabriela fondly spoke of eased the tension. It was the love he saw in Gabriela's eyes, as Ignacio peered through a haze of smoke, that seemed to open up a sentimental door found deep within Ignacio's heart.

"Your aura, it speaks to me in ways of muses. I'm completely entranced from the radiant energy emanating out, just from the thought and words spoken about your child. It says a lot about how powerful the idea of love can be. Not too long ago, this room was filled with hate and fear, which now seems to have been completely washed away, just from expressing the affection you have for another. I can see now why, in your eyes, it doesn't matter who the father is, since the love you share with your child seems to completely eradicate the void. It seems so pure and real, that the love you two share blossoms an eternity of fulfillment."

Ignacio's words filled Gabriela with reassurance as she silently sat with a slight smile. No matter how dark and mysterious Ignacio's deception made him appear to be, in Gabriela's eyes, at the moment it seemed she was able to pierce the surface of his persona with a simple act of affection.

"The little things, that's what makes our love for one another so real and everlasting. The little things, like the way she would say certain words or do particular things. Those things always seemed to be more fulfilling than money or possessions. Sometimes, that's all anyone ever needs in life, the little things, like a smile, a simple kiss, laughter, a simple gesture, or . . . or even the way someone may look at you or say something. That lost art of humanity seems to be forever gone. It's a shame, too, because, besides the little things, which are sometimes not recognized, the true love people seek isn't out there in the material world, but right here, deep within ourselves, in our heart and soul. From in here, that's where all the love and truth is, always and forever."

"This is true. I can see the passion in your eyes. Even with all the love you share with your child, even after all you have been through in life, especially after finally leaving the dark life you once lived far behind, still, you went back into the shadows, to the same horrible people you had left, for help?"

"So I assume that's why I'm here now."

"Clever girl."

As a haze of smoke was left wafting between them, Ignacio admired Gabriela's demeanor. Gabriela looked away and refocused her attention on Ignacio's left hand, holding the cigarette between the pointer and middle finger. Like the gleaming rings of Saturn, the platinum ring wrapped around Ignacio's ring finger was a reflection of love.

"So, do you love her?" Gabriela provoked Ignacio. He stared at her, looked down at the wedding ring on his finger and then deep into Gabriela's eyes, with a smirk. Gabriela smiled.

"Any children?"

"Two. *Dos niños.* One boy, and one girl." Ignacio then took a drag from his cigarette, leaving Gabriela in a state of awe. "See, I'm not such a bad guy."

"No, you're not. You just seem to try so hard to be one."

"You know, we'd make a great couple."

"Maybe in another life, when we are both cats."

"Meow."

After the flirtatious exchange, Ignacio checked his watch, finished his cigarette, dropped the butt on the concrete floor and put it out with his foot as he stood up.

"Well, it's about that time," Ignacio said as he walked towards the door.

"So who was he? The man you spoke of before, who risked everything for a dream?"

"He goes by many names, but if I had to give you one name to remember him by, it would be . . . the Mujerjuego," Ignazio said as he stood in the open doorway and looked back.

It wasn't the answer Gabriela was expecting, but she could see how important of a man the Mujerjuego must be, and how much he meant to Ignacio. Most importantly, whoever he was, his image seemed to provoke Gabriela to carry on and endure her solitary confinement. Ignacio admired Gabriela's beauty one last time before abandoning her, leaving her only with a smile. After Ignacio disappeared behind the door, Gabriela closed her eyes. Even though darkness consumed her, deep within there was an illumination of faith.

<u>36</u>

Gabriela walked through the streets of Union City apprehensively. All thanks to Eva the nurse, Gabriela was provided with food, money and shelter. Her services were only temporary, until Gabriela was sent to meet her real benefactor. He was a very powerful and respected man within the Latino communities of North Jersey. Someone also known in the three metropolitan counties of New Jersey—Essex, Hudson, and Union, which all bordered New York City. That man was Don Fernandez.

Don Fernandez was known as the godfather of the Latino communities in North Jersey. If a Latino immigrant needed a job or a home, Don Fernandez provided one. If an illegal immigrant needed proper credentials or identification, such as a green card, visa, Social Security number or a driver's license, it was taken care of. Even if someone needed Don Fernandez's help to traffic family members into America illegally, so they could be with each other, it could be done.

Los Unidos, a Cuban restaurant nestled in the heart of Union City, was where Gabriela would meet Don Fernandez. Inside, as Cuban music echoed out, Gabriela was greeted by an exotic, voluptuous Cuban hostess who guided her past a long line of waiting customers and then through the dining area. Gabriela noticed the vast restaurant was architecturally laid out like the streets of Havana. Ceilings that rose up towards the third floor, and many people Salsa dancing on the open cobblestone dance floor.

Eventually, the Cuban hostess led Gabriela towards the back of the restaurant and then all the way up to the third floor, to a private area that overlooked the entire restaurant. After the hostess sat Gabriela at a table, she walked away into a private room, then returned to inform Gabriela to wait patiently for a few more minutes before turning to say goodbye.

Soon after, Don Fernandez emerged out from the double doors of the private room. Don Fernandez was an overly robust man with an expanding waistline, standing just over six feet tall, who walked with a slight limp on his left leg. As he approached Gabriela, she observed his massive presence, concentrating on his intimidating, yet sincere face and a thick black mustache that was complemented by his short, wavy black hair. Even though Don Fernandez's physical presence gave the illusion of laziness, his materialistic façade symbolized power and success. Designer pants, a purple button-down designer shirt with the top two buttons left undone, revealing his chest hair and gold chain, along with an old Mickey Mouse watch that didn't work and gold rings on five of his ten fingers—the pinky and ring finger of his right hand, and the pinky, ring finger and index finger of his left hand.

Don Fernandez symbolized the success and wealth of an immigrant. He was a man who had lost his whole family in his home country of Cuba, due to their political differences with the government's Communist party. Eventually he had immigrated to the United States of America, a seven-year-old refugee with no one and nothing but the clothes on his back and a bag filled with some personal possessions. The possessions included a family photo, a Mickey Mouse watch given to him by his late father, and a Bible.

Don Fernandez had gained power and success through hardship and discipline, and now he tried to take care of those who had been down the same path as him, those who walked in his shadow and who had the will to live the dream. Even if it meant he had to live an unconventional life on the side, working against the law.

As Don Fernandez approached Gabriela, she stood up to show respect. Don Fernandez was taken away by her beauty. He took Gabriela's hands within his big bear paws and slowly raised her one hand to his big, lush lips to kiss it. He held his lips on her hand for a few seconds while gazing up into her beautiful dark eyes, before taking both her hands in his. After their introductions, they both sat down.

"Before we begin to talk business, *bonita*, would you like to have a drink, or perhaps something from the menu? I prefer the Churrasco a la Cubana, it's quite exquisite," Don Fernandez said in a deep baritone voice.

"No, *gracias*." Gabriela looked away from his penetrating eyes. The waiter who stood beside the table then left to get Don Fernandez a bottle of his favorite aged red wine. Once the waiter had left, Don Fernandez stood up.

"*Bueno.* Well, since this meeting was arranged on such short notice, please pardon my sudden departure for a moment, but I must finish with a very important client of mine. She's waiting for me in my private room. It should only take a minute or two. The both of us just have to sign some documents. In the meantime, enjoy your drink, until I return."

Inside was Marta Mendoza, who was putting on her blouse and buttoning it up. The now fifty-three-year-old, was done making love with Don Fernandez. She was also having Don Fernandez sign off on a new shipment of cocaine, which had come in from Colombia.

"So, the girl is here?" Marta spoke with a raspy, hoarse voice.

"*Sí, sí*, the young Mexicana who needs some help." Don Fernandez walked towards Marta, who handed him a pen. He leaned down to sign off on the documents, which had the inventory information about the shipment of cocaine he had received from Colombia. After he signed the documents, Marta took them, put them inside her leather briefcase, and then began to passionately kiss Don Fernandez, who responded by groping Marta's oversized breasts and ass. The two were secretly involved in a heated love affair, which was a dangerous venture for the high-ranking Nada Mas officials. In the eyes of Don Fernandez, it was a politically charged power move. At the end of another romantic session, both Don Fernandez and Marta Mendoza began to walk towards the exit doors.

"It's always a pleasure doing business with you," Marta said with a smile.

"*Claro, claro*," Don Fernandez said as he stepped into the private area with Marta. Gabriela curiously looked at Marta, who stared at her, causing Gabriela to look away.

"This is my associate and business partner, Marta Mendoza, and this is Gabriela."

Marta shook Gabriela's hand with a grin. Marta felt jealous of Gabriela's beauty, but remained kind to Don Fernandez's guest. Gabriela could see hatred in Marta's dark eyes and felt uncomfortable.

"So, this is the Mexicana who needs some help?" Marta said with a catty smile.

"*Sí.*"

"So, Gabriela, you shouldn't be so scared. Don't worry, Señor Fernandez treats all women like queens, if you're indeed one of the fortunate ones, of course." Marta turned back towards Don Fernandez to flash him a smile, to let him know who the one and only queen was. "Who knows? Maybe someday we'll have the pleasure of doing business together. I'm always looking for young girls who have ambition. You know, the ones who have nothing to lose, especially young Mexicanas who came to the United States as you have. If not, maybe our lives will cross paths again sometime in the future. Until then, *buen dia.*" After Marta left, Don Fernandez sat back down to join Gabriela.

"*Bueno*, so, back to business. What is it I could do for such a beautiful *chiquita*?" As Don Fernandez spoke, the waiter returned to fill his small glass with wine, leaving the bottle on the table.

"I—I don't ask for much, Señor Fernandez. As I'm pregnant, all I ask for is a place to live on my own, and a secure job. Something I'll be able to do while I'm pregnant. That's all, nothing more."

As Don Fernandez sipped his wine, he noticed the scars on Gabriela's wrists, but then focused on every aspect of her essence of beauty. Gabriela's full, lush lips stimulated him, and her cleavage bulging out of her button-down shirt aroused him. Also, in Gabriela's eyes, he saw an ocean of ecstasy.

"For work, I have something in mind for you, *bonita*. I have a friend who runs a sewing factory in Newark. He could use an extra hand, and it will be a perfect job for a pregnant woman. You sit all day as you work, so there is no stress on the back or legs. As for a home, you're in luck, since I just got started in the real estate game. I have some property in the area, some nice apartments you may like. I think that we could arrange a day for you to take a look at some I have available for you. It will be fun, like house hunting."

"*Sí, sí, Señor Fernández. Muchas, muchas gracias.*"

"The pleasure is all mine, *bonita*, and in return, well, I think that we can work something out."

Don Fernandez gazed into Gabriela's eyes and then reached out to hold both of her hands to caress them. Gabriela knew what to expect. She'd been down that path before, except this time, she was much wiser and understood the game well in order to get what she needed to, then freely leave it all far behind, forever.

Don Fernandez helped Gabriela up and guided her into his private room, caressing her lower back. Gabriela looked back over her shoulder and focused on a mural of Latin American history and culture that filled the wall, in the likeness of Diego Rivera's famous murals. The image was of a Latin American woman, holding a newborn child in her arms. She was with a group of other Latin American immigrants, all guiding or holding children and possessions as they migrated together. Behind them were homes and family waving goodbye, as they walked further down a path towards large modern-day buildings— industrial factories. Further ahead in the distance was a metropolis, which was illuminated by light from the sun, rising between two mountain peaks. Before Gabriela was able to savor the inspiring image of hope and new beginnings, she found herself slowly walking closer towards the doors of the private room. Cuban music continued to rhythmically echo throughout the open vastness of Los Unidos. She walked through the doors and into darkness.

37

Gabriela and Sarita walked hand and hand down Newark Avenue, on a picturesque summer day, until they reached the historic downtown district. The post office was the reason for Gabriela and Sarita to make the long walk from The Heights, which was a monthly bonding journey meant for family.

Gabriela held a package, while Sarita carried envelopes. They were gifts for Gabriela's mother, brother and relatives. Inside the envelopes were letters written by Gabriela and Sarita, along with pictures. There were pages filled with details about what they'd done for the past month. Gabriela's relatives always wanted to know every little thing about her life, Sarita's life, and America. Sometimes they would want to know more than they should, but Gabriela didn't mind letting her emotions out to tell all. She was a good storyteller, and her relatives, especially Tío Emilio and Tía Rosa, were never disappointed. They were always left desperate for more.

Every package that Gabriela sent back to Mexico each month was filled with either clothes, drawings made by Sarita, or small gifts, but there was also money, extra money that wasn't wired to an account in Mexico. Gabriela always made sure to save plenty of American money each month, enough to send to her mother and relatives in Mexico, so that they could live comfortably each month. Gabriela's mother and relatives felt very blessed to have Gabriela take care of them every month, from America. They felt that Gabriela was sharing the American Dream with them.

From the post office, Gabriela and Sarita went to the Exchange Place

Seaport. It was one of the many locations found in Jersey City and its bordering cities, such as Hoboken and Weehawken, found on the western banks of The Hudson River, being overshadowed by the New York City skyline. Bringing the letters and package to the post office reminded Gabriela of her home in Mexico, while the New York City skyline reminded Gabriela of how far she had come from Tehuacán, Mexico. Most importantly, it reminded her of the American Dream.

After resting and enjoying the New York City skyline, Gabriela and Sarita then began to go home. For Gabriela and Sarita, being back in The Heights felt refreshing, especially when the Clearview apartment complex came into view. Home was their sanctuary. After collecting the mail from the lobby mailbox, Gabriela and Sarita walked up to their fifth-floor apartment.

Gabriela held the mail in one hand and the key in the other hand. As she turned the key, nothing happened. She then took the key out and put it back in. Still the door wouldn't open. She tried again and again, and still the door wouldn't open. Gabriela then handed the mail to Sarita and put the key in with both hands, turning the knob as she leaned her whole body into the door. She began to lean in harder and harder each time, slamming her body into the door. Still the door didn't open, causing Gabriela to bang on the door with her hand.

"*Mierda!*" Gabriela then turned towards Sarita and shrugged her shoulders. Suddenly from out of the shadows came an arm and hand. Gabriela and Sarita shivered as they turned around.

Standing behind them was Dante, the mysterious, reclusive man from next door. Dante glanced at both Gabriela and Sarita. Even though Dante's hair hung down over his face, they were able to see his eyes. Dante had big crystal-blue eyes, a chiseled, scruffy face, and a slight smile. Without saying a word, he stepped between them while Gabriela and Sarita slowly separated. They looked at each other and then at Dante. Dante then took the key out of Gabriela's hand, put it into the keyhole and twisted the knob in a strange way as he leaned into the door. In one try, the door opened. Dante took the key out and placed it back into Gabriela's hand, and then closed her hands around it with his. Without saying a word, he walked back into the shadows and back into his apartment.

Gabriela and Sarita stood still as they watched Dante walk away. They couldn't believe what had just happened.

"Thank you," Gabriela said. There was no response as Dante walked away into his apartment, shutting the door behind him. Gabriela and Sarita looked at each other and didn't say a word. They then quietly walked into their apartment.

<u>38</u>

Gabriela and Sarita were silent as they settled in and set up the kitchen table with leftovers of chilachilas, black beans, rice and taquitos. The chance encounter had sparked an array of thoughts and emotions, which were now displayed in the eyes and smiles of Gabriela and Sarita.

Sarita's curiosity was now beyond her greatest expectations. The enigma of who the mysterious, reclusive man could have been was now washed away with relief. Sarita's fears were forever gone. As for Gabriela, she fiddled around and looked away while trying to hide her adolescent smile behind the rim of the glass she drank from.

"Um, so, do you like him?"

Gabriela removed her glass of wine from her lips and tried to hide her slight smile behind the rim of the glass. "Like him? What do you mean?"

"Um, well, you've been smiling ever since we came inside."

"I don't know what you're talking about," Gabriela said, taking another sip.

Sarita leaned forward. "You do, don't you? I can tell by the look on your face. But don't worry, Mama, I, won't tell anyone."

"Well, maybe a little, Chor-tee. He did have really nice eyes, and a nice smile."

"So, why don't you go talk to him, 'specially since he helped you?"

"Because, sometimes . . . sometimes things are best when left alone, Sarita. When you're older, you'll understand." Dante and who he had once been remained on Gabriela's mind.

Sarita then focused on the scars on Gabriela's forearms. The cigarette scars were a haunting reminder of a darker time from Gabriela's past, a part of Gabriela's life that Sarita had learned the hard way never to question ever again. Sarita began to readjust herself on her chair while eating and humming sweet nothingness. Gabriela admired Sarita's innocence and then focused on Sarita's scuffed-up untied red high-top Converse All-Stars.

"Sarita, why must you treat your shoes like that?"

"Like what?" Sarita looked down at her shoes.

"Like that. Like one of your art projects that you draw all over. It looks like graffiti."

"Um, no, it's not graffiti. It's like my name, some words, a smiley face, and all different kinds of designs and other things. I tried to make them look different from other people's shoes," Sarita explained, sitting on her left leg as she held her left shoe hanging over the edge of the chair.

"I understand what you're trying to do, Sarita, but you need to appreciate your things. I worked very hard to pay for those shoes. You've only had them for about a month, and look at them. Besides all the artwork you drew on them with marker and pen, they look like you've had them for a year. Look, they're all scuffed up, they have holes in them, and . . . and they're all faded and worn out. It's a shame, Sarita, because some children aren't fortunate enough to have nice shoes like you, and if they did, they would appreciate and take care of them. They would have some sense of self-respect, to appreciate themselves and the little things in life. When I first came to America, I only had one pair of shoes. They were just as bad as your shoes now, except that I had mine for a very long time. I walked many miles in my shoes. They earned their wear and tear of holes and abuse. Every step I took, every time my feet felt sore, all I could think about was the day I would get a new pair of nice, comfortable shoes. When I finally did, I appreciated them and took care of them. I can still clearly remember those shoes; they lasted a very long time," Gabriela said, gesturing passionately.

"I do appreciate my things, Mama. It's just my way of showing . . ." Sarita let out a volcanic burp, causing Gabriela to remove her glass of wine from her lips with disgust.

"Sarita! How about learning how to appreciate yourself first? How many times do I have to tell you how inappropriate that behavior is? Sarita, it's not funny. Do you want people to disrespect you and look at you like you're some kind of animal? Because that's what they're gonna think if you keep going around acting like that," Gabriela lectured Sarita, who tried to control her laughing.

"I'm sorry, Mama. I won't do it again, promise," Sarita said. Gabriela didn't say a word. She just shook her head from side to side. "But, do you wanna hear a joke, Mama?"

"A joke, now, Sarita?" Gabriela yawned.

"Um, yep. It's a new one," Sarita said energetically.

"All right, Sarita, all right, go ahead."

"Um, okay, so what's something a poor man has, something a rich man doesn't need, and if you eat it, you'll die?" Sarita leaned forward, rested both her arms on the edge of the table, and observed Gabriela, who contemplated and sipped her wine. "Soooooooooo?"

"Easy, Sarita, easy. I'm still thinking." As Gabriela proceeded to contemplate, Sarita began to tap her fingers on the table. "Well, it looks like you stumped me again, Sarita, I can't think of anything. So, what is it? What is it a poor man has, a rich man doesn't need, and if you eat it you die?"

"Nothing, get it?"

"Ya know, I think it's good how you're always making jokes, Sarita, constantly being creative and using your mind. You have a great imagination and know how to use it to create something from nothing, something you like. Not too many children your age like to write jokes, stories and enjoy art like you. It really means a lot to me to see how enthusiastic you are with what interests you," Gabriela praised Sarita.

"Um, yeah, well, if I'm gonna be a famous actress someday, then I'm gonna need to know some good jokes."

"Yes, you're right, Sarita. It will help you to know some good jokes. But don't forget the little things, the things matter most in life, especially when you want to succeed at something. Hard work, discipline, patience, respect. They're just some simple traits. They mean a lot and will go a long way on whatever path you choose in life. They are essential elements which help along a journey when chasing dreams. No dream is too unrealistic or too far to reach. If you can imagine a dream, it can be lived. You just need to be strong from within, never allow other people or their opinions to control your life or interfere with your decisions and beliefs. As long as you believe in yourself, follow your heart and never lose hope, no matter how hard the path you choose may be, or whatever obstacles stand in your way, never, ever give up. Always have hope and finish whatever you start."

After Sarita savored all of Gabriela's inspiring words, she began to think of a dream which had plagued her mind for many years.

"Quien es mi padre?"

Gabriela froze. "Excuse me?" She said as she slowly removed the empty glass from her lips.

"Um, have you ever found out who my father is yet?"

Echoes from a dark and haunting past suddenly manifested. Even if time had eroded over a single night of blind conception, Gabriela could only humor Sarita's curiosity after pouring herself another glass of wine.

"I'm sorry, Sarita, but like I've told you many times before, I still don't know. Trust me, none of the men in my life were good anyway. Like I always say, some things are best left unanswered. When you're older you'll understand."

Gabriela looked away from Sarita's eyes. Keeping Sarita in the dark was for her protection, but seeing the emptiness in her eyes was too hard to bear, especially when watching Sarita sit with her chin resting on her arms, crossed on top of the table while looking up, like a sad, lost puppy dog. But Sarita wouldn't submit. Her will was strong.

"Someday, Mama, I'll find out, I will."

Sarita was determined to find the truth. Gabriela and Sarita finished their dinner in silence. Sarita then went to her room to preoccupy herself with art and fall asleep. As for Gabriela, she remained at the table with her last glass of wine and her thoughts.

Dante was on Gabriela's mind. Even though Dante's life inside his apartment was a complete mystery, his eyes were windows into the past, a past that Gabriela was willing to put back together.

Love would provoke Gabriela to follow her heart further into the night. She grabbed a new bottle of wine and went to Dante's apartment door. She closed her eyes and imagined the life that could have been and the life that could now become complete, and knocked. The silence echoed an eternity, yet only a few minutes passed without an answer. Gabriela then pressed the side of her face with the palm of her hand against the door and then closed her eyes and began to sing a Spanish lullaby.

Dante was pressed up against the door on the other side. Before he even had a chance to consider bringing closure to a past left unfinished in order to rewrite the current state of time, Gabriela stopped. She then pushed herself off the door, kissed her hand and touched the door with her fingertips.

"*Buenas noches.*" After saying goodbye, Gabriela left the bottle of wine on the floor. As Dante watched Gabriela walk back into her apartment through the peephole, he was filled with regret, yet his heart flowed with desire. Dante stepped back from the door and went to his couch to lie down. He closed his eyes and imagined the past and all that could have been.

39

Sarita sat cross-legged before Dante's door while humming. Even after knocking several times without an answer, Sarita still refused to leave.

"Sarita, *qué estás haciendo? Ven aquí*," Gabriela called out.

"But—" Sarita slowly turned her head.

"Pero. Cuantas veces te he dicho, Sarita? Déjalo solo. Vamos, adentro."

Sarita turned her head back around and rolled her eyes, sighing. From the other side of the door, Dante watched through the peephole as Sarita turned around and ran past Gabriela into the apartment. Gabriela followed behind Sarita, shutting the door behind her. Dante then stepped back from the door.

Inside Dante's apartment, the oscillating fan slowly rotated, the wind chimes echoed out transcending ambiance, and the soothing winds blew in the open windows. Dante walked into the kitchen, grabbed the brand-new bottle of red wine Gabriela had left for him, opened it and began drinking.

Each sip felt refreshing. Dante looked around, and then at the plane ticket to Mexico, still attached to the refrigerator door. Dante reached out to grab the ticket and hold it in his hand. Aero Mexico flight 1203 from JFK Airport to Mexico City was only a few days away. It was Dante's ticket to freedom. Even though Dante was on the verge of escape from his daunting past, at the moment it felt secondary. Nada Mas, and all Dante had once been involved with, no longer filled him with fear. There was life, and Dante's source of illumination was outside his door. Sarita was the one who was able to revive Dante from his decaying cocoon and give him the inspiration to move on with life and his art.

No matter how much Dante knew he needed to leave America and go to Mexico for his own safety, if he was to stay behind, Sarita would be the reason why.

After contemplating leaving everything and heading to Mexico, Dante put the plane ticket back on the refrigerator door, took another sip of wine, and then walked towards all his unfinished paintings. Ever since Greco's last visit, Dante had been able to swim back up from the bottom of a bottle and finally move on without guilt or reason. He was able to finish more than two-thirds of his work, which would complete his one-man show. Redemption for all that seemed to have been lost, forever.

The dream was a reflection in Dante's eyes as he sat on his stool to finish an unfinished painting, while intensely painting in his original, unique style with intense, swift, thick brushstrokes, manifesting his original creative genius. As Dante continued to put all of his heart and soul into his work, the persistence of time would become nonexistent. Day turned to night, his hands became numb and filled with blisters. He knew when he was done, not by the enslavement of time, but by an intense euphoric kundalini sense of bliss and fatigue such as someone would experience when they were done making love.

After finishing, Dante dropped his paintbrush down to the floor and reached for his bottle of wine. He put it to his lips, only to have nothing come out, and then just sat while holding an empty wine bottle, filled with the same emptiness and drainage as his soul.

Soon after, there was knocking at the door. At first Dante froze and held the empty bottle up in a defensive manner, fearing his daunting past had arrived. But once Dante crept to the door and looked out the peephole, he lowered the bottle down by his side. It was his past, but not the threatening presence he was expecting to arrive someday. It was Gabriela; she was back. As much as Dante wanted to hide away again, he knew deep in his heart he couldn't. He removed the chain, unlocked the door and then slowly opened up.

"Hey," Gabriela said as she tucked strands of hair back behind her ears.

"Hey, how are you?" Dante opened the door a little bit more.

"I'm fine. Don't worry, you don't have to invite me in. I won't be long," Gabriela said as she crossed her arms. "After all these years of living next door, you've dodged me, avoided me and hid in your hole of an apartment. I get it. I'm not upset about that, and I appreciate you sliding money under my door every month to help out. But after Sarita seeing you face-to-face for the first time, I feel she needs to know about us."

"Oh yeah? And how much are you willing to tell her now? I thought we agreed to wait until she was eighteen. You know it's dangerous for both of us, especially for her if we tell her now."

"I know, I know. We both made bad decisions in the past, getting involved with Nada Mas, but you and I both know it was all we had during such desperate times in our lives. And then we found each other. I don't know about you, but I believe in fate, that people are brought into each other's lives for a reason. I also believe that it was fate that brought Sarita into our lives."

"I guess, but why now? Why tell her now?"

"I—I don't know. It just feels right. Anyway, I'll let you go for now. Now that she has seen you face-to-face, please try to make an effort to get to know her. Not for me, for her. Well, maybe for you too."

"I'll see. Once I find out it's safe to come out of hiding, maybe I can take her out for ice cream or something?"

"That would be nice, and maybe I'll able to see you sooner than later, instead of once every four to six months. It feels like my yearly doctor visits."

"Hey, it's the life we chose for her. That's how it is. Not only shouldn't we be living close together, but being seen together is even more dangerous."

"Yeah, anything for love, I guess. Anyway, be well," Gabriela said. She glanced up into Dante's eyes, stepped back and then turned around.

As Gabriela slowly walked away and then back into her apartment, Dante watched. No matter how uplifted Dante felt from completing his paintings, the truth was eating away his heart. The livelihood of Gabriela and Sarita was worth more than all of Dante's art. With only a small window of time left to choose what mattered most, Dante stepped back into his apartment with conflicting thoughts, and then shut the door.

40

All that had been created and erected into a dominant force was now beginning to crack and fade away from the cancer slowly manifesting from deep within the heart of Nada Mas. Nada Mas was no longer what it had once been. It had changed since the beginning and was now on the verge of a vast transformation. All of those who had been at the core since its birth were all slowly breaking apart. Nada Mas was now at a crossroads between life and death, and it was only a matter of time before the cancer within would consume and take control.

Everything that Marta Mendoza had helped create and secure would soon face the beginning of its demise inside of a lavish, undisclosed penthouse apartment located within the heart of Manhattan.

"Something's not right. Benny's gone completely underground. I haven't been able to contact him lately, and Coughlin and Rosenthal both canceled our meeting at the last minute, which is extremely unusual for those two. I came all the way from Mexico to New York just for this important meeting, so that we can justify the future of Nada Mas. It's not even safe for me to be in the United States right now, considering I've been on the FBI watch list lately. They're watching my every move. The last thing I need right now is to get arrested and extradited. I'm very concerned right now, about everything."

Marta Mendoza nervously vented to Don Fernandez on her cell phone, pacing around the open space near the high loft windows that overlooked midtown Manhattan.

"I wouldn't worry too much," Don Fernandez said as he sipped his wine while sitting in his private room in Los Unidos. "There's been a lot of political tensions worldwide. A big push by these bureaucratic lawmakers to pencil-push these corrupt bills into laws in order to limit operations and cut ties between all those involved. If Benny is the intelligent man you claim he is, then he's probably just lying low till things calm down. As for Coughlin and Rosenthal, like I just said, with the way things are right now, they're on call 24/7, so I wouldn't get sick over their sudden absence."

"Well, I wish that I could be as positive as you, but I just have a feeling that something's wrong from within. Lately, numbers don't add up. There's been a lot of negative talk within the ranks, and there's been a lot of raids and arrests throughout the States. Whatever it is, I . . . I have to get back to Mexico. I can't stay around here any longer, it's not safe for me here."

"Okay, well, if that's how you're feeling right now, just make sure you go straight to the airport."

"Don't worry, my bags are already packed. Let me get going, I'll call you when I get back to Mexico."

"Okay, *mi amor*, okay. Just be careful. You know, trust no one, and have a safe trip."

"Okay, mi amor, besos."

"Besos."

After Marta Mendoza and Don Fernandez said their goodbyes, Marta hung up the phone. She scurried into the bedroom to get her luggage off the bed, only to be stopped by a knock on the door. Marta jolted up and dropped her cell phone. She only thought the worst as she picked up her phone and slowly walked towards the door. Before Marta even had a chance to answer it, federal agents kicked the door in, storming in with guns drawn. Marta stood frozen with her hands held up as the federal agents read her her Miranda rights and handcuffed her before taking her away.

# # #

As the world around continued to move on after Marta Mendoza was apprehended by federal agents, Suarez and Salas slowly walked side by side through an undisclosed Latin American butterfly garden.

"So now that Mendoza is in custody, what's our next move?" Salas said.

"For now, we remain idle. After setting up Mendoza, everyone within the ranks will be on edge until matters cool down. There will have to be a new mediator to fill in for Mendoza. That's when we'll come into the picture. But first, we need to play our cards right in order to regain faith and trust, and win over the hearts and minds of those who doubted us from the very beginning—before we meet to determine the fate of Nada Mas," Suarez said passionately, as butterflies flied around him.

"What about Benny?"

"I wouldn't worry about Benny. With Mendoza out of the picture, after he makes contact with all high-ranking officials, and when a new mediator is chosen, he will be forced to come out of hiding to conduct business. He will choose his new mediator—which will most likely be me, given he started out with my parents and is an extremely loyal and traditional person. After the amount of revenue I have been able to bring in for Nada Mas, choosing me will be the right move both financially and businesswise. After that, Benny will be forced to come out of the dark, and that's when we'll take him out, eradicate all he has created and replant the fate of Nada Mas."

"And what if you're not chosen?"

"I doubt it, but if he does pass me up and chooses someone else, then we take back Nada Mas by force. In the meantime, I have moles within the FBI gathering intel on anyone associated with Nada Mas and Benny. My best assassin has been and still is gathering information on, hunting down, and taking out anyone who was close with Benny and knows him personally."

As Suarez spoke such grim words, he envisioned a new Nada Mas. All that Suarez had help create and felt such bitterness towards was soon going to be completely cleansed and left for the taking. It was the end of all Nada Mas was born and molded into, and from out of the ashes of everything that once was, a phoenix of dominance would rise throughout the globe.

<u>41</u>

Gabriela silently sat at a table in the back corner of Café Amoritas, where she worked. While sipping her coffee and gazing out the window, she was at peace, free from all the troubles in the world. Sometimes, though, even within walls of comfort, there was someone who could diminish all the love with negative influences. Wilmer, a short, stumpy Dominican who had a fade with a well-groomed goatee and chinstrap scruff, with sleeve tattoos on both arms, approached Gabriela, sitting down to join her.

"*Hola*, Gaby," Wilmer greeted Gabriela with a deceiving smile.

"*Hola*, Wilmer, how are you?"

"I'm good. So, you're done for the day?"

"Yes, finally. I can't wait to get home so that I can relax. How about you, are you almost done?"

"Nah, not yet. Unfortunately, I have to close again," Wilmer said, sounding disgruntled. He looked away from Gabriela and reached down into his backpack.

"Really, again? I can't believe Nathan still hasn't put you back on your normal shift, all because of what happened," Gabriela said, humoring Wilmer. She knew that he deserved his punishment for showing up late, and for being rude to customers. Even when Wilmer sat back up and placed a package the size of a hardcover book wrapped in brown paper on top of the table. No matter how much Gabriela disliked Wilmer, she smiled and gave him her full attention.

"Yeah, yeah, yeah, I know. I can't believe it either. And after all I've done—ya know, cleaning, baking, even making soup of tha day when I don't have to. All tha extra things I do for this place, still he screws me and puts me on closing shift. Anyway, I don't wanna talk about it now, I have to get back soon, but before I go, there's something I wanted to ask you." Wilmer, spoke quickly with a thick Spanish accent as he looked around and fiddled with a pen.

"Oh, yeah? Well, before you ask me, I wanna know, is this for me?" Gabriela reached out to hold the package, only to have Wilmer take it away and place it back down on the table.

"No. Well, I mean, yes and no. Listen, I need you to do me a favor."

Gabriela could sense what was coming next. She knew Wilmer all too well, not because they were coworkers, but because he was a reflection of the criminals and gang members she had once been associated with. The gleaming gaze of desperation seen in his eyes, and his sense of paranoia, was evidence that Gabriela would somehow be brought into darker waters.

"*Mira*, I need you to take this to a friend of mine. I would bring it myself, but I'm stuck here all day."

"So, what is it I have to bring to your friend?"

"That's not important. What's important is that my friend gets this."

"How do you expect me to bring something to your friend if I don't know what it is, huh?" Wilmer began to tense up and nervously look around again, and then he leaned in closer to softly speak in a firm manner.

"Okay, okay. But before I tell you, promise me you'll tell no one, *comprende*?" Wilmer said. Gabriela nodded. "It's money. I'm not gonna tell you how much, so what I need from you is that you get this to my friend. He's gonna give you something for me."

"If it's drugs, Wilmer, then no, I'm not getting drugs for you."

"Oh, really? That's funny hearing that from you. Aren't you the expert at transporting money and drugs, huh? Do you really want me to talk about your past and get into details?" After being silenced, Gabriela looked away and then sat back. "Good. And don't worry, because my friend doesn't live far from you, so you can stop by his house on your way home. Here, this is the address."

Wilmer wrote an address and name down on a napkin and handed it to

Gabriela, who began to read it. Wilmer then reached into his backpack again.

"And I also need you to hold on to this for me. I'll pick everything up from you after work."

Gabriela could see desperation deep within Wilmer's eyes as he securely placed a soft round item in the palm of her hand. After Wilmer pulled away, she brought her hand closer and slowly opened it up to see what was inside. She wasn't surprised at all to see it was drugs, an eight ball of cocaine. The sight of it was a reminder of the past, causing Gabriela to look away.

"You owe me. After all the favors I've done for you. Working double shifts and covering for you so that you could spend more time with your little girl. Loaning you money, lying for you and keeping your past secret from everyone here, huh? What do you think would happen if everyone here knew that you lived a life worse than mine? C'mon, this is nothing compared to what you've done with your life. It will take five, ten minutes. All you're doing is dropping off a package, picking one up and holding on to a few grams of blow for me until I'm done here and I come pick it up, that's it."

As much as Gabriela wanted to tell Wilmer no, she knew that everything he told her was true, and that the truth gave Wilmer the advantage.

"Okay, okay, but just this one time. No more after this, never again, okay? Promise me that."

"Of course, of course. I promise, okay? If you need anything, anything at all, don't hesitate to ask, okay?" Wilmer said slyly. He checked the time on his watch, picked up his backpack, and stood up. "Okay, well, I gotta get back to work. Thank you, and don't worry, you'll be fine, okay? Take care."

After Wilmer said goodbye and left, Gabriela placed her cup back down and then gazed out the window. Where the road ahead led, Gabriela wasn't sure. Even if it was just a taste, just a little reminder of working as a mule, Gabriela knew what to expect, and she wasn't going to allow the daunting lifestyle to ruin all she'd sacrificed and worked so hard for. Gabriela knew to always expect the unexpected and to trust no one, so before leaving, Gabriela closed her eyes and prayed to the Virgin Guadalupe. After opening her eyes, she stood up with her bag and departed with vigilance.

<u>42</u>

After a twenty-five-minute bus ride and a three-block walk, Gabriela stood before the front door of a dilapidated two-family home. She looked all around while she waited for Wilmer's friend to answer the door. Every second felt like an eternity. Even the ice cream truck melody heard in the distance and barking dogs brought discomforting urgency. Gabriela banged on the decrepit storm door, left hanging on one hinge again, as she adjusted her handbag while trying to look in through the elongated narrow windows running up alongside the entrance door. She was unable to see beyond the stained curtain, but she was able to hear stomping feet. A pair of beady eyes peeked out from behind the curtain, which was quickly pulled back again. Gabriela stood in the open, waiting to be greeted. A raspy Spanish voice called out from inside.

"Who is it?"

"It's Gabriela, I'm Wilmer's friend. He asked me to come here for him to drop off a package. I have something for Nelson."

There was no response, only sounds of multiple locks being unlocked, followed by the opening of the door. The door only opened a third of the way. Gabriela was able to get a glimpse of her host, who looked out beyond her and then beckoned her inside, shutting and locking the door behind.

As Gabriela walked inside the aged home, across the stained carpet and into the living room filled with used furniture covered with dust and dog hair, there was a stench of musty dog piss baking in the humid summer heat. Even the paraphernalia left lying around was evidence that the home wasn't a setting for a family but a front for illegal activities and operations. Gabriela knew the setting all too well, and as discomfiting as all within the walls was, Gabriela was unfazed. It resembled the safe houses she had lived in when she had first come to America. But before Gabriela even had a chance to adjust and settle into the unsettling domain, her host stepped before her.

"So, where is it?" Nelson said impatiently.

"Are you Nelson?"

"Yeah, yeah, yeah. C'mon, where is it? Where's the package?" he mumbled as he scratched the side of his scruffy face, his buzz-cut head and neck while looking around. Nelson was a tall, thin, frail Honduran, wearing faded jeans and a stained white wife beater. Gabriela focused on his dark, crusty decaying skin, flawed from addiction and uncleanliness, as she reached into her handbag to get the package.

"It's all here, right?" Nelson said, sounding psychotic as he snatched it away.

"I guess so. Wilmer is the one who wrapped it and gave it to me."

"Yeah, yeah, yeah." Nelson turned around and walked into the kitchen, mumbling. Gabriela was left with a pretty young Latin American girl who sat quietly on a couch in the living room with a sleeping baby cradled in her arms.

"*Hola*," Gabriela said kindly.

"*Hola*," the petite young girl said with a smile. She had long dark hair, pouty lips, and doe eyes, and she wore old, worn-out purple shoes, faded jeans and a purple tank top. Sounds of barking dogs from outside, the beeping of an old smoke detector filled with dead batteries, the creaking of wooden floorboards from people walking around on the second floor all echoed out. Gabriela looked into the kitchen. She could see Nelson counting the money from Wilmer's package and all the paraphernalia and assortment of other illegal drugs, pharmaceutical drugs and packaged narcotics left lying all around. She stopped to admire the girl and the baby, then walked towards her.

"Is he yours?"

"No, no, I'm too young to have a baby, not until I'm like twenty-seven, twenty-eight or in my thirties. It's someone else's; I'm just taking care of him until his mother comes back."

"Oh, okay, well, good practice for you. Especially with him. He's so quiet and so beautiful."

"Yes, yes, you're right. I'm very lucky he doesn't cry all time." The giddy young Latin American girl's smile grew bigger as she spoke.

"So, what's his name?"

"Paulo."

"Aw, what a pretty name. And how old are you?"

"Seventeen, but I'll be eighteen in three months."

"You're so young. How come you're living here in a place like this. Don't you have a home with family and parents to love and take care of you?"

"Yes, but not here. They're all back home in El Salvador."

"Oh, okay. Well, I'm from Mexico. I know what it's like being so far from home. You must miss them, very much."

"Oh, wow, yes, very much. I try to talk to them as often as I can."

"Yes, I know it's hard being so far away, but in time you get used to it. So, how come you're here?"

The young El Salvadorian girl then brushed her hair back, momentarily revealing bruises on the left side of her face that had been covered with her hair. Then again, as her hair came hanging down along the sides, Gabriela, also noticed bruises and scratches on the undersides of her arms.

"Oh, well, ya know, to live a better life, babysitting and make money to send home to take care of my family."

Gabriela had lived the life and walked in similar shoes, and it was heartbreaking to see such a young girl living the way she had, but also a haunting reminder of the life Gabriela lived.

"It's okay, you don't have to hide who you are. I've lived a similar life, I know."

The girl looked all around, and then down at the baby. After the girl finally found the strength to look back up at Gabriela, Gabriela revealed her cigarette scars on her forearms.

"Listen, I understand that some of the things you may do in here are because you don't have a choice, or it's the only way for you to live at this time in your life. As hard or scary as it may seem to just leave all this, it's not. In fact, if you want, I could take care of you. All you have to do is just walk away."

As the barking from the dogs outside intensified, the girl looked over her shoulder at Nelson, who was preparing a package, and then back at Gabriela, angst in her eyes.

"I—I can't. They'll find me if I leave. They always find those who leave, and when they do, only the lucky ones are left with scars, while the others, well for them, *muerte*."

Gabriela understood the girl's situation, but decided she would make one final attempt to offer her help. Gabriela took out a piece of paper and a pen to write down her name and phone number, which she gave to the girl.

"I understand, but if you ever need someone to talk to, or if you need anything, anything at all, don't hesitate to call."

"Oh, okay, thank you. *Muchas gracias*," the girl said as she took the piece of paper.

"Yes, *de nada*. I'm Gabriela. And what's your name?"

"Martina," the girl said with a smile.

"Martina, what a pretty name," Gabriela said as she admired Martina and the baby.

Martina seemed like a desperate immigrant searching for solace, but Gabriela was able to see something pure and strong deep within Martina's beautiful doe eyes. At that moment, Gabriela was willing to help Martina in any way.

As the barking from the dogs in the backyard intensified, Nelson finished. Martina looked over her shoulder, then turned back towards Gabriela and hid the piece of paper with Gabriela's name and phone number in her pocket.

"Here, this is for Wilmer. Make sure he gets this as soon as possible. Tell him that Nelson said everything is cleared and that we're good to go in two weeks, okay?"

"Okay."

"Make sure you remember to tell him, don't forget," Nelson demanded.

As Gabriela took the package, she could hear pills rattling around in bottles and a sudden uproar of scampering on the floorboards upstairs. Gabriela looked into Martina's eyes, and then at Nelson, whose face became pale. Gabriela could sense danger. Nelson took the package back, ran and stormed out the back door. Gabriela turned towards Martina, who had jumped up, causing the baby to cry. ICE officers came barging in through the front door with guns drawn, causing Gabriela to fearfully turn around towards the ICE officers and face the horrors of illegal immigration, which left her in a frozen state of vulnerability.

43

For love—or that's at least what Gabriela convinced herself while she slowly bobbed her head up and down, her full, lush lips wrapped around Don Fernandez's thick oversized cock. The pain in Gabriela's jaw would always be overwhelming, but it was the thought of the baby in her stomach that motivated Gabriela to get past the horrific experiences and finish the job. This job was now routine to her, since Don Fernandez had provided Gabriela with bogus credentials, citizenship documents, an apartment, and a job. Gabriela had never imagined being in such a desperate situation, but she was at least in caring hands. Don Fernandez always coddled Gabriela, no matter what dehumanizing fantasies were being manifested in his mind. Sometimes, Don Fernandez would palm Gabriela's head like a grapefruit, or savagely pull on her hair like she was a whore, all depending on his mood. Either way, he was at least generous, always providing Gabriela with a thick, soft towel to kneel on, and a cup of water and wash rag to use for cleanup.

Fortunately, Don Fernandez was easy to arouse and make cum very quickly. Usually four to eight minutes, all depending on how motivated Gabriela was feeling. In the end, Gabriela, didn't have to worry about facials, since those were for the unworthy whores. Gabriela was put on a pedestal, so Don Fernandez enjoyed having Gabriela swallow his cum, because it created the illusion of love. It was the only part of the routine Gabriela despised. Don Fernandez would usually cum more than a mouthful, and would gag Gabriela with his cock, forcing her to swallow. Some of it would usually overflow out her mouth and dribble down her chin. When Gabriela went to use the bathroom after finishing up, she would force herself to vomit.

Today was a special day, though. After finishing and cleaning up, as Cuban music resonated, Gabriela sat in Don Fernandez's private room, caressing her stomach, filled with an eight-month manifestation of Sarita. She visualized her departure. Gabriela could still taste the saltiness of Don Fernandez's cum, but she focused on the final act of an eight-month period of secretly plotting an escape, with help from Luz and Anna Marie, who worked with her in the sewing factory. They also helped set Gabriela up in an apartment in Jersey City and a new job at a café, both of which would be waiting for Gabriela when she was ready to make the right moves to eventually leave Don Fernandez. It was as Don Fernandez freshened up in the bathroom that Gabriela had a window of opportunity.

Gabriela focused on the centerpiece resting in the center circle of the room, a statue of Prometheus. Prometheus who had tricked the gods and stolen the fire, divine knowledge, from them, rested on top of a square emerald-toned marble base with a height and width of three feet, which was the outer layer of a safe. Inside were important documents, such as names and emails of corrupt business associates, along with paper trails of their phone and online communications, domestic and overseas bank account records and transactions, and records of illegal business activities—important documents that would expose Don Fernandez's connection to Nada Mas. All of it could be used to blackmail Don Fernandez. There was also a loaded gun, and cash—lots of cash, about six figures. Gabriela acquired the combination, with stealth tactics and patience, since she was unable to get all the sequential numbers at once. Now it was finally time for Gabriela to open up the safe.

As soon as the small window of opportunity opened up, Gabriela got up and walked over towards the statue of Prometheus. She thought about how much the myth of Prometheus meant to Don Fernandez, but most importantly how long it took Don Fernandez to finish freshening up in the bathroom.

As Gabriela knelt, she felt around the edges of the marble base until she found the grooves to open up the marble panel, to reveal the door to the safe.

She quickly rotated the knob clockwise and counterclockwise, to each of the intended sequential numbers, only to grunt and hit the base with an open hand after failing to unlock the safe twice. Gabriela paused and started over, when she heard the toilet flushing.

Gabriela's heart beat rapidly as she tried to refocus and dial in the correct numbers. As the flushing water from the toilet faded away and flowed into the running faucet water, Gabriela thought of Sarita, growing in her stomach, and that motivated her to successfully open the safe. Gabriela's eyes lit up. Her small window of opportunity began to close as the running water from the faucet stopped and the bathroom doorknob turned. Gabriela then took all that was of utmost importance, closed the safe door and the marble panel, and ran back to the couch, stuffing all she had taken into her handbag as the bathroom door slowly opened.

As Don Fernandez stepped out of the bathroom, Gabriela sat still. Each slow step Don Fernandez took brought greater despair. Don Fernandez stood before Gabriela and reached out to hold both of her hands to help her stand up. He caressed the side of Gabriela's face as he gave her a kiss. As their lips locked, Gabriela looked over Don Fernandez's shoulder into Prometheus's eyes of stone.

After savoring the kiss, Don Fernandez pulled away. Gabriela gazed deep into Don Fernandez's cold, dark eyes one last time, before she would leave him forever.

44

Rays of sunlight illuminated Dante's hand as he gracefully glided the paintbrush across the unfinished canvas. For seven days and seven nights, Dante had slavishly completed painting after painting like a master artist racing against time to fulfill obligations for a high-profile commission. Even though Dante wasn't painting for the infamous Medici family or for the pope, his talents were beyond even the expectations of this elite class of clients.

Although fatigue and lack of sleep could be seen deep within Dante's eyes, along with the bags of darkness framing them, Dante still found the strength to keep his eyes open and stay focused in an attempt to finish what he had started. Each gesture of the paintbrush felt fulfilling as he brought closure to another abstract masterpiece. Finally, Dante's paintbrush dropped down to the floor. He got up and walked into the bathroom.

Dante wailed out as the ice-cold water rained down onto his bare skin. He reached out with outstretched arms to lean on the tile wall and brace his freezing, limp, fatigued body. Once Dante's body adjusted to the temperature of the water, he opened his eyes and focused on the water dripping down, swirling around his feet and down the drain. Dante felt rejuvenated.

After freshening up, Dante slowly paced back and forth while taking drags from his cigarette. He carefully observed each of the paintings spread out all over his apartment. Although Dante was his own worst critic, it was the thought of those who had devoted their lives to a craft, who had been able to not only inspire the hearts and minds of mortals, but also change the world. They were the innovators, the dreamers, and the artists who had walked the same path as Dante. But above all else, what motivated Dante to get his art the respect it deserved, what gave him the reason to live, were the muses who had come into his life. The thought of muses was what had fueled Dante through a week of insomnia and inspired him.

After reflecting on all that inspired him, Dante he returned to his stool to continue painting. He picked up his pack of Luckys, took another one out and lit it up. Each drag felt revitalizing as he leaned in closer to observe the painting on the easel, while running his fingertips through the wet paint, smearing it in an attempt to perfect his illusion of art and beauty.

Just as Dante's eyes continued to shift back and forth between the canvas and the open window, a Monarch butterfly flew into the apartment and landed on the windowsill. The butterfly filled Dante with solace as he observed it, slowly reaching out his fingers towards it. To Dante's surprise, the butterfly didn't fly away, but slowly stepped onto Dante's paint-stained fingertips. The spiritual attraction filled Dante with a mystical uprising, as he held his fingertips before his eyes with the butterfly resting on top. Eventually, the wind scared the butterfly away. As Dante watched the butterfly fly out the open window, he was attracted and drawn towards Sarita.

# # #

Outside, Sarita slowly rocked back and forth on the swing, while twisting her scuffed-up untied red high-top Converse All-Stars around in the dirt. Softly singing a Spanish lullaby, Sarita was lost within her mind. She opened her eyes and focused on Dante's window.

"Who are you?" Sarita said. Her burning desire to confront Dante and find out who he was consumed her.

# # #

As for Gabriela, while the curtains flowed amongst the currents of the wind that blew in through the open window, she remained in the comforts of home, dancing to her own rhythm. Gabriela was at peace and free as the faucet water flowed through her fingertips while she cleaned dishes. There were no worries or reasons to fear the world around her at that moment. Gabriela was safe and content within her thoughts. Mexico, America, and even all of those who had come into Gabriela's life, the ones who had filled her with joy, consumed her mind. But above all else, the two that overshadowed all within Gabriela's mind were Dante and Sarita.

# # #

Dante smoked the final remains of his cigarette while he continued to observe his paintings. He dropped the butt down onto the floor, adding to the other butts, put it out with his foot, and then lit up another Lucky. As Dante continued to admire his masterpieces, his focus faded away as he sensed an unknown presence approaching from outside his apartment door. Dante's attention was then drawn away from his paintings.

# # #

As Sarita continued to observe Dante's window, even though he wasn't there anymore, his presence still invoked her. Then a sudden sense of nausea struck and slowly built up, causing Sarita to hold her stomach and look up towards the windows of her apartment.

# # #

As Gabriela continued to clean dishes, she softly sang a Spanish lullaby. Thoughts of Sarita still occupied her mind. The love they shared, and the life they had built together, seemed strong and everlasting at the moment. Emanating from outside the comforts of home, however, was an unsettling presence.

# # #

As Dante crept towards the door, the unknown presence he felt from beyond the other side of the door became stronger. Dante took a drag from his cigarette and leaned in closer against the door with outstretched arms as he looked out the peephole.

# # #

Slowly emerging from the darkness, further down the hallway, were three men dressed in black. As they walked side by side, their malevolent presence became more intense the closer they got to Dante's apartment door.

# # #

Dante watched the three men in black standing in front of Gabriela's apartment door. He pulled back his eye from the peephole to refocus his vision and then placed it back to get a clearer look at the men in black. After Dante was able to see that they weren't there for him and didn't pose a threat, he removed his eye from the peephole. As he pushed himself away from the door with a sigh of relief, he turned away from the door while taking a drag. As Dante ran his fingers through his hair, he walked back to his painting.

###

Sarita continued to look up at the kitchen window of her apartment while holding her stomach. Time became nonexistent. Gabriela's presence in the kitchen window, yelling out to Sarita, seemed overdue to Sarita, yet her intuitive sense of concern would quickly be overshadowed by Dante, who returned to his window. Once again, as Sarita gazed up at his window, only seeing Dante's silhouette through the curtains, she became relaxed.

###

As Gabriela continued to clean dishes and softly sing a Spanish lullaby, instantaneously, the ghosts from a dark and haunting past came storming into the apartment. The plate held in Gabriela's hands came crashing down onto the floor, shattering into fragments. Before Gabriela even had a chance to react and defend herself, the three thugs pounced on her.

The first one grabbed Gabriela and tightly held her from behind, with one hand over her mouth and the other around her waist. The second thug stood in front of Gabriela with his gun pointed at her. The third thug stood guard near the door. Gabriela trembled as she gazed deep into the eyes of the thug pointing the gun at her. They took her away. All that remained was the drops of water from the kitchen faucet, slowly dripping down, and fragments from a broken plate left scattered all over the kitchen floor like broken dreams.

###

After hearing the disturbance, Dante got up from his stool and trotted towards his door to look out the peephole once again. Dante was instantly filled with shock and concern as he watched the three men in black forcefully hold and push Gabriela out of her apartment and down the hallway with guns drawn.

After the three men and Gabriela made their way further down the hallway, vanishing from view, Dante quickly went towards his open window to see if Sarita was still outside. She was. Dante became so confused. He stepped away from the open window and paced around in circles while trying to gather his thoughts and figure out what was going on and what he should do.

# # #

After Dante disappeared from sight, once again, Sarita got up from the swing. As Sarita slowly walked towards the apartment, while still gazing up at the emptiness of the kitchen window, she was filled with delirium and stopped in the courtyard. Sarita could see three men in black inside, forcefully pushing and guiding Gabriela with guns drawn, coming out of the stairwell door and into the lobby.

# # #

As Gabriela was forcefully being pushed and guided, she gazed up through her strands of hair. She focused on Sarita for a moment, only to have the three men force her to continue walking through the lobby and towards the front entrance doors. Gabriela was only able to look back over her shoulder for a final glimpse, with tears in her eyes.

# # #

"Mama . . . Mama." After softly calling out, Sarita approached the courtyard entrance doors, walked inside and then through the lobby towards the front entrance doors. She watched as the three men in black pushed and guided Gabriela further away down the entrance path. As Sarita stood before the entrance doors with her body and the palms of her hands pressed up against the glass door, she watched the three men push Gabriela, into the back of an unmarked van.

"Mama! Mama! Mama!" Sarita yelled out with tears in her eyes.

After the unmarked van vanished, Sarita sobbed. At last, she backed away from the door with tears in her eyes and began sprinting through the lobby, up the stairwell, while stumbling over the laces of her shoes and then down the hallway. The only person she could think of going to for help was Dante.

After Sarita made it to the fifth-floor hallway, she slowly walked towards

Dante's door. Sarita then began to knock, while calling out for help with tears dripping down her cheeks.

"Pleeeease . . . mister . . . open up . . . pleeeease . . . help . . ."

Dante walked over towards the door to look out the peephole and became hesitant when he saw Sarita. Dante battled with his heart and mind over what was right and wrong, but his compassion overcame all. Dante slowly opened the door, reached out, and took Sarita by her hand. After pulling Sarita inside, he looked out into the hallway and then shut the door.

<u>45</u>

As Gabriela silently sat all alone in solitary confinement, thoughts of Sarita filled her mind. The thoughts would fade away when she heard a storm of stomping boots on the other side of the door. Gabriela opened her eyes and listened until it stopped, then focused on the clinging and clacking of bolts and locks, and then finally on the creaking of the door, slowly opening. Ignacio emerged, and then Don Fernandez stepped into the cell. Don Fernandez sat down on a chair, resting before Gabriela.

"So, do you miss me, *bonita?*"

Gabriela didn't say a word.

"Well, I take your silence as a sign of forgiveness, and even after all these years, even though you may still look like an innocent little angel who's been lost and abandoned, desperately searching for some sort of security from another, a saint in the eyes of others, you and I both know that you're no angel, and you're especially no saint. Your selfish actions and disrespect still humors me to this day, to imagine how you thought that you could actually take from me and safely leave me forever. Luckily for me, you didn't go too far, and I know a lot of birds in the area and in high places, who do a lot of chirping. It's unfortunate for you, though, that you got caught up in the middle of a random roadside raid conducted by ICE. At first, when I heard the news, I was surprised to hear that you were there. Then again, knowing your past and what you've done to me—well, karma is sweet revenge. Now, with that said, is there anything you would like to say before I continue and explain why you are here and what will happen with you?"

"I had my reasons to take all that you gave me and then just suddenly disappear from you forever."

Gabriela's words amused Don Fernandez.

"In a way, I have some respect for your boldness, yet it's a shame how your actions have come back to haunt you. My personal vendetta for you is an overwhelming thirst for blood, but your life will be spared because of a situation which has suddenly arisen during the time of your absence. And luckily for you, you have been found during this time, so that your life will become compensation and not eradicated." Don Fernandez paused, leaving Gabriela in the dark. "An associate of mine, someone whom I believe you briefly met in the past, just once, La negra corazón , who you may remember as Marta Mendoza, is in some trouble. Now it seems that you're the answer to what problems have suddenly arisen for my associate."

The thought of the darkness in Marta's eyes, and the façade of malevolence painted all over her wrinkled, makeup-covered face, haunted Gabriela. To hear Don Fernandez continue and speak of her current situation only brought Gabriela more heartache and pain.

"Anyway, Marta's connected with Nada Mas, as am I, and is someone who I have been doing business with for many years. She is due for deportation within the next two days. This is someone who is very close to me, like family. Normally, what I would do is use my status and contacts within higher places to delay the deportation process, or just simply have the case disappear, giving my associate immunity. What makes this situation extremely interesting is the fact that, the day I began negotiations, I also found out about your whereabouts. So knowing you were back in my life has changed things. The anger has come back, and my first instinct was to have vengeance. I could have easily killed you, like that, but something inside me told me no, that there is another way of handling you and the situation. Since negotiations aren't going so well, that's when it dawned on me what to do with you. Death is bliss indeed, but to go on living, living against your own will, without freedom, without choice, and without the ones you love—well, in my eyes, that's vengeance. So instead of me simply killing you, you will instead fill in the shoes of Marta Mendoza and be deported within the next two days. Is there anything you would like to say before we say our final goodbye?"

"What if I refuse to cooperate?"

"Don't worry, *bonita*, because you have no choice."

After Don Fernandez finalized Gabriela's fate, he turned towards Ignacio, who checked his watch and gave him a nod. Don Fernandez then turned back around to face her. He savored the beauty and disappointment seen deep within Gabriela's eyes for a moment before getting up to step towards Gabriela and run his fingers through her hair and hold her head as he gave her a final kiss goodbye on both cheeks. As Don Fernandez began to walk out the door, Gabriela asked one final question.

"What about my daughter? What will happen with her?"

"Don't worry, you'll see your daughter again. You will see her in the afterlife."

Don Fernandez's words crippled Gabriela. After Don Fernandez finished savoring the loss of hope seen on Gabriela's face, he exited the undisclosed holding room. Ignacio stood in the doorway, admiring Gabriela one last time with a slight smile, then shut the door behind him. Gabriela was left all alone, once again, and closed her eyes.

II
Intermezzo:
Bonded by fate

46

~Pure Intentions~

Even though I regret getting involved with Don Fernandez, my intentions were always pure. My life at the time was so fragile, and all I needed was for someone who would be able to help hold it together, and provide, not just for me, but for my unborn child at the time, Sarita. And no matter how flawed everything being provided for me was, or how sinful my actions were in order to pay off my debt, in my heart and in my mind, everything I did was out of pure intentions, to benefit Sarita and give her a better life. My involvement with Don Fernandez was the foundation to the life I now have. And even though that road, which seemed so liberating in the beginning, led to a dead end, unexpectedly bringing Don Fernandez back into my life and separating me from my hermosa, in the end, all that fatefully unfolded eventually brought me back down a fulfilling path, uniting Sarita and I once again, bonding both of us together with the source of our trinity of one.

Sarita paused and then placed the open journal facedown on her lap. The memory of being separated from Gabriela brought back a gut-wrenching feeling; emotions buried long ago that Sarita had never imagined experiencing ever again. There seemed to be a sudden impulse of pain twisting, biting, and tearing away at Sarita's heart and soul, but it would be the thought of Sarita's savior at the time of her separation from Gabriela that would purify all.

Dante, who at one time seemed to be so terrifying, yet had been the only trustworthy person to go to in a time of distress, filled Sarita's mind and began to summon her. Sarita stood up from the old wooden chair with all three of Gabriela's journals in her arms and began to walk out of the dilapidated apartment, once called home, now left abandoned throughout the years. She walked to the end of the hallway, towards the door to what used to be Dante's apartment. There was no doorknob on the paint-chipped door, only a gaping hole that revealed a glimpse into the past. After reflecting on all that she'd once feared to be on the other side, Sarita pushed the door open and stepped in.

All that remained was the paint-stained floor and empty bottles of beer, liquor, and wine. They weren't Dante's. They had been left behind by the homeless who had vacated the abandoned apartment, and teenagers and drifters who had occupied the empty space for socializing or a temporary residence. Along with the trash, old, deteriorated furniture was left behind from the last tenant who had lived there as well. Graffiti was painted all over the walls, such as various gang tags, like the infamous Nada Mas, the anarchy logo, with the words *Anarchy Now* and names of lovers, along with holes in the walls. As for the windows, they were all boarded up, except for the one Dante would always be near. The top and the bottom portions of the window were boarded up, but the middle was left open, allowing sunlight to shine in through the gaping hole, along with other holes and cracks in the boards that covered the other windows, allowing sporadic beams of sunlight to shine into the dimly lit emptiness.

Sarita began to walk around, imagining the way it once was, being within the same apartment as a child, under the tutelage of Dante. She envisioned the now-bare wall that had once been filled with paintings, both hanging up and leaning against it, but also the empty space where all of Dante's paints, easel, art supplies, sketchbooks and sketches used to be. But what intrigued Sarita the most was the partly boarded-up window that used to be the link between Dante and Sarita. The window was now a portal into the past, which summoned Sarita. She began to caress the windowsill and look out the window. Outside was an abandoned yard, engulfed with unkempt vegetation and garbage. Nothing remained from the past except for the old rusty swing set. It used to be Sarita's playground, and now it filled Sarita's mind as she imagined from behind her closed eyes all that had manifested, from being bonded by fate.

47

As time slowly elapsed, the cooling winds blew in through the open window, laced with the oscillating fan and wind chimes, melodically echoing out a symphony of soothing comfort. Dante sat on his stool, sedated, as he took sips from his bottle of cheap red wine while observing Sarita sleeping on the couch like a putto, unconsciously laid out in the Garden of Eden.

Dante battled with pixies of good and evil. After a dualistic array of selfish and selfless motives regarding what to do with Sarita were conjured up, Dante's attention was drawn towards his cell phone. It seemed to be his only hope. Dante reached for the cell phone. He dialed Virgil, an old artist friend, from his contacts and took another reassuring sip as the phone rang in his ear. Just before Dante was ready to hang up, Virgil answered.

Virgil was shocked to hear from Dante, whom he hadn't seen or spoken to in years. He spent a few minutes speaking over Dante to catch up on lost time before Dante was able to explain himself, asking Virgil for advice and help as to what to do with Sarita. Virgil was no help. His advice was just as cruel as Dante's selfish thoughts. His only advice was to not get involved. To just dump the kid off on a street corner in some neighborhood, and that Dante was way too talented to have to deal with the situation at hand. After Dante hung up, he focused on Sarita. Dante felt desperate and all alone.

He got up and walked around his messy studio, searching through garbage, his desk filled with completed works of art and beauty and art supplies, for charcoal sticks and pastels. Dante then walked over towards Sarita and gently lifted up the couch cushion her head rested on, reached under and grabbed his sketchbook, lowered the cushion back down, and walked back to his stool.

Opening up the old sketchbook caused dust to waft out. Dante scanned through the pages filled with art until he found some blank pages. Sarita's anatomical features stirred Dante in the way of muses as he sketched out portraits of Sarita from many different angles and perspectives.

Dante sketched with the endurance of a driven art student, yet he was broken and needed to find his rhythm. After resurrecting his artistic skill, he beat out sketches with perfection until becoming completely drained. The sketchbook in his dirty charcoal-and-pastel-stained hands and forearms was now filled. After regaining some strength, Dante got up, tore out pages, and laid them out all over the floor and coffee table to critique. Dante stood with one arm held across his chest and the other held up with his fingers held around his chin. Sarita then began to wake up.

Sarita readjusted and stretched out, yawning and cracking joints before letting out one last yawn like a lion, finally opening her eyes and sucking her gums. After Sarita adjusted her vision, she looked at Dante with bewilderment.

"Where… where am I?" Sarita said as she sat up.

"Well, let's just say you're not in Kansas anymore, Dorothy."

Sarita squinted. "Um, my name isn't Dorothy. It's Sarita. And what's your name?"

"Well, it's a pleasure to finally meet you, Sarita. My name is Dante."

"Dante . . . it's a pleasure to finally meet you," Sarita whispered, and then the realization of what had happened to her mother overcame her. "Wait! Where's my mother? What—what happened to her? Where did they take her? I want my mother!"

Dante's smile quickly faded away. "Whoa, whoa, wait. Wait a minute, kid. Calm down, no need for the waterworks. Everything's gonna be all right. Your mother is fine." Dante stumbled while walking towards Sarita, who then began to move away from him.

"Leave me alone! Don't touch me. I, I want my mother!" The feminine wrath ignited once again as Sarita began to yell at Dante, who held her down by the shoulders while Sarita squirmed around and slapped him.

"Hey, calm down, kid. There's nothing we can do right now. All I know is you aren't gonna be able to see her anytime soon. For now you're stuck with me until we figure out what to do with you."

"Who are they, and, and why would they take my mother away?"

"Just relax and listen to me, so we can figure out what's going on and what to do with you, okay, kid?"

She sat back down, curled up in a ball, and then wrapped herself up within a blanket. As tears slowly flowed from Sarita's eyes, Dante sat down on the coffee table.

"But, but why? I don't understand. What about me? What will I do without my mother? Who will take care of me?"

"Well, it looks like I'm your guardian for now, kid, so I suggest you relax and make yourself at home, okay."

Sarita looked around the dirty apartment and then looked at Dante, with his shaggy dirty-blond hair, scruffy face and dirty old clothes, realizing she was no longer in the comforts of home, but now in the home of the mysterious, reclusive man, Dante.

"You, take care of me? Look at this place. Look at you."

"Well, I'm sorry to disappoint. I know this isn't the Ritz, and I'm no Johnny Depp, kid, but for now you're stuck here with me, so try to make yourself comfortable and try to at least get used to me since we'll be together for the time being." After Dante spoke, Sarita lay back down and covered herself up with the bedsheet. "Good idea, kid. Go back to bed. Hopefully when you wake up, you'll be a bit more relaxed, so we'll be able to talk things over."

Sarita silently thought of her mother and what would happen with her, until finally closing her eyes and eventually falling back to sleep.

"Goodnight, kid," Dante said as he stood up and ran his fingers through Sarita's hair.

He walked into the kitchen to get himself a much-needed beer before passing out.

<u>48</u>

Sarita slowly opened her eyes to the blinding rays of light shining in through the open window, sat up on the couch, and scanned the space around. All that was horrid was overshadowed by original pieces of art created by Dante, who was unconsciously laid facedown on a small bed.

It would be Dante's sketches of Sarita that would beckon her. Sarita was impressed as she held up each one, but they were only a taste of Dante's mastery. Across the apartment, hanging up and leaning against the far wall, were all of Dante's completed and unfinished paintings, which attracted Sarita away from mere blueprints of artistic genius.

As Sarita stood before it all, she was inspired. All of Dante's paintings, painted with an array of emotions, which created a balance between fear and love, the feminine and the masculine, and the duality of man, all had an ageless, universal, yet simple abstract appeal. They had the ability to move those who appreciated such work. The diverse range of colors, smeared all over in thick layers, splattered on the canvases, created a sense of fluidity. Along with a variety of abstract and contemporary images, there were women in the nude, and women clothed in the likeness of goddesses but Sarita's curiosity would draw her attention toward unfinished and covered paintings.

As Sarita reached out to remove the cover from one of the paintings, she was interrupted by Dante, who moaned and squirmed around. Sarita became startled and stopped. Quickly, she pulled back her outstretched hand and then turned to see if Dante woke up. He didn't.

Sarita then tiptoed towards the refrigerator, which she looked inside of for something to eat, but there was nothing, only beer, condiments and smelly old food. Sarita shut the door and then noticed a plane ticket attached to the door. She took it off and studied it. Aero Mexico flight 1203 from JFK Airport to Mexico City. This fascinated Sarita, since her mother was from Mexico. Sarita thought, "Why is Dante going to Mexico?" But what was even more interesting was that the name on the ticket wasn't Dante's name. It was a bogus name, Thomas P. Daniels. It was odd, but one of Dante's paintings was calling her.

After Sarita put the plane ticket back, she walked towards the open window. It was where Dante seemed to always be while observing Sarita and the other children, but more intriguing was the easel with a covered painting resting on it. As Sarita stood before all that seemed hidden and enshrouded in enigmatic mystique, she became breathless. She imagined what kind of painting deserved such secrecy, before slowly reaching out her hand to grasp the corner of the cloth, only to have a confronting presence fall upon her from behind.

"Hey, what do you think you're doing, kid?" Dante grabbed Sarita's hand and turned her around.

Sarita silently stood with her hands held together behind her back while twisting her right foot into the floor, biting her bottom lip and looking all around.

"Um, I, I, was, just . . . ."

"You were just snooping around and looking in places where you shouldn't be. Have you ever heard the saying 'respect another person's privacy'? Well, this is my private stuff, which isn't for the eyes of other people, especially noisy little girls. Okay, kid?"

After speaking, Dante pulled Sarita away from the painting and then adjusted the cloth covering it, making sure it was on tighter than before.

"Um, so you're a painter?"

"You're pretty smart, kid. So, how'd ya guess?" Dante said as he walked away from Sarita while picking up garbage from the floor.

"Um, I, I think that you're very good. You have pretty paintings, I like them very much."

"Well, it's always good to have a critic who thinks so highly of my work, so I accept your compliment, kid."

"Um, my name is Sarita. Or or did you forget already!" Sarita said defiantly.

Dante squinted, sensing that Sarita was going to be more than a handful.

"Sarita. Well, don't you have a nickname, something that would be easier to remember?"

"Um, yeah. Um, Chor-tee."

"What?"

"Chor-tee."

"Chor-tee . . . chorr . . . shorrr . . . you mean, Shorty?"

"That—that's what I said."

"Shorty. Well, thank you for the compliment, and now that you have finally calmed down, how about some dinner? I'm sure you're hungry. I know I am."

"Um, sure."

Dante began searching for pots and pans, throwing stuff, until he found an old grimy skillet and pot. He went into the refrigerator and sniffed everything. All of the bad food, such as rotten fruits and vegetables, expired cold cuts, and leftover fish, he tossed into the pile of garbage in the corner, leaving him with nothing but a refrigerator filled with beer and condiments. Dante then went into the freezer, which was filled with nothing but icicles and a few bottles of vodka and hard liquor. Sarita walked into the kitchen.

"Um, would, would you like some help?"

"Sure. Here, you can set the table," Dante said, handing Sarita paper plates, old stained glasses and twisted-up utensils.

Sarita thought to herself, "How could a grown man live like this?" as she set the table. She sat down and waited for Dante, who then began to look through drawers, cabinets and piles of paper for some sort of restaurant menu so he could order in food. After unsuccessfully finding one, Dante slammed drawers and cabinets shut while mumbling obscenities.

"Looks like I'm gonna have to go to the store real quick to get us some food."

"Um, so, are, are you gonna leave me here all alone?" Sarita said with a sad puppy dog face.

"Well, now that I think about it, no. You're coming with me, so hurry up so we can get this over with. Well, c'mon, I don't have all day."

Sarita slid off her chair and walked towards Dante, who guided Sarita over towards the door, looked out the peephole, and then led Sarita out.

Dante made it out of the front entrance of the apartment building without being seen. Mona then came creeping in from the courtyard. She could clearly see Dante and Sarita from inside the lobby. Seeing them together seemed odd, and very suspicious, in Mona's opinion. Mona carefully watched their every move as she continued to smoke her cigarette, even though there were numerous No Smoking signs hanging up near the entrance. After Dante and Sarita vanished from Mona's sight, she then ran to her apartment. Mona frustratingly tried to open up her apartment door with her cigarette of half ashes hanging down from her lips.

"C'mon, ya motha's ass, open up!"

As Mona leaned into the door while turning the key, she forced the door open and then ran towards the window that faced out towards the street in front of the apartment. Mona's apartment was filled with a bona fide sense of discomfort, with Post-its hanging all over with little reminders and inspirational messages, such as "remember to try the bikini wax tonight," "collect rent from shit bag in apartment 213," and "don't let any man use you like a disposable utensil, you're worth more than that." There were also stacks of tabloid magazines, newspapers, many ashtrays filled with cigarette butts, and as Mona ran through the TV room, there was a VHS tape recording all the daytime shows, such as *The View, Tyra Banks, The Wendy Williams Show* and *The Young and the Restless*. Mona watched Dante walk down the sidewalk with Sarita, peeking out from behind the curtains as she continued to smoke her cigarette. Mona then picked up the phone, which rested next to a shrine of burning candles and a twenty-four-by-twenty-four inches portrait of Frankie hanging above on the back wall, with a rosary hanging on the edge of the frame, to call the police.

"Hello, this is Mona Molina from the Clearview apartment complex. I'm cawling out of suspicion of a tenant of mine, who fits tha profile of one of those, whatcha cawl it, doe . . . domestic terrorist, that's it. Ya know, tha type that keeps to themselves. And I've been saying it for years now, that he's up to no good, anyway. I just now saw him leaving tha apartment complex with tha girl, one of tha kids from tha building, during tha day, mindja, which is extremely suspicious, since tha creep only comes out at night. God only knows what goes on up in that apartment all day. And otha tenants have always been and still are suspicious of him . . . No, of course not, my late husband, Frankie, took care of him years ago when he moved in . . . Wha, what tha hell ya tawlking about? I'm concerned ova here. Not only do I have high blood pressure, but I'm terrified for tha well-being of tha child, and God only knows what tha creep has done to tha motha, who I haven't seen in days . . . Yeah, that's right, I haven't seen tha motha in days, eitha . . . Who tha hell knows? Right now I'm only concerned about tha child, and tha creep she's with . . . Yeah, mm-hmm . . . Wha eva, tha sooner, tha betta . . . Apartment 101, I'll buzz ya in . . . Yeah, yeah, I appreciate it too. Thank you, take care."

After Mona hung up the phone, she turned away from the window and lit up another cigarette. She then grabbed the sunblock she'd originally intended to get from the kitchen countertop and then left her apartment to go back outside to join the other two brujas with a sinister grin. She felt fulfilled for taking advantage of an open opportunity to report the mysterious, reclusive tenant, Dante, with good reason and intent. Mona could only patiently wait for now to see justice be served in her likeness.

49

Resting on the tabletop before Sarita was a bowl of Campbell's tomato soup, saltines and a burnt grilled cheese sandwich. As Sarita leaned forward to observe the effortlessly made dinner, she cringed.

"What, what is it? My cooking's no good?"

"Um, well . . ."

"I know I don't cook like Paula Deen over here, but you could at least try it."

Sarita then said an exaggerated prayer in Spanish before taking a spoonful, which was just warm enough and tasted strange because of all the extra spices and salt that Dante had added to it. The vile soup then triggered Sarita to spit up all over Dante. Soup dripped off Dante's face as he wiped it dry. Sarita started laughing. Dante gave her a sincere look. Suddenly they could hear someone knocking on the door.

"Shit!" Dante took Sarita by the hand, dragged her into the bathroom, put Sarita in the bathtub, told her to "stay still and be quiet, like hide and seek, play dead," and then closed the curtain. Dante then ran back to the kitchen, put both bowls of soup in the sink, placed both grilled cheese sandwiches on top of the two plates stacked together, which he put on top of the counter, and put his bottle of beer into the refrigerator.

Dante then began to walk towards the door, only to stop after realizing he had left Sarita's glass of milk on the table. He raced back. The knocking on the door intensified. Dante stood with the glass of milk in his hand, unsure what to do, until deciding to chug the milk, put the empty glass in the sink, and trot towards the door while wiping the excess of milk left on his mouth with his forearm.

Dante looked through the peephole and tensed up seeing two Jersey City police officers. He opened the door.

"Hi, sir, how are you? I'm Officer Moreno and this is my partner, Officer Christianson. We've just received a report about a missing child who lives in the building, whose mother apparently appears to be absent too. They live in the apartment next to you. As of right now, we're just sweeping through the building, and asking tenants if they have seen or spoken to the mother or the child within the past couple of days. So, with your cooperation, if you don't mind, could we step inside for a moment to ask you a few questions?"

"No, not at all, come in."

As the two police officers entered and walked through Dante's apartment, they covered their noses and then removed their hands as they stood before Dante's paintings.

"Wow! These are good. I've never seen anything like these before. You're a real original," Christianson commented.

"Yeah, they're pretty damn good. Any for sale?" Moreno asked.

"Thank you. No, not at the moment. They will be when I finish them and put them in my one-man show, which is coming up soon."

"Oh, yeah? What gallery?" Christianson asked.

"The Red-Light Gallery."

"Yeah, I think I've heard of that place. You must be really successful to have a show there. Big money is put into that place."

"Yeah, can't you see how successful I am?"

The two officers laughed and then began to walk around and observe Dante's paintings. Dante bit down on his bottom lip while he watched Christianson slowly walk by the bathroom and then begin to step in, only to walk out since the smell was so unbearable. Dante felt relief but then noticed Moreno nonchalantly looking down at all of the sketches of Sarita scattered all over the floor, which Dante then scampered towards and began to pick up.

"Sorry about the mess, but I've been very busy lately," Dante said while running his fingers through his hair.

"It's not a problem. You seem like you have a lot of work on your hands," Moreno said. He bent down before Dante to pick up one final sketch left underneath the coffee table. He turned it upside down and looked at it, leaving Dante in an utter state of anxiety.

"So, who's the girl?"

Dante lifted his head and looked Moreno in his stern eyes as he took the sketch and then turned it over.

"Oh, her, she's . . . she's just someone who modeled for me one time," Dante said. Moreno then took the sketch back, to show Christianson.

"Check her out," Moreno said childishly to Christianson, who then walked over towards Moreno, holding the sketch.

"Damn, where you'd find her? That's Bunny Ranch material. I mean, my God, look at the size of those tits," Christianson said.

"Oh her, I found her in some café in the East Village." Dante smiled.

"Sure she's a she? You gotta be careful over there, ya know," Moreno joked.

"So I hear."

"Anyway, we really don't want to take up any more of your time, so if you don't mind, I just have a couple of questions to ask. Since you live next door to the mother and daughter who are apparently missing, have you seen or spoken to either one within the past few days?"

"No, neither one. In fact I hardly ever see them. They're usually very quiet and keep to themselves. What I do know is that the girl usually plays out back with the other kids who live in the building. As for the mother, well, she works a lot and is hardly ever around. I usually hear her come home sometime in the evening, like sevenish or sometimes even later, all depending on the day. That's pretty much it. I hope that's enough to help you in some way."

"That's fine. That should be enough for now. I think we're done here. Thank you for your cooperation. If you do see the girl or the mother anytime soon, don't hesitate to call us. Keep your eyes open. If the girl's not with the mother, she may be with someone else she shouldn't be with."

"Okay, no problem, Officer. I'll keep my eyes wide open."

"Okay, thanks again for your cooperation, and good luck with the show." Moreno pointed to the paintings, handed the sketch back to Dante, and then walked out with Christianson.

After they left, Dante shut the door, walked into the bathroom and opened up the shower curtain. Sarita stood silently with her arms wrapped around her body. Dante reached out his hand, grabbed Sarita's, and dragged her back out to the kitchen, where they both sat down at the table.

"Listen, Shorty, I can't keep you here any longer. I need to get rid of you before those guys find out I'm keeping you up here with me and think that I did something to your mother. They'll lock me up and put me in jail."

"Get rid of me? Are you crazy? What would you do? Leave me all alone in the streets?"

"Well, it did cross my mind, Shorty, but I'm not that cold. I have a heart, and I'm willing to take you to someone who could take care of you. So, do you have any family, friends, or know anyone who's friends with your mother?"

Sarita scanned the apartment as she thought. After contemplating the few people in her life, she came to the conclusion that Dante would be the one.

"So, is there anyone you can think of, anyone at all?"

"Um, you."

"Me?"

"Yes, you. You're the only person left in my life who could help me get back to my mother. There's no one else."

"Whoa, whoa, wait a minute, Shorty. I can't take care of you. First of all, kids are very dirty and creepy, and very annoying, which I want nothing to do with. Second, I have to finish my work. I have a very important one-man show coming up, and plus I plan on going on a very, very long vacation soon, very far from this place. And besides all of my personal endeavors, I can't get involved and look after you. Someone else will have to do that. Do you understand what I'm telling you? That the only thing I will be able to do is to find someone else to take care of you and do what needs to be done? Or probably what I should do is take you to social services and then they'll be able to find your mother, or set you up with a nice family and keep you in a good home until they do so."

"I don't want a nice family! I want my mother! I want to be with my mother again, p-please. Dante, help me. You said you have a heart. Well, well, show me your heart. Please, my mother is all I have, and from the looks of it, I'm all you have right now. Please, help me get back to my mother," Sarita bellowed out with tears in her eyes.

As Dante watched Sarita sob, he felt a tingle in his heart. Sarita seemed to have suddenly begun to fill in a void, an emptiness within, which had been haunting Dante. In Sarita's eyes, Dante saw a hint of previous muses who had inspired and fueled his heart. As much as Dante wanted to get rid of Sarita, leave everything behind and go to Mexico, deep within, he knew that he couldn't let go, not yet.

"All right, all right, relax. I guess, since I'm responsible for you now, I can try to find a way to get you back to your mother. First, you need to calm down and relax. No crying, not on my watch. Second, you'll have to understand that it won't be that simple, okay, Shorty?"

"You mean it? You'll help me get back to my mother?" Sarita choked with each breath as she wiped away tears.

"Yeah, I'll try to help you get back to your mother."

Sarita turned her frown into a smile, got up and walked over towards Dante to give him a hug.

"Okay, Shorty, okay. Let's not get too mushy. Now that you're a bit more relaxed, do you think that you could at least try to eat the soup I made you, even though it's not up to your standards?"

Dante pushed Sarita away, got up, got both bowls of soup and the plates with grilled cheese sandwiches, and set them on the table. He got his beer and poured Sarita another glass of milk.

"So, how will you help me get back to my mother?" Sarita asked as Dante ravenously ate his soup.

He stopped, leaned back, and then sipped his beer. "Well, since I can't take you to the authorities, who will be able to help find and get you to your mother, since you don't know of anyone who could take care of you and take you to the authorities, the best thing that I can think of is to take you to one of my friends."

Dante humored Sarita and created a sense of security. It was the best thing Dante could come up with, since his so-called friends were nowhere to be found, or the ones who were would want nothing to do with Dante and wouldn't help at all. Hopefully, though, Dante thought, at least one who was around would be willing to help.

"Really, your friends will help me?"

"Yeah, but let's not worry about that right now, okay? Tomorrow when we wake up, I'll take you to my friend. So finish your food so you can get some sleep. I plan on leaving at sunrise tomorrow, okay, Shorty?"

"Um, but, but I'm not tired. I slept all day."

"Well, you're gonna have to try to fall asleep."

"Okay," Sarita muttered under her breath.

"Good."

As Dante continued to eat his soup and sandwich and sip his beer, Sarita was filled with fondness. Not only was Dante willing to help, but she was in the presence of a great artist. There was a spiritual connection that filled Sarita's stomach like butterfly wings.

"So, since you'll be spending another night in my apartment, let me lay down the laws of the land, since you've already violated some. First rule, which is the first rule you broke, don't touch anything. The second rule, ask for permission for anything, and the third and final rule, don't touch anything, *comprende?*"

Sarita looked up through her hair and deep into Dante's eyes while biting down on her bottom lip.

"What? What is it? Why are you looking at me like that? Hey, listen, if you have a problem with my rules, sorry, Shorty, but this isn't a democracy."

"Um, nothing. I, I just feel funny, down here." Sarita slowly reached down to gently caress her stomach.

"Well, if you're sick and have to throw up, hurry up and go to the bathroom before you start throwing up all over the place."

"No, I'm not sick. It feels good, like butterflies flapping around in my stomach, like I'm being tickled inside. Um, maybe . . . maybe it's love," Sarita said childishly, causing Dante to spit up beer and lean forward while wiping his beer-stained lips.

"Love, butterflies, or whatever it is flapping around in there, just make sure you don't throw up all over the place."

"Um, well, whatever it is, you're the one who makes me feel this way. I used to be scared of you, like all the other people, but not anymore. Now I guess it's because you're gonna help me, or something. I don't know, but since you're gonna help me, then I should help you, like, be your assistant."

"Well, I appreciate your offer, but I'm fine on my own. I don't need any assistance, especially any help from some little girl."

"From the looks of it, you do! I mean, look at this place. Look at you. You're all alone and have no one. How come? How come you live like this by yourself? How come you never let anyone into your life, like my mother? What are you scared of? And who's Thomas Daniels, and why is he going to Mexico?"

Sarita looked past Dante to the Aero Mexico flight 1203 plane ticket from JFK Airport to Mexico City, still on the fridge. Dante looked back as well. Then he turned back and sipped his beer while contemplating why he lived alone, why he had kept to himself for the past thirteen years, and why he was planning on leaving everything in his life far behind; most importantly, why Sarita was kept in the dark.

"There are many reasons, many reasons you wouldn't understand, as to why I live alone, why I don't let people like your mother into my life, and why Thomas Daniels plans on going to Mexico. It's all because of a life I once lived that would come back and hurt those in my life. All this, what you see, isn't what it once was," Dante said passionately, opening up his arms.

"But, you're a painter, aren't you?"

"Yeah, and?" Dante looked all around.

"Well, you're very good. I like your paintings a lot. And I, I don't know, but now knowing that you're not the scary person I once thought you were, I feel good coming to you for help."

"Well, try not to get too attached, Shorty. I like my space. Anyway, finish your food."

Sarita timidly looked away and continued to eat. Dante watched as she ate. How she readjusted her body in her chair—from sitting on one leg, to crossed legs, up onto her knees, and back again—all while softly humming sweet nothingness as she ate and tapped the edge of the table with her fingers. Whether it was fate, or the creator, who had sent Sarita, Dante accepted the hand he was dealt. Not only did Dante see that Sarita was his responsibility, but her demeanor was that of the muses who he devoted his life to. He would try to find in Sarita reason to commit his life to her, but it would be Sarita's innocence that would eradicate all.

"Hey, stop that, that's a nasty habit, especially for a little girl. Trust me, there ain't no gold up there, Shorty," Dante said with disgust.

"Um, but, but . . . ."

"But, but, it's nasty! Don't do it again. Anyway, you all done?" Dante stood up and cleared the table, then guided Sarita towards the couch.

"Um, Dante?" Sarita said as she lay down while Dante covered her with a blanket.

"Yeah, what is it, Shorty?"

"Um, pr-promise me I'll get back to my mother."

Dante ran his fingers through his hair, looking away and then back into Sarita's eyes.

"I promise. C'mon, get some sleep. Tomorrow is gonna be a long day. Goodnight, Shorty."

"Goodnight, Dante."

As Dante walked away, he ran his fingertips through her hair, leaving Sarita all alone. She gazed across the vastness at Dante's paintings while caressing her stomach, then closed her eyes.

<u>50</u>

The full moon shined down upon New York City and Dante. He paced back and forth on the rooftop while drinking from a bottle of cheap merlot. As Dante gazed out across the horizon at the New York City skyline, like so many times before, he was filled with visions of the past and the future. New York was the city where Dante had found failure and success, which was now nothing but an image of memories frozen in time. It was a place he wished never to return to, but now it was his destination; not for redemption, but for a child. As Dante continued to pace back and forth while drinking the cheap merlot, he only hoped that the city would be welcoming, not for him, but for Sarita.

"Why have you forsaken me . . . why . . . for what . . . for muses?"

As Dante yelled up towards the heavens above, laced with a numbing sense of drunken bliss, like so many times before, deep within the eye of Dante's mind, was an abstract array of ageless questions. What was it all for? Why had God sent him a child? Dante then stopped and laughed as he guzzled more wine, which ran down his chin and onto his shirt.

"Sarita . . . light of my life . . . fire of my loins . . . ha-ha . . . for muses . . . for love."

On the eve of Dante's return, he raised his bottle up and gazed out across the horizon, at the New York skyline. The city he forever wished to leave far behind. He took an everlasting sip for muses, but most importantly for Sarita.

51

It was the beginning of a new day. After waking up, Sarita cleaned the dirty dishes, scrubbed down the countertop, and began to arrange and organize all of Dante's art supplies. Sarita hummed sweet nothingness as she continued, while Dante stood before the bathroom sink, wearing only his old paint-covered jeans. He leaned down, drinking running water from the faucet like an exhausted dog drinking from a puddle of water.

When Sarita finished, she sat down on the couch, put her feet up on the coffee table, and sighed. Although she wasn't in the comforts of her own home, she felt safe and free, especially without the strict rules imposed by her mother. For a tiny moment, the absence of Gabriela felt refreshing. Sarita felt independent, capable of going out into the world on her own. But her innocence would avert her.

Once again, Sarita was drawn towards the covered-up painting resting on the easel. Sarita's curiosity beckoned her towards the painting. There was a sudden surge of euphoria as Sarita reached out towards the cloth draped over the painting. Sarita felt like Eve taking the sacred fruit from the tree of knowledge of good and evil.

Just as Sarita was about to reveal the painting that was hidden and enshrouded with mystery, Dante crept up behind her, his shadow cast down upon her while he reached out and grabbed Sarita by the wrist. Sarita froze and was spun around. She stared at Dante with a flabbergasted look on her face. Dante had fire in his eyes, while Sarita looked up at him sincerely, swaying her hips from side to side, twisting her right foot into the floor.

"What do you think you're doing?" Dante goaded out.

"Um, I, I woke up, and then I was cleaning, be, because I was waiting for you to come out of the bathroom."

"Sure as hell doesn't look like you're cleaning. You look like you're snooping around again and up to no good. Didn't I tell you before not to touch anything?"

"Um, yes, but, but . . ."

"But, but, but; zip it! I don't wanna hear any more excuses, *comprende*?"

Dante paced around while picking up garbage and organizing papers, journals, and sketchbooks. Eventually Dante moved back towards the kitchen while reading a comic strip from the comic section of an old newspaper with a smile. Before throwing it out, he reached into the refrigerator to get a beer for himself and milk for Sarita.

"Here, drink this before we go."

Sarita joined Dante. As Sarita sipped her milk, Dante left his half-empty beer on the table and went to put on a pair of scuffed-up black boots. He started searching through his apartment for a bag, clothes and whatever items he would need, such as his forging kit. Inside were the necessities needed, such as X-Acto knives, razors, clear tape, Teslin—a waterproof synthetic printing medium used to forge bogus IDs—credentials, camouflaged passports, novelties that could easily be forged into real ones. Dante then found an old military bag in the back of his closet and started stuffing it with clothes, plus a few personal items.

"That's it? That's all you're bringing?"

"Yeah, that's it. We're not going to Rio, Shorty."

Dante then went searching for money he had stashed away. He searched cabinets, jars, desk drawers, underneath the couch cushions and the mattress, and gathered up whatever money he could find. Before leaving, Dante opened up an old sketchbook and took out a napkin with Benny's phone number on it. It had been preserved within the pages for many years. Then he grabbed an old five-inch-thick Webster's Dictionary from the bookshelf and opened it. Inside was a .35 revolver, which Dante stuffed into his pants. He walked into the kitchen, took the Aero Mexico flight 1203 plane ticket off the refrigerator door, and proceeded to fold it and place it into his wallet. Dante guided Sarita towards the door. He hesitated, standing in the doorway for a brief moment. He looked back at his apartment, at all his finished and unfinished paintings, knowing that he was leaving everything forever. There wasn't going to be a one-man show.

Dante and Sarita walked towards Sarita's apartment and crept in. Everything was as it had been, including the fragments of the dish Gabriela had held when she was abducted, left broken and scattered all over the kitchen floor. As Dante slowly walked through the foyer, he abruptly stopped, holding out his arm across Sarita's torso for protection, hearing the subtle clicking noise of a gun cocking.

As the wooden floor creaked further ahead, around the corner in the connecting room, Dante pushed Sarita up against the sidewall. He quickly moved forward around the corner and grabbed the hand holding the gun, which reached out from around the corner. Dante wrestled the anonymous man. He slammed him up against the wall three times, causing pictures to fall off the wall and the gun to fall out of his hand. Dante then wrestled him down to the floor like a mixed martial artist. He punched him and slammed his head onto the floor, while both tried reaching for the gun. Eventually, Dante was able to gain a better position. He grabbed the gun and then held the barrel up against the side of the man's head.

"Start talking."

"Pha, pha . . . fuck you mon . . ."

Dante slammed his face into the wooden floor again, breaking his nose, which caused him to cry out in Spanish. He began to speak, with blood dripping out of his nose and down his face.

"My, my name is Santiago . . . I—I'm here to terminate the girl."

"Who sent you?" Dante furiously lashed out, twisting Santiago's arm.

"D-D-Don Fernandez . . . the mother did business with him."

"Where's the mother?" After Dante questioned Santiago, he remained silent. Dante twisted his arm even more while still pressing the barrel of the gun up against the side of his head, even harder. "Speak . . . speak you fucking piece of shit. Where's the mother? Tell me where the mother is."

"Ah, ah, she—she was deported. Sent back to Mexico as compensation for disrespectfully leaving and taking from Don Fernandez . . . she filled in for an associate of Don Fernandez, who was due for deportation . . . since the mother was out of the picture, I was sent to terminate the girl."

Dante looked back over his shoulder and gazed deeply into Sarita's eyes, while she peeked around the corner of the wall. Dante then turned back, knocked Santiago unconscious with the butt of the gun, and stood up.

"Hurry up and get your things, Shorty, we're leaving."

Sarita trotted into her room. She grabbed a dark khaki-toned messenger bag adorned with an array of pins and patches. She packed clothes, briefly searched through her old storage trunk and old wooden cigar box. She packed away a sketchbook, pens and pencils, friendships bracelets, some money and some candy. Sarita also took the framed photograph of her and her mother that had been given to her on her birthday, and her rosary. Sarita quickly fed her fish and went into her mother's bedroom, taking an address book and a map of Mexico. After Sarita finished packing, Dante put Santiago's gun into his bag and then guided her out the apartment, leaving the past behind, to embark down a path paved with redemption.

52

Darkness filled the midnight sky with a soothing sense of gothic delight, and enclosed within the overcast of darkness was New York City. Being in New York City was the beginning of a dream, but also a reminder of a past that never had been, and a future that might be someday. It was the journey, the path least taken, which would bring fortune. Within the labyrinth of New York City was one of the lost and abandoned seekers of success, Dante.

Like so many great artists before him, Dante had come to New York City with high hopes and great expectations. He had left it all behind now. He'd given up trying and making up excuses and elected to grow up to pursue a dream others said didn't exist and couldn't be reached. He no longer lived his life by the advice or opinions of others, but instead had learned to follow his heart.

Dante blindly walked through the streets of New York. Within the darkness of the apocalyptic flood rains, he was filled with courage and perseverance for the unknown path which now lay ahead. All he had with him were the clothes on his back, a bag, and a portfolio case. Dante would travel from New York City's Penn Station further uptown, through the theater district, until reaching the crossroads of the world: Times Square. The mythic setting that Dante had only known from pictures brought him a numbing sense of liberation. He was now standing within the image of his dream and took the time to savor the moment.

It rained like hell, but it felt like heaven as Dante stood there all alone. As he did, he felt nonexistent to the herds of people who blindly walked around him. He appeared to be the only one who was awake and fully aware of his own existence. Standing there in the rain appeared to purify Dante's soul. It felt like a rebirth of life. After Dante made peace with his own existence, he continued on to West Forty-Third Street and found his final destination for the night: the Hotel Carter.

The Hotel Carter would be home for now, even though it lacked beauty, comfort, class and style. Inside, there was a sense of solace within the emptiness, as water rhythmically dripped down from Dante's saturated clothes, which hung draped over the bare shower curtain rail. Lightning sporadically flashed in through the hotel windows, illuminating all of Dante's preeminent pieces of art. Laid out all around the hotel room were all the paintings, drawings, and sketches which had fit inside Dante's portfolio case, along with photographs and slides of all the artwork he had been unable to bring along with him.

As water continued to drip down to the tile floor, within the decaying walls of the bathroom, Dante stood in the nude, with only a towel wrapped around his waist. He leaned up against the edge of the sink with both of his outstretched arms, as he stared at his reflection in the mirror. His reflection stared right back. It was someone he didn't recognize anymore. Dante was no longer who he once had been, or at least not who he had thought he was. He was someone else. His long dirty-blond hair hung down before his smooth chiseled face, poised with ambition. His crystal-blue eyes contained hope. But deep within, it was his soul that burned with desire.

53

As the dawn of a new day illuminated the New York City skyline and the industrial urban landscape of North Jersey, waiting to go out and conquer the day within the depths of the Journal Square PATH station of Jersey City were Dante and Sarita, standing beside each other on the station platform. The PATH train bound for New York City arrived, and Dante and Sarita boarded. The train departed, eventually coming to a halt in the heart of the World Trade Center terminal. Ground Zero wasn't what it had once been—a symbol of American commerce and the Mecca of world trade and corporations. Now it was just an empty abyss of foundation, machinery and construction.

Dante guided Sarita through the crowds, up multiple levels of stairs, into the main level of the vast terminal and towards the rows of escalators which rose up to the streets. In front of them stood a massive black monolith; the Millennium Hilton, which stretched up towards the heavens above where darkness kissed the illumination of the rising sun.

Dante dragged Sarita away, past people passing out fliers for restaurants and tourists attractions and free newspapers, through crowds of tourists taking pictures of Ground Zero, young and old Tea Party supporters, We Are Change advocates, 9/11 Truthers, wearing inside job and infowars.com t-shirts and other informational Internet website t-shirts, and others, such as Architects and Engineers for 9/11 Truth, Scholars for 9/11 Truth, NYFD, NYPD, and first responders for 9/11 Truth, representing truth and veterans, both old and young, who joined together as one to inform and open up the minds of the blind, and the blind mortals who renounced them. As Sarita walked beside Dante, further up Church Street and deeper into a world of good and evil, they approached a monument of steel beam frame remains from the World Trade Center. It was twisted into the shape of a cross, fifteen plus feet high, as a symbolic structure of hope. Dante waved down a cab.

As the cab drove through the heart of New York City—a loner's paradise, up Park Avenue—everything seemed to be surreal. Slowly rising above the horizon was Grand Central Terminal. Grand Central was one of the many Meccas of New York City that brought business, immigrants and travelers from all over the world. It was also home to the Greek god, Mercury, Hermes.

The massive statue of stone that was beautifully carved into the likeness of Mercury rested at the central peak of Grand Central's façade. Mercury was the son of Zeus, the god of commerce, exercises and thieving, which required both skill and dexterity. Mercury was also the messenger of Zeus, who wore a winged hat and winged shoes and held a rod entwined with two serpents and wings, called the caduceus. While Mercury was considered cunning and dishonest, he was also helpful to mortals. He was a patron to travelers and wayfarers and caused a reflection in Dante's eyes as he gazed up at the massive statue of stone, of Mercury, rising up high into sky.

Dante and Sarita ended up in the Upper East Side, home to high society, the wealthy, liberal elites, and globalists. After stepping out of the cab, Dante and Sarita stood before one of the elite high-rise apartment buildings, home to Dante's old business partner and friend. He was the man who had discovered Dante, recognizing his talents and helping cultivate Dante's success as an artist. He was also a corrupt con man in the art world, as an art dealer who sold fake paintings, forged certificates of authenticity, and blackmailed other dealers and clients. To him, the art world was criminal. It was power, and it was greed, an excessive lifestyle for those who could see within the darkness and be free.

"Um, is this where your friend lives?"

"Yep," Dante said as he looked up at the façade of the massive apartment building. He guided Sarita through the entrance doors, which the doorman held open, into an enclosed part of the lobby filled with intercoms and mailboxes.

Dante rang one of the intercoms.

"Good day, may I help you?" a clean, crisp voice said.

"Alex, it's me, Dante. Remember me? Your favorite artist. Tell Sonny that I'm in the neighborhood, and I thought of him and how I wanted to stop by to say hi to an old friend."

"Dante! How are you? I'll let Sonny know that you're here. Hold on for just a moment." Five minutes elapsed before Alex returned. "Dante! Sonny is very happy to hear from you and that you thought of him on your visit to the city. I will buzz you in now."

"Okay, thank you, Alex."

"You're welcome, Dante," Alex said, and then the buzzer to the lobby entrance door unlocked. Dante and Sarita walked into the lobby, along the marbled floors, past the expensive furniture and décor, towards the back elevator that went right up to Sonny's penthouse apartment.

Dante tapped his thigh as he looked up at the elevator floor numbers lighting up above the door. Sarita watched Dante with concern. Eventually, the doors opened. A skinny middle-aged man in a suit, with a well-groomed slicked-back haircut and pencil-thin mustache, stood before them, smiling.

"Dante, it's so nice to finally be able to see you after all these years! How are . . . oh, and I see you brought a friend with you. Very pretty little girl." Alex firmly shook Dante's hand with both hands, and then guided them into the apartment. "Come along, Sonny is just finishing up some paperwork and will be done shortly. You two can relax and wait for him here. Is there anything I can get you two? A drink, or some food perhaps?"

"No, thanks, I'm fine."

"Anything for the pretty girl whom I haven't been properly introduced to yet?" Alex said with a slightly offended demeanor.

"Oh, sorry, this is Sarita."

"Sarita, what a lovely name. Anything for you, dear?" Alex hissed like a snake as Sarita leaned in closer to Dante.

"Um, no, thank you, I'm fine."

"Well, then, it's been a pleasure to finally see you after all these years,

Dante. Take care for now. Nice to meet you, dear. I'll let you two be. Sonny should be out in just a moment. Bye for now."

Alex turned around and left Dante and Sarita in a massive Romanesque great room that had marble floors and marble columns rising up to the high cathedralesque ceiling, along with the huge windows overlooking Central Park. As Dante waited in the lounge area, Sarita strolled back towards the vast entrance hallway lined with multiple columns, and the walls adorned with an abstract array of priceless paintings. As Sarita admired the exquisite art, she ran her fingertips gently along the surface of the paintings. Dante stood before an immense fireplace, poised with mixed feelings. The painting hanging above the mantel, a portrait of a woman in red of heart-stopping beauty, was an idol of worship in the eyes of mortals. But to Dante, the painting was a window into a past, a reminder of the day he had painted it, and the woman, Sonya, an old muse, his true love and soulmate, who was now gone. And now there was Sarita to fill in the void.

As Sarita joined Dante and gazed out the windows that overlooked Central Park, double doors opened up, and footsteps echoed in the distance. Dante and Sarita simultaneously turned their heads to look further down the hallway that connected into more rooms. They saw a man, in his early forties, who had a chiseled, clean-cut baby face, piercing dark eyes, a slight smile, and spikey black hair, wearing black imported Italian designer pants and leather boots and a white designer button-down collar shirt with the sleeves slightly rolled up, walking towards them.

"Dante, you son of a bitch! It's been, what, thirteen years of exile? And out of all the places and faces to come back to, you chose me. Now I don't know if I should feel turned on by the fact you came to me, or cautious that you're only here for something. So what is it, old friend? A rekindling of an old friendship, or do you need me to get you back on your feet again, huh?" Sonny gave Dante a big hug. "Oh, and . . . and I see that you brought a little friend. What happened? One of your models surprised you with a gift, and now you need help taking care of it, huh, Dante?"

"Well, sorta. Sonny, just listen and let me explain myself."

"Okay, I'm listening. Take a seat so you can explain yourself, and . . ."

"Sarita," Dante said.

"Sarita, have a seat, dear."

Sarita walked away from the window and sat down next to Dante. Alex came back after Sonny insisted Dante share a drink with him, getting Sonny a glass of brandy and Dante a glass of Jack Daniels on the rocks.

"So I haven't seen or heard from you in thirteen years, and now you come back to the city you told me you wanted to leave behind, forever. Visiting me with a child? So, I'm listening. What's up, old friend?" Sonny said obnoxiously.

"Well, first of all, I'm sorry for what happened thirteen years ago, but I had my reasons."

"Sorry! You had your reasons! Dante, we were blood brothers. We both came from nothing and turned into a great success together, then suddenly you get feelings and develop a conscience—because of a girl."

Sonny looked up at the painting of the beautiful woman dressed in red hanging above the fireplace mantel. Dante then looked up at the painting of Sonya as well.

"And what happened, Dante? Do you remember what happened? You got introduced to Greco by that blood-sucking whore, and what happens? You leave our lifestyle behind, the only one you ever knew, for a girl! As for you, you're the one who was still able to move on with his life. And me—remember what happened to me? I got thirteen years in the can, and you went off with some whore and backstabber to try and continue your career, your life, the right way! Last I heard, the right way hasn't been working out for you, brotha. Looks like I'm the one who continued to succeed and you're the one who is back where he started from, in the gutter with nothing! Remember that guy?" Sonny said as he looked past Dante at one of Dante's self-portraits, hanging on a back wall. Dante turned to look as well.

It was an abstract self-portrait, painted on a two-foot-by-two-foot piece of inch-thick wood left at a construction site in Manhattan, with stolen acrylic paint. The dreary purple, blue, and dark background reflected the state of the world Dante had once been in. But in his big crystal-blue eyes, there was light, a radiance, which gave life to such a piece of melancholic beauty.

"I miss that guy. Ya know, the loyal, talented artist, who wasn't afraid to live life, and take risks. And now look at you. So, I hope that your reason for being here today is good?"

Dante took a sip while contemplating the fact that Sonny was right.

"Once again, I'm sorry. I regret what I did, but right now I need you to please just listen to me and hear me out. See this girl with me now? I'm looking after her for the time being. I'm her guardian until I can figure out what to do with her. Her mother was suddenly abducted by some gang she used to be involved with. Supposedly, they sent her back to Mexico, anyway, with that said I have to get this girl to social services or to the authorities. I'm all she has right now, so I'm asking you to help not me, but this girl. Sonny, please understand."

Sonny took another sip as he studied Dante, then looked over at Sarita before speaking.

"So he's your guardian now?"

"Um, yes. He's gonna take care of me and help me get back to my mother." Sarita's eyes were turned up, and her lip quivered.

"I see. And do you trust this man—Sarita, right?"

"Yes, I trust Dante."

"Do you realize that this man is a con man like me, that his real motive is for himself and not you?"

"Um, no, that's not true. He's good to me," Sarita said blindly. Sonny chuckled.

"You were always better than me, Dante. Even though you could care less about children, you know that I adore them and would do anything for a child, especially one who lost their mother." Sonny paused and then looked into Sarita's eyes. "You wanna know the biggest secret, Sarita? Do you wanna know what Dante really is? He's an artist, and artists are the best con men, the greatest. Artists need to be con men to convince the blind souls that the bullshit they create is actually worth something. That's what we did, Sarita, we conned the art world, and they bought our bullshit. The difference between Dante and I is that Dante was the creative genius and I was the one with the silver tongue.

Dante created visual bullshit that caught someone's eye, and while they were blinded by his so-called beautiful art, I reeled them in with my silver tongue. We were a good team. We convinced them all, except that I was the one who at least had a heart. So, Sarita, you're lucky I like children, because I'm willing to help you to a point. As for Dante, it depends. So what's your price, Dante?"

"I've always had a heart, Sonny, but only for the ones I loved. Even though I dislike children, this one I care about. I'm willing to give up everything to take care of her, even give up on my next one-man show and Greco, which leaves me with nothing. So I'm giving it all up for this girl. How much are you willing to give, not only for an old friend but for an abandoned girl?"

Sonny thought for a moment. "For the girl, I'll give whatever finances are needed. As for you, well, I'm willing to consider giving you a second chance, since it's been thirteen years, and I don't hold grudges for that long. So, if you promise to come back and be my partner again, like in the beginning, and have your next one-man show in my gallery, like old times, friend, we'll convince them all. In return, promise me you'll get Sarita back to her mother safely. You know how much I adore children. Ever since my parents got divorced when I was a child, I know the feeling of being separated from a mother. That's one of the reasons I donate a lot of my money to children's charities and children in need. So, giving you financial security is the best I can offer you right now. I'm sorry I can't do more. I just got out of prison not too long ago, and I'm leaving today to go to Europe for a month to look for new talent and make some business deals. You're a genius, Dante. You'll figure something out, and remember that you still have old friends in the city who could also help."

"Thank you, Sonny, you won't be disappointed. She's in good hands right now. All I need is enough money to support her and me until I figure out what to do with her. And yes, if you're willing to give me a second chance, I'm willing to reunite and convince them all again."

Sonny smiled as he raised his glass with Dante to share one last sip before standing up and shaking hands. Sonny then left to go into another room and returned with a bag, which he handed to Dante.

"That should be plenty. So good luck, and we'll get together when I return from Europe, and then we'll begin our new life in the art world, together again. As for you, Sarita, I hope you get to your mother soon. I know the feeling of being separated from a mother, and believe me, when you finally reunite, it will feel like heaven. You're in good hands. Dante won't let you down. So, good luck to the both of you."

Sonny escorted Dante and Sarita to the elevator, gave Dante a big hug goodbye, and then dropped to his knees to look Sarita in the eyes to say his final farewell before leaving Dante and Sarita to continue to carry on in search of support and answers.

<u>54</u>

As a Yellow Cab drove Dante and Sarita down to the West Village, Dante remained optimistic, while Sarita fueled her curiosity.

"So what does your friend, Sonny, mean when he says that you're a con man?"

"He's just joking around. Ya know, because of how convincing my artwork is. I'm an artist, not a con man, and besides, con men aren't even good people, but I'd be lying if I didn't say that I had to do a little hustling with Sonny to make it in the art world. It's very hard to explain, and you're way too young to understand the art scene and the corruption we've dealt with, but that's the way it was, and it is what it is."

"Okay, but who's Sonny, and how is he your friend?"

"Well, first of all, me and Sonny go way back, Shorty. We were both young struggling people in the art world. I was a poor struggling painter and he was a struggling art dealer who owned a little gallery in SoHo. He put everything he had into that gallery and couldn't find good enough artists to represent. I mean, it got to the point where he was on the verge of bankruptcy and would be out of the gallery and in the streets, until I came along at the right time. After I came to New York City, every gallery I went to turned me down. Fortunately for me, someone helped me get started, and find clients, but I ended up having a falling out with them and ended up in the streets, with nothing but one painting. That's when Sonny and I ran into each other. Call it fate, destiny, or whatever, but after we met, we hit it off right away and became good friends.

243

He loved my work and knew that I was good enough for him to convince the people in the art world with big money to buy my work. So that's what he did. He convinced those people to invest in me, my work and himself. After that, the rest is history, Shorty. We both gained the success we wanted, and then I met someone who took me away from Sonny, breaking up our friendship and business partnership. A girl. Anyway, this girl convinced me that what we did was wrong, that I was better off without Sonny and should be working with someone else—a man named Greco, who wasn't what he appeared to be. At the time, I didn't realize how manipulative and selfish she was. But none of that matters now, because I still love her, and most importantly, I still trust her. It's unfortunate, because she was the sweetest person, who just got caught up with bad people, a bunch of crooks who manipulated her and turned her into this, this . . . anyway, to make a long story short, I'm the one who lost, and Sonny is the one who won."

"And what about this girl?"

"Well, let's just say I owe her an apology."

"Is that where we're going now? To see this girl?"

"Yep. Not only do I owe her an apology, but she is the only person that I can think of right now that I know here in the city who can help you."

"Um, okay."

Dante and Sarita ended up in the West Village. It was Dante's old home, a place he once loved. After getting out of the cab, Dante and Sarita walked along an old cobblestone street, West Twelfth.

"Wait here."

Dante left Sarita on the sidewalk and then walked up the stairs to a green door and rang the bell. There was no answer. He rang it again and again. There was still no answer. Dante turned around with his head down and slowly walked down the stairs to Sarita. He put his arm around her and began to walk away.

"Wait! You can't just leave and give up that easily. What about your apology? You promised." Sarita stopped walking and then took off her messenger bag.

"It's a lost cause. She's not home, and we can't sit around all day waiting for her."

"Um, well, we don't have to wait. Why don't you leave her a letter?"

"A letter?"

"Yeah. You have to apologize somehow, so since she's not here, leave her a letter," Sarita insisted.

"And how will I leave her a letter without any paper or pen, huh?"

Sarita then reached into her bag and took out her sketchbook with a pen and handed them to Dante.

"All right, just give me a few minutes, okay, Shorty?"

"Um, okay," Sarita said with a smile.

Sarita stood on the sidewalk and watched Dante write while he sat on the front steps. After about twenty minutes, Dante finished. He folded up the letter, slid it into the mailbox, walked back down towards Sarita, and guided her through the West Village.

"So, what's her name?"

"Sonya."

And then that was it. They continued to walk in silence and roam until they reached Washington Square Park. It was right in the vicinity of NYU, coffee shops, small restaurants and bars located within Greenwich Village. It was a beautiful clear summer day. The park was filled with an array of people who went about their daily lives. Unbeknownst to Dante and Sarita, though, as they walked past the massive stone fountain, an old friend from Dante's past was leaning up on the edge of the fountain while talking on his cell phone, smoking a cigarette, and watching Dante walk by, blind to the world around.

Meng Tzu Xing, who was known as Sue, had layered spiky black hair with frosted tips and a clean-cut chiseled face with a few chin hairs, a dirt-lip mustache and very thin, narrow Asian eyelids. Sue was all smiles as he talked on his cell phone. He was a stylish kind of cat with flavor, was wearing tight, faded feminine-looking hip hugger jeans with a tight red t-shirt that had the stars of the Chinese flag. It was one of his many different outfits, that ranged from hip-hop to punk rock. Today, Sue had gone with his classic, casual look. He was never too underdressed or too overdressed for any occasion. Even when Sue went to bed, his style was fresh and intact. Sue even had black tattoos on both of his inner forearms to compliment his multiple flavors of style. On his right forearm, written in Chinese characters, were the symbols for fear and love, and on his other forearm was the symbol that represented his family name and its honor.

Sue had been sent to America from China to live with a family friend so that he could live a better life. His father was single and poor and didn't want Sue to live in poverty. At the age of thirteen, Sue had arrived in America to pursue the American Dream. Unhappy and all alone, Sue had become one of the lost and abandoned at a young age. While living in Chinatown, he had run away from his guardians and ended up living on the streets. Sue was a hustler at thirteen and found a Chinese restaurant owner who took him in. He worked as a delivery boy for the restaurant but also delivered and sold goods for older street hustlers who took him under their wings. Sue didn't go to school. His school was the streets, and his teachers were hustlers. Hustling was all Sue knew, and while not in school, one of his favorite hangouts was an Italian restaurant, Bella Notta's.

Sue and the owner, Bella Notta, hit it off from the very beginning, and eventually, as Sue got older, Bella offered him a job. Now Sue was the eyes and ears of Little Italy. He knew everything and everyone within the perimeter of Little Italy and Chinatown. He also kept an eye on other parts of the city, such as SoHo and the East and West Village. Sue was also known and had contacts all over the five boroughs.

"Okay, okay, you bring me . . . No, no, it okay, I still be here den . . . Anyding you wont . . . C'mon, you know Sue, I only have the newest and freshest styles . . . Tell you what, if you come up wit double you have already, I throw in someding extra for you . . . In fact I also hook you up wit fresh new hunny I know . . . Free of charge, anywhere, anytime . . . Anyding you wont for however long you wont . . . Trust Sue, you won't be disappointed . . . She let you cream dat face and let you in dat back door . . . She make you explode like volcanic eruption, you won't forget, you be back for more . . . What chu wont, blonde or brunette, leather and chains, pleasure and pain, oil and toys, c'mon there's noding she won't do, she fulfill all your fantasies . . . Okay, okay, dat will cost, you don't get two fresh hunny for free . . . How much you willing to pay to fulfill all you fantasies? . . . C'mon, these professional hunnies, dey the best at what dey do, you don't find hunnies like des for dat price anywhere . . . Okay, sound good, you won't be disappointed . . . Okay, I catch chu later brotha . . ." Sue spoke very high and fast. After watching Dante and Sarita walk through Washington Square Park, he then got on the phone with Bella Notta.

After leaving Washington Square Park, Dante and Sarita continued to walk through the heart of the West Village, and then further downtown into SoHo. Dante didn't say a word as he guided Sarita. Knowing he had brought Sarita to New York City with a reason and a promise he swore he wouldn't break, Dante tried to hide the fact that he was out of options. His only option now was to continue moving forward. But Sarita could see it on his face that he was nervous, scared and not sure what to do. And after walking many blocks, Sarita began to drag her feet. Dante pulled Sarita by the strap of her bag as she stumbled along.

"C'mon, keep up!" Dante bellowed out as Sarita stopped in place and then kneeled down to tie her shoes. "C'mon, hurry up!"

"Um, wait. First I, I have to do the bunny ears, and then the loop da loop," Sarita said as Dante panted. He looked around until Sarita finished, then stood up. "And I'm tired, Dante. My feet hurt. We've been walking for a long time now. I, I can barely stand up. Can we please stop to rest?"

"Hold up, Shorty, I don't even know where we are right now, I haven't walked these streets in a long time."

"Um, well, what about that café over there?" Sarita said, pointing across the street at a small mom-and-pop café.

Unbeknownst to Dante and Sarita, they had been stalked since passing through Washington Square Park. While Dante and Sarita stood on the street corner, debating where they should go next, a black Cadillac Escalade pulled up to the curb. Two wise guys in suits and sunglasses simultaneously got out and then quickly approached Dante from behind and in front.

"Um, but I'm not in the mood for pizza."

"What do you mean, you're not in the mood for pizza? I never said you had to eat pizza, it's just a place to . . ."

"Hey, look who it is," the wise guy said as he approached Dante.

"Hey, Dante, remember me?" the other wise guy said as he walked up behind Dante.

Dante turned around and stood nose to nose with the first wise guy to approach him. He stepped back only to freeze as the barrel of a gun was jabbed into his lower back.

"Don't even think about it, lover boy. You're coming with us. We're gonna go for a nice little ride."

"Let's go, Dante, nice and easy."

Both the wise guys then stood on either side of Dante while they held both his arms, with the gun still jabbed into his lower back. They then began to drag him to their SUV. Sarita, who was completely ignored by the two, watched with shock and then began to push and kick the wise guy without the gun.

"Hey, let go of him, leave him alone."

"Che cazzo!" the wise guy cried out as he turned around to confront Sarita, who began to kick him in the shins.

As Sarita continued to kick him and step back, Dante tried wrestling his way free, but was subdued by the fear of the gun jabbing harder into his lower back. The brute strength of the wise guy apishly pulled Dante closer to the SUV and then forced Dante into the backseat. Sarita began to scream out and was silenced by the wise guy. He finally restrained Sarita, covered her mouth, and then dragged her into the back of the SUV. After both the wise guys got into the SUV with Dante and Sarita, it pulled out into the narrow side streets, dodging pedestrians, who ignored the incident. It continued, cutting off cars, and then sped away.

<u>55</u>

In the beginning, the dream was a nightmare. The term *struggling artist* was now a reality filled with a lot of heartache and pain. For six months, Dante had experienced the spiritual high of fulfillment, brought from great gratitude and praise towards his work, but he was unable to sell a single painting. The reality of not selling a painting caused Dante to question his own motives and ambitions and his reasons for coming to New York City to live the dream of becoming a successful artist.

After failing to sell a single painting on street corners, in subway terminals, Union Square Park, and being rejected by more than two dozen art galleries within Manhattan and Brooklyn, Dante walked out of the last art gallery disheartened, broke and filled with doubt. He felt like a hopeless pawn in a game of chess, constantly being overshadowed and ignored. He felt like a victim being brushed to the side, only to be left alone, to wither away and die. He was right back where he'd started from, walking through the city streets with only the clothes on his back, a bag, a portfolio case and hope for a future unknown. Except this time, he was broke and had no place to live. All Dante had was enough money to have one last meal and buy a train ticket out. After blindly walking throughout New York City, Dante ended up on Mulberry Street, in the heart of Little Italy, inside a nook of a little secluded Italian restaurant.

As Dante sat all alone, finishing what he considered to be his last supper within New York City, he looked around into nothingness, lost within a numbing state of drunken bliss. Dante appeared to be nonexistent, like a pawn who was left behind, who was ignored by all watchful eyes except for those that hid in the shadows. From across the half-filled dining area, Dante was being watched. As day turned to night, and the dining area became empty, there was curiosity lingering within the shadows.

Bella Notta, the watchful eyes that hid in shadows, sent someone over to wake Dante. Dante lay facedown on the table, unresponsive to the pair of hands that shook him by his shoulders. Eventually he did wake, only to be informed that he was being thrown out. Matters then became worse when Dante was unable to pay the bill. Soon more men were sent, who began to beat Dante as they stood him up. Before Dante was thrown out, paintings from his portfolio case were taken out to be destroyed, only to be saved.

"Aspeta!" Bella Notta was entranced by the beauty of Dante's paintings. What had been ignored and banished by the eyes of the art world was praised by Bella Notta.

"In life, we are just pawns, meaningless pawns, who live to someday become kings and queens," Bella Notta stated before bringing Dante underneath his wing. He believed that Dante was a great artist. As for Dante, any doubts he had as an artist, or in life, were soon absent and suddenly replaced with hope.

# # #

The dream was now a reality. For the next six months, Dante was able to live as a successful artist. Bella Notta provided Dante with an apartment, paints, canvases, clients and living expenses. Dante was also provided with a part-time job running numbers and illegally selling pharmaceutical drugs, which was how Dante repaid Bella Notta for his care.

In time, Dante made a name for himself but still felt that he wasn't where he wanted to be. He wanted it all, the fame and fortune, except that the path Dante was following wouldn't take him there. Dante knew this, and even though Bella Notta was like the father he had never had, Dante didn't want to succeed under Bella Notta. He wanted nothing to do with the underworld he had been forced into, and longed to become successful on his own. He understood that the only way out was to play the game, which he eventually learned and played well. Just when he was ready to respectfully leave it all behind, she came into his life, an adolescent angel.

As Dante peered around an unfinished canvas, there, standing in the doorway were Bella Notta and an untainted muse. She was so young and naïve, wearing a clever mask to deceive. She was just a giddy schoolgirl, an innocent sixteen-year-old. But she wasn't innocent, she was an old soul laced with sin. She had curves like tides in all the right places, and her endlessly flowing locks of beautiful long, dark, thick hair flowed down around and between her perky round breasts that had fully developed early. As she gazed up through her strands of hair and deep into Dante's eyes, biting down on her full lush bottom lip, Dante was lost within her poetic eyes. Dante wasn't going anywhere. He was staying.

"This is my daughter, Lola."

56

Classical Italian opera played throughout Bella Notta's, a bohemian nook filled with class and an intimate sense of amenity. Dante and Sarita were escorted through the dining area, along the wall filled with vintage Italian movie posters, past multiple tables adorned with white tablecloths, and then through and out the back atrium, by the two wise guys and Sue.

Outside, the patio was enclosed by stone walls of tenements, connected by intertwining clotheslines with clothes attached, which rose up high into the sky. Just above the patio was a canopy made of wooden frames garlanded with greenery, flowers and vines of an olive tree.

As scattered beams of light shined through gaps in the canopy throughout the patio, they illuminated pieces of art and life—eyes of stone, water flowing down from a stone fountain, leaves of plants, a statue of a Roman goddess, angel wings of stone, and a relief sculpture of a lion's head hanging on the back wall. Laid out in the patio area were square tables covered with white tablecloths, while symmetrically spaced along the stonewall perimeter were Roman columns that had statues of putti resting on the capitellum tops. In the back right corner, hidden within the shadows, was Bella Notta.

Sue walked up to Bella. He was sitting at a table, indulging in the final remains of his late lunch: fresh veal parmesan, drenched in Bella Notta's homemade gravy, with his face turned down towards the bowl. Only the top of Bella's head, with its receding hairline, its thin, short, curly, black-and-gray hair that was brushed back, could be seen. After taking his final bite, he looked up towards Dante and Sarita as he wiped his mouth clean and tossed the gravy-stained napkin into the bowl and then handed it to Sue. As Sue held the empty bowl, he nodded to Dante to come over.

After being relieved by the wise guys, Dante slowly walked towards Bella with Sarita by his side, while staring into Bella's eyes. Bella had big dark owl eyes that hid in the shadows of his big, thick bushy black-and-gray eyebrows, which stared back with great intensity and penetration. His stare could see right into a man's soul, and Bella could see that Dante was nervous. The wrinkles on Bella's forehead weren't lines of age but lines of stress and restlessness. They were the marks of his myth and aura showing that Bella was a true artist of his craft, a man who never slept or left Little Italy, a man who was known as an enigmatic recluse, a very powerful and respected businessman.

As Dante and Sarita approached and stood before Bella Notta, Bella didn't say a word. Sue then handed Bella's empty bowl to a waiter who came from the kitchen, said his goodbyes, and went back outside to stand in front of Bella Notta's storefront once more to continue his neighborhood watch. Dante and Sarita took a seat across from Bella, who rested his elbows on the table, clasped his hands, leaned forward, and silently stared at Dante with great intensity as he began to slowly peel an orange. The canopy cast patches of shadows down upon Bella. As the soothing wind blew and the running water from the fountain flowed, even though the air was cool, Bella's presence brought warmth. Soon after, the waiter returned with a chilled bloody mary, which Bella held and slowly stirred with a celery stick. Bella's hand was so warm that the frost on the glass quickly melted away as he ate the celery stick, lifted the glass to drink, and placed it down.

"*Come stai?*" Bella asked in a soft yet powerful voice.

"*Bene.*"

"Good." Bella held his drink slightly off the table and slowly twirled it. "You see this bloody mary?" Dante nodded. "*Che!*" Bella slightly raised his voice.

"Yes, Bella, I see it."

"Good, because you have until I finish this bloody mary to explain to me why you are here after you were told to never return. *Capisce?*" Bella Notta firmly said.

"*Capisco.*"

Bella smiled and then raised the full glass to his lips and began to drink. When he finished, he put the glass down.

"Well, I'm listening, Dante, and from the looks of it, you better be quick and to the point. It's hot out and I'm very thirsty. I love washing down a meal with a chilled bloody mary."

Dante looked at Bella and then down at the half-empty glass and the half-eaten peeled orange. A bloody mary was one of Bella's favorites, but not during the summer. Usually a glass of red wine or ice-cold homemade lemonade was Bella's drink of choice for the summer heat. The orange and the bloody mary were just two of the symbolic psychological messages he used. Dante understood the message of both. It was a warning, that if you weren't able to gain forgiveness from Bella, which didn't happen often, or to convince him to give a favor by the time the glass was empty, there would be vengeance.

"First of all, Bella, I don't mean any disrespect towards you or your family. I didn't come back here for me. I came for this girl."

Bella then turned towards Sarita. Sarita turned away and looked down towards the floor. She then slowly lifted her eyes up towards Bella in hopes he wasn't looking at her anymore, but he was, and the staring was more intense. Bella smiled.

"So, after you disrespected me, my family, and you were banished and told never to return not only here, but the entire city, you come back for this girl?"

"Well . . . Bella, I came back hoping to find someone to look after her. I mean, I haven't had a chance to see all the people I know who may be able to help me out, like . . . like your daughter . . ." Dante ran his fingers through his hair as he boldly spoke of Lola.

"*Aspeta!*" Bella raised his voice, causing Sarita to tense up. Dante feared for the worst. Bella's daughter was the last person he wanted to mention in front of Bella. But she was also probably the only one left who would be able to properly take care of Sarita, so he felt he had to, and take the risk that Bella would be forgiving.

"First of all, my daughter should be the last person you speak of before me. There is no reason for me to get into that. Second, I assumed the reason you would even consider mentioning my daughter as someone who could help you is either because all your friends got wise and abandoned you, or your secret little dirty past has caught up to you." Bella's soft voice gradually rose and then became soft again. "So, Dante, I'm curious. Is she yours, or did someone leave you with responsibility, something that you fear most and want nothing of? You're selfish, Dante. Your selfish actions are what ruined our relationship."

"It's a long story, Bella, but yeah, someone left me with the responsibility of looking after this girl unwillingly, which, ya know, I'm willing to do, but I have other obligations that need to be met. So, what I'm trying to say is that I just need someone I trust to look after her."

Dante then reached into his bag, pulled out a stack of money, and placed it on the table. Dante's stomach turned. It was a lot of money that had just been given to him, and even though the money was all Dante had to support Sarita and himself, it was also all they had to protect them from being the victims of vengeance.

"Here. I know it's not much, but this is to bury our past and buy immunity for me and the girl. You'll never see or hear from us ever again."

"So, do you care for this girl as much as you cared for my daughter?"

"Yes, Bella, yes. I care for her just as much as I did for your daughter," Dante said. He looked away and down as he ran his fingers through his hair, and then slowly lifted his head to look at Bella.

Bella smiled, looked over at Sarita, and then reached around the round table, grabbing Sarita's hand. He slowly lifted her arm up with his to stand her up and pull her towards him. Sarita looked back over her shoulder at Dante and could see that Dante looked even more scared.

Sarita stood just a few inches below Bella's eye level, and nervously looked up into his big, dark eyes that hid in the shadows of his big, thick, bushy black-and-gray eyebrows as Bella brought her beside him. Sarita was able to get a closer glimpse of the man in the shadows and see that the wrinkles in his forehead were deep like mountain ridges, and his gray stubbly beard with his brushed-back mane of receding black-and-gray hair created the mask of an ageless lion. Sarita was now face-to-face with the lion. She stood still, wishing she was still in the hands of Dante, even if he seemed hopeless and unable to help her.

Bella then sat face-to-face with Sarita as he let go of her hand and then began to run his fingers through her hair. Sarita was out of Dante's reach and helpless, and all she could do was to just stand there and allow the lion to do whatever he pleased. Dante leaned forward and rested his arms on the table as he watched Sarita stand hopelessly within Bella's grasp.

"*Bellisisma . . . Bellisima*," Bella softly said as he continued to run his fingers through Sarita's hair and caress the side of her face with the outer edges of his fingertips. Sarita's eyes followed the movement of Bella's hand, which adroitly grazed the surface of her skin.

"So young and naïve, and so innocent. Just an innocent little angel who ended up in the hands of someone so selfish. It's so unfortunate, but that's life. Right, Dante?"

"Right, Bella, right." Dante played along with Bella's rhetoric. The maestro was in the middle of orchestrating a symphony, a libretto, a tragic opera, and his audience had no choice but to sit quietly without interruption and listen to such tragedy and misfortune.

"So, my little angel, what is your name?"

Sarita's eyes continued to follow Bella's fingertips as they caressed the side of her face. Finally, Bella removed his fingertips from Sarita's face, and her eyes lifted up towards Bella's.

"Sarita," Sarita softly said.

"Sarita. Well, Sarita don't be so shy. Come, come closer."

Bella leaned forward in his chair and reached out his right arm to put around Sarita's shoulder, then turned Sarita around and pulled her in closer. Sarita looked into Dante's eyes for comfort. Dante saw the fear in Sarita's eyes. He knew at this point from Bella's taunting smile and demeanor that the man wasn't willing to negotiate. All Dante could do was flash Sarita a reassuring smile.

Bella held Sarita closer, so that their heads rested closer together as Bella's right arm now reached around Sarita's right shoulder across her upper chest and neck so that he could caress her left cheek with his fingers. Bella's fingers brought coldness upon Sarita. As Bella spoke, he looked down towards Sarita and then up towards Dante.

"So, Sarita, do I scare you?"

"Um, no," Sarita said, her voice cracking. She looked up and deep into Dante's eyes.

"It's okay, Sarita, I won't hurt you. You can be honest. Go ahead, tell me how you really feel," Bella said softly into Sarita's ear as he continued to tauntingly stare at Dante.

"Um, yes, I'm—I'm scared." Sarita stuttered and shivered.

"Anything else?" Bella softly asked.

"Um, no, that—that's all," Sarita said softly.

"What about Dante? Do you trust him?" Bella smiled as he looked deep into Dante's eyes.

"Um, yes."

"Even now that he has left you in the hands of someone you fear?"

"Um, y-yes."

"Do you want to know a little secret, Sarita?"

Sarita remained stoic.

"Well, I'm gonna tell you a little secret anyway. Dante here was once a close friend of mine, very close. In fact, I used to take care of him. We had a very close friendship, but it soon ended. He did something bad, Sarita, something selfish. He took something away from me, something that could never be replaced. Now is that the kind of man you trust, Sarita?" As Bella spoke, he continued to caress Sarita's left cheek. Her eyes filled with tears.

"Um, yes." Tears slowly rolled out Sarita's eyes and down her cheeks. Bella then stopped caressing Sarita's cheek and pulled Sarita in closer, tighter, to hold her by the throat.

"Remember the feeling you brought me, Dante, remember what

happened!" Bella's voice steadily rose to a crescendo as he looked down upon Dante, who remained in a vulnerable state. More tears rolled out Sarita's eyes and down her cheeks as she began to frantically pant.

"Yes, Bella, I remember and I'm sorry. I'm sorry for what I did. I still regret what I did. Please, Bella, don't hurt her. It's not her fault. She had nothing to do with our past." Dante serenely spoke, hoping to calm Bella, but Bella squeezed Sarita's throat even tighter.

"Yeah, well, how does it feel now to hopelessly sit there and watch someone who you love so much have their life threatened by someone considered to be a trustworthy friend? How would you feel if I took away her innocence just like the way you took away the innocence of my daughter? How would you feel to live the rest of your life with the blood of the innocent stained on your hands? You see, Dante, seeing you here now after I've forever banished you from the city, and my presence, doesn't bother me. The years have healed. Yes, I am willing to forgive you, but to have the audacity to step foot in the city, and think that you could just blend in without being seen? Sorry, Dante, but your presence and this girl you're with hurts me. It hurts my heart, especially since she is a reminder of my daughter's loss of innocence, and a reminder of what tore us apart!"

As Bella's voice reached its peak, it began to slowly descend and get softer.

"So, Dante, since I am a businessman and must make decisions, even with the people whom I have a bittersweet relationship with, I will still produce. So, I will spare this little girl's innocence, and her blood on your hands, but I will also give her back to you."

Bella removed his hand and arm from around Sarita's throat and upper chest. As Sarita stood beside Bella, free and in tears, Bella ran his fingers through her hair and caressed the back of her head. Sarita looked up at Bella as she wiped away her tears, and then Bella gave her a little push on her lower back to walk back towards Dante. Dante stood up, embraced Sarita, and waited for Bella to declare his final judgment upon him and Sarita. Bella then reached for his half-filled glass and slowly drank the remains and then put the empty glass down on top of the table.

"She was and still is your responsibility. Knowing how responsibility is your weakness, and something that you fear and do not want—well, life is worse than death, Dante. The situation you find yourself in now, I feel to be better than vengeance."

Bella then reached out to pick up the stack of money Dante had left on the table and ran the bills through his fingertips as he counted.

"I also accept your compensation. Now, take this girl with you and get out, and never return. I never want to see you again or hear from you ever again. Like I told you once before, you're dead to me. And if I do, you can guarantee there will be blood. *Capisce?*"

"*Capisco.*" Dante picked up his bag. It was just Dante and Sarita from here on out. Dante was now out of options. He knew that he had to stay strong and needed to carry on. Before departing, Dante looked deep into Bella's eyes as a final farewell, then turned around and guided Sarita out, leaving Bella alone forever. Dante and Sarita then continued further down the unscripted path, without options or any sort of support.

<u>57</u>

After leaving Bella Notta's, there was no turning back. Even if Dante currently had no one else to go to for assistance, he carried on with Sarita by his side. New York City, which had once been Dante's desire, where he was able to plant the seeds of his dreams, was now an addiction he wanted to leave far behind. Sue, standing on the street side, smoking a cigarette and talking on his cell phone while balefully looking at Dante, was a reminder of the dark past Dante had overshadowing him, a past he needed to desperately get away from, but Sarita was the anchor slowing him down.

Even if Sarita was able to open up Dante's heart once again, being lost in such a distressful situation seemed to provoke Dante to take desperate measures. Dante was willing to abandon Sarita. Mexico was calling, and Dante's plane ticket in his pocket felt liberating. Even more maddening was the daunting fact that Dante's past, Nada Mas, was justification for leaving NYC, the tristate area, and escaping to Mexico without Sarita.

For now, though, after leaving Little Italy, Dante guided Sarita down Grand Street and then up Centre Street. Just as Dante was about to conjure up a scheme, Sarita tugged on his hand.

"Now what? What is it?"

"Um, Dante, could we please stop to eat? I'm so hungry, I—I haven't eaten all day."

As Sarita sympathetically looked up into Dante's eyes, Dante was lost for words. Dante saw a glimpse of Sonya, her trust in him that washed over any remnants of malicious intentions.

"C'mon." Dante gave in, and continued to walk up Centre Street with Sarita. They walked onto Broome Street and came to a stop at the corner of Broome Street and Broadway, the "Canyon of Heroes." It was here, as Dante watched a sea of people pass by, that he was willing to leave Sarita. To slip away, and disappear in the crowds, in Dante's mind, would feel less heartless. "Why not? Children get lost and separated from parents in crowded places, right?" Dante thought to himself.

"All right, you have two choices, Shorty. Hot dogs or sandwiches?"

Sarita looked across Broadway at a hot dog vendor parked on the street corner, and the SoHo Café located across Broome Street, on the opposite street corner.

"Um, hot dogs, with—with ketchup. Lots."

"That's it?"

"And—and soda."

"Coke?"

Sarita nodded. Dante walked Sarita to an entrance door niche located between a corner shop and a clothing store. He brought her onto the stoop between two rising squared-off columns of red brick, before the green wooden-framed glass door that rose up an extra half of a door's length above, numbered 486. It was a perfect place to leave Sarita and then blend in with the crowds and disappear forever.

"Just wait here until I come back, okay, Shorty?"

Although Dante's words came out in such a sincere manner, deep within, guilt was eating away his heart. As for Sarita, not knowing her fate was bliss.

Just as Dante turned around to walk away, Sarita called out, "Um, Dante, you—you won't leave me, will you?" Sarita's innocence was tempting, but Dante could only tell Sarita sweet lies.

"No, I'll be right back."

"You promise?"

"I promise."

Dante looked away and ran his fingers through his hair as he humored

Sarita. He then looked into Sarita's eyes one last time before turning away. Sarita's heart was filled with trust. As Dante walked away and crossed Broadway without looking back, his heart began to freeze over. Fear would overshadow and convince Dante that there was nothing else he could do. Dante would give into the coldness deep within his heart and abandon Sarita. Cutting the strings of attachment and leaving his past far behind not only felt right at the moment, but also redeeming.

After crossing Broadway, Dante was finally free. Or so he thought. All of the fear and malice that had suddenly corrupted Dante's heart and soul became diluted. Dante could feel an energy force beckoning him from across Broadway. When Dante turned around and looked across the sea of people, Sarita was able to pull him back.

Fate, or the life in which Dante thought he was destined to live, alone, was suddenly abolished by the beauty of watching Sarita. Sarita walked back and forth along the curb of Broadway with outstretched arms. The way she was so innocently playing as she waited for Dante fueled his heart and soul. The only other woman who had ever been able to overcome such malevolent thoughts and emotions was Sonya. The love Dante had for Sonya was the absent love Sarita had never had but needed. Dante felt responsible now, not because Sarita had suddenly come into his life, but because there had never been a father in her life. Watching her playfully wait, blind to his cruel intentions, was enough to spur him to carry on with Sarita by his side. In the end, the reality of the situation would overcome Dante.

As Sarita continued to walk along the curb, she heard a comforting voice. Sarita opened her eyes and turned around to see Dante standing before her with the hot dog and soda she had ordered. After Dante gave Sarita her food, they both took a seat beside each other on the stoop. Sarita ate her hot dog and drank her soda while watching the crowds in front of her walk by, as Dante thought about where to go with Sarita.

"So now what, Dante?"

"I don't know, Shorty. Just relax for now, okay?" As Dante spoke he turned away.

Sarita could see that Dante was in a state of distress. "Mama, where are you? I hope that wherever you are, you're okay, and I 'specially wish you were here now. If you were here, I wouldn't be sitting here. We'd probably be going for a walk or something. But even though Dante was the only one I had to go to for help, and none of his friends were able to help, I still trust him. He smells like dirty laundry and acts weird sometimes, but, it seems like he needs some help from me. I just don't know what to do. Please, if somehow, some way, you can hear my thoughts and know how I feel, send me a sign, or someone to take us away, and bring us to you. Please, there has to a way to help me get back to you," Sarita thought to herself.

As Sarita looked away from Dante, an answer appeared. As a tourist stood before Sarita, she focused on his map. It reminded her of the map of Mexico she had brought with her. Most importantly, Sarita's mother was in Mexico. She reached inside her bag, pulled out the map of Mexico, and then reached towards Dante, who curiously looked down at the map.

"What is that?"

"Um, it's a map."

"A map? A map of what?"

"Mexico."

"Mexico? Why are you showing me a map of Mexico?"

"Because, since you weren't able to help me, and you don't seem like you know what to do next, I'm gonna do something, I'm gonna help you get away from whatever you're scared of, and I'm gonna help us get me back to my mother. I saw your plane ticket to Mexico. Isn't that where you want to go anyway? So why don't we go together? That way, I can get to my mother, and you can go to wherever it is you want to go in Mexico."

"Yeah, I know that's where your mother is, but—"

"But what? Isn't that where you want to go? And besides, you don't seem like you have any more friends left to help us. We have nothing to lose."

Sarita's tenacity seemed to suddenly provoke Dante. It was a fire that Dante hadn't felt since he had first come to New York City as a struggling artist with nothing to lose. All the passion and desire that Dante had once felt was now the fuel he needed in order to carry on, especially since Mexico, seemed so far away, and a ludicrous place to go to with Sarita right at the moment. Mexico would now be a haven for them.

Though Dante possessed the appropriate materials needed to forge bogus credentials and passports, using them for Sarita was risky. Dante's bogus identity, Thomas P. Daniels, was already implemented into the system, while there was nothing for Sarita. The airport security system would identify Sarita's bogus passport right away. The only other option Dante could think of was to make a bogus passport for Sarita that could be used at a US-Mexico border checkpoint. It seemed a crazy idea for Dante to suddenly abort his plane ride to Mexico and take Sarita to the border, but it was now an astute one. Sarita was now a very important asset for Dante, and he wasn't ready to cut the strings of attachment, not yet, since she could be used as collateral, if needed.

"Mexico? And where would we go in Mexico?" Even though Dante felt that Mexico was where he should bring Sarita, he still wasn't one hundred percent convinced.

"Well, first of all, that's where my mother is, and second, not only is my mother there, but I also have family there. Here, look, there's a whole address book that shows where my family lives in Mexico."

Sarita then took out an address book from her bag and held both the address book and map before Dante. Dante stared at them before taking them out of Sarita's hand. He still wasn't convinced.

"How will we get there? Did you think about that, Shorty?" Even though Dante already concluded that he would bring Sarita to the border, Dante humored Sarita. In a strange way, he was trying to find a reason not to take the risk, but the unanswered questions would be unable to hold Dante back.

"Um, I-I don't know?" Sarita shrugged her shoulders as she spoke.

Dante turned away. Once again he thought about how security at the airports was too tight, so flying wasn't an option. Hitchhiking or taking a bus cross-country would take too long, and by then Nada Mas would catch up to them. The best form of transportation that Dante could think of at that moment was a train.

Dante was willing to take the risk. In order to get there, he would have no choice but to go back down the darkest path he'd ever known. He would need to get help one last time from another old friend connected to Nada Mas. He was the link between Dante and his true friend, Benny, the mastermind behind Nada Mas, who would be able to help Dante and Sarita safely cross the US-Mexican border without any problems from the authorities.

"All right, all right, I'll take you to Mexico," Dante said. Sarita smiled as Dante handed her the address book and the map of Mexico. After Sarita put the them back into her bag, she embraced Dante.

"Thank you, Dante."

"Hey, hey. Easy, Shorty, you're welcome." Dante shied away as he spoke.

As much as Dante was willing to abandon Sarita, he knew deep within his heart that he couldn't. Sarita was a part of him, and she was now his charge.

<u>58</u>

After spending the night in a cheap hotel resting inside Penn Station, located underneath Madison Square Garden, Dante and Sarita sat at a small square table in the back of a food court that branched off from the Penn Station boarding terminal for the Amtrak trains.

"Um, so, where exactly is Too . . . Too-sca . . . Tooscalll . . ."

"Tuscaloosa. It's in Alabama, in the Deep South, near the Gulf of Mexico."

"It's near Mexico? Like, right next to Mexico, like New York City and New Jersey?" Sarita slightly raised her voice.

"No. Mexico is nowhere near Alabama. The Gulf of Mexico isn't Mexico, it's the name of the body of water that Alabama and Mexico are surrounded by, like the way the Atlantic Ocean surrounds New York City and Jersey. Once we get to Alabama, we'll only be halfway to Mexico. Don't they teach you geography in school?"

"Yeah, but I don't like that stuff. I like art. So why are we going to Alabama. Why don't we just go straight to Mexico?"

"Because we can't. There's no train that goes straight to Mexico from here. If there was, believe me, Shorty, we'd be on that train. Unfortunately, we have to go to Alabama and then get on a different train. I had no choice. It was the only train going west with open seats right now," Dante explained.

As Dante sipped his beer, Sarita reached down to open her bag, pulled out the map of Mexico, and then reached out across the table. Dante took the map.

"Um, well, how will you get me into Mexico?"

"I have an old friend that lives in Arizona who could help us. For now, let's not worry about that. Let's just worry about getting to Alabama. Okay, Shorty?"

"Um, is he a friend like Sonny, or—or a friend like Bella?"

"A friend like Sonny."

"So, we should be fine, then, right?"

"Right."

"How far do we have to go once we get to Mexico, to where my mother lives?"

"Hold on, give me a second to figure this out."

Dante continued to study the map while sipping his beer. Sarita pulled out a roll of money from her pocket. As Sarita counted her money with her hands tucked in closely to her chest, Dante looked over the top of the map. Dante squinted, placed the map down, rested his elbows down on top of the table and then leaned forward.

"Hey, whose money is that?"

"It's mine," Sarita said as she looked down at the money.

"Your money? How do you have money? You don't work, you're just a kid. There's only two ways for a kid your age to get money—either from their parents, or from stealing. Your mother isn't around to give you any money, so that only leaves one option."

Sarita put the money back into her pocket and crossed her arms on top of the table as she leaned forward.

"Um, I didn't steal it, I won it," Sarita said with a smile.

"What do you mean, you won it?"

"I won a bet."

"A bet? Aren't you too young to bet for money? And if it is a bet, what kind of bets are you making?"

"I bet the boys in our building that I wasn't scared to knock on your door." Sarita spoke with a slight smile as Dante held his bottle of beer before his lips while sucking and biting his bottom lip.

"So, you're the one who's been knocking on my door and running away. Anyway, what kind of bet is that? Why would you be scared to knock on my door. I live right next door to you."

"It was a type of dare, because everyone in our building is scared of you. All the boys thought that I was the most scared of you, and I was even more scared to knock on your door." Sarita leaned in even closer.

Dante then slowly leaned back in his chair and held his beer before his lips. "Everyone?" he asked softly.

"Everyone," Sarita whispered.

"Well, I don't see why."

"Well, maybe if you came out more often and talked with people, then maybe no one would be so scared of you."

"First of all, I told you before that I had my reasons for living alone, reasons you wouldn't understand. And for all those people from our building who are scared of me, that's their problem, not mine. In life, people fear the unknown. When you get older you'll understand. And since all of this came up because of some silly little bet you made, let me give you a little advice on betting. Never make a bet you can't afford, okay, Shorty?"

"Why not?" Sarita inquired.

"Because bad things could happen," Dante elaborated.

"Like?"

"Like . . . like, I don't know, like you could lose something very valuable, or priceless, like a friend or family member. Or even worse, you could lose your life. Ya know, end up dead."

"So is that the reason you never leave your apartment? Because of a bet?"

"Something like that," Dante answered vaguely as he brought his beer down from his lips. "But, anyway, we have more important things to worry about right now, okay, Shorty?"

Dante lifted up the map of Mexico and looked at it again. As he did, Sarita imagined what the future held for her and Dante. Dante then glanced over the top of the map to see what Sarita was up to. Her silence gave Dante reason to be suspicious, but her demeanor was that of Sonya.

As Sarita tucked her hair back behind each ear, having a few strands come out and hang down, and innocently looked up at Dante with her head slightly tilted down while she sucked on her lips and then bit down on her bottom lip, Dante saw Sonya. Sarita mimicked the way Sonya would look up at Dante, and she reminded Dante what his purpose was in life, even now, as he sat poised with a map of Mexico and a train ticket, understanding that his life was now devoted to her.

"Dante, when we get to Mexico and I'm with my mother again, are you gonna stay with us, or are you gonna leave us?"

"Well, when we get to Mexico, I'll let you know." Dante ran his fingertips through the hairs on the back of his head. Even Sarita's words were a reminder of Sonya.

"I don't want you to leave me, even when I'm with my mother, because I like having you in my life. So can you promise me that you won't leave me, ever?"

Dante closed his eyes and thought about the responsibilities that had been bestowed upon him, and how in the end, no matter if Dante decided to stay or leave, all he wanted was for Sarita to be happy. Even if Sarita's origin was kept secret, Dante would continue to humor her.

"I promise," Dante said as he opened his eyes and removed his fingertips from his hair.

"Do you swear it?"

"I swear it," Dante said, even if his heart was being corroded with remnants from his past.

"Then pinky-swear it." Sarita sat up on her knees and reached up before Dante with her pinky sticking up in the air. Dante gazed into Sarita's eyes, looking down at Sarita's pinky and then back into her eyes as he reached up to wrap his pinky around Sarita's.

"Um, double-swear it."

"What?"

"Double-swear it."

Sarita leaned forward over the table, reached under her arm with her other arm, and then stuck up her other pinky. Dante crossed his arm under as well and then locked his pinky with Sarita's. It was a promise Sarita didn't want broken.

Dante became overwhelmed by the look in Sarita's eyes. After both felt reassurance, they left the dining area, blended into the crowds of the Penn Station boarding area, and boarded the train.

<u>59</u>

Sarita sat with her arms wrapped around her knees, which were held up in front of her chest like the child she had once been, composed. Being here, in what used to be Dante's apartment, smiling and beaming with adoration over what had become of taking such an unmapped path, with someone who seemed at the time to be so unworthy, was liberating. Sarita was now free, free from abandonment and torment. Imagining being with Dante was fulfilling, remembering how gentle he had been with her as a child, and everything he had been willing to sacrifice in order to not only help and protect Sarita, but attempt to reunite her with her mother. It was now the thought of Gabriela that would take Sarita away to the pages filled with the life of Gabriela once again. After Sarita picked up one of the three journals that were resting on the floor beside her and rested the open journal up against her knees, she began to scan through its pages. Looking at random words and sentences filled Sarita with an array of emotions, provoking her to close the journal. But it was stumbling upon the following pages that stimulated Sarita with a craving for more.

~Beyond Here and There~

Being here now with my hermosa, Sarita, cradled in my arms and looking back on everything that once was, how here used to be there, a better life I've always imagined, which is what I now have, yet it seems that ever since I came from Mexico, being here and being there, no matter how flawed the path I've taken has been, or how big the dream I'm constantly chasing is, my there always seems to become my here, the end, the goal or the dream or whatever it is I'm chasing and searching for in life. But, the end isn't the end, it's the beginning, the beginning of something new. And that's where I now find myself once again. All alone. Except that I now have my reason to live. I now have Sarita. Where we go from here, I don't know. I can't predict the future or guarantee our fate, but like always, I will imagine living a better life, building from here to there, to here to there, until eventually completely fulfilling the American Dream, which is what I've sought since the beginning of this journey. And no matter how many heres and theres I have to climb, I will always love Sarita and give her the world. Most importantly, after spending many years of helping and guiding her from here to there, throughout the constant cycle of it all, I want to someday sit back and watch her go from here to there, chasing bigger dreams than me. And when she finally gets to the end and reaches whatever it is she's chasing, in the end, I want her to be happy.

~Thirteen~

Thirteen. There were thirteen of us. Thirteen strangers who fatefully came into each other's lives for the night. All of us came from different parts of Latin America, some from Mexico, some from Guatemala, some from El Salvador, and some from Ecuador and Peru. And even though we all came from different places and had different backgrounds, we were all chasing the same dream. With our differences, we were one, one family, for one moment in time. And it's funny, remembering being together in the back of the van, how cramped together we were within the darkness, and the silence that lasted the entire ride.

Even though I only vaguely remember what each person looked like, or what their names were, or what their plans were once they got into America, what I do clearly remember was the look on everyone's face. There was this sense of fear on everyone's face, yet there was hope in their eyes. After all these years, after everyone went their separate ways, I still always think about where everyone has gone, and what they've been doing with their lives.

The middle-aged couple from Peru, who spent their entire lives working in fields—they were two of the lucky ones who made it that night, along with the abuelito from Chiapas, two of three young friends from Guatemala, and Rodrigo, whose name I remember because of how selfish of a person he was that night, in the van, and when we were all trying to get across the river and up the ravine. But there's nothing that can be done. It was his fate to make it.

As for what they've been doing in America, and where they went, I don't know, but I wish I did and that I could see them. Even though the seven of us that made it that night were strangers, the experience we shared is something that changed all of our lives, forever. But I also feel so sad for those who didn't make it, like Fabiola, and I especially feel so sad for Elena and her child, who I brought here with me. She should be a young girl by now. What has become of that night—well, it wasn't without reason. Its effect on all of us was everlasting, and no matter where they all went or what has become of them, God was there that night. I felt it. God brought us all together. For what, I still can't figure that out, but what I do know is that each person, each moment of that night, somehow changed me. It changed us all.

<u>60</u>

At first, there was complete darkness. No one was able to see, not even a few inches before their faces, until eventually, their eyes adjusted. Even after being able to see, though, along with having the moonlight shine in through the windows of the van, past the openings in the curtains, within the dimness it was still hard to clearly see. But the light was enough to see the twelve other migrants cramped together in the back of the van.

Gabriela sat on a wooden milk crate behind the driver's seat, with her back against the side of the van. She silently observed each of the migrants as she readjusted her body and rubbed her lower back. She tried to soothe the pain inflicted by a screw sticking out from the wall behind her, and her torso, which was aching from the prepackaged cocaine tightly taped onto her. As uncomfortable as it was for Gabriela to be sitting on an unstable makeshift seat, squeezed between two other migrants, rocking and bouncing around, along with it being as hot as the sixth circle of hell, it was the least of Gabriela's worries at the moment. For Gabriela, the unknown path she now took was frightening, and being there now was surreal, but felt emancipating.

As Fabiola dozed in and out of consciousness, the other migrants that sat along the perimeter of the back of the van, and on the floor in the middle, felt calm. Most of the migrants were stoic. No one spoke or moved. For a trip that seemed like an eternity, there was this long silence, except for the roaring of the engine and the howling winds blowing in through the slightly open window, which rattled as the van bounced around. Even though they were all strangers searching for the same dream, the unknown that awaited them seemed to instill a sense of fear in them all. Gabriela would find solace from the *gordita* woman who rocked her baby, wrapped in a *rebozo*.

"Hola, cómo estas?" the *gordita* woman softly said.

"Bien, y tú?" Gabriela kindly replied.

"Bien," the *gordita* woman said with a smile.

"So, what's her name?"

"She doesn't have a name yet. I'm waiting until we get to America to name her."

"Oh, okay. So, do you know what you want to name her yet?"

"Ah, sí. America."

"That's a pretty name, especially for a girl who will grow up and live in America. I'm Gabriela."

"Mucho gusto, yo soy Elena. So, where are you from?"

"I'm from Tehuacán, in Puebla State, but I lived with my aunt and uncle in Sonora State before I ended up in this van."

"Ah, Mexicana. Me too, I'm from Mexico City." Elena smiled, which brought Gabriela warmth. "Those two over there, they're from Peru. The three *amigos* are from Guatemala, and the *abuelito* is Mexicano, he's from Chiapas. The other Mexicanos, I'm not sure where they're from, but that one, Rodrigo, is very rude and selfish."

Both Gabriela and Elena observed Rodrigo who sat with his legs straight and elbows out to create more space for himself. His face cringed with bitterness, but he remained sedated amongst the others.

"Stay away from him. The others, I'm not too sure where they're from, but it doesn't matter where we're all from because we're all going to the same place, and when we get there, we all get to start over again. So, it doesn't matter who you were before you get to America, because once we all get there, you can become whoever you want to be and do whatever you dream of doing with your life."

Gabriela forced out a smile. Inside she was still unsure of what would become of her exodus to America, but Elena was able to see beneath the surface and bring her hope.

"It's okay, *chica*, you shouldn't be so scared."

"Well, it's not that I'm scared. It's more like being nervous, not knowing what to expect when we get to wherever it is they're bringing us."

Elena reached over to hold Gabriela's hand. "You shouldn't worry, *chica*, because wherever we're going, once we cross that border, everything will be gone, all your fears. You need to be strong, *chica*, have faith, have faith in God. God is looking out for all of us. He will be there with us and help us get across the border and into America," Elena said in hopes of inspiring Gabriela.

Gabriela looked into Elena's comforting eyes and then at the baby cradled in her arms. "I hope so. There's nothing for me back home. America is all I have right now. I'm very fortunate to be here right now, and I hope to make it to America."

"You will, *chica*, you will. Stop worrying; be strong, and don't worry, because I'm right here with you," Elena said, squeezing Gabriela's hand.

"*Gracias*." Gabriela smiled.

"*De nada*," Elena said, and after Gabriela and Elena said their final words, the baby began to wake up. Elena then turned away to comfort the baby with soothing words while rocking her.

"She's very pretty."

"Gracias. Que Dios protega a mi niña bonita."

"I hope to have a baby like her in America. First I need to find the right person to have one with."

"You will, you will."

"I hope so." Gabriela smiled and turned away, imagining living a better life in America and having a baby of her own.

<u>61</u>

Gabriela silently stood before ICE officers, her makeup smeared across her face from her tears. Her beautiful long dark hair, normally well-groomed, now hung down unkempt in front of her face, like a modern-art masterpiece—dreadful. As Gabriela repositioned her body like a slave who was being auctioned off, with each captured digital image of her profile and the handcuffs wrapped around her wrists, her sense of dehumanization and imprisonment filled her with failure, regret and despair.

After the photographic identity process was over, Gabriela was then led into another room. Here Gabriela's true identity would be recorded into the system she hadn't been a part of ever since she had come from Mexico, a little more than thirteen years ago. The shadows that Gabriela had been living in ever since were now being slowly eroded.

As each of Gabriela's fingertips were pressed down and scanned into the biometric system, everything was now being revealed. The shadows were gone and the curtains were being pulled open. Any freedom Gabriela had or felt was gone.

Gabriela stood with her head bowed down, looking up through her hair at the powers that be. Even though the majority of ICE officers show amnesty towards illegal immigrants, the two who stood on either side of Gabriela showed her no remorse. It didn't matter that Gabriela was female, because in their eyes, illegal immigrants, whether male or female, were just pawns, cancer, who gave the patient—hardworking, loyal, legal immigrants—a bad name. Especially the ones who committed criminal acts, acts of violence, or who were involved with drugs and gangs. Being caught in a safe house that was only a front for drug trafficking didn't give the ICE officers a good impression of Gabriela.

Once Gabriela's fingerprints were scanned into the system, like two henchmen, the two ICE officers guided her into an office area filled with multiple desks, more ICE officers, and other illegal immigrants who had been caught and brought into custody. Amongst the illegal immigrants were the few who were brought in with Gabriela, including Martina who had been apprehended during a surprise roadside raid.

Gabriela was led to an empty desk and told to wait for another ICE officer. She fixated on the handcuffs wrapped around her wrists and began to fiddle around with them, but then focused on the Latin Americans and other illegal immigrants being interrogated. There were tears in the eyes of both men and women. Even if some of the men tried to hide their pain behind a stern face, the tears painted a clearer picture of all that was felt in their hearts. Gabriela thought it was unfortunate to watch the illegal immigrants with pure souls and intentions, being demonized and compared with the criminals, who were the cancer crossing the border illegally. The hardest thing was not that these brave souls had failed at their only attempt at being able to live the American Dream, but that they had failed their families and any promises they had made. Most importantly, they had failed their children. For some, their children were one of the most important reasons to risk all. Even those who didn't have children risked all to someday provide for their unborn children.

Eventually, an ICE officer arrived. Georgio Verrello was a tall, somewhat built man with olive skin and short salt-and-pepper hair who could pass as a Hispanic man at first glance. His black designer suit pants with a matching white designer button-down shirt and a complementary wine-red tie gave the impression of a successful man.

Georgio was also an immigrant, from southern Italy, who had come from nothing. He was in his fifties, but looked ten years younger. There was sympathy in his eyes, and comfort felt from his presence. But Gabriela found it difficult to give in to the serenity Georgio brought.

Georgio opened up a leather portfolio and began to look through files and folders. He glanced up at Gabriela and gave her a subtle smile, but Gabriela wasn't buying it. She knew what would happen to her, and no smile at this point was going to take away all the fear. Gabriela played the game, though, and smiled.

Soon, another ICE officer, Ignacio, approached Gabriela. As he handed Georgio an envelope, along with files and papers, he observed Gabriela's exquisite features, such as her dark eyes and perky breasts, with a slight smile. Gabriela could sense his aura of malevolence.

"*Cálmate, cálmate.* It's okay. Don't worry, everything is going to be all right. We're not here to hurt you, we're here to help you," Ignacio said with a slight Spanish accent and a taunting grin, but Gabriela remained silent. "*Mira, mírame.*"

Gabriela slowly raised her head, only revealing a glimpse of her face to satisfy Ignacio, who looked deep into Gabriela's eyes before Georgio handed him some documents. Ignacio observed Gabriela's beauty one last time before giving Gabriela a slight smile as his final farewell.

Georgio reached into the envelope, pulled out items and then tossed them onto the desk. He leaned forward, rested his elbows on top of the desk, and clasped his hands together.

"So, do you know what these are?"

Georgio spoke with a clear, smooth voice as he lifted his hands up to emphasize his words. Gabriela brushed back her hair with her fingertips to reveal the rest of her face and looked down at her bogus Social Security card, green card, visa, and eight ball of cocaine.

"Yes."

"Good, because according to these, you go by the alias Christina Rodriguez, you're from Elizabeth, New Jersey, and you live in Jersey City. We both know that this is not true. Now, before you tell me where you got all this from, and before we get into why you were with Nelson Lopez, and how you know him, I first need you to tell me what your real name is and where you're really from."

Gabriela was hesitant. She was only able to focus on all the items, and the other illegal immigrants being interrogated, but then found composure from deep within her heart and soul.

"My name is Gabriela Olivia Del Sol. I was born March first, 1975, in Tehuacán, Mexico. I came to America by myself thirteen years ago, with a group of people brought in a van by coyotes. I first lived in California, then I spent some time in Texas, and then I ended up in Miami, where I lived for about a year and a half before coming to New Jersey, which is where I've been living since."

"So, Gabriela, how come you moved around so much? Why didn't you just stay in California or Miami? What made you decide to come to New Jersey, knowing that New Jersey is very far from Mexico. Wouldn't it have been easier for you to just stay in California?"

"Yes, but I wanted to get as far away from Mexico as I could to start a new and better life."

"Well, that may be, but I need you to explain to me why you were with Nelson Lopez, and how you know him, and where you got all of this. And, please, be honest. I'm only trying to help you, because I know you didn't get any of these on your own. Someone provided these for you, and whoever it was, you know and I know that they aren't good people and that they really don't care about what will happen to you now that you've been caught."

Gabriela shied away and looked down at her handcuffed wrists, and then glanced over at the other illegal immigrants once again, focusing on a tattooed man who appeared to belong to a gang. He reminded Gabriela of all the thugs she'd been associated with since she had come to America. It was a part of her life that she wished to leave behind, but which now haunted her, and Don Fernandez was the ghost who threatened her livelihood.

"Listen, Gabriela, I'm an immigrant myself. I moved here from southern Italy with my parents and two brothers when I was seven. I grew up in Orange, New Jersey, and you know what? It doesn't matter if I came from Italy, Mexico or even China, because in America, Gabriela, most immigrants struggle with life and sometimes are not treated as equals.

"As for illegal immigrants like yourself, Gabriela, I understand that it's harder for you to make it in America and that not all illegal immigrants are bad people. I know because I deal with illegal immigrants every day and a lot of them find themselves in the same situation that you're in now. The only way for them to get started in America is to get involved with bad people who do bad things, and when these good-hearted illegal immigrants like yourself get caught, they're scared of what these bad people might do to them or their families, and what we will do to you.

"I understand that you did what you did to survive—and, hey, as a once-struggling immigrant, like my father, I had to hustle and bend a few rules to make it myself. But I also knew what the consequences were at the time, and to this day I regret doing what I did. That's one of the reasons I'm where I am now—to help people like you.

"So before you tell me who provided you with all this, I need to know if you have any children. If you do have children, or any family that these people could hurt, I promise we'll protect them and you as well. Anything that you tell me is confidential, and when we do get to the legal process, I could promise you immunity and leniency in your sentence based on any decision you make."

Georgio watched Gabriela with great concern as he emphasized his words with dramatic hand motions. He had dealt with many different illegal immigrants throughout the years and had a keen eye and a good sense of characters. He was good at picking out and punishing the thugs and criminals who deserved to be imprisoned or sent back. And for the ones who meant well, like Gabriela, he would use all his power to try to delay or avoid their deportation.

In the end, if Gabriela was to reveal how she'd ended up in Nelson Lopez's safe house during an unannounced ICE raid, and Sarita and use her as an anchor child, the deportation process would most likely be delayed or eradicated for the well-being of the child. But either way, Gabriela felt that she wouldn't be able to live in the shadows anymore. She would have to forever live her life under the government's watchful eye and would no longer have the freedom she was used to.

An alternate route for Gabriela would be to turn in Don Fernandez, but she and Sarita would then forever be targets of vengeance. To Gabriela and other illegal immigrants, it was easier to skip the hassle of the legal process and just voluntarily return home, especially for Mexicans, because ninety percent of them would illegally cross the border into America again and just start over, which seemed easier than going through the legal process. But Gabriela would play the game and reveal glimpses of her involvement with criminals.

"I got all this from a friend I know who is in a gang. In return, I had to hold on to drugs and bring them to Nelson. I don't even know who Nelson is; I was just doing a favor for a friend."

After Gabriela spoke, the reassuring aura that Georgio created soon faded away as he looked down towards Gabriela. Georgio could tell that she was spinning the truth.

"I see. And this friend of yours, does he have a name?" Verrello inquired.

"Um, I'd rather not say."

"Well, in order for me to help you, I need a name."

Gabriela glanced down at her handcuffed wrists, the thought of Don Fernandez and Sarita plaguing her mind. Gabriela was now at a stalemate, and knew that she had to quickly conjure up a prime figure in order to move on. But, all she was able to do at the moment was look up and focus on the eight ball of cocaine, one of the reasons she'd ended up where she was now.

"Wilmer. My friend's name is Wilmer."

"Wilmer. So, do you consider Wilmer to be a very close friend of yours, someone that you see and speak to all the time?"

"No, not all the time, but he is someone I keep in touch with. Anyway, he isn't the one who got me all this. It was someone in his gang that I don't even know."

"Okay, so what gang is Wilmer in? The Bloods, the Latin Kings, MS13, Nada Mas? Remember, I'm only here to help and protect you, so don't be afraid to tell me the truth."

"I'm not sure. The Bloods, I think. I can't remember," Gabriela said nervously.

"You can't remember. Well, I find that hard to believe. Let's see, maybe if we call your friend Wilmer now, he could help you remember. Here, you can use my phone."

Georgio held the desk phone out towards Gabriela, who remained silent as she stared at it. The humbling attitude and comforting feeling that Georgio had brought with him was now completely gone, but his motive was still the same. Whatever happened from here, he was willing to help Gabriela the best he could.

"*Mira, mirame.*" Georgio provoked Gabriela even more. Gabriela slowly lifted her head and sat up. "Listen, Gabriela, I know that you're lying to me, and lying is only going to make all of this take longer, and it will hurt you in the end. Do you understand me?"

"Yes."

"Good. Now, I'm going to start from the beginning again, and you're going to answer my questions and tell me the truth, because if you don't, this time, any kind of amnesty I promised you will disappear. So, Gabriela, are you going to cooperate?"

"Yes."

"Okay," Georgio said, putting the phone back and resting his elbows on the table as he leaned forward. "So, who got you all of this?"

Gabriela became filled with fear, knowing that by revealing Don Fernandez, she was putting her own life and Sarita's at risk. But at this point, Gabriela had to take away all types of reason and accountability. Even if fear was Gabriela's only god, she had to find the strength to overcome it and understand that she was now in better hands.

"Don Fernandez."

"Don Fernandez? So who is Don Fernandez?"

"He . . . he's a restaurant owner from Union City."

"I see. And what's the name of this restaurant?" Georgio asked. Even though, deep within, Gabriela felt overwhelmed with fear, she would give in, just to bring closure, so that she could move on with her life.

"Los Unidos. That's it. That's all I know and all I can tell you. I don't know anything else, just that he's the one who provided me with all this. Can we just end this now, please?"

"I thought that he was your friend, that you knew him?"

"A friend, yes, because he helped me. I never really knew him, I hardly ever saw him after he helped me."

"That I find hard to believe, because people like your friend, Don Fernandez, don't just do favors for nothing. I know you didn't pay him money or bake him a cake, because when men like Don Fernandez do something for women like you, especially the pretty ones, they usually want sexual favors in return."

The reminder of the sexual favors that Gabriela used to give to Don Fernandez brought back haunting memories. Gabriela could still taste the skin of the man she had sold her body to in order to survive; to be able to someday live a better life. Suddently, she had an unyielding urge to go back to Mexico.

"I . . . I . . . yes, I . . . gave sexual favors to Don Fernandez in return. I don't wanna be here anymore, please. I wanna go home. None of this is worth all the pain I feel. Please, I'm done, I . . . I wanna see a lawyer. I know my rights. I wanna go home and see a lawyer."

Gabriela wiped away tears, choking up with each word. Everything Gabriela had been through for the past thirteen years living as an illegal immigrant, all she had hidden and kept bottled up, all came out at once.

"It's okay, Gabriela, it's okay. Calm down. Here, take these. You need to be strong, okay? I know that what you did was very bad and that you still bear all the scars and haunting memories, but remember that you did what you had to do. I understand that. And right now, I will guarantee that we will find this Don Fernandez and give him what he deserves. As for you, Gabriela, with this information that you're giving me, I promise you that I . . ." Verrello handed Gabriela tissues.

"Please, stop! I . . . I just wanna go home. I don't wanna be here anymore. Being here is a reminder of all the bad people I've been with and bad things I've done." Gabriela's voice cracked with anguish.

The displeased look on Gabriela's face was one that Georgio had seen many times before. It was heartbreaking to see illegal immigrants break down emotionally with desperation. Even harder than that was seeing families separated and torn apart. Illegal immigrants were human beings like everyone else, and Georgio had no intention of ever using his authority in a dehumanizing, intimidating manner to serve justice. Even if it was unfortunate that both criminals and those with morals were looked at through the same lens—that illegal immigrants were just meaningless pawns who all deserved to be sent back where they came from. Gabriela was just another human being in distress, who sought forgiveness and help.

"I'm only here to help you, and with the information that you have given me, I promise you that I will delay the next stages in the legal process and that—"

"Please, stop. I understand what it is you're trying to do, and I thank you for that, but look at me. I have been through a lot in the past thirteen years, just to survive. I've been through hell and back, and I just wanna go home. So please, send me home. Get me a lawyer, and . . . and send me home."

"Very well, but before we continue, I need to know if you have any family or any children."

All Gabriela could focus on at this point was how she was nothing but a failure to Sarita, and how her dark and haunting past would threaten Sarita's life. Gabriela didn't say a word, and Georgio could tell she was hiding something from him, but he respected her present state of being. And as Georgio looked down to write, Gabriela fought to hold back all of the bottled-up desolation, which began to burst out.

All the tears that she held back began to flow out. Gabriela tried to wipe away each tear, one at a time, but there were too many to control. Gabriela had to cover her mouth as she choked up, then sat back in her chair in an attempt to compose herself.

After Gabriela was able to control her emotions, she focused on the illegal immigrants who were now a reminder of the life she'd dreamed of, now lost. But a woman holding a child seemed to be the center of attention. The child, especially its calm smile, lost within a room of chaos and pain, reminded

Gabriela of Sarita; reminded her that there was hope.

As a percussion of thunder slowly rose up in the distance, and lightning from the darkness of the midnight sky sporadically illuminated Gabriela within the dimness of her new, yet aged apartment, she sat composed, writing memories from her past down in her journal. Ever since crossing the border, after taking many daunting and unpredictable paths, Gabriela was finally living the life she had always dreamt of. After Gabriela wrote down her final words, she closed the journal, placed it down, and then lifted up her six-month-old baby, Sarita, who was resting on the couch beside her. Gabriela walked around the open space, with Sarita cradled in her arms as she began to cry. Gabriela softly sang a Spanish lullaby while gently rocking Sarita to sleep. Once Sarita became calm, Gabriela lowered her voice down to a whisper.

"I love you very much, Sarita, very much. Someday, when you grow older, then will you know what you truly mean to me. If it weren't for you, Sarita, we wouldn't be here today. Because of you, I now have the hope and strength to move on for you, to give you what I came here for, to live a better life. Someday, Sarita, someday, you will have the opportunities and chances I never had. Someday, someday, you will live the American Dream."

Gabriela began to softly sing a Spanish lullaby one last time while gazing out the window into the darkness of a midsummer's night, filled with visions of everything that had been once and everything that might be.

62

After traveling many miles from the Elizabeth Detention Center in New Jersey, and US Immigration and Customs, Gabriela gazed out the bus window. The vast, empty desert wastelands and grandiose mountain ranges of the ever-changing Mexican landscape flashed before Gabriela's eyes, and she felt sorrow and regret in her broken heart. But to Gabriela, it wasn't the end, but the beginning. Facing failure at this point wasn't submission to a daunting fate, but a necessary feat to overcome in order to spiritually grow and continue on a path least taken so that she could fulfill her destiny and finish what was started long ago. There were many miles of misery traveled. Although arriving in Mexico seemed unpleasant and devastating without Sarita, it was, in fact, what she needed in that moment to lift her up and encourage her to pick up the pieces of her broken heart. She needed to find a means to reconnect with Sarita.

Sonora State now seemed like a decaying fountain left far behind with a distant trail of flowing water that had been stained throughout the sands of time. Gabriela stood frozen like a putrefying statue of stone filled with heaviness and disappointment. She stared at the antique black rotary phone, and it reminded her of Sarita. Since Gabriela's confrontation with Ignacio and Don Fernandez and being deported back to Mexico, Sarita's whereabouts and well-being were still a complete mystery. The Mexican authorities had contacted Gabriela to inform her that Sarita had been kidnapped. In a way, Gabriela was relieved to know that Sarita's abductor wasn't Don Fernandez, but she still feared for the worst.

All Gabriela was able to do was frantically pace around while biting her nails, waiting for either Sarita or a call from someone to let her know that Sarita was safe. Gabriela was blind to Sarita's fate, but deep within her heart, there was faith.

<u>63</u>

The Clearview apartment complex of Jersey City, New Jersey, was now the center of a crime scene investigation. FBI vehicles lined the streets outside the apartment complex. Inside, and outside in the courtyard in the back, were groups of curious and confused tenants. FBI agents mingled amongst them, going from individual to individual in an attempt to gather as much information as they could with intense, strategic interview sessions. Two of the FBI agents assigned to the case, also the two in charge of the task force investigating the case, were FBI Special Agents Alec D. Donovan and William W. Walsh. Donovan and Walsh were outside in the back courtyard with the three brujas.

Mona stood in front of Martha and Mable, wearing a flower-patterned scarlet nightgown that still had the price tag attached to it. As a haze of cigarette smoke languidly lingered between Mona and Donovan and Walsh, ash rained down on top of her clear plastic sandals and ingrown toenails, with pink nail polish on half her toes. Around her and the other two brujas, scattered on the weed-infested brick courtyard grounds were dozens of cigarette butts. As Donovan stood with his yellow Have a Nice Day stress ball completely squeezed within the palm of his hand, Walsh took notes in his little black notebook while Mona spoke.

"Those goddamn local police do nothing but eat and sleep all day. Ya don't think I know what goes on all day? Well, I do. I know what goes on. And if they would do their goddamn job, we wouldn't be in this situation right now, am I right?"

Martha and Mable simultaneously nodded and groaned in agreement, observing as ash fell onto Donovan and Walsh's well-polished black boots. Mona took one long drag to finish her cigarette, then tossed it down onto the ground. She lit up a new cigarette with her plastic BiC lighter and blew the smoke into Donovan and Walsh's faces.

"I hope the FBI aren't like the goddamn locals. I hope you'll listen to me and do your jobs. Honestly, I could care less about that creep from apartment 515. All I care about right now is my dignity, and that justice will be served," Mona complained.

"Ma'am, I understand that you're upset about how the local police treated you and how they didn't do their jobs. The FBI are well-trained professionals. It's our job to deal with high-profile criminals, along with federal and national security issues, and we take our jobs very seriously. There's no monkey business with us, you can trust us. What I need you to do for us right now is to calm down and please cooperate with us, okay?" Donovan said.

"Upset? You think I'm upset? This *is* calm. For a widow, a victim of tha 9/11 attacks, who is still emotionally traumatized and a victim of being used by some creep from apartment 515, I'm calm, and believe me you don't wanna to see me upset."

"Hmm, she's right. We're all victims here," Martha added.

"Hmm, that's right. We're Americans," Mable agreed. Walsh could see that Donovan was beginning to lose his patience and felt that it was the right moment step in.

"Ma'am, you're right. You are a victim, and we're all Americans here. Listen, I feel horrible about the way the locals treated you, and I give you my sympathy and support for your past tragedies. As for my partner and I, we're professionals, and we're the best at what we do. That's why we're here. With your cooperation, we'll be able to get things done quicker, and then we'll all be on our way. We'll leave with the information we need, and you can live the rest of your life knowing that the FBI was good to you."

Mona stood in silence as she slowly exhaled smoke from her mouth, looking at Walsh, then at Donovan, then back at Walsh. Walsh and Donovan looked at each other with anticipation as they waited for Mona to speak. Donovan squeezed his stress ball tighter as he stared at Walsh with relief that he hadn't said something stupid to upset Mona. As for Walsh, who felt that he'd smoothed things over with Mona, he slipped Donovan a wink.

"So, you're tha rookie, huh?" Mona questioned Walsh.

"No, ma'am. This is my third year on the job," Walsh said nervously.

"So you're a rookie. Then why in the hell am I speaking to you? Who's in charge here?"

"I am, ma'am. As I told you before, I'm FBI Special Agent Donovan, and I'm also in charge of this task force, so it's okay for you to speak with me."

Donovan stepped forward through the haze of smoke and in front of Walsh so he was now face-to-face with Mona. She continued to puff on her cigarette, and ash, sprinkled down onto his boots.

"Okay, so I guess that means I can trust ya, that ya won't treat me like a piece of shit like those goddamn locals did. Ya know they cawlled me crazy? Well, I'm not crazy. I know what I saw. I still have 20/20 vision, mindja. It was that creep from apartment 515."

"Yes, you mentioned that before. Now this tenant of yours, from apartment 515, you say you saw him leave with the girl from next door. What do you know about him?"

"Well, first of all, when he first moved in thirteen years ago, my late husband Frankie took care of him and all his paperwork, God rest his soul."

Smoke wafted out of Mona's mouth as she spoke. She made the sign of the holy trinity with the cigarette in her moving hand to pay illusory respect for Frankie. Martha and Mable also made the sign of the holy trinity for Frankie and their late husbands.

"I never interacted with any of tha tenants when Frankie was alive. When Frankie left me, unfortunately, I was forced to, and tha creep from apartment 515 is still tha only one I hardly eva see or tawk with. He would slip tha rent money under my dowr in tha middle of tha night, and occasionally I would see him come in and out of tha back stairwell that goes up to his apartment, between dusk and dawn."

Mona puffed on her cigarette and blew more smoke into the faces of Donovan and Walsh. Donovan squeezed his stress ball, while Walsh turned away and took notes.

"There was this one time, though, after he first moved in. I caught him coming in from tha front entrance. He looked scared and nervous, and very dirty. He smelt bad too, mindja. Anyway, he was late with his rent, which was unusual—I give him that, though, he did pay his rent on time, unlike some of tha otha lowlifes who live here. Okay, where was I? Oh, yes, so I hollared at him about tha rent money. Tha son of bitch didn't say a word, just stared at me like I was speaking anotha language, and then he reached into this bag, this green backpack—tha same one I saw him with when he left with tha girl. So, as he reached into tha bag, I leaned forward and took a peek inside . . ." Mona then leaned in closer towards Donovan and whispered, "It looked like drugs. What's that white stuff? Coke, coka?"

"Hmm, tha cocaine," Martha jumped in.

"That's it, tha cocaine, ya know, a big block of it. And then he pulled out all this money for me. Cash, mindja. He didn't even count it, just gave it to me and left without saying a word." As Mona spoke, Walsh wrote quickly while Donovan stopped squeezing his stress ball.

"Cocaine?" Donovan questioned Mona.

"Yeah, tha cocaine. Hey, listen, Deputy Dan, I know what I saw. It was tha cocaine and it was tha creep from apartment 515," Mona said defiantly. Donovan squeezed his stress ball even harder. "Now, eva since tha creep from apartment 515 and tha girl lived here, I've never seen them together. Like I said, last week was tha only time I've eva seen tha two togetha. That's why I cawlled tha goddamn locals, because I found it to be suspicious to see them leave tha apartment complex togetha."

"What about the mother? Do you know if the mother had any kind of relationship with him, or if she wanted him to take care of her daughter?"

"How tha hell would I know what goes on behind closed doors? Listen, I just collect tha goddamn rent. I don't get into tha personal lives of my tenants, okay? Now, are we through? Can we go?"

"That's understandable, ma'am, but I just need to ask you one more thing. What about the proper documents needed for the tenants to fill out to get an apartment, with all their personal information? Do you have any of this information kept on file?"

"Of course I have all dat information kept on file. Whacha think this is, a goddamn soup kitchen I'm running ova here?"

"Okay, ma'am, okay. Walsh, I think we're done here. Thank you for your time, ma'am. We appreciate all the information you've given us. And now, if you don't mind, we'll need to look over all the documents you have on the tenant from apartment 515. I'll have one of our agents kindly escort you to your apartment and look over the documents."

"That's all? I just have to show ya tha documents and then ya guys will be done and leave?"

"That's all, ma'am, and we'll need to search apartment 515."

Mona then led the way back inside the apartment complex, while Martha and Mable followed behind her, along with Donovan and Walsh. They crossed paths with Agents Johnson and Martin. Donovan stopped everyone inside the entranceway to quickly talk to the other FBI agents. Mona stood with her arms crossed, tapping her foot. She looked at Donovan with disgust and felt used by Donovan. He had abandoned her after getting all the information from her. Johnson and Martin then went with the three brujas to look over the documents on Dante.

Donovan and Walsh made their way up to apartment 515. They covered up their noses when they stepped inside. A rancid odor of garbage, paint and alcohol filled the air. The oscillating fan was on, and cooling winds blew in through the open window, playing the wind chimes. There was a pile of overflowing garbage in the kitchen, and whatever empty bottles of alcohol and pieces of paper Sarita and Dante hadn't cleaned up were still left lying all over the floor and furniture.

Donovan and Walsh walked through the apartment kicking garbage, empty bottles and paint cans. They searched through piles of papers, in cabinets, in the closets, and underneath the couch cushions and mattress. They found nothing useful. The two then came together around the couch and coffee table and stopped to stare at all of Dante's paintings.

"Wow! These paintings are pretty damn good. This guy paints like van Gogh," Walsh stated.

Donovan took out his stress ball and squeezed it as he studied Dante's paintings. Donovan wasn't a man with any interest in the arts or culture. To him, they were just paintings. "Yeah, real good, Walsh, but what do you know about paintings and art?" Donovan said as he put away his stress ball and then took out his pills. After taking his pills, he walked up closer to the paintings to look through the ones leaning up on the wall. Carefully and meticulously, he ran his fingers along the surface of each painting, its frame, looking behind each one.

"Well, I know a little. I used to date an art student when I was at American University. She used to make me go to museums all the time. This guy is definitely one of those abstract expressionism guys, like Poe-lock."

Donovan peeked up from behind a painting. "Don't you mean Pollock?"

Walsh stood with his arms crossed as he looked up towards the cracked, spiderweb-covered ceiling and then at a painting on the wall.

"Pollock? That's right, Jackson Pollock. They used to call him Jack the Dipper."

Donovan stood up and walked by Walsh, patting him on the shoulder. "That's Jack the Dripper, because he used to drip the paint onto his canvases, not dip them."

"You know what I mean."

"Yeah, but what could you tell me about painters of today, who are still alive? Do you recognize any of this guy's work?"

Walsh studied all of Dante's paintings, digging deeper and deeper into his mind to pull out information about the artists his art student ex-girlfriend used to tell him about. The paintings looked familiar, but he couldn't remember the guy's name or the painter his ex-girlfriend use to love.

"Nothing. I only know about the dead painters, sorry."

"That's okay, Walsh, that's okay," Donovan said as he began to walk across the apartment, towards the kitchen. Walsh turned around to watch

Donovan walk away while kicking garbage, only to stop and pick up a multicolored friendship bracelet left behind by Sarita and some pieces of paper from the floor and coffee table. He continued to walk with one held in his hand. As Donovan stood near the kitchen table, Walsh joined him.

Donovan focused on the kitchen table. Walsh stared at Donovan, who stood poised, smiling, and then he looked down at the table as well. There was a half-empty bottle of beer and a half-empty glass of milk.

"Well, it looks like that crazy landlord was right, Walsh."

"What, that this guy kidnapped the girl?"

"Well, we're inside his apartment, he's missing, and his table is left set for two. Check this out." Donovan showed Walsh the friendship bracelet and Dante's sketch of Sarita, which he picked up from the floor.

"The bracelet looks like something a girl would wear, and that looks like the picture we have of the girl. But what about all the drugs that crazy landlord said she saw, and the mother?"

"Well, so far he's clean on possession of narcotics. We looked through everything, there's nothing here. The landlord said she saw him with drugs some years ago, but who even knows if it was drugs she saw? That lady's nuts. It was probably something else, or nothing at all. As for the mother, well, we need to get more information on her and this painter. Something should come up soon, I'm sure. Anyway, we're done here. C'mon, let's get out of this shithole." Donovan began to walk out of the apartment while Walsh followed behind.

As the two came to the door, Johnson and Martin arrived with the tenant documents Mona had about Dante. Donovan scanned through Dante's files and then walked away with Walsh as the other FBI agents finished searching Dante's and Gabriela's apartments.

"Before we get back, Walsh, I want a list of witnesses we could bring in to interview later on. I want this entire complex tightly secured. I want units here night and day watching this place, watching who comes in and who goes out, along with any other place this guy may frequent. Then later today, we need a forensic team up here scanning for prints. I wanna get phone taps on anyone we can find who is associated with this guy and the mother. Also, find out who the mother is, where she's from, and what her relationship is with this guy. I want to get as much information on this guy as we can. I want to know where he's from, what he's done, who he knows, who knows him. I even want to know what color underwear he wears and if they're boxers or briefs. I have a hunch, and I'm not buying the whole painter thing. There is more to this guy than what we see."

"He seems like he goes commando."

Donovan stopped walking, giving Walsh an agitated look as he tightly squeezed his stress ball. Without saying a word, he put his head down while shaking it and then continued to walk further down the hallway and out of the apartment complex.

# # #

The eight-fingered Colombian assassin dressed in white crept through the darkness of Dante's apartment. He'd entered the Clearview apartment complex undetected in the middle of the night, before FBI units were set up to watch over Dante's apartment. After receiving a lead from moles within the FBI who pledged allegiance to the Suarez drug cartel, Octavio, Suarez's best hitman, had been sent to terminate any original affiliates from Nada Mas. Suarez was eager to eradicate what was left of Nada Mas little by little, and eventually take it over, by any means.

Octavio continued to scan through Dante's apartment in hopes of finding something useful to help track down Dante, something the FBI might have missed. He picked up a sketch of Sarita with his three-fingered hand, looked at it, and put it in his pocket. And after searching through documents, books, and papers, Octavio finally found something useful: a printed receipt for Aero Mexico flight 1203, and, kept wedged between sketchbooks, a small black leather pad filled with contact information of a handful of friends and associates. It wasn't much, but it was something Octavio could use to track down Dante, in order to not only kill him, but find the mastermind of Nada Mas, Benjamin Bradford.

64

After the train departed from the Tuscaloosa train station, Dante and Sarita walked down Greensboro Avenue, which ran through the heart of Tuscaloosa. They searched for some sort of food establishment where they could rest, eat, and kill some time before their departure. After walking many miles, Dante and Sarita settled down inside an old diner. They chose a window booth, hidden in a nook near the back corner. After receiving their meals, they began to eat and indulge in deep conversation.

"That's why the Internet is the greatest invention of the twentieth century, Shorty, because it's a library filled with infinite information. Not only that, but also, for the first time in human existence, all humans throughout the entire world are connected and can communicate with each other through various websites and social media networks." Dante dramatized his words with his hands.

"Um, but with the cell phone, you can talk to anyone at any time. Like, if there is ever an emergency, you can save someone's life from wherever. And don't forget that a cell phone is both a phone and the Internet, so that's why it's better, because not only can you call someone from wherever and use the Internet, but it can also fit in your pocket. You can also take pictures, film videos, play games, listen to music and watch movies from wherever you are," Sarita explained as she tried to pour ketchup onto her french fries out of a brand-new glass bottle of Heinz.

Dante watched with aggravation. Since their debate had started, Sarita still didn't support Dante's opinion that the Internet was a better invention than the cell phone, and the greatest invention of the twentieth century.

"Hit the fifty-seven," Dante said as he watched Sarita continuously hit the bottom of the upside-down ketchup bottle with the palm of her hand.

"Um, fifty-seven? What are you talking about?"

"Here." Dante grabbed the ketchup bottle from Sarita's hands. He hit the 57 on the side of the bottle with the palm of his hand to loosen up the ketchup and then rolled the bottle within the palms of his hands to pour ketchup down in a glob beside her french fries.

"Um, on—on the fries," Sarita innocently ordered Dante, who looked up with annoyance at being talked to as if he was her personal servant. "Um, more." Sarita sat up on her knees. "Um, some—some more, Dante."

"More?"

"Uh-huh." Sarita nodded as Dante poured out the final drops. Dante then began to pour ketchup onto his cheeseburger—which was cooked rare and not well done like he'd asked for—and fries. Sarita began to devour hers, together with the grilled cheese sandwich, which she filled with fries and dipped into the ketchup-filled plate.

By the time Dante took a few bites of his bloody cheeseburger, which oozed out the sides and down his chin, Sarita was already halfway done with her food.

"Hey, Shorty, slow down. This isn't a pie-eating contest. You're gonna choke to death if you keep eating like that. Didn't your mother teach you any manners?"

Sarita nodded as she continued to eat quickly. After finishing her grilled cheese sandwich, she took a gulp from her glass of milk, wiped her mouth with her forearm and then began to eat the last of her french fries.

"Um, do you want my pickle? I hate pickles."

Dante didn't say a word. He just continued to stare at Sarita with irritation. She completely ignored him as he reached out, took the pickle from Sarita's hand and placed it next to the pickle on his plate.

Dante observed Sarita as he continued to eat. How she constantly shifted her body while she ate, the way she ate her french fries with her ketchup-stained fingers, and even the way she was able to gaze around through her hair, while simultaneously chewing her food like a cow and humming sweet nothingness. Somehow she was able to switch over instantly from conversation with Dante, zone out, and drift away into a world of imagination, while continuing to eat. She reminded him of Sonya.

"Hey, Shorty, what did I just say about manners?" Dante said with disgust after Sarita let out a volcanic belch and then wiped her ketchup-stained mouth with her forearm. The image of beauty and innocence was tained by her lack of manners

"Sorry, Dante, but that was a good one," Sarita said with a smile as she chuckled.

"Well, I hope you don't do that stuff in front of strangers. It's a nasty habit. It makes you look like a *maiale.* You need to learn how to present yourself like a little lady. Ya know, have some self-respect."

"What's a *maiale?*" Sarita asked with a mouthful of food as she repositioned her body. Dante rested his elbows on top of the table with outstretched arms and spoke with dramatic hand motions.

"A pig."

"I'm not a pig! I'm just a kid." Sarita leaned forward and rested her arms, crossed together on top of the table.

"Kid, adult, it doesn't matter how old you are, Shorty. If you want people to respect you, you first need to respect yourself."

Sarita smiled. Having Dante try to present himself like a fatherly figure filled her with adoration.

"You need to act like a little lady. Ya know, say please, thank you, respect your elders. That way, people will treat you with respect and take you seriously. If you go around acting like a *maiale* or like some of these other kids I see roaming around, acting like they're a bunch of hoodlums—ya know, the troublemakers who use foul language and talk back to adults—no one will ever take you serious when you try to talk to them, and no one will want to be your friend. Would you wanna be friends with someone who burps and farts all the time, Shorty? Huh?" Dante explained.

"No, but that stuff is funny," Sarita laughed as she tried to speak.

"Well, funny for a kid, maybe, but not when you're an adult, Shorty. That's why you need to act like a little lady now, because if you grow up farting and burping, picking your nose, or doing whatever else, no one will ever want to be with you. And the ones who do want to be around you, well, they won't take you serious. They'll pretend to be your friend because it's funny. You'll just be a joke to them. They will take advantage of you because they will have no respect for you, and just use you like a tramp."

Sarita squinted. "What's a tramp?"

Dante sat back with his glass of water in hand. "It's someone who roams around, like Chaplin, but in this case, like—well, ya know, a sleaze, a hooker, roaming around making money off men, but degraded and treated poorly. Anyway, what I mean is, I don't want you to grow up acting in a negative way, and have people treat you in a degrading way," Dante elaborated.

"Um, but what's wrong with roaming around, Dante?" Sarita sat up as she inquired.

"Well, nothing. Anyway, you're missing the point of what I'm trying to tell you, Shorty. Act like a little lady, and respect yourself, so that other people respect you, got it?"

All Sarita could think of was the word *tramp*. "You mean like Julia Roberts in *Pretty Woman*?"

"How old are you?" Dante squinted.

"Um, ten. But, but I've seen a lot of movies, and remember all the good ones. Someday, I'm gonna be a famous actress," Sarita responded confidently.

"First of all, you're bit too young to watch movies like that, and second, the day you become a famous actress, Shorty, is the day Mexicans take over America."

"You watch, Dante, someday I will. I will."

"Keep dreaming, Shorty. Besides, you have a lifetime ahead of you, so try not to fill your head with false hopes at such a young age. The older you get, the more you'll realize how disappointing life is." Dante leaned in closer. "And if you want some advice from a once-struggling artist who had big dreams like you, Shorty, well, you need to have a lot of patience, and you also need to expect failure and be able to accept it. Failure is a precursor to success. Nothing in life is just given to you. You need to earn what you want. You need to set your goals and dreams high, but also be realistic, very ambitious, disciplined, hardworking and strong mentally, because if you're not, you'll give up and fail. You won't push yourself harder to achieve your goals and reach your dreams. And you can't allow someone to tell you what you can and can't do in life." Dante brought his glass of water before his lips while he spoke his final words. "And have faith in yourself. Okay, Shorty?"

Dante's words were an echo of Gabriela's, and her soul of comfort was a reflection in his eyes.

"Um, you mean like hope, Dante?"

"Yeah, like hope, Shorty." Dante ate the last of his cheeseburger and french fries, while Sarita sat with her arms crossed on the table, smiling.

"So, what are all of those on your wrists?"

Sarita rotated her wrists. "These are my friendship bracelets, Silly Bandz, ties for my hair, and good luck charms."

Dante held Sarita's wrists as he ate fries with his other hand. Sarita pulled back her hands and began to take off one of her friendship bracelets.

"Um, here, give me your wrist."

Dante smiled as he held his left wrist out before Sarita. "So, does this make us BFFs, Shorty?"

Sarita tied a black-and-blue homemade friendship bracelet around his wrist. "Uh-huh. And it will also bring you good luck."

Dante studied the friendship bracelet on his wrist. "Thank you, Shorty, I feel honored," he humored her.

"Um, you're welcome," Sarita said with a smile.

Dante admired Sarita as she presented herself and spoke like a little lady. He was proud. From this point on, Dante was willing to continue on, even if it was through the fiery depths of hell, in order to protect Sarita and fulfill his promise.

<u>65</u>

Hell's bells rang out as Dante and Sarita stepped into an antique shop hidden within the heart of Tuscaloosa, Alabama. The shop was filled with a labyrinth of various items that time had abandoned and left behind. It was a hoarder's paradise.

All around there were items of caution, history, knowledge, useful and useless possessions, aged military fatigues, weapons and memorabilia from every American war. There were clocks, clothes, appliances, furniture, mirrors, religious relics, Elvis memorabilia, pictures, paintings, toys, street signs, old tools, license plates and tons of other miscellaneous junk. Deeper within the antique shop, there were bookshelves filled with old bare hardcover books.

"Hey, Shorty, don't forget that we have a train to catch. Remember we're not here to go shopping. We're just killing some time. Fifteen minutes, that's all, okay?" Dante informed Sarita as she walked away.

She looked back over her right shoulder. "Uh-huh," Sarita responded nonchalantly, continuing to walk away alongside the front display case.

In the front of the antique shop, in the belly of the wooden display case that stretched the length of the shop, were a variety of valuable antiques, such as jewelry, watches, occult relics, guns, knives and other weapons and torture devices. The items within were a reflection of the shopkeeper.

She was an angel laced with sin and blood-tipped wings, filled with mystique and gothic delight. Her elbows rested on top of a fetish magazine, *Bizarre*, as she leaned forward on the counter. Her full, lush lips sucked on a

302

cherry Blow Pop she slowly twisted in and out of her moist orifice of sin. Her seductive simulation of fellatio was infused with even more eroticism by her pierced tongue, which slowly caressed the circumference of the sucker. Her arms had black tattoos. A bed of roses stained her right shoulder and wrapped down the rest of her arm along with thorns. A nude pinup model posed on her left forearm, which was complemented with black occult symbols tagged above on her shoulder. Her straightened jet-black hair was layered down to and around her shoulders with cropped bangs. A modern-day Bettie Page, bop top. As she silently leaned forward, she seductively gazed out with her piercing green eyes adorned with black eyeshadow.

Dante was lost within her eyes. Her mystique and sense of gothic beauty moved him in the ways of muses laced with sin. For a moment, he was lost in a deep trance, and then an aura of lust and temptation, as he slowly stepped closer. He stopped and pretended to look at items in the front of the antique shop, but focused on her.

As Dante peered around at various items, she continued to seductively gaze deep into Dante's eyes while sucking on her cherry Blow Pop. Everything about her gothic beauty, such as her hourglass frame, voluptuous breasts that bulged out of her short, and tight black *Night of the Living Dead* V-neck T-shirt, easily aroused Dante.

Even her nipple ring, which could clearly be seen through her shirt, and matching lip and nose rings held Dante in a state of bondage and stimulated his senses. Just as Dante controlled his emotions and built up enough aggressiveness to approach the temptress, hell's bells rang once again. Dante froze and came back to reality as a stranger walked into the antique shop.

As the bells from the entrance door rang, Sarita stood before a collage of mirrors, staring at the reflection of her scuffed-up untied red Converse as she slowly turned from side to side, rotated and posed. She made funny faces and observed how her body appeared broken apart from different perspectives within the overlapping mirrors. Sarita looked like a Picasso portrait.

Dante pretended to look at trinkets while gazing at the shopkeeper through notches and openings in the shelf of the aisle he stood in. He also looked back over his shoulder at the man who walked in and suspiciously stared at him from the back of the aisle. The bearded stranger, with shaggy hair, wearing blue jeans and a faded red mom-and-pop business t-shirt with a matching faded red hat, stared at Dante like a vulture. Every time Dante looked away, he could feel the stranger's gaze burn into his back.

Finally, the stranger walked down another aisle, and Dante turned his focus back to the shopkeeper. She leaned down to reveal even more cleavage while sucking on her Blow Pop with an increased sense of intense fellatio. Dante once again slowly approached her. Just as he mustered enough courage to greet the temptress, it was eradicated by the innocent.

"Dante, come here for a sec. I want to show you something. It's really cool," Sarita said enthusiastically. The shopkeeper didn't move, just continued to suck on her cherry Blow Pop. Dante slowly looked away and turned to Sarita with aggravation.

"What? What is it, Shorty? Can't you see I'm busy?"

Sarita bit down on her bottom lip as she held both of her hands together behind her back. She looked around and twisted her right foot into the wooden floor.

"Um, I'm sorry, but you really need to see this."

Just as Dante was about to respond, he noticed the stranger in his peripheral vision, standing a few feet to his right in the aisle. Dante once again became cautious.

"Can't you just tell me what it is?" Dante gazed between the points of the triangle: the shopkeeper, Sarita, and back at the stranger, who slowly edged closer towards him.

"Yeah, but it's better if you see it," Sarita pleaded. The stranger then walked right up beside Dante and cleared his throat.

"'Scuse me, sir," the stranger said in a deep Southern accent. Dante looked him up and down and then stepped to the side so that the man could get to the front counter.

"And what if I go over there and it's something I really don't wanna see?" Dante looked back at the stranger, who was asking the shopkeeper about the military memorabilia.

"I bet you a million dollars you'd like it."

The angel of sin stood up to look through an inventory book behind the counter, and the stranger turned around and watched Dante and Sarita suspiciously as he waited.

"Remember what I told you about making bets you can't afford, Shorty?" Dante looked away from the stranger who stared intensely while chewing on his gum.

"Um, yeah, but trust me."

"Hey, don't I know you, boy?" The stranger held his arms crossed across his chest. Dante slowly turned around, looked the stranger's unfit frame up and down, and then looked sternly into his eyes.

"Nah, sorry, you must be mistaking me for someone else." Dante turned back around, and Sarita looked around him at the stranger, who stepped towards Dante.

"Nah, I never forget a face, boy. I've seen you before, and that girl too," the stranger said confidently.

Dante turned around to find the stranger, who now stood a foot away from him. The stranger focused on Sarita's profile, then studied Dante's demeanor.

"Like I just said, you must have mistaken me for someone else." Dante turned around again, only to have the stranger grab his shoulder to turn him back around.

"Hey, don't turn your back on me, boy, I'm not done talking to y'all."

Dante clutched his fists. The stranger chewed his gum. "Yeah, you are him. That's what I thought." The stranger looked at Sarita. "And you's that border jumper's little girl whose been kidnapped by this anti-American boy here. I've seen y'all's faces on tha TV." The stranger then stepped closer to Dante to get around him to grab Sarita.

"Hey, man, what in the hell do you think you're doing? Just back the fuck off!" Just as Dante turned to square himself up between the stranger and Sarita, the stranger, who was now nose to nose with Dante, began to perform his gestapo tactics, preparing to make a citizen's arrest to protect the homeland.

"Y'all ain't going anywhere, boy. Y'all just wait here while I call tha police." The stranger tightly grabbed Dante's wrist while he reached into his pocket to get his cell phone.

"Hey, don't fucking touch me, man!" Dante removed the stranger's hand and pushed him away. Sarita stepped back and peeked around a shelf for protection. The shopkeeper turned around and then leaned forward on the countertop.

"Hey, hey! What in tha hell do you two think you're doing? Get the fuck outta my shop if you're gonna fight like little schoolboys! Take that shit outside!" The angel of sin's high, piercing voice rapidly rose to a crescendo as the stranger and Dante wrestled back and forth and then into an aisle, where they separated, and the stranger was able to punch Dante's left eye.

As the stranger swung a third time, Dante blocked it with his outstretched arm, turned his body to the right to rotate himself and the stranger 180 degrees and then pushed the stranger up against the shelf behind him, causing some trinkets to fall to the floor, along with clocks and mirrors that came crashing down to the floor on the other side.

Dante connected four punches to the stranger's face, breaking his nose, and then punched him twice in the gut. As the stranger bent over, sucking wind, Dante kneed him twice in the gut and then once in the head, causing the stranger to drop to the floor. The angel of sin rushed out from behind the counter to take matters into her own hands. Sarita screamed.

As the stranger lay unconscious, Dante bent down over him, holding his head up by the hair as he delivered his final blows to the stranger's bloody face. When the man was unconscious, Dante stood up, held his bloody hands together, and wiped blood from the cut above his left eye. Seconds later, he found himself unconsciously lying on top of the stranger.

The angel of sin, adorned in a pair of black leather knee-high military-style platform boots, stood silently above the unconscious bodies of Dante and the stranger with a blackjack in her hand. She observed them both emotionlessly, slightly tilting her head from side to side.

Sarita stepped up behind her. The angel of sin turned around and dropped to her knees to comfort Sarita, who was in tears, and choked up.

"Shh, shh, it's gonna be all right, sweetie. I'm gonna get us some help, okay?" She said softly as she ran her fingertips through Sarita's hair.

"What's gonna happen to us?"

"Nothing. Nothing at all, because I'm gonna take care of you, sweetie."

The angel of sin stood up and walked away. Sarita slowly stepped towards Dante and the stranger. She wiped away tears and tucked her hair back behind her ears.

The angel of sin returned. She came up behind Sarita and covered her mouth and nose with a chloroform-soaked rag. Sarita slipped away into unconsciousness and dropped to the floor beside Dante and the stranger.

The woman walked to the entrance door of the antique shop and locked it. Peeking outside, she turned the sign in the window over to read "Out to Lunch" and then closed the blinds. She walked back behind the front counter.

As she leaned forward on the countertop, seductively observing the three unconscious bodies lying on the floor with a slight smile, she took out her pink-and-black leopard-patterned cell phone and dialed a number. The phone rang numerous times before there was a voice on the other line.

"Pooh Bear, it's Jezebel. I have a couple of sheeple ova here, and . . . and a butterfly . . . Nah, you don't have to do anything, they're already unconscious . . . . I'll explain later, just get your ass ova here, now."

As the sunlight shined in through the blinds, there was a knock on the door. The angel of sin peeked through the blinds and then slowly opened up the door for Pooh Bear.

"Goddamn, Bonnie. I told you never to call me during tha day. This better be a good catch!"

Pooh Bear turned to look at Bonnie. He had the appearance of a biker, about six feet tall, well-toned, with dirty brown shoulder-length hair and a handlebar mustache, complemented with facial scruff. He was dressed in biker boots, tight jeans with a wallet chain, and a tight, faded green graphic tee, and both of his arms were painted with tattoos.

"Hey, fuck you, Ronnie. I'm doing you a fava ova here, okay? Goddamn!"

Bonnie shut the door, locked it and turned around.

"How many times have I told you don't talk down to me? Fuck! Now, where they at!"

"Fuck you, they're ova here!" Bonnie guided Ronnie toward their prey.

Bonnie and Ronnie stood side by side, she with both of her hands on her hips, he with both of his arms crossed, observing Dante, the stranger and Sarita.

"So, what happened?"

"Those two came in, looked around for a little bit, and then that one came in and asked me to look up some prices for him. As I was doing that, he told tha otha two that he knew them. He said he recognized them on tha TV or something. Whateva, I don't watch tha TV, but after that, those two started fighting. That one knocked that one out, and then I knocked that one out. After that, I knocked out the little butterfly. Did you see anything on tha TV, Ronnie?"

"Nope."

"Well, anyways, tha sheeple are mine, I can definitely use them. In fact, I can use them now. So, you gonna help me bring them down?"

"Fuck, Bonnie, and what about me, huh? What, I'm only here to do y'all's dirty work!"

"Fuck, Ronnie, no! I was gonna see if ya wanna join in, huh?" Bonnie caressed Pooh Bear's chest and slowly slid her hand down and grabbed his bulging crotch as she spoke. Ronnie pushed her hand away and turned towards her.

"Not now. As for the butterfly, I can bring her over to Ducky. He'll be able to use her."

"Ducky, that sick fuck. Goddamn, Ronnie, you so selfish!"

"Fuck, Bonnie, y'all wanna make this shit happen?"

"Yeah!"

"Well, then, shut tha fuck up and let's get moving."

Pooh Bear stepped forward and began to move Dante's unconscious body off the stranger. As he did, Bonnie walked over towards the entrance door, peeked out the blinds, closed them completely, and shut off the lights, and then there was darkness.

~Addendum~

The road to all you desire isn't paved easily; you must first go through hell . . .

66

The secret gulag was dark, damp, musty and only dimly lit around the perimeter. Surrounding the empty vastness were candles of various shapes and sizes, laid out on the ground, kept on candlesticks and wall shelves, corroded over with dried candlewax, along with a ceiling light creating a circular illumination of light in the center. There was also a cold draft blowing in through the cracks of the stone walls as water dripped down from an old, rusty pipe.

Dante regained consciousness and opened his eyes, only to be blinded by a black blindfold. He couldn't see, but he could feel his imprisonment. In the likeness of cattle hanging down from the ceiling in a slaughterhouse, slowly swaying from side to side, in the nude, as Dante stretched up with his fingertips, he could feel the extended chain hanging down from the ceiling, along with the leather cuffs digging into the flesh of his ankles and wrists. He felt the cold, concrete floor under his toes and could hear that he was not alone.

As loud industrial rock music resonated, loud smacks of flesh hitting flesh could be heard, along with agonizing cries. Tears dropped down to the floor, along with drops of blood. The stranger looked at his reflection in the high French mirror as Bonnie fucked him in the ass with a big black forearm-thick, eighteen-inch strap-on. He stood bent over a horse bench with his arms strapped down, each thrust causing him to bite into the pony-bite gag he wore.

"Yeah, you like that big black dick in your ass, don't ya, ya fucking hairy-ass pig? Ya fucking honky-tonk dick-in-tha-ass mothafucker. Ya, Mama likes how you sweat so good. C'mon, ya fucking hillbilly. C'mon, let me hear ya beg for more. Tell Mama ya like it. C'mon, let me hear ya. I wanna hear ya scream for more, big daddy!" Bonnie yelled psychotically as she rapidly penetrated the stranger's tight, hairy anus like a rabid dog in heat. The stranger's fingernails dug deep into the horse bench as he cried out for her to stop.

After Bonnie pulled out half of the big black strap-on from the stranger's swollen anus, blood seeped out his asshole and dripped off the tip of the strap-on. She stood before a table filled with various sexual torture devices as the stranger watched with tears in his eyes.

At the sound of all the horrors happening beside him, Dante began to squirm around like a hopeless fly trapped in a spider's web. He pulled down on the chain connected to the leather cuffs with all his body weight, trying to loosen the bolts from the support brackets attached to the ceiling.

As the bloodstained strap-on lay on the floor in front of the stranger, Bonnie stood behind him. He stared at the reflection of the fetish queen, who stood with both legs spread apart. She wore knee-high black leather platform boots and a black garter belt which rose up further to a perfectly proportioned round apple ass. A pair of leather panties hugged her tight ass, which curved out around and back into the thin hips of a perfectly proportioned hourglass figure. Left exposed was the flesh of the lower back, which curved up into the bottom of a tight black leather corset, with black leather laces looped in and out of the back, the center of the corset tightly hugging the hourglass frame up to the bare shoulders, where the leather laces were tightly knotted together. Just above the pair of bare shoulders were tips of jet-black hair.

Bonnie now held in her hand a wooden paddle lined with rows of metal studs. As she took two long, slow wind-up swings, bringing the surface of the paddle close enough to the stranger's bare white hairy pimple-laced ass that he could get a little taste of things to come, he whimpered. Like an initiation into a fraternal order of secrecy, the first whack was only a love tap, causing the stranger to bite down on the pony bite gag, but every following whack, with three-second intervals in between, became more intense than the last.

"Yeah, yeah, you like that, you dirty little pig, yeah! C'mon, tell Mama you like it, tell Mama you like it, you little whore, you fucking pig whore! Let me hear ya beg for more, fucking cry out for Mama, you fucking pig face!" Bonnie yelled with an exasperated, erotic sense of superiority.

As the stranger panted like a dying dog, Dante continued to squirm around and pull down on the chain to loosen the bolts from the support brackets attached to the ceiling even more. Bonnie then removed the blood-and-pimple-pus-stained paddle from the stranger's aching red ass and walked back to the table to put it away and pick up another instrument of erotic sin used for pleasure and pain.

When Bonnie returned, she stood behind the stranger once again, rolling a rounded metal pig tail anal plug in the palm of her hand. She still wanted more, to fill in the void within her empty heart of black and gray, with control. Bonnie reached out and grabbed the stranger's left shoulder tightly as she stepped closer and shoved the anal plug up into his tight anus, twisting it.

"That's right, piggy, squeal. Squeal for Mama! Fucking squeal some more! Yeah, that's right, that's right, piggy. You like it in that ass, you fucking pig face, fucking pig whore! Piggy, piggy, pig, oink, oink, oink. Squeal some more, piggy, squeal! Fucking squeal louder, piggy!"

Blood slowly seeped out of the stranger's sodomized anus down the pig tail of the anal plug and the crack of his bloody, swollen, hairy ass. With his eyes closed, he continued to bite down on the pony bite gag and sob. At last, he passed out, lying limp over the horse bench, condemned like Jesus Christ before his crucifixion.

As Dante hung down blind and sedated, he heard multiple metal door locks being unbolted, an array of keys jingling, unlocking maglocks and unhinging of metal padlock plates, and then the opening of an industrial-sized metal door.

Then there were the bootheels stomping on the concrete floor in the likeness of a Nazi storm trooper, followed by an unrecognizable array of subtle mechanical movements and sounds—the grinding of metal being dragged across the floor, metal or some kind of heavy objects being put together and moved around, metal chains and a continuous annoyance of clicking sounds. Soon after, there was silence, which then faded into the irritating squeaking of rusty wheels, with one limp wheel being dragged and rattled around as some sort of pushcart was being pushed.

The fetish queen stood before Dante. Beside her was a pushcart with a white cloth draped over a variety of objects of different shapes and sizes. Bonnie slowly caressed her hand over the cloth and then removed it to reveal a variety of instruments of erotic sin and nightmarish medical utensils.

As loud industrial rock music came on, Bonnie began to caress Dante's cheeks, neck, chest, stomach, and ass and then fondle his genitals. All that Dante felt was then complemented by Bonnie's full, lush lips kissing Dante's cheeks, down to his neck, his chest and nipples, with teeth, all the way down his torso, and then back up again. She ended with a lingering, luscious kiss on Dante's lips, which she extended and savored as she slowly pulled back, sucking on Dante's bottom lip, pulling and stretching it out between her lips until finally separating, leaving a strand of saliva. From behind the darkness of the blindfold, Dante's blind sense of arousing discomfort was then overshadowed by multiple, open-hand slaps across the face, followed by stinging slaps from multiple straps of a bull hide flogger slapping against his bare chest, back and ass, leaving red marks all over his body.

Bonnie brought the edge of a surgical scalpel towards Dante's cheek and slowly and gently grazed the edge of the blade down along the flesh of his throat, to his bare chest, down to his stomach, and then further down to his genitals. Cold sweat began to drip down from Dante's forehead. He shivered until Bonnie removed the blade, and then he began to squirm around and pull down with all of his body weight on the chain, trying to loosen the bolts from the support brackets attached to the ceiling once again.

Clothespins were then applied onto each of Dante's nipples. He began to squirm around even more, but stopped when hot candlewax dripped onto his chest, slowly oozing down to his stomach and eventually hardening.

"Fuck you . . . you sick fuck!"

Bonnie slowly wiped away her facial of Dante's saliva with her fingertips and then licked it all away. She then stepped away and returned to tightly hold Dante's throat with one hand while slowly grazing the razor-sharp edge of a straight razor along his cheeks, and then down to his exposed throat. As much as Dante wanted to confront her once again, he knew that his silence was now better. He needed to be mentally and physically strong.

All sense of contemplation became overshadowed by the sharp paper-cut-sized incisions Bonnie cut into his neck. Dante began to breathe heavily and speak obscenities while Bonnie sucked on the blood oozing out. Soon after, Dante screamed as Bonnie rubbed peroxide-soaked gauze along the incisions on his neck.

Bonnie dropped down to her knees, causing Dante to squirm around once again. He pulled down even harder on the chain and felt the support brackets give away slightly as Bonnie began to give him a blow job. Even though Dante was being pleasured and aroused, he instantly stopped resisting when he felt sharp teeth begin to slowly graze around the soft, sensitive flesh of his cock, reminding him of who was in control. When Dante became fully aroused, Bonnie put a rubber band around his genitals and began to slowly graze the flat side of the razor along his manhood.

When Bonnie leaned back and removed her mouth from around Dante's dick, along with the razor, to catch her breath, Dante decided to take advantage of the small window of opportunity. With all his strength, he quickly pulled up his knees, kneeing her in the chin. Bonnie bit down on her tongue and dropped the straight-edge razor. As she sat on her knees with a mouth full of blood, Dante reached out with his legs and wrapped Bonnie's head between his knees, pulling her in closer. Bonnie began to gag for a breath of air as she tried to pull Dante's legs apart. She slapped Dante's stomach, only provoking him to squeeze even harder. Bonnie tried to pull Dante's legs apart, but she couldn't breathe. Dante then snapped her neck.

When Dante realized that Bonnie was dead, he released her head from his legs and felt her lifeless body slide down onto the floor. Dante then pulled down on the chain with all his strength, until eventually, the bolts holding the support brackets to the ceiling detached, freeing him. As he lay beside Bonnie's lifeless body, he removed the blindfold and the clothespins. At first it was just a blur, but after he opened his eyes, he was able to clearly see the secret gulag. He unbuckled the leather cuffs from his wrists and ankles.

Before attempting an escape, Dante grabbed his clothes from the floor and put them on. His attention was then focused on the bloody, condemned, unconscious body of the stranger. Dante unstrapped the unconscious stranger from the horse bench. After seeing that Sarita wasn't present, he turned to leave.

Just as he was about to walk out, he noticed film production equipment beside the door. There was a desk with a computer on top of it, and on either side of the desk were tripods with digital cameras. As Dante slowly walked past the equipment, the final minute of NIN's "Closer" played. Dante also observed the live webcam feed of himself and the secret gulag scene on the computer screen. He looked at each camera and then, in a fury, smashed the computer and the cameras. There was then complete silence after pieces of the film production equipment shattered throughout the dimness.

Dante stumbled up the stairs and then through the antique shop. Even though Dante was now free from his state of bondage, he was filled with a numbing sense of fear for the unknown. Sarita was nowhere to be found, and Dante was left with no clues as to where she might be. Even worse were his worries for Sarita's safety and how the horrific scene left behind was a reflection of what state of bondage Sarita might be in. As Dante left with his and Sarita's bags, hell's bells rang one last time.

67

As a spider crept in front of Sarita's shoes, she pulled her feet back. Thick rope was wrapped around Sarita's ankles and up her shins. Her knees and thighs were pressed together as she sat in a chair. Her wrists were bound to the arms of the wooden chair with more rope. Like so many missing children held captive, Sarita had been taken within the darkness of an underground subculture, controlled and conducted by some of the most heartless and soulless individuals in the world—all part of a sadistic branch of Nada Mas.

Sarita awaited her fate with a red rubber ball gag stuffed into her mouth as she looked deep into the eyes of evil. The darkness she could see in his eyes was a reflection of his character. Even the big dark bags and wrinkles underneath his eyes revealed a glimpse of his true nature. There was also the skull-and-bones buckle of his leather belt, which wrapped around his expanding waist line. The hairs on the forearms, which were held crossed against his chest, resting on top of his belly, were gray, while his stubby fingers were adorned with silver rings. He had a tattoo of Donald Duck on his flabby tricep, and full lush lips that hid within the black-and-gray hairs of his beard as he chewed tobacco. In the eyes of the innocent, his presence could be seen as a reflection of a malevolent Santa Claus, but in the eyes of his associates, he was known as Ducky.

The darkness in Ducky's eyes reflected the cold blood that pumped from his black heart and flowed throughout his soulless vessel of gluttonous degradation. He didn't give a damn about the families of the innocent or the children who were the victims of the dehumanizing and evil acts of exploitation that he personally conducted and controlled.

"So, whaddya think? Should we call tha Rev?" Pooh Bear asked. Ducky continued to silently observe Sarita while chewing his tobacco and then spat a wad onto the concrete floor.

"Yep."

"All right, but remember, he ain't that easy to negotiate wit."

There was a moment of silence. Ducky's contemplative state was part of his wicked aura of visualizing the horrific acts of evil he would conduct. Before negotiating with the Rev, it was a necessity, since the Rev had been dehumanizing and exploiting innocent children well before Ducky or Pooh Bear were even born. The Rev was not only one of the evilest sons of bitches in the underworld, but he was also one of the most successful in using and selling innocent children for slave labor, prostitution, and child pornography. He was a prolific asset within the pedophilia rings connected to Nada Mas.

"Yep." Ducky spat out another wad of tobacco after breaking the silence. "But before we negotiate, let's make her a star first. Betta go git tha spider boy."

"Tha spider boy?" Pooh Bear said with a sense of fear.

"Yep," Ducky said with malice burning deep within his eyes, then spat another wad of tobacco down onto the floor.

"Now?" Pooh Bear asked as he turned towards Ducky.

"Nah, not yit."

Sarita trembled as she watched Ducky spit out another wad of tobacco. She closed her eyes. The horror of what Ducky and Pooh Bear might do to her filled her mind, but what was even more frightening was that she might never see Dante or her mother ever again.

68

Overcast clouds slowly drifted across the darkness of a cold and dreary midsummer's night. FBI Special Agent Alec D. Donovan silently sat inside an unmarked black SUV that was parked across the street from the Clearview apartment complex. He was tightly holding and looking at Sarita's multicolored friendship bracelet. Donovan's focus was like that of a physicist who slowly paced around in figure eights, lost in deep thought, unfazed by the world around. Even as drops of rain began to slowly rain down, rhythmically splattering down on the hood, roof and windshield of the SUV until they eventually sped up to a downpour, Donovan's eyes remained fixed on Sarita's bracelet. The bracelet was a reminder of the separation of souls, and all the challenging and enigmatic scenarios Donovan had been involved with throughout the years. Although on the surface of everything slowly unfolding, there seemed to be a façade of doubt and failure, Donovan would remain strong and stay focused on what his next move would be. His concentration was interrupted by Agent Walsh, who opened up the passenger-side door and quickly got in.

As Walsh sat down and closed the door, Donovan put Sarita's multicolored bracelet back into his pocket. Walsh, who was soaked from head to toe, shivered as he handed Donovan a cup of coffee.

"Here's your coffee, black with five sugars, and your turkey, ham, and Swiss sub," he said, reaching into a plastic bag.

"You told them to hold the onions, I hope, right?"

"Yep, hold the onions, and add extra turkey and ham."

"Good, good." Donovan finished unwrapping his sub and began to eat while Walsh took out his sandwich and lottery scratch-offs, which he handed to Donovan.

"And, some scratch-offs."

"Mmm, nice . . . let's hope we win this time," Donovan said while watching Walsh take out and unwrap his sandwich, which he then began to eat. "So, what you got there, Walsh?"

"Tuna salad."

"You on a diet, Walsh?"

"Nah, I've just always liked tuna fish since I was a kid, that's all. Anyway, listen to this."

Donovan continued to eat his sub ravenously, causing excess to fall down onto his lap while he tried to simultaneously scratch the scratch-off that was leaning on the steering wheel and listen to Walsh speak.

"When I was paying for everything in the convenience store, I was talking with the guy ringing me up. He said he saw the suspect with the girl the day before they disappeared. He said he came in with her to buy some food, and that it was odd seeing him with the girl, since he's never seen him with the girl or the mother before, and that the girl usually comes in with the mother or alone. This guy said that the suspect didn't seem threatening, that he was nice with the girl, he offered to buy her whatever she wanted, and even ended up buying her some candy. He said the girl didn't seem scared or threatened at all."

"Well, I suppose that our boy, Dante, was very sweet and nice with the girl, but that's probably because he was in a public place, ya know, with people around, watching. He's gotta put on a good show . . . dammit! Goddammit, I needed one more to get the fifty thousand dollars!" Donovan tore up the scratch-offs, which he handed over to Walsh. "Next time you get scratch-offs, Walsh, don't get the shitty leftover holiday ones. Ya gotta get the five-dollar win-for-life ones. Stop getting cheap with me. These dollar scratch-offs won't win you jack shit. Anyway, where was I?" Donovan took out a cigarette, lit it up and began to smoke while eating the rest of his sub and sipping his coffee.

"Dante being in the convenience store with the girl the day he abducted her."

"Yeah, well, like I was saying, there's more to this guy. He's smart, and has to be connected to something big. There's no reason for him to just take the girl, just because. We gotta find more people who know the guy and get more intel on him. And as soon as we hear back from ICE and get more intel on the mother, find out where she is, the dots will start connecting between Dante and the mother, and we'll start to get a clearer picture of everything unfolding. Hey, Walsh, what are you doing? Shut the damn window, it's drafty in here. You want me to catch a cold or something!"

Walsh coughed. "Sorry, Donovan, but it's too stuffy in here. As far as witnesses go, no one in that building knows anything about Dante or the mother, and I'm still looking for more people in the New York art scene who may know this guy personally. Hopefully someone shows up tonight to try and contact him."

"Let's hope so, Walsh. Ya know, that's why we're here." Donovan focused on the Clearview apartment complex while smoking. "That crazy fucking landlord has been standing in that window all day and night, smoking cigarettes and watching us, and look, there's the other two. They're staking us out like we're the suspects. What a piece of work those three are."

Walsh leaned in closer towards Donovan to look out the driver-side window. After seeing a silhouette of the three brujas in the windows, all on their phones, Walsh leaned back and opened up a bag of Swedish Fish.

"Want one?"

"What are those?"

"Swedish Fish."

"Nah, I'll pass."

Walsh turned on the radio and scanned through various stations until finding a song, provoking him to turn up the volume.

"All right, nice." Walsh bobbed his head back and forth with the rhythm of the song. Donovan, who was unamused, quickly removed the cup of coffee from his lips, put it down, and then reached out to turn off the radio, which was blasting N.W.A.'s "Fuck Tha Police."

"What the hell are you doing, Walsh? Shut that shit off, it's irritating my ears!"

"N.W.A. is classic rap," Walsh said in an attempt to sound hip.

"You call that music," Donovan said, blindly degrading the music he knew nothing about.

"Well, it's not bad."

"Not bad? You kiddin' me? Anything is better than that crap you call music. Next time I'll bring my CCR tapes and play some real music for you. Anyway, Smitty, you there?" Donovan said into his radio.

"Yep, still up here hanging out in the stairwell," Smitty said sarcastically.

"Any activity up there yet?"

"Negative, it's been quiet for the past two hours. How about you guys, anything happening out there?"

"Negative, same thing out here, all's clear. I think we're gonna call it a night. Smitty, why don't you get down here so we can get outta here?"

"All right, Donovan, sounds good, I'll be right down."

"Okay, Smitty, over and out." Donovan contemplated his next move, while Walsh played with his cell phone apps.

"Did you fart, Walsh?" Donovan winced in disgust as he turned towards Walsh, who hesitated and fumbled around with his cell phone.

"Um, I, I think so," Walsh said nervously.

"What do you mean, you think so? It sure as hell wasn't me, or Casper back there."

"Um, sorry, I couldn't hold it in," Walsh said innocently.

Donovan didn't say a word. He just turned his head, took a drag from his cigarette, and then opened up his window to vent out the SUV and let in some fresh air.

69

Watching Sarita on her own, running around the playground with other children, playing tag, racing across the monkey bars, and whooshing down the spiral slide, was comforting. The acts of conceiving, giving birth, nourishing and raising a child were magical; to push them out into the world and watch them cope, adapt and evolve on their own was fulfilling. Letting go was true love, and following everything Gabriela had been through since coming from Mexico, to witness pure benevolence, and the unprejudiced bonding between such a diverse group of children playing together, brought a sense of peace. There seemed to be no sense of direction visible in the eyes of the innocent, but while the children continued to frolic throughout the park, everything that Gabriela had created, guided, helped grow, and watched flourish and evolve into a butterfly soon came before her.

"Mama, Mama!" Sarita called out. The energetic five-year-old with pigtails, dirty knees and scraped-up limbs, wearing a purple-and-blue flowered dress, leaped into Gabriela's open arms.

"Aw, *mi amor*," Gabriela said with a smile, while sitting on a bench.

"Did you see? Did you see me go? Tree, tree times, tree times I went across the monkey bars!" Sarita said excitedly as she looked around, swaying her hips from side to side and twisting her foot into the ground.

"Yes, *mi amor*, I saw everything you did with the other children. I'm so proud of you" Gabriela tucked loose strands of Sarita's hair back behind her ears.

"Mama, could you come with me to the swing so that you could push me again?" Sarita reached out and grabbed Gabriela's hand.

"Okay, okay, *mi amor*, let's go. One more time before we go home."

Gabriela stood up and began to follow Sarita towards the swing set while holding her hand. Gabriela lifted Sarita up onto the swing and began to push her. The power behind each push was gentle but gradually built up as Sarita ardently called out for Gabriela to push her higher and higher. As Sarita reached up towards the sky with her outstretched legs, Gabriela was filled with adoration. It was the little things in life that Gabriela, appreciated and cherished most. And although the moment wouldn't last forever, it would become an everlasting memory, frozen in time, a place to someday go and hide.

But even though everything seemed so peaceful and perfect, at that moment, it was just a dream, an escape from the horrors of the present. The beautiful light from the heavens above shined down upon Gabriela, blinding her with revelation. Everything that once was soon vanished and withered away, leaving behind echoes of Sarita's soothing voice, subtly fading away in the distance...

# # #

All there was now was bittersweet silence as Gabriela lay limp on the bed. She gazed up at the ceiling and focused on a beam of sunlight that shined in through the window and stretched across the room. In the likeness of Frida Kahlo, Gabriela was confined to a bed, left alone with her thoughts. Unfortunately, though, all that was being painted in her mind didn't last forever. Heartening dreams were now gone, but after reflecting on the good in her life, Gabriela found what little strength she had left to get up and creep out of the bedroom.

She staggered into the dining room to join her tía and tío for breakfast. Unsure how to greet Gabriela, Tío Emilio silently ate his atole while Tía Rosa poured Gabriela a mug of her own, which she then gave her along with some pan and chilachiles. Still Gabriela didn't move or react. She remained silent as she gazed down through her hair and focused on the creamy cinnamon-laced atole while her tía and tío looked at each other for answers. Tío Emilio eventually found the courage to confront Gabriela.

"Good morning, Gaby, how are you? Did you sleep well?"

Gabriela remained unresponsive.

"It's okay, sobrina, it's okay. You don't have to talk now, we understand, but try to eat some food. You need to eat something. It will make you feel much better, especially the atole, which I know you love," Tía Rosa added kindly.

Though Gabriela remained silent, Tía Rosa's cunning words were able to magically spark some life back into her. She began to eat her atole with a spoon, dip some pan into it, look up and speak with a slight smile.

"It's good." Gabriela didn't say much. She just needed more time to heal the wounds. Her smile had quickly vanished, but Tía Rosa and Tío Emilio wouldn't give up on their niece, who was like a daughter to them. The three continued to eat in silence. After allowing enough time to pass for Gabriela to settle in more and become more relaxed, Tío Emilio questioned Gabriela's future ambitions.

"So, have you decided what you want to do yet?"

Gabriela remained silent while she looked down and ate. "What do you mean?" She finally asked.

Tío Emilio and Tía Rosa stopped eating, looked at each other, and then turned to study Gabriela's daunting demeanor.

"If you want to go back home to Tehuacán—" Tío Emilio started.

"No! No, I don't want to go back home to Tehuacán! I want to stay here and be as close to Sarita as I can be!" As Gabriela's motherly wrath erupted, she looked up at her tía and tío, who were stunned by her juvenile tone. Gabriela looked back down and continued to eat. Knowing how hurt and confused Gabriela must be, Emilio decided to leave it for now.

There seemed to be no sense of closure, so all three continued to eat in unsettling silence. As time ticked away, Gabriela watched as spoonfuls of atole were repetitively scooped up and dripped down into her mug and Emilio and Rosa finished their breakfast. Emilio and Rosa cleared away their dishes, gave Gabriela a kiss on the forehead and their blessings—as she remained sedate— and departed for the day.

As Gabriela sat alone, Sarita occupied her mind. She found the strength to lift her head, eat and look out across the table. She imagined Sarita sitting at the table with her. It was an enduring cure Gabriela needed to momentarily fuel her to carry on until the day they meet again. Once Gabriela finished, Sarita's image faded away. Gabriela was left alone, once again. After clearing the table, Gabriela would spend the remainder of the day confined to her bed in the likeness of Frida Kahlo, devoted to the power of prayer and hidden away in her dreams.

<u>70</u>

Although the night was filled with mystifying dreams, Gabriela woke again without Sarita by her side. Instead only a pillow lay tightly clutched within her arms. As haunting as it seemed to be, this time Gabriela wouldn't lay limp. She would rise up and find the strength to shed the pain in order to continue with her life and all that lay ahead. Like a newborn, the first few steps out of bed was a struggle, but once the light of day illuminated Gabriela with warmth and rejuvenation, she stood tall and steadily walked into the dining room, towards the uplifting scent of atole, pan, chilachilas, and warm tortillas left on the table. There was also a note leaning up against a vase filled with flowers.

Gaby,

    Good morning, sobrina, we hope you slept well last night. We had to get up early today for work, so we will not be able to join you for breakfast. Don't worry, though, because we didn't forget about you. We made your favorite, so enjoy. After you eat, try to keep busy today, no more bed. Try to stay active—it's good for the mind. There's a lot to be done around the house, so feel free to do some work, such as clean the dishes, clean the floors, clean all the furniture and organize things around the house, and you could try to bring life back to the garden, which hasn't had much since you left long ago.

    Also, there's a little surprise waiting for you in the bedroom. There's an old trunk filled with all your old belongings you left behind when you went to America. There's a lot inside to go through, and some old treasures which may spark some more life back into you. For now, enjoy your breakfast and enjoy your day. And remember, God is always with you, no matter how misguided your life has been. Take care, many blessings and we'll see you tonight.

Mucho besos

Tío Emilio y Tía Rosa

Gabriela smiled. She felt warm. And although it was exhausting to clean, dust and organize each room, it helped her to refresh her mind. An array of memories resurfaced. Gabriela felt revived going from room to room. But it was Gabriela's bedroom that would be filled with some of her fondest memories.

It was here where she would lie in bed every night, dreaming of a better life. At the time, the idea of going to America, living a good life and having her own family had seemed impossible. But being back in the same room again after so many years had gone by, even without living the life she'd imagined in America, she felt stronger, wiser and more spiritually fulfilled. Especially after opening the old decrepit trunk and looking through all her old possessions that she had left behind.

Inside the trunk were all of her clothes, dresses and handcrafts made by Mexican artisans, photographs of her and family from her childhood, and her old flute, which she would sometimes play in the garden alone or with her uncle, who sometimes joined her with his guitar. There were also her favorite books to read. Tucked away at the base of the trunk was her old brown leather-bound journal, which she had forgotten to bring with her to America.

The journal dated back to the time when Gabriela was living in Tehuacán with her mother and brother. It was worn out, but inside, scribed all over the creased pages, was life. Gabriela scanned through the pages filled with her deepest thoughts and feelings from her teenage years. She felt a sudden convergence of mixed emotions forming. She could remember being young, and the days when she was foolish and in love, innocent and naïve, yet had sinned and dreamed of leaving behind a little world filled with misfortune and pain in order to take on the unknown. Even though Gabriela's fearless quest had brought her back to her past, there were no regrets, not even when she looked back into the shadows of the past.

# # #

Tommy Tutalo

~All That's Left of Me~

Even after all the love I gave, he left me, and all I now have as I sit here all alone are the stars, the moon and the heavens, which look down upon me. I lay back here in tears, dreaming of the day when I can leave it all behind. Maybe I'll find love once again, or even the one who could mend my broken heart and take me away to a better place. And no matter how daunting this life may seem, somehow there always seems to be some way out of the darkness, an escape found deep within the little things in life. A simplistic reminder of how something so small and simple could freeze all of time and wash away the pain. Like the little things I saw at the market today, such as a little girl's smile, laughter, or even a simple kiss, which brought back life in my heart, giving me hope and reason to live and move on, so far away, that somewhere beyond the deserts, there is a better life that awaits me."

After Gabriela read bits and pieces of a passage from her past, she closed the journal and held it close to her heart. Inside were the memories, the fuel that had once inspired Gabriela, and now it was her amulet to continue on.

<u>71</u>

Café Solano was an eccentric little nook; an artist's retreat, a cozy setting for friends, lovers and all those who just wanted to get away and be alone while in the company of others. The atmosphere was filled with electrifying Spanish *guitarra* riffs and hypnotic vocals from a musician's heart and soul, an abstract array of voices, laughter and even applause. For Gabriela, it was a sanctuary to go to and get away from her tribulations.

Gabriela was like a ghost in the crowd, seeking redemption without distraction. She sat in the back of the café, sedated and unfazed by all the excitement while sipping her cup of coffee and browsing through her journal. Inside the journal, Gabriela found solace and a reason to move on with her life. It was as she looked into the pages of everything that once was that Gabriela would be able to relive the moments that had changed her and her life forever.

~New Beginnings~

Starting over from a seed of doubt at first seemed to be so foolish and unfulfilling, but now, on an open road taking me to an unknown destination, it's easier to see beyond the deserts and the infinite horizon where the sun no longer sets but rises. It illuminates my path ahead, where I leave behind my shedded skin of miseries and misfortunes and sprout my wings of hope and desire. All that I lost is now my strength, and all that I leave behind is now my inspiration. When I blend the two together from within my heart, I strive and rebuild from the tainted seed of doubt, a tree of life. Even within the deserts of the unknown, I will somehow find a way to pick up the pieces and grow. Where I go from here, I will leave up to God, but I know that even though I can't see the road ahead or what the future holds, I will be ready. I'm in control of my fate and take with me no more hate, but love, hope, and faith.

~Mi Casa Nueva~

At first everything seemed so strange, but like my father and my first love, Tío Emilio had a very welcoming presence, and he's also a musician, but more modest. And even though he is quiet, a man of few words, when he does speak, he has a compelling way of intriguing and inspiring those he speaks to. His words somehow fill the heart with love and devotion and stimulate the mind in a provoking manner, leaving you in wonder, and like rain, his words feed the mind, which grows into a euphoria of enlightenment.

He treats me like the daughter he's never had, always caring, catering to, teaching and guiding me in the right direction. For an uncle I've only known from pictures and stories I've been told, each day he tries to make up as much lost time as he can, and he does it with such grace and understanding, giving me the space I need and want, yet always leaving me wanting to come back to him for more—more company, more comfort and more wisdom. I don't know what the future holds for me, and I'm not sure what each day will bring, but for now, I know that he is my male counterpart, the balance to my feminine obscurities and misleading intentions. He keeps me in line, yet lets me go out into the world all alone, to discover not what's out there, but what's in here, hidden and lost in my heart.

And even though leaving Mamá behind was the hardest thing to do, there are no regrets, because there was a strong understanding between the two of us that it was the right thing to do. She understood that I was young and ambitious, someone who always had big dreams to go out into the world and conquer whatever feats awaited me. Our love is strong because of the trust and respect we have for each other, and the understanding that no matter how far away we are from each other, or how long we are separated from each other, we will never forget each other and will always take what we learned from each other to make us stronger and help us in life and the many paths we take separately. As for Tía Rosa, my mama's sister, she will never replace Mamá, but she has been like another mother to me. *Everything I left, I now have, the love, the way of life, the bonding, and the support and respect for me and the life I choose.*

Although I no longer have the peaceful, secluded mountains of Oaxaca to get away to, or the familiar city of Tehuacán, where I have all of my closest family and friends to spend time with, I now have my new family and my new home. I'm now in the north, Sonora State, which is filled with so many people, yet I am all alone in a sea of faces. Although I'm here to start over, experience life, and find my calling and path in life, I'm also here to look for work. At first finding work was difficult, but my tía helped me get a job in a small sewing factory.

Although it's not a life I've ever imagined, I am grateful to have this job and the money I make from it, and even though it's not much, I know that in time, I will save my wages and spend my money wisely and move on to bigger and better things. I still dream of going beyond the deserts to America. I don't know how or when, but I know I'm destined to be there. This is only a stopping point, a place where each day is spent working in the factory and enjoying the company of my tía and tío, especially playing music in the garden with my uncle and spending time with the few neighbors who I consider friends.

But what I like about each day is the free time I spend alone, endlessly wandering the city streets and getting lost in the vast markets. My favorite place to be is Café Solano, a little place where I can relax, listen to good music, enjoy good food, and drift away in my thoughts, which I spend a lot of time doing, always putting my deepest feelings into my journal. I imagine, I dream of a better life, and no matter how many times my past comes back to haunt me, I'm always able to see the light in the darkness that was meant to bring me here, to live a different way and guide me so far away.

~Fabiola Flores~

Since I've known Fabiola from Tehuacán, she's always been like night and day. Every time I was with her, I never knew who I was with. One moment, she was my best friend, and then in another moment, she suddenly changed into my most hated enemy. Sometimes she's a saint, sometimes she's a sinner, posing as both a whore and the Virgin Mary, someone who constantly lies and *exaggerates, yet always speaks the truth and says what's on her mind.*

She's a fearless girl, willing to say or do whatever it takes to be on top, succeed and get what she wants in life. She is unique and wise, in the most unconventional way, a friend who shares the same dream as me, America. She wants in just as much as I, except she knows the right people to get there and has the right personality to survive on her own. I'm still living in a crack, little shell of comfort, and I feel that Fabiola brings out the lion in me, that courageous, fearless attitude I need to get into America and survive.

Although I don't accept or agree with the lifestyle she's lived, the truth is that since I've known her, I've learned so much from her: how she used to use teachers and students to benefit herself in our school days, and how she would run away from home and spend days alone in the streets. She always found ways to make money and buy food. That's how I've learned how to live in the streets all alone, and how to use people and get what I want and what I need. And although I don't agree with all her methods she has taught me, I've become somewhat of a female hustler like her. I lack her experience, of course, but I've become someone who doesn't seem to be that modest book-smart girl from Tehuacán but someone who is now free from her shell of captivity and fear and has blossomed into a streetwise butterfly, like a bandida on the open deserts.

I've learned the art of lying, stealing and using others for self-gain, yet staying morally pure and true to my heart and God. A sinner, yes, but forever a saint, doing what's necessary to reach my dream in order to benefit my family and friends. All I do is in the service of others. Fabiola is blinded by excess and materialism. She has helped me awaken and grow into a stronger person in order to live and survive in this place called hell. To Fabiola, I am her guardian, and savior, someone who has found and exposed her weaknesses and teaches her about modesty and the importance of family, love and devotion, and being true to your heart, that it's okay not to constantly wear a mask, because all the mask is is a façade to hide all the fear, the darkness behind the blinding mask. It's when removing the mask that the light shines through, exposing truth, love and happiness, all of which she needs, and I provide them for my ticket into America.

72

The touch of her skin was transcending, and the taste of her lips was moist with life. But it was her innocence that infused Dante with an energetic uprising. As Dante kissed, gently caressed and groped Lola Notta's perky round breasts and body while removing her clothes, there was a static sense of forbidden bliss felt all around. After Dante removed all of Lola's clothes and finished warming up her untainted body, the two lovers now sat on the edge of the bed and gazed deep into each other's eyes.

"Um, it's—it's my first time. Are you sure it's going to be okay? I mean for you, ya know, what we've spoken about?"

"Don't worry. Age is just a number, and we can't allow fear to control our lives, and any decision that we make." Dante ran his fingertips through Lola's beautiful long dark thick hair. "For us, all we need is love. Love trumps all, even the law of man. And our love is strong."

Lola's innocent sense of devotion was like putty in Dante's hands, and her trust in Dante allowed him to penetrate her innocent bed of roses. In secrecy, Dante and Lola engaged in a heated love affair that lasted all day and night. When resting from the many hours of sex, Dante painted his innocent muse, who was in awe of her ageless lover.

As the night began to slowly drift away into the dawn of a new day, Lola once again modeled and stood in the likeness of a Renaissance muse who was carved from the hands of divinity for her master artist. All of her eternal sense of divine beauty, from her head to her toes, posing with contrapposto, created an everlasting image of art and beauty.

Her poetic eyes seductively gazed across her shoulder while she bit down on her full, lush bottom lip, her locks of hair flowing down around her shoulders, down the curving crease of her back and in between her fully developed breasts. Her silky-smooth olive-toned skin was flawless, and down in between her legs was her innocence lost. Even though she was only sixteen, she was ageless and divine to the eye.

Lola was more than a paramour, she was Dante's muse. She was his passion's drive, fuel for the soul, the only thing meaningful and worth sacrificing for since he had come to New York City. Lola was worth the risk of putting not only his art career on the line, but his life as well. Like Bella Notta, Dante now lived his life in shadows, but for muses.

The essence of it all was an everlasting bond filled with beauty and mystique. In the eyes of those blindly led, it was a forbidden sin, but in the eyes of those who could see, it was love.

Love, whether the love for a muse or another, was one of the most powerful of all human emotions. Love was ageless and blind; it had no borders or prejudices. It was an everlasting driving force of passion for the heart and soul. There were absolutely no strings attached and no limits for love. Love had the ability to drive a human being to the edges of existence, and sometimes love was a pathway to death. Together, love and death were the two most powerful of all life experiences, and Dante was willing to sacrifice one for another.

After more passionate sex, Dante painted Lola once again. Before he could get one last glimpse of all the love and devotion seen within her eyes, he was drawn away. Standing in the doorway behind Lola Notta's nude body were Bella Notta and three of his wise guys.

Lola Notta was taken away forever, and Dante was left all alone with Bella Notta and his three wise guys. They beat Dante to the point of near death, destroying all of his life's work, leaving him on the fish-infested street of Mott Street, where his apartment was, and forever banishing him from Little Italy and New York City with absolutely nothing.

# # #

For the next seven days there was no sun. Only darkness existed as Dante spent each day and night recovering in alleys, on street corners, on park benches, in subways, inside churches and inside 24/7 corporate fast-food chains. Dante had nothing but his heart and soul, which were both now bruised and destroyed.

It was the beginning of the end. As the night sky filled with gothic delight, flurries sprinkled down, and along with the numbing winds howling through the empty snow-covered streets, what had once felt like heaven now felt like the frigid depths of hell.

Dante eventually arrived at the doorstep of St. Thomas Church. He gazed up at the French high gothic-style façade filled with redemption. Dante wasn't a man who believed in faith, but for the moment, he felt the need for forgiveness of his sins. He was willing to spend his last days with an illusionary God whom he had renounced long ago.

Carved within the side of the gothic architectural entrance arch, alongside Dante on either side, were six snow-covered jamb statues of stone saints. As Dante slowly ascended the stairs, he looked into the stone eyes of the statue of St. Thomas that stood between the entrance doors. The presence of a saint felt comforting as Dante opened the gothic doors and entered St. Thomas.

Dante rested his aching legs and freezing, fatigued body as he sat on one of the soft maroon cushions next to one of the high-rising gothic-style stone columns. The gothic interior was of cathedral proportions, and within the dimness of it, were two architectural elements that filled Dante with a spiritual uprising.

Behind the altar, was the nave vault, which rose up ninety-five feet to the medieval stone rib-vaulting ceiling. It was a massive wall of limestone and sandstone, which was carved into numerous statues laced with similar gothic architectural design of flat walls behind altars of Medieval England cathedrals. Just above the altar was a depiction of St. Thomas kneeling before Christ, with nine Old Testament prophets foretelling the coming of the Messiah, the Virgin Mary, St. John and the Twelve Apostles carved into the lower part of the rising wall of stone, which was also carved into early saints, martyrs, noted bishops and missionaries. Behind Dante, above the entrance of St. Thomas, was the symbolic image of the sacred feminine—a rose, a massive stained-glass rose window.

Dante silently sat all alone. He was overshadowed by the overwhelming presence of a spiritual entity. Father Michael, who suddenly appeared, welcomed Dante with open arms and sat beside the troubled soul. As the numbing winds continued to howl through the empty snow-covered streets of New York City, Father Michael would be the cure Dante was searching for. Dante would spend the rest of the night engaged in deep, soul-lifting conversation with Father Michael and end up spending the night inside St. Thomas Church. There would be no departure from the city of dreams and new beginnings, New York City. Before Father Michael left Dante all alone for the night, he left him with inspiring words of redemption for a future unknown. There was hope.

"Failure is the absence of faith . . ."

<u>73</u>

Dante staggered out of the antique shop and continued to stumble across the street while pressing his bloodstained shirt against his stomach with the palm of one hand, carrying Sarita's bag in the other. Even though Dante was now free from the bondage situation, the memory of the horrors of being physically dehumanized and violated poisoned Dante's mind; he would forever be mentally and physically scarred.

Dante was blind to the world around. He was lost. Continuing on without direction, he eventually submitted and sat on the curb of a side street. His head hung down within his hands, and blood slowly dripped from Dante's forehead and splattered down onto the ground. It was a reminder of the sacrifices he had made for Sarita, who now occupied Dante's mind.

Even as police sirens shrilled in the distance, Dante focused on Sarita and her bag, which he then opened. Reaching inside, Dante took out Sarita's leather sketchbook with her initials engraved into the cover and scanned through the pages. A spark of life filled his heart. He ran his hands over Sarita's clothes and combed through the items inside the bag. Dante held up the well-defined polished wood rosary that Gabriela had given Sarita. He weaved it in and out between his fingers until the end came out from the bottom of his hand and dangled down in the air.

"Failure is the absence of faith." Father Michael's inspiring words filled Dante's mind.

Dante clasped the rosary and squeezed so tightly that the beads dug into his bloodstained hand, creating tiny round indentations. He took the rosary and placed it in his pocket and then reached back into Sarita's bag. He took out a picture frame with a photograph of Sarita and Gabriela, the one Sarita had received on her birthday.

Dante touched the glass with his fingertips. He could see the love and happiness deep within their eyes. Dante became even more inspired to continue on, wanting to reunite a mother and daughter. And after taking a moment to reflect on the past and where to go from here, Dante put the picture back, closed the bag and stood.

Sitting up against the wall behind him was a bum. He was an older man with a big bushy white beard and long, nappy white hair who wore a military jacket with medals and patriotic patches and pins such as, Semper Fi, POW/MIA, Fourth Marine Division, Ron Paul, infowars.com, END THE FED, Don't Tread on Me, Tea Party, and 9/11 truth, and a pair of old jeans with military boots. Beside him rested a trash bag filled with all his possessions, and in his hand he held an old coffee cup filled with loose change.

"Hey, boy, y'all seem to be lost. If y'all can spare some change and some food, Murphy will gladly be of some assistance to y'all," the bum spat as he mumbled like a pirate.

"Here, it's all I have. I appreciate your kindness, but I don't think that you'll be able to help me. Sorry, but thanks anyway," Dante said, dropping some change into Murphy's coffee cup.

"Ha-ha-ha, y'all can count on ol' Murphy here, tha good ol' Lord trust in me and so y'all can trust Murphy, ha-ha-ha."

Murphy let out a wheezing laugh with a gaping smile and a wafting stench of foul breath and liquor. Dante covered his nose. Murphy reached out his hand for Dante to help him to his feet. Dante was taller than Murphy, who was about five feet tall. The police sirens got louder, and Dante turned his head and moved closer towards the wall and storefronts.

"Ha-ha-ha, running from tha law, I see, ha-ha-ha. Murphy had his share of law running and hiding from Charlie, ha-ha-ha. Tha good ol' Lord bless me and was always wit me, ha-ha-ha. Murphy spent six months in tha bush, and one year running from smokey, ha-ha-ha. And here Murphy be, still standing, ha-ha-ha, tree purple hearts and one divorce, ha-ha-ha. And tha missus was more torturous than running from Charlie and smokey, ha-ha-ha. And if y'all lookin' for where Pooh Bear may be, Murphy know where he be."

"Pooh Bear?"

"Ha-ha-ha, yep, that damn fool who walked outta that there ol' antique shop I saw y'all and that girl go into. He carried her on outta there ova his shoulder, ha-ha-ha." Dante turned around to look.

"Could you please show me where he took her?"

"Ha-ha-ha, well, Murphy is sure that tha good ol' Lord has blessed y'all, ha-ha-ha, and is tha reason for Murphy being here for y'all assistance, ha-ha-ha. And tha good ol' Lord tells me we will find what y'all lookin' for, ha-ha-ha."

Murphy picked up the trash bag filled with his possessions and began to guide Dante through side streets and down alleyways. And after traveling incognito, Dante and Murphy came to a stop, and Murphy pointed to a candy shop.

"Ha-ha-ha, well, here we be, Ducky's home, ha-ha-ha. This where y'all be able to find Pooh Bear, ha-ha-ha, inside in tha basement, ha-ha-ha. Well, bests of luck gittin' involved wit Ducky and Pooh Bear for a girl, ha-ha-ha. Women, tha cause for tha rise and fall of man, ha-ha-ha, tha reason for our unthinkable acts of stupidity and courage just so we can win their hearts, ha-ha-ha, for love, ha-ha-ha, tha good ol' Lord's greatest magic trick for deceiving humans, all for laughs and his own entertainment, ha-ha-ha. Love tha poison and cure for tha heart, ha-ha-ha, especially tha love for a child and what y'all getting involved wit, it worth blindly going in there for her, ha-ha-ha."

"Thank you, Murphy," Dante said with gratitude.

"Ha-ha-ha, don't thank Murphy, thank tha good ol' Lord, ha-ha-ha. Y'all don't owe Murphy nuttin, Murphy is glad to be of some assistance for y'all, ha-ha-ha."

Dante paid Murphy to watch Sarita's and his bags and walked across the street. His head was still full of disturbing thoughts about being sexually violated, and thoughts of what horror might await him in the candy shop. Blood seeped out from between Dante's fingers, tightly clutched into a fist. He stood before the candy shop's double wooden red doors and held the doorknob. He felt overwhelmed with a sick feeling because of what he might find waiting for him on the other side. After escaping from the horrors of a secret gulag, the lingering memories filled Dante with fear. He worried about what condition Sarita might be in, or if she would even be inside. Dante summoned the strength to open the doors and blindly stormed into the unknown, fueled by the desperate desire to find Sarita.

Inside the candy shop there were numerous shelves, plastic and glass cases filled with a variety of corporate and homemade candy. Dante paced towards the back and then past the front counter. The young, tall, skinny, blond shopkeeper leaning on the countertop stared at Dante with bewilderment. Dante began to look for a door to the basement, opening up an employees-only door. The shopkeeper stood up straight.

"Hey . . . hey, can I help you?" the shopkeeper said as he walked towards Dante. Dante didn't say a word. He just ignored him as he began to walk into a back room behind the counter. "Hey, I'm talking to you. Where in tha hell do you think you're going?"

As the shopkeeper tried to stop Dante, Dante punched him down to the ground and then got on top of him and beat the shit out of him until he was unconscious. Dante went into the back room. It was only an office with no other doors. Dante wasn't convinced or willing to give up that easily. He calmly took the time to think, meticulously observing his surroundings. He found what he was looking for. Underneath Dante's feet was a piece of carpet. He removed it, and hiding underneath there was a hatch that opened up to the basement.

The darkness of the stairwell reminded him of the horrors he had experienced. He was wiser now and knew not to step down into the unknown unprepared. Before going down into the basement, Dante looked around for a weapon. He found a black wooden cane with a golden duck head handle leaning up against the wall behind a desk. He smiled as he walked over and grabbed it. Sarita's lingering presence then beckoned him down the stairs.

After descending down the steep, dark stairwell, Dante slowly and silently peeked around the corner to his right to try and get a glimpse of what awaited him within the light. He slowly stepped around the corner.

To Dante's right, one half of the room was set up with film equipment similar to that from the antique shop basement. There was a desk that had a computer on top of it with a webcam, and on either side of the desk were tripods with digital cameras and stage lights. On the other side of the room there was an elaborate set consisting of a child's dream bedroom filled with a variety of toys, stuffed animals and animated characters, a home entertainment system with multiple video game systems, and a king-sized bed with a trunk-sized toy box at the foot. The bed rested in the center of the mock child's bedroom. Dante could only imagine the horrific dehumanization and exploitation that must've taken place within the room and feared for Sarita's innocence and her safety.

Before Dante could do anything further, he noticed a half-closed door on the opposite side of the room. Dante walked to the door but froze when he heard kicking and scratching around. He focused on the toy box. Whether it was Sarita or not, whoever was locked inside was now aware of Dante's presence and had begun to moan for help. Dante began to step towards the toy box to free whoever the innocent soul was from captivity but then stopped. Muffled voices were coming from the other side of the door, which confirmed that it wasn't Sarita locked inside the box. Sentences were unclear, but the word *she* was all Dante needed to hear. Even though there seemed to be an innocent child locked inside the box, Dante had no choice but to abandon the hopeless soul for now to continue on for Sarita.

Dante walked towards the closed door and peeked into the dimness. He was only able to get a glimpse, but it was enough to see three men. He listened to their conversation and heard them making degrading and dehumanizing sexual comments about Sarita. Dante tightly clutched the black wooden cane and then quietly and slowly began to open up the wooden door some more.

As Dante crept in, he was able to see the back of Pooh Bear, the Rev, who stood to the right of Pooh Bear, and then Ducky, who stood to the right of the Rev. After Dante stepped up behind them, Sarita slowly lifted her head, opened her eyes, and saw Dante. Sarita's eyes lit up. Dante put his finger to his lips, motioning her to stay quiet. Sarita was already unable to speak since she was gagged with the red rubber ball of a leather S&M gag in her mouth, but she didn't move or blink.

Pooh Bear sensed a presence. He turned to look back over his shoulder, only to get blindsided on the side of his head with the golden duck head handle of the cane. Sarita closed her eyes as Pooh Bear was knocked unconscious and dropped to the ground. Blood slowly seeped out of the gash in his head and flowed through the cracks of the concrete floor. After being surprised, the Rev quickly turned around, only to be confronted by Dante, who swung the cane like he was swinging for the fences. The golden duck head handle smashed the Rev's glasses and broke his nose, causing shattering glass and blood to spray out in all directions. As the Rev held his bloody face, Dante hit him three more times across the face until he dropped to the ground. Blood dripped down from the golden duck head handle.

"Cock sucker mothafucka, I'll kill ya!" Ducky yelled, lunging towards Dante with outstretched arms as Dante turned towards him. Dante stepped to the side and swung for Ducky's face, only to have Ducky grab the golden duck head handle. Ducky then grabbed the top of the cane with both hands and pulled Dante in closer. He held on to the cane with both hands while Dante gripped the cane with one hand and the golden duck head handle with the other. Ducky tried to pull it away from Dante. Dante then kicked Ducky between the legs, causing Ducky to wheeze and stand still. Dante kicked Ducky in the stomach as he moaned. Dante managed to hold the golden duck head handle, the top part of the cane, as it detached from the bottom, which Ducky held in his hands. After Ducky was able to regain some feeling between the legs, he quickly went after Dante with the bottom part of the cane, only to have Dante stab him in the side of his belly with the knife attached to the golden duck head.

Dante stood inches away from Ducky, seeing the agony in his eyes. He let go of the handle and then stepped back as Ducky began to spit up blood. Ducky held the golden duck head handle with both hands as he looked down and then up at Dante. He slowly dropped to the ground and lay limp on his back. The bloody golden duck head stuck up in the air from Ducky's belly, and the blood from the wound flowed down Ducky's belly and then through the cracks of the concrete floor.

With her eyes closed, the silence filled Sarita with concern. Her concern was replaced with comfort as she felt the warmth of fingertips caressing the side of her face and running through her hair. Sarita opened her eyes and saw Dante wipe his hand clean on his pants, then remove the gagger from her mouth.

Dante sent Sarita up the stairs to wait for him in the office. He then went about destroying the film production equipment and then opened up the toy box and freed the spider boy, a conjoined twin freak. He consoled him and left him alone in the basement. Before leaving with Sarita, Dante dialed 911 on the office phone and then left the phone off the hook so that the authorities could come to arrest the psychotic criminals. The spider boy and other innocent children would eventually be helped, protected and saved. Soon Dante and Sarita would find themselves blindly going further down a path of the unknown, together, again.

74

Inside the office there were papers and files scattered all over the desk, and on the floor. The filing cabinets overflowed with more files and papers. There were also newspaper clippings, files, pictures and a giant map of the United States with pin markers and marker lines tagged all over the map hanging up on the wall behind the desk. On top of the desk lay coffee cups, fast-food bags, and wrappers with leftovers. Sitting behind the desk, talking on the phone, was Special Agent Donovan. Walsh quietly walked up and patiently stood waiting in the doorway.

As Donovan spoke on the phone, he gestured with his outstretched hand for Walsh to walk in and take a seat. After Walsh sat down, he began to pick at leftover fast food as Donovan continued to talk on the phone. Walsh held a half-filled container of french fries in his hand as Donovan hung up the phone.

"Do I walk into your office and start eating food off your desk?"

Donovan put Sarita's multicolored friendship bracelet back inside his pocket. He then reached over and took the container of french fries out of Walsh's hand and began to eat.

"No, but it didn't seem like you were going to finish them," Walsh said as he chewed.

"Never assume, Walsh, it will only get you into trouble." Donovan leaned back while eating his french fries. "You still have a lot to learn, Walsh. You're young and cocky and you think you've figured it all out already. I know I was once in your shoes, sitting where you are now. Someday you'll be like me, but for now just listen and have some patience, okay? And ask before you take."

"Okay, Donovan, I know, sometimes I can go a bit too far over my head." Walsh motioned to ask Donovan if he could take a half-finished chicken sandwich. Chewing his french fries, Donovan gave him the okay with a nod. "I'm sorry about interviewing those witnesses without notifying you first . . . good sandwich . . . and it won't happen again, I promise."

"I know you meant well, but you had no right to question those people without my authority. But that isn't the reason I called you up to my office. I just got a tip from the Tuscaloosa Police Department down in Alabama. They found the girl, well, sorta . . ."

"And the suspect?"

"Relax, Walsh, just be quiet for a minute and listen carefully, okay?"

As Walsh continued to eat Donovan's chicken sandwich, he leaned back in his chair with his legs spread apart, resting his elbows on the arms of the chair.

"First of all, what I can tell you is that the Tuscaloosa Police Department weren't the ones who came into contact with our girl and boy. Nah, they got their information from some local and a homeless guy, and what they were told—well, you may want to finish that sandwich and hold on to something tight, know what I mean?"

Walsh leaned forward as he finished chewing the final remains of Donovan's chicken sandwich. Donovan rested both of his elbows on top of his messy desk and then continued his debriefing with outstretched hands.

"Well, our case has just gotten a lot bigger; in fact, it's a fucking mess right now. Honestly, I don't know where to begin. The thought of it makes me sick."

"Okay, okay, calm down. Why don't you try starting with what happened first?"

"An antique shop, that's where this local recognized our boy and girl. He felt the need to take matters into his own hands when he recognized the two, only to get himself abducted and kept as a prisoner in the basement along with our boy."

"What? How?"

"As of right now, we're still in the process of gathering more details, but what we do know is that the owner of the antique shop is some Internet porn star, like . . . like Traci Lords, or wait, let me think . . ."

"Eighties? It's the millennium. Wouldn't she be more modern, like Lisa Ann?" Walsh asked with a stimulated sense of interest.

"Quiet, Walsh, you're missing the point. What I'm trying to say is that being an Internet porn star was her way of making money, in a sick psychotic way, to fulfill her fetishes. Anyway, she kept this local and our boy prisoner in the basement of the antique store, torturing and sexually abusing them while broadcasting it all over the Internet using a live webcam feed."

"Dominatrix," Walsh added as he leaned in closer with an even more aroused sense of interest.

"Whatever, I didn't get too much detail, but somehow our boy escaped. And from what this homeless guy told the Tuscaloosa authorities, he ended up in some candy shop, which was where our girl was being kept hostage."

Walsh became even more intrigued.

"This is where this whole situation gets even more bizarre, not only for our boy and girl, but for me. It brings back haunting memories from old child abduction cases I investigated that never ended well. Anyway, our girl was held captive by a group of psychotic pedophiles who were running a network of child pornography and selling children on the black market for prostitution and slave labor. This group was connected with the fetish queen from the antique shop and had their own secret sex dungeon in the basement of the candy shop, but for children! How ironic. They used it to broadcast child pornography live over the Internet also. From what the Tuscaloosa authorities know as of now, our boy confronted these three men and then left with the girl. Where they went and what their motive is now, not a clue. What I do know is that we have a lot of shit to clean off our hands."

"Well, what about the mother? And anything else on the suspect? Ya know, now that we know about his past."

"Nothing yet on the mother, we're still waiting to hear back from ICE. As for the struggling artist, this guy has a history of violence and misdemeanors. I mean, look at this intel we've gathered, from Indiana, New York and Jersey. Stealing from various retail stores, pharmacies, homes, assault, assault on a police officer, drug trafficking and his connections to Nada Mas. As for the few people we were able to get in touch with who knew him, it's the same old story; this guy is quiet and shy, very smart, and a very talented artist, the last person you would think of who would kidnap a girl."

"It's always the quiet ones, the loners, ya know," Walsh added.

"Yeah well, this isn't your ordinary loner. He's lived the life of a successful artist. All of this is still hard to process and understand at this point. There's gotta be someone else out there who knows more about this guy and his past. He's gotta be connected to something bigger with Nada Mas, but first, before we can get any more units out collecting and connecting more pieces to all of this, we gotta worry about cleaning up this mess in Bama. Once we gather up more information, touch base with the DEA and other branches within our agency, then hopefully we'll have a better understanding of our boy and where he may have taken the girl. For now, Walsh, pack your bags. We're going to Bama."

"The south. I hate the south, it's too hot," Walsh grumbled like a child.

"Well, then, don't forget to bring some comfortable clothes. If you don't have anything comfortable to wear, you could borrow some of my old stuff. Hey, it may not be fashionably up to date, but it will do. I have some extra light material shirts, like silk, good quality. Besides that, don't forget your underwear. I don't need you leaving skid marks in mine again. And most importantly, don't forget your purse and you'll be fine."

"Yeah, sorry about your Fruit of the Looms, but thanks, Donovan, you're the nicest."

"We need to hurry up so we can catch our flight to Bama. Go home, pack your bags, and clean yourself up. Ya look like a horse's ass. I'll pick you up in one hour, so you better be ready. I don't wanna show up and catch you rubbing one out again," Donovan joked with Walsh, who stood up. Walsh grinned as he walked over to the door, followed by Donovan, who put his arm around Walsh's shoulders and then guided him out of the office.

75

Not too long after Marta Mendoza was apprehended, all high-ranking officials of Nada Mas were contacted by Benjamin Bradford and ordered to meet at a safe site. Tensions were high and everyone was on edge due to the sudden seizure of Marta Mendoza and the future fate of Nada Mas. All were willing to risk their own lives by migrating out to an undisclosed location, hidden deep within South America. A dilapidated hotel located on the river's edge of the Amazon River was where they would gather. All the high-ranking officials checked in and traveled by riverboat down the Amazon River, deeper into the heart of the Amazon, until they reached their final destination, hidden deep within the rainforest, secluded from civilization.

Secretly built and left abandoned throughout the years was an old redundant military outpost that the Nazis had built and fled to as refugees at the end of World War II. It was discovered while Nada Mas was expanding its drug-manufacturing operations in isolated areas in Latin America. Inside, the massive deteriorated warehouse, blanketed over with vegetation, was filled with unopened crates, rusty oil drums, and an array of file cabinets and files scattered all over. The high-ranking officials made the best of what they had. In an organized effort, they made a makeshift conference table with chairs and benches out of plywood, scrap metal, airplane parts, ammunition boxes, and MRE boxes. After setting up their meeting table, all members sat down, and each took out and opened up an issued laptop—used for Nada Mas purposes only. They waited for their laptops to boot up. There were a few Nada Mas guardsmen, along with the native guides who had come along to fend off wild Amazonian animals, such as anacondas, poisonous frogs, various oversized insects, and other predators. Finally, after all laptops were booted up, connected to the Internet, and logged in to an independent communications system created for Nada Mas, there was a wave of anticipation.

After everyone's screen came into focus, a live webcam feed revealed a dark figure sitting in shadows. It wasn't what everyone expected to see, but they all knew who it was. Benjamin Bradford, the mastermind behind Nada Mas, their superior host for the evening, would remain anonymous, and they all gave him their utmost attention.

"Gentlemen, welcome. I hope that your travels weren't too treacherous, but then again, we are living in darker times and need to remain as isolated and alert as possible. In the post 9/11 era, security is much tighter and highly advanced, and it is becoming even more draconian with each passing year. Not only are the liberties of the free people being slowly eroded, but our way of conducting business is being threatened as well. Therefore, all that Nada Mas has created must now change with the times. As you all know, one of our highest and most loyal officials has recently been apprehended by the American authorities. Her fate at this point is still uncertain, which means that one of you will have to fill her shoes and not only fulfill her duties but be able to help rewrite the path of Nada Mas. Not only am I looking for someone with devoted loyalty, but someone fresh, mentally strong and creative to help take all that has been created, mold it, and bring it into a new era."

As Benjamin Bradford spoke sternly, his disguised robotic words pierced through the hearts and minds of all the high-ranking officials with a sense of revelation. There was a wave of silence as all sat in a contemplative state as they waited for Benny to continue.

"Now, knowing where we stand, and why we are all here now, I'm sure there has been a lot of talk about who will replace Marta Mendoza and how that selection will be conducted. I assure you that rumors of a vote are not true. There will be no democracy in this selection. I have put a lot of time and thought into who should replace Marta, long before this council was created. Fortunately for the lucky one, they have not only surprised me in many ways, but they have gone beyond the call of duty and surpassed many of you with revenue and expansion of operations. Before I continue any further, is there anything any of you would like to say? The floor is now open."

After Benjamin Bradford brought closure to his opening statement, all high-ranking officials silently stared at one another. There was an exchange of caution, jealousy and resentment.

Viktor Vyhovsky stroked his white beard as he stared at the shadow figure on the screen of his laptop. The Americans—Timothy T. Townsend, Jeffrey Rothstein, Calvin Coughlin, Eric Edwards and Randel Rosenthal, who sat together at one end of the makeshift conference table—softly schemed amongst themselves. Carlos, Mariano Cruz and Don Fernandez passionately spoke with their hand gestures, while the Reverend Jefferson C. Collinsworth and Sven Schaffert calmly spoke like the intellectual gentlemen they were. Gang Gao silently sat as an army of one, lost in deep thought and concentration as he keenly scanned all of his equals and paid close attention to Suarez and Salas, who silently watched with slight smiles. Suarez and Salas already knew the fate of Nada Mas.

"Well, I take it that everyone's silence is a sign of expectancy for who amongst you will be selected as the new mediator . . ." Benny paused. There was a wave of stoic eagerness as everyone leaned in closer towards their laptop screens. After a buildup of suspense, Benny continued, "Sebastian Suarez, you will be the new mediator and coordinator of this council."

There were many gasps and a side chatter of neglect amongst those who disagreed with the final decision. Suarez and Salas looked at each other and smiled. All those who resented him looked away in disgust or glared at him with fury in their eyes.

"To your parents, who were there from the very beginning, helped build the foundation of Nada Mas, helped mold Nada Mas into what it now is, I owe my loyalty to their allegiance. Not only that, but you have proven yourself worthy of the new reins I am passing down to you. Your network brings in a revenue that surpasses your counterparts, four, sometimes five times greater than anyone's expectations. It was a unanimous decision based on the facts and what I know from working with your parents, what you are and will be capable of executing for Nada Mas. In closing, I hope that all of you will accept my decision with dignity and respect and that all of you will follow orders from our new mediator as expected. If not, the same rules apply for all those who choose not to abide by the philosophies and order that are Nada Mas. This debriefing is now over. I hope that all of you will enjoy the remainder of your stay and hope to set up another meeting with all of you as soon as your new mediator and I begin the new phase of Nada Mas. Thank you for your time, and be well."

Benjamin Bradford finished speaking and logged off, and the live cam web feed went black. Everyone then simultaneously logged off, shut down, and closed their laptops. After the selection, everyone packed up their laptops, and those who disagreed with the decision spoke out in defiance.

"So, the spoiled little cocky rich boy is now going to tell all of us what to do," Eric Edwards said sternly as he stood up. He looked Suarez in the eyes as he continued, "If your parents were still alive to see what you have done with their wealth and the network they built from nothing, you'd be sitting in a corner in a wet diaper sucking your thumb. But if that's the way it's going to be, to have to take orders from a baby with the keys to the kingdom, then so be it. Just make sure you don't fuck it up for all of us. Remember, I got my eye on your every move. If you try to step out of line, the second you do, I'll have your balls hanging down from my mantel as Christmas ornaments. I'll see you on the boat."

Eric Edwards walked away with the other Americans. Viktor Vyhovsky, the Reverend Jefferson C. Collinsworth, and Sven Schaffert slowly followed behind while muttering under their breaths in resentment and acceptance. Gang Gao continued to silently sit alone, lost in deep thought and concentration, while ferociously staring at Suarez. Don Fernandez, Carlos, and Mariano Cruz stood up.

"Well, there is nothing that can be done to alter Benny's decision. It is what it is, but remember, all that you have done to get to where we are now, someday that will come back to you. All that has happened to Marta will come to you," Don Fernandez said firmly.

"Is that a threat?" Suarez asked with a smirk.

"No, consider it a warning to you, to watch your actions. Anyway, congratulations, my friend. Enjoy the new role, I'll see you on the boat." Don Fernandez walked away with Carlos, Mariano Cruz helped Gang Gao stand up, and then the four walked away, leaving Suarez and Salas all alone.

"So, now that you're in control, what's our next move?" Salas said as he watched the others walk away.

"We play along, play fair, gain back their trust and seduce their hearts and minds with all I will give to them. After we gain their love and devotion, that's when we go in and take it all. All we need is a little patience, and in time, when the moment is right, that's when we'll take back Nada Mas," Suarez said with confidence.

There was a storm of passion and determination forming in his eyes, and a chemical combustion of courage and perseverance burning deep within his heart of gray. It was the end, the shedding away of the old guard and the beginning and birth of the new age of Nada Mas.

<u>76</u>

New Orleans and the Super Dome weren't what they had once been, since Katrina had changed the appearance of both. After porting upon the shores of New Orleans, Dante and Sarita had some time to kill before boarding another train that would bring them closer to Mexico. For now, Dante and Sarita walked along Bourbon Street and through the heart of the French Quarter incognito while admiring the French architecture, Cajun culture, exquisite jazz music and local restaurants, shops and settings enshrouded with voodoo and vampire lore. Dante and Sarita waded through crowds of people to Jackson Square Park, home to the St. Louis Cathedral, where they admired the abstract array of local artists' work being sold by street vendors. There were also horses that pulled carriages. Sarita got a reading from a street-side psychic—keeping all that she was told a secret from Dante. Dante and Sarita then continued into the cathedral, where Dante found a priest to confess his sins to while continuing to guide Sarita underneath his wing.

The two eventually ended up sitting along the banks of the mighty Mississippi River. As they silently sat beside each other, Dante took out a Lucky.

"Do you know those are bad for you, that they kill millions and millions of people a year?"

Dante laughed as he lit the Lucky resting between his lips.

"If I want to kill myself slowly, then that's my free will," Dante said blandly.

"Well, you are killing those around you too."

"Goddamn left, right politicos," Dante mumbled and then held up his cigarette before her. "Listen, Shorty, even though cigarettes may be laced with a chemical imbalance of harmful addictive toxins the corporations created and use to profit off an individual's addictive tendencies, which cause health problems and even death—well, it's not the cigarette that's the problem, it's the individual. The individual who has the choice to ingest any harmful substances they want to escape from reality by sedating their senses for pleasure. As for those who feel harmed, uncomfortable or threatened in any way by the presence of cigarette smoke or smokers—well, either respect my choice and space, or find a smoke-free area to be in, or spend your time someplace else. So, if this is bothering you so much, Shorty, why don't you go take a walk? Actually, I could use some alone time."

Dante passionately spoke with outstretched arms as he emphasized his words with his cigarette held between his two fingers. Sarita stared at him, at a loss for words. After all she had just been through, to have the person she trusted to take care of her be so cold was eating away her insides.

Sarita turned away, holding her stomach while kicking her feet back and forth. Dante looked over with anger in his eyes as his mind became plagued with all the sexual torment he'd been through. Once he noticed the bruises and scaring on Sarita's ankles and wrists, he recoiled.

For a little girl to experience what Sarita had, to be held captive by such filth, the disease and parasites of humanity, to imagine all they had done to other children filled Dante's heart with sympathy.

"Sorry, Shorty, I didn't mean to speak so bluntly," Dante said and rubbed Sarita's back. "I get it, what you and I have just been through is sickening, but I don't know what to say."

"It's okay, you don't have to say anything. Just sitting here with you is all I need right now. Thank you for rescuing me," Sarita said sincerely as she looked across the river.

The two enjoyed the silence, the breeze blowing off the river, the smell of Cajun food wafting from nearby restaurants, and most importantly, each other.

"Ya know, that's why it's so important to live life. Don't be afraid to take chances and risks in life. You never know when an opportunity will be taken away, or your life. Believe me, you wouldn't be here right now, Shorty, if your mother never took the risks she did in life. It's funny, I can still remember when we first met . . ." Dante paused to look deep within Sarita's eyes. "You probably wouldn't be here right now. Anyway, what I'm trying to say is that you shouldn't wait for life to come to you. You need to live the life you want, now, and don't wait till tomorrow, or for yesterday to fade away, because you'll end up living your life with regrets and fear. Don't allow others to control and manipulate your life, no matter how big or powerful they are, because you will always be stronger just by not being afraid to live the life you want. Okay, even during dark times, like what we've just gone through, you gotta carry on and keep living life to the fullest."

Dante took another drag from his cigarette before he continued.

"I'm telling you all of this because I don't want to see you grow up in a world with borders and limitations, a world without freedom and have to live within a world of bondage. You're the future. You're the one who can change all of this someday, or be the one who can prevent it. Learn to be yourself in life, an individual, not a follower, but follow your heart, question everything in life, learn to become knowledgeable about every facet of life and then be able to look at everything from many different perspectives, so that you can make your own judgments in life without the prejudices or opinions of others. To live life blindly in a box, while only being able to view the world through one small lens—one perspective—is death. You are as precious as one drop of water—everyone in life is. It only takes one drop, one person, to make ripples, to make waves, to create change, to bring down walls, to change the world forever and create peace and harmony, oneness amongst the people."

As Dante finished his cigarette, Sarita silently stared at him with a sense of respect and watched as Dante flicked his cigarette butt out before him.

"I just don't want you to grow up blind to the world around you. Someday when you're older, you'll understand." After Dante concluded his warm monologue, there was a moment of silence.

Dante's cell phone rang. He checked to see who it was. It was Greco. Dante didn't answer the phone. He only stood up and walked over to the edge of the Mississippi River, staring at the phone for a moment before throwing it into the river. Dante then took out his Aero Mexico flight 1203 from JFK to Mexico City plane ticket out of his pocket, tore it up, and threw the shredded pieces out into the wind, which then blew away. At this point it was useless; his flight had already left.

This is the end, Dante thought; the end of compleating his one man show, and association with Greco. Thirteen years spent in purgatory was gone. It was all over—his career, his life. He only knew that he had to move on and bury the rest of his past, to leave it all behind for the love of another. Even give up his ticket to safety and freedom in order to escape the ghosts of his past and the threat of Nada Mas.

Dante walked back to Sarita, put his arm around her shoulder, and then began to guide her back to the train station. Sarita was the future, and Dante's last hope of doing anything good with his life. They needed each other.

<u>77</u>

For Dante, life was better after Bella and Lola Notta were left far behind. He was now free from the shackles of corruption and temptation. Two years after coming to New York City to live as a successful artist, it all seemed to be in jeopardy now. But Dante still believed, even now with nothing, that he would be able to make it.

As Dante strolled aimlessly within the heart of New York City's Grand Central terminal, underneath the massive ceiling painted with the constellations of the zodiac, there seemed to be hope. Roaming around New York City, searching for a cure, and seeking inspiration seemed to be the only way. Whatever possessions Dante was able to salvage, he kept in his backpack. Cradled in his arm was his newest painting, the only one he was able to complete after being left on the streets.

It was an abstract self-portrait. It was painted with stolen acrylic paint on a two-by-two piece of one-inch-thick wood left at a construction site. The dreary dark purple-and-blue background reflected the state of the world where Dante now found himself. But in his big crystal-blue eyes there was light, a radiance that gave life to such a piece of melancholic beauty.

Dante's self-portrait was his only companion as he spent each day roaming around the streets of Manhattan, thinking, dreaming, and imagining the life he wanted. His resurgence of life was what kept him grounded, and the flow of life that he swam through brought him back to Central Park on a cool, sunny day.

Strawberry fields felt like a sanctuary, and after passing by memorials of multicolored flower petals and strolling by beams of sunlight shining down through the canopy of trees that lined the walkway of the mall, through the Bethesda terrace arcade, Dante spent the remainder of the day sitting on the edge of the massive stone Bethesda fountain.

The whole world seemed to pass by as Dante silently sat all alone, like a ghost in the crowd. A bride and groom embraced each other, a mother and a child walked by holding hands, an elderly man crept along with a cane, musicians played eccentric music and sang, and people old and young from all walks of life seemed to be at peace in such a convergent setting. The circle of life seemed to be center stage, and Dante sat as an audience of one.

He was ignored by all who walked by, as was his painting leaning against the base of the fountain. But Dante didn't mind. The simplicities of life seemed to consume his mind, with an antidote of love. Just as Dante was ready to leave it all behind, a presence was felt standing before him.

"Excuse me, sir?" A stranger said kindly.

As Dante held up his hand in an attempt to block out the blinding light, the stranger stepped closer and blocked out the sun so that Dante could see.

The man in black was very young. He had a clean-cut, smooth, chiseled face with spikey black hair and wore fashionable imported designer clothes. Hanging down from his shoulder was the strap from a leather messenger bag, and in his other hand was a red notebook.

"Sorry to just creep up on you, but I couldn't resist coming over here after I noticed your painting—from all the way up there—from the top of the stairs. Did you paint this? Are you a painter?" the man said ardently.

"Um, oh, yeah. Yes, I'm a painter. I painted this," Dante said with bewilderment.

"This work, this is really good. I haven't seen anything painted with so much emotion in a long time." The man reached into the pocket of his messenger bag and pulled out a business card, which he handed to Dante. "Anyway, I wish that I could stay and chat some more, but I'm late for a meeting. I'm an art dealer, I recognize talent. Well, it's my job and I have to. Anyway, you got it, you got something special here. As much as I want to stay and talk with you, I can't. Sorry, but I gotta go. Give me a call, we'll do lunch," the man said as he walked away.

Dante watched curiously as the stranger disappeared into the sea of people. He flipped over the business card and looked at the name of the art dealer, Sonny Sosa, with a childish grin. Higher forces were at play. Even within the mist of darkness, light was able to shine through and find Dante.

78

The dream was now a reality. After many years of living as a struggling artist, Dante had finally made it. He became the best-known, most-respected and sought-after artist in the New York City art scene that eventually ended up expanding to Europe and Asia. Dante's success was way more than he could have ever imagined. Dante felt very blessed and fortunate, but with all he had gained he also felt that he had great responsibilities. But for Sonny, all the success he shared with Dante wasn't enough. Sonny wanted more; he wanted the world.

The light from the rising sun shined in through the massive industrial windows of Dante's loft studio in an old Manhattan factory. His half-covered nude body was illuminated as he lay half-awake on his king-sized platform bed. In the distance there was a crescendo of dissonance. Outside within the labyrinth of New York City was a muffle of chaotic traffic and inside there was a relaxing ambiance; an oscillating fan, running water, pigeons flapping their wings as they flew in through broken window panes, and soon an elevator rising in the distance.

Dante slowly got up and sat on the edge of his bed with his head hanging down in the palms of his hands, lost within a numbing state of drunken bliss.

Soon after, an exotic voluptuous Latin woman came walking towards Dante from the open concept kitchen with a mug of freshly brewed coffee. She stood before Dante and helped him drink it while running her fingers through his hair. After Dante finished sipping his coffee, she embraced and kissed him as a final farewell before leaving. As she walked towards the industrial elevator doors, they opened. Sonny stepped out and walked past her with a smile, looking back over his shoulder as she made her exit.

As the elevator doors closed, Sonny turned his head back, continuing to walk towards Dante while rubbing the palms of his hands together. Dante was oblivious to Sonny's presence as he sat on the edge of his bed with a bedsheet draped over his lap, sipping his coffee.

"Hey, Dante, wake up, you son of a bitch."

Dante looked back over his left shoulder and watched as Sonny walked around the bed until he stood in front of him. Dante sat sedated, his eyes glazed over as he looked up at Sonny.

"Well, I can see that, that Mexican whore did you in real well last night. She's a nice little thumper," Sonny said with a childish grin.

"She's not Mexican," Dante mumbled.

"Well, Mexican or not, she's a real fine piece of ass, definitely one of the sexist women I've seen you have up here," Sonny said. He reached down to the floor to pick up Dante's torn-up paint-stained jeans and tossed them on the bed. "Here, put some clothes on." Sonny turned around and walked away to look at all of Dante's finished paintings, which were spread out all over the loft. Dante slowly lifted himself up from the edge of his bed, put his pants on and then crept towards the kitchen with his coffee.

"So, which one is the last one you've been putting the finishing touches on?"

"The big square one on the back wall," Dante said as he walked into the kitchen with his back to Sonny. Sonny walked around the studio space filled with paintings until he stood before the painting Dante was talking about. "You wanna cup of coffee?" Dante called out.

"Nah, don't bother, I'm not staying. I only stopped by to see your progress on this final painting," Sonny explained as he keenly observed the painting. Dante walked towards Sonny, shirtless, while sipping his coffee. He stopped and stood beside Sonny's right side. The two then silently observed Dante's final painting for his upcoming one-man show, which would be his biggest to date.

"So, who is she?"

"Some girl."

"I see that. Is she someone I know?"

"Nah, I don't even know who it is. She's just someone from my imagination," Dante said as he passionately stared at the painting of a beautiful woman created from his subconscious.

"Well, with an imagination like that, too bad she's not real."

"Yeah, too bad."

"Well, it looks finished to me. What else do you have to do?"

"Not much. Well, I mean, it's pretty much done. I just wanted to let this one sit a little longer, ya know, see if I still feel the same about it after some time goes by," Dante explained.

"Well, how much time has gone by?"

"Since I last saw you."

"A month; and you did nothing else but stare at this for a month?"

"Yep."

"Well, let's hope that this one is worth a month. Your show is in one week. Everything needs to be done in two days so we can start setting up, so make sure that you're satisfied with this by the end of the day, okay?"

"Yeah, I know."

"Good. Okay, well, I have to get going, I have a lot to do today to prepare for next week. After next week we'll move on to bigger and better things. I've been looking into expanding to the Internet. Ya know, create one of those websites for you to sell some work. We'll make affordable art for the average consumer. And in my eyes, Dante, we have to. You're the last of a dying breed of artists. The modern-day artist no longer goes to New York City or any other big city to make it. The modern-day artist goes to the Internet, to get discovered and find their success. A few years from now, 2006, 2007, many artists will be finding their success on the net. We need to change with the times. That's our next move after this show." Sonny stepped behind Dante and held his shoulder, then walked away.

"But before we get there, you need to finish that last one. So, as soon as you finish, give me a call. I'll be waiting, the sooner the better. Remember your last show, Dante, we sold out, we convinced them all." Sonny's words resonated as the elevator doors closed.

Dante was left all alone with his final painting. As Dante sipped his coffee, he focused on the portrait of one of the most stunning women Dante had ever seen, except that she wasn't real, only an image from his imagination, an unknown woman who had possessed Dante's mind.

Who are you? Dante thought. For months, her image of beauty and mystique had been like an everlasting dream. She was only an image in his mind, but she moved him in the ways of a muse. She was like an angel sent down from the heavens above, laced with a divine sense of art and beauty, who mesmerized Dante with her poetic eyes and beautiful long, dark, thick wavy hair, who was now only laid out on the canvas before Dante's eyes, wide open.

# # #

The image of a woman from Dante's imagination was now the center of attention. Within the enormous Romanesque gallery, symphony strings reverberated soothingly while all around were Dante's finished paintings. Within the heart of the gallery were the elites—globalists, politicians and important people of the art world, not only from New York City but all over the world. The pinnacle of Dante's success was filled with big money, corruption, deception, greed, illusion, and vanity. It was a world filled with gods and demons, and Dante, who had once been lost, a quiet, shy loner, an introvert, was now the center of attention.

The wolves all blindly roamed around admiring Dante's paintings, while scheming. Dante hid within the shadows as he observed this so-called comedy of life unfolding before him, watching as all his hopes and dreams were lost within a world of illusion. He leaned against a pillar in the corner of the gallery while sipping his cocktail. Even though he had fulfilled his dreams, he was plagued with regret; everything that was supposed to feel rewarding felt fake and excessive, as if a nightmarish cloud of darkness had descended over his dreams. Nothing now appeared as he'd once imagined it to be.

Dante's relationship with Sonny was magnificent, and Sonny was a part of

Dante's success, but they had their differences, which had finally boiled over. What was considered to be the most important day in both their lives and careers was also the beginning of the end.

After Sonny made business deals with people throughout the night, Dante wanted nothing to do with it. He wanted to finally leave it all behind—the excessive, exploited lifestyle of a successful artist—and go back to living a simple, quiet life in the shadows. Dante had finally been ready to sacrifice it all, until she had come into his life.

Like an enchantress from an Arabian night, deep within her mesmerizing poetic eyes was all the love in the world. Not only did she bear angelic wings, but she also had beautiful long, dark, thick, wavy hair that flowed like Botticelli's *Birth of Venus*, as well as captivating features that were able to freeze time. In the eyes of mortals, she was like a flawless fashion model, but to Dante she was a goddess. Unfortunately, though, she was lost within a world of illusion, lies and madness, and on either side of her were two of the most manipulative crooks of the art world. There was Virgil, her lover and the rival artist of Dante, and Greco, rival art dealer of Sonny.

She looked back between Virgil and Greco with her head slightly tilted down while looking up through her hair and biting down on her full, lush bottom lip. As Dante gazed across the crowded gallery and became lost within her eyes, an internal storm of melancholy suddenly washed away. There was hope. When she was finally left all alone, Dante didn't hesitate for a second; he felt and realized that she was the one.

As symphony strings played an uplifting melody, Dante made his way across the vast gallery, through a sea of people, towards the woman wearing a flowing backless red dress. Dante ended up standing face-to-face with her, before the portrait of an imaginary woman whose appearance was similar; he was lost within her poetic eyes. Deep within, Dante saw the same instant love and devotion he had for her. After she found the strength to look away and embrace Dante, she whispered sweet words of adoration into his ear, but all Dante was able to comprehend was her name.

"Sonya . . ."

<u>79</u>

As the scorching sun dominated the midsummer day's sky, Donovan and Walsh walked away from the Tuscaloosa Police Department.

"So where do you think they went?" Walsh said as he drank his cup of coffee.

"I don't know, Walsh. Right now, I can't even think straight. After talking to those sick fucks and seeing what they do and what they've done, and getting no help from that idiot who tried to take matters into his own hands! Why couldn't that idiot just have kept his mouth shut? Nothing would've happened, and we wouldn't be wrapped up in this fucking mess! Now we're stuck in Alabama until another unit shows up to clean up this mess, so that we can move on, fuck. Goddamn, it's fucking hot! How in the hell are you drinking coffee right now!"

Donovan tightly squeezed his stress ball. He stripped his jacket and tie off, unbuttoning the top three buttons on his shirt, which was soaked in sweat. Walsh tried to keep up without spilling his coffee.

"I need my fix at least three times a day. It doesn't matter if it's hot or cold out. I can't function without it. If you're that hot, I can give you your shirt back. You're right, this light material keeps you cool in this heat. I'm starting to like the south."

"Enough, Walsh, just listen up for a minute!" Donovan cut in, and then lit a cigarette.

"You know that those are bad for your health. If your wife finds out that you're smoking down here, after you promised to cut back—"

"My health isn't important right now, and my wife is my problem! What's important is where this Dante character went with the girl, and if she is okay. Not only that, but they have a couple of days on us. They could be anywhere, within a few miles or as far away as California. If they were able to make it this far without a trace, who knows where they might have ended up? We need to get the word out to the media again. They helped us before, so they'll be able to help us again."

"I agree, but shouldn't we secure the US-Mexican border checkpoints first? Seems logical to me that he may try to leave the country, passports or not. Knowing who he is, and what he's done in the past, it's definitely a possibility. He could attempt to get himself and the girl across the border, especially if he got this far."

Donovan stopped and studied Walsh. "You're right, that would be a logical thing to do. You're getting better each day, Walsh, good for you; it's a shame that I can't continue to watch you grow like a child. Someday you'll be nearly as good as me."

"Or better."

"Hey, let's not press your luck."

Donovan took a drag as the two of them stood on the sidewalk across the street from the police station. Both silently pondered their situation.

"Ya know, I should be on a beach in Mexico right now, drinking margaritas and fishing off the coast of Baja."

"You want your shirt back, don't you?"

"Nah, don't worry about the shirt. What I mean is that the way everything is unfolding right now, it's starting to get underneath my skin, ya know? How unpredictable everything has been so far, it's starting to scare me a little bit."

"Maybe you should take your pills. They'll help calm you down a li'l bit."

"Forget the pills, I don't need any pills right now. I'm fine, just fine. What I'm trying to say is that I've been in this unpredictable situation before, I know the feeling, and it's starting to come back. Like I've told you once before, Walsh, I don't wanna end my career and end up on a beach in Mexico thinking about my last assignment as a tragedy. I want to remember it as something to be proud of. Ya know, putting this guy in his place and safely reuniting the girl with her mother. That would be a perfect ending, the cherry on top."

"Well, you shouldn't worry, Donovan. After working with you for the past three years, not only have I learned so much from you, but you've made me a better person. It's because you're the best at what you do and always find a way to successfully bring closure to whatever case you're working on, or find a way to handle any difficult situation in life."

"Ya know, you usually never say the right thing, Walsh, but those were very kind words. Thank you, I really appreciate the support. Somehow you're able to bring out the youth in me that I had thirty-five years ago, the feeling that helps me get through these tough, stressful situations. I'm very lucky to have you as my partner and very grateful to have you as my last."

Donovan and Walsh both savored the moment as they looked at each other with gratitude. Donovan put out his cigarette and Walsh removed his sunglasses to show respect. The short moment shared soon came to an end by a presence, which suddenly crept up from behind Donovan and Walsh, causing them to turn around.

Standing before them were two federal agents, both dressed in matching suits. The younger agent standing before Donovan was clean-cut and well groomed, drinking an iced coffee, while the older agent standing before Walsh had short snow-white hair and squinty, piercing bright blue eyes. He wore cowboy boots and held a cigarillo between his grinning teeth. The two agents introduced themselves as they pulled out their FBI badges. They were from separate branches within the FBI's pyramid structure of compartmentalization, two separate entities within a whole system of one. Even though both branches were searching for the same suspect, because of the compartmentalization, each FBI unit had its own individual source of information on Dante, who each unit was looking for, for different reasons.

"Gentlemen, I'm Special Agent J. P. Qubish and this is my partner, Special Agent E. B. Von Burton. We're working on the drug-trafficking case that involves a nationwide crime syndicate and drug-trafficking network we've been hunting down for the past eighteen years. It appears that one of our prime suspects, whom we've been hunting down for the past thirteen years, is now on the run with an abducted child. Coincidently, well, it seems that we're both looking for the same guy. So with your cooperation, we're gonna need to discuss whatever intel you have on this guy," Qubish said in a very cocky, demanding manner, as if Donovan and Walsh were under his command.

"Well, before I can disclose any confidential information, am I guaranteed you'll be able to disclose useful information to us, which we currently don't have, and—"

Donovan was cut off by Von Burton, who waved his hand before Donovan's face.

"Sorry, Walsh, but this is a high-profile criminal we're dealing with. No way we're gonna be able to disclose any more information, so if you will just cooperate and give us the information we need, then we'll be on our way," Von Burton said obnoxiously.

Donovan tensed up as he looked at the hand girlishly waving before his face.

"First of all, I'm Special Agent Alec D. Donovan, Von Burton."

"It's Special Agent E. B. Von Burton," Von Burton said with a smirk.

"Whatever. Why should we just hand over useful information if you two won't share information with us? The way I see it, we're on the same team, we should be helping each other out, right?"

"Sorry, Donovan, but that's not the way it's gonna be, not with this case. There's certain confidential information that we're just not going to disclose to you, or any other agency at the moment—"

"Well, without us, you guys wouldn't have been able to find one of your prime suspects. You guys couldn't find him in thirteen years and it only took us a couple of days. What happened?" Walsh asked.

"He was an asset linked to one of the biggest nationwide crime syndicates and drug-trafficking networks, who you might have heard of—Nada Mas. Anyway, he played an important role and went into hiding. Luckily for us, another suspect connected to Nada Mas who we apprehended was able to give us some more insight as to who he was, and eventually be used to help us bait him. Unfortunately it happened that we found out his whereabouts when the abducted girl and mother came into the picture. So before you start accusing me about not doing my job, I think that you should worry about doing your job. Aren't there over a million illegal immigrants in the United Stated right now? Your little abducted girl is the spawn of one of them, so shouldn't you worry about getting your expendable seed child and sending her back to Mexico with the rest of the border jumpers, Wash?" Qubish said in a calm, stern manner as he stepped towards Walsh, blowing smoke into his face.

"It's Walsh," he said as he choked on the excess of smoke.

"Whatever, just stay out of our way. We'll handle this situation, okay?" Qubish said.

"Listen, Qubish, if you want to act like it's your show, fine, just stay out of our way," Donovan said calmly.

"No, you make sure to stay out of our way," Von Burton instigated.

"Don't you talk down to me, Burton." Donovan stepped closer to Von Burton, who wore a taunting smirk. "I'm a thirty-five-year veteran, and you look like you're still wearing a diaper. So I suggest you take your mocha latte and—"

"It's E. B. Von Burton, and don't worry, I'm sure we'll get to our guy and your girl first," Von Burton said spitefully. Qubish then stepped in between Donovan and Von Burton.

"Hey, hey, c'mon, you two. Enough of this schoolyard bullshit. We're professionals, we should be acting like gentlemen." Qubish seemed to speak only to Donovan, which Walsh took as offensive and disrespectful. So Walsh stepped before Qubish with his hands held up before him.

"Hey, step back, Qubitch. Why don't you just relax, okay? Let's all just go our separate ways?"

"Don't touch me, Walsh. Just step back, before you get hurt," Qubish demanded. All four agents then stepped back, separated from each other, staring with the least respect, and then took a moment to relax.

"Okay, now that we're all calmed down, I hope, I think that this is where we go our separate ways. Qubish, Burton, it was a pleasure to meet you two, and as strange as this may sound now, I hope we see each other soon," Donovan said in an attempt to bring peace.

"Don't worry, Donovan, we will, and I'll make sure to keep your girl company while we wait for you two." Qubish smacked Von Burton on the chest as Von Burton made his wiseass remark, and then they said their goodbyes and walked away.

"Oh, it's on, we'll be waiting for you at the finish line, Qubitch," Walsh said as Qubish and Von Burton walked further away. Donovan looked at Walsh and shook his head.

"We'll be waiting for you at the finish line? What the hell is that, Walsh?" Donovan said as he turned towards Walsh while shaking his head from side to side.

"They started it."

"Yeah, I know. Don't let it get to you, okay? It's over now, it's time for us to get back to business," Donovan said. The two began to walk away.

"Well, I guess I overreacted a little bit, sorry."

"We all did, Walsh, we all did. It's all right, don't worry about it. C'mon, let's get outta here," Donovan said calmly, bringing closure to a long, stressful day.

<u>80</u>

Sergio Serrano sat dignified with zeal gleaming in his piercing green eyes as he waited within an office area of an undisclosed FBI facility for his superiors to summon him into their private office for an essential meeting. Awaiting Sergio amongst the chaos of ringing phones, chatter, Internet and flat-screen television news feeds, and various FBI agents walking by and working at their desks was praise and promotion. Sergio was blind to his advancement, but he had come dressed for the unexpected. Sergio's newly bought slim-cut gray designer suit, white button-down shirt, and matching dark gray tie were all ironed and pressed, and complemented his well-polished black Italian designer boots. Even Sergio's fresh fade and smooth clean-shaven face were a reflection of preparedness for the unknown. But as multiple agents from various branches within the FBI continued to walk on by Sergio, he stood alone as a minority of one. A Latino who was a devoted agent filled with morality, willing to make the necessary sacrifices for family, country and the Federal Bureau of Investigation.

As Sergio imagined what would become of his career, one of his superiors came out from an isolated side office. Special Agent E. B. Von Burton was the higher-ranking agent to call upon Sergio Serrano. After Sergio was briefly greeted, he stood up, walked across the open floor towards Von Burton, shook hands, and followed him into a private office.

Inside, the spacious office looked like a model office on display in an upscale furniture store. Everything was immaculate. Sergio's modest upbringing seemed to be overshadowed by the lavish desk, leather chairs, and couch, and his status eclipsed by the collage of degrees and certificates and shrine of gold, silver and crystal medals, statuettes, plaques and awards mounted on the wall space behind the desk, where Special Agent J. P. Qubish stood talking on the desk phone. Qubish's stature was endowed with graciousness as he gave firm orders over the phone and summoned Sergio into the office, commanding that he take a seat with his outstretched hand and index finger.

After entering the office, Sergio silently and respectfully took a seat in one of the leather chairs resting before the desk while Von Burton stepped to the side. The quality and smoothness of the leather chair felt rewarding, a giant leap from the unstable, chipped wooden chairs Sergio had grown accustomed to in the Bronx tenement he had grown up in. To have Von Burton and Qubish stand above and look down upon Sergio filled him with not only intimidation, but also honor at being in the presence of such decorated men of valor. Sergio felt welcomed into their circle of valiant and prestigious agents of the FBI.

"So, this is the kid?" Qubish said to Von Burton while he hung up the phone.

"Yep, straight from the womb," Von Burton said sarcastically.

Qubish smiled and stepped forward, leaning over the desk to shake hands with Sergio Serrano.

"Just the way I like them, innocent and blind to the horrors that await them." Sergio stood up to show respect. "No need to get up, son. Sit, relax, and get comfortable. We have a lot to go over."

Sergio sat back down.

"So, I hear you served in the Corps, two tours in Iraq and Afghanistan."

"Yes, sir, that's correct. I was in the First Marine Division and was a part of Operation Iraqi Freedom and Operation Enduring Freedom."

"Is that so? So, how was it? Did you see a lot of action out there in the asshole of the world?"

"I guess you could say I saw my share of action, mostly in Baghdad and Fallujah, where I dealt with a lot of insurgents. But after taking over Baghdad and Tikrit, I ended up in Afghanistan, where things weren't as chaotic, since I helped lead a multinational coalition and worked alongside the Afghan National

Security Forces."

"That's good that the storm cleared away, especially since you were deep in the shit, but I'm sure you got your licks in and blew away some Al-Qaeda shit bags and took out some sand monkeys while you were over there. Doing humanity a favor, ya know, help keep the population down without those fucking savages. I know what you must've been dealing with over there. Shit, I had my share in Korea and Nam, I still got scars from those fucking zipper heads."

Qubish display of psychotic patriotism left Sergio unsure how to respond.

"So, how was the hijab pussy out there? Nice and sandy, enough to make your dick come out like a chicken cutlet?" Von Burton said.

"Don't they keep their ghost rags on over there and cut three holes in it, one for the mouth, one for the cunt, and one for their hairy butthole?" Qubish added.

"Nah, that's the Amish."

"Amish don't fuck, it's tha Orthodox, those fucking Jews. Don't be fooled, they were spawned from the same desert those fucking savages run amok in," Qubish stated, then turned towards Sergio, who remained silent. "Anyway, enough small talk, back to business. So, Mr. Serrano, you're here with us today because we've been looking for someone like you. We need someone to help infiltrate a nationwide crime syndicate known as Nada Mas, a group I'm sure you've heard of." At the mention of Nada Mas, Sergio reached up to caress his left shoulder and became filled with terrifying flashbacks.

"Yes, I've heard of Nada Mas. One of my first assignments with the FBI was out in California, working undercover with small-time street thugs who were connected to them."

"Yeah, that's right, Operation Friends Till the End. It's all here on your file." Qubish held Sergio's personnel file in his hand, then placed it back down on the desk and began to tap his index finger on top of the desk. "It didn't end too smoothly, did it?" Qubish pointed at Sergio's left shoulder.

"No, it didn't. Unexpected circumstances came into play during a sting operation, and all hell broke loose."

"Oh yeah? So, what happened?" Von Burton asked.

Sergio looked up at Qubish, who nonverbally gave Sergio the okay to discuss the event.

"Well, my partner and I were assigned to befriend two small-time thugs who worked for the Suarez drug-trafficking syndicate based in Colombia. They were connected to Nada Mas, which at the time was only in its infancy. The assignment was only supposed to last a few months. My partner was supposed to be the one who befriended these small-time thugs, and I was only supposed to sit back, follow them and keep a close eye on both of them and my partner. Anyway, one day while my partner and I were out having some coffee, he got a random call to meet up with one of them, just to get together and hang out. I followed them to a restaurant and waited in the parking lot. When they came back out, they had a woman with them. She had a baby, and by the way she was being forced to walk, it was obvious that she was abducted—for what, I didn't know at the time. It wasn't until I followed them to another restaurant that I found out why she was taken."

"Listen to this shit," Qubish interrupted. Von Burton smiled like a teenage girl wanting to hear more gossip and then gave Sergio his full attention.

"So, after I followed them to another restaurant, I decided to go inside to see what was going on. After they got inside, they joined another thug and then ordered some food. I ended up getting a table not too far from where they were sitting, someplace isolated from suspicion, yet in the open for my partner to see me. Not only was my partner able to see me, but he was in a position where he could exchange text messages with me and give me some intel on what was going on, since all the attention was now on the woman. It turned out that she was just some mule working for the Salas drug-trafficking syndicate. The thugs knew about it from a friend they knew who worked in the restaurant where she made the money and drug drop-offs. After I found out who she was, everything became more intense, especially when another guy showed up, a Colombian who was there to collect the score this thug made with my partner. After the collector checked the goods, that's when negotiations began and the unexpected began to unfold."

Sergio paused, readjusted his body, and then continued with melodramatic hand motions.

"Since the fat thug who was waiting at the restaurant, was in the bathroom the entire time, the other thug went to go check on his friend in the bathroom, but quickly came back without him. That's when the Colombian began to panic. From what I remember, my partner looked up at me, gave me the *be ready to get involved* look. As he did so, the Colombian caught my partner signaling me, which provoked him to stab my partner in the hand with a steak knife. As he reached for his gun, suddenly, out of nowhere, these other two sitting at the bar—who we later found out worked for the Salas syndicate and just happened to be there—opened fire. Everyone in the place panicked. Innocent people got shot, along with the thug, the two from the bar, and me." Sergio reached up to hold his left shoulder again. "Shot by some patron who was carrying and felt the need to get involved without knowing who was who."

"There's always a fucking cowboy in the crowd, looking to get involved in hostile situations when they don't know their dick from their gun. Fucking stains of the NRA, that's what they are," Qubish added passionately.

"Anyway, after the two random Salas gang members were taken out, along with the Suarez street thug and my partner, the Colombian left with the girl and the baby. He used them as hostages and took the exchange bag as well. Later on, after leaving the scene, the Colombian ended up losing control of his car and crashing. He was stabbed in the throat with a pen by the girl, who ended up surviving the crash and left with the baby. Ironically, she left all the money in the exchange bag, in the car."

"Talk about being at the wrong place at the wrong time. Small world, right? And what ever happened with the girl?"

"No one knows. All we were able to find out was that she was some illegal who obviously got scared and fled into hiding. Still, to this day I think of her and the baby. Ya know, hoping wherever she ended up going with the baby, she's okay."

"Well, unfortunately, there's not much we can do for people like her, but what we can do is protect them from the thugs who use them for profit. That's why you're here today. We need not only good agents to infiltrate these drug gangs, but Latinos such as you who will be able to blend in."

Qubish lifted Sergio's personnel file and opened it.

"Based on your file, your name is Sergio Serrano, a Mexican American from the Bronx who served four years as a Marine in Iraq and Afghanistan. After being honorably discharged, you ended up going back home to New York City to work for the NYPD as part of their street crime tactical unit, infiltrating MS13, and most recently served two years in the FBI, working alongside Cristiano Castillo, also known as Chato, in operation Friends Till the End, infiltrating the Suarez crime syndicate connected to Nada Mas."

Qubish closed Sergio's file, placed it back on top of the desk and then continued.

"Before we move on any further, as you already know, Nada Mas is a major crime syndicate within the United States. It's involved with drug and human trafficking and connected to institutions such as the banking system, major corporations, media outlets, and pretty much anything people depend on. But the root of this evil, and the head that needs to be cut off, is the drug trafficking syndicates it's connected to. They span to the tip of South America and all the way across the globe to the far ends of Asia. Fortunately, most of the head drug lords and players at the top of the pyramid of Nada Mas have either been detained or killed off by rival gangs or people within. Basically, Nada Mas is on the verge of collapse. After hunting these bastards down for the past eleven years, we're finally in a position where we have an opportunity to get to the mastermind behind Nada Mas, Benjamin Bradford, aka Benny. Since he's been able to successfully run everything from the shadows, it's been difficult to get to him. After detaining various members, gathering intel, and putting the pieces to the puzzle together—well, the picture is much clearer, and there are two big pieces that we need in order to get to Bradford."

Qubish handed Sergio two profile folders, one on Dante and the other on Stanley Albert Paul, aka Daffy, which Sergio then opened and perused.

"As you can see, the closest link to Bradford is his best friend, Dante De Luna, a very successful artist who basically lives off the grid and has been difficult to track down. But the other link, who we've had an eye on for a very long time, is Stanley Albert Paul, also known as Daffy. This guy's a computer hacker who helped Nada Mas out tremendously in the early years, then took his earnings and basically went on a permanent vacation. Lucky for us, he's kept tabs on everyone within Nada Mas, and most importantly, he will be easy to tempt and bring into custody. And that's where you come in. Well, if you're interested. But before you make a decision, let me give you the lowdown on what you'll need to do. Daffy keeps his nose clean legally, covers all his illegal activities so well that we have no way of legally detaining him, and we have not been able to locate him after all these years. All we know is that he's living somewhere on the West Coast. We'll need someone with your skills and experience to get to him. So before we get to Daffy, what we need to do is to get to his most trusted friend within Nada Mas, a street thug from Jersey named Indio Iglesia. So, basically, you'll be assigned to spend one to two years working undercover in Jersey, befriending Indio, building a strong relationship, and then moving out west—with the help of Indio—to locate Daffy and hook up with him. After that, we'll be able to lure Daffy in and set him up on a sting operation, detain him and get him to 'fess up. With all we have on him, he'll give in and give us all we want."

Sergio caressed his chin in contemplation, looking down at the open files resting on his lap and then up at Qubish.

"And this Indio is the only person close to Daffy? There's no one else at all who lives on the West Coast?"

"That's right. The only other person close to Daffy was Dante, who we have been unable to locate. He cut ties with both Daffy and Indio a long time ago. He's the only one who may be able to make contact with Bradford and know where to find him, but the only way we'll be able to get to him is through Daffy. But ever since Daffy got involved with Nada Mas, he cut all ties with family and friends, and since Indio was the one person he was always with and dealing with all the time, Daffy built a very good trusting relationship with Indio, and it was through Indio that Daffy befriended Dante. So by detaining Daffy, it's a win-win situation. Not only will we be able to locate and eventually detain Dante, who has been involved with Nada Mas, through Daffy, but he is the final link that could get us to Benjamin Bradford."

"So, basically, it's a puzzle we're putting together and the three final pieces are Indio, Daffy, and Dante." Sergio closed the files and leaned forward to hand them back to Qubish, who smiled.

"Yes, that's correct, and Benjamin Bradford is the big picture we're putting together." Qubish turned towards Von Burton. "I like this kid. You got good taste, E. B."

"I told you I like them smart. No type A, easy to get in the sack, mind trap beauty queens, although you are kinda cute with that Latin flavor you got going on."

"You're not so bad yourself. So, if I decide to play along and take part in this operation, how's it going to work out?"

"Well, if you decide to jump on board, you'll be provided a new alias," Qubish explained. "IDs, documentation, birth certificate, passport, anything you may need to live as your new persona, which will be Andres Alvarez. You'll be set up in an apartment in New Jersey and provided a script for your new identity: family history, schools you've attended, and the life you've lived as Andres Alvarez, which you will need to know like you know your own dick. Unlike your last undercover assignment, you will not be overseeing another agent. You will be the one playing best friend. You'll have a team of agents overseeing everything and watching your back. That shit that happened with Operation Friends Till the End won't happen on my watch. I'll make sure that you're protected at all times, especially if you end up in a heated situation. So, Mr. Serrano, do you have any questions?"

Sergio thought for a moment before speaking. "Sounds like a good assignment. This is something I've been waiting for for a while. My only concern is the time I will be doing this. Ya know, for how long?"

"Well, we can't guarantee a specific duration of time, but we do know you should be able to get what we want within a window of one to two years, where you won't be able to contact any family or friends except through us."

"That's one of the things I was concerned about. Ya know, since I have a big family, and family is everything to me," Sergio said with concern.

"Hey, listen, we all have family, but the good thing is you're willing to make the necessary sacrifices to support them and honor them, just like you did when you spent four years in Iraq and Afghanistan, which was more dangerous than what you'll be doing for us."

"E. B. is right, and the good thing is that you're single, with no wife and no kids, so there is no need to have to worry about their safety, to feel guilt or to have to lie and make excuses for never being home. I've seen many divorces happen because young, ambitious agents such as yourself step up for one of these gigs, and I've also seen many good men become so detached from their lives that they lose everything. Not only are you smart, kid, but you have a good head on your shoulders. That's what we like about you. You do this gig and get the job done, the two years or so you sacrifice will benefit you and your family tremendously in the future. So, what's it gonna be, kid?"

Sergio was left in the limelight. He was not only a very humble and loving individual, but an honorable agent, willing to sacrifice for family and the men of valor he had served with and those he now worked beside. Bringing down Nada Mas was like slaying Goliath, and Sergio was willing to be David, against all odds, to throw the rock that brings down Nada Mas, which had negatively affected many families and individuals with their crimes against humanity. After thinking about the bigger picture and what he was in a position to do, Sergio confidently leaned forward.

"Okay, I'm in."

"Good, I'm happy to hear that, son. You're gonna be fine. Before we begin with the necessary arrangements, let's set up another meeting so that we can debrief you on the assignment and then take it from there. It was a pleasure to meet you, Mr. Serrano." Qubish stepped towards Sergio, who stood up to shake hands.

"No, the pleasure is all mine. Thank you for this opportunity."

"You've earned it, kid."

Sergio smiled and then turned towards Von Burton to shake his hand and then say farewell before leaving the most important meeting of his career.

Sergio Serrano was a minority of one, a Latino who was now in a position to represent Latinos in a positive light by being the force that would eventually take down Nada Mas. He felt honored to bring down a crime syndicate that had not only adversely affected many but had used, harmed and profited off of the souls of Latinos such as himself.

81

After eighteen months spent living inside a studio apartment in Bloomfield, New Jersey, the metamorphosis was almost complete. Sergio Serrano was no longer warm and safe within his cocoon of love and security but was now in the wild, an agent of man, who had finally shed his chrysalis skin and evolved into Andres Alvarez. Andres wasn't a modest, slim, clean-cut specimen of peace but a toned, bulked-up fearless warrior, waiting for the right moment to spread his wings and fly with the vultures.

For now, though, every day was exactly the same. After securing a job as a waiter at Riviera Azul, the restaurant Indio Iglesia helped managed and oversee in the Ironbound section of Newark, Andres lived a very strict and regimented lifestyle. When not working, Andres spent each day learning the neighborhoods and gathering as much intel as he could on Indio and all his associates. He frequently visited places within Essex, Hudson, and Union counties, learning about who Andres, the persona that Sergio Serrano had become, was, and above all else, he kept his mind, body, and soul fit.

Around Andres's studio apartment, as he did yoga, pull-ups, push-ups, and sit-ups, there were limited possessions, just the necessities to survive the time spent living in solitude, such as a bed, a table, chairs, a futon, a dresser, a coffee table, kitchen utensils and other essentials. Scattered around were books and magazines left stacked up in various spiral piles, which were used as a source of entertainment since there was no television to resort to to distract and close the mind. Also, all of his clothes were neatly folded and placed inside the dresser or hanging up in the closet. The most important items in the apartment were left resting on the table: a laptop, a cell phone, an issued 9mm gun, folders filled with the profile records of Andres Alvarez and Indio Iglesia, and photographs and notebooks filled with important information collected and gathered on Indio, the world in which he lived and Nada Mas.

After finishing a rigorous workout, Andres stood stoic in his black-and-orange trunks. Fatigued and blissful, he studied his reflection in the full-length mirror, able to see clearly that everything around him was an illusion. Andres Alvarez, the bulked-up body reflected in the mirror, wasn't the true persona behind the mask.

Sergio Serrano's soul was pure. The body was his temple, and like the sacred sanctuaries of worship, Sergio's body was clean from negative influences and energy, such as hate, fear, and edible toxins. It was his alter ego, Andres Alvarez, who needed to be fed harmful vices in order to fit into the character who shared the same body. Smoking cigarettes, consuming alcohol, and moderately taking cocaine were necessary during the duration of the undercover assignment in order to build tolerance and the experience so that Sergio could play along as Andres Alvarez with Indio and other criminals. After working out and stretching, Sergio stepped into the kitchen, did a line of cocaine, poured a glass of Johnny Walker Red, and lit up a cigarette. He then stepped out into the middle of the vast open studio apartment, smoking his cigarette and sipping his whiskey as he contemplated, straddling two dueling personas.

It was a parallel world, and Sergio was stuck in the middle. The only thing that remained from his past was the scar on his left shoulder from his last assignment. In the bare dust-covered door mirror, there was Andres Alvarez, while in the well-polished dresser-mounted mirror with pictures of Jesus, the Virgin Mary, and the Virgin Guadalupe attached to the edges, a rosary hanging down from the upper right corner of the frame, there was Sergio Serrano.

As Sergio smoked and sipped his whiskey, he acted the part of his alter ego in the full-length mirror, then held the cigarette and whiskey behind his back as he looked at the reflection of the upper half of Sergio Serrano, standing without any sense of vice.

"Who are you?" Sergio scowled at his reflection in the mirror on the door. He took another sip of whiskey and drag from his cigarette.

"C'mon, mon, you know who I am. I'm Andres Alvarez, from Jersey. Ya know, the one who's gonna bring down Nada Mas . . . oh no, and why is that . . . because I don't have the fucking balls to . . . ya hear this fucking guy telling me I don't have the fucking balls too." Sergio turned away from the mirror and then looked back at his reflection. "Listen, shit bag, I got balls as big as your fucking head, ya understand me? Matter of fact, how 'bout I cut off your fucking balls and feed them to you? How about that, huh?"

Sergio took another sip of whiskey and a drag from his cigarette and then turned and looked at his reflection in the dresser-mounted mirror. He held both the glass of whiskey and cigarette down behind his back and only focused on the upper half of his bare, well-toned upper body and the religious relics.

"*Mamá . . . Mamá*, I know that the things I have to do are sinful, but remember what I told you, that these sacrifices I make are for you, to give you and Papá a better life. That's why I risk my own life every day, so that your lives will always be safe from the criminals who try to harm the innocent, and so that you two can live in comfort . . . I know, I know, don't be tempted by vice and sin, my soul is pure and at any moment it is subject to be poisoned by the damned . . . *Mamá*, you're the one who taught me to be strong from within, and not with these." Sergio touched his heart and held out his fists as he spoke. "*Mamá*, please, don't worry, you know that I love you very much, and we will see each other again, sooner than you think. Remember, I have my friends with me always, okay?"

Sergio paused to savor the spiritual presence of Jesus, the Virgin Mary, and the Virgin Guadalupe. There was an overwhelming sense of peace, which was then suddenly interrupted. Sergio slowly turned his head and looked back over his shoulder at his reflection in the door mirror. He took a sip of whiskey and a drag from his cigarette and then turned around and stepped towards the mirror.

"What . . . whatchu say 'bout my motha . . . what, that she's a what . . . a little louder . . . *puta madre!*"

As Sergio furiously lashed out, he quickly stepped up to the mirror so that he was nose to nose with his reflection. The mirror fogged up with every breath. Sergio didn't back away from his reflection. He firmly stood his ground and gazed deeply into his own piercing green eyes. He smirked and slowly stepped back, finishing his whiskey and the cigarette, which he dropped to the floor and stepped on with his bare foot.

"That's what I thought, mothafucker! Andres Alvarez is king here. *El rey,* mothafucker! Consider this a warning, 'cause next time, I won't cut off your fucking balls and feed them to you, I'll fucking tie you down and fist-fuck your motha in front of you! Ya hear me?"

After Sergio Serrano finished his thuggish dramatics, he silently stood in the open in front of both mirrors. He was no longer Sergio Serrano; he was Andres Alvarez. A brutish, thuggish animal who was streetwise and showed no fear. A menacing warrior with a soul of purity trapped within. But even though, on the surface, Andres Alvarez was the dominating force, deep within the reflection of the piercing green eyes was the soul of Sergio Serrano, the life force behind the character who was prepared to go out into the wild.

82

Riviera Azul was a Latino bar and restaurant nestled within the heart of the Ironbound section of Newark. It served various Latin dishes from Central and South American cultures. Tucked in between various Brazilian and Portuguese restaurants on Ferry Street, it stood out amongst them all, an eye-catching muse with secrets hidden deep within. Inside, amongst the Latin and modern interior décor, were a variety of satisfied customers from all walks of life. To the blind, it was a trendy, hip classy Latin setting, but for those who could see, it was an underground front.

After working for eighteen months as a waiter, Andres Alvarez knew the ins and outs of Riviera Azul. Every day was exactly the same. But it wasn't the customers Andres kept a watchful eye on; it was the small-time drug dealers picking up supplies and returning earnings, representatives of various crime syndicates associated with Nada Mas, and most importantly, the comanagers, Otto and Indio Iglesia, whom Andres had been studying for the past eighteen months, and befriending.

For now, Andres Alvarez played his role as the loyal and hardworking waiter. He was diligent, steadfast, and friendly to customers. The animal within remained asleep; it was waiting to wake up. It was only a matter of time. After studying the routine within Riviera Azul while waiting tables throughout the day, Andres knew it was in the evening hours that Indio Iglesia would make his appearance. As usual, on Tuesday nights at around seven p.m., just as the dinner crowd began to flow in, Indio came walking in. The young, lanky, handsome

Uruguayan slowly walked in wearing all-black designer clothes, with a black knee-length raincoat. He greeted the voluptuous Hispanic hostess and a few regulars and sat down with Otto at the bar.

Andres keenly watched from across the restaurant after taking his last order for the night. As always, when Indio visited, he had a drink at the bar until one of his drug runners or business associates came in. When they did arrive, Indio went into the private room adjacent to the bar with them. But not tonight. As Indio and Otto chatted with the young drug dealer who arrived at the bar, tensions rose. Not only did he refuse to go into the private room with Indio, but he began to yell and make a scene. Indio and Otto both tried to calm him down, while other employees tried to redirect patrons' attention. No one was able to prevent the drug dealer from taking out a brick of cash and cocaine, which Indio tried to take and hide.

Andres seized the moment. The cash was unbound and tossed into the air, which caused it to rain down, and the brick of cocaine ripped open and exploded, antiquing Indio, Otto and the entire bar and floor. This caused Indio and Otto to scuffle with the drug dealer. Andres ran up behind the dealer, grabbed his gun and took him down to the ground.

As patrons stood up to look—and a commotion began—Andres restrained the drug dealer with ease. Knocking him out, he removed the clip from the gun, discharged the bullet from the chamber, tucked the gun and clip into his pants, and then lifted up the drug dealer and dragged him into the back room. Indio and Otto watched with amazement, quickly cleaning up the cash and cocaine, calming patrons down, and then joining Andres in the back room.

# # #

Everything fell into place like clockwork. After the police were notified, they came in to question employees. Andres gained Indio's respect and trust through his actions and was now in a position to be taken under Indio's wing. The moment was right. After work, as Andres stood outside underneath the awning, smoking a cigarette while torrential rain came down, he patiently waited and watched Indio through the front windows. Indio said goodbye to employees and then walked out of Riviera Azul. He greeted Andres and took out a pack of cigarettes. Andres held out his pack of cigarettes and offered Indio one.

"Thank you, brotha . . . Andres, right?" Indio said as he took a cigarette.

"Yep." Andres lit the cigarette for Indio.

"I owe you one, brotha," Indio said after taking a drag. "And ya know, I also want to thank you for all you did the other day. After seeing how you handled the situation—besides knowing you were in the military, you kept your mouth shut."

"No problem, I was just trying to help out."

"Yeah, I appreciate it, but to be honest, I'm curious. Ya know, how come you didn't say anything to the police about what happened? 'Cause, quite frankly, not only are you kinda new here, but you're not as invested as the others who work here. Well, not yet."

"I don't know, just being a loyal employee, that's all."

"So, they teach you about loyalty in the military, I guess, right? Gung-ho, gung-ho," Indio joked.

"Of course, we live and die for our country and our brothers in arms we fight alongside. It's also in the blood, ya know, being loyal. I was raised to be a loyal person," Andres added.

"That's good to know. As for you working here for me, after seeing how you are, I got bigger and better things planned for you. You won't have to live off of table scraps and loose change people leave you anymore, ya understand what I mean? You proved to me you're worth the upgrade."

"Yeah, yeah, I gotchu. Thanks, I appreciate it." Andres smiled.

"Good, that's good. Anyway, I can't believe this rain. All day it's been like this. It's depressing, and the cold isn't helping either." Indio paused and took a drag. "So, where'd you park your car?"

"I don't have a car, I take the 11 bus from Penn Station."

"Really, and no umbrella either?" Indio studied Andres. "You can't walk from here to Penn Station in this rain." Indio flicked the half smoked cigarette out into the street. "Where you live?"

"Bloomfield."

"Bloomfield, that's not far from here. C'mon, I gotchu, get in."

"You sure?"

"Of course, I can't let one of my best waiters get sick." Indio opened the passenger-side door to his fully loaded black Range Rover Sport, shut it behind Andres, and walked around the front. Andres smiled as he sat in silence. After Indio got in, they left Riviera Azul and drove out into the darkest part of the storm.

<u>83</u>

Although outside it rained like hell, inside the impeccable Range Rover Sport it felt like heaven. The techno trance music playing, the cleanliness, the new-car smell, and Indio's welcoming persona made Andres feel at ease. And even though Andres didn't know where the road ahead led, he knew that he was one step closer to completing his assignment.

"So, if I remember correctly, you're from south Jersey, right?" Indio said as he drove with his hands at ten and two.

"Yep, Galloway Township."

"Oh yeah, that's right. So, what made you decide to move all the way up north?"

"Just a change of scenery. Ya know, after a majority of my closest friends all moved out of state, and with no other family around anymore, I felt that it would be best to move up north to start fresh," Andres recited from his script with ease.

"Any brothers or sisters?"

"Yep, just me and José back there," Andres joked as he looked back over his shoulder. Indio looked in the rearview mirror at the empty backseat and smiled.

"So, I guess that makes you an only child. What about your mom and dad?"

"Dad left when I was four, and Mom passed away not too long ago. She had heart problems her whole life. Ya know, it was just her time to go."

"Sorry to hear, but why Bloomfield?"

"I don't know, it was one of the first places I found for rent when I was looking, and I just decided to jump on it."

"Like fate or something," Indio added.

"Perhaps. Who knows, right? But I can say that the only reason I ended up finding Riviera Azul is because no other restaurants in Bloomfield or Montclair were hiring. So I took a bus down to Newark and ended up on Ferry Street. Out of all the restaurants there, Riviera Azul was the most appealing."

"That's right, that's why we do such good business down there. Anyway, I gotta make a quick stop. You don't mind, do ya?"

"Nah, not at all."

"Thanks, I just gotta see a friend real quick and pick something up, that's it. It should only take a few minutes."

"Yeah, that's cool, no problem. I'm in no rush to get home."

"Okay, nice, so it works out for the both of us; we're almost there now." Indio turned off the main street, down narrow, secluded side streets. Eventually, he approached an overpass and then stopped for a moment underneath.

"Okay, here's the deal. Ya see that two-family house at the end of the street?"

"Which one, that white one?" Andres wiped the condensation off the window with his hand and leaned forward to get a better look.

"Yeah, that's it, 101," Indio said as he pointed at the house. "Listen, I was expecting to come here on my own, but now that you're here, well, you could help me out. I have to go inside and pick something up from a friend of mine. Here's the deal, though. If I don't come out in ten minutes, and I mean ten minutes, no more, no less, you come in to get me." Indio took out a pad of paper and wrote something, then handed the note to Andres. "Here, this is the password to tell the guy at the door so that you'll be able to get in."

Andres looked at Indio curiously. "So, what is it, a boys' club?"

"Something like that, but without getting into too much detail, this shit bag, Ángel, some small-time pimp, some real fucking creep, owes me some money." Indio shut the light off and drove out from under the overpass into the pouring rain and the darkness of the night, further down the secluded dead-end street, and then parked two houses down.

"All right, check the clock. Remember, ten minutes, no more, no less." Indio reached into his inner jacket pocket, took out a gun, checked the rounds, put it back, and then reached across Andres and opened up the glove compartment. "Don't be scared, it's only for my protection. And this one is for you, just in case you have to come in for me. If you do, there'll be a guy standing at the base of the stairs. Just tell him that you're meeting me and Ángel, that you have something for us. You're an ex-Marine, so you should know how to use one of those."

"Yeah, but . . ." Andres pretended to be nervous.

"Listen, not only are you an ex-Marine, but ever since you broke up the drug deal gone bad in the restaurant, seeing how you were able to handle such an unpredictable situation and, most importantly, keep your mouth shut for the police, I know that I can trust you now. Consider this a test. Ya wanna make more money, well, you help me now, you won't be waiting tables and mopping the floor anymore, got it? So, be ready, okay?"

"All right, no worries, I gotchu."

Indio flashed him a smile and then exited the Range Rover. As Andres watched Indio trot towards the house, he contemplated his situation. Everything that was now unfolding was playing in his favor. Where the road ahead led, Andres didn't know, but he was sure that it would get him to where he wanted to go sooner than later. Only time would tell.

After seeing that ten minutes had passed on the digital clock, Andres took out a small Virgin of Guadalupe card to admire and pray to. He put it away, took out the gun from the glove compartment, and looked at his reflection in the visor mirror. In the mirror was Andres Alvarez, the animal who was willing to make the necessary sacrifices and commit whatever sin was needed to fulfill his assignment. Deep within the piercing green eyes was Sergio Serrano, the modest soul trapped in a world of heaven and hell.

After reflecting on his dueling personas, Andres exited the Range Rover. As he stood out in the pouring rain, he tucked the gun into the waistband of the back of his pants and reached inside his inner jacket pocket. He took out his issued 9mm, checked the rounds, put it back inside, and then trotted towards the two-family house.

Andres stepped up to the door on the left side of the two-family house. He knocked, then waited for someone to answer. He gave the password and, to his surprise, without any inquiring as to who he was, was welcomed in by the obese man guarding the entrance.

Flashbacks of urban warfare in Iraq and Afghanistan consumed Andres's mind as he blindly stepped into the unknown. He took a moment to observe his surroundings as he slowly walked from room to room. It was evident that the duplex was a front for criminal activities. In different rooms were men from all walks of life, indulging in alcoholic drinks, drugs, gambling, and musing over the many Latin women who catered to their every need. It was nothing new to Andres's eyes, but being a stranger in an unknown place, Andres knew to be vigilant, especially since he didn't know where Indio was exactly and whether or not he was in danger.

Although Andres was curious, he had to let his inquisitiveness go and carry on with his assignment. Returning to the base of the stairwell, Andres spoke to the person Indio had instructed him to talk to.

"Hey, brotha, how are you?"

"What's up?" The short rat-looking street thug was wearing a red Puma jacket, standing with his hands in his pocket inauspiciously.

"I'm here to see Indio and Ángel. I have something for them."

The street rat sternly stared Andres up and down and then reached out his open hand. Andres smiled, shook his head and reached into his pocket, taking out a twenty-dollar bill, which he then handed to him. The street rat stepped to the side to let Andres up the stairs.

"They're on the third floor in the room at the end of the hallway."

"Thanks, brotha; keep the change," Andres said as he began to walk up the stairs. The hallway of each floor had Latinas walking in and out of rooms with satisfied customers, and up and down the narrow stairwell past Andres. Andres walked with his head down so that no one would see his face. This unfortunately kept Andres blind to one of the most important pieces of the puzzle the FBI was trying to find.

As Andres walked up to the third floor with his head down, Dante De Luna walked down the stairs past Andres with one of the Hispanic whores. They brushed shoulders. Just like that, the most important piece of the puzzle that could lead Andres and the FBI to Benjamin Bradford, the mastermind behind Nada Mas, was gone.

Andres walked to the end of the third-floor hallway. As he crept past each room, he could hear whores being fucked, funk music playing, and a variety of conversations. Andres stepped before the door at the end of the hallway. Before entering, he put his ear close to the door to hear what was going on. All the voices coming from within were muffled, but from the subtle uprising, Andres was able to confirm there was a confrontation. Being the ex-Marine Andres was, he took out the gun Indio had given him, assumed an offensive stance and prepared to storm into the unknown.

But the street rat from downstairs had stalked Andres and was now pushing the barrel of a cocked gun against the back of his head.

"Don't even think about it."

Andres froze. He felt stupid that he'd let his guard down and been caught by the little rat-looking motherfucker. The street rat took the gun from Andres and walked into the room.

Ángel stood with his gun pointed at Indio, who stood with his hands up. There was another street rat standing beside Indio with a gun, who the thug in the red Puma jacket handed Andres's gun to, and a Latina sitting on a bed in the nude beside Ángel.

"Shiiiiiiiiit, whose tha fuck is this mothafucka?"

"He's a friend of this one."

"Shiiit, so who's this? Tha drug mans yous told me was waiting in ya car for yous with all tha shit? Shiiiiiit, and eyes thought yous were lying, shame on me." Ángel turned towards the whore and looked at everyone as he continued. "Shit, now wees have a party. Fiesta, mothafuckas, ain't that right, baby girl?" Ángel caressed the cheek of the Latina with the outer edges of his elongated fingertips.

"So, what's yous name, mothafucka?" Andres remained silent. "Shit, what, yous deaf or something, or yous just some dumb Forrest Gump mothafucka? Shiiiiiit, eyes ain't got time for that silent shit." Ángel pointed the gun at Andres. "Now, what's yous names, yous Corky ass mothafucka?"

"Andres," he said softly.

"Andres. Shit, yous sounds like yous wanna sucks my dick like this baby girl rights here. So, Andres, whys yous wit this damn fool? Shiiit, don't yous know hes thinks hes big times cause hes all up in Nada Mas's ranks? Shiiiiiit, eyes makes more profit wit my owns independent operations sets up all up in heres. Shit, ain't that right, baby girl?"

"So, why you'd come to me to do business?" Indio said calmly.

"Whos tolds yous to talk, mothafucka? This is my show."

Andres could clearly see the unstableness in his eyes and the decay of drug abuse all over his fragile body, and was just waiting for the right moment to take control of the unpredictable situation.

"See how you are? This is why you will fail in the end, you're unprofessional. Look at you, I'm doing you a favor with what I'm offering you, and you can't see that. What you're paying for, all I'm giving you, is a bargain. It's like Christmas for you right now and you can't see that?"

"Shiiiiiit, and whos the fucks is yous, Santas Clause, mothafucka? Shiiiiiit, eyes do business hows Ángel does business, eyes takes what eyes wants when eyes want." Ángel looked down at a mound of cocaine and a cut brick of it resting on top of the coffee table in the center of the room.

It was now evident why Indio had brought Andres with him at the last minute. It was clear that Ángel wasn't some regular buyer, that he was a new customer who couldn't be trusted.

"Shiiiiiit. Knows what, Rojos? Whys don't yous leave Forrest and Santa here wit me? Ramirez, yous can wait outside the door, eyes got these two in check."

Both the street rats, Rojos and Ramirez, left, and Ángel wiped the excess of cocaine off his nose with his gun pointing at Indio and Andres. He felt empowered.

"Now, here's hows wees gonna conduct business, nows that yous friends is here. One of yous is gonna stays here wit me and baby girl, while the otha one of yous goes and gets me more powder for our fiesta. What yous think about that?"

"Why would we do that?" Indio questioned Ángel.

"Cause eyes says so, plus, yous ain't got no choice, cause if one of yous don't go wit Ramirez to get more cake mix, shit, eyes kills yous both right now."

Ángel pointed the gun at both Indio and Andres. Just as he looked away for a moment, Andres rapidly drew his gun from the inner pocket of his jacket, shot Ángel in the stomach, and then turned around and shot through the door, hitting Ramirez. The Latina screamed as Ángel's blood was splattered all over her nude body, and his limp body lay across her lap.

"Fuck!" Indio yelped.

"Hurry up, get the *perico!*" Andres yelled. Indio put the drugs into a leather bag and picked it up. He walked up to the Latina, who curled up into the fetal position.

"Where's the money? Where's all the money?"

The Latina remained frozen. Andres picked her up and once again demanded to know where Ángel kept all his money. She crawled into the closet and came out with a gym bag filled with cash. Andres looked inside, showed Indio all the cash, and then ran to the window. Indio went out and down the fire escape first.

"Hold on, I'll be right there," Andres yelled out the window to Indio, who didn't even look back. Andres checked on Ángel, who was still breathing, wrapped a bedsheet around his wound, and then checked on Ramirez, who held his wounded leg. Just as Andres turned back around to leave, Rojos came storming up the stairs and began to run down the hallway, managing to scare Latina whores and their customers with his gun drawn. Andres went out the window, down the fire escape and deeper into dark waters.

<u>84</u>

Two years after patiently investigating and befriending Indio Inglesia and unexpectedly being brought into the lower ranks of Nada Mas, Andres Alvarez was finally in a position to bring closure to the assignment, inside Riviera Azul, where it had all started. Andres and Indio, sat side by side with a drink in hand, reminiscing over the short time they'd shared together. No matter how attached Indio seemed to get, Andres couldn't allow his conscience to overcome his faceless exterior, even as Indio continued to muse over his presence.

"Ya know, I'm really gonna miss you when you leave." Indio took his fourth shot of tequila and a sip of his draft beer. "Seriously, in the little bit of time we've spent together, I feel like we've gotten really tight."

"Really? Well I feel honored, so I'll drink to that," Andres humored Indio as he raised his glass of Johnny Walker Red.

"Yeah, well, I also won't miss how vague you can be, especially with all those women you get numbers from."

"Hey, I don't fuck and tell, my friend. You want another drink?"

"Yeah, right. Sure, yeah, I'll take another. Hey, Raquel, one more, *por favor*." Andres played along with Indio's jealousy and made sure to keep him loose and talking with more drinks. After Raquel, the gorgeous Brazilian bartender, gave Indio another drink, he took a sip and then continued to speak openly. "But, in all seriousness, what I'll really miss most when you're gone is all you've done for me. Really, all the shipments you've delivered and all the money you've collected from all those shit bags. There'll never be another like you, my friend. Ya know, someone I can rely on and trust."

As Indio slurred his words with his drink in hand, Andres smiled as he looked at Indio's tipsy reflection in the mirror.

"I don't know about all that, but what about the people you used to work with when you first got involved with Nada Mas? Weren't they the bigshots who got everything started over here? You kinda make me feel superior to them."

"Which people?" Indio garbled out with a slight smile.

"Ya know, the hacker who set up shop in Jersey City, and that artist friend of yours you've told me about once before. Weren't the three of you the core of operations at one point?"

"Oh, you're talking about Daffy and Dante. Didn't I tell you about those two before?" As Indio spoke with a drunken sense of alertness, Andres smiled and then continued to orchestrate and pull Indio's strings.

"Yeah, but you just mentioned that they just got started with Nada Mas when you did, and you never really got into too much detail about them."

"You sure?"

"Yeah, I'm sure."

Indio took another sip of beer. "All right, I guess. So, yeah, Daffy, he was this genius computer hacker brought in to set up shop here in Jersey, even though he was fucked up in the head. I mean, this guy was some sick fuck. He used to enjoy having women fuck him in the ass with a strap-on."

Andres listened with a smile and then incited Indio to share more. "Seriously?"

"Yeah, I'm not making this shit up. And as fucked up as he was, he was extremely diligent and great at what he did. He had everything organized, ya know, like the daily operations, finances, inventory, funding. He basically created a whole database for Nada Mas from scratch and kept tabs on everything and everyone. He was a dysfunctional prodigy."

"No shit. And what about the other guy?"

"Who, Dante?"

"Yeah."

"Dante, well, he was good people, ya know. I guess you could say I had a close relationship with him, even though he was an introvert and he was quiet and kept to himself. The only reason I got close with him was because it was my job to pick him up from the airport and pick up supplies from his shit apartment he was living in at the time in the East Village."

"Is that so?"

"Yeah, actually it's sad how he ended up there. He used to be some really successful artist and have some amazing girlfriend; I mean, this girl he was with was like a supermodel. She was like his muse or something, ya know, someone he idolized. All he ever did was talk about her, but the sad thing is, once he got brought into Nada Mas, she ended their relationship, broke his heart, and that's pretty much how he ended up where he did in the Village." Indio took another sip of beer.

"So where he is now?"

"Wish I knew. I haven't seen or spoken to him in years. After the first wave of operations was complete, I got reassigned to a different location, and Dante ended up moving. He just packed up and moved out without telling anyone."

"Really, and has anyone else seen or spoken to him since?"

"Nope."

"And Daffy wasn't able to locate him?"

"Nah, it was as if he disappeared from existence. Actually, what's funny is that Daffy was heartbroken. He had a thing for Dante. He was like a little kid when he was with Dante, ya know, how a younger brother can be with their older brother. I swear to God, Daffy would've probably sucked Dante's dick if he'd told him too." Both Andres and Indio laughed and then took a sip from their drinks. "But, in all honesty, knowing Dante, he's probably dead. I wouldn't be surprised if he killed himself over his girl. He probably left the country to get as far away as he could and either drank himself to death or jumped off the roof of a skyscraper."

"Interesting. And what about Daffy, you still keep in touch with him?"

"Yeah, somewhat. Ya know, not as much as I use to. He's living out west now, not too far from where you plan on going. I'm pretty sure he's still in Tucson. That's not too far from Phoenix, right?"

"Nah, I don't think so. Anyway, ya know, once I'm out there I'll make the best of it, starting fresh again like I did here."

"Well, if you do need a friend while you're out there, or you, ya know, need some help, I can always hook you two up."

Andres's smile grew bigger. Indio was finally baited and hooked.

"Yeah, sure, I'd like that. Especially since while I'm out there, with all I learned from you, I plan on starting up my own operation, then maybe the both of us can get something going. I'll be right near the Mexican border, and I have some old friends who know people living in the north of Mexico," Andres said smoothly as he held his drink in his hand.

"Of course, of course. We'll get some little side hustle going between us. And remember, like I told you before, I owe you for all you've done for me, remember that, so anything you need, while you're out west, I got your back."

Indio patted Andres on the back and then sipped his beer while Andres watched Indio's reflection in the mirror with a slight smile. Indio was a lost soul who was easily led on. In two years, it hadn't taken much to get close with Indio and gain his trust. Indio was a gullible pawn who was easily manipulated and conquered. The game was set from the very beginning, and now Indio lay limp in checkmate.

As for Andres, who sipped his beer and then placed his pint back down, he looked away from Indio and stared at his own reflection in the mirror. The metamorphosis had finally come full circle. Andres Alvarez no longer saw the brutish fierce animal reflected in the mirror, but the modest and prudent agent who was willing to sacrifice his life for the good of family, country and the Federal Bureau of Investigation. Sergio Serrano, the life force behind the mask, still remained, living deep within the piercing green eyes reflected in the mirror. It was the heart and soul of Sergio Serrano, which had evolved and would continue to fuel the alter ego reflected in the mirror, Andres Alvarez, to get to the final puzzle pieces, far away on the West Coast, in order to finally bring an end to Nada Mas.

85

Since the beginning, Dante's lonely life had been a spiritual test of character, both internally and externally. It had been a journey that had taken Dante from the pits of an impoverished life to the peaks of success, and then back down into an inferno of failure and regrets. It seemed that after shedding away the past and blindly carrying on with Sarita by his side, Dante was now in a better place, even if he seemed to be lost. The road ahead was vast. Both Dante and Sarita appeared to be free from their predecessors, but like the last pieces in a game of chess, they were now in a stalemate, somewhere within the heart of Texas.

As the sun and the moon ascended and descended during the long train ride through Texas, a majority of Dante and Sarita's time was spent in conversation, looking through Sarita's sketchbook, sketching each other, making abstract origami creations, playing intense games of poker, go fish, and war, daydreaming out the windows of the moving train, and every now and then, taking a nap.

"B-L-U-E . . . five . . . 1-2-3-4-5 . . . you will end up in hell," Sarita said with a smile as she read Dante's fortune from a handheld diamond three-dimensional shaped out of paper, which could open up into two different sections, each revealing a series of numbers and colors and then, underneath all the flaps, a fortune.

"Give me that, that's not what it says." Dante reached out and grabbed the fortune-telling origami diamond out of Sarita's hands. Dante's inner child brought out laughter from Sarita, and then Dante performed his own fortune. "Seven . . . 1-2-3-4-5-6-7 . . . green . . . G-R-E-E-N . . . eight . . . 1-2-3-4-5-6-7-8 . . . ha, now that's better. You will grow old and healthy with lots of money. Now that's what I call a good fortune."

Sarita reached out to take it back, but Dante held it up high so she couldn't reach.

"Give it back. It's not fair. You cheated, you checked all the fortunes before you gave yourself one. Cheater, give it back."

"You're imagining things. I never cheat, I live my life by the book."

"Liar, give it back." Dante and Sarita laughed and childishly played with each other. Dante handed Sarita her origami. Sarita then let out a yawn like a lion resting in the plains of Africa.

"Hey, hey. Easy, Simba. It looks like it's time for you to go to bed."

"Um, I'm not ready for bed. I'm just catching my breath. C'mon, Dante, let's play cards again." Sarita yawned, fighting to keep her eyes open as she spoke before drifting away. "Um, Dante, what do you think my mother is doing right now?"

"She's probably doing what you're doing right now—lying down somewhere in Mexico and thinking about what you're doing."

"Dante, could you sing me a song? It helps me fall asleep. It's something my mother does for me before I go to sleep at night."

"Well, sorry to say, but I'm no Sinatra."

"Um, how about a bedtime story?"

"Well, I guess so." Dante didn't sound too enthusiastic.

"Okay, good, but nothing scary, like . . . like 'La llorona,' 'The Bruja of Monterrey,' or 'The Chupacabra.' My mother would always tell me those when I was bad, so nothing scary, okay?"

"Okay, Shorty, whatever you want."

"So what are you gonna tell me?"

Dante thought for a moment before he spoke. "Have you ever heard of Agartha?"

"No, who's that?"

"Agartha's not someone's name. It's a place, a mythical place. A utopia, like Atlantis."

"Really?"

"Really."

"So, where is it?"

"It's hidden somewhere deep within the hollowed earth."

"You mean like, like somewhere inside, like the center of the earth?"

"Yeah, something like that. But not only is it hidden somewhere deep within the center of the earth, but it also exists in here." Dante touched Sarita's chest with his finger. "Deep within the heart."

"Really?" Sarita's voice gradually rose as she caressed her chest along with Dante.

He nodded. "All you have to do is close your eyes and imagine. Imagine a world where time doesn't exist, where there's no end and no beginning, a place where there's no borders, no laws, no governments or religions, a place where there's no belief in anything, but yourself. Imagine a place where the four seasons are all one simultaneous, endless cycle, a place where the sun and the moon no longer exist, they are only perceived as illusions in an infinite twilight skyscape, and because the cycle of time is just an illusion, within Agartha, there is no such thing as age or getting old. People just grow and evolve and stay forever young. And even though Agartha is a physical place hidden deep within the hollowed earth, which already exists as is, consciously, from behind closed eyes, Agartha exists in your own likeness, a manifestation of your imagination, where you are in control and can go wherever you want—past, present, future, all as one, in the now. And when you do open your eyes, remember that Agartha, the world created from within, is projected out before your eyes. The entire world is yours, from behind closed eyes."

Sarita closed her eyes and imagined a better place as she dozed off. Dante paused to admire her, then continued.

"So, whenever you feel alone or afraid, just remember to close your eyes and imagine. Imagine a better place and time. Imagine Agartha, because Agartha is whatever you want it to be." After Dante finished there was a moment of soothing silence.

"Right now, I see my mother, and she's singing to me, like this." Sarita began to sing a Spanish lullaby. Dante was moved, and soon Sarita's voice became softer and softer as she slowly fell asleep.

Dante silently admired Sarita as she dozed like a sleeping beauty. But then, all sense of solace was soon disrupted by an uncontrollable act of nature.

"Aaa-chooo."

"God bless you," a voice was heard as Dante wiped away the excess of snot from his nose with the sleeve of his shirt. After Dante childishly cleaned his nose, he turned towards the man, who suddenly appeared to be sitting in the seat across the aisle.

"Thank you."

"You're welcome," the skinny, balding middle-aged man wearing a black suit responded humbly. "I must say, sir, that you have a very lovely daughter over there. She's pretty and is a very vibrant young girl, everything a father could ask for in a girl."

"Thank you."

"Floyd, my name is Floyd."

"Floyd. Well, I'm Dante, and I appreciate your kind words, but she's not my daughter. I'm her uncle. Her father's mother passed away, and my sister, her mother, took the first flight they could get to California. They didn't want their daughter to worry, so I'm looking after her. We're on our way to meet up with them and spend a few days together in California," Dante coyly stated.

Floyd leaned in closer gazed deep into Dante's eyes. His piercing dark eyes could see beyond Dante's deceptive mask and deep into his tortured soul.

"Well, I'm sorry to hear. Do give my condolences to the young girl," Floyd said sincerely. He put his newspaper down, took out a flask from the inner pocket of his suit jacket, and then handed it to Dante.

"Sure will, Floyd, sure will." Dante took a sip, and after the taste of bourbon touched his lips, he began to take an everlasting swig. "Ah, that's good. I like your style, Floyd. I needed that, especially now, since traveling through Texas seems like we're slowly moving towards the galactic center, like we're being sucked into a black hole or something. I feel like I've been stuck on this train for an eternity." Dante reached out to return the flask to Floyd, but Floyd pushed Dante's hand back and insisted he have more.

"Well, Texas is one of the largest states in the United States."

"This is true, Floyd, this is true."

"And some feel that Texas emulates purgatory, a sort of stalemate of life, if you don't mind me saying. It creates an illusion of elapsed time and an illusion of entrapment, but sometimes those purgatorial states are good for the mind. They create a time to critique one's own life and motives. It can cleanse the soul and help people change and find themselves." Floyd's mystical words echoed, and Dante stared enigmatically at Floyd while sucking his bourbon-stained lips and then taking another swig of bourbon.

"You're a wise man, Floyd. Those are very philosophical words, my friend, very philosophical."

"Why, thank you, Dante, I only speak the truth."

"Well, I like you Floyd, you're a good man." Dante handed the flask back to Floyd, who put it away and folded up the newspaper. He leaned in closer towards Dante.

"Anything to help a friend in need," Floyd said with an ambient sense of esoteric nostalgia. And in the likeness of the watchers, Floyd gazed deep into Dante's eyes with an enigmatic smirk as he stood up and handed Dante his newspaper.

Dante was then left in an utter state of confusion and curiosity. After he watched Floyd slowly walk away, he turned back around to look at the newspaper. He turned the newspaper over to reveal the front page, with the headline "Dante's Inferno." The article began, "Abducted child still in the hands of the sinful after being brought through a hellish underworld of sex, drugs, and pedophilia . . . ," and was accompanied by a picture of Dante. Instantly, Dante was filled with a chilling uprising of fear, causing him to look back at Floyd, who silently stood at the back of the aisle.

Floyd gave Dante one enigmatic smirk and nod as his farewell before leaving Dante all alone to critique his life and motive, to use the time alone to cleanse his mind and soul. Dante turned back around and sat still while gazing out into nothingness and looking at his reflection in the window. Everything that once had been and everything that might be was suddenly an empty void, a tainted unscripted reality, an everlasting illusion left lingering deep within the eye of Dante's mind as his reflection stared right back. Dante's reflection was unrecognizable. It was someone he didn't know anymore. He was no longer who he once had been, or who at least not who he'd thought he was. He was someone else.

III

Amor Vincit Omnia

(Love conquers all)

<u>86</u>

There was an internal storm manifesting within Dante, who sat all alone like a decaying statue of stone. A disappointing past consumed his mind. Dante's reflection in the mirror, lined with blow, resting on top of the coffee table filled with prescription drugs, empty bottles of beer, liquor and wine, stared right back, someone he didn't recognize anymore. After losing Sonny and Sonya, Dante was lost himself. The absence of both brought out his demons, and Dante's only escape was found with sin. One sin led to the next, and eventually, from out of the darkness, Dante ended up slothfully rotting in the back of a cab driving down route 21 towards Newark, New Jersey; Dante's escape from all his troubles. Inside a three-story two-family home located at the end of a dark, secluded dead-end street, he would find a cure.

After Dante stepped out of the cab, he stood sedated with confusion. Lightning sporadically flickered and flashed while an uprising of a percussion of thunder and apocalyptic flood rains poured down on him from a passing storm, echoing out in the distance like a symphony of the night. He staggered towards the door marked 101 and knocked three times. The door cracked open.

"Yeah, what can I do for you?" a deep baritone voice said.

"Claro de Luna." The door shut, followed by a dissonance of multiple locks unlocking, and then the door slowly opened. After Dante walked inside into a foyer, an obese man shut the door, locked all the locks, sat down on a chair, which was next to a shotgun leaning on the side wall, and picked up the *Hustler* magazine left on the floor underneath the chair.

From outside, the two-family home appeared as two separate entities, but within it was a whole, since the dividing wall was removed, creating an opening that joined the two as one. Dante began to walk through the foyer towards two staircases, one from each home, and then to his left, into a vast room filled with an array of people. Dante approached and joined three gentlemen lounging around a table placed before a grand fireplace with drinks in hand. They greeted Dante with open arms and continued their conversation while Dante sat.

"This country was stolen, built and is still controlled with corruption and fear, my friends. We are nothing but pawns. The only way for the little guy like us to make it in the so-called land of the free is by living outside the box. We need not to be afraid to step out, to bend the laws of man, to live unconventional lives in order to truly be free. The average man is blind, he is a slave to society, a sheep. Me, my eyes are wide open, and I can see right through the cracks and past the curtain. I can see what goes on backstage. That's why I live the way I do. That's why I am free, my friends, that's why I am who I am." Virgil, the tall, thin, balding, impudent independent artist, then had his optimistic philosophies interrupted by the individual who sat to his right.

"Yeah, you're an artist. The master of all con men, a perfect con artist."

"Well, at least someone here can agree with me that it's one of the best ways to live life freely. Right, Dante?"

Dante stared across the table at Virgil with his hazy bloodshot eyes. "*Carpe diem* . . . seize the day, my friend," Dante slurred his words.

"Ha, that's why I love you, Dante. You understand, not like all these blind sloths and gluttonous slaves who waste each day of their lives and go about their dull daily routines like zombies. Cheers to that, my friend." Virgil raised his glass and took a sip. Gabriel, who quietly sat to Virgil's left, put his hand on Dante's shoulder.

"Hey, Dante, you all right, brotha? You don't look too good. You want a drink or something?" Gabriel called over one of the Latinas who were serving drinks while Pablo, who sat to Virgil's right, rubbed his nose with his finger.

"I think you might have had a little too much angel dust before you came here, Dante."

Dante noticed Pablo's gesture and wiped his nose clean.

"Why waste your own supply, Dante? You know there's plenty of that here, and that you're good for a few grams. I'll talk to Ángel for you, or I could just get you some myself, you know that. Not only do I operate more diligently, but I have a lot of supply to share with those close to me," Virgil said.

"There he goes again, egotistically preaching his successful schemes and greediness," Pablo interrupted.

"Hey, there's nothing wrong with greed. It's a precursor to pride and power. But I won't get into my philosophies on greed, I'll spare you the opportunity to recollect and use my own philosophies for your benefits."

After Virgil's egotistic rhetoric concluded, a Latina came over with Dante's usual drink, Jack on the rocks, and then left. They all silently savored their drinks. Even though Dante and Virgil were rival artists, it was the place they found themselves in now that brought them closer together and created a sense of friendship. In the eyes of mortals, it was a cesspool of sin, filled with blind, lost and abandoned souls, but in the eyes of those who were consciously awake, aware of their own sense of existence, and could see, it was an escape from the dull, daily routine of life.

And it seemed at the moment that, amongst the whores, greed, and corruption, there was a dualistic battle between good and evil. Inside where those who were allowed and trusted could go to for a late-night drink, gambling, drugs, and lust, there seemed to be no sense of morality. It was an abode where the blind felt they could see, a place for the abandoned to feel loved, a place for the lost to feel found, where the corrupted could feel pride, and the damned could feel blessed. It was a sanctuary for all, a place that brought the illusion of hope.

Dante saw no hope or life deep within their hollowed eyes. They were lost, the forgotten, an array of businessmen and blue-collar guys, accompanied by exotic Latin whores, lounging around amongst greed, lust, slothfulness and excessive amounts of mindless self-indulgence. But as Dante gazed across the vastness at the masquerade, there was hope, a sudden convergence of the law of one and the law of attraction, manifesting from the fated skies as the stars aligned.

From one of the Latinas, there was an auric sense of adoration emanating that pierced through Dante's burning heart of passion and desire like thorns doused in elixir, cleansing all the misery felt within with a euphoric uprising of love and peace, attracting and entrancing Dante.

Dante was instantly infused with alluring devotion as Ángel guided her through the crowded room. She was a dove lost within a sea of cancerous parasites. Even though she was a complete mystery, it was when she glanced up that Dante was filled with a sense of knowing, the moment she looked into his eyes. As she became flushed over with a shimmering surge of ecstasy, Dante, who was lost within her dark, exotic eyes, became overwhelmed with amity. She reminded Dante of Sonya. And in the likeness of Sonya, not only was she able to heal Dante's tortured soul and seduce him with the glance of an eye, but she was forever gone. Ángel pulled her away.

"It seems that Dante has been blinded by the beauty of a woman, just another victim of lover's eyes," Virgil said.

"Huh . . . what?" Dante mumbled as he turned towards Virgil.

"Don't worry, Dante, she has that effect on everyone who sees her for the first time. She's Ángel's new Mexican *novia*. I think her name is Gabriela. Anyway, the name doesn't matter. She's just another devil with angel wings. She'll break your heart and leave you broke, if you're able to get to her, that is."

"There's always Beatrice, the blind whore," Pablo said with a grin.

"She's old pussy, but she was probably one of the best models I've had out of half the whores here."

"Cheers to that, Dante. *C'est la vie, c'est la vie.*" Virgil raised his glass.

"Well, Beatrice is one of the whores from Tijuana, and we all can agree that the best pussy comes from Tijuana," Gabriel added. All agreed and raised their glasses to drink.

"So, Dante, how is it working for Greco now, since Sonny got locked up? What did he get, seven years?" Gabriel said.

"Not the same, Gabe. Nah, he got thirteen years. As for Greco, well, he's too demanding. Me and Sonny, we were perfect for each other. We were on the same page, we shared the same vision and had a better relationship," Dante explained.

"So I guess that means you regret leaving Sonny for that whore," Virgil said sternly.

Burning in Dante and Virgil's eyes was vengeance. The two shared the same models, and Sonya was one of them. The three were trapped within a love triangle. Dante ended up stealing Sonya away from Virgil, and then Sonya eventually left Dante, which left both heartbroken. Even though the brothel brought them closer together, their past emotions for each other sometimes resurfaced. But it was their respect for each other as artists and their understanding of each other that created peace.

"Not a day goes by, but I don't need you to remind me of my past mistakes. We all make mistakes, right, Virgil? Don't you regret stealing ideas from those poor unknown art students of yours? Don't you owe them for your success?"

"Touché," Virgil said softly as he smiled.

"Do you two have to act like a married couple all the time?" Pablo said with a smile while Dante and Virgil stared at each other for a moment, each wearing an unyielding poker face.

"I believe that perception is a necessity for both of us," Virgil said.

"Enough. I think what you two need is some angel dust and pussy from Tijuana. So what's it gonna be, huh?" Gabriel said.

Dante's depression, anxiety, and poisoned mind ignited into a burning fury. The demons were back, and Dante knew that he needed to feed them in order to feel a sense of control. Pussy sounded sweet, but he needed something more, something pure, something that could take him away, further down the spiral and deeper into the dark abyss.

"Some angel dust sounds nice," Dante said.

"Good, same here. You two gonna join us, or do you prefer some *mamacitas* tonight?"

"*Mamacitas* sound nice to me," Pablo said with a smile as he finished his drink.

"You boys go have fun. I prefer the voyeuresque setting as I enjoy and finish my final drink alone before I depart for the evening," Virgil said with a smile as he stared at Dante.

Dante, Gabriel and Pablo stood up, and said bye to Virgil. Pablo went up to the third floor where the whores were. Dante and Gabriel went up to and entered a second floor room after paying the supplier at the door for access and blow. Before Dante took a seat, he went to use the bathroom.

Dante's distorted reflection in the cracked mirror was the portrait of his life. Everything that had ever been good in his life was now crumbling and fading away. Sonny was now in jail and wouldn't be released for thirteen years, and Greco, wasn't the man he appeared to be. As for Sonya, she had abandoned him and broken his heart. All Dante had left now was melancholy and angst. Dante was standing on the edge of a great divide. One path would lead to Dante's demise, and the other would lead to growth. All Dante had to do was to find deep within his heart the answer, which was to live his life with fear or with love.

<u>87</u>

Temptation had brought Dante back into the heart of darkness. Dante had all he ever needed to wash away the pain within the comforts of home, but he couldn't keep away or resist the urge for more. The itching and internal hive of hurt crawling deep within his tainted skin was too overwhelming. Dante was a slave to addiction and needed more to stimulate the senses and the mind, something that could cover a tortured soul with a blanket of tranquility. Dante sought mindless self-indulgences and lust as an escape from his internal wounds, but being within the heart of the echelons of forbidden sin and temptation once again would not only provide Dante with all he'd ever imagined, but open his eyes so that he could see and find love in such a hopeless place.

At first, love was nonexistent. Dante was just a ghost in the crowd as he sat in the corner of the brothel all alone, sipping his Jack on the rocks and observing his surroundings. The usual artists Dante would frequently share his miseries with weren't present, nor were the regulars. The atmosphere was filled with life, rooms were filled with men indulging in their favorite narcotics, gambling and lusting over the many Latin whores who catered to every man's desires, but Dante still felt loneliness. In a world filled with so many souls, Dante was alone, but above all else, he was destined to find a cure. Standing all alone, seductively gazing across the crowd and deep within Dante's eyes was Gabriela. Dante was once again lovestruck. Even when she shied away and ran her fingertips through her hair, Dante continued to muse over her, until finally, after being rejuvenated with life, Dante found the strength and assertiveness to get up and approach the

Latin angel who had suddenly come into his life.

"*Hola, senorita,*" Dante slurred his words as he stepped up beside Gabriela with his drink in hand; she looked away with a slight smile, pretending she didn't hear Dante, but then turned towards Dante when he pinched her tricep.

"*Hola.*" Gabriela looked deep into Dante's eyes. Inside she could see gentleness, which moved her like no one else before. Gabriela tried to hold back her smile but couldn't hide the fire igniting in her heart. No matter how many times Gabriela had been deceived since coming to America, there was a soul connection felt with Dante. She was willing to give him a chance.

"*Tu o-joes, muy bonita.*"

Gabriela smiled even more as Dante's monotone American accent glazed over the beauty of the Spanish language with decay.

"*Ojos,*" Gabriela said with a smile.

"*Ojos . . . tu ojos, muy bonita,*" Dante said with confidence.

"*Gracias, tus ojos también son muy bonitos, eres muy misterioso, siempre sentado con una bebida, un artista con alma torturada, me encanta verte.*"

"*Um, sí, sí, gracias,*" Dante said as if he understood what Gabriela said.

"*De nada,*" Gabriela said with adoration in her eyes.

"So, how come you're all alone tonight. Where's your watch dog who's always with you?" Dante said sarcastically.

"Who, Ángel? Ángel has business, he'll be gone for the next few days." Gabriela bit down on and sucked her bottom lip.

"Is that so? So, are you allowed to speak with another man now that you're free?"

"It depends," Gabriela said with a smile as she nonchalantly turned away.

"On what?" Dante questioned Gabriela, who turned back.

"What do you want to talk about?"

"Well, a lotta things, but first of all, what's your name?" Even though Dante already knew Gabriela's name, he wanted to ask her properly.

"Gabriela. And you?"

"Dante." He reached out to shake Gabriela's hand.

"Dante," Gabriela said softly. "So, why do you come to such a place?"

"Why do you work in such a place?" As Dante reflected back the question to Gabriela, she held back her smile, ran her fingers through her hair, and then became sterner.

"I don't work here, I live here, and trust me, I don't like living here or being with Ángel, but it's all I have right now until I figure out a way to get outta here."

"Would you like some help?"

Gabriela crossed her arms and looked away, then back again at Dante. "Help . . . from who, you?"

Dante smiled, then sipped his Jack on the rocks and continued to look into Gabriela's eyes as a way to show her his offering.

"I don't think so."

Even though Gabriela remained stern with Dante, the fondness was igniting deep within her heart and beaming out of her eyes.

"Why not?" Dante asked childishly.

"Because, the men who come here only come here for three reasons— drinks, drugs, and women," Gabriela said to test Dante's devotion.

"Well, that may be, but I'm not here for any of that."

"Oh no? Then why are you here?"

"To get away."

Dante's simple words pierced through Gabriela's heart like one of Cupid's love-stained arrows, provoking Gabriela to show her beaming smile once again.

"So, I guess we have something in common, because that's why I'm here, to get away."

"Oh yeah? So what is it you're trying to get away from?"

"My past."

"Aren't we all?" Dante took another sip. "C'mon, I'll take you to a much better place than this."

"Oh yeah, and where is this much better place?"

"My studio."

Dante's musing and his humble invitation caused Gabriela to turn away to observe her surroundings. The hellish walls of sin she was trapped within were only a stopping point in life, and life seemed once again to have sent someone to take Gabriela away from her tribulations. Before leaving with Dante, Gabriela checked on each of Ángel's trusted men, who watched over the brothel while he was gone and were also supposed to watch Gabriela. Fortunately for Gabriela, they were preoccupied with Latin whores and unaware of Gabriela, who then turned back towards Dante after seeing she had a window of opportunity to leave unnoticed.

"You have a car?"

"No, but we can take a cab. It'll take about twenty minutes or so." Dante filled Gabriela with adoration, provoking her to smile, look away and then back again at his boyish smile.

"We could walk if you want."

"No, the cab is fine."

"Okay, well, let's go, then." Dante reached out his hand to take Gabriela's. The cab would then drive Dante and Gabriela to Dante's studio. The taboo attraction and risky venture would take them away from their miseries and misfortunes. Their daring hearts were now the guiding light seen in both Dante and Gabriela's eyes. The illusion of love, as crazy as it seemed to blindly follow it, would bring both Dante and Gabriela everything they'd ever imagined. Before long, it would all begin inside Dante's apartment in Jersey City, his studio, where they soon arrived.

After exiting the cab and walking up the five flights of stairs, like two adolescents running away to a secret place to engage in foolish acts of lust, both Dante and Gabriela joked and laughed. Dante struggled to open his apartment door with the key until he put his weight into the door, which then creaked open. At first, as Gabriela stepped into Dante's apartment, she felt nervous—like a virgin on prom night—but once Dante put on the lights, Gabriela's eyes lit up with awe. All around, there were finished and unfinished paintings, rolls of canvases, cans of paint, paintbrushes, an easel, sketchbooks, sketches, photographs, and an assortment of art supplies. Gabriela was seduced by Dante's original works of art. He focused momentarily on the stack of shoebox-sized packages filled with cocaine and pharmaceutical drugs, which he walked towards to cover up with a bedsheet, and then went to the kitchen.

"So, would you like a drink, some wine or something?"

"Um, yes, please, some wine is fine."

"I only have red, is that all right?"

"Yes, that's fine. So are all these paintings yours? They're wonderful."

Dante got Gabriela a glass of wine and himself a bottle of beer. Gabriela walked up closer to the paintings to study them.

"These are so beautiful. How long have you been painting for?"

"Thanks. Since I could walk and eat on my own. Let's just say I never had good table manners."

"Well, it shows, but it works. Everything looks so sloppy, but it's so clear to see, and beautiful. These are so original, I've never seen anything like it before," Gabriela said joyfully.

She then began to study each painting like she was inside a museum. As Dante watched her, he was awestruck. There was something special about her. What it was, he didn't know, but it felt good. It filled in an emptiness that had plagued Dante's life ever since Sonya had left him; she was now the cure to his void of pain. Dante felt free and alive.

"So, who's this woman?" Gabriela said curiously.

"Just someone I used to be with, but you shouldn't worry about her. She's long gone."

"Oh yeah? Is that why most of the paintings of women are of her? Pretty much all of the paintings here," Gabriela said sarcastically, turning towards Dante.

"She's the subject of a one-man show I'm working on. Things didn't work out with us, so this is my way of saying goodbye." Dante walked up to Gabriela.

"Is that so? Well, besides the many paintings of this woman, and these beautiful paintings, these four paintings I find to be very interesting."

The four mixed-media paintings were windows into Dante's heart and soul. They were four individual representations of Dante's troubled life. The first canvas was layered in thick coats of grout, then glazed over in deep wine-red oil paint, with a big black-and-blue heart, torn apart but stitched together with leather strips in the center. It was a reflection of Dante's early years as a struggling artist living in New York City, lost and seduced by sin and temptation. Dante's life at the time was bruised with decay, but love would bring Dante a sense of fulfillment. The second painting was a representation of Dante's love for another who had filled Dante's heart with completion, then taken it away and destroyed it. On the canvas of this painting, there were layers of paper-thin wood, painted over in the same wine-red oil paint, with a hollowed heart in the middle and a pile of debris and crumpled-up heart at the base of the empty heart. Painting two represented an extremely daunting time in Dante's life.

The third painting showed some life and rebirth. A similar wine-red background was layered in acrylic, but the heart in the middle was filled with jigsaw puzzle pieces. Even though the heart was about seventy-five percent completed with puzzle pieces, it showed a sign of life. But the painting that fascinated Gabriela the most was the fourth painting. This painting stood out amongst the others. Like the first painting, the canvas was layered in grout and glazed over with wine-red paint, but the heart in the center was painted like a human heart pumping blood. Not only was the realistic-looking heart unique, but all the many different old keys attached to the base, all around the bottom corners, and up the edges of the canvas, with one final unique skeleton key hanging down from the top center of the canvas by a string before the heart, created an extremely enigmatic representation of someone being lost and found, with love, but not yet. The key to Dante's heart was found, but waiting to be taken by a soul mate, his twin flame.

"Well, the keys were part of an art project that never was, of collecting lost keys. To me, there's something interesting about lost keys. Each key has a story to tell, every one original and unique, with different owners, either used to open doors, a safe, or some sort of lock. And now they're just what's left of a past long gone. As for why I chose to use them for this particular painting, well, I guess the keys fit the whole theme of the collection of paintings. We all have doors to the past, and all these keys represent a past long gone, ya know, letting go and moving on."

"And what about that one key there? How come that one is hanging down before the heart that looks more real than the others?" As Gabriela, questioned Dante's artistic integrity, she innocently crossed her arms, tilted her head from side to side to study the painting more precisely, and then uncrossed her arms to take another sip of wine and look over at Dante.

"Well, that key is waiting to be given to the right person, someone who could open the door to the heart."

"And whose heart is that supposed to be?"

Dante took a sip of beer, stepped forward to untie the key from the string, and then stepped up to Gabriela and looked her in the eyes. The exchange of energy was powerful. Before their hearts could burst out, Dante took Gabriela's hand, opened it, placed the key within and then closed her hand. Dante then began to run his fingertips through Gabriela's hair, caressed her face, and then slowly moved in for a kiss. The softness of Gabriela's full, lush lips infused Dante with ecstasy. Gabriela became flushed over with warmth and overwhelmed with a surge of energy rising up from her root chakra, all the way up her spine to her crown chakra, activating her kundalini into an orgasmic explosion of salvation. Everything felt as one, infinite possibilities manifested by the union of two souls. Even when Dante pulled away to look Gabriela in the eyes, the auric field of love remained around the two.

"Mine."

Gabriela then fell limp in Dante's arms. He began to grope and kiss her. Dante was gentle. As she momentarily looked over Dante's shoulder at his paintings, she became overshadowed by Dante's past. All over were portraits of Sonya, and here Gabriela was, enclosed within the arms of the man she was foolishly falling for, yet she felt she wasn't the only woman in his life, nor was she the one above all the rest. It seemed that the mystery woman, Sonya, whose face was all over, was the number one woman in Dante's life, and no matter how hard it was for Gabriela to see this and accept it, she wasn't going to allow Dante to have a chance to think of her tonight. Even if this would be their first and last night together, Gabriela wanted to be the woman of the night, and above all else, Dante's only true love.

"Wait, before we go any further, I want you to paint me. Like that woman over there, but I want you to paint me better than her. Make me feel like I'm all you have."

Gabriela's enticing words caused Dante to pause. He thought of Lola, and Bella Notta, and what had become of him after getting involved. But at this point in Dante's life, to engage in another heated lust affair was worth the risk. Death was knocking on Dante's door, and he wanted to enjoy life before it was his time to go.

"Okay." Dante held out his hand to take hers and guided her to an open space. Everything was already set up, such as the easel and a couch that was pressed up against the bare wall used as a backdrop. Dante stood Gabriela near the couch, left her alone for a moment to set up a blank canvas on the easel and gather an assortment of paints and brushes, and then returned to Gabriela, who he began to position in various poses. As Dante's hands caressed Gabriela's body, Gabriela felt loved. There were no more worries. Just before Dante began to position Gabriela on the couch, while they were nose to nose, Gabriela moved in for another kiss. As they pulled back, Dante began to unbutton Gabriela's blouse, but stopped, only to have her pull him closer.

"It's okay, you can paint me with no clothes."

Dante then began to remove Gabriela's blouse, only to have Gabriela stop him again so that she could remove the rest of her clothes. Dante was awestruck. Once Gabriela was fully nude, Dante began to position her and draped a red blanket around her, exposing glimpses of her exotic body and Latin curves. Dante returned to the easel, took a sip of beer, and then began to paint Gabriela.

As Dante peered around the canvas, he was mesmerized, and no matter how many times he looked away, Gabriela's beauty pulled him back. As for Gabriela, for the first time since coming to America, she felt a soul connection. There was something about Dante that made her feel a sense of peace. Even though being with a stranger in an intimate setting appeared on the surface to be taboo, to Gabriela, it was a leap of faith, a door that led to a better life, and Gabriela had the key to get there, the key to Dante's heart.

Dante would glance at the shoebox-sized packages filled with cocaine and pharmaceutical drugs, and then at the portraits of Sonya, but Gabriela would always take him away. There was something beyond reason, or even the cosmic order of fate, that made Dante feel a sense of nirvana with Gabriela. But even though Gabriela had the key to Dante's heart, Sonya could never be replaced, except for tonight. Gabriela wouldn't allow Dante to be possessed by Sonya tonight. Tonight, Dante was Gabriela's. She needed him, even if just for one night, and she could see in Dante's eyes that he needed her too. Gabriela moved Dante in ways of muses, but it was like a hypnotic spell, a connection of two lost souls searching for something—empathy, true love and meaning. Whatever it was, both felt the spiritual connection and urge to unite their souls, to manifest something pure and true. What was only one night of lust and passionate intercourse felt like an everlasting dance with destiny. It didn't matter if they never saw each other ever again, because both felt fulfilled and gave each other the strength to carry on with their miseries and misfortunes.

88

~Amor~

Love, it was love . . . love, love, love, love, love . . . love, which I thought was forever gone, I was able to find in such a horrible place. And that's just the way love is. It seems to come into our lives when we least expect it. For me, I had to come all the way from Tehuacán, Mexico, to the far ends of the United States to find love. Love in New Jersey, and it's funny, because I've never heard of New Jersey until I came to the United States, and from what I heard, it wasn't a pleasant place to go to, but that's okay now, because underneath the negativity of it all, I found love. In a time when I felt so alone and lost, he came into my life and took me away from everything I was running away from. Everything about him was so amazing, but those eyes, oh my God, those eyes. He had the bluest eyes, and when I looked into his eyes, I was lost in an ocean of love. I drifted away to a better place. There was something about those eyes. They were a window to a safer place, found in his heart and in his soul, and I was the fortunate one who was given the key to his heart, which I still possess today. After meeting each other and spending one magical night together, then going our separate ways, the love we shared, would last forever. It was our fate, and it was also destiny that brought us back together again, and gave us the greatest gift anyone could receive, life.

As echoes from the heart and soul of Gabriela were left ringing in Sarita's ears, she admired the key to Dante's heart held in her hand, which Gabriela had kept preserved within the pages of her journal. Sarita was beaming with life as she continued to pace around within the heart of what was left of Dante's apartment, while holding the open journal in one hand and the key that was the link between, Dante, Gabriela, and herself in the other. It would be a euphoric uprising of love, brewing deep within Sarita's heart and soul, that would bring her to a sudden halt. She continued to scan through the pages of Gabriela's past and admire the key to Dante's heart. Sarita imagined the way Gabriela must have been, being in such a romanticized situation, and how Dante must have wooed her and treated her. But whatever had happened on that magical night, above all else, the remnants of love were left lingering around. Sarita could feel it.

Sarita then closed the journal, clasped the key to Dante's heart in her hand, and began to walk back towards the partly boarded-up window Dante used to peer out from and observe her while she sat on the swing set as a child. As Sarita looked out the window into the past, she was instantly overwhelmed with love. Innocently swinging back and forth on the swing was Sarita's daughter, Mariela. For Sarita, to stand there and admire her seven-year-old daughter the way Dante once had done with her was surreal. It was a convergence of the past and the present, and that which linked everything together was Gabriela.

Gabriela, who was no longer physically in the now, was not only spiritually present but could be seen in Sarita's daughter. Mariela had Gabriela's eyes and hair, but Mariela's inquisitiveness and innocent curiosity had been passed down by Sarita. All while Sarita spent the time alone, reading through the pages of everything that once had been and reflecting back on a life lived within the decaying walls of the past with Gabriela and Dante, Mariela spent the time exploring the remains of the Clearview apartment complex. As Mariela swung back and forth on the swing, filled with life, love and what became of all that now was, it brought tears to Sarita's eyes.

As Sarita wiped the tears away, watching Mariela while tightly clasping Gabriela's journal and the key to Dante's heart, love it seemed became the force that was able to withstand the sands of time. But death would be what would unite the past with the present. The thought of Gabriela coming back to Sarita's mind provoked her to step away from the window, leaving Mariela alone for a moment, and then step back into the heart of what had been Dante's apartment.

Sarita brought both the key and the journal close to her heart, closed her eyes, and imagined how death was able to bring back life, a rebirth of love and happiness within the walls of the past. Even if it seemed at times there wasn't a God, at the moment, Sarita felt a higher force looking over her.

<u>89</u>

Within the darkness, while penetrating beams of light shined in through the stained-glass windows and in through the cracks of the small claustrophobic confession booth, illuminating one of the sinful, there was an aura of anguish.

"Bless me, Father, for I have sinned. It has been three weeks since my last confession."

"*Dime hija. Cuales son tus pecados?*"

"Well, Father, I fear for my child's well-being because of my past sins. I have done terrible things in the past, terrible things that I regret doing. But . . . but these terrible things were for my survival. It was the only way for me to help take care of my child. I, I'm so sorry, Father. I'm sorry, please forgive me."

"My child, God forgives all those who have sinned, especially those who have sacrificed for the love of another. May I ask you respectfully, my child, what it is you have sinfully done wrong, and why is it you now fear for your child's well-being?"

"Yes, Father, of course. Several years ago, I went to America illegally. In the beginning, I had nothing. I lived with bad people who used me to profit from sin. Eventually, I left those bad people and had a child, but I ended up going back to other bad people to profit from sin to support my child. It was the only way for me to take care of my child at the time. It still haunts me to this day, Father. I regret it all; it has brought me nothing but heartache and pain."

Gabriela sat with her head bowed down within the darkness and began to choke up. As she lifted her head back up within the light, her eyes filled with tears. A single tear slowly came out and slid down her cheek.

"Calm down, my child, calm down. Everything is going to be okay, because God forgives you, and God is and will always be with you, my child."

"But my child, Father. I have failed my child. I have failed my child, and she is all alone now and in danger because of my sins, Father."

"Please, my child, you must try to find the strength from within. You say your child is now alone because of your sins. Where is your child now?"

"She is still in America. I was sent back without her because of my association and involvement with very bad people."

"Is she living with family or a friend now?"

"No, no. I have been informed that she has been kidnapped, and now I still feel so much pain and regret because I'm not there with her. Please, Father, I only want forgiveness for my sins, so that God will look over and protect my child. Please, promise me this, Father."

"Well, my child, God is not only with you, but also with her and will protect her. The path you have chosen may have been sinful, my child, but your sacrifices for another are why God not only forgives you but will always be with you and your child. What will be best for you now is to go home and rest. Worrying will only make you feel worse, and for your sins, you are forgiven. Now go home and do three Hail Mary's, three Our Father's and pray to the Virgin Guadalupe."

After the padre spoke, Gabriela wiped the tears away and then found the strength from within to speak calmly, and then carry on.

"Mucho gracias, padre, muchas, muchas gracias."

"De nada. Now, *en el nombre del padre, del hijo y del espíritu santo, amén."*

"Amén." Gabriela made the sign of the holy trinity.

She stood up and then made her way through the house of God. The presence of God shined in through the stained-glass windows, illuminating the path before her, and the warmth brought Gabriela a feeling of redemption and contentment for her sins and the safety and well-being of Sarita.

<u>90</u>

Gabriela felt purified and filled with serenity as she walked through the *zócalo*. The Mexican authorities were able to gather more information on Dante and inform Gabriela earlier in the day, and everything appeared to be all right at the moment, but Gabriela still needed to get away and preoccupy her mind. Walking with no direction seemed to be the only cure to the reality that, even though Gabriela knew Dante many years ago after spending one intimate night together and having been fatefully brought back into each other's life, the man she knew now was a complete mystery, along with his past and connection to Nada Mas, known for kidnapping for ransom and killing for profit. No matter how unpredictable the path ahead was and what would become of Sarita, Gabriela confidently carried on.

Gabriela casually walked down a long open road filled with locals, artisans, musicians, and street performers, she remained isolated from the world around and immersed in her mind. Being here and there and back here again, coming full circle and ending up right back where she'd started from, wasn't failure, but was liberating. Gabriela was at peace, like a Buddhist monk in a meditative state of being and acceptance, as she walked without anger or judgment. Walking by artisans, musicians, and street performers, it was an object of affection that stopped Gabriela with awe.

"*Para ti, mujer bonita,*" said Guillermo, a soft-spoken middle-aged man. He stepped up before Gabriela and handed her a heart-shaped wooden pendant glazed over with multicolored Mexican graphics and designs, which made her smile. "Something to go with your pretty smile."

"This is beautiful. Did you make it?"

"*Sí, sí,* I carved it from the finest wood in Mexico and painted this one, and all the others. Here, look, try it on." The artisan took the heart-shaped pendant, untied the lace, and then stepped around Gabriela to put it around her neck.

"It looks very good. I like it," Gabriela said as she looked in a hand mirror the artisan gave her.

"*Sí, sí,* but would you like to try one of the other ones on?"

Gabriela glanced down at the others and then back up again, knowing she wore the right one.

"Um, no, I really like this one a lot. ¿Cuánto cuesta?"

"Diez pesos," Guillermo stated. Gabriela gave the mirror back and then paid Guillermo the ten pesos. "*Gracias, gracias,* now you have the heart of Mexico."

"*Sí.*" Gabriela smiled as she held the pendant in her hand. "So, what's your name?"

"Guillermo Gonzalez, and you?"

"Gabriela, Gabriela Olivia Del Sol."

"Del Sol? Gabriela Del Sol? Are you related to Emilio Del Sol?"

"*Sí,* Emilio is my tío."

"Ah, *sí,* I know Emilio. He lives not too far from me. We often see each other at the market. He always has good things to say about you."

"Really? What a small world we live in."

"*Sí, sí,* small enough to keep inside your heart."

Guillermo's cunning words illuminated Gabriela with hope and great expectations for better days.

"*Sí,* I agree. Well, *gracias, Señor Gonzalez,* maybe I'll see you around again. *Adiós.*"

"*Sí, sí,* if it's meant to be, we will see each other again. *Adiós.*"

As Gabriela said farewell to Guillermo, she held the heart-shaped pendant in her hand and smiled. She then continued to walk with no direction.

<u>91</u>

Café Solano would become Gabriela's final destination for the day. During the time of putting together the pieces of the past and moving forward, Gabriela found solace within the café. Inside Gabriela sat all alone at her usual back corner table with a cup of coffee, the heart of Mexico now hanging down from around her neck, and her journal opened up to a fresh new page. With a pen in hand, pouring words from her heart and mind, Gabriela would be able to put the pieces of her life back together again, to see herself and the world around in a different light. As time slowly pass by, within Gabriela's mind—where there was an infinite realm of possibilities—the perception of time ceased to exist. There was no end or beginning, only an ocean of freedom and love, as she spilled words onto the blank pages of her journal.

~The Puzzle of Life~

What a puzzle this life has been, since leaving Mexico to go to the United States and then ending up right back where I started from. In the beginning, everything was so unclear, like jigsaw pieces scattered all over the table, a chaotic disorder of all the places I would go to, all the people I would meet and all the choices and chances I would take laid out before me. At first, none of it made any sense, neither my life nor the choices and chances I made. But as time passed by, and I lived my life day by day, slowly, pieces were beginning to become flipped over, organized, grouped and slowly put together. My life slowly began to make some sense. Even if some of the experiences and the people in my life were terrible at the time, so daunting, now, looking at the bigger picture of my life, without the bad, there wouldn't be the good. The picture I now see wouldn't exist. It's big and full of life, and no matter how dark or bright pieces of my life have been, they all fit together. The balance of the negative and positive experiences in my life is what created the picture. At the center of it all is the biggest piece of my life, Sarita. She is the heart and soul of my life, and even though we have been separated, the picture is still kept together. Initially it was devastating, but now, reflecting back on it all, I understand and accept where we both are in life. Not only do I have this understanding and acceptance of what has become of our lives, but above all else, what has kept it all together, love. Love is the most powerful force on this earth. After all I've been through, it was always love that got me through the darkest of times and gave me the strength to carry on and live the life I want to live. None of the injustices of immigration, the law, or borders could stop the power of love, especially as a Mexicana who crossed the border illegally. I had heard so many stories of migrants living in the United States. Once I saw all the hardships and injustices they faced, I'm proud to be who I am and where I am now. Even though the United States is big and powerful, based on what I've experienced, it seems to have a lack of love, or not enough love. And that's the secret. That's why so many Mexicans and Latinos who migrate to the United States make it. They live and they love. When you love life and have a passion and drive fueled with love, anything is possible. Even right now, as I sit here all alone, reflecting back on the pieces of my life I slowly put together, looking at the bigger picture—even though it's missing one piece—love is what still holds it together.

# # #

Love would carry on over into the night. It was all Gabriela now had, and she wasn't going to let it go. As Gabriela stood outside her uncle's home in the desert, exhausted and all alone, with a blanket wrapped around her, the love she had for Sarita wouldn't wither away in the night. The full moon that filled the night sky and illuminated Gabriela was not only a beacon of hope but the only link between her and Sarita. Every night that Gabriela spent in Mexico since their separation, she would gaze up at the moon, knowing that wherever Sarita was in the world, she must be looking up at the same night sky and moon. Even if Gabriela and Sarita were far away from each other, the moon was what kept their hearts close together and their love for one another alive.

Gabriela would softly sing a Spanish lullaby, and when she finished, she would open her eyes, look up at the full moon, and imagine Sarita looking up at the same moon, somewhere far away.

"Buenas noches, Sarita."

After Gabriela had said her farewell to Sarita for the night, she would then walk through the desert back to her home. She would lay down in bed all alone and try to go sleep and dream of Sarita, hoping to wake up with Sarita by her side. For now, even though they were separated by distance, both would sleep underneath the same moon.

92

Cigarette smoke from Dante's Lucky rose up into the air as he leaned on the railing of the second-floor balcony of a cheap hotel in Tucson, Arizona, while looking up at the full moon.

"I'm all done, Dante, you can go in if you want to."

Sarita walked up behind Dante. Her hair was still wet from her shower. She wore a pair of Mexican national team soccer shorts with a Hello Kitty t-shirt. She stepped up beside Dante, got up on her tippy toes and leaned up on the railing with both of her arms crossed. Dante took one last drag of his cigarette, and then flicked the butt down onto the parking lot.

"You smell pretty good, Shorty."

"Thank you, it's the conditioner I used," Sarita stated and then took a whiff of Dante, who hadn't showered since they'd left New Jersey. Sarita scrunched up her face and pressed her nose against her forearm. "Um, I think you should take a shower now."

"Why, do I smell funny?" Dante lifted up his arms and smelled his armpits.

"Um, no, it's, it's just better to shower at night. That way you don't have to in the morning. We'll be able to leave early and not waste any time. You can use my conditioner," Sarita offered.

"You're right, but I'm not a shower-at-night type of guy, I'm a shower-in-the-morning type of guy."

"Um, okay, but I, I was just suggesting."

"Sorry, but thanks."

"Um, you're welcome."

Dante and Sarita observed the night sky together. They were joined as one, a oneness of consciousness. The night sky filled with stars, and full moon was soon smeared with a brushstroke that suddenly swept across it. Dante and Sarita both watched in awe as a shooting star skipped across the twilight sky. Sarita's soul lifted as she tippy-toed her body up higher to get a better look.

"*Mira,* Dante! *Mira!* Look! Did you see that! The shooting star!" Sarita grabbed Dante's arm and then pointed up towards the night sky.

"Yeah, I saw it too, Shorty."

"You're supposed to make a wish!"

"I know, I know, I've seen *Pinocchio* before."

"So make a wish!"

"Relax and give me a chance."

"Um, okay!"

Dante looked up and made his wish while Sarita looked at Dante with a smile.

"So did you make one?"

"Yeah, I made my wish, Shorty."

"Good, but don't tell me. It's bad luck to tell."

"I know that."

"Okay, my turn." Sarita looked up towards the night sky, as she tilted her head to focus on a star. When the right star was found, Sarita closed her eyes and bit down on her bottom lip to make a wish. She then opened her eyes.

"So, did you wish for something good?"

"Um, sorry, but I can't tell you."

"Oh, yeah, right, I forgot. It's bad luck."

Sarita nodded. The two turned their heads to look up towards the night sky again. As thoughts of Gabriela lingered deep within Sarita's mind, she focused on the full moon, feeling a spiritual connection. It was as if the moon somehow, by some unknown force, linked Sarita and Gabriela's souls. It felt like being home.

"Ready for bed?" Dante said. Sarita nodded. The two turned away from the railing, Dante guided Sarita to her bed, and helped tuck her in.

"Um, Dante, is your friend really gonna be able to help us get to my mother?"

"Yeah, like I told you before. He's like Sonny. He's someone we can trust." Dante ran his fingers through his hair.

"Do you promise?"

"Yeah, I promise," Dante continued to run his fingers through his hair and look away.

"Do you swear?" Sarita looked deep into Dante's eyes.

"Yeah, I swear." Dante looked away once again.

"Um, swear on your life?"

"I swear on my life." Dante turned back towards Sarita.

"Swear on your life, and, and pinky-swear." Sarita reached out her hand and extended her pinky finger. Dante wrapped his pinky around Sarita's.

"I swear on my life." Dante looked past Sarita. Sarita smiled, as the two let go of each other's finger, and then yawned.

"Can you tell me another bedtime story?"

"Sorry, Shorty, but I'm all out. How about you? You got anything?"

Sarita pouted. "Well, I don't have any stories to tell, but I have a joke."

Dante smiled, knowing that she had the best of him.

"That's fine, just as long as it's short and sweet, and something clean, nothing dirty."

"Um, yep, so, okay . . . um, okay, so, so there are two muffins in an oven. As they both sit side by side, the oven temperature slowly begins to rise. Eventually it gets hotter and hotter, until it reaches four hundred and fifty degrees. As it starts getting hotter, one muffin says, 'Oh, gosh, it's getting hot in here,' and then the other muffin says, 'Oh, for peeps sake, there's a talking muffin in here.'"

"A talking muffin," Dante said softly with a smile.

"Do you like it?"

"Of course. In fact, I would actually like to hear another one tomorrow, okay?"

"Okay, but not tomorrow. Tomorrow it's your turn, okay?"

"Okay, deal. Now, time for bed." Dante got up, caressed Sarita's forehead, and then ran his fingers through her hair. "Goodnight, Shorty, I'll see you in the morning."

"Goodnight, Dante."

"I'll be right outside, having one last smoke before bed, okay?"

"Okay."

Dante shut off the lights and stepped outside. Sarita rolled over on her side, closed her eyes and thought of Gabriela. She imagined that her mother was lying in bed with her while she tightly clutched a pillow.

Outside, Dante leaned on the railing as he smoked. He thought about tomorrow and the path that lay ahead, which led to a door Dante had promised himself he would never enter again. This time, he didn't have a choice. He had to go through that door for Sarita. On the other side of the door was the gatekeeper, the man who would be able to get Dante and Sarita into Mexico safely. That man was Benjamin Bradford, the founder of Nada Mas.

As Dante smoked his cigarette, memories from his past began to manifest while he tried to focus on the men across the street in the other parking lot. They were warehouse men who were unloading boxes, crates and long, narrow mirrors and paintings onto the back of a truck. It reminded him a bit of his involvement with Nada Mas. Dante stared long and hard at the men, closed his eyes, and then drifted away to another place and time.

<u>93</u>

As Dante strolled down the wide whitewashed hallway of an undisclosed storage facility located in the industrial backyard of Jersey City, New Jersey, he was overwhelmed with heartache. Dante staggered with fatigue. He was jet-lagged and slightly drunk, walking beside Indio. After making their way through a labyrinth of hallways and corridors lined with garage-size doors, Dante and Indio finally came to a halt before a door numbered 2323. Indio typed in a numeric password and then used a key to unlock and open the door.

Inside the storage garage, stacked against the back wall were boxes filled with cocaine and pharmaceutical drugs, and in the center was a long rectangular table. The table was covered with an array of equipment: multiple laptops, police scanners, an ID/passport-forging machine, stacks of money, and a cash-counting machine resting on top. Sitting at the table was Stanley Albert Paul, also known as Daffy. He was a five-foot-eight, two-hundred-and-thirty-five-pound, thirty-one-year-old male with dark, wavy, unkempt shaggy hair and a beard, who was a hacker with a history of cybercrimes, working as a freelance hacker for various corporations and investment bankers.

"Hey, there he is. The legend, back from paradise. Huh, so how was it?" Daffy joked with Dante as he typed on two separate laptops.

"Paradise? I wouldn't call it paradise, it's just business."

"Yeah, well, you were in Mexico. You had to have some fun while you were there, right?"

Dante focused on all the boxes filled with cocaine and pharmaceutical drugs while running his fingers through his hair.

"Not exactly, since I'm locked up in a studio all day working on paintings with armed guards. I can't even take a piss without guys with guns standing behind me! In fact, I'm not allowed to go anywhere. Just straight from the airport to the studio, that's it."

"No shit. Well, at least you get to get outta the city for a bit. This fucking cold weather is relentless. Another fucking storm is coming in later this week, can you believe that shit?" Daffy said while he typed and focused on the laptop screens.

"Really? Well, that sucks for you. For me it's no problem, 'cause I gotta go back to Mexico soon so I can finish up the last set of paintings. Know what? If it makes you feel better, I'll make sure to think of you while I'm sipping margaritas in the warm sun."

"What a fucking prick!" Daffy stopped typing. "Anyway, so what do you think?"

"Think about what?"

"C'mon, man, you know, all of this." Daffy opened up his arms and looked all around.

"Well, everything looks the same, except for your office space."

"You like it? It was my idea to set up shop here, so that I don't have to go back and forth all the time. Like this, I can spend a few hours here, and make sure pricks like this one over here don't try to steal anything." Daffy looked at Indio with a slight smile.

"Ha, that's funny calling me the thief. You're the one who launders money and taps into people's personal savings accounts," Indio stated.

"Yeah, well, it's just business."

"Hey, the same with me, right, Dante? Wasn't I on time every time I picked up a package from your apartment in the village? And I have never been short one cent, for you, you paranoid burnout. You need to stop smoking grass."

Indio removed a messenger bag from his shoulder. He opened it up and took out three stacks of money, each worth $25,000. "Here, here's this week's earnings."

Daffy snatched each block of cash from Indio's hand and proceeded to put it into the cash-counting machine.

"Let's hope it's all here." Daffy continued, "All is good. Anyway, why in the hell are you here, Dante, with this loser?" Indio smiled and laughed.

"Indio here picked me up from the airport."

"Oh, yeah? Which one, JFK?"

"Yep, and he's then gonna bring me back in two days."

"Yeah, 'cause I'm the lucky chauffeur."

"Oh yeah? Two days? You wanna hang out? Ya know, like last time, at what's that place you took me to last time, that underground brothel in the village with all the Spanish whores? Ya know, it's in the basement of that coffee shop. C'mon, this may be the last chance I have before I move out west to Arizona. Benny wants me working from there soon," Daffy said with childish enthusiasm.

"Oh yeah, is that so? It's called The Bean, and yeah, if you wanna go one night before I head back to Mexico, I'll talk to my friend to see if he can get you in again."

"Yeah, definitely, that was the best time I've ever had."

"Why, 'cause you actually got laid?" Indio joked with Daffy.

"Hell yeah, motherfucka, I banged two chicks in one night. Fucking wild, man. One had one leg and the other one had one eye and no teeth. I was able to fuck them for however long I wanted if I let them shit and piss on me."

"Has anyone ever told you that you're a sick fuck?" Dante shook his head.

"Yeah, all the time, but at least I know how to enjoy life. I owe you bigtime, Dante, for getting me into that place. Anyway, I spoke with Benny today, and he wanted me to give you something." Daffy reached down under the table and picked up a cardboard box, which he then placed on the table. He stood up to open it and took out all the contents.

"So, who exactly is Benny? I mean, besides me and him exchanging emails, and the few times I get to talk to him on the phone, I've never met the guy before, and from what I hear, no one else has ever seen him before. Rumor has it you're the only one who has ever seen him and spent time with him." Daffy finished arranging and organizing all the contents he had taken out of the box.

"Well, that's why they're just rumors."

"Yeah right. Anyway, check this out, Benny's gift for you."

On the table was a printer size ID forging machine, a smaller one, and various kinds of forging materials.

"What's all of that?"

"It's a forging machine that creates bogus IDs, passports, birth certificates and any kind of documents that need to be forged. It's the same as the one I have here." Daffy put everything back into the box and then handed it to Dante. "Here, all this is yours. Inside the mini kit you have the necessities needed to forge whatever you need, from home or on the road if needed, in case of an emergency, if you lose an ID and need to make one last minute and you're not home." Daffy paused to open a smaller box and pulled out identification cards, which he then handed to Dante. "Here, these are real cool, an official Nada Mas identification card and, ha-ha, business cards. Be careful who you give those to."

"Real cute, I guess this makes me an official member. Did you get one of these too?" Dante said while looking at his Nada Mas ID card and business cards with a slight smile.

"Of course, along with everyone else," Indio joked with Dante, then turned towards Daffy. "Anyway, where's my week's worth of supply?"

"I got it over here, ya prick, hold on." Daffy got two cardboard boxes filled with pharmaceutical drugs and two shoebox-sized boxes filled with cocaine. He handed them to Indio, who handed two to Dante.

"Hey, before you guys go, you wanna do a hit?"

"Nah, I'll pass," Indio said as he waved his hand.

"Limp dick mothafucker. How about you, Dante? At least you're hung and got some balls."

Dante shied away as Daffy offered him a hit of blow.

"C'mon, one hit, not like you gotta go someplace important."

"All right, just one."

"Now we're talking." Daffy got out a mirror, which he placed on the table, then poured out two lines of blow. Dante leaned in with Daffy to take a hit, then leaned back and looked up as he sniffed and savored the sudden surge of ecstasy.

"Wow, this shit gets better each time." Dante wiped excess blow away.

"New shit from Colombia. Only the best comes from there."

"Sounds nice. Anyway, let's get going. I'll see you next week," Indio said.

"All right, you prick. Dante, I'll call you tomorrow so we can go to that place, all right?"

"Yeah, sounds good, talk to you tomorrow."

Dante picked the boxes up and then turned around to join Indio. Dante and Indio left the storage room and Daffy closed the door. He began to walk back down the wide whitewashed brightly lit hallway of an undisclosed storage facility located in the industrial backyard of Jersey City, New Jersey.

94

Being back in Mexico for Nada Mas was burdensome, yet liberating for Dante because it was the end of the painting project he had been working on. The last of the series of paintings that were being used to smuggle drugs across the US-Mexico border were finally complete, and Sonya was drifting further away. Dante's absence since getting involved with Nada Mas was tearing them apart. Benny, who stood poised in shadows with his back to Dante, looking out a wide office window overlooking the inside of an undisclosed drug-packing warehouse, was the wedge that was splitting Dante and Sonya apart.

"It's amazing how, from just one simple thought, an idea that seemed so crazy and impossible to pursue, all of this has been created. Of course, I had to make the right connections first, but looking back on all of it now, no matter how dangerous or difficult it was in the beginning, it seems so simple now. You know, how I was able to turn an idea into an empire." Benny was tall, thin, had well-groomed dark hair and facial scruff, wearing solid green military fatigues. Only a silhouette of his stature could be seen in the dimly lit office.

Down below, on the open warehouse floor, was a crew of workers. They were busy packing drugs into various items, such as canned food, statues of Jesus, the Virgin Mary and the Virgin Guadalupe, bags of coffee beans, furniture, mirrors, tiles and concrete bricks. Even pallets loaded with supplies had drugs packed inside the hollowed-out wood frames, which were then loaded onto big rigs with forklifts.

"All thanks to you, my friend. Picking up and holding on to all those packages of pharmaceutical drugs, cocaine and marijuana, and helping me establish a foundation on the East Coast. From you and the first crew I set up, I was able to expand up and down the entire East Coast, even more than I ever envisioned. And not only that, but this silly little scheme—with smuggling drugs in your paintings—has worked out better than I thought. Especially with the previously done paintings, which we bought, reframed with the cocaine-filled frames and sold again for a bigger profit. After the coke gets sold and new frames are put back on, it's a brilliant little side hustle," Benny said as he turned his head slightly to look back over his shoulder, revealing a glimpse of his face in a beam of light shining down from the single fishbowl-shaped ceiling lightbulb.

Dante stood stoic with his arms crossed and head tucked in as he coyly observed the contents on Benny's desk. Benny then took hits of cocaine lined on a compact mirror he held up to his nose. On the oversized desk were stacks of file folders filled with documents on Nada Mas's drug-smuggling operations, such as logistics, inventory, contracts, bank accounts, and documents on high-ranking officials within Nada Mas.

"Even after becoming bigger than I could have ever imagined, fuck, I can't keep track of how much money I make per hour each day, with all the inventory, and profits, along with when transactions are made. One mistake with the numbers can fuck everything up. It could even get me, or someone like you, killed," Benny said with a grin as he wiped an excess of cocaine off his nose. "Even if you are still the only person I trust in this world, don't think that your life is safe from all of this."

Dante glanced up at Benny, who took another hit of cocaine. The shadows Benny stood in, with his back to Dante, kept Dante in contempt.

"Don't worry, I'm just kidding. Besides, it's probably that girl of yours—what's her name? Sonya?—who would kill you before I do. But, if I ever were to, believe me, I love you and trust you so much as a friend that I would stab you in the heart and look you in the eyes, make it Shakespearian, rather than stab you in the back like she would. Anyway, your final paintings are down there, getting ready to be shipped out. After they reach their final destinations, you'll be compensated for your services, and as agreed will be free to go back to your normal life," Benny stated as he took another hit of cocaine.

Dante was now tense with agitation. As Benny spoke, Dante focused on all the important documents on Nada Mas that lay in front of him. After having his life threatened, all the documents seemed to be priceless information that could someday be used as collateral.

"Yeah, that sounds like true love to me. But isn't it funny how because of all this, our lives were brought back together, and now, we'll be going our separate ways again?" Dante said as he looked up at Benny, who looked back over his shoulder again.

"You know, you're right. All of this brought us back together, but even though we will be going our separate ways, remember, wherever you go from here, you'll always have a watchful eye looking over you, so I'd be careful," Benny firmly stated with fire in his eyes. He turned away once again to take another hit of cocaine.

"So, I guess this is goodbye, then." Dante focused on all the documents again.

"Yes, this is our final farewell. Once again, thank you, thank you for everything. Esteban is waiting for you outside the office. He'll escort you out of here and take you back to the airport. And remember, if you ever need anything, anything at all, feel free to contact me at the number I gave you. Be well." Benny did another hit of blow.Dante then walked out of the office.

Esteban, a short, scruffy Mexicano wearing military fatigues, greeted Dante as he stepped down to the base of an extending steel staircase. Dante quietly followed behind Esteban through the warehouse, all the way to the back exit near the loading docks, where Dante watched his paintings get loaded onto the truck like so many before. Dante's heart felt numb as he watched the final painting get loaded onto the back of the truck. It was a portrait of Sonya.

The portrait of Sonya was one of Dante's most successful paintings ever completed. It was Dante's *Mona Lisa*, and in the likeness of da Vinci, Dante was attached to the painting. Not only was the painting a reminder of one of the most intimate nights Dante had ever spent with Sonya, but it was also a reflection of his love and devotion. Love on canvas, which had been taken away from Dante by Sonya after they separated. Sonya had given it away to an art dealer, who began a chain reaction of sales in which the portrait of Sonya would be bought and sold numerous times and passed around the world. Eventually, the portrait ended up in Mexico, to be stripped away and reframed with cocaine-laced frames and shipped to the United States, to its new and final owner, Sonny. Sonya on canvas would end up on the wall space above the fireplace mantel in Sonny's penthouse located on the East Side of New York City. Sonya was the light of Dante's life, but as the portrait of Sonya was packed into the darkness, a feeling of emptiness fell upon Dante, and all sense of love, devotion, and hope for a future unknown was lost, forever.

95

Upon Dante's arrival and return to Tucson, Arizona, Dante cautiously guided Sarita underneath his wing through dauntingly familiar realms, in search of Benjamin Bradford. Dante seemed desperate, but he was willing to find and reunite with Benny in order to be provided safe passage into Mexico.

Walking for many miles, Dante and Sarita approached an old gas station nestled on the outskirts of town. Since Dante no longer had a cell phone, he would use a pay phone to call Benny. Dante stepped inside a phone booth and took out the napkin with Benny's number on it while Sarita patiently waited. Dante began to dial in the number, but the phone was out of service. It caused Dante to slam the receiver against the phone box numerous times, causing loose change to spill out. Dante then stepped out of the booth with his head bowed down. He began to pace back and forth while trying to figure out what to do next.

"What's the matter, Dante? What's wrong?" Sarita asked.

"Everything. Everything is completely fucked! I'm sorry, Shorty, but it all ends here. I can't help you anymore. Not without my friend who will be able to help us! Without him, we don't get into Mexico and we don't get to your mother!" As Dante vented, Sarita's heart became crippled, and she could see the end of all things to come deep within his eyes.

"But you promised me. You promised me that I would get to my mother and that you would bring me to Mexico to see her!"

"Yeah, I promised you, Shorty, but I make a lot of promises that get

445

broken! What do you want from me? I got you this far. There's nothing I can do without my friend. It's over! It ends here!"

Sarita's hopes dashed, she began to push and hit him with tears in her eyes. She turned around and began to walk away. Dante then reached out to grab Sarita.

"Hey! Where do you think you're going!" Dante held Sarita by the arm; she hit him harder in a desperate attempt to get away.

"Let go of me! Don't touch me! You're not my father, and you never will be!"

"Well, right now, it looks like I'm the closest thing you have to a father, and I'm all you have right now!" After Dante lashed out, Sarita turned around and began to hit him again.

"I hate you! I hate you! You're a liar! I want my mother, Dante! I just want my mother, and I wanna go home! I wanna go home."

After ferociously lashing out, Sarita panted. Dante then embraced Sarita, and as he tightly held Sarita within his arms, he looked around in search of an answer. To Dante's surprise there was an object of inspiration left out in the open that caused Dante to push Sarita away. Dante slowly walked forward as if in a trance. There was hope.

"Relax, Shorty, everything's gonna be all right. I think I just found what we're looking for." After Dante calmed Sarita down, she slowly walked up towards Dante to stand beside him as he pointed. On the opposite side of the street from the gas station was a billboard with half an advertisement on it, which read:

Eden of Hell

Where temptation is limitless

And nothing is forbidden

Along with the slogan on the billboard, there was half an address, a phone number and half of a pinup stripper, left from the other half of the advertisement, which had been torn off the billboard.

"Um, Eden of Hell? What's that?" Sarita curiously asked.

"Where we'll find another one of my friends who can help out, c'mon."

Dante then continued on with Sarita. After walking for about an hour, Dante and Sarita finally arrived at their destination, hidden in a secluded back lot, Eden of Hell. The building was painted all black, adorned with red letters that read Eden of Hell above a double-door entrance. Dante and Sarita walked through a half-empty parking lot towards the entrance doors and stepped inside. It was dimly lit and the small lobby had a stool on one side and a life-sized cardboard cutout of a stripper with devil horns, a devil tail and flames around her, with a bubble coming out from her mouth that read, "Welcome to Hell."

Directly in front of Dante and Sarita was a thick red curtain that muffled out sounds echoing out from the room on the other side. Dante guided Sarita into the room without being abjured, since there wasn't anyone present checking IDs.

"Tush" by ZZ Top loudly played throughout as they walked through a haze of smoke alongside a long dance stage that stretched further down the vast rectangular room. On the outside of the room there were barstools and tables, and at the opposite end of the room was a big bar area. Inside, three strippers danced on the stage, while twelve early bird regulars sat around the stage. As Dante guided Sarita to the bar, her eyes lit up. The stimulating atmosphere provoked Sarita, who could barely walk and keep up with Dante, until a stripper did a spread eagle right in front of Sarita, causing her to freeze. Dante looked down at Sarita and then at the holiest of holes before him. With a slight smile, he covered up Sarita's eyes with his hand and then dragged her along. Sarita tried to remove Dante's hand as they continued walking, and then a stripper approached them just before they got to the bar.

The stripper was wearing a black thong and knee-high leather platform heels. She had a mane of long, thick dark hair, dark skin, big dark eyes, thick, pouty lips, and huge fake boobs, and she spoke with a very loud and seductive voice.

"Hey, doll. So, what happened? You got lost taking little miss cupcake to tha daycare? She don't belong in here. Why don't you leave her outside? Then you could come back in here and I'll show you my little playroom where me and you could have a good ol' time, doll. And by the way, I'm Evangeline, and trust me, doll, you'll only get tha best with me," she said, caressing Dante's chest. Dante removed her hand.

"Sounds tempting, but I'll pass. I'm here to see Rocco, is he here?"

"Yeah, Rocco's here. He's in the back. You want me to get him for you?"

"Could you? And tell him that Dante's here."

"Dante. Okay, you two can wait at the bar."

"Thank you."

"Oh, you're welcome, doll," Evangeline said and then guided Dante and Sarita to the bar. She walked down a dark hallway that ran alongside the bar into a private area.

As Dante and Sarita waited at the bar, a patron sitting next to Dante, who had a pint of beer in hand, and a shot of whiskey resting on the bar, turned towards him.

"Heeey, *guapo*, what happened? Huh, it looks like you got left with all the baggage." The Mexicano with short unkempt black-and-gray hair and a goatee slurred his words as he patted Dante on the back. He reeked of alcohol.

"I guess you could say that, but I don't mind the company." Dante looked around and then studied the Mexicano's rugged demeanor.

"I know what you mean," the Mexicano said with a smile as he deviously stared at the young, voluptuous female bartender wearing short shorts and a cut-off V-neck belly shirt. She gazed up through her dark wavy hair while she scrubbed down the bar. "So, since we both enjoy the company of others, how about a shot?" the Mexicano offered as he reached out to grab his shot.

Dante looked around and past the bar down the dark hallway and then turned towards the Mexicano.

"Sure, why not?" Dante said with a smile.

"*Órale*, I like your style, *guapo*. Hey, Rhea, another shot, *por favor*, for my *guapo gringo* friend over here." Rhea, the young exotic bartender, then poured and handed Dante a shot of whiskey. "For living life on the road, with *compañeros*," the Mexicano said as he raised his shot up towards Dante's.

"And to the interesting ones we meet along the way," Dante added.

"*Sí, sí.*" The Mexicano took a shot with Dante.

"So, *mi amigo*, what is it you do with your life?" Dante said as he patted the Mexicano on the back.

"I'm a musician, I'm here with my band." The Mexicano turned away from the bar and pointed out all his bandmates, who looked like a band of bandidos, lounging around, drinking and enjoying the strippers.

"Oh yeah? So what's the name of your band?" Dante asked as he turned back around.

"Valdo y Sus Amigos," the Mexicano stated.

"So, let me guess, you must be Valdo."

"Claro, claro."

"So, you guys any good?"

"C'mon, mon, we're the best band in the Southwest. Listen, we just finished playing to a sold-out crowd in Phoenix, and now we've got a gig in Mexico, just over the border in Sonora State," Valdo said passionately.

"Mexico, huh? That's funny, that's where I plan on going," Dante said coyly.

"¡*Órale, viva México*! So, why you going to Mexico? What, you got some mamacitas down there who are gonna treat you like you're some papi chulo?" Valdo nudged Dante while he swayed from side to side in drunken bliss.

"Something like that."

"Well, too bad you have all that baggage with you." Valdo then leaned in closer and said softly, "If not, ya know, we've got lots of female fans down in Mexico. You could have a little piece of the action, plus"—Valdo then opened up a cigarette case filled with blow—"all the cake mix to party like you're in the clouds, *mi amigo*."

Dante smiled and studied Valdo for a moment.

"Oh yeah? Well, I'd be careful crossing the border with all that," Dante provoked Valdo.

"Hey, mon, there's no need to worry about some smokey gringos or drug-sniffing dogs. Whenever we bring a little coke over the border, especially a tiny bit like this, we seal the cocaine so airtight that no dogs are able to sniff a scent. Plus, we're a well-known band with a big tour set up already, and with our manager here . . ." Valdo called over a clean-cut, skinny Mexicano with curly hair and glasses, who was dressed casually in jeans, a sports jacket, loafers, and a fedora. "Pinto over here is our manager, who always deals with security before we even get to the border checkpoints. It helps save us time. Also, between you and me, if needed, we have hidden compartments in the floors of the vans for storing extra instruments, big enough to smuggle three to four migrants. If we wanted to, ya know." Valdo sipped his beer before continuing, "So, what are you doing with the *niña*?"

Dante became cautious. He looked down the dark hallway once again, hoping to see Rocco, who wasn't there yet, and was forced to carry on.

"Just to, ya know, spend a couple of days there and enjoy the markets and the food, something different, ya know. But still not sure how we're gonna get there yet," Dante said as he ran his fingers through his hair.

"Oh, yeah? Well, listen, if things don't work out, you two can hitch a ride with us. Yeah, then you can tell everyone about how good Valdo y Sus Amigos are to the people, since we're the people's band," Valdo said as he patted Dante on the back with a drink in hand.

"Okay. Okay, thanks, I'll keep that in mind. So, when do you plan on leaving?"

"Not till later in the day."

"Oh yeah?" Dante keenly studied Valdo's drunken state before continuing. "Hey, you wanna do another shot? C'mon, this one's on me." Dante then offered Valdo a shot as a means of gaining his friendship and trust. He might be a potential benefactor, if needed.

"*Claro, claro*. Hey, Rhea, another round of shots . . . damn she's fine. A little more work, and I'll be able to convince her to come to Mexico with us," Valdo slurred nonsensically as Rhea poured two shots and gave them to Dante and Valdo.

"Well, to new friendships."

"*Sí, sí, por mi amigo, viva la vida.*"

After both Dante and Valdo took their shots, Pinto got off the cell phone, leaned towards Valdo, and then whispered into his ear, before stepping away.

Valdo turned back towards Dante. "Okay, *mi amigo*, I gotta talk some business." Valdo reached into his pocket, took out a business card, and handed it to Dante. "Here, this has my personal cell phone number. If you and the *niña*'s plans don't work out, give me a call before the end of the day, and you two can travel with us." Valdo stood up and patted Dante on his back as he said farewell. "Okay, *mi amigo*, adiós, and remember, *mi amigo*, not only will you enjoy our company, but remember to tell everyone about your travels with Valdo y Sus Amigos, the people's band." Valdo staggered away to join his bandmates.

Dante turned back around with a smile and then saw Rocco walking out from the dark hallway. He was a beer-bellied biker-looking guy with shaggy dark gray hair, a gray beard, and pudgy hands and arms covered with tattoos. Rocco walked behind the bar and stood before Dante and Sarita.

"Dante, you old dog. You're the last person I would've expected to see in this place. So what brings you here, and what's with the kid?"

"Listen, Rocco, I don't have time for bullshitting. You're a smart man, so don't make me have to beg you," Dante said firmly.

As Rocco leaned back, the fake smile faded. He became stern, and then he told Rhea to get them both a Jack on the rocks.

"Listen, Dante, you know you shouldn't be here. We don't need you bringing all the Feds and DEA back here. Right now I'd be very careful, because they're probably still hanging around the area. They were here the other day asking about you and Benny. Even after all these years, they're still looking for him, and I'm sure you came to me because you know that I'm the only person who knows where Benny is and how to get in touch with him. With the shit you're in, it seems that Benny is the only one who can safely get you out of this mess you got yourself into. Why, Dante? What's this girl worth to you?"

"It's something you wouldn't understand, and besides, I made a promise."

"A promise. Since when do you keep promises, especially for a kid? I hope you do realize that Benny isn't happy with you right now and probably will want nothing to do with you. You're the reason the Feds and DEA now know who he is. They are not only still looking for him, but getting closer."

"Well, I hope you and Benny realize that you two owe me a favor after what I did for both of you. I put my career on the line, my whole life on the line for you two. C'mon, Rocco, do the right thing. I know you're a good man and a respectful one. Call Benny for me, for this girl."

Rocco silently observed Dante's demeanor, and then Sarita's essence of innocence. He looked around, finished his glass of bourbon, took out his cell phone, and then walked away. Dante finished his drink as he waited for Rocco. Rocco stood at the end of the bar while talking to Benny on the phone. When he hung up, he walked back over to Dante, reached behind the bar, pulled out a pen, and took a napkin from the bar top.

"Listen, Dante, Benny said he's willing to see you, even though he didn't sound too happy about you being here or wanting to see him. In fact, he didn't want to see you or want me to tell you where he is, but I convinced him otherwise. He's a mess right now, Dante. He's scared, paranoid, a real ticking time bomb, so you be careful when you get to him. You know how he can get when he's like that. Here, this is where he is and how to get to him. Here's the keys to my truck, it's in the back. Be careful, Dante, and good luck, brotha."

After Rocco finished writing on the napkin, he handed it to Dante along with the keys to his truck. Dante stood up, stuffed the directions into his pocket and then said goodbye to Rocco. Dante and Sarita walked out of the Eden of Hell and made their way to the back, where Rocco's truck was located. It was an old white four-door Ford pickup truck, with paint that was faded and peeled off. The two got inside, and before starting the truck, Dante stopped to look at an angel ornament hanging down from the rearview mirror. Dante was Sarita's guardian and knew that where they were going now, he would need a guardian for himself. Dante started the truck and drove off into the empty, vast desert wasteland in search of Benny.

96

It was just another ordinary day; a cool beautiful autumn afternoon. The transition into a new season brought great expectations and hope for the remaining months of the year and the future. Dante was now at the pinnacle of his career. He was living the dream as a successful, financially secure artist who had gained the recognition and respect he deserved within the art world and amongst his peers. But all the success Dante gained was nothing when compared to his greatest triumph, Sonya. Sonya overshadowed all. She was Dante's everything, his guiding light, the only one who had ever been able to bring his burning heart, the mending feeling of true love and attachment. Dante was lost without her. But Sonya's love for Dante was beginning to fade away, and she was slowly drifting away.

Dante was in a very vulnerable state. He felt lost and alone and was now an easy target for the vampires who knew him best, the ones who knew to take advantage when Dante was at his weakest. He could barely stand up. Another self-destructive night of insomnia was spent drinking away his miseries. A half-wilted rose felt like redemption in one hand, and the pack of Lucky's Dante bought felt like escape in the other.

Dante stood all alone. He was being watched. From the other side of the glass, Dante was being stalked by someone from his past. The tall, thin, scruffy man with a shag patiently waited for Dante to walk out of the convenience store in Greenwich Village. Each drag of his cigarette was complemented with deep concentration. This was it, the moment of a strategically planned attack. The man outside the window hid in shadows like a bishop lurking in the corners, waiting for the pawn to blindly step into the opening light.

As Dante walked out the door, the man outside put out his cigarette with his foot and prepared to make a move. Dante turned left out the door and walked with his head down while he brought a Lucky to his lips. Dante only thought of Sonya, but then suddenly all visions of Sonya were gone.

"Oh shit . . . hey, buddy, are you all right? I'm so sorry, man, I wasn't paying attention, I apologize."

Dante held his head with his hand. As Dante began to lift his head, the man reached down to pick up the rose.

"I'm really sorry, man. I was in a rush, I wasn't paying any attention to where I was going, and . . . here, here's your rose, man. I'm so sorry, you're all right, though, right?" the man said apologetically.

Dante glanced up at the man as he took his rose back and then reached down to pick up his cigarette. "I'm fine, no need to apologize. It's okay, we all have our foolish moments. In fact, I should be apologizing to you. I was the one daydreaming and not paying any attention to where I was walking," Dante said. He stood up, placed the cigarette back between his lips, patting his front pocket, then in his back, searching for his lighter. The man reached out his hand with his Zippo, lighting Dante's Lucky. Dante took a drag and then lifted his head and analyzed the man. He had a familiar face from Dante's past, but Dante couldn't match a name with the face.

"Hey, listen, man, I'm really sorry; I feel like such an idiot. I'm in a rush, I'm lost. My mind's not where it should be," the man said nervously as he looked around.

"Hey, relax, it's gonna be all right. I'm fine, there's no need to worry. And if you're lost, maybe I could help you out. I live around here." Dante took long drags while studying the man's face.

"Well, I'm not from around here. I'm visiting someone in the city. I have to meet them at . . . " The man then pulled out a piece of crumpled-up paper and began to read from it. "I have to meet someone at their apartment near Eighty-Eighth and Third Ave. Is that around here?"

"Nah, sorry, man, you're not even close. That's all the way uptown near Central Park. You're definitely not from around here. Where is it you're from?"

"I'm coming from New Mexico, but I'm originally from Indiana. I have some new clients I need to meet with and . . ." The man gazed deep into Dante's eyes and saw vulnerability. Dante was completely clueless and unaware that he was just a pawn being led on. "Wait a minute, I think I know you, you look very familiar. You're a painter, aren't you?"

"Yeah, that's right. And you say you're originally from Indiana. Where in Indiana are you from? Because I'm from Indiana too."

"Dante? Holy shit, it is you. Dante, it's me, Benny. Remember? We grew up together. Wow, this is fucking strange, man, like we're in the fucking Twilight Zone or something. What are the chances that we go years without seeing or speaking to each other, and now we unexpectedly run into each other on the streets of New York City, the center of the fucking world? Holy shit." Benny acted surprised. He wore an illusionary smile.

All the memories of Benny suddenly came back to Dante. The recognizable face now had a recognizable name. Benny was an old childhood friend from Indiana.

"Benny? I knew I recognized your face. I just wasn't sure. Ya know, it's been a long time since we last saw each other or spoke, and yeah, this is fucking weird, like fate or something brought us together. When do you have to meet this client of yours?"

"Not for another three hours, but since I have no clue where I'm going, I figured I'd use the extra time to find the place. What's up with you, what are you doing now?"

"Well, I was gonna go see someone, but that can wait, they're not expecting me anyway. I haven't seen you in years, man. You wanna sit down for a quick drink and catch up on lost time?"

Benny's illusionary smile grew bigger.

"You sure? Seeing that rose in your hand tells me that you have a girl you wanna surprise, or you want to make amends with."

"Well, honestly, things haven't been going too well lately, but it can wait till later. C'mon, you were never one to pass up a drink, especially a free one. It's on me. C'mon, let's go get a quick drink."

"Are you sure, Dante?"

"Yeah, Benny. C'mon, let's go." The two began to walk through Greenwich Village. As Dante guided Benny, he offered Benny a cigarette and then returned a light before Benny could pull out his Zippo. Benny accepted and then smiled with relief and accomplishment. He was halfway done.

The beautiful clear autumn afternoon soon withered away as the two now found themselves tucked inside of a local dive bar hidden deep within the heart of Greenwich Village. The dark faded, lacquered aged wooden bar and interior gave the illusion of an old stylized Irish pub, while the dimness and darkness created a comforting, yet isolated atmosphere. Hiding away in a nook of the bar were the two old friends, now reunited, sharing a drink and lost time. Each held a pint of beer in one hand and a double shot of bourbon in the other.

"Here's to old friendships and new beginnings," Dante said as he raised his glass of bourbon up to Benny's.

"Cheers to that, brotha," Benny said, and then the two old friends slugged back their bourbons. Each still wore a childish smile like the two schoolboys they once were, who would get together after school. Dante felt at ease to be sharing a drink with an old childhood friend. It took away the bitterness and on-edge emotions he'd been experiencing lately with Greco and Sonya. As for Benny, he was just as relaxed, but wore a deceptive mask and remained poised, with deep concentration.

"So what's it like, Dante? To be living in the big city as a successful painter?"

Dante shyly looked down with a smile as he lifted his pint of beer to his lips.

"Well, it's not as glamorous as you may think. First of all, being a painter brought me a lot of heartache and pain. And the city—well, don't believe the hype. New York City is not what it is said to be, and it isn't what it appears to be. It's also a very expensive place to live in, and to make it in this city, especially as an artist, you need a lot of luck. A lot. You could be the most talented person in the world in whatever it is you do, but without luck, brotha, you're just another victim of broken dreams. I'm one of the lucky ones who came here with nothing to lose." Dante looked down at the pint of beer in his hand and then looked up at Benny, who was leaning forward while sipping his beer, giving Dante his full attention.

"Well, what you call luck, I call fate. You were always a great artist, since we were kids. Remember those murals of graffiti you would do in the streets and under bridges? Especially that one you painted on the side of Old Man Gaines's barn when we were in junior high."

"Yeah, I remember that. I also remember how he chased after us with his shotgun." Dante smiled.

"Ha-ha, yep, we used to always fuck with Old Man Gaines. The problem with you, Dante, was that you never believed in yourself or had any hope, man. Well, not until you left for New York."

"I just never thought I was good enough to make a living as a painter or as anything else in life. I was rejected by every art school I sent slides to, and I didn't have the grades to get into a decent school, man. I guess that painting houses and barns after high school gave me the drive and hope to go to New York City, the center of the art world, to see how I stand, and here I am now, still standing. How about you, Benny? You were always smart and had direction. How was college?"

As Benny sipped his beer, he wore a deceptive smile. The comfort Benny created made Dante even more vulnerable.

"College, well, don't believe the hype. College wasn't what it was said to be and not what it appeared to be either. There were no twenty-four-seven orgies and it wasn't a twenty-four-seven party." The two laughed. "It was tough, man, especially for someone who was as smart as I was. I barely made it out in four years."

"Four years, some people barely make it out in six. Well, look at it this way. All the bullshit classes are over with, and now you're in the real world, making real money."

"Yeah, well, the real world is just as hard. In fact, it's harder."

"Well, I wouldn't know because I've never had a real job where I made real money. I went from living at the bottom of the barrel straight to the top. So what did you get your degree in? What is it you do now?"

Benny's smile grew bigger with fulfillment. The sense of accomplishment grew stronger with every passing moment.

"Business. I'm a businessman. Well, an independent businessman. I started up my own business and I'm looking to expand, that's why I'm here in the city."

"Business? What kind of business do you have?"

"Well, it's kinda hard to explain. I import and export," Benny said vaguely as he looked down into his beer in his hand.

"Well, what exactly are you importing and exporting?" Dante sat like a child waiting to have a Christmas gift revealed to them, and whatever Benny was about to reveal to Dante at this point, he was willing to accept and believe in anything Benny told him. Acceptance was inevitable. They were old childhood friends, and Benny was well aware of the close relationship they'd once had. This was an asset that would play in Benny's favor.

Inside the dimness of the pub, the comforting, yet isolated atmosphere created the perfect mood for deception. Benny was usually calm, but was now on edge and felt the need to look back over his shoulder to observe the half-empty vastness of the pub. Even from the little back corner table in the nook of the pub, Benny felt the need to check for eavesdroppers and observant eyes. He wasn't taking any chances, especially at this point. As Dante silently sat with his back to the wall, he could see the paranoia and change of mood on Benny's face. Benny's tall, thin, lanky body hunched downward like Larry King and leaned closer towards Dante while he rested his elbows on the table and clasped his outstretched hands together as he gazed up at Dante with his depleted, bloodshot eyes.

"Well, I really shouldn't tell you exactly what it is I import and export, but we're old friends, and I trust you, Dante. I can still trust you, right?" Benny's ruse now had Dante hooked. Dante leaned in closer, like a child pressing their face up against a candy store window, trying to see what was on the other side of the glass.

"Yeah, of course you can trust me, Benny. Like you said, we're old friends, and friendships never die, right? Remember all the time we spent together in Indiana?"

"Okay, you're right, the roots of our friendship are deep."

"So, what's the big secret?" Dante inquired. Benny then turned his head and looked back over his shoulder. As Benny turned back around, he took another sip of beer. Dante joined him. Benny then placed his pint back down as he sucked his beer-stained lips. The dramatic suspense that Benny was orchestrating was hypnotically pulling Dante in even more.

Benny leaned in closer, his soft tone coming down to a near whisper. "I import and export narcotics." To Dante's surprise, his eyes opened up wider.

"What! What are you trying to tell me? That you're a drug dealer? That you smuggle cocaine?" Dante slightly raised his voice with the revelation, and Benny quickly raised his hands and waved them before Dante's face to quiet him down. He looked back over his shoulder once again. Dante quietly watched. This time he knew why there was paranoia and could now see that Benny didn't appear to be the man he once was or who he at least thought he was.

"Be quiet. I don't need the whole bar knowing my business." Benny rested his hands on the table and looked over his shoulder again. Dante watched Benny's hands and then looked up into his eyes as he turned back around, leaned in closer and spoke in an even softer tone. "Listen carefully, Dante. In simple terms, yes, I'm a drug dealer. Well, actually, I was a drug dealer, and now I'm a drug trafficker," Benny said while dramatizing with hand motions as he tapped his index finger on top of the table.

"Wait, slow down, Benny. You're way ahead of yourself. I think that you need to start from the beginning and explain yourself some more. So you leave Indiana and you end up going to college in New Mexico. Explain to me how someone like you goes to college to get a degree and ends up being a drug smuggler," Dante asked, and then patiently waited for a response as Benny slowly raised his pint of beer to his lips to take one more refreshing sip.

The thought of Sonya now pierced through Dante's mind like a crown of thorns. He looked down at the half-wilted petals of the rose of redemption meant for her, laid on the table. Dante was filled with emotions as he thought of how this day was meant for Sonya, and now here he was, standing before two doors—love and friendship.

As Dante lifted his eyes from the half-wilted rose, Benny also raised his eyes from the rose as well. Their eyes aligned and Benny then glanced down at the rose again and then looked back into Dante's eyes with a slight smile, which quickly faded away.

"Well, Dante, where I think it will be best for me to begin would be New Mexico, Albuquerque, New Mexico, which is where I went to school. This life change of mine started at the beginning of my junior year. It was at an on-campus party where I met this guy through a friend, who was a drug dealer for a drug cartel working out of Tijuana, Mexico. The Mendoza drug cartel. He started telling me about his life and how he made a living by selling drugs to college students in New Mexico. He made friends at all the colleges in New Mexico, and these people were his contacts, which is where he would meet them and make a deal. This guy wasn't some dumb fucking bubblegum gangster, selling dope on the city streets, asking to get caught. Nah, not this guy. This guy was fucking smart. He was streetwise and book-smart. This guy had a whole fucking system that was flawless. So me and this guy hit it off right from the beginning. We both shared the same intellect and we both were on the same page. He saw this in me and didn't hesitate to say yes when I told him that I wanted in. So for the next two years, I was one of his contacts at school. I helped this guy make deals and get clients. I did this until I graduated, and it was during the summer after graduation when I convinced this guy to take me to the source so I could learn what goes on behind the scenes. The two years I spent as a drug dealer was like having a second major, like learning a new craft. I was outside the doors, I was at the end of the line and I wanted in badly."

Benny continued to passionately speak. His eyes burned like fire and his hand motions and tapping of his index finger on top of the table became more dramatic. The thought of Sonya was gone as Dante leaned in closer.

"So, this guy trusted me and believed in me and my ideas. After graduating, I ended up spending that whole summer in Mexico, making contacts and creating relationships with some of the head guys from this drug cartel in Tijuana that the guy introduced me to. Through them, that's how I was able to meet the twins, Martin and Marta Mendoza, the two who founded and ran the Mendoza drug cartel, the key players I needed to get in good with—to make it. After spending some time together, even though things didn't seem to work out in the beginning because of my ideologies at the time, and being that I was some fucking gringo who had no business in Mexico, or running my own network, I was wise enough to eventually build a great trusting relationship with Marta, since the brother didn't trust me. Luckily for me, after slowly building a relationship for about three months, Marta was able to convince her brother to trust in me, and after that he would do business with me. I convinced them then to take me to the source. I spent two fucking weeks in the fucking Yucatan and deserts of Mexico until I got to the source. Dante, there were fucking endless fields of this shit, hidden in small, isolated villages, deep within treacherous mountain ranges and inside storage bunkers, like the endless fields of corn back home in Indiana. All of it for this one fucking cartel."

"Fuck, Benny, I would never have imagined you doing all of that. Even right now, I'm finding it all too hard to register. So you end up in the fucking jungle and desert with fields of this shit. What next? How the fuck did you get all of that shit out and into the States?"

"Relax, Dante, I was just about to get into that. So I'm in the fucking jungle and desert, the middle of nowhere, with all this shit, and I convinced Marta and Martin to let me take kilos of this shit, over one hundred fucking kilos of this shit. They don't even trust their own guys with that much, and here I am, just a fucking gringo with money, contacts, brains and a fucking convincing idea. You see, Dante, those two years I spent as a drug dealer were my establishing years. I was paying my dues and saving my money. I wasn't some fucking hack job drug dealer who exploited himself with useless amounts of excessive material goods. Nah, no way, that's how you get fucking caught. I never touched the shit either. I was always clean and had a clear mind. So I used all the money I saved to buy my first kilos of supply from the Mendoza cartel. As for importing and exporting all of it, I had a friend who was a pilot who lived in Arizona and flew one of those small prop planes. He would fly back and forth from Arizona and Mexico all the time. He worked for some private agency that had security clearance with the border airspace, so I started off small, using just the plane and this abandoned airfield in the desert of Arizona. Soon I started making a lot of money and went from just smuggling marijuana to smuggling marijuana and cocaine. I ended up getting more people to work for me and expanded my business. I went back to the schools, to the college kids, who were my biggest source of consumers, and ended up running a network out of Arizona that distributed to all the big colleges and universities in California, Nevada, Arizona, New Mexico and Texas. The more I sold, the more demand for supply came. Soon I needed new creative ways to smuggle the shit in, so I made more contacts. I became partners with the Colombians, the Suarez cartel, which was connected to the Mendoza cartel, and I also got in with the border patrol from various Arizona and Texas border checkpoints and got in real good with a few who work at some of the biggest checkpoints in those states. I use trucks that get free passage by the border patrol guards I have on the payroll, I transport shit hidden in floor tiles, furniture, concrete bricks, toys, canned foods, frozen fish, and grocery supply trucks. Nowadays I have a tunnel system that runs under the US-Mexican border, to these little safe houses, and small businesses I own. I even have these fucking tiny fiberglass U-boats that can make it through the Gulf from Colombia to the States undetected. And now here I am in New York City, looking to expand my network to the East Coast and come up with new creative ways to smuggle in more shit. Besides expanding to the East Coast, though, along with all the drugs I've been trafficking in from Mexico and Colombia, I've been slowly getting involved with other business ventures, such as pharmaceutical drugs, which are big now. So not only do I ship in shit from Mexico, but I'm in with some pharmaceutical companies, and out in Cali, the porn business is huge, so I have my own production company set up. And lately, I've been getting involved with human trafficking. Ya know, working with coyotes who take these migrants in over the border. Anyway, it's all connected and just business, *nada mas*. Ya know, nothing much, which has kinda stuck, the ideology and name, Nada Mas. I have that shit patented and branded. Even if I did borrow it from the Colombians, it's mine now. Nada Mas."

Dante, who was now hunched down lower than Benny, peered up into his eyes like a puppy dog filled with curiosity. "Fuck, Benny. So you're like some fucking kingpin now, like some fucking Pablo Escobar, dealing with the fucking Colombians! The Colombians don't fuck around, Benny, they'll fucking kill anyone and everyone involved." Dante spoke like a child sharing a conversation with the older rebellious kid who was streetwise and used his illusionary bragging rights to lure in the gullible youth.

"Nah, I wouldn't say that, though I am successful in my own right." The pint of beer in Benny's hand was now half-empty, and his slight smile now revealed half a mouth of teeth between the side of his lips.

"Well, exactly how successful are you? How much money have you made?"

Benny's smile grew bigger like a wolf, filled with greed, hungry for more. "Over two hundred and fifty million dollars. I have a hundred and twenty-five million spread out and stashed away in banks in Ecuador, Panama and Switzerland, and the rest I keep in a safe place in Arizona. Along with all the money, there are all the getaway spots I have around the world. I have a villa on a beach in Mexico and an estate in Arizona." Benny's hand gestures grew more theatrical as he spoke.

"And with all this money, you have come all the way to New York City to try and make more?"

"Exactly, greed. Do ya wanna know what greed is? Greed is true love, greed is power, and with power you can be and do anything you want. You become invincible, like Superman. This country was built on greed. America is the fucking symbolic Mecca of greed and power. If you live your life like a fucking sheep, like the majority of Americans, you won't get too far in life. You need to be a wolf like me to become as successful as I am. You can't live your life blindly. And New York City, well, New York City is filled with wolves like me. Wall Street is filled with packs of 'em. Just like when I went to Mexico for the source, expanding to New York City is like going to my source of consumers. The college kids are easy consumers to get, but to have the businessmen of New York City and eventually the politicians from D.C., that's fucking big money. New York City and D.C. alone are worth more than all the colleges I deal with on the West Coast. If I can expand my network to the East Coast and make the right moves, fuck, Dante, not only will I be the most powerful drug trafficker in the US, but the most powerful and successful businessman. I'll be bigger and make more money than the Bush and Clinton crime families and the CIA combined, and then I'll be the one who controls the drug war and the whole political system."

Dante looked Benny up and down as Benny sat back while gulping his pint of beer with a big smile. Beer flowed out the sides of his mouth and oozed down his chin like a gluttonous pig drinking from a trough. Benny no longer appeared to be the man Dante had once known. The soft-spoken, humble intellectual was gone.

"Benny, how the fuck do you think you're gonna be able to get all that shit across the country? You have over one thousand miles to cover. That's not like flying a prop plane across the border and driving past border patrol on the payroll."

"Well, like I told you before, Dante, lately I've been smuggling shit in trucks with the shit hidden inside of tiles, furniture, and canned foods. So far it's worked, and I see no reason why it won't work because of distance."

Dante was buying every word that Benny had been selling him so far, and Benny was finally ready to now cash out. The fire in Benny's eyes now burned like an inferno. While Dante listened, Benny leaned in closer as he held his pint of beer just a few inches off of the table.

"What about you, Dante? You're the creative one. I'm sure that you must have a ton of ideas that could work," Benny said as he looked into his pint of beer, took a sip and then looked up at Dante. Dante had never smuggled drugs in his life and knew nothing about drugs or the lifestyle. The only thing that Dante had ever smuggled were tubes of paint out of art stores and fruit from street vendors. That was a pocket-and-run business. To actually smuggle mass quantities of illegal goods over a great distance would take more than five fingers and a pocket.

"I don't know, Benny. What do I know about smuggling drugs? I know absolutely nothing about what you do."

Benny sipped his beer. He then slowly twirled the beer around at the bottom of the glass, looked down into his pint and then up at Dante.

"How about paintings, Dante?"

Dante squinted. It was a dramatic change of subject and the last thing Dante would have ever thought of. It was just what Benny had been orchestrating the entire time. Like the maestro he'd been playing so far, Benny was now ready to commence his orchestrated dramatics.

"Paintings? What do paintings have to do with smuggling drugs?"

"The frames, Dante. I was thinking about the frames, like how big could frames be, how thick?"

Dante could see how desperate and motivated Benny was.

"I don't know, Benny. It all depends on how big the painting is. And don't you already smuggle shit inside of wood you use for furniture?"

"Yeah, Dante, but I don't wanna just transport the hollowed-out frames filled with shit. I wanna transport the whole fucking painting. Do you understand what I'm talking about? If I have whole paintings with a legit destination, that would take away any kind of suspicion, and if the truckload is stopped and checked, there should be no worries. The authorities wouldn't check a truckload of paintings, especially for narcotics. Do you get what I'm talking about?"

"Yeah, I understand what you're trying to tell me, Benny, but where are you gonna get enough paintings to smuggle all the shit you plan on smuggling?"

Benny sipped his beer and looked up at Dante with a persuasive smile.

"Me?"

"Yes, you. You would only have to make enough for a one-man show. What's a one-man show, like twenty to thirty paintings?"

"Yeah, for a big publicized one."

"Whatever, that's fine, because I only need to do the painting scheme once."

Dante squinted once again. Benny wasn't making any sense. Here was a smart businessman who'd created his own drug-trafficking network and now he wanted to risk everything with one truckload of drugs smuggled in frames of paintings. Benny then held the rim of his pint of beer before his lips.

"Because I was wondering if you could help me out afterwards, help me get started on the East Coast."

Dante sighed. Benny was an old childhood friend who he would help out when in need, but to get involved in drug smuggling and drug dealing had Dante questioning his true friendship and his persona.

Who am I? Dante thought to himself. That shy, good natured farm boy from Indiana was long gone. Ever since Dante came to New York City, his path in life had become darker and darker. And as much as it was something he didn't want to get involved with, deep inside, there was a part of Dante that would do anything for a friend in need.

"Benny, I can't get involved. It's not my thing, and what if I get caught?"

Benny rested his pint of beer on top of the table. "You won't get caught, Dante. Just listen and hear me out. I just need a contact I know and trust to help me get started on the East Coast, that's all. I don't know anyone over here, and right now you're the only one." Benny orchestrated his speech with his hands. He had Dante in check and was now ready to bring closure.

"What about your business associate you came here to meet?"

"Well, you're my business associate. It was just blind luck, like you said, fate, that I ran into you on the streets. I was gonna look you up when I got here. Listen, Dante, I only need you for a little bit, just to help me get my feet wet and get started on the East Coast. I already planned the whole thing out. All the truckloads that I send over, I'll store all the shit in a storage garage. All you have to do is pick up one package at a time from the load and hold on to it until one of my guys comes to pick it up. You'll only have to help me get rid of one, maybe two truckloads. By then I should have enough of my men set up and organized," Benny explained.

"And what about these paintings you want?"

"Well, honestly, it was just a way to bring up the topic, but if you really want to, we can do it. I planned it out. You would come to Mexico to paint in a studio I have set up. I would fly you in, and you would only have to come once or twice a week to work. I mean, how long would it take you to do about twenty to thirty big abstract paintings?"

"I don't know. If I keep it simple and work all day for one or two days a week, I guess two to four months."

"Whatever, that's fine. There's no time limit. It's just something different I thought of. Once I get the paintings into the States, I'll switch the frames. That way the paintings won't go to waste. I'll be able to profit off the paintings as well. So, are you in?"

Dante remained silent as he thought about Sonya and stared at the wilted rose resting on the table. Benny noticed Dante. He wasn't going to allow anyone or anything to get in the way of his master plan, especially a woman.

"Forget it, Dante, if she's gonna get in the way," Benny said nonchalantly, leaning back while holding his pint of beer and giving Dante a look he couldn't refuse.

Dante stared at the wilted rose once again. Sonya was Dante's greatest triumph in life, his muse, his everything, and the thought of her was overwhelming, provoking Dante to risk all.

"I'm in. And you don't have to worry about her. She won't get in the way," Dante said softly as he slowly lifted his head and eyes.

"Are you sure? You need to be one hundred percent sure. There's no getting out. These guys don't fuck around. Once you're in, you're in. Because if you aren't, and she gets in the way—"

"Don't worry, Benny. She doesn't have to know anything. Just remember that you owe me bigtime for a favor like this," Dante said as he looked into Benny's eyes and then looked down as he reached for his beer. "So explain to me again how everything is going to work out."

Benny's smile slowly grew bigger, like the Grinch.

"Of course, Dante, of course. If there is ever anything you ever want or need help with, don't hesitate to ask." Benny then leaned forward as he placed his pint back down and sat with his elbows resting on top of the table and his hands held up before his face once more as he dramatically orchestrated his speech. Dante was finally in checkmate, and Benny was now ready to bring closure to his strategically planned scheme.

"So, here's the deal. Right now I have one truckload coming in from Mexico, stocked with furniture filled with cocaine. After the load gets to New Jersey, I have a storage garage in Jersey City to store everything. Once my men unload everything in the garage—" Benny grabbed a napkin and gestured for a pen from the waiter who passed by, and then wrote his phone number down. "Thank you . . . here, this is my contact number, it's a secure line." Benny handed Dante the napkin. "Every time a shipment comes in, when all the supply is gone, you contact me. All you have to do is, each week, hold on to a week's supply to give to one of my dealers, and then collect the profits. Once I get a trusted team set up, you won't have to do much, and . . . and if you ever need anything at all, feel free to call. Just make sure no one ever sees or gets this number."

As Benny concluded, Dante sat stoic while he stared at the phone number on the napkin held in his hands. Eventually, Benny and Dante would leave and go their separate ways. No matter where the road ahead would lead, whether into a barrier of despair, or into a state of evolution and redemption, above all else, in Dante's heart, his motive was for Sonya.

<u>97</u>

The sun slowly rose over the horizon as Dante drove across the empty vast desert wasteland into southwestern Arizona. Although Dante was blindly revisiting his daunting past, he would remain self-assured. The thought of Sonya and Sarita was what kept Dante grounded and vigilant. They were all that was good in his life, and worth dying for. At that moment, they were the inspiration Dante needed to carry on in order to bring closure to a haunting past and his present state of tutelage for Sarita.

After traveling a great distance, Dante eventually turned off the main road onto an adjacent dirt road that stretched out further into the middle of nowhere. Hidden from the main road was an abandoned airfield and air hangar. As he pulled up and parked, clouds of dust from the desert sands, left wafting, slowly faded away. Dante saw in Sarita's eyes the trust she had in him, which fueled his tainted heart and soul, the fire needed to erode away any fear that still remained.

"No worries, Shorty. Everything's gonna be all right, I promise."

Sarita opened the door and stepped down out of the truck. Dante turned around and reached into the backseat to grab his bag and his gun, and Santiago's gun. Dante stepped out of the truck and tucked Santiago's gun into the front of his pants and his own gun into the back of his pants, hiding both under his shirt and standing behind the door so Sarita didn't see.

Dante joined Sarita at the rear of the truck and began to walk beside Sarita, towards the entrance doors of the abandoned air hangar. One of Benny's minions, dressed in black, stepped out and greeted them. He attempted to check

Dante for weapons, but Dante took out Santiago's gun, voluntarily handing it over to Benny's minion, who accepted Dante's peace offering and escorted Dante and Sarita into the hangar. Inside there was a small prop plane and beams of light shining in through holes in the ceiling and windows.

Towards the end of the hangar, they approached Benny, hunched down over a long rectangular table. Laid out horizontally in front of Benny were bricks of cash, various police scanners, and radios, cell phones, multiple laptops and cocaine. While Benny was doing lines of cocaine, another one of Benny's minions stood behind the right end of the table. Benny lifted his head up and back to savor his last hit of blow, then slowly lowered his head, closing and then opening his eyes.

"For a ghost I haven't seen in years, well, ya look all right, Dante. Like, like a portrait hanging up in an ancient gallery. Yet it's so amusing to see you here now, after all these years, so desperate, so alone, yet still trying to hide behind a mask of audacity. Like a lion in chains, your heart of valor burns like fire, yet it seems that you're still so fragile and broken inside, so trapped and all alone, so dependent. Isn't that why you're here now, old friend? Because you have no one, no one else to go to. You came back to the hand that feeds for guidance, for more, for escape. And because of your fucking insecurities and broken dreams, and rancid trail of idiocracy, not only do the fucking Feds and DEA know what my true identity is, but they are now looking for me, and sniffing right outside my door. You were an asset I should've killed a long time ago," Benny said furiously.

Dante could see paranoia deep within Benny's depleted, bloodshot eyes. Benny wasn't the man he once was, a soft-spoken humble intellectual, turned high-profile headstrong criminal mastermind. The man that stood in front of Dante now was a train wreck. Benny now had dark shoulder-length hair and a beard. He wore military boots with worn-out solid army-green military fatigues, the top buttons of his shirt left open. He looked like a mentally and physically drained POW.

"Why didn't you?"

Benny paused, sniffed and wiped away the excess cocaine from his nose before continuing. "Friendships never die, right? So you could at least thank me for sparing your life after all these years."

"Don't you still owe me for all I've done for you? From what I remember, weren't you the one who came to me for help first? Wasn't I the one you needed, the one to help you get your feet wet, and set up a foundation for your empire on the East Coast?"

Benny laughed at Dante's words.

"Yeah, you're right. I did go to you first for help, to help me set up shop on the East Coast, since it was you and only you I trusted. But now, my whole operation of living and controlling all in exile and disappearing off the grid, from existence, like, like David Copperfield, is all over, because of you cutting the cords and bringing down the fucking curtain, showing the whole fucking spectrum of authority and federal agencies and the whole fucking world who I am and where the fuck I hide. Underground, in tunnels, or, or even sometimes in the open, for all to see. Well, now the whole illusion and façade I created, the whole fucking magic show is over!" Once again Benny's words erupted like a storm.

"Well, sorry for being the jester who brought down the whole house of cards, but you had it coming, Benny, sooner or later. Everything you created, this whole Nada Mas network, it was only supposed to be some modest scheme, not this monster you've created. It has its tentacles connected to big corporations, the pharmaceutical industry, banking, politics, and even worse, it's connected to networks involved with trafficking human beings and using them as slave labor and prostitution. Even children are forced into sexual submission because of Nada Mas, from this nightmare Nada Mas has become. It's still hard to believe how big you've become and how long you lasted. Not too many people become as big as you and get as far as you. And who knows? Maybe you were allowed to become what you became and helped by an unseen hand, ya know. But either way, it doesn't really matter, because that's the game. That's the pyramid. Without the ninety-nine percent holding you up anymore, you crumble and fall. Guess that I'm the kick start to your demise. It's for the better, though. Sometimes the eye in the sky needs to be shown who they really are.

Nothing but insecure, dependable, soulless pieces of shit," Dante said passionately but remained poised.

"That may be, that may be. But sometimes, sometimes it's much better to pick up the pieces and rebuild a dream, start all over again, fresh. Ya know, like a blank canvas waiting to be crafted into something new, something beautiful. My new canvas of dreams is waiting for me. That's why I'm leaving the country. I'm going to Mexico. My paradise of dreams awaits me, and my angel wings over there will take me, G, and Q there. Shortly after we, well, we bring closure to all of this, friendship, and, and whatever the fuck it is you want to talk to me about. So, make it quick, and don't expect any promises, either."

"Mexico? That's why I came all the way across the country to see you. Not for me, but for this girl. She's the one I need to bring to Mexico. Just take us with you. After we land, we'll go our separate ways. You'll never see or hear from me, ever again," Dante requested desperately.

"Bring you to Mexico? What are you, out of your fucking mind! Besides the fact that me and you are done with each other, there's only room for me, G and Q."

"What about your contacts at the border, the border patrol you have on payroll? Can't you get them to give us safe passage across the border into Mexico?" Dante pleaded.

Benny was filled with disbelief, as he sniffed and wiped away excess cocaine. "Nah, sorry, I don't do charity work for invalids and little girls I have no association with. Sorry, Dante, but you're fucked. You're on your own from here on out."

Benny's final words poisoned Dante's heart. As Dante stood still, sedated with confusion, he looked back at Sarita, who watched with concern. Benny smirked as he looked at how hopeless Dante and Sarita appeared to be, did a hit of blow, and then crept around the table.

"Q, why don't you be a gentleman and escort our friend here and the young lady out of here. Once you get them outside, well, kill them both." Benny gestured to Q, who began to walk from around the end of the table while drawing his gun.

"Dante," Sarita called out and began to slowly step backwards when she saw Dante gesture with his hand to do so.

"Ya know, isn't it poetic, Dante, that after all you've been through in life, all the struggles and hardships you've dealt with before, during and after living as a successful artist, that your life will end here, in the middle of nowhere? Au revoir, my friend, au revoir . . ." Benny stepped towards Dante and wiped his nose. Q now stood before Sarita with his gun pointed at her, and G now stood just behind Benny, off to the side with his gun drawn.

In Sarita's eyes, there were tears as she began to quiver all over and sob. Dante tried to calm Sarita with his gaze as he attempted to conjure up a way out. Being outnumbered and outgunned wasn't playing in Dante's favor. He needed a miracle.

"And as for this poor child you brought along with you, Dante, well, she . . ." As Benny stepped before Dante while trying to find the right words, Dante was drawn away by a gleam coming from the rafters, causing Dante to look up with an outstretched hand to shield his eyes from the blinding light now shining down.

Bang! Bang! Bang! Bang! A wave of bullets from Octavio, the eight-fingered assassin dressed in all white hiding up in the rafters, penetrated Benny's back, causing Benny to drop forward onto the ground. Sarita rushed towards and hid behind an oil drum while both G and Q turned with guns drawn to fire at their unknown assailant, who shot both of them to death. Dante drew his gun and was able to pull off a couple rounds before running for cover behind multiple wooden warehouse crates that were stacked like Lego blocks.

As the assassin continued to fire at the crates, Dante looked across the open floor at Sarita, who sat curled up in a ball behind the oil drum. After the assassin paused for a moment, Dante crept around the side of the crate to look, but quickly pulled his head back as a bullet came inches away. Dante was able to get a glimpse, and that was all he needed.

Dante then fired a shot from the other side of the crates, causing the assassin to fire there and focus on that spot. Dante quickly shuffled back to the first side, boldly peeked around it, and unloaded his gun into the assassin's area.

Luckily, one of the bullets hit the assassin, causing him to fall back off the rafter and down onto a platform that was about ten feet below him. Dante could see that the assassin was hit and wasn't getting up, so Dante came out from behind the crates. He then stepped in front of Benny's limp body, lying facedown in a pool of blood, and turned him over. Benny was still breathing but coughing up blood.

"Sa, son of a bitch, I'm . . . I'm fucking d-dying," Benny cried out.

"Don't die on me. Not now, I need you now more than ever before! C'mon, Benny, stay strong. Breathe, keep breathing!" Dante said as he held Benny's head up.

"M-m-mothafucker, I . . . I can't be, believe this fucking sh-shit . . . " Benny coughed up blood as he forced out his words.

"Benny . . . Benny, don't die on me, Benny!" Dante began to shake Benny in order to keep him conscious just a little bit longer.

"Ya, ya . . . na, need, to, to . . . ." Benny struggled to speak. He coughed up more blood and began to gasp for air.

"Need to what? Need to what? Benny, don't fucking die. What is it I need to do, Benny?"

Benny gasped out his last breath and then fell completely limp. He was dead. Dante wiped Benny's blood off his forehead and looked over to Sarita, who was still sobbing behind the oil drum. Dante stood up, took notice of Sarita's traumatic state, looked up at the assassin lying still on the platform up in the rafters, and frantically looked for an escape. He dashed towards the prop plane and jumped inside, but then jumped out.

Knowing that he didn't know how to fly, Dante trotted back towards the table and began to pace around. There was desperation in Dante's eyes and uncertainty in his body language. Once Dante calmed himself down, he refocused his thoughts and came to a halt. Dante stood behind the table filled with bricks of cash, various police scanners, and radios, cell phones, multiple laptops, and cocaine, and reached into his pocket. Dante took out Valdo's business card for his band, Valdo y Sus Amigos, and then looked up at Sarita with a smile.

98

In the calm of the night, Daffy debauchedly watched the strippers dance the night away on the center stage of the Booty Trap strip club while he sipped his bottle of beer and waited for a client to arrive. Inside the decrepit poorly lit strip club were a variety of night owls, perverts, and men both old and young, seeking pleasure and a sense of companionship from one of the many strippers who roamed around the open floor. They sought lonely men willing to give away all their money just for a taste and a few minutes spent with a woman. Although Daffy was easy to persuade, he kept a safe distance from the center stage and watched from a back corner table located off the path that the strippers prowled on while on the hunt for an easy score. As difficult as it was for Daffy to resist the temptation, he stayed focused on his beer and his iPhone while tapping his fingers on the edge of the table until his client arrived.

From out of the shadows of the club, a young, discreet Hispanic male with a well-defined scruff and piercing green eyes, wearing baggy jeans, scuffed-up Timberland boots, an oversized gray Ecko Unltd hoodie, and a New York Yankees hat slightly tilted down and to the side, maneuvered his way pass a gauntlet of aggressive strippers. He approached Daffy from behind, patting him on the shoulder as he stepped around and sat down beside him. Daffy jerked up but then became calm when he saw who it was.

"Easy, brotha, it's only me."

"Andres. Fuck, I thought you were one of those pocket whores, know what I mean? They'll do anything for a dime or two," Daffy said as he looked around along with Andres at all the strippers going from guy to guy.

"Well, these pockets are deep, so I can spare some of these ladies the charity later on when we're done."

A petite Colombian stripper with modest-sized breasts and a tight round ass walked up to both Andres and Daffy.

"Hey, babies. So which one of yous want to take me for a ride, huh?" the Colombiana said as she sat on Andres's lap, caressing his chest.

"Well, first of all, I'm not allowed to go anywhere with strangers, and second, how much does a sexy mami like you cost?"

"Please, I'm no stranger, baby. I'm Abiliana, but you can call me Abilia. How much you willing to spend for all of this, huh?"

"Everything I got in my pocket."

Abiliana ground her ass on his crotch, giving him a hard-on.

"Mmm, I like, baby. You got a lot, but I charge you good. One hundred dollars for one hour. C'mon, we can get started now." Abiliana got up and took Andres by the hand, who let go.

"Sounds good, *mami*, but I need to have a few drinks first before we get started."

"Okay, baby, okay. I come back soon." Abiliana gave Andres a kiss on the cheek and then left.

"Don't go too far. I wanna be able to keep my eye on you." As Abiliana walked away, she shook her ass for Andres and then blew him a kiss.

"You fucking pig, you just got here and already you're giving into the first one that comes onto you," Daffy said as he turned away from Abiliana.

"Yeah, well, pussy's pussy, and from what I saw after walking in here, she's one of the few worth spending money on. Anyway, cheers, brotha. Here's to a good night." Andres lifted up the beer Daffy had waiting for him and took a sip along with Daffy.

"Yeah, well, I prefer one of those Asians over there, not some fucking Spanish *mami* flytrap. From what I hear, they'll let you fist-fuck 'em while twisting a beer bottle up their ass."

"You're a sick fuck. Anyway, here's all the information you asked for."

Andres took out a folded-up piece of paper, which he handed to Daffy.

"Okay, okay, this looks good. It's actually more information than I needed, but with all this, I should be able to get what you want by the end of the week."

"Good, good. That works out perfectly, because after all the transfers are made, there's the weekend to lay low before anyone realizes what happened to their accounts."

"Yeah, well, it's still risky, but with all this data I now have, and the system security encryptions, we should be fine, no worries," Daffy said after scanning through all of the bank account information of top Wall Street investors and corporate investors. "So, how long have you known Indio?"

"For about two years now. After I spent some time in Jersey, working in his restaurant down in Ironbound, Indio took a liking to me. Ya know, we hit it off right away and became good friends. He's the one who brought me into Nada Mas."

"Oh, yeah? I worked out of Jersey for a little bit, for Nada Mas before it blew up into the monster it once was. I'm not surprised that it's all broken up like it is now, either. It's not what it was when I worked for them. Well, that was a long time ago, way before you ended up in Jersey. So how come you're out here on the West Coast? Why didn't you stay in Jersey?"

"Just a change of scenery. I like to move around a lot. Plus, Jersey's too fucking cold. That's why I moved out west. Lucky for me, I have a few people I know who live just over the border in Mexico, that I'm gonna start doing business with, maybe hook Indio up and get him involved in some way as well. Anyway, Indio's the one who told me about you, how you're like some computer genius who can hack into anything. After I got all this information from an insider from Silicon Valley connected to Wall Street, that's when I contacted Indio and asked if he knew anyone who could do something with the information. So he told me about you, and how you were living out here in Arizona, not too far from where I live now."

"Yep, kinda laying low for a while, since Nada Mas isn't what it once was. It's a dying dynasty. There's too many big egos and no more trust and loyalty like in the old days. So, lucky for you, I never had a problem with Indio, he's good people. After he told me about you, at first I was hesitant, since I don't know you and I only work with people I know, but after he told me what good friends you were, well, lucky for you I trust Indio and his judgment."

"Yeah, Indio's like a brother, and you shouldn't worry, because after this score, well, you'll get a nice big piece of the pie."

"Well, I hope so, after all these accounts you have me hacking into. But you know the deal. I'm sure Indio gave you the heads-up, I want a down payment before I touch any of this. So, with that said, you got that appetizer for me now? No pre-meal, no deal."

After Daffy stated his fee, Andres's smile grew bigger. He then sipped his beer as he gazed deep into Daffy's gullible eyes. "Of course, I have it right here." Andres reached down to pick up a messenger bag. He then handed it to Daffy, who placed it on his lap, took a sip of beer, looked around the club, and then discreetly opened and peeked inside. Inside was $50,000 cash.

"Looks tasty," Daffy said with a smile as he closed up the bag and then placed it down on the floor beside his feet. He picked up his beer and finished it. "Well, it's always a pleasure doing business with a friend of a friend. Like I said, give me a week or so to process everything and make the transfers." Daffy began to stand up with the bag of money, only to be held back by Andres, who blocked Daffy's path with his outstretched arm.

"Whoa, where you going so fast? Don't you want to enjoy the moment? C'mon, how about a little fun before both of us leave? It's on me, anyone you want."

"Well, maybe another drink."

"A drink—c'mon, I see the way you keep watching those Asians over there."

Daffy looked across the strip club at the two exotic Asians dancing together, seducing Daffy with their gaze. Andres smiled as he watched Daffy become easily persuaded.

"Aren't those the ones you said will let you fist-fuck 'em and stick a beer bottle up their ass? C'mon, my treat, you can stay with them for however long you want. I'll go with the Colombiana until you're done." Andres stood up and wrapped his arm around Daffy's shoulder and began to guide him across the strip club towards the Asian strippers.

"Well, I hope you have no place to go, because I may be a while," Daffy said.

"That's what I'm talking about, time to enjoy the night," Andres said and then brought Daffy over towards the two Asians, who guided Daffy upstairs to a private room. As the three walked away, Andres watched with a smile and then made a phone call. "Moby Dick is hooked and reeled, send in all units," Andres said and then hung up.

Daffy sat on a couch in a private room with his pants down, stroking his average-sized cock, while the two Asians groped, kissed and danced with each other. Just as the two Asians began to give Daffy a blow job, FBI agents came storming in with guns drawn.

"Hands up, get your hands, up!"

"Down on the ground, down on the ground!"

The two Asians panicked, and Daffy remained still. He had his cock in his hand and premature cum glazed all over his hand and pants. The final agents to come storming in were Qubish, Von Burton and Sergio Serrano, aka Andres Alvarez. After Andres stepped into the room, Daffy looked at him as if he was seeing a ghost. Daffy shook his head as the FBI agents apprehended him and began to forcefully walk him out.

99

Dueling guitar riffs blasted out improvised Mexican-style music intertwined with rock as Gio and Gia played alongside each other in the back of the traveling van. It was a white 1982 Dodge van with advertising graphics painted on the side, transporting Valdo y Sus Amigos towards the US-Mexico border. Sitting all along the perimeter of the back of the van were the band members. Chango, the drummer, banged on a bongo drum, and Rafa, the bassist, patted his thigh to the rhythm, both sitting alongside the door side of the van. Across from Chango and Rafa was Dino, the pianist, Paulo, who played the panpipes, and Adrian, who played the accordion. Valdo drove the van, and Pinto, the manager, sat beside him in the passenger seat. Two other vans filled with all the instruments and stage equipment along with the stage crew and technicians followed behind. Dino and Adrian stomped their feet on the rug-covered floor. Dante and Sarita lay cramped together underneath in a gutted storage space used for extra instruments.

Valdo y Sus Amigos were like a band of bandidos out on the open road, unafraid to conquer all that lay ahead. As they continued to travel down Interstate 19 South from Tucson, Arizona, to the border of Nogales, spirits were high. The exchange of beautiful upbeat music kept all in an optimistic state of mind. The drive to the border was long and unsettling, but the music seemed to erase all of time, until they reached the border checkpoint in Nogales.

"Hey, hey, *muchachos*, everything okay down there? We're at the border checkpoint, so stay quiet, *comprende*?" Rafa advised Dante and Sarita after he

480

stomped his foot on the floor to get their attention.

Dante, lying in the fetal position, muttered obscenities under his breath as he tried to adjust his body. Sarita was fully stretched out on her back and she remained still. Her eyes were red and glazed over from crying as she remembered witnessing people being shot.

Valdo y Sus Amigos stayed in a calm state of being as they looked out the windows and watched the lines of idling cars and multiple US Border Patrol agents walking around from car to car with drug-sniffing dogs. As the van slowly drove closer towards the end of the line, underneath a massive white tent towering across three lanes of traffic, a US Border Patrol agent stepped up to the driver-side window.

"Good afternoon, sir, how are you?" US Border Patrol agent Fuentes, a Mexican American wearing a solid green authority uniform kindly asked Valdo.

"Very good, very good. Hey, I'm alive and well, you're alive and well, my *amigos* are alive and well, and God is good, *si*?" Valdo said passionately in a very animated manner.

"*Claro, claro*, my friend, I agree. But what brings you and all of your friends to Mexico?" Agent Fuentes held one hand on his hip and the other on his shoulder radio, receiving other agents' chatter.

"We're Valdo y Sus Amigos, the greatest band in the Southwest. We're finishing up our southwestern tour in Sonora State. Have you not heard of Valdo y Sus Amigos?" Valdo said proudly.

"Nah, can't say I have. Are those other two vans with you?" Fuentes asked.

"Yes, all our instruments and stage equipment's in there," Valdo said.

"Okay, that's good. Just do me a favor. Could you and your entourage of vans please pull over to the side over there?" Fuentes directed.

"Hey, we're on a tight schedule. I've already notified the proper authorities to let them know that we're coming through so that we don't get held up," said Pinto, exasperated as he leaned across Valdo.

"Okay, that may be, sir, but still, all vans, trucks, and any vehicle that exceeds a certain weight must proceed to the side to undergo further inspection," Fuentes firmly stated.

"Hey, there's no need for that!" Pinto lashed out.

"Excuse me, sir, but I'm not asking you, I'm ordering you to proceed further to the side, now." Fuentes stepped closer towards the window with one hand held on his gun. "Pull the vehicle over to the side, now!" Fuentes pointed with his other hand.

There was then side chatter amongst the bandmates as Valdo pulled the van over towards the side, where three other agents awaited them, one accompanied by a drug-sniffing dog. Everyone was ordered out of the vans. Underneath the floor, Dante tensed up as he tried to hear what was going on, and Sarita began to choke up on the excess of gravel left behind from the bottoms of everyone's shoes. As one of the US Border Patrol agents questioned Pinto, who showed him all the proper credentials needed for everyone, the other agent searched the two vans with the instruments and equipment first, then stepped inside the van all the bandmates were in.

As more gravel began to trickle in through the tiny gaps in the floor, Sarita continued to choke up, then turned over on her stomach and lay facedown. Fortunately, at that moment, the agent was focused on the rearrangement of the three standard van benches, which were placed around the perimeter. But then, after feeling around the surface and inside the creases, he was drawn towards the rug on the floor. And without any hesitation, the agent began to move the three van benches, which were not bolted to the floor, and feel around the edges of the rug. As the agent felt around for openings in the rug, which was securely attached to the floor, and looked underneath each of the benches, Sarita began to cough into her forearm. Dante struggled to keep his burning eyes open from the sweat seeping down his forehead and into his eyes. He began to shush Sarita as her coughing became worse. And then, Sarita began to cough uncontrollably into her forearm while the agent's head lay inches away on the other side of the floor. The other agent who was outside the door called the agent out of the van.

After the agent joined the other agent outside the van, Valdo y Sus Amigos were free to go. All of the bandmates then filed into the van and freely drove off into Mexico. It still had to pass through the Mexican checkpoint.

"Hey, *amigo*, how you doing down there?" Rafa said to Dante as all of the others leaned in to hear Dante respond.

"Well, besides sweating my ass off, my balls feel like they're gonna crack open like a pair of walnuts. Are we in Mexico yet?" Dante yelled out.

"Ha-ha, don't worry, *mi amigo*, we're almost there. Hey, if you want, Chango here will massage them for you when you come out." Everyone laughed out loud and then sat back and patiently waited until they approached the Mexican checkpoint.

Although the Mexican checkpoint was similar to the American side, passing through it wasn't conducted in the same manner. Vehicles needed to drive up to a traffic light, which would randomly flash green or red. If the traffic light flashed green, vehicles were allowed to freely drive into Mexico. If it flashed red, then the Mexican authorities would stop the vehicle, question the passengers and then inspect the vehicle. Fortunately, though, all three vans received the green light and passed the random voluntary selection process.

After freely passing the Mexico checkpoint and driving into Nogales, Mexico, the bandmates opened up the compartments in the floor and helped Dante and Sarita out. Both were given water.

"Well, *mi amigos*, we made it. You're in Mexico," Valdo yelled out as he drove the van through the city streets.

"*Órale, mi amigo*," Rafa said as he patted Dante on the back.

"So, what song do you wanna hear, *mi amigo*?" Gio asked Dante as he tuned his acoustic guitar.

Sarita remained still, in a traumatized state as she watched Dante chug water, then wipe the excess off his chin and shirt.

"How about something from the Stones? You know any Rolling Stones songs?" Dante asked as he looked out the window.

"*Sí, sí*, I've got the perfect song . . . *uno, dos, uno, dos, tres* . . ." After Gio counted out, he began to play the Rolling Stones' "Wild Horses," and then, after the guitar solo introduction, Gia began to sing the lyrics.

As the soothing guitar riffs and voice of Gia echoed out, Valdo y Sus Amigos, along with Dante, who held his arm around Sarita, now felt at ease, smiled, enjoyed the music and their freedom as they drove further into Mexico.

100

As voices and camera clicks echoed throughout the abandoned aircraft hangar, Donovan and Walsh walked in. Walsh walked a few steps behind Donovan as they got closer to the circle of FBI agents. The few men closest to them then separated from the group, breaking the circle and leaving a semicircle of agents. On the ground before them were three dead bodies lying in a pool of blood. After Donovan and Walsh joined the semicircle of agents, directly across from them were Qubish and Von Burton.

"Well, look what the wind blew in. So, what happened? You two get stuck in traffic? We've been here for an hour already," Von Burton said with a smirk.

"Hey, relax, Von Burton, we just found out ten minutes ago," Donovan said as he wiped sweat off of his forehead.

"So where's your guy and our girl? I thought you said you would keep her company if you got to her first. All I see is three dead bodies. Better hope our girl doesn't end up like these two," Walsh said to Von Burton.

"Or what, Walsh?" Von Burton raised his voice.

"Hey! Enough of this schoolyard bullshit. Let's act like the professionals we're supposed to be, okay? You see those two dead pieces of shit lying in each other's blood? They're G and Q, two loyal servants of this big piece of shit the FBI have been trying to find for a long time, Benjamin Bradford, also known as Benny, the head of Nada Mas. Now you're probably wondering what his connection is to our guy and your girl. For starters, Dante helped Benny get started on the East Coast, and most importantly, he knows Benny personally and

484

is someone who could give us more intel on Benny and Nada Mas. For now a former member of Nada Mas who we apprehended and now have working as an informant was able to get information on Dante's whereabouts, which led us here. Unfortunately as you can see, we were too late. Someone else got here first. From the shell casings and the trajectory of the bullets, there was another gunman up in the rafters. Who he or she was, what this person's motive was, and the connection to Benny and Dante is still unclear. As for who shot first and Dante's motive for contacting Benny? It's still unclear as well, but based on who he is and what he's caught up in, there are several possibilities as to why he kidnapped the girl and still has her with him, alive—well, we hope."

"What do you mean, we hope?" Donovan said.

"Well, knowing his past, the kind of people he's dealt with, his connection to Nada Mas, and what has happened here, who knows? It's just a possibility right now, until we can gather more information," Qubish said as he puffed on his cigarillo.

Donovan tightly squeezed his yellow stress ball while Walsh bit his lip as he looked at all the blood and dead bodies. Walsh felt dizzy and nauseous.

"You don't look too good, Walsh. What is it, your first time seeing a dead body?" Von Burton said.

Walsh then began to have that vomit taste run up his throat as he gagged and held his mouth.

"Yeah, it's my first time. Not only that, but there's three."

"Well, congratulations, you broke your cherry. Kudos on the three-for-one. What about you, Donovan? Have you been a virgin for the past thirty-five years, or do you just look like you are?" Qubish said.

"I broke my cherry a long time ago, Qubish, and believe it or not, I've seen a lot of dead bodies in the past thirty-five years, more than you may think. When dealing with child abductions for that long, you get to see a lot of gruesome shit, shit that makes hell seem pleasant."

"Is that so? More border jumpers than homegrown, I hope."

"That's so wrong, Qubitch, how can you say a thing like that?" Walsh said.

"What's a matter, Walsh, can't take a sick joke? You better toughen this kid up, Donovan, especially if he wants to do thirty-five years like you," Qubish, the most professional out of all of them, added to his childish antics.

"He's still learning, Qubish, but don't you worry, he'll be as tough as nails real soon. So, Qubish, since you're the brains, what possibilities have you come up with?"

"Many, Donovan. First one, and the one that I believe to be correct, is that our guy got nervous. He knew that we were hot on his trail and getting close to him, so he needed to get someplace far away. The girl, I believe, was a hostage he would use if we happened to get to him before he got to wherever it is he plans on going. Now, you're probably wondering, why would he come to Benny? One possibility is that maybe he needed Benny to help him get to where he was going by providing him with money and safe passage. My guess is Mexico; it seems logical to me, since he came all the way here from New Jersey. For him, it's risky to stay in the States. Plus, in Mexico, as it's out of our jurisdiction, he's a free man there. As for what happened, who knows yet? Maybe Dante and Benny were negotiating an escape. Maybe they had a falling out. Or, what I think happened, whoever this mystery person is that showed up, it must either be someone from within Nada Mas, or someone from another cartel or gang who couldn't get to Benny. I'm guessing whoever it is must've trailed Dante to get here and then taken Benny out. Right now anything is possible, but based on the facts we have now, I'm pretty sure that our guy is on his way to Mexico."

"Well, besides this mess we have here and this mystery person, is there any more information or theories that we don't already know, to help us better understand why he has our girl other than using her as a hostage, and that he's on his way to Mexico?" Donovan said to Qubish. More sweat began to pour down his face as Walsh looked at him with concern for his well-being.

"Sorry, Donovan, that's all I have right now, the same information and theories you have about your girl. I was actually hoping that you would have more information on your girl by now. It appears that we're on the same page. Want to know what works for me when I'm stuck on a case and find it hard to get answers? I go back to the beginning. I clear my mind of all I know and look at a case in a completely different way. I don't look at the facts, assumptions, or opinions of others. I try to get different results by approaching the situation with a completely different sense of consciousness. I'm abstract, I use my imagination. Einstein did. Maybe he's just using the girl as his ticket into Mexico, and as insurance, but looking at this with an abstract sense of perspective, who knows? Maybe the girl went to him for help—ya know, since we know the mother did have a history with different gang organizations."

"Of course, the idea of our girl going to your guy for help crossed our minds," Walsh said. "But with all the eyewitnesses, interviews and facts, nah, there's no way—"

Von Burton cut off Walsh. "Shouldn't you two have more information on your girl than we do? Oh, yeah, I forgot. You're just the new guy."

"Hey, watch your mouth, Burton. You're still a diaper dandy yourself. Don't worry about us. Just let us do our job and we'll figure this out before you two," Donovan firmly stated.

"Remember what I said, gentlemen. Go back to the beginning, be abstract and use your imagination. Gentlemen, once again, it's been a pleasure," Qubish said as he and Von Burton walked away and out of the abandoned aircraft hangar.

"So what do you think, Donovan?" Walsh said as he turned his head away from the three dead bodies. Donovan put his stress ball away.

"A lot of things. Qubish may be a stubborn bastard, but he makes a good point. I think we should go back to the beginning, look at what we know in a different way, and see if we can get more information on the mother other than what ICE relayed back to us."

"So, you're gonna go take Qubitch's advice?"

"As of right now, yeah, until we get more information. Things may change. Have a little faith, Walsh. Let's get out of this shithole, c'mon. First thing I wanna do is go over our witness reports, contacts, everyone and anyone who knows the mother, and trace back our trail. We may find something we didn't see before. As soon as we're done with that, we'll have a better idea as to where to go from here."

As Donovan spoke, he walked towards the exit as Walsh followed behind, trying to keep up his pace. As the two FBI agents came to the doors, they walked out into a blinding light and a sea of media reporters and cameramen. They were now stuck working on the case behind the biggest news story in the country. Donovan's nerves and stress were now beyond controllable. He pulled out Sarita's multicolored friendship bracelet to hold for relief and motivation. Failure was not an option, and the stakes and pressure were higher than before. Hopefully, Donovan thought, all would end in Mexico, the case and his retirement, in a positive manner.

101

Being in Mexico felt liberating as Dante and Sarita stepped out of Valdo y Sus Amigos' van and into an OXXO convenience store parking lot. There was a brisk sensation of amity and redemption in the air as Dante looked around and then up into the sun, savoring his freedom, while Valdo y Sus Amigos said their farewell. Chango shut the side door and Dante walked around to the driver-side window.

"Hey, Valdo, thank you again. You don't know how much we both appreciate your help," Dante said as he firmly shook Valdo's hand.

"*Claro, mi amigo, con gusto;* hey, remember if you two want to come back to the States with us, just give me a call. You still have my number, right?"

"Got it right here." Dante took Valdo's business card out of his pocket to show Valdo and then put it back.

"*Muy bien.* Don't forget to tell everyone you see how good Valdo y Sus Amigos was to you. Remember that Valdo y Sus Amigos is the people's band. Adiós, *mi amigo*," Valdo said passionately and drove off. The rest of Valdo y Sus Amigos all yelled out their goodbyes while playing music from the back of the van.

That was it. Dante and Sarita were on their own once again. They stood in the middle of a vast, congested urban border city. They were now free from their predecessors and on an open road, which now should lead to Gabriela. Somewhere within the city was Gabriela, waiting to finally reunite with Sarita. Before that time would come, Dante and Sarita needed to find their way.

"Um, so, now what?" Sarita asked Dante, who observed the city.

"We walk from here." Dante then began to walk and guide Sarita out into the narrow city streets. There seemed to be a sense of peace within the hearts of Dante and Sarita as they walked with no direction along the open road, but then came a storm. All around, there was a chaotic dissonance of chants, cheers and drumbeats. Sarita was intrigued by the commotion and crowds of people holding banners, flags, and posters, who filled the streets, while Dante remained vigilant.

"Dante, what's going on? Why are there so many people yelling and cheering?"

"I don't know. Just stay close to me, okay?" Dante put his arm around Sarita's shoulder while guiding her through the crowd. Eventually, they both became engulfed by the herd of sheeple and unwillingly forced in one direction. As a chaotic storm of chants, cheers and drumbeats slowly rose to a crescendo of one thunderous voice, it was evident as Dante and Sarita followed the flow of the herd into a massive zócalo filled with a sea of protesters that the well-organized peaceful uprising was at some point going to be forcefully silenced by fear and tyranny. Amongst the massive uprising, there was an army of Mexican federal police officers, fully equipped and armed, wearing militarized police uniforms and riot gear, strategically positioned throughout the city square. As Dante struggled to safely guide Sarita through the massive crowd of people, away and out of the zócalo, a few blind and misled nonviolent protesters, unwelcome anarchists, and undercover provocateurs, dissenters and disobedient ones began to instigate police officers, throw rocks, become violent and light fires, inciting riots and triggering the police state to bring its iron fist down upon the innocent nonviolent protesters.

As the Mexican police force began to clash with protesters and make lawful and unlawful arrests, Dante and Sarita were able to retreat down a secluded side street. The chaos seemed to be left far behind as Sarita walked beside Dante and onto the safety of an empty street, but the storm of people caught up. A stampede of protesters eventually fled the failed uprising and chaotic injustices unfolding within the city square, scattering down adjacent side streets while trampling over the slow and the weak, who hopelessly fell to the ground. Then they started to rush down the side street where Dante and Sarita momentarily found refuge. As a tsunami of protesters came rushing towards Dante and Sarita, simultaneously, on the opposite side of the street, a wall of Mexican police officers held their ground, armed with militarized weapons, and took aim on the hostile crowd rushing towards them, who were throwing rocks, bottles and fire bombs. As a chaotic uproar of violence unfolded, Dante and Sarita stood in the middle of a crossfire between the police and the protesters. Without any sense of hesitation, Dante lifted Sarita up, cradled her in his arms and turned his back towards the Mexican police officers to protect Sarita from the wave of rubber bullets and tear gas which were fired upon them and the crowd of protesters. As rubber bullets battered Dante's flesh and tear gas slowly rose up into a cloud of darkness, Dante staggered, then dropped to the ground unconscious. Sarita fell out of Dante's limp arms and was pushed deeper into the crowd of people, who either rushed forward towards the Mexican police officers to stand their ground or scattered in all directions.

As Sarita lay on the ground all alone within the heart of the chaos, she slowly lifted herself up, only to be knocked down to the ground again by a stampede of people running in all directions. She stood again, calling out for Dante, and then was knocked down to the ground once more.

"Dante . . . Dante," Sarita whimpered as she slowly lifted herself up again to stand up, frozen, with tears in her eyes, to cry out for Dante again while people ran by her, knocking her from side to side.

"Dante! Dante! Dante!"

As Sarita desperately yelled out, Dante was nowhere to be seen. As Sarita stood abandoned and all alone within the chaos, hands from a stranger fleeing the uprising reached down lifted Sarita up and then carried her from out of the violence.

102

In the distance along the horizon were the final remains of a crime scene investigation, and within the emptiness of the vast desert were Donovan and Walsh. As they walked side by side, Donovan squeezed his stress ball while Walsh watched him like a child waiting for the right opportunity to interrupt a parent's angry state of being.

Donovan's scruff was thick and the ridges in his forehead deep. Walsh's innocent face became flush with weariness and his eyes filled with concern as he observed the visible tension of Donovan's physique. The veins in his neck and hand that tightly squeezed the stress ball bulged out like the blood-pulsing veins of Michelangelo's statue of David. Donovan then put away his stress ball, took out stress pills, took two, and then took out a cigarette.

"So, what do you think, Donovan?"

"Right now, Walsh, nothing, nothing at all . . . well, actually, I think that the best thing for me to say is that I'm clearing my mind. Ya know, reevaluating our situation from a different perspective."

"So, you're taking Qubish's advice, being abstract and using your imagination like Einstein."

"Well, sorta, Walsh, but more like putting myself on the other side of the game, looking at everything from the perspective of our boy, our girl and the mother." After speaking, Donovan began to pick up his pace. Walsh quickly followed behind.

"Well, after all that's happened so far and all that we know, do you think that it's safe to say that they're probably going to Mexico, or that they're already there?" Walsh asked.

As Donovan listened, he came to a stop. Walsh stepped a few steps ahead of Donovan, but then stepped back beside him.

"Mexico, I feel, is definitely their final destination. Whether they're there or not, well, that's the real question. With nothing on the Amber Alert we sent out, I think it's best to start securing the border by getting units set up along border checkpoints in the Southwest. If he's still in the States somewhere, then the girl is definitely still with him and still alive. I strongly feel that he has her hostage and kept safe for good reason, because right now she's a very important asset to him. Now, if they are in Mexico already, well, there isn't much we can do, it's out of our jurisdiction. But if he did bring the girl with him, in my opinion, with the way everything has unfolded, I don't think that he will kill her there, because there doesn't seem to be any reason for him to go all the way to Mexico and then just kill her. No way, she was or still is his ticket into Mexico and nothing more."

"So, what do you think he will do with the girl, Donovan? Just abandon her? And what about the mother?"

"It's a possibility, Walsh. It's definitely possible. As for the mother, from what ICE told us, now that she's back in Mexico, we have to wait until we can contact the Mexican authorities and hopefully have them cooperate and work with us by looking over the mother and wait to see if Dante shows up with the girl. But right now, it's too early to jump to conclusions. Right now, the most important thing for us to do is to meet with Qubish and Von Burton. Dante's history with Benny is definitely a big piece of the puzzle, especially now that he's dead. After we gather more information on the relationship between them, then we'll have a better idea as to where he may be going and what his motive is and hopefully figure out who this mystery gunman is and why Benny was killed. Right now, let's just hope that we get to Dante before he gets into Mexico."

"Don't forget about the informant that used to be a part of Nada Mas, the one Qubish said they were getting information from. I'm sure that he'll have some useful information for us too, right?"

"Yeah, ya know, you're right Walsh. What am I gonna do without you, when I retire?"

"Aren't you gonna be living in Mexico with your wife? Remember, you told me that you'll be drinking margaritas on a beach and fishing off the coast of Baja?"

"I know that, Walsh. I didn't mean it literally. What I meant was that without you by my side, who will remind me of my absentmindedness?"

"Probably your wife. She has a very good memory and is always on top of things, or I'm sure that there will be some good locals around your retirement home who would be willing to help you."

Donovan then reached into his pocket and pulled out a folded-up piece of paper.

"Ya know, you're like the child I've never had, Walsh," Donovan said as he handed Walsh the paper.

"I know, Donovan, you tell me all the time." Walsh opened up the paper. It was a picture of Donovan's retirement home, a two-story beachfront villa. In the foreground was a dirt path, lined with stone pots filled with high-rising plants, leading to the front of the villa. In the distance behind the villa was the Pacific Ocean, with the setting sun descending behind the horizon. The rays of light from the setting sun shined down across the ocean and illuminated the villa.

"Well, it's so that you never forget," Donovan said as he admired Walsh like the child he'd never had. Walsh just silently stared at the picture of the villa without even acknowledging or realizing what Donovan's deep emotional words truly meant to him.

"Don't worry, I won't. So, this is it Donovan, paradise." Walsh glanced over at Donovan and then back down at picture.

"Yeah, so what do you think?"

"Well, you definitely set yourself up real nice. I'm feeling kinda jealous of you right now. I mean, look at this place. It's perfect. It's in Mexico, it's right on the beach, and you even have a dog, which is funny because I thought you hated dogs. I guess that retiring and going to live in a place like this in Mexico changes a man, huh?"

Donovan tensed up when Walsh pointed out the dog. He'd hated dogs ever since the horrific, tragic accident in which his late partner, Special Agent Wilson, and his entire task force had fallen victim due to a stray dog. Donovan instantly lost his smile, flicked his cigarette to the ground, and then grabbed the paper out of Walsh's hands to see for himself.

"What! What are you talking about? Let me see that." As Donovan stared at the picture of his villa, he pulled out his stress ball with the other hand and then tightly squeezed it. Within the picture was a dog hidden in the shadows next to the side of the villa, near a bush.

"Son of a bitch," Donovan said softly as he squeezed his stress ball even tighter. "That's not my dog. It's gotta be some stray dog, who better not be there when I move in."

"Oh yeah? Well, it looks like he's leaving you a nice big welcome-to-the-neighborhood gift." Walsh leaned in closer and pointed out the stray dog, which was squatting in the shadows. As Donovan clearly saw the stray dog taking a shit, the veins in his hand began to bulge out as he squeezed his stress ball, folded up the piece of paper, and then put it back into his pocket.

"Well, as much as I hate dogs, Walsh, it was a dog that brought us closer together." The dog in the picture reminded Donovan how Walsh had come into his life.

"Yeah, you're right, Donovan. I remember that day like it was yesterday. What a tragedy."

"Well, yeah, of course it was a tragedy, but don't forget that because of that day, that tragedy, Walsh, we wouldn't be here together right now. And I hope that you come and visit me in Mexico. I never thought I would say these words to you, Walsh, but I'm really gonna miss you when I retire."

"I'm gonna miss you too, Donovan, and of course I'll come visit you in Mexico. In fact, I have a lot of vacation time saved up, so I may even be able to spend a month with you."

"Hey, I said I'm gonna miss you when I retire, but not that much. Don't think that I'm gonna be like some Holiday Inn Express, okay?"

"Well, maybe for a week or two, but when I do come, we're definitely gonna go fishing off the coast of Baja, right?"

"Of course, Walsh, of course."

"Ya know, isn't it kinda funny how we started out in Jersey, how this assignment began in Jersey and how it will all probably end in Mexico, your career, our partnership and this assignment?"

"You're right, Walsh, you're right, but don't forget that our friendship will last forever."

Donovan's words uplifted Walsh. Donovan and Walsh then silently stood side by side while they looked out across the horizon as the sun set, like a father and a son reminiscing.

<u>103</u>

After the chaotic uprising cleared away, all that remained was Sarita's messenger bag. It was left torn open, her clothes scattered all over the street, her sketchbook left open as the wind blew through the pages. The frame that held the picture of Sarita and Gabriela together was left sticking halfway out, flapping around in the wind, the glass broken. It was also left in the debris filled streets. As for Sarita, she was lying in a bed with a blanket wrapped around her.

Sarita awoke, sat up, and opened her eyes as a soothing voice sang a Spanish lullaby. Across the dimly lit room was a little old Mexican woman sitting in shadows, singing with a rosary held within her fragile hands. After the little old Mexican woman finished singing, she slowly lifted her brittle body up from the chair, crept across the room towards a table, poured some water into a glass from a pitcher, and then went to Sarita. After giving Sarita a glass of water, the little old Mexican woman sat beside Sarita on the edge of the bed and ran her fingertips through Sarita's hair while softly speaking words of comfort.

Eventually, a middle-aged Mexican man—Guillermo Gonzalez, the artisan who had met Gabriela and sold her a heart-shaped pendent—walked into the room to join Sarita and the little old Mexican woman. After Guillermo joined the two, he began to question Sarita, who dramatically responded and illustrated with her hands all she had been through. Her stories intrigued her audience of two with utter amazement and shock. Then, as if the fated skies had aligned, in response, Guillermo revealed that he knew Gabriela and her family.

104

The persistence of time became nonexistent, while a repetitious symphony of mechanical gears, pedals, and sewing machine needles moved like clockwork as illegal immigrants worked within a metropolis of broken dreams, enslaved with compliant sedation. All the illegal immigrants who worked within the sewing factory were finally free, beyond borders, from the injustices and poverty experienced within their homeland. The illusion of freedom, and safety and security within the United States was overshadowed by the slave labor all were dependent upon for their survival and as a stepping stone to someday live the American Dream. Even though, in the eyes of the elites and globalists, they were perceived as a hive of busy bees, just pawns, expendable assets used for profit and gain, in the eyes of mortals, some had the hope and will to someday rise up to become kings or queens in their likeness. Beyond all shadow of a doubt, as the illegal immigrants continued to focus and work like blind mules, Gabriela silently sat with her eyes closed before her sewing machine while focusing on and caressing her once flat, empty stomach that was now a small hump filled with a rebirth of life and new beginnings. There was hope.

"Hey, Gaby . . . Gabriela . . . wake up . . . cómo estás?"

As Luz, an illegal immigrant from Peru, spoke, Gabriela opened her eyes. Gabriela then focused on her scarred wrists, wrapped in bandages. Just as Gabriela regained consciousness, and turned towards Luz to speak, Ana Marie, who sat on the opposite side of Gabriela, said, "*Mira*, Gabriela. If you keep rubbing that thing, it's gonna pop out too soon."

Ana Marie, who was also from Mexico, spoke very loudly as she shook Gabriela by the shoulder. As Gabriela turned, Luz and Ana Marie stopped working for a moment so that they could talk to Gabriela. The two had been working in the sewing factory in Newark for just over a year and taken Gabriela, who had only been there for a few months, under their wing. As Luz and Ana Marie stared at Gabriela, who sat between them, and lifted herself up from her chair to sit up straight, Ana Marie leaned forward to nonverbally express to Luz, "This Gabriela girl needs help and needs to loosen up." Gabriela then sat up and looked at Ana Marie and Luz, who sat back. Ana Marie smiled as she looked Gabriela up and down.

"I'm fine, *chica*s, just fine." Gabriela smiled.

"Are you sure, Gaby? You seem like you're not feeling so well, like something's bothering you," Luz said, but Gabriela remained stoic.

It wasn't that Gabriela wanted to hide everything from Luz and Ana Marie, who had been nothing but generous and helpful since she had begun working with them. It was just that Gabriela didn't want to burden them with her troubles and baggage, or reveal the truth about her dark and haunting past.

"No, no, I'm fine, honestly. I was just, ya know, daydreaming, drifting off a li'l bit. But I'm back now, so everything will be okay. I'm with you two now."

Gabriela tried to humor Luz and Ana Marie so that they could just leave it as is and get back to work. Unfortunately, that wasn't going to work because Ana Marie, being the little gossip butterfly that she was, wasn't going to leave any short conversation as is and never passed up an opportunity to gossip, even if it meant taking a topic and turning it into a completely off-subject conversation.

"Hey, *chica*, listen, we all daydream, except that I can work and daydream at the same time. That's what you need to learn to do, because if *Panzón* over there catches you, he's gonna be up ya ass all day. And don't think that he's gonna be easy on you, *chica*, just because you have a turkey in tha oven or because you're pretty, okay?"

Ana Marie wore too much makeup and cheap jewelry. Her face was a completely different color than her arms and the rest of her body, and the liner on her lips was so dark and thick that it looked like someone had pasted a pair of wax lips on her foundation-covered face. The cheap fake gold rings that she wore on every finger and her long, faded, chipped press-on fingernails complemented her big hoop earrings and her fake gold necklace, which had her name on it so that whatever man she was with would remember who they were with. Ana Marie was all about vanity and indulgence. Her ambitions in life were to look good at all times and to find an American man with money, lots of money, someone who could take care of her. That was Ana Marie's American Dream.

"Hey, *chica*, I know that it's a beautiful and wonderful thing to be pregnant, to know that you're gonna be a mama, but you shouldn't think about that all the time. It's not healthy, especially for the baby. You don't think that your emotions reflect onto your growing child? With all the stressful problems you have, *chica*, that baby's gonna come out like some loco. What you should be thinking about is who is gonna take care of you and that baby. You need to find yourself an American man, one with money, lots of money. And if you wait till after that baby is born, *chica*, then how are you gonna take care of yourself and a baby, working in this sweatshop? If you want, I'll introduce you to some good men, men who will take care of you. But remember, *chica*, even if you find an American man with lots of money, you still need to be a strong woman. Don't you eva let any man own you like a dog and carry you around by a leash. Uh-uh, no way, *chica*, not in today's world. In today's world, women have the upper hand. We're the strong ones, ya know why, because there are three things in life that rule the world, *chica*. Who ya know, money and vagina. You don't know anyone, you have no money, but you have a vagina. Be a strong woman."

Ana Marie talked very passionately, loud and fast, and stopped sewing to emphasize her emotions with her dramatic body language. Gabriela was so used to Ana Marie's pro-woman crazy talk that it didn't shock or surprise her anymore, so she learned to just smile, nod and agree with everything Ana Marie told her, since she knew that if you ever questioned her opinion or disagreed, Ana Marie would continue on until she won you over. Gabriela just pretended to listen as she continued to sew because Ana Marie was being so loud that *panzón*, the supervisor, was now looking over at them.

"Shh, shh, Ana, keep your voice down. *Panzón* is right over there, looking at us," Luz whispered.

Ana Marie then shut up and looked over her shoulder at *Panzón*, fatty, her supervisor. *Panzón* stood in the main aisle, which ran between the two sides of the factory filled with rows of sewing machines. He was only about five rows behind Gabriela, Luz, and Ana Marie, while standing with an irritated look on his face as he stared at Ana Marie with his two hands resting on his expanding waist. Like always, Ana Marie just gave him one of her illusionary smiles, turned around, put on a mocking puss and then began to silently sew again.

Gabriela, Luz and Ana Marie then looked forward and silently worked. Their silence was used to reflect, and only whispers were used for conversation, since it was forbidden during working hours but was a necessity for morale. Throughout the factory, during working hours, many of the illegal immigrants would have secret conversations. Their whispers were a part of a lifestyle that was lived in shadows with fear.

Eventually, *Panzón* walked by Gabriela, Luz and Ana Marie. He glared hard and long at Ana Marie, then Gabriela and then Luz. Each girl pretended to look down at their sewing machines as they worked but were really looking at *Panzón* out of their peripheral vision. Except Ana Marie. Ana Marie gave *Panzón* another one of her fake smiles and looked him up and down in a seductive way. *Panzón* knew what Ana Marie was trying to do and wasn't buying her sorry look. He just shamed the girls by pointing and shaking his stubby finger at the three and pointing to his one eye, letting them know that he was watching them. *Panzón* then walked to the front of the aisle and then across the front row of sewing machines. He stared at the three girls until he walked into another part of the factory, where he couldn't be seen anymore.

"*Mira, mira al Panzón*. He waddles around like a walrus all day, pointing his stubby finger at all of us like he's better than us, just because he's supervisor. Let me tell ya something, *chicas*. *Panzón* came here the same way we all did, illegally, except that *Panzón* had to kill a man to get here. And the funny thing is he's been here a lot longer than us, he's supervisor and he still lives in poverty like most of us. What a fat, lazy waste of space, bastard, *maldito Panzón*."

"Did *Panzón* really kill someone so he could come to America?" Gabriela asked.

"Nah, *chica*, but he did refuse to give up his spot for four children who had nothing, only an aunt who lived in America who would take care of them. All *Panzón* had to do was give up his spot and wait a month until he would be able to go again with the coyotes."

"That's it?"

"That's it, *chica*, just one month so four children who had nothing would have a chance to live a better life in America. Last I heard, those four children, even now that they're all grown-up, still live in the streets of Mexico. To me, *chica*, that's killing someone."

"It's true, so I hope that when you have your baby, you make sacrifices and do whatever is necessary to take care of your child and give it the world," Luz said.

"Yeah, don't be like *Panzón*, *chica*. Anyway, you have some time to relax before you need to worry about taking care of a baby. In fact, why don't you come out with us tonight, *chica*? There's a place in Elizabeth we're going to, you'll like it. I'll help you find an American man with lots of money, *chica*. Well, after I find one for myself."

"What about Billy, and Charles too?" Luz joked.

"*Mira, chica*, Billy is for Tuesday and Thursday, Charles is for Monday, Wednesday and Friday, and Saturdays are for whoeva I find. And Sundays, well, Sunday is for God," Ana Marie said. Both Luz and Gabriela laughed.

"Someday, Ana, someday you're gonna get caught, and then what will you do without an American man to take care of you?" Luz said.

"There's always *Panzón*," Gabriela said with a smile.

"Agh, no way, *chica*, I'd rather live the rest of my life alone with cats." Ana Marie cringed while all three girls smiled and laughed. "Anyway, *chica*, if you're feeling up to it later, you're welcome to come with me and Luz. You have our numbers, just give one of us a call when you get home, okay, *chica*?"

"Okay, Ana, I'll let you know later." Gabriela nodded.

"Sounds good, *chica*. All right, time to get back to work. Work, work, work, work, work."

All three girls then looked forward and continued to silently work. Gabriela caressed her stomach, filled with a rebirth of life and new beginnings, once again. She then closed her eyes and drifted away from the walls of bondage and into a better place and time.

# # #

As the mechanical symphony continued, all the dependable and unfortunate exploited victims of corporate greed worked within a corporate-controlled facility. From behind closed eyes, Gabriela silently sat before her sewing machine while caressing her now flat, empty stomach. Even though a dark and haunting past and fear of the unknown began to corrode Gabriela's heart, there was still a glimpse of hope. The thought of Sarita was inspiring, but unfortunately, all sense of comfort would become silenced and washed away by the final work bell and the supervisor's voice, bringing closure to a long workday. Gabriela then opened her eyes and focused on her hands, holding her stomach for a moment before looking up across the vast facility filled with sewing machines. Mexican women stood up, stretched, and began to walk, leaving the walls of bondage far behind for the day.

Gabriela stood up and began to walk with the flow of women out of the sewing factory, like a herd of sheep. After exiting, Gabriela stepped to the side to gather her thoughts and emotions as women walked around her. Eventually, when Gabriela was left all alone, tears began to slowly flow out her eyes and down her cheeks. Before Gabriela even had a chance to get herself back together, a soothing voice was heard in the distance.

"Mama . . . Mama . . . "

Gabriela was infused with a surge of life. Across the open square, Sarita trotted towards her with open arms. Like two monarch butterflies that blindly departed from a pupa of security to embark on a journey into the vast unknown, only to return and bring closure to a life that had finally come full circle, there was now a sense of peace and fulfillment. It was the end to a spiritual journey as

Gabriela dropped to her knees and embraced Sarita while tears began to flow out of her eyes. Their hearts and souls were bonded and mended together once again. This time Gabriela wasn't going to let go or allow any other outside forces to separate them. Not now, not ever.

105

In the eyes of Dante, it was love as he peered around the canvas while painting Sonya. But to Sonya, it was just another conquest of status and repertoire. As Sonya stood before Dante, draped in a flowing red dress while posing like Mona Lisa, standing in contrapposto and gazing back over her left shoulder with her beautiful long dark hair hanging down over her left eye, her right eye left exposed, there was an enduring surge of energy flowing throughout Sonya's body. Sonya was a soul deceiver who fed off the energy of others and always needed to be in the company of very powerful alpha males, those who were at the top of the pyramid in business, banking, politics, fashion, and the arts and entertainment world. She was a groupie of the elite, but a product of manipulation. Dante was blindly seduced by Sonya's divine essence of beauty, in the likeness of Aphrodite.

As if carved by the divine hands of Bernini, Sonya was perfect in every way, giving Dante reason to idolize her and worship the ground she walked on. Sonya's poetic eyes were gateways into heaven. Her smile lit up a room, and her auric presence filled the atmosphere with love. Unfortunately, it was a love that possessed the minds of man. Before the sun would set, Dante would complete his masterpiece, then passionately fuck Sonya all night long. After Dante and Sonya climaxed with an orgasmic explosion of kundalini, Sonya would roll over onto her side, fall asleep and leave Dante all alone on the other side of the bed. He wasn't done for the night. Dante had bigger plans.

As time slowly withered away into the night and the half-moon ascended,

Sonya woke up without Dante by her side. At first it was nothing new, since Dante would usually wake up in the middle of the night to paint, but this time it was different. As Sonya opened her eyes while lying on her side, she was greeted by a Post-it stuck onto the palm of her hand, which had a message written by Dante.

"I hope you slept well, *bella*, and now that you're up, follow the white rabbit."

Sonya smiled as she sat up in bed and then was drawn towards another Post-it, which was sticking onto the lampshade of the lamp resting on the nightstand with a picture of a cartoonish white rabbit and an arrow pointing out into the vastness of the industrial loft behind the bed. As Sonya turned around, she was instantly hit with an aroma of freshly made Italian food. But it wasn't the freshness or the seducing scent that warmed Sonya's insides. It was the sight before her. All over were lit candles that illuminated the open space along with the moonlight shining in through the industrial-size windows, red rose petals scattered all around, and more Post-its, left sticking to the support pillars that rose up to the ceiling, and on furniture, in strategic order, numbered and laid out in a well-planned path for Sonya to follow. And all the way on the opposite side, in the open concept kitchen, was Dante, putting the final touches on a surprise dinner.

Sonya was awestruck. After savoring the moment, Sonya wrapped herself up in a blanket, took a picture of everything with her cell phone, and then began to walk around the illuminated vastness and pick up all of the Post-its laced with messages and pictures of a white rabbit. Once she had collected all of the Post-its, she walked into the kitchen and took a seat at the dinner table, which was all set. On top of the square table, covered with a red tablecloth, were two place settings, two big pasta bowls tightly covered with tinfoil, a pitcher of mango-flavored water, Italian bread, a bowl of various kinds of olives, Caesar salad, shrimp cocktail, a block of parmigiana cheese and a cheese grater, and a bottle of red wine. And at the center of the table were three lit candles resting on top of a three-tier candleholder. After Dante finished sautéing some bacon-wrapped scallops, he placed a plateful on the dinner table, embraced Sonya, gave her a kiss on the lips and forehead, and then sat down at the table.

"So, you made all this while I was sleeping?" Sonya said with a smile.

"Yep, good thing you sleep like a rock. Well, except for the snoring," Dante joked.

"Oh, please, stop it. I don't snore." Sonya's voice rose with affection.

"Like a motorboat."

Sonya smiled. "Well, at least I didn't wake up to find you passed out drunk as usual, or attempting to jump out the window to kill yourself."

"All thanks to you, I'm now a changed man. You give me reason to live."

"Well, besides your charming words, I'm a very lucky woman to have a man who not only enjoys cooking but cooks so well. Mmm." Sonya tasted some of the bacon-wrapped scallops and then looked at the Post-its Dante had left for her. "My God, so good. Thank you so much for all this, and my cute bunny wabbit."

"You're welcome. Here, let me show you how it works." Dante leaned across the table to pick up all the Post-its laid out before Sonya. He stacked them together and flipped through the pages, creating a moving image of the white rabbit jumping.

"Oh my God, that's so amazing. I love it!" Sonya said as she took the Post-its from Dante and flipped through the flip book. "So, I'm curious, what's the special occasion?"

After Sonya spoke, there was a long uncomfortable silence. Dante sipped his beer, ran his fingertips through his hair, and then looked all around as he began to speak and look into Sonya's eyes. She ate bacon-wrapped scallops and olives and sipped her flavored water.

"Well, besides it being one year since we've met . . ."

Sonya choked on her flavored water, and then put her glass down.

"Has it been that long? Wow, I can't believe I forgot all about it."

"Yeah, well, at least I'm grateful you're still here." Dante poured Sonya and himself a glass of red wine and then handed Sonya hers, which she held up with Dante.

"I'm so happy to be with you too. But I don't know where my mind's been lately. I seem to have been forgetting a lot lately. Like, I misplace my keys all the time now. Anyway, I'm with you now, and I'm so happy."

"Me too, *bella*, me too. Tonight is all for you, my love, my everything; cheers to a long enduring year and many more to come."

"Cheers," Sonya added, and they toasted. "So, what's for dinner?"

"One of my specialties." Dante removed the foil from the bowls of pasta to reveal fettuccine with lobster meat and shrimp, doused in Dante's specialty vodka sauce.

"Oh my God, oh my God, I hope it's what I'm thinking of!" Sonya said, only to yelp when she saw what was inside. Inside the pasta bowl, Dante had all of the pasta kept around the perimeter of the bowl with tinfoil, creating a doughnut shape, while in the middle was an engagement ring. As Sonya sat frozen with her hands held over her smile, admiring the ring, Dante got up, picked up the ring and then got down on one knee.

"Sonya, before I met you, I was just a seed, drifting in the wind. I had no direction or reason to live. And now that I found you, you are the ground, my foundation to grow and live a life of love. Because of you, I now have direction and reason to live. You are my light, my guide, my everything, and from this bond, I hope to grow a tree of life and everlasting love. Sonya, will you marry me?" As Dante's musing words flowed out like a soothing breeze, Sonya choked up once again, shed some tears and then accepted Dante's hand.

"Yes! Yes, I . . . I will!"

Dante slid the ring onto Sonya's ring finger, stood up to embrace her and kiss her, and then sat back down. The engagement ring gleaming in the light was a twisting white gold band laced with smaller diamonds, which had an octagonal diamond at the center. The ring was slightly bigger than Sonya's ring finger, but Sonya made sure the ring stayed on. Admiring the engagement ring, Sonya then began to take many pictures of the ring with her cell phone and then posted the pictures to multiple social media websites to show the world.

As for Dante, he sipped his glass of red wine while admiring Sonya. There was something about her that possessed Dante's heart and soul, something he couldn't resist or take his eyes off of, even if Sonya was completely ignoring

Dante during such a special moment. To muse over and admire Sonya's smile and giddy body language was fulfilling to Dante, who was blinded by love.

"So, are you happy?"

"Huh? Oh, yeah. Yes. Yes, I'm so happy. Oh my God, this ring is so gorgeous. Where did you get it!" Sonya, who was focused on the ring, struggled to find the right words.

"From a jeweler a friend of mine recommended."

"Well, whoever he is, he's very good!"

"Yeah, well, he did a lot better than I thought, since, ya know, I designed that and gave him a sketch to use as a blueprint."

"Did you really? Oh my God, I love it even more now. I can't wait to show it off to everyone!"

"Well, before you exploit our engagement to the world, how about we enjoy this moment, together, before the—" Before Dante could finish speaking, he was cut off.

"Oh my God, hold on . . . hello, Angie . . . wait, wait, guess what, guess what? I'm engaged! Yes, Dante just proposed to me! I know, I know, I can't believe it, it was soooooo romantic! . . ."

Dante watched her as she stood up and began to walk away from Dante and throughout the industrial loft studio space. Sonya disrespectfully cut Dante off and left him at the table all alone, but Dante was still completely entranced by her mesmerizing presence. But, unfortunately for Dante, who sipped his glass of wine, he was just another victim of Sonya's vampirism. Even if he thought his bond with Sonya was everlasting, in the hands of fate, all that was mended together with a blind sense of love would eventually fade away.

<u>106</u>

A three-story brownstone, nestled within the bohemian nook of the West Village along the cobblestone street of West Twelfth Street, was now home. Dante had given up his industrial loft and independence to settle down in a traditional family setting and live a more domesticated lifestyle with his muse— his fiancée and soon-to-be wife, Sonya. Dante and Sonya had secured their love with materialistic objects of affection, but the reality of their current situation was that it was only a prop wedged between the two. They weren't a union of one. They were two separate entities, slowly drifting further away from each other. Sonya lived in Dante's limelight. She slowly worked her way up the pyramid while leaving Dante behind in the shadows. Dante was blind with love and became a victim of Sonya's devious ways. Dante's own success led him back into darker waters, while Sonya lived off his success and life force. The two opposites were slowly being pushed further apart. Without Sonny, Dante was a minnow in a shark tank, swimming around with sharks like Greco, who was ruthless and unreasonable with Dante, and Benny. All Dante had was Sonya, who was furious with Dante's recent absences, due to his personal demons and involvement with Benny and Nada Mas.

"I can't! I can't do this anymore!" Sonya lashed out with tears in her eyes as she paced back and forth with her hands tensely held up beside her head, tucking her hair back behind her ears and then dramatically throwing her arms up. Dante followed behind her in an attempt to calm her down.

"Listen. Listen, Sonya, we can fix all this and make it work. Just calm down so that we can sit down and talk things over."

Sonya stopped pacing, turned around to face Dante, and silently stared at him for a moment before unleashing hell.

"How! How are we gonna fix all this, Dante, huh? What, you're gonna start doing all the things you've promised me? Like, like, let me see, let's start with how you always tell me we're gonna go away for a long vacation somewhere in the Mediterranean. Or do the little things, like fix the toilet you promised you would fix three months ago, after refusing to pay a plumber, or change the lightbulb in the living room!"

"I told you, I'll do it when I'm free—" Dante calmly stated, but was then cut off by Sonya, who became even more agitated.

"Oh, now, when you're free! Are you kiddin' me with when you're free? For God's sake, Dante, you have more free time than the bums in Bryant Park. Or wait, I got it, we're gonna actually go out and eat at a nice restaurant, instead of having to sit inside the house all the time! Even if you are a good cook, I feel like a prisoner, Dante! You never want to go out, and the sad thing is, it's not like you're poor and don't have the money or the time! Dante, I can't keep playing this muse for the lonely, sad, victimized artist anymore. Okay, wait, I'm sorry, artiste!" Sonya passionately spoke with sarcasm and aggressiveness, her voice intensely rising and falling like the tides.

"Anyway, something's up with you, Dante. You haven't been the same lately. You know the tortured soul romantic, who used to hug me and kiss me all the time, leave me little love notes and sketches under my pillow for me to wake up to! I wish I knew where that person is. Ya know, the one who gave me this!" Sonya held up her hand to reveal her engagement ring to Dante. "Because, right now, this man standing before me, I don't know who he is! Who are you, and why are you here right now? Ya know, since you're never around anymore, you never answer your phone or emails, or my forty-something messages I leave you each day!"

After Sonya spoke, once again there was a long uncomfortable pause as Sonya stood with her arms crossed while staring like Medusa at Dante, who childishly looked all around for the right words. "So, where is it you go all the time, huh? What is it, another woman you're seeing!"

"No, no, it's not another woman. It's, I can't—"

"Don't even try to give me that 'I'm a Pisces and I need my solitude to escape from all the chaos and negative energies in the world so that I can rejuvenate my soul and focus on my work' bullshit!" Sonya spoke with dramatic hand motions as she mimicked the way Dante spoke. "And if there is someone else in your life, well, don't worry. You don't need to tell me, because, because there's someone else... I'm seeing another man, someone who's committed, who's always around, and someone who loves me. Someone who really loves me and isn't with me just for inspiration!"

As Sonya's passionate words penetrated Dante's heart and soul, he froze. All Dante could think about was being absent from Sonya's life because of a sudden storm cloud of depression and creative block that had suddenly crept back into his life, taking Dante back down into his old ways of misery and misfortunes, provoking him to be alone. Not only that, but Dante was deeply involved with Benny and Nada Mas, and unbeknownst to Sonya, his absence was for her protection.

"You're never around anymore. I get lonely. I need someone to hold me and love me. I used to have that with you, but lately, I feel like I don't even know who you are anymore." Sonya began to sob harder.

"Who is it?" Dante sternly questioned Sonya. "Who is it? Is it Virgil?"

Sonya didn't say a word, just turned away and wiped her eyes. Dante was faced with betrayal. In a final, desperate attempt to win back Sonya's heart, he walked up to her to offer a hug and kiss, only to have Sonya's feminine wrath ignite once again.

"Don't touch me. Don't touch me, leave me alone! Leave me alone!"

Heaven's not far when a woman is loved, but when scorned, hell is even closer. Sonya's wrathfulness became so intense that, when it came to a final crescendo, Sonya began to smack, punch, and push Dante away in a fury, and then retreated to sit down at the kitchen table. Dante stood frozen with bewilderment as he wiped blood from his nose, and then he stormed out of the West Village home.

As the soft light from the setting sun filled the kitchen, Sonya sat at the kitchen table. She lifted her head from the palms of her hands while still sobbing. She wiped away tears with her fingertips and sat in silence as she continued to sob some more. Suddenly she slammed both of her arms down on the table while screaming out like a madwoman in severe pain. She stripped off her engagement ring, threw it against the wall, and swiped the centerpiece off the kitchen table, sending it crashing down to the floor. She then dropped her face into her crossed arms and continued to sob.

Water slowly flowed through the cracks of the wooden floor from the broken glass jar. Within the scattered debris was a wilted rose of redemption, along with the engagement ring. Everything that had once been was now forever gone, and everything that might be was now a blank canvas waiting to be painted.

<u>107</u>

As echoes from the past, a chaotic storm of *violencia*, and the ghosts of everything that had once been faded away, Dante sat all alone within the shadows, leaning forward with his arms wrapped around his knees and his head bowed down. The thought of Sonya and Sarita consumed his mind while he held Sarita's rosary within the palm of his hand and slowly rolled the beads in and out of his fingers.

As Dante firmly clasped Sarita's rosary, the jail cell door opened and two Mexican guards entered. Even though Dante didn't understand, Spanish, one word he knew brought back hope: *libre*. They then helped Dante up, guided him out of the cell, out of the holding area, and then towards the police station exit.

After exiting, as his eyes adjusted to the blinding sun light, across the street, standing within a crowd of people passing by, were Gabriela and Sarita. Dante admired and savored their presence for a moment. He then walked across the street, causing Sarita to let go of Gabriela's hand. Sarita walked towards Dante with a slight skip in her step, gradually increasing her speed until reaching Dante. He dropped to his knees in the middle of the street to embrace Sarita.

Dante and Sarita tightly held each other, and after they pulled back, Dante looked into Sarita's eyes while running his fingertips through her hair. They got up and walked towards Gabriela, who had tears in her eyes. Gabriela reached out her hand to shake Dante's, only to receive a kiss on the cheek and a hug. Even though the love they had for each other was taboo and long gone, now it seemed right. Dante was the final piece to a trinity of one.

108

The air was dense as Daffy silently sat all alone in the center of an undisclosed holding room. Even though Daffy's ankles were shackled together, he remained stoic. Daffy's handcuffed hands rested on the table. He fiddled around with his thumbs while he stared at his reflection in the double-sided mirror that lined one side of the bare walls. Whatever fate awaited Daffy was uncertain, but he was prepared to defy his masters. Special Agents Qubish and Von Burton walked in and stepped before Daffy. Qubish firmly looked down upon Daffy with his piercing blue eyes, while Von Burton, who stood with his arms crossed, looked at Daffy with a taunting smirk. Daffy, who wasn't fazed, sat back while stroking his beard with his cuffed hands.

"Good evening, Mr. Paul. As of right now, it's my understanding that you have been in this situation before, so I'll be brief with the cute introductions." Qubish opened a file folder and scanned through Daffy's personal records and profile.

"Based on your files, your legal name is Stanley Albert Paul, you go by the pseudonym Daffy and the hacker alias Asmodeus. You're a forty-four-year-old male, an elite computer hacker with a long history of cybercrimes and misdemeanors, who has worked as a freelance hacker for various corporate agencies, investor bankers, associates, the common man, and the international crime syndicate known as Nada Mas. Mr. Paul, you have been detained due to your involvement with Nada Mas. Now, before we get into your current legal status and continue on any further with the legal process, what we need is for you to cooperate with us and explain to us everything you know about Nada Mas, Benjamin Bradford, and Dante De Luna."

Daffy slowly leaned forward. "I'm not saying shit till I speak to a lawyer."

"Listen, right now, you're in no position to remain silent. We have so much on you that your silence is only going to create more problems for you and make this process take longer for all of us." Qubish closed the folder, stepped closer, and tapped his finger down on top of the table.

"Is that so? Well, I guess the both of you fuckers better make your selves more comfortable. Why don't you go sit on grandpa's lap, you fucking cupcake?" Daffy taunted, leaning back.

"Hey, watch your mouth!" Qubish said firmly.

"Huh? Watch my mouth? Why don't you go fuck your mother? You don't scare me with this SS shit."

"Hey, what did I just tell you? Watch your lip, son, before you dig yourself a hole."

"Ha, watch my lip." Daffy slowly leaned forward once again and gestured with his finger, beckoning Qubish to step closer, which he did. "Why don't you go tell that bitch of a mother to ice her lips? They're swollen from my big fat cock, and I'm not talking about these lips right here." Daffy pointed to his lips.

Qubish slammed the file folder down on top of the table, turned towards the double-sided mirror and gestured with his hand across his throat in a slicing motion to the FBI agents watching all from the other side of the mirror. The red recording light on the surveillance camera turned off, and Qubish took off his jacket, rolled up his sleeves and then stepped towards Daffy. Daffy childishly looked up at Qubish with a smirk. Qubish looked down on him with fury in his eyes. Qubish then took out a handkerchief and wrapped it around his ring laced fingers, making a fist and then sucker-punching Daffy three times in the face.

"Hey, what the fuck? You fucking Nazi!" Daffy wailed out after getting hit. Qubish put his handkerchief away and then pushed Daffy back, making him fall back down to the ground.

"Why'd you make yourself fall down? C'mon, get up, you fucking worthless piece of shit." Qubish lifted Daffy back up in the chair.

"Hey, what the fuck is with this Guantanamo Bay torture shit, man? This is so unconstitutional. Once I speak to a lawyer, your ass is done, you fucking, agh, agh . . . ."

Qubish began to choke Daffy from behind with his tie. "What's that? speak up, I can't hear you. Something about unconstitutional." After choking Daffy for about a minute, Qubish removed the tie and then pulled Daffy's head back by the hair and furiously spoke into his ear. "Listen, you fucking shit bag, I don't want to hear anymore disrespectful remarks from you. I want cooperation, do you understand me, you fucking monkey's ass? If you step out of line again, I will fucking cut out that fucking tongue of yours and feed it to you. Do you understand?"

"Yeah, yeah." Daffy struggled with each breath as he talked.

"I can't hear you, you fucking maggot."

"Yeaaa, yeaaa, yes, yes, sir." After Daffy submitted, Qubish released him and stepped back around to the front of the table, gestured to the FBI agents behind the mirror to turn the surveillance camera back on, and turned towards Daffy to continue with the interrogation process. Daffy caressed his neck.

"Okay, okay. Relax, man. Fuck, what is it you want to know?" Daffy muttered.

"How about an apology?"

"What? Sorry. Sorry about insulting your mother. Fuck, that hurts."

"Apology accepted. Now, for starters, why don't you start with how you got involved with Nada Mas?"

"I first heard about Nada Mas while I was living out in Arizona in my early twenties. It was after I spent some time in Sedona, and I ended up living in Tucson. I used to go to this strip club all the time, Eden of Hell. That's where I heard about Nada Mas. Ya know, after spending enough time there, I became a regular and got real close with the girls that worked there and the staff. But it was the owner, Rocco, who I became very close with, who informed me about Nada Mas."

"Sounds cute, but why would Rocco tell you about Nada Mas?"

"Because Rocco was close with Benny, and Benny was looking to expand his network out on the East Coast, but didn't know anyone from the East Coast he could trust, except for Dante. After Rocco told Benny about me, that I was born and raised in Jersey and that I was a computer hacker, Benny was ecstatic. Not only was I from the East Coast, but I would be able to help out with setting up operations in Jersey, and use my hacking expertise to create a system database for Nada Mas, which would organize and protect inventory, logistics, emails, bank accounts. Basically anything being done electronically by Nada Mas, I was conducting and overseeing."

"Interesting. But what was Benny like? What was your relationship like with Benny?"

"I never met the guy before; I only communicated with him through Rocco, and via emails and phone conversations in which his voice was disguised."

"How come you never tried to hack into personal records to find out who he was?" Von Burton questioned Daffy.

"I did, many times. There's nothing on him. He's like some ghost, like he doesn't even exist. I checked everything, from his parents, his birth certificate, schools, any personal information kept on record. There's nothing. It's as if he was just created out of nothing. I think he had someone within Nada Mas, one of his high-ranking officials connected to a government agency, erase him from existence."

"Okay, so Benny is some ghost, yet you remained loyal and continued to work for someone you've never met or didn't even know? How come?"

"Because of the perks, man. I was being paid exceptionally well."

"Okay, but how come you didn't stay in Jersey? Here on file, I have that you were only in Jersey for a few months and then went back out to Arizona."

"Since I was no longer needed after shop was set up in Jersey, I went back out to Arizona to enjoy life, man. I was set financially."

"Doesn't look like it to me," Von Burton said sarcastically.

"Yeah, because the flashy ones are the ones who get caught. I chose to look poor, but live rich in order to remain anonymous. And by the way, shouldn't you cowboys know who Benny is and where he is by now? Aren't you one of the alphabet agencies who have been investigating Nada Mas, searching for Benny since before he blew up into the mastermind he now is and went into hiding? Bunch of posers," Daffy said as he sat back with his arms crossed while obnoxiously looking at Qubish and Von Burton.

"Whatchu say, you little shit? You want another fresh one!" Qubish made a fist and stepped towards Daffy, only to be held back by Von Burton. He then calmly continued.

"Well, from what we know, the NSA offered you a job when you were only eighteen years old. How come you passed on that offer? It doesn't make any sense since you would've been set for life. All of your juvenile records, your cybercrimes at the time, would've been wiped clean, and if you chose to get a college education, you would've been able to go anywhere you wanted for free. So, why not except their offer?"

"Maybe 'cause I didn't want to work for a corrupt system, especially since with all I could do, I didn't need anything they offered me. And no matter how many times they tried to blackmail me or convict me, they had nothing against me, because I'm not some poser hacker. I know how to cover my trail and remain anonymous."

"Oh yeah? That's funny since we were able to get to you and bring you in," Von Burton added.

"Well, it sure as hell took you shit bags long enough."

"Hey, watch your lip, Bluto, and don't think that all your cybercrime trails are covered, 'cause—well, I wouldn't cream my pants again just yet. Let's just say that all we have on you will get you at least twenty-five years." Qubish opened up Daffy's files again and began to scan through them. "Stroking cock and smoking pot to child porn, endangering the welfare of a child, and engaging in sexual intercourse with multiple minors, numerous times." Qubish then put the open files down on top of the table before Daffy.

"Who—what the fuck is this shit? Another setup?" Daffy dramatically waved his arms out before him as he leaned forward and spoke with astonishment. "I've been through this setup bullshit numerous times before. Why don't you go wipe your ass with this?"

"Listen, fucker, you're face-deep in shit right now. You should've thought twice before distributing and downloading all that kiddie porn and fist-fucking all those illegal teenage girls and Brazilian trannies working at Oh La La's."

"You've been NSA'd for a long time, buddy, and all those false aliases, firewalls, and system protection programs you've been hiding behind—well, it was only a matter of time before we were able to tag you and watch your every move. After that, all we needed to do was to bait you in, and lucky for us, our bait was good, so you better start talking before we detain you indefinitely and you end up getting anally fist-fucked from behind bars," Von Burton assertively stated.

Daffy leaned back and stroked his beard. "Andres, that fucking narc. Indio too?" Daffy said softly.

"Sorry, but Indio's just a gullible fish out of water. Lucky for us, you trusted him, and we were able to get to him in order to get to you. Now you're our final link to Dante, and the ringleader of Nada Mas, Benny. So, if you want to limit your sentence when we're done with you and keep fists and cocks out of that tight asshole of yours, you better start cooperating and tell us everything you know about Dante De Luna." Qubish once again firmly tapped the top of the table with his finger. Daffy silently sat like a deer in headlights, and then after taking everything in, he began to speak.

"I met Dante when I was overseeing operations in Jersey. Indio would always pick up packages from Dante and bring them to me, but one day Dante came along for the ride. I guess you could say he was a cool guy. Ya know, he had the same sense of humor I had, and after the three of us went out for drinks that night, we became pretty close. We kept in touch and went out for drinks together."

"How cute. So did you hold his cock while he took a piss?" Von Burton said.

"What a fucking faggot. Yeah, I still got it, right here, Mary fucking Poppins." Daffy flashed Von Burton the middle finger. Von Burton smirked, and then Daffy continued, "This fucking guy. Anyway, I wouldn't say I knew Dante well. We were just associates, ya know, drinking buddies. I've been to his place once, and I walked out thinking this fucking guy has some real issues, ya know, based on the paintings I saw inside his shithole of an apartment he was temporarily living in down in the East Village, since his girl kicked him out of their posh house."

"Well, what about when you two were out drinking? What was he like?" Qubish asked.

"Any of you daisies have a cigarette?" Qubish looked over at Von Burton, who opened up his jacket, took out a pack of American Spirits, and held out the open pack before Daffy, who took one cigarette, which he then placed between his lips and began to smoke after Von Burton lit it with his Zippo. Daffy took a couple of drags before he continued to speak.

"He was fucking quiet, and believe it or not, I did all the talking, but I liked his fucking style. He had this sly demeanor. He'd sit back, quietly drink his drink, and attract all these women, which I didn't mind since I was getting some action from the leftovers."

"So, you used Dante to help you get pussy?" Von Burton said.

"Fuck yeah. Best pussy I've ever got, that's one of the reasons I hung out with him. When he did talk, it was fucking depressing. He'd go on and on about this girl who he was fucking obsessed with, the same one that kicked him out, what's her name . . . oh yeah, Sonya. How he fucked up a good thing with this Sonya chick, and he would constantly question what he was doing for Nada Mas, and how fucked up America is and life in general."

"So, he's some sappy philosopher?" Qubish asked.

"A smart one," Von Burton added.

"I don't know about smart. The motherfucker couldn't even use a computer and would forget shit all the time, especially his wallet."

"Ha, maybe because you were just a dumb pawn he was playing around with."

"Why would he fucking use me, huh?"

"Because he's smarter than you think. He knew what he was involved with when he agreed to help Benny and work for Nada Mas. He kept tabs on everyone within Nada Mas he was associated with, or learned from others, including you, Captain Lou Albano," Qubish said.

"Whatever, who the fuck cares? And I doubt that he's ever seen Benny, or knew Benny at all."

"I wouldn't push my luck just yet. Dante and Benny were childhood friends, in fact, best friends growing up. That's why Dante was brought into Nada Mas, and that's why Dante was the only one who ever knew where to find him." Qubish filled Daffy with revelation.

"No shit. Well, I wouldn't say he's the only one who knows where to find Benny."

"Look who finally caught on. That's why you're here now." After Von Burton spoke there was a moment of silence. Daffy puffed on his cigarette.

"You're here because not only are you one of the few within Nada Mas who hasn't been brought into custody or killed off, but we know how smart you are, and that you are a final link to Benny, with an idea as to where he is, and at some point, Dante will contact you for help." Qubish explained.

"So, I'm gonna be used as bait?" Daffy said.

"Eventually, but first we want to know where the fuck Benny is."

"I have an idea, but the only other person who knows where Benny is, besides Dante, is Rocco."

"We know that, but Rocco won't talk, and he's clean. He has no connection to Nada Mas and lives his life like a saint. With that said, you're gonna help us find out where Benny is by getting Rocco to give up his whereabouts and eventually help us bait Dante."

"Is that so? And what if I refuse to play ball?" Daffy said firmly.

"If you refuse to play along, I can guarantee that you'll spend the rest of your life behind bars."

Daffy silently smoked his cigarette and contemplated.

"Listen, we know that you have been slowly distancing yourself from Nada Mas, and that Nada Mas is falling apart, so it's in your best interest to play ball with us. It doesn't make sense for you not to, since we know you have no personal attachments to Dante, Indio, or anyone else within Nada Mas. Why risk your own life for something that doesn't mean anything to you, something that was only a passing point in life?"

There was a moment of silence after Von Burton spoke. Daffy continued to smoke his cigarette and stroke his beard and thought for a moment before speaking. "Well, first of all, what am I guaranteed, as far as a plea deal?"

"If you play ball, your sentence will be limited, and we can probably get you out early on probation."

"What do you mean probably?"

"Listen, an exact sentence isn't guaranteed right now. We won't know until you go through the legal process. What we can guarantee is that if you work with us, you will serve a hell of a lot less time in federal prison, and that you'll get out earlier. If you refuse to play along, you could serve twenty-five to fifty years. That's a lifetime, so do you understand now?"

"Take the deal. In the long run, you'll benefit from it, and everyone wins." Once again, after Von Burton spoke, there was a moment of silence as Daffy smoked his cigarette and contemplated his decision.

"Okay, I'm in."

Qubish and Von Burton turned towards each other and smiled.

"I believe we're done for now," Qubish said. "As for you, Daffy Duck, enjoy the cigarette, because after you're done, we'll take you to a detention room, and then from there we'll continue on with a debriefing on what it is you'll need to do."

"Such warm and welcoming words," Daffy said sarcastically.

"If you're lucky, maybe we'll give you a pair of slippers, and a pair of scissors and a razor blade to chop and shave that bird's nest off your face." Daffy laughed as he stroked his beard and smoked his cigarette. Qubish and Von Burton then said goodbye to Daffy before exiting the undisclosed holding room and leaving Daffy all alone in a state of bondage.

<u>109</u>

Dante, Gabriela and Sarita ate their first and final meal together at a table on the outside patio of Gabriela's aunt and uncle's home. The shadows of a dark and haunting past were left far behind, and while the internal and external scars still remained, deep within their hearts there was now solace.

As Dante admired Gabriela and Sarita, he thought of the life he'd never had, a domesticated lifestyle he'd never dreamed of, yet seemed to regret never creating and sharing with Sonya. But everything was going to be all right. He now shared that with Gabriela and Sarita as they ate, laughed, and told stories.

Gabriela watched Dante and Sarita bond. To see Sarita so emotionally attached, for the first time in her life, to someone who filled the empty shoes of a male figure in her life was fulfilling. Dante was eccentric and unique. He was different from all the others who'd tried in every way to win Sarita's heart and complete a trinity. Dante had been absent for many years, but he was still able to easily connect with Sarita. There was untainted devotion in his heart. Gabriela could see the trust Sarita had towards Dante deep within her eyes. Her radiant smile was comforting.

"So, what happens with us when we get back to America?"

After Dante spoke, there was stillness. Dante then leaned forward to reiterate his vague sense of optimism.

"Well, since I was able to get you this far, Shorty, seeing how well the three of us connect and how happy the three of us all seem to be together... Well, I don't know how to say it, but why don't we all go back to America to live the life we've all wanted to live there? This doesn't have to end here."

Gabriela and Sarita looked into each other's eyes for answers.

"Listen, Dante, Sarita and I are very grateful and thankful for all you have done for us, very, very much. Words can't even express the feelings I have for you, but we can't go back to America. We can't. I'm sorry, but it's not safe for us anymore."

Gabriela was right, and being logical, but Dante wouldn't accept her pragmatic opinion, even if he was also better off staying in Mexico.

"Honestly, I can't explain the way I feel right now either. I don't know, but just being here with you two now has somehow changed me, changed me in a way that it just feels right, in here," Dante said passionately as he firmly held his hand over his heart.

"To risk everything. All of this. Us being here now. To risk my life, for something I feel and know is right. I don't know, maybe, yeah, it sounds crazy, but after all I've been through, for you two, I don't know, you've both changed me. I'm not the man I once was. Nah, no way. We wouldn't even be here right now discussing this. I don't know, but you two give me this feeling no one in my life has ever been able to give me. You two complete me, fill in an emptiness I can't explain, and it's because of this void you two fill that not only am I willing to risk everything in order to safely help you two get into America, but I'm risking everything, and doing all of this for you two, to give back what was taken away, so that I can share that with you. We can start a new life, back home in Jersey, together, where all of this started, to finally be able to live the dream you dreamed of living in America."

Even though Gabriela was filled with adoration, there was still a thorn of doubt embedded within her heart, which still needed more to remove any sense of fear.

"I don't know. It all sounds so good and wonderful to hear all these things you say, but what if we can't? What if it doesn't work out, and something goes wrong? And how will we even be able to get back into America? What would we do, pay coyotes?"

"Failure's not an option. No, we won't have to. If Valdo and his band were able to get us into Mexico, then they'll be able to get us back into America."

Gabriela looked away from Dante's eyes and then into Sarita's eyes and saw all the love and trust Sarita now had for Dante. Sarita then reached out her hand to hold Gabriela's, which won over Gabriela's heart and soul. In the likeness of the monarch butterfly's precursor, to blindly go into the vast unknown, beyond borders, once again, Gabriela was filled with strength, courage, hope and perseverance. At this very moment, like when Gabriela had first embarked on a blind journey into America, in search of the American Dream, it felt right to risk everything for a dream, but this time for the love of another, Sarita. Gabriela then reached out with her other hand to run her fingertips through Sarita's hair before turning away from Sarita towards Dante.

"To America," Gabriela raised her glass of wine, as did Dante, and Sarita raised her glass of milk as a toast to their final departure, back to America, for love.

Eventually, the first and final meal shared between Dante, Gabriela, and Sarita would finally conclude. Sarita would become sedated, tucked away into bed, and then she would fall asleep. And for the rest of the evening, Dante and Gabriela would walk beside each other through the city and zócalo, underneath the twilight sky, like two adolescents in love, walking with no direction. Finally, in the heat of the night, all the love they had bottled up for each other came bursting out at once like a bottle of aged wine.

Dante and Gabriela spent the night making passionate love, the kind of love a soldier would make with their spouse whom they hadn't seen in a year or more. Except that, for Dante and Gabriela, their absence seemed to be an eternity. Dante and Gabriela fulfilled their burning desire for one another. The two then slept within a blanket of love, underneath the full moon. Their hearts were bonded together once again, and now Sarita was what inspired them to carry on, for love.

110

On one side of the border there was Mexico and on the other side there was the United States of America. In America, on the outskirts of the Nogales border, were Qubish and Von Burton. The two silently stood in an empty, secluded lot overlooking the border checkpoint. Qubish stood firm while he smoked a cigarillo. Von Burton stood tall with a cup of freshly brewed iced coffee. They were like two knights in a game of chess who patiently waited for the right opportunity to go on the offensive and capture the hopeless pawn. Eventually, arriving from behind in the distance were Donovan and Walsh.

Donovan tightly squeezed his stress ball, and Walsh took sips from his third cup of coffee, as they approached Qubish and Von Burton.

"Gentlemen, I didn't think you two were gonna show up. I was starting to get nervous over here. So, what happened?" Qubish said.

"Sorry about the delay, fellas, but I had to make a quick emergency pit stop." Donovan put his stress ball back into his pocket and held his stomach.

"Cramps?" Von Burton said with a smirk.

"Nah, I don't bleed like you, Burton. It's a slight stomach virus."

"Oh yeah? So what did you have last night? The fish or was it—"

Donovan turned back towards Qubish. "Neither. I think it was the soup of the day special I had."

"Well, the service was good, I hope, right?"

"Oh yeah, the restaurant and the service were excellent. It was definitely a good recommendation on your behalf, but as soon as I got back to the hotel room, Jesus Christ, it was like Hiroshima, know what I mean?"

Walsh cringed up his face as he nodded. He then began to feel nauseous like the night before and got that sudden taste of vomit in his throat.

"Poor thing. So did you hold his hand all through the night, Walsh?"

"No, why? Why would I do that?" Walsh said with a sense of disgust.

"Well, he is your partner. Or did you help wipe his ass instead?"

"Unlike you and Burton, who still wear Huggies and Depends, we don't bond like that. We wipe our own asses."

Qubish smiled as he looked at Von Burton. At this point in the game, all four agents were all on good terms. Despite their differences, they were one, a unity of sacrifice and trust, a brotherhood that was now on the same page and ready to move forward with their agenda together.

"Well, I hope you at least washed your hands. Here are the files you asked for." Qubish handed Donovan a file folder. Donovan took it with his right hand and reached out with his left hand and put it up before Qubish's nose. "Real cute, but remember, not only do you owe me for this, but you also owe me for being late to your own meeting, which you set up, right?"

"Me too," Von Burton added with a smirk, causing Donovan to shake his head and smile.

"I'll make it up to you, Qubish. How about lunch? And for you, Burton, a spoon full of Gerber's," Donovan said as he opened up the file folder, which he then began to scan through.

"Only if it's a five-star restaurant," Qubish replied and then gave Donovan a chance to read through the files on Benny, Nada Mas, all the connected crime syndicates and drug-trafficking networks, and its high-ranking officials, Dante and Daffy—who they now had in custody.

As Donovan mumbled to himself while he scanned through the files, the other three agents patiently waited.

"It's all there, everything you asked for. The files on Benny, the files on Dante, and I even threw in a pyramid chart of Nada Mas, with profiles on each high-ranking member," Qubish added. "As you can clearly see on the pyramid, a majority of Benny's top soldiers, captains, and high-ranking officials are either in our custody or dead, and Benny, King Tut, at the top of the pyramid, is now dead himself. One of the major players who isn't in our custody or dead is our boy Dante. Now you two already know that we have been looking for Dante for a very long time, and that he is, or was, a very important asset to us. And right now, you two are probably wondering why Dante was so important to us and why have we been looking for him for so long, even though he's at the bottom of the pyramid. That's because he was the only one who knew Benny personally and was able to contact him directly."

"So, you're telling me that Benny organized and ran the biggest and most successful crime syndicate and drug-trafficking network in the history of the United States of America, without any of his high-ranking officials ever knowing who he was, and where he was, but allowed a meaningless rat dweller from the bottom of the pyramid to? Sorry, Qubish, but don't take this the wrong way when I tell you that I'm really finding all of this hard to believe."

"Why? Why is it so hard to believe that all of this is real, that it's the truth? Well, gentlemen, in life, sometimes the truth is more unbelievable than the lies. Truth is stranger than fiction, and all of it is real because Benny wasn't some fucking dumb, blind, egotistical drug lord. He was mentally stronger than that. He was a reclusive genius. It all worked because he made sure that everyone was loyal to him but also feared him and that they never knew where he was. Benny had a whole system, and if there were any problems, he had his ways of taking care of any problem with fear, and he had contacts everywhere, and of every status. He was able to do all this from behind closed doors because of modern-day technology, the Internet, hacking into systems and paying hit men from Columbia and other parts of South America very well to terminate anyone within his network who he felt was a threat or unable to do their job. He never hesitated to do so, or felt any sense of remorse for them or their families. He's massacred tons of families and ended many bloodlines. Benny basically had everyone marked and tagged and played the role of God. He had to, because he knew that there was always a chance that someday, someone would either fuck up and reveal everything or try to kill him. Benny had this whole philosophy on corruption, that corruption only worked within small walls and never worked within big walls because there are too many eyes and ears within the big walls. Someday, someone would see or hear something they didn't like and bring down the walls. The idea of the name Nada Mas was borrowed from the Colombians. It was after Benny got involved with the Mendoza cartel that Nada Mas was created and officially became his. That's why, when Benny became bigger than he could have ever imagined, he went into exile and became a recluse, to run and control everything from behind closed doors. It was during this time when Nada Mas became the monster that it was. Its tentacles stretched out all over the Americas, Asia, Europe, parts of Africa, and was deeply connected to and did business with various drug cartels, domestically, from Central and South America, corrupt politicians, CEOs and high-ranking officials in banking, pedophilia networks, human trafficking, prostitution, pornography. I mean, this list goes on and on, all the way down through both state and local governments and into the school systems throughout the country. Since Benny was involved with so much and had so much influence in so many different fields, he created a lot of enemies and had no choice but to become a shadow figure. He's even had numerous doppelgangers used as stand-ins to act as his decoy, not only with the authorities and his own enemies, but even to fool people within his own network."

Donovan and Walsh stood stoic with revelation. What they knew or what they thought they knew about Benny was only the surface. To Donovan and Walsh, the Benny they knew was like a king of kings, and now they could clearly see deep within Qubish's eyes that he was more than just a king. He had once been immortal.

"Kinda like bin Laden," said Walsh, who was in awe of the legend of Benny.

"Yeah, if you believe that bin Laden did what he did and is still alive. Benny has a whole myth about him, but he's not a myth. He's the real deal," Qubish said.

"Yeah, but why Dante?" Donovan asked.

"Relax, I was just getting to that. Well, because they were childhood friends, but after Dante was used and they went their separate ways, one of

Benny's loyalist friends from his college years became his new BFF, and that would be Rocco," Qubish stated.

"So, why didn't you just go to Rocco? Wouldn't it have been easier?" Donovan inquired.

"We did, many times, but he wouldn't talk, and we couldn't hold anything against him because he's clean and has nothing to do with Nada Mas or Benny. Luckily, the important member of Nada Mas we apprehended and used as an informant was able to find out from Rocco that Dante went to see Benny at the abandoned air hangar. Unfortunately, as you already know, it was too late, since we're about two days behind our boy, Dante."

Donovan then scanned through the remaining files and stopped on the file of Stanley Albert Paul, aka Daffy.

"This Daffy character is now the one who can get us to Dante, or at least he's the only person we know of that Dante has left and will most likely go to for help," Qubish added.

"So, how much does he know, and how big of an asset will he be for us?" Donovan asked.

"Well, he knows a lot more than we anticipated. This guy is a selfish little screwed-up genius. He made it his own business to know everything about everyone in Nada Mas, and as big of a burnout as he was, he was good at playing the game. He was able to convince people that he was nothing more than a worthless slacker, when in fact he's a very manipulative street hustler and computer hacker. Like I said before, since Rocco was the missing link to Benny, Daffy was able to get Rocco to speak. They were all under the impression that Daffy was some sick, perverted burnout who was no threat. Well, don't they all now wish that they weren't so judgmental, because it is now them who will be judged."

"Okay, all this is good, Qubish, but what other kind of useful information did you get besides an analysis on Benny, Nada Mas, this Daffy character and the connection between all of them and Dante? What about our girl and the mother? Were you able to get any useful information on them from your sources connected to Nada Mas?" Donovan closed up the file folder.

"Yes, I did, from Daffy. He came through for us. The information he got from Rocco is that our boy is definitely going to Mexico with the girl. He's taking her to her mother. And get this, Daffy was able to get information on people associated with the mother and everyone the mother was involved with since coming to the States illegally. While she was living in Jersey, she got involved with a high-ranking official of Nada Mas, Don Fernandez, some big-time underground boss who runs illegal operations in Jersey. Well, he had a falling out with the mother, who I give credit to, since she took important documents from him, records of all the illegal activities he was involved with, documents she was going to hold on to as collateral after leaving him. And get this, one of Don Fernandez's associates, Marta Mendoza, also known as the Black Heart, a female boss who was the head of the Mendoza drug cartel based in Mexico that helped Benny get started—she was also the head of Nada Mas's operations and oversaw high-ranking officials under Benny's command. While she was in the States doing business after getting set up by the Suarez drug cartel based in Colombia and getting apprehended by authorities during a nationwide takedown of Nada Mas, just as she is going through the legal process and was due for deportation, Don Fernandez finds out from an insider in ICE that the mother was picked up on a random roadside raid. Long story short, after the mother is given a trial date and released from custody, Don Fernandez finds the mother, gets her, and with his connections within various agencies, is able to deport her in place of Marta Mendoza. He then unsuccessfully tried to terminate the girl, who ended up with our boy, Dante, who was feeling the heat and getting ready to get out of Dodge."

Donovan and Walsh felt relieved.

"So, now what?" Walsh said.

"For now, we secure all the borders. Hopefully he didn't get into Mexico yet, and we wait to see if he goes to Daffy for help."

"What if he's already in Mexico?" Donovan said with concern.

"If so, we have the Mexican authorities notified already. If Dante makes contact with the mother, they'll take care of him. As for now, gentlemen, we just play the waiting game. I hope that those files painted a bigger picture for you. If you have any more questions or come up with anything else, well, you know where to find me. Well, gentlemen, I believe that this is where we go our separate ways. Donovan, Walsh, once again, it's been a pleasure. Hopefully we see each other real soon. And make sure you take care of that tummyache."

Qubish gave Donovan a love tap on his stomach. As Von Burton followed behind, he smirked as he handed Walsh his empty cup. After they were gone, Donovan and Walsh turned back to each other.

"So, what do you think, Donovan? Do you think he's already in Mexico?"

"Without a doubt, Walsh. Along with all the facts we now have, the two and a half days he has ahead of us is more than enough time to get there," Donovan stated as he took out Sarita's multicolored friendship bracelet. "I just hope that if this Daffy character is right, our boy is bringing our girl back home to her mother, that nothing goes wrong and no one gets in the way. Ya know what I mean, Walsh? Until he gets her safely to her mother, anything can still happen."

"Well, hopefully the Mexican authorities get to him first."

"That's one of the things I'm afraid of."

"Well, what else could happen?"

"Like I said Walsh, anything."

Before leaving, Donovan and Walsh looked out into the distance. In the distance was the Arizona-Mexican border checkpoint, and further out was Mexico. Beyond borders, anything was now possible. At this point, nothing could be done but be patient and play the waiting game.

<u>111</u>

Nada Mas was no longer the entity it once had been. The giant, which had been poisoned by cancerous affiliates from within, was slowly being taken apart piece by piece. Suarez and Salas, who had been carefully plotting a coup d'état since the very beginning, were finally in a position, where they could initiate the demise of Nada Mas. By eradicating all high-ranking officials, they would bring an end to the old guard, plant new seeds and begin to rise with the new.

After notifying authorities and sending out assassins, there was a wave of arrests and bloodshed throughout the globe. None of the original council of fourteen, including Marta Mendoza, would remain alive or active after the death of Benjamin Bradford was announced. Only the two cancerous thorns embedded within Nada Mas since the very beginning, Suarez and Salas, would remain. All would simultaneously be taken out of the picture without warning.

Timothy T. Townsend, the American entrepreneur born into a bloodline of wealth, whose family had founded one of America's biggest pharmaceutical companies, Curatio, would be blindsided. As Townsend was giving a keynote speech at a World Health Organization convention held in Atlantic City, federal agents came marching into the conference room, disrupting the attendees, and apprehended Townsend while he was in the middle of speaking. He was confronted and removed from the facility before his most devoted peers.

# # #

Calvin Coughlin, an American investment banker and politician with ties to D. C. and Wall Street, was detained by federal agents while on the floor of the United States Senate. All was captured live on C-SPAN, even the tears in Coughlin's eyes.

# # #

Randel Rosenthal, Nada Mas's official lawyer, was visited by federal agents as he was walking out of the temple after attending a Saturday morning Shabbat. All the temple's worshipers looked on in shock and fear as the well-loved, devoted and biggest temple donor got confronted and taken away at gunpoint. All that was left of Randel Rosenthal was a trail of urine.

# # #

Jeffrey Rothstein, an important player in the entertainment industry, with links to major Hollywood studios, record companies, social media networks, and various production companies, would be detained during a long night spent inside the Nobu Hotel of Caesar's Palace, indulging in gambling, sex and drugs. Inside the exquisite David Rockwell–designed ten-thousand-square-foot three-bedroom rooftop villa, while Rothstein was in the Italian-made hot tub with four Vegas hookers, doing blow, sipping martinis and smoking a Cuban cigar, federal agents came storming in from the sky deck Zen garden with guns drawn. The four hookers panicked and jumped out of the hot tub while Rothstein was left all alone with his cock in his hand as federal agents surrounded him.

# # #

Eric Edwards, the fit and toned retired Sgt. Major Marine with ties to the CIA and other federal agencies, would face the culmination of his fate on the open road. As Edwards enjoyed a drive on a beautiful sunny Sunday afternoon, the brakes of his Jeep Grand Cherokee—which had been sabotaged—failed while he drove down the Red Mountain Pass in the San Juan Mountains of southwestern Colorado, along the winding and treacherous US-550, the Million Dollar Highway. Just as Edwards was at the pinnacle of the snaky mountain road, he lost control, veered off the road with no protective guardrails, and plummeted down the rocky mountain terrain into an explosive burning inferno.

# # #

Viktor Vyhovsky, the white-bearded, neurotic Ukrainian who trafficked Eastern Europeans across the Atlantic Ocean to the East Coast in cargo ships, would be executed out in the middle of the frozen Siberian Tundra. As Vyhovsky was hunting musk ox with a very close friend connected to Nada Mas, he would be betrayed. After a long trek through the permafrost terrain, as Vyhovsky took aim at a musk ox with the scope of his rifle, his assassin shot him in the back of the head. Vyhovsky's brains and blood would be left splattered all over the white terrain.

#

Carlos, the older, unfit, humble boss who owned and helped run a chain of bars and restaurants up and down the East Coast, would see his final sunset. As the sun descended beyond the Miami skyline while Carlos was partying on the deck of his sixty-foot yacht with a plethora of beautiful Hispanic women, Nada Mas assassins pulled up alongside the yacht on Jet Skis and unloaded their clips. Carlos, along with many women and men, were mowed down by a wave of bullets. After Carlos's hefty frame, squeezed into a pair of hot pink speedos, was pumped full of lead, he fell over the bow of his yacht and into the bay. All that was left as Carlos' body floated facedown in the blood-filled water was a chaotic storm of women screaming and yelling for help.

#

Mariano Cruz, the Mexicano who conducted a successful coyote and drug-running operation along the West Coast border states, would be laid to rest in the comforts of his own establishment. As Mariano Cruz was urinating in the bathroom of Casa Roja, one of his loyal servants, who had now pledged allegiance to Suarez and Salas, poisoned Mariano's mezcal. After Cruz came back from the bathroom, he thanked his loyal servant, who only gave a nod as a final farewell. Cruz then picked up his glass, walked over towards the banister on the second floor, looked down at the cantina on the first floor and all its patrons, and then slowly drank his mezcal. At first it felt refreshing, but after the poison kicked in, Cruz became numb all over, dropped his glass, held his heart, and then fell over the rail down onto the bar on the first floor.

#

The Reverend Jefferson C. Collinsworth, the broad six-foot-five African American from South Carolina, with a well-groomed black-and-gray head of hair and beard and an empowering presence and voice, who was associated with many ministries and Christian sects and the NAACP, a civil rights activist with ties to the FBI and CIA, would meet his demise in the house of God. After Collinsworth gave a passionate sermon, he was confronted by one of Nada Mas' assassins while in his private chambers. Collinsworth's skull was smashed from behind with the base of a large bronze altar crucifix. His body was left on the bloodstained marble floor alongside the crucifix.

#

Sven Schaffert, the Swiss banker who kept the hard-earned money of all the bosses and high-ranking officials of Nada Mas safe in a Swiss bank, would be ambushed by two assassins, a black bag pulled over his head as he walked out of a Swiss bank. Sven wouldn't see the light of day until he was brought to an undisclosed location and the bag was removed from his head. All Sven was able to see was the city street from the rooftop of an eighty-eight-story building. And before Sven had a chance to see his abductors or plead for his life, he was tossed over the edge. Sven Schaffert's body ended up on the sidewalk before the entrance to the building, twisted up in a pool of blood for all onlookers to see.

#

Marta Mendoza and Don Fernandez, the Cuban refugee restaurant owner who conducted drug-trafficking operations in New Jersey, would both be taken out while spending an intimate night together. As Marta's chubby frame ground on top of Don Fernandez's broad-built hairy body while his oversized cock penetrated Marta's swollen hairy pussy and her oversized saddlebag tits flopped up and down to the passionate rhythm and sweat put into the long enduring act of sex, their last dance with love would soon come to an end. After an assassin came creeping in through a window of the bedroom and silently stepped into the moonlight as Marta moaned out, the assassin shot Marta in the back. As blood sprayed all over Don Fernandez, he sat up in a panic, and then he was shot in the face and multiple times in the chest. Both bloody bodies would lie limp together, and the two lovers would be left in a pool of blood.

#

Gang Gao, the frail, quiet, yet strong and fierce Chinese man who trafficked Asians across the Pacific Ocean in cargo ships to the West Coast, would have his final battle with life. As Gang Gao sat cross-legged in a Zen garden with his eyes closed in meditation, an assassin slowly crept up behind him with a knife. Just as the assassin was about to slit Gang Gao's throat, his intuitive senses awakened him and he grabbed the assassin, tossed him over his shoulder, and then stood up. Gang Gao stood poised in a crane position and patiently waited for his killer to make the first move. After the assassin dressed in black wiped blood from his nose, he charged at Gang Gao. Gang Gao defended the assassin's thrusting attack, knocked the knife out of his hand and then exchanged a series of blows to the face, chest, stomach. Gang Gao got the assassin on the ground. As he sat on top of his killer, strangling him with his brittle hands, the assassin stretched out to grab his knife, which he then used to slice Gang Gao's face, forcing Gang Gao onto his back. The assassin then got on top of Gang Gao and began to drive the knife down towards Gang Gao's chest, which Gang Gao used all of his strength to hold back, inches away. And then, just as the tip of the blade pierced Gang Gao's chest, drawing blood, Gang Gao spat in the assassin's eyes, blinding him and giving Gang Gao an opportunity to push the assassin off. Once the assassin was pushed down to the ground, Gang Gao stood up, above his killer.

"You fight like fool, and now you will die like dog."

And then, just as Gang Gao stepped before the assassin, the assassin, who pretended to lay down unconscious, swept Gang Gao's legs out from underneath him, causing him to fall back down to the ground. The assassin then stood up again with the knife and then quickly came down, penetrating Gang Gao's chest with the knife. Gang Gao wouldn't die, not yet. As the assassin came nose to nose with him Gang Gao spoke his final words.

"If death is . . . is what you bring, then . . . then death is what you will . . . will receive."

After speaking, Gang Gao head-butted the assassin, stunning him, and then took the knife out of his chest, which he then drove into the chest of the assassin.

The assassin fell limp next to Gang Gao. Both would die beside each other in a pool of blood, and both of their spirits would ascend into the higher realms of the karmic cycle of life and death within the blissful setting of the Zen garden.

# # #

After the final pieces of Nada Mas were all taken out, the two remaining power figures that were left in control of all, Suarez and Salas, communicated over the phone from undisclosed locations.

"The final piece has been eradicated," Suarez said as he held up and massaged a black marble king chess piece, while on the chessboard before him, the white queen lay toppled over.

"So, who's left before we take over Nada Mas and have complete control?" Salas asked.

"The artist, Benny's loyal servant and friend. Although Benny was taken out, the artist survived," Suarez said sternly.

"Is he even a threat at this point?" Salas inquired.

"No, but no one from the beginning remains alive," Suarez stated as he reached out and tipped over the white pawn, which was the remaining piece left standing on the chessboard.

<u>112</u>

In the beginning, all there was for both Dante and Gabriela was faith and love. And now, as they stood side by side on a street corner with their bags packed, they had each other and Sarita by their side. Life for both of them, which had previously seemed to be such a desolate journey, was now hopeful. Sarita was the driving force behind their blind leap back into a world of dreams and opportunities which they had left far behind. America.

Even if they were safe and free in Mexico, America was the foundation in which they seeded the roots of a life they had not only imagined and wanted but had created and grown. And all that had grown from the seeds of a better life was Sarita, their priority, who deserved to live in the land of opportunities where she was born. It was only a matter of time before their return, and it was when Valdo y Sus Amigos arrived that the future seemed promising for Dante, Gabriela, and Sarita.

"*Hola, mi amigo.* I didn't think you would show up," Dante said to Valdo as he stepped up to the driver-side window.

"*Lo siento, mi amigo*, but we all had a late night," Valdo stated as he turned back towards the band. "Isn't that right, *muchachos*?" Valdo y Sus Amigos all grunted and groaned as they sat back, sedated with drunken bliss. Valdo then turned back around. "*Hola, señorita, que bonita es usted.* What are you doing with such a free spirit?" Valdo said with a smile to Gabriela, who shied away. "So, I guess you're the extra person *mi amigo* spoke to me about. Since there are now three, one of you will have to ride in the last van alone with all the equipment, since there's only room for two in this van."

"That's fine, I'll ride in the last van," Dante said.

"Nah, sorry, *mi amigo*, but the floor space in the last van isn't big enough for an adult. The *niña* will have to ride alone," Valdo stated.

"No, no, wait. Sarita can't go by herself," Gabriela said as she stepped in front of Dante and up towards the driver-side window.

"I'm sorry, *señorita*, but there is no other way. If all of you want to safely come back to the States with us, it's the only way," Valdo explained. Gabriela then turned back towards Dante, hoping he would have an answer or a better way to ease her concerns.

"Don't worry, she'll be fine. Like I told you before, we had no problem getting into Mexico, so there should be no problem getting back into the States." Dante forced out comforting words as he ran his fingers through his hair.

"It's now or never, *señorita*," Valdo firmly stated. Gabriela then turned towards Sarita, who reached out her hand.

"Don't worry, Mama, I'll be fine," Sarita spoke such calming words, but it was the look in her eyes that filled Gabriela with the confidence she needed to carry on.

"Okay, okay, let's go," Gabriela said and then turned away to face Valdo.

"Okay *mi amigos, vamos.*"

Dante and Gabriela walked Sarita to the last van, where one of the stage crew technicians helped Sarita into the small floor space. After Sarita settled into the space, Gabriela looked into her eyes one last time to give Sarita all her love.

"*Te amo,*" Gabriela said before the floor cover was put back on, enclosing Sarita in her temporary confinement of solitude. For now it was a burden for both Gabriela and Sarita, but a necessity that would bring them back the life that had been taken away from both of them. Valdo y Sus Amigos were very humble and welcoming as Gabriela stepped into the back of the van and was sealed inside her temporary tomb beside Dante. Sarita was still on her mind.

"Hey, don't worry. Everything's gonna be all right, I promise," Dante tried to comfort Gabriela.

Not even the roaring of the van engine, the rattling of the windows, creaking from the van benches, and a dissonance of Mexican music and business propaganda being spoken out through megaphones and microphones interrupted Gabriela's contemplative state of being, devoted to the safety of Sarita. The silence in which Gabriela lay cramped within was her sanctuary.

Valdo y Sus Amigos drove north in silence until reaching the Nogales border checkpoint. For Valdo y Sus Amigos, the undertaking of passing through the Mexican checkpoint went smoothly, not because they were only leaving Mexico, but being that Sonora State was considered a free trade zone, there were no proper procedures to comply with. It was only when Valdo y Sus Amigos approached the United States checkpoint that tensions rose. Due to the influx of illegal drugs and migrants being smuggled over the border, the atmosphere at the US border was more intimidating.

All along the line of idling cars underneath the massive white tent towering over and across three lanes of traffic, multiple US Border Patrol agents walked up and down the lanes of cars with drug-sniffing dogs. And at the end of the line, before crossing over into the United States, inspections and questions were conducted in a very intrusive manner. Especially if there were any signs of suspicion, such as timid individuals, or vehicles which could have been converted in a manner to smuggle and transport illegal drugs or migrants. So as Valdo y Sus Amigos drove up to the front of the line and a US Border Patrol agent stepped up to the driver-side window, all the bandmates remained silent.

"Good afternoon, sir, how are you?" Border Patrol Agent Porter said sternly.

"Okay, my friend, okay. It's a wonderful day to be alive, *mi amigo*," Valdo said as he tightly held the steering wheel, squeezing and twisting his hands while also looking away.

"Yes, it is. So, how was your stay in Mexico? Did you and your friends enjoy yourselves?" Agent Porter said robotically as he looked inside the van and into the back where the bandmates were, who remained silent.

"Fine, fine, my friend. Ya know, we had a show in Sonora State," Valdo vaguely stated.

"Hey, listen, here's all of our paperwork. This is Valdo y Sus Amigos, a well-known band from the Southwest, okay?" Pinto said arrogantly as he reached across Valdo with all of the band members' proper documents along with the vehicle's registration.

"Sir, I am not speaking to you, nor have I asked for any identification or documents," Agent Porter said firmly as he stepped back from the window with his hand on his gun. He held his open hand up before Pinto, who then cut back in.

"Hey, listen, Officer . . . Porter, I'm just trying to make things easier for you. We've got a tight schedule to follow. All of these guys are exhausted from a long tour and their final show from last night," Pinto said loudly as he leaned across Valdo, who was trying to hold him back.

"Excuse me, sir, but I'm going to need for you to please control yourself and sit back. There is no need for the attitude. I appreciate your thoughtfulness, but all you need to do right now is to remain silent. There's a lot of vehicles we need to properly inspect without any interruptions, sir," Agent Porter said in an extremely authoritarian manner with his hand still tightly held on his gun and his other hand firmly pointed at Pinto. "Now, all I need to know right now, sir, is if you and any members of your party are bringing anything into the United States from Mexico."

"No, no, *amigo*, nothing at all," Valdo stated.

"Okay sir, and what about the other two vehicles behind you? Are they with you?" Agent Porter asked as he pointed back at the other two vans.

"Yes, they're with us. They're transporting all of our instruments and stage equipment," Valdo said as he looked back out the window along with Porter. There was then a long unsettling pause as Porter studied the two vans.

"Okay, okay, that's good. Okay, well, I hope that you all enjoyed your stay in Mexico. Carry on," Agent Porter said as he removed his hand from his gun.

"Okay, *amigo*. Thank you very much, have a good day," Valdo said. As Valdo drove away, Agent Porter then began to speak into his shoulder radio while he waved the second Valdo y Sus Amigos van forward.

Not only was the US Border Patrol presence more beefed up and abrasive, but as Valdo drove the van past the checkpoint and further down the road, the sweltering heat from the sun began to heat up the confined spaces Dante, Gabriela, and Sarita were tucked inside of. Dante squirmed around in an attempt to relax his strained muscles, while sweat seeped down his forehead and down his back. As for Gabriela, she tried keeping her arms tucked into her body and away from the hot metal. At the moment, their silence felt like an eternity, but once they heard all the bandmates talking, they were rejuvenated with a surge of life.

"Hey, we made it, *amigos*. We made it!" Rafa said excitedly as he stomped on the floor. Dante and Gabriela smiled. They were almost home. But then, after the van came to a halt, there was an unsettling wave of silence.

"Come on, come on," Valdo said softly as he watched in the rearview mirror, seeing the US Border Patrol agents signal both of the other two vans to the side, where they would be properly inspected.

"What's wrong? What's going on?" Rafa yelled up to Valdo.

"They're checking the other two vans," Valdo said.

"What's going on?" Gabriela said to Dante.

"I don't know, maybe they're waiting for the other two vans to catch up," Dante said.

"Well, I hope so. It seems to be taking a long time," Gabriela said nervously.

"Don't worry, just be patient," Dante said as he tried to wipe sweat out of his eyes. Gabriela didn't say a word. She turned away and thought of Sarita.

As for Sarita, she tried to remain calm and silent as she heard equipment from the van being removed and someone walking around just above her. In the distance, she could hear drug-sniffing dogs barking, and underneath the van, she could hear someone probing, scraping and scratching around on the metal underbelly. And then, when there seemed to be no end to the probing and barking, there was a moment of silence. Each slow, relaxing breath Sarita took filled her with peace, but then there was a sudden knock and grind on the floor just above her, which startled her. As the agent crawled around searching for anomalies in the floor, Sarita cringed, and tears began to slowly seep out of her eyes. And before she even had a chance to calm herself, another agent stepped inside the van and there was intense banging on the undercarriage. Blind to the fate that awaited her, Sarita then covered her mouth to muffle her panting and closed her eyes to hide within the darkness.

Gabriela continued to think of Sarita and tried to convince herself that everything was going to be all right. Even within the heat and uncomfortable confinement, Gabriela tried to remain calm, but after hearing the doors to the van open and members of the band moving around and exiting the van, Gabriela looked into Dante's eyes for solace. But then the floor opened. Light blinded Gabriela, who froze, thinking it was the authorities, but once her vision adjusted and she was able to see, she became numb with joy as she looked into Sarita's eyes.

Sarita smiled as she stood above Gabriela, who remained still while Dante began to crawl out. After Dante got out, Rafa reached down and helped Gabriela up and then settled down on one of the van benches beside Sarita, who she then hugged.

"We made it, Mama," Sarita said as Gabriela ran her fingers through her hair.

"I know, Sarita, I know," Gabriela said as tears began to trickle out of her eyes.

Dante didn't say a word. He just thought about the beauty of reuniting and giving back to two of the most important females in his life. And as they drove further down the desert highway, all of Valdo y Sus Amigos began to sing and play. And as soothing music blanketed all, faith and love filled the hearts of Dante, Gabriela, and Sarita, who had overcome internal and external barriers and were now free to rewrite the life they'd all dreamed of someday living together in America.

113

If there was a cure for all that had been lost, it was Valdo y Sus Amigos, who uplifted everyone's heart, mind, and soul with their music. Happiness was found once again in the eyes of Dante, Gabriela, and Sarita as Valdo y Sus Amigos continued to inspire their souls and drive them to their final destination. Being back in America was liberating, but there was still one more stop to be made before their final embrace. It was after a long trek north that all roads eventually led to an apartment complex nestled on the outskirts of Tucson, Arizona, where Dante would reunite with Daffy in hopes of gaining some financial support.

As Valdo y Sus Amigos' three vans idled outside the apartment complex, the music concluded, and all of them gave Dante, Gabriela, and Sarita all of their love and blessings for all that lay ahead, and then helped them out of the van. After getting out and stepping down on American soil, Dante then walked around to the driver-side window.

"All right, *mi amigo*, thanks again for everything. Who knows, maybe our lives will cross paths again," Dante said as he shook Valdo's hand.

"*Claro, claro, amigo.* We'll see each other again, I'm sure, but before we meet again, don't forget to tell everyone you see how good Valdo y Sus Amigos was to you. Remember, Valdo y Sus Amigos is the people's band. Okay, *adiós, mi amigo.*" Valdo said and then waved to Gabriela and Sarita. "*Adiós, bonitas,* farewell." Valdo y Sus Amigos then drove off into the setting sun, leaving Dante, Gabriela and Sarita all alone on an open road.

"All right, so here's the deal. This is where one of my friends lives who can help us. I'm gonna go in real quick to talk to him and see if he can loan me some money, so you two wait here. I'll be right back, okay?" Dante said.

"One of your friends? Are you sure? Isn't it better if we just go off on our own? Ya know, start heading back to New Jersey? Or we could go to Los Angeles. At least there are still people there I can trust," Gabriela explained.

"That may be, but this friend of mine is someone from my past, someone I know for a fact I can trust. Plus without any money, we aren't going anywhere. This friend of mine will be able to give us some money, enough to live off of and lay low for a few months until things cool down, okay? So, you two wait here, I'll be right back, okay?"

"Okay," Gabriela said as she reached down to hold Sarita's hand. She then watched as Dante trotted across the street and then walked through the apartment complex.

After Dante found Daffy's apartment, he silently stood in front of the door for a moment. This was it, his last link to a past he wanted to leave behind forever. It was either going to be beneficial or blow up in his face. But at this point, to risk all was worth what he might gain and be able to give to both Gabriela and Sarita. After contemplating the many different scenarios that could unfold from opening up another door from his past, Dante reached down to see if the doorknob had been left unlocked. It had. Dante knew Daffy all too well, and after opening up the door, Dante slowly walked into Daffy's apartment.

As Dante crept deeper into the apartment, faintly echoing out from a TV left on in the background was the song "The End," by The Doors, scoring the opening scene to the film, *Apocalypse Now*, with Martin Sheen's character sitting in a Vietnam hotel room in a contemplative solitary state of confinement as he awaited his fate. He could also hear an oscillating fan as he walked in and found Daffy passed out on the couch. He was dressed in a wife beater and boxer shorts, with a crumpled-up bag half-filled with marijuana, a marijuana bowl, empty and half-filled bottles of beer, multiple laptops, a police scanner, and a cell phone resting on top of the coffee table. Dante cautiously walked up to Daffy, putting his hand over his mouth, picking up a half-filled bottle of beer, and then pouring the final remains onto Daffy's crotch, waking him up. As Daffy jolted up with confusion and paranoia, Dante shushed him and then removed his hand from Daffy's mouth after he calmed down.

"Dante, what in tha hell are you doing here? I thought that—"

"Shut up and just listen to me. I need some money. Give me some money, Daffy. C'mon, I know you have at least six figures stashed away somewhere."

"Money, for what?" Daffy played ignorant.

"Don't play dumb with me. Besides the situation I'm in right now, after all I've done for you, you owe me. C'mon, give me some money!"

Just as Daffy began to get up, his cell phone ringtone, Santana's "Oye Cómo Va" played.

"Who's that?" Dante asked.

"It's, it's . . ."

"Well, whoever it is, answer the damn phone!" After Dante lashed out, Daffy continued to nervously stare at the ringing cell phone. Dante then lifted Daffy up by his shaggy hair, dragged him into the adjacent kitchen, and then grabbed a knife left on a cutting board.

"Hurry up and get the money, before I fillet you like a fucking fish!" Dante held the knife up towards Daffy's throat.

Daffy staggered away, went into a bedroom, got money from a secret stash, and then quickly returned, handing Dante a brown bag filled with $25,000 cash.

"What about a car? Do you have a car?" Dante said as he looked at the cash inside the bag.

"Yeah, yeah, it's parked right out front. The blue Nissan Sentra, it's an older model."

"Okay, well, where are the keys?" Daffy looked around for the keys. "Where the fuck are the keys?"

"O-over there, on the counter," Daffy said as he pointed past Dante towards the kitchen counter. Dante then turned around and grabbed the keys. "Sorry it had to be this way."

"So am I," Dante said as he looked into Daffy's deceitful eyes one last time, and then left.

Outside Dante looked for Daffy's car and wasn't surprised to see it was a clunker, a four-door 1990 Nissan Sentra with faded blue paint. Dante got inside it and drove out of the apartment complex towards Gabriela and Sarita, who then got in. Dante then peeled out and drove down a desert highway. As Dante drove off, he looked up into the sky, into the rearview mirror and back over his shoulder. Gabriela could clearly see the fear in Dante's eyes. After she looked inside the bag that Dante gave her and saw all the money, she knew that the freedom they had finally resurrected was now in jeopardy.

<u>114</u>

All that was built from faith and love would soon come to an end in the desert, but not yet. For now, it was only a thought in Dante's mind as he continued to drive further down the open desert highway while constantly looking into the rearview mirror, up into the sky, and around. After driving for many miles, further ahead, towards the vanishing point, slowly rising up over the horizon was a decrepit old truck stop. It seemed to be a safe haven, an escape from all that was threatening to the livelihood of Dante, Gabriela, and Sarita. Although they were free in America, besides Dante being a fugitive on the run, there were still remnants from the past that posed a threat to their future.

Dante parked the car in front of the truck stop diner. He turned off the car and tightly wrapped his hands around the steering wheel while he looked into the reflection of his eyes. Deep within, Dante no longer saw an introvert within his tortured soul, a blindly led artist who never quite knew what he wanted. No matter how successful the life Dante lived seemed to have been, Dante was now able to see that his life, his purpose, was only meant for those who had been able to open his heart. Those who possessed the key at the moment were Gabriela and Sarita, who patiently waited for Dante. Not only were they the fuel for Dante's heart and soul, but they were special, they were a part of his flesh and blood. And in this final moment, Dante was willing to sacrifice his own life to preserve theirs.

"Um, Dante, are we stopping to eat?" Sarita asked as she leaned forward from the backseat. Dante looked at Sarita's reflection in the rearview mirror, turned around, and then, as he looked into her eyes, he was reminded of his true calling in life.

"No, Shorty."

"But I'm hungry," Sarita said. Gabriela then turned around.

"Shhh, it's gonna be okay, Sarita. We'll stop someplace else later, okay?"

"Um, okay." Sarita nodded while holding her stomach.

"Listen, before we leave and start heading east towards Jersey, I'm just gonna go inside to make a quick phone call." Dante looked at Sarita's reflection in the rearview mirror and then turned towards Gabriela. "For now, take Sarita and the money, go across the street to the farmers' market to buy some food, and wait for me there, okay?" Dante explained.

In Dante's crystal-blue eyes, Gabriela saw sadness. Not the sadness you see in someone being convicted or mourning over the loss of a loved one, but instead the bittersweet desolation of someone losing everything. Dante didn't have to say goodbye. Gabriela could see it in his eyes and could see deeper within that all the love he had for her and Sarita would soon be gone.

Gabriela turned away to bend down for the bag of money. Even though money was the only means of security Dante was able to provide at the moment, in his heart, he felt it was the best he could offer in such a predicament. He wanted to do more. He wanted to carry on with both Gabriela and Sarita, but the past held him back. Instead of living a life in shadows with the ones he loved, whose own lives would be threatened by his past, Dante had to let them go. After Gabriela sat back up and looked Dante in the eyes again, he was convinced that he was doing the right thing. Especially when he looked away into the rearview mirror and into the reflection of Sarita's eyes. Dante was willing to give the world, security and life to the cure to his heart and soul.

After admiring both Gabriela and Sarita, Dante reached into his pocket and pulled out Sarita's rosary. He turned around and reached out towards Sarita with the beads and cross hanging down from the palm of his hand, holding it out as it dangled down in the air before Sarita.

"I believe this is yours, Shorty."

Sarita then reached out to hold the crucifix of the rosary within her fingers to admire one last time. After savoring it, Sarita then slowly raised the rosary up towards Dante's hand with the beads coiling within the palm of her hand. Then, as Sarita brought her hand to Dante's, with the rosary pressed together between both their hands, she rotated her hand and Dante's hand around until her hand was on top, causing the rosary to return to Dante's palm. Sarita pushed Dante's hand back.

"Um, no, Dante, you keep it, as something to always remember me by."

Sarita's words filled Dante with jubilation. Dante then put the rosary back into his pocket. Knowing that this would be his final moment shared with Gabriela and Sarita, he reached into his other pocket and pulled out a key, holding it out before Sarita.

"Here, take it," Dante stated. Sarita took the key and held it in the palm of her hand.

"What's this for?"

"My apartment. You'll find something inside to always remember me by. And, and maybe something you've been looking for, for a long time now," Dante said as he looked at the key and then into Sarita's eyes.

As Sarita sat poised with curiosity, Dante turned towards Gabriela and smiled. Gabriela could clearly remember her first night spent with Dante many years ago, and what had manifested from it.

"But aren't you coming—" Sarita asked, but was cut off.

"Shhh, it's gonna be okay. Go on, go with your mother."

As Gabriela admired Dante while he was looking back at Sarita, tears began to form in her eyes. No matter how much she wanted Dante to stay with her and Sarita, she knew that he wasn't going to. Even if it was their fate to separate once again, Gabriela wasn't going to allow Dante ever to forget her. So, as Dante turned back towards Gabriela, she removed her heart-shaped pendant from around her neck and placed it in Dante's hand.

As Dante held the pendant, in Gabriela's eyes he saw an ocean of love. He reached out to run his fingers through Gabriela's hair and then slowly brought his hand down to hold the right side of her face. Dante caressed the side of Gabriela's face until she reached up to tightly hold Dante's hand.

Gabriela felt like heaven. She was moist, warm with ecstasy, from down between the knees and up to her blood-pulsing heart filled with euphoric ambiance, which was now rapidly beating beneath the raised surface of her skin. All she wanted was one final kiss, but deeper within, she knew that her love for Dante was worth more than a simple kiss or holding on to the one you love, that true love was letting go. As Dante slowly pulled away, Gabriela bit down on her bottom lip to savor the moment, knowing that it would be their last. Dante then looked into Gabriela's eyes one last time, turned away, opened the door, and then stepped out of the car.

"*Vamos, Chor-tee,*" Gabriela said as she looked back over her shoulder. She then opened the door and stepped out of the car, followed by Sarita.

As Gabriela and Sarita began to walk away from the car, Dante watched them one last time. Gabriela and Sarita walked further away towards the farmer's market. Sarita looked back over her right shoulder at Dante with an innocent sense of abandonment in her eyes. Dante smiled, and then that was it. She was forever gone. After the trinity of one separated and went their separate ways, Dante turned around and walked away.

After Dante, Gabriela and Sarita were seen separating from a distance, the numbing coldness in Octavio's eyes, hidden behind dark sunglasses reflecting in the rearview mirror, was that of Abaddon, the angel of death. As Octavio patiently waited for the right opportunity to deliver his final message, he slid the loaded clip into the gun with his left hand, which was missing the pinky and ring finger. His bullet wound and bloodstained white shirt, from being shot in the torso in the air hangar, were a reminder of failing to terminate his final target. And now, as Dante stepped out into the open, Octavio was determined to kill him this time.

Before Gabriela and Sarita crossed the street, as Gabriela patiently waited on the edge of the road for cars to pass, a sudden shadow of fear fell upon her. Gabriela felt as she had when she had first come from Mexico and lived a life in shadows. When Gabriela began to cross the street, she held Sarita's hand tightly. As Sarita followed, she could see in Gabriela's eyes that she no longer appeared to be appeased and buoyant that they were now free, but instead she seemed like she was scared. Of what, Sarita didn't know. Sarita only held Gabriela's hand even tighter, as she looked forward and found herself lost within the eyes of a stray dog. As the stray dog crossed the street and walked past Sarita and Gabriela, Sarita watched the stray dog as it walked past them, and then focused on the farmer's market before her. Further away in the distance, from behind the front glass window of the diner, Dante watched as Gabriela and Sarita crossed the street while talking on a pay phone. It would be Dante's final farewell to Sonya and final dance with fate.

Gabriela and Sarita walked side by side as they picked out fresh produce from the farmer's market. The cooling winds and wind chimes hanging down from the farmer's market tarp reverberated soothing ambiance. Sarita then left Gabriela's side and began to walk alongside the bins while softly singing a Spanish lullaby and running her fingers along the wooden frame of the bins and through pieces of fresh fruit. Sarita stopped before a bin filled with fresh red apples and began to look through them for the biggest and freshest one. As Sarita stepped up on her tippy toes to reach for the apples in the back, away in the distance, sirens could be heard, slowly rising like a storm. Sarita then grabbed a big, fresh red apple. After stepping back down, she stood before the bin with the apple in her hand and then turned around to look back down the desert highway that stretched further away into the empty, vast desert wasteland, where the sirens became louder.

As Dante opened up his heart and soul to Sonya, in the distance, a chaotic uprising of sirens echoed out like a tsunami, slowly building up to a crescendo. And no matter how urgent the sirens were as he heard them get closer, Dante wouldn't allow anything to disrupt his final moment with Sonya.

As the sirens became louder like rolling thunder, further away in the distance, rising above the horizon, were unmarked black SUVs. Gabriela and Sarita, who were standing side by side, watched as Dante walked out of the diner and then stood in the parking lot. They then looked back down the highway at the SUVs, which drove faster and faster towards them. Before they had a chance to cross the street to join Dante or to just simply walk away, the SUVs came screeching into the diner parking lot.

Simultaneously, Octavio stepped out of his car. His black snakeskin boots glistened in the sunlight. Dante looked over to his right at the black SUVs parked just a few yards away. Through the front windshields, he could see no amnesty in the eyes of the FBI agents. Dante then turned away, only to be faced with the Colombian assassin aiming his gun at him, and then there was darkness.

Sarita dropped the red apple to the ground as the eight-fingered assassin delivered his final message to Dante, who fell to the ground after bullets pierced through his flesh. At the same time, the FBI agents came storming out of their SUVs. As the eight-fingered assassin paced across the parking lot towards Dante while getting off his first few rounds, Qubish was the first agent to storm out, both his guns drawn. Qubish fearlessly stepped out into the open and paced towards the eight-fingered assassin with outstretched arms, unloading his clips with a cigarillo still held between his grinning teeth. As Qubish fired his guns in the open like Wyatt Earp, Von Burton fired his gun from behind the open passenger-side door of his SUV, like he was hiding from enemy fire in the trenches of World War I.

From one of the other SUVs, Donovan jumped out to join Qubish, only to get shot by a single bullet after pulling off a few rounds of his own. Walsh tried to get out with Donovan but had trouble unbuckling his seat belt and then opening up the door. By the time Walsh stepped out of the SUV to join Donovan, he fumbled his gun around until it fell to the ground, just as Donovan dropped to the ground, holding his wound. As quickly as everything built up to a storm, there was then silence.

There was a haze of gun smoke left languidly lingering all around within the calm of the storm. Octavio lay dead on the ground. Von Burton along with other FBI agents went over to see who he was. Qubish strutted towards Dante as he put both his smoking guns away. Walsh, who was caught up in the excitement, ran past Donovan with other FBI agents.

"We got 'em, we finally got 'em, Donovan . . . Donovan—" Walsh cut himself off when he noticed that Donovan wasn't standing beside him. He then turned around to see Donovan laid out on the ground in a pool of blood. As Donovan squirmed around like a hopeless insect, crippled and trapped within a spider's web, Walsh dashed over to him.

From across the street, Gabriela held Sarita as they watched. Sarita cried out and then began to attempt to dart across the street, only to have Gabriela hold her back and embrace her.

As FBI agents took care of the eight-fingered assassin and Dante, Walsh sat and cradled Donovan in his arms.

"It's gonna be okay, Donovan. Everything is gonna be okay. As soon as the ambulance gets here, they'll have you all fixed up and ready to go—"

"Shut the fuck up, Walsh. You're not making this situation any better! Fuck, a bullet, one fucking bullet, on my very last day on the job!" Donovan coughed up blood as he spoke.

"Egh, my new shirt," Walsh shrieked as he jerked back.

"It's not even yours. It's mine, fuck! This is it, Walsh, so I'm only gonna be able to ask you once to do me a favor. Tell . . . tell my wife that . . . that I love her . . . ."

"This stain will never come out. Wait, no. No, don't say that, Donovan. You're fine, you'll be able to tell her yourself," Walsh said. Donovan then coughed up even more blood on himself and on his shirt that Walsh was wearing as he removed his hand from his wound to show Walsh how fatal it was. Walsh gagged and looked away. And when Walsh found the strength to look back, he held Donovan's hand.

"Anything else you want me to tell her?"

"Yeah, tell her . . . not to dye her hair anymore, for me, that . . . that I always loved her natural hair color, her . . . her dark, thick hair, even more now with her gray streaks, be . . . because it's her natural beauty that I love, how . . . how she ages like a bottle of wine, her . . . her natural beauty becomes better with age, and . . . and when she's in Baja, well, first make sure she still goes, that . . . that I'll always be with her, to . . . to look up at the stars at night because I'll be looking down at her, and . . . and do you wanna know a secret, Walsh?"

"Sure," Walsh said nonchalantly with tears in his eyes.

"My wife, she . . . she fucking laughs like a donkey . . . it aggravates the shit out of me, be . . . because she does it all the time, she . . . she laughs at the stupidest shit, and it's so fucking loud, and . . . and fucking lingers in my head forever, I . . . I can never get her irritating laugh outta my head, and . . . and it's fucking embarrassing when we're in public places, all . . . all my life I spent with her, I put up with it, and, . . . and I never had the heart to tell her, to . . . to confront her and tell her how I really feel, be . . . because that's why I love her . . . the little things . . . the little things about someone and . . . and the little things in life, that . . . that's what I always remember . . . those little moments and . . . and little things that are worth more than words or anything else . . . and one more thing be . . . before I'm gone, I . . . I love you, Walsh."

"So, you're coming out of the closet?" Walsh choked up with tears.

"No! When I say that . . . that I love you, Walsh, it's . . . it's because you're like the son I've never had . . ." Donovan spoke from his heart as he struggled to breathe.

"I, I know, Donovan, you always tell me. I never forget because you're like the father I never had." Walsh held Donovan's hand even tighter as he laughed and then choked up, with tears in his eyes, once again. There was then a moment of silence. "Donovan . . . Donovan . . . ." Donovan's hand then fell limp and slid out of Walsh's hand.

After the haze of gun smoke slowly cleared away and the FBI agents began to cordon off the crime scene, Gabriela took Sarita by the hand and began to walk away. Neither said a word as they walked down the desert highway towards a small town.

As Walsh held Donovan in his arms, he looked all around with tears in his eyes. Walsh then noticed Sarita's multicolored friendship bracelet that came out of Donovan's pocket, lying on the ground, which he then picked up. As Walsh held Sarita's friendship bracelet, he looked out, further ahead across the street, and smiled when he saw Gabriela and Sarita walking away in the distance. And as the illuminating light from the setting sun shined down upon Gabriela and Sarita, in a time of samsara, there now seemed to be a sense of peace and liberation felt within their hearts and souls.

# # #

Sonya,

My Light, My Fire, My Burning Desire to live Another Day, As Always you give Me reason to live, And As Much As A Surprise this letter May Be to Receive this After Many Years of My Absence, Believe it or Not, this is Not A desperate Plead for Help, Because I Screwed up Again, its Because Someone Actually Came to Me for Help. Don't worry, eventhough you Are the Only One left in My life to go to, Who would Be Able To Help, I'm Not Asking for that, instead, Consider this A long Awaited Amends.

It's funny, What Drove us Apart, Has Now Brought Me Back to you. Whether it Was Fate, Destiny, or Just A Coincidence, Being Here Now, Sitting on Your Front Steps Writing this letter feels right inside. I feel the Way I Did When I first Met You, that love No Matter How Misguided or tainted it Has Become throughout the Years, it Has Never Burned out. Maybe thats What true love is then, letting go, And Moving on, Allowing the One You love to grow And evolve Without Any Sort of Attachments. Being Seperated By time And Distance Has fueled My love for You, And No Matter Which Path You or I Have Been Down throughout the Years Knowing that You Have Come into My life, that our Hearts & Souls Have Been Bonded By fate, or By Some Higher force is fullfilling. My life feels Complete

Where we go from Here I Can not Say, But whatever road You And I take, whether they run Parallel or in Different Directions, know that My love for You will grow More And Never Die out. I wish Nothing But the Best for You, And that whatever it is You choose to Do with Your life that You're Happy :)

By the time You read this I will Be Gone, But Maybe Someday Further Down the road our lives will Cross Paths Again. Until that Day Comes know that You Have Changed Me for the Better. You Are Nothing less than My everything.

Ciao Bella ♡

Dante

115

As Sarita stood before Dante's apartment door, although the key held in her hand wasn't the key to Dante's heart, it would be the love left behind that would mend together all that was torn apart. At the moment, everything seemed to be so surreal, yet meant to be, and after remenicining about the past, accepting the present, and looking forward towards a future unknown, Sarita stepped towards the door, unlocked it, and then slowly stepped into the shadows of the past.

As the wind blew in the open window, through the curtains, the wind chimes melodically echoed out, and the oscillating fan was left standing still, without any life. The sunlight shined in through the open window, illuminating Sarita while she walked throughout Dante's apartment. Everything remained the same. The leaky faucet, the empty bottles of beer, liquor, and wine, the garbage and cigarette butts lying all around, and sketches of Sarita left scattered all over. Each one that Sarita picked up to admire was a reminder of her time being with Dante and how all that she held in her hands was all that was left behind from a stranger Sarita had once feared, who had become a friend and a companion and was the reason for her to even exist in this life. But the sketches were only mere blueprints when compared to what awaited Sarita near the open window.

Across the apartment was the covered-up painting and easel, resting near the open window, where Dante had once sat to observe Sarita whenever she was outside. It was able to beckon Sarita, provoke her curiosity and attract her away from the sketches. Sarita stood frozen with anticipation for a moment before all that seemed hidden and enschrouded in enigmatic mystique. All Sarita could think of was Dante, and after reflecting on all she'd once feared and all that she now knew of Dante, Sarita reached out to remove the cloth and reveal the forbidden painting that Dante had once told her not to look at.

At first, Sarita was overwhelmed with joy, but most importantly, there was an understanding as to why Dante had always watched Sarita from the window. Sarita ran her fingertips across the canvas glazed over with thick layers of paint, smeared and splattered on, forged into a portrait of Sarita sitting on a swing. In the eyes of Sarita, all that she had once feared made sense now. Sarita was the subject of Dante's painting, his muse and inspiration, which he slaved over. But it didn't compare to what awaited Sarita on the other side of the apartment.

As if being called on once again by Dante's mastery, Sarita's attention was pulled away from her portrait and drawn towards all of Dante's paintings left leaning up against the back wall. Some were exposed, while others were covered in bedsheets. After walking across the apartment, Sarita stood before Dante's exposed paintings but was then provoked to uncover and reveal each of the other paintings, which were paintings of different women posing in the nude. And although each woman's beauty was appealing, the promiscuous character of each painting was inappropriate for the innocent, causing Sarita to look away. All except for the final painting, which Sarita slowly uncovered. After revealing the last painting, Sarita stood still with bewilderment. The face on the canvas wasn't some stranger. It was someone Sarita knew very well. Her mother. As Sarita reached out to touch the painting, Gabriela's presence was felt.

"Do you like it?" Gabriela walked up behind Sarita as she spoke. Sarita seemed lost, then looked back over her shoulder and deep into Gabriela's eyes in search of answers, only to turn back to observe the portrait of Gabriela. As Sarita continued to stare at the painting, once again, Gabriela stepped up behind Sarita and embraced her. Gabriela and Sarita then admired the portrait of Gabriela, a masterpiece laced with an abstract appeal of revelation and truth, created by the divine hands of a master artist, Dante.

In the likeness of Picasso's "Les Demoiselles d'Avignon," enschrouded in enigmatic mystique, like the Mona Lisa, was Gabriela's portrait, an abstract image of Gabriela in the nude, her seductive curves of sin covered with a red blanket, sitting with her back and her upper body turned towards the viewer while seductively gazing out into the eyes of mortals with a slight smile. It echoed an eternity of forbidden sin and truth. After Sarita studied Gabriela's portrait for a moment, she then turned to look up into Gabriela's eyes to speak and then back to cherish the masterpiece once again.

"Mama, I don't understand. How does Dante have a painting of you when you two have never been together before?"

Gabriela leaned in closer towards Sarita and softly spoke into her ear.

"Once, Sarita, only once. Remember the time I told you when we met for the first time, when I walked into his apartment, when his door was left open?"

"Um, yes, I remember."

"Well, that wasn't the end of the story. It wasn't even the beginning." Such words of revelation opened Sarita's eyes to the truth. And even though the truth of who she was and where she came from was hard for the innocent mind to fully conceive all at once, it was liberating. All Sarita could do at the moment was smile and adore Dante's gift for her, while Gabriela tightly held Dante's gift to her. Although the trinity of one was broken and seemed to be forever gone, in the eyes of Gabriela, their love, no matter how tainted, was everlasting. Gabriela, Sarita, and Dante, the trinity of one, would live on forever.

# # #

~In the End~

In life, is it the unknown that we all fear, or is it the truth? And whichever one it is, as terrifying as both can be, when we do find the strength to dive into the unknown or face the truth, in the end both are liberating. If I never found the strength or the courage to go out into the unknown, to face all that awaited me beyond borders in the United States, I wouldn't be where I am now in life.

And as hard as it was for me to accept who I was and the life I lived, the truth, no matter how flawed or terrifying it was, opened my eyes so that I could see the little things in life that mattered most and set me free. And as I sit here all alone, thinking about my life, I'm not going to hide in the past any longer and fool myself with how peaceful and pleasant life back in Mexico was or how evil the United States could really be. This is only one opinion, from one life, out of many in this world.

So, no matter how good or bad life was back in Mexico or here in the United States, it doesn't matter. Nothing in this world matters except for the ones you love, and as we carry on with this life, it's only what you make of it and create for yourself. So it's important to appreciate the little things when so many have none, take the time to admire the sun, the moon, the stars, and all of life, nature, animals, and of course, humans. Yes, it is a mystery as to who we really are and why we are here, but when you're able to live a life without fear, fear of the unknown, fear of what others do or think, fear of yourseslf and fear of the truth, the possibilities in life are limitless, borderless.

I'm here now because I've shed the fear I once had and found love, not only in the world, but in myself. So if being fearless of the unknown and the truth sets us free, then it is love that brings us all together. I don't have all the answers and I don't know where I'll be tomorrow, but when I'm gone and I leave this world, I don't want to be remembered for who I am or what I did. I want to be remembered for what I left behind in others, those who were a part of my life, and those who helped me become who I am. I want to be able to forever live on in others, because in the end, the physical things left behind won't matter. Money, big houses, fancy cars, certificates and awards won't be able to do what words and love can do to a human's heart, mind and soul. Those words, and the love you give, live on forever in others. They become the seeds of the future, which will someday grow into the trees of a fulfilling life.

Echoes from Gabriela's final words read from the last page of the third journal pierced through Sarita's heart, mind, and soul, with an infusion of love as she silently stood before the boarded-up window within what used to be Dante's apartment. The thought of Gabriela and all that had once been filled Sarita's mind. After reflecting on the life of her mother and the love they shared for each other, Sarita slowly closed the journal. There was then a long, peaceful wave of silence. And although the doors to Gabriela's life were now shut, all that remained locked inside was now a part of Sarita. Sarita was the flower erected from Gabriela's womb, and even though the trinity of one was separated throughout the years, all came together within the walls of the past. But most importantly, from all that has come and gone, there was life.

"Um, Mama? Mama?" Mariela's soft, sweet soothing voice echoed throughout the emptiness of everything that had once been. Sarita smiled and then turned around to face the light of her life, her daughter. The seven-year-old was petite, with long, dark flowing hair, tied into pigtails which hung down past her shoulders. She also had a gapped smile. And in Mariela's beautiful dark eyes, Sarita was able to see Gabriela, and when Mariela began to innocently walk and skip along the floor of the past towards Sarita, she saw herself.

"*Mi chiquita, besos,*" Sarita said as she kneeled down to give Mariela, a hug and a kiss, and then while she continued to talk to Mariela, she stood up before her and began to run her fingertips through Mariela's hair. "So, how was it, exploring the building Mama used to live in, my little Dora the Explorer?"

"Um, well, it's a little creepy. I think some of the rooms are haunted, but it was fun. Speshially the swing." Mariela twisted her right foot into the floor with her hands held together behind her back as she gazed all around into nothingness and then up into Sarita's eyes.

"Okay, *mi chiquita*, okay, that sounds good," Sarita said with a smile.

"Is it time to go yet?"

Sarita looked all around what remained of Dante's apartment, with Gabriela's journals held in her hand. "Yes, it's time to go, c'mon." Sarita reached down to hold Mariela's hand and then began to walk her towards the door and guide her out from the walls of the past, leaving behind the remnants of everything that had once been.

<u>116</u>

Illuminating light from the heavens above shone down while the brisk, cool winds echoed out an ambiescent symphony of soothing solace, wistfully blowing through the leaves and branches of autumn trees laced with an abstract array of vibrant auburn, orange, and yellowish earth tones and through the bed of roses left resting on top of the coffin. There was an auric essence of love and affection, tainted with meloncholy and infinite sadness, left lingering around as the priest said his final farewell to the faithful departed, along with a few last mourners. Soon after, Sarita and Mariela were left all alone with Gabriela, who was finally at peace and free. Even though, in the eyes of mortals, Gabriela appeared to be deceased and forever gone, it seemed that after finally completing her spiritual cycle of samsara, Gabriela was finally home amongst the cosmos and would live on, forever.

Down on earth, though, there were no more soothing songs or dances with fate. The union of one was forever gone, along with walks along the Jersey Shore, or gazing out across the North Jersey landscape at the city lights of the New York skyline underneath the midnight sky and the illuminocity of the full moon. Only memories and broken dreams remained, along with remnants of Gabriela's spiritual presence, as Sarita tightly held Mariela's hand. Sarita and Mariela would accept their fates, leave behind the past, stop worrying about the future, and live in the now, admiring Gabriela's final resting spot as a last farewell to the sacred feminine. Tears of sorrow began to trickle out of Sarita's eyes and down her cheeks.

"It's gonna be okay, Mama. Grandma will be safe in heaven." Mariela reached up to hold Sarita's hand. Sarita choked up, wiped away her tears, and then looked into Mariela's eyes for relief. After savoring the untainted love seen deep within Mariela's eyes, Sarita looked away. Sarita and Mariela stepped forward and each placed a rose on top of Gabriela's coffin. Then, after leaving behind a token of love and savoring Gabriela's final resting place and her spiritual presence, Sarita and Mariela walked away.

As Sarita and Mariela walked along the cemetary path, underneath a canopy of trees, there was a familiar presence felt from a distance, which beckoned and attracted Sarita. At first, Sarita became numb with confusion. She was blind with curiosity and uncertainty, but then, as the ghost of the past slowly approached her, Sarita smiled.

In the likeness of an aged master artist, shriveled up with fatigue and adorned with chest-length hair and a wizard-length beard like da Vinci, Dante walked towards Sarita, eventually embracing her, tightly holding on, bringing Sarita comfort and his condolences until finally letting go. Dante then looked into Sarita's eyes while running his fingertips through her hair.

"Well, look at you, Shorty, all grown up now. You look good, more beautiful than the last time I saw you." Dante's alluring words infused Sarita with joy. She shyly looked away and gazed all around with a vibrant smile.

"Thank you, and you look really good, too."

"Well, knowing otherwise, I accept your compliment. So, who's this little *camarón*?"

"This is Mariela."

"Well, nice to meet you, Mariela." Dante reached down and rubbed the top of Mariela's head and then ran his fingertips through her hair as he spoke to Mariela, who shyly stepped closer towards Sarita. "Amazing how much time has gone by since we've last seen each other. So much has changed, yet it seems as if a day hasn't gone by."

"I know, I know. You're right, and it's only been twenty-two years."

"Only," Dante responded sarcastically. Sarita laughed. "Well, if it has been twenty-two years, time sure hasn't affected you much. As for me, well, let's just say I'm no bottle of wine. Even though so much time has passed, things will no longer be the same now without your mother. You two were all I've ever thought about throughout the years, my light in the darkness, my dreams and drive to live another day. You two were the only thing good in my life. The thought of you two, especially your mother, well, she was the only truth in my life, my untainted inspiration, and now all that's left is you, my little winged dove, my angel from above, my heart, my light, my everything, the purest thing in my life, always and forever," Dante said affectionately.

Sarita struggled to find the right words. "And she loved you just as much. She fought for four years, but unfortunately, the cancer got the best of her."

"I know. I could see her love in your eyes and feel all the love you have for her in your voice. Anyway, I wish we had more time, but . . ." Dante turned around and looked out across the empty vastness at two federal agents who were waiting and watching Dante from a distance. They signaled to Dante that his time was up and it was time to go. Dante turned back around. "Unfortunately, our reunion must be cut short."

Dante stepped towards Sarita, embraced her, and then whispered loving words into her ear. After savoring Sarita's essence, Dante stepped back and gazed deep into her eyes one last time while gently running his fingertips through her hair. Dante turned towards Mariela and looked into her eyes and ran his fingertips through her hair as well as his final farewell before turning around and walking away, leaving behind the ghosts of everything that had once been, and his greatest masterpiece, forever.

As Sarita and Mariela watched Dante walk away, three monarch butterflies, a trinity of one, flew around in the open while the light from the heavens above shined down upon Dante, illuminating his divine essence of his enigmatic mystique as he departed into the vast unknown, forever gone. After Dante vanished from existence, Sarita took Mariela by the hand, turned around, and slowly walked away.

"Mama, who was that man?"

Sarita smiled. "Tu abuelo," she said softly." Her smile grew bigger.

"*Mi abuelo?*" Mariela said with bewilderment.

"*Sí.*" Sarita gazed deep into Mariela's eyes while running her fingertips through Mariela's hair as she continued. "And remember what I always tell you, Mariela, what your grandmother taught me and what helped both your grandmother and me in life . . . even during the darkest of times, inside your heart are all the answers, all the truth and love needed to carry on and live the life you want to live. All you have to do is believe, and have hope . . . *esperanza* . . . ."

~Fin~

Tommy Tutalo

<u>About the Author</u>

Tommy Tutalo is an independent author, writer, photographer, painter, and visual artist, whose work is considered to be diverse, and universal. A native of West Orange, New Jersey, Tommy comes from a hardworking, and loving blue-collar family, and grew up in an ethnically diverse community. Both Tommy's up-bringing, and the melting pot he grew up in have been two influential factors in his life and the arts. At an early age Tommy discovered a love for both the arts and the beautiful game, soccer. Soccer would become Tommy's first outlet, and craft he would nourish and pursue, putting the arts off as secondary. Tommy's hard work ethic, devotion, and perseverance with soccer, would enable Tommy to play at a very high level during his adolescent years, becoming one of the most decorated and recognized players in New Jersey, and eventually sought by, and play for The Richard Stockton College of New Jersey, where he would win a DIV III National Championship with the 2001 team. This would be the pinnacle of Tommy's soccer career, and the foundation for the next phase in his life. As one door shut, another door opened, and Tommy would then pursue the arts, learning many different art mediums during, and after graduating from college, with a Bachelor of the Arts degree, Art History, and by any means devote his life to living as an independent artist and author.

www.tommytutalo.com

Tommy Tutalo

www.ingramcontent.com/pod-product-compliance
Lightning Source LLC
Chambersburg PA
CBHW020455020726
47493CB00001B/36